KU-175-294

M. S. Power was born in Dublin and educated in
Ireland and France. He has worked as a TV producer
in the United States, but now lives in Galloway,
Scotland, where he devotes his time to writing. His
story, *Mr Apple Seeks the Light*, was the winner of the
Hennessy Short Story Award in 1983 and his first
novel, *Hunt For the Autumn Clowns*, was published in
the same year to critical acclaim. His three novels
comprising *The Children of the North* trilogy, *The Killing
of Yesterday's Children*, *Lonely the Man Without Heroes*
and *A Darkness in the Eye* has been made into a major
BBC drama series, and a further two of his novels are
available in Abacus, *Bridie and the Silver Lady* and *The
Crucifixion of Septimus Roach*. His most recently
published works are *Crucible of Fools* and *The Summer
Soldier*.

'Power deserves credit for his accomplished handling
of an ingenious plot, and its recherché elements'
London Review of Books

'What lifts the book out of the bogs of thrillerdom and
propaganda is its whimsical blend of farce and tragedy'
Observer

'A strangely uplifting and attractive book about
"ordinary people trying to survive against the odds"'
Books and Bookmen

'Power's narrative is vividly disturbing . . . brilliantly
controlled'

Daily Telegraph

'To succeed in balancing reality and fantasy in a
contemporary setting like this is no mean feat. Power
knows exactly when to swing from one to the other'
The Times

'The plot has many twists and turns and is entirely
convincing; the dialogue is sharp and believable. But
what is so remarkable is that Mr Power manages to
show how in the end terrorism totally degrades
everyone, and to do this without preaching'
Daily Telegraph

'One of the most penetrating novels about Northern
Ireland yet to appear'
Time Out

'An edgy, topical *roman noir* enhanced by the sheer
quality of its writing, which is impressively good'
Irish Independent

Also by M. S. Power in Abacus:

BRIDIE AND THE SILVER LADY
THE CRUCIFIXION OF SEPTIMUS ROACH

M. S. POWER

CHILDREN OF THE NORTH

THE KILLING OF YESTERDAY'S CHILDREN

LONELY THE MAN WITHOUT HEROES

A DARKNESS IN THE EYE

An *Abacus* Book

First published in Great Britain in three separate volumes
THE KILLING OF YESTERDAY'S CHILDREN Chatto & Windus
Ltd 1985 © M. S. Power 1985
LONELY THE MAN WITHOUT HEROES William Heinemann Ltd
1986 © M. S. Power 1986
A DARKNESS IN THE EYE William Heinemann Ltd 1987
© M. S. Power 1987

This combined volume first published in Abacus by
Sphere Books Ltd 1991

All characters in this publication are fictitious
and any resemblance to real persons, living or dead
is purely coincidental.

The right of M. S. Power to be identified as author of this work
has been asserted by him in accordance with the Copyright, Designs
and Patents Act 1988.

All rights reserved.
No part of this publication may be reproduced,
stored in a retrieval system, or transmitted, in any
form or by any means without the prior
permission in writing of the publisher, nor be
otherwise circulated in any form of binding or
cover other than that in which it is published and
without a similar condition including this
condition being imposed on the subsequent purchaser.

Printed and bound in Great Britain by
Cox & Wyman Ltd, Reading

ISBN 0 349 10255 4

Sphere Books Ltd
A Division of
Macdonald & Co (Publishers) Ltd
Orbit House
1 New Fetter Lane
London EC4A 1AR
A member of Maxwell Macmillan Pergamon Publishing Corporation

THE KILLING OF YESTERDAY'S CHILDREN

For my friends
Ken and Jeanne

... and it was from the grey and menacing sea that it seemed to come, dark and threatening and evil, moving languidly in that sinister bodeful way that presages only sorrow and death but mostly sorrow, invading the souls of men and planting there the seeds of hate and revenge yet disguising these as good and right, nay as holy and glorious and by this awful deception turning man against his brother, gloating in the grim and terrible slaughter, exulting in the destruction of those who only yesterday were children.

The Visions and Visitations of Arthur Apple

A swirling, ominous cloud of acrid black smoke rose from behind the ornate spire of St Enoch's Church. Seeming to carry in its billows the echoes of the explosion that had just shattered the nervous, expectant quiet of the city, it curled and dispersed into the grey, heavy sky. Almost theatrical, thought Colonel Maddox; the next thing to appear would be a genie with a hollow laugh. Like daemonic incense, decided his companion, Mr Asher, and found the allusion highly satisfactory. The two men stood side by side at the narrow, heavily screened window, watching with curiously detached relief. Both were dressed in civilian clothes and looked ill at ease, the Colonel tugging from time to time at his jacket, straightening imaginary creases; their neat, grey suits invited a familiarity neither of them wanted. It was, appropriately enough, Good Friday.

As the smoke thinned out and the plangent sounds of lamentation and fury (the inevitable aftermath of all explosions) grew louder, the two men turned from the window in unison, as though their remote participation in the privacy of sorrow and outrage were an intolerable intrusion. Only when the screams and wails and the accompanying threnodic keening of the ambulances had diminished, to be replaced by the clamour of dustbin-lids being clattered in protest and the heavy rumble of military vehicles moving in, did Colonel Maddox pour two stiff drinks from a bottle produced, with a wry, guilty smile, from one of the filing-cabinets that lined the small office. He pushed one across the desk to his companion. Mr Asher emptied his glass in one swallow closing his eyes and holding his breath for a few seconds as the liquid burned its way to his stomach. He was a small, thin man in his early fifties, and both his height and age worried him: to compensate for his lack of stature he was excessively aggressive; to overcome any sign of ageing he employed a battery of creams, lotions and dyes which might have tempted one to regard him as effeminate, had not his actions been entirely masculine and his reputation with women such as to dispel any such thought. Although a high-ranking if somewhat maverick officer in the R.U.C., he was always referred to as 'Mr Asher', and in an odd way this civilian title seemed to enhance his rank and endow him with a certain mysterious potency, making him one of those shadowy, slightly sinister creatures more accredited to fiction than fact. Mr Asher, however, was very much a fact, and certainly more than slightly sinister.

Colonel Maddox poured himself another drink. Apparently lost in reveries of his own, he was oblivious to Asher's glass, automatically proferred but quickly withdrawn with a little cough of embarrassment. A deep flush suffused Asher's face, as though the Colonel's unintentional snub had been a conscious chastisement for overstepping the mark of familiarity. He placed his empty glass with exaggerated care on the desk and proceeded to make a great show of blowing his nose.

' – still simply cannot understand it', penetrated Mr Asher's trumpeting.

'I'm sorry, Colonel, you were saying?'

'Oh – that I still simply cannot understand why the wretched man allowed himself to get caught up in such a ghastly business.'

'Ah, that again,' Asher said, sighing with mild frustration. 'He knew exactly what he was doing.'

'Come, now, he can't have known – '

'Oh, he knew,' Asher insisted dogmatically. 'If you ask me he *wanted* to – '

'To die?' the Colonel interrupted in amazement, as if the idea were new to him.

'In a way. He had notions of nobility. Sacrifice. That sort of thing,' Asher found himself explaining, uncomfortably aware that he cared little for such matters.

Colonel Maddox stared into space for several minutes, allowing the remark to mature in the hope that it would decant itself into some semblance of clarity. 'You seem to be saying he *planned* the entire thing.'

'I wouldn't go that far. I think he recognized it as the only possible conclusion to the events he had set in motion. I also believe there was more between him and Deeley than we know.'

'You've read his diary, I suppose,' the Colonel remarked.

'Bits,' Asher admitted, his high-pitched intonation indicating that to have bothered to read the whole thing would have been a waste of valuable time.

'I've read it all,' Colonel Maddox confessed. 'Twice. Every terrible word. Frightening.'

'He was sick. Nothing more, Colonel. Just plain sick,' Mr Asher announced, with that peculiar emphasis that somehow makes illness sound obscene.

Colonel Maddox seemed to think about this for a while, making miniature whirlpools with the whiskey in his glass as his long, bony body swayed to and fro. 'There is an awful sickness, John, that affects that part we used to call the soul,' he said finally, in a vague, distant voice. The idea seemed to awaken something strange and upsetting in him.

'Huh,' grunted Asher.

Maddox finished his drink and returned to the window. Resting his hands on the sill he gazed down and around, his vision blurred by the thick wire screen that protected the glass: the almost deserted streets, rutted and uneven, their paving-stones long since requisitioned as ineffectual ammunition; row upon row of small, mean houses, all lightless, the graffiti on their walls proclaiming hatred and differing shades of patriotism (and demanding freedom, too – little enough to ask); and the upended rubbish truck, remnant of an overnight barricade, where three lean and nervous mongrels now scavenged, unable to believe their luck. Two armoured cars rumbled across his vision, the sound of their grinding motors powerful and menacing – and comforting, too, to the soldiers they carried, as they faced another wet, dreary night filled with the promise of death. What had happened just one week ago should have been forgotten by now amid this constant, continuous tragedy. One would have

3

thought that the death of one insignificant man would be swallowed up and lost in the unending litany of bereavement. It was not so, however. Horror and destruction were now regarded as appallingly normal, but it seemed one was still permitted to single out one individual life, hold it in some regard and mourn its loss. The Colonel fumbled in his pocket, found his cigarettes and lit one. Far to his left, beyond the spire slowly fading in the gloom, a brilliant flash of light shot across the sky. Maddox automatically started counting, waiting for the sound of another explosion. A small, tired smile affected his mouth as he recalled his mother telling him to count between the lightning and the rumbles to know how far away the thunder was. He had reached only six before the noise thudded across the city and rattled the window.

'Bloody boyos are restless tonight,' Asher remarked fatuously.

The Colonel nodded without turning, amazed at the small grin on his own lips.

'Anyway, it's not our worry tonight, Colonel.'

'No.'

'And I must be off.'

'Must you? Have another drink before you go.'

'Well – a quick one, sir. I have someone – ah – waiting,' Mr Asher confessed smugly, always pleased to advertise his prowess.

'God, I wish I could be like you, John,' Maddox said in a quiet voice, his head shaking in disbelief. 'You can switch off just like that,' he said, snapping his fingers. 'None of this affects you one little bit, does it?'

'Should it?'

The Colonel's mouth framed the beginning of a reply, but he restrained himself. He poured two more drinks before finally answering.

'Perhaps not. Perhaps you've got the right idea.'

'I don't know about the right idea, sir, but I can guarantee you this: nobody survives here if he gets too involved.'

'But we *are* involved.'

'No, we are *not*,' Mr Asher interrupted firmly. '*You're* not, at any

4

rate. You've simply got to do your job and get the hell out of here as soon as your tour is up. No attachments, Colonel. And when they send you home, forget Belfast. Throw that part of your mind away.'

'Throw away your mind,' the Colonel heard himself saying. 'Funny,' he continued, looking up and staring at Asher intently. 'Somebody else said that to me once.'

'They were right.'

'Perhaps. And you?'

'Me?'

'Yes, you, John. What do you do?'

Mr Asher pursed his lips for a moment, then allowed them to relax into the semblance of a smile. 'I do nothing, Colonel. I've lived with this chaos all my life. I'd only be lost if it stopped. That's when my problems would start, if it all suddenly stopped.' Asher sipped his drink before adding, 'But it will never end; so I've nothing to worry about, have I?'

Colonel Maddox watched his companion drink again, the slender, well-manicured fingers tilting the glass, the small, hostile eyes peering into it.

'So, in a sense, you have thrown away your mind, John?'

'The day I was born.'

The Colonel nodded, taking the cigarette, long since extinguished, from his mouth.

'Light?' Mr Asher conjured a flaming lighter from his pocket so rapidly it must surely have been ignited there. He moved the flame back and forth under the Colonel's cigarette. 'You're still brooding about Apple, aren't you?'

'He haunts me.'

Asher shook his head incredulously. 'He turned on us, dammit.'

'That's not the point, John. He did what he thought was right. He was honourable,' the Colonel said emphatically, straightening his back. Reference to honour demanded a rigid spine.

'Honour be damned – '

'And he wasn't a coward,' the Colonel remarked irrelevantly, in a tone of vague significance.

'He was nothing but a stupid old fool,' Mr Asher decided, pocketing his lighter at last and glancing at his watch. 'Now I must be off,' he said, joining the Colonel at the window. 'You've been here long enough, sir. Too long. That's what's getting you down. It always happens at the end of a tour. I've seen it a thousand times.'

'I don't think – '

' – and the nights are always the worst,' Asher continued, determined to forestall any further discussion. 'I had an old aunt once. She used to swear night was sent for only two things: making love or reviewing our errors. So I leave you,' Asher concluded, putting on his coat and knotting a dark blue scarf about his neck, 'to the latter. Me, I have high hopes of – '

Maddox rounded on him swiftly and grabbed him by the shoulders. 'You terrify me, John. Nothing touches you. You're just like those animals out there. No compassion. No – no – *feelings*.'

Asher seemed for a moment stunned by this outburst. Removing the Colonel's hands from his coat he held them for a second in his own, without speaking. Then he dropped them and rubbed his own together, saying tightly: 'I'm not paid to have feelings, Colonel. Neither are you.'

Colonel Maddox closed his eyes and nodded like a man willing to agree with anything. Then he laughed, a wry, mournful strained laugh.

While they had been talking the rain had started again, and it now pattered in drops as hard as rice on the window. The demonstrations that always followed the bombings would be postponed, and the soldiers on foot patrol would pull on their waterproof capes and feel a little safer.

'Well, you go on home, John. I'll stay here for a while. I still have a few things that need to be done.'

'Right. I'll see you in the morning. And remember: we're here to do a job. That's all.'

'I'll remember.'

'And try and get some sleep. You look all in.'

'Sleep?' the Colonel asked mildly. 'Ah, yes. Yes. Yes, I will.'

6

'And forget about Apple and that,' Asher said, indicating the thick exercise-book – several exercise-books, in fact, crudely bound with tape to form one enormous volume – lying on the desk.

'Yes.'

Asher paused by the door and turned. 'Colonel,' he said, in a voice uncharacteristically gentle, 'there's one thing you have to understand. When a man dies here, soldier or terrorist or civilian, it is as though he never even lived. He dies, and that's an end to it. He leaves nothing behind. He takes even the memory of his life with him. They get us or we get them – whichever way it goes, the result is the same. However,' Asher added, his cold humour returning, 'we just have to make sure it's us who get them first.'

Suddenly, the Colonel found himself shaking with laughter. He threw back his head and roared until the tears rolled down his cheeks. Asher was shocked. 'I didn't know I said anything funny, Colonel,' he said softly.

'You didn't, John,' the Colonel confessed, wiping the tears from his face with a large white handkerchief that had his initials neatly embroidered in one corner. 'You certainly didn't. I was just thinking how stupid it all is. Here we are talking so damned philosophically about something neither of us understands, and both of us should be dead.'

'You, perhaps, sir. They never had any intention of killing me. They need me alive to bargain with.'

'Well, me, then. But here I am alive and well, drinking my whiskey and supposed, according to your way of thinking, to have no feelings.'

'You were lucky.'

'Perhaps. Life is not always the greatest favour fortune bestows, you know. Anyway, I'm sorry for laughing. I *am* tired. Forgive me, John. Off you go and enjoy yourself.'

'Good night, sir.'

'Good night, John.'

Alone, Maddox slumped into the old, worn leather chair by his desk and listened to Asher's receding footsteps. As they disappeared with the slamming of a distant door, he leant forward and rested his elbows on the desk, head in hands. His fingers pressed hard into his temples as if to ease some excruciating pain or erase a disquieting thought. And it seemed to work, for he threw back his head and yawned loudly and luxuriously, allowing himself a smile at the mild vulgarity. He was still smiling when his eyes came to rest on the bound exercise-books before him. Slowly, almost reluctantly, like a small child reaching towards a familiar yet still alarming jack-in-the-box, he stretched out to flick open the cover, and started to read again the baleful words printed in large capitals: I AM I SAID. I AM I CRIED; and under these in script so tiny that the Colonel was forced to lean even closer to decipher the words: *The Visions and Visitations of Arthur Apple*.

He started to turn the pages, letting them fall through his fingers as though searching for some particular passage, a passage that would be revealed to him by whatever power allowed the pages to come to rest. 'He was no fool,' he heard himself say aloud. Under different circumstances, indeed, he would have been considered an extremely brave man. An example to us all. Maddox sighed deeply. An example to us all. How he had yearned to hear such words used of him! He decided to risk another small drink and sat for some time unmoving, his eyes fixed on the open book in front of him, the strange horrors and agony it contained seeming to radiate from the pages and taunt him. And yet, he thought, it was not all horror, not all agony. There was hope there, which was good; and comfort, which was something the Colonel knew he could use himself at that moment; and there was even a sense of fun, though whether the writer had been laughing at himself or at some prospective reader was unclear. The Colonel noticed that the pages had stopped moving beneath his fingers, and he leaned forward to read.

... haunted so often by the thought of songs, of warmth, of innocence, of simplicity, of comradeship, of all these and more that you speak of on your journeys here from Tetragrammaton to console me. If only they could know you as I do, understand the wonderful mission you have given me. You have ordained me, created of me a High Priest, nay, a god; through me you have chosen to save so many and I rejoice in the goodness I have been chosen to perform. Ah, my friends, my spirits of light and peace, my souls of Divine and Sefer, in the raising of my petrified spirit you have determined my salvation and through my efforts the salvation of ...

Colonel Maddox, for obscure reasons of his own, refused to turn the page, despite a longing to read again the story of Arthur Apple's attempted salvation. Instead, he closed the book and leaned back in his chair. 'Light and peace'. How dreadful it was that such passages, which held out nothing but the promise of serenity and hope, could be sullied and misconstrued to justify accusations of madness and evil. But then everything decent one did in life was twisted and misinterpreted and held to ridicule, was it not? Suddenly the Colonel felt the urge to cry, in anger more than in sorrow. He sighed as a strange, unfamiliar and overpowering sense of longing possessed him: he longed to have spoken with this shy, gaunt man in different circumstances; longed, too, to have had Arthur Apple explain to him how he had survived, how after all the injustices and belittlements he had remained capable of such great, if misplaced, sacrifice.

In the late afternoon of the last day of January 1979 two men, well muffled against the cold, penetrating wind, made their way past the two security guards into the hotel. One of the guards motioned as if to halt them, but changed his mind abruptly when he spotted the tiny warning signal from his colleague, and the hand that he had intended to use in restraint gave instead a salute that hinted at respect and brotherhood.

Inside, the two men walked briskly across the open foyer and made for the residents' lounge: as they entered, the head-waiter's eyes flickered in recognition and he gestured them to a table in the corner. Having taken their coats – each of which he gave a sharp shake to remove the last unmelted snowflakes – he hovered respectfully.

'Oh, a brandy, I think, Declan. Cold as the Arctic outside,' Seamus Reilly, the smaller, older of the two men said. His voice was quiet and precise, but friendly enough.

'A whiskey for me,' Martin Deeley decided. He would have preferred beer, but beer went straight through him when he was nervous.

'Oh – and Declan – '

'Mr Reilly?'

'Something to pick at.'

'Certainly, sir. Anything in particular?'

'Whatever you have handy.'

'Very good, sir.'

The waiter glided away and the two men sat in silence as Reilly took inordinate care over lighting a small, thin cigar. He blew the first lungful of smoke towards the ceiling, watching it as it curled upwards to join the painted clouds inhabited by grim-faced cherubs on the domed roof of the lounge. Finally: 'We're pulling you in for a while, Martin,' he announced casually, but in a tone which warned there was no room for dispute.

'I see.'

Reilly raised his thin eyebrows and smiled. 'You do?'

'No. I don't.'

'Ah.'

Deeley waited a few seconds for an explanation, but when none was forthcoming he leaned forward and said in a low, urgent voice, 'I thought I carried out – '

Seamus Reilly raised a small hand on which he knew he wore too many rings, halting further conversation as though stopping traffic, and gave the waiter the benefit of a thankful nod as the drinks and assorted nuts were placed carefully on the table. When the waiter had left Deeley tried again. 'I thought I carried out – '

'You did, Martin. I can assure you we have no complaints on that score. You have, as a matter of fact, been almost too successful,' Reilly conceded, swilling his brandy in his glass and sniffing it like a connoisseur. 'And so,' he continued, adopting the slightly arrogant, condescending tone he enjoyed using when delivering the orders of his superiors, 'our information is that the Brits are getting a little too interested in you.'

'Oh.'

'Well, to be truthful, not in you precisely; but they've been circulating a description which fits you pretty accurately.'

'Oh.'

'And, as I said, it has been decided to pull you in for a while. In out of the cold,' he added with a little smile, pleased with his literary touch.

'I see.'

'Also, there are some on the Committee who feel – and I am not one of them, I hasten to add – who feel that perhaps you enjoy killing too much, and that a little rest would be in your own interest.'

'That's bullshit, and you know it.'

'Me?' Reilly said in mock surprise and amazement. 'Me? I *know* nothing, Martin.'

'Not much, you don't. Nothing goes on but you know of it. Anyway, so what if I like doing what I'm good at?'

'Like?'

'Well – '

'Let me tell you something, Martin – and this is between you and me, a little friendly information, you can call it. You're supposed to get sick to the pit of your stomach every time you kill. I don't care who it is that's the target. The day you stop puking when you take someone's life you're no use to anyone. Least of all us. You get so you can't stop. You get careless, and that means trouble for everyone.'

'Jesus, I don't *enjoy* it, Seamus. I – '

'I think we'd better leave it there. The decision has been made.'

Martin shrugged his shoulders. 'That's that, then,' he said bitterly.

'Yes. That's that.'

'So what do I do? Sit on my – '

'Oh, don't worry. You are not about to sit on your arse all day as you were about to suggest. Far from it. We have something else we want you to do. Something that needs to be done and will keep you out of the way for a while. Out of the limelight,' Seamus Reilly explained, and gave another thin smile. 'Cheers.'

'Cheers.'

Martin Deeley lay back in the overstuffed, uncomfortable armchair and sipped his whiskey, one part of his mind taken up with wondering what job Reilly had in store for him, another, rather more energetic part furiously refuting the suggestion that he had in any way enjoyed performing his successful assassinations. The trouble was, and he was well aware of this no matter how he tried to convince himself otherwise, that although, doubtless, it had not reached the ecstasy that Seamus Reilly had intimated, there was indeed some truth in the accusation: there was, after all, something curiously pleasurable in the sensation of causing death, even if –

' – for the bookmaker's at last.' Seamus Reilly's voice suddenly penetrated his thoughts.

'What did you say?'

'I said,' Reilly replied testily, 'we have found our man for the bookmaker's at last. I wish you would listen when I speak, Martin. You know I hate repeating things.'

'Bookmaker's?'

'You see? You don't listen. We discussed this at length last month.'

'Oh, that. Yes, I remember.'

'Good. Anyway, we have our man to run it and we want you to work there and keep an eye on him.'

'Me? In a bookie's? Me?'

'That's right, Martin. You. In a bookie's. I'm sure you'll enjoy it no end. You will be his assistant, and it will be up to you to let us know if he shows any sign of – eh – changing his loyalties. We don't, of course, expect any complications, but you never know. And we need that shop to clear our funds.'

'Christ, Seamus, I don't know a damn thing about bookmaking. The only time I go near those places is to put something on the National.'

'You don't have to know anything. Anyway, you're a bright lad. You can learn. Think what an interesting interlude it will make when you come to write your life-story.'

'God Almighty! A bloody bookie's!'

'All you have to do is keep a watchful eye on our Mr Apple.'

'Oh, God, no. Not Arthur Apple.'

'Yes, Martin,' Reilly admitted.

'But he's a freak, Seamus.'

'Mr Apple – and you will kindly remember always to call him *Mister* Apple – may have his peculiarities, but he certainly is not a freak.'

'But he – '

Seamus Reilly once again raised his bejewelled hand to command silence, the corners of his mouth twitching peevishly. He was not a man who enjoyed having Committee decisions questioned or criticized.

'Mr Apple may well have left Her Majesty's diplomatic service under a small grey cloud, he may even be regarded as strange – eccentric, if you will – but he is invaluable to us.'

Deeley shook his head in disbelief.

'Furthermore,' Reilly continued, 'the fact that he is widely regarded as somewhat batty places him nicely above suspicion, and that is all that matters as far as we are concerned.'

'He's a bloody freak,' Martin insisted.

'Have it your way. He's a freak. But he's a freak you are going to work with. And you are going to show respect for him. We need him, Martin.'

'Jesus, we must be in a right bloody state if we need the likes of Apple.'

Reilly's eyes went cold. 'We can get any number of young killers to replace you, Martin,' he said, icily. 'It is much more difficult to get the right person to launder our funds, and we have that person in Mr Apple. He is an almost perfect cover for our operation.'

'Well, that's just bloody marvellous. You want me to – '

Reilly placed his glass on the table and leaned forward. 'We don't want anything, Martin. We are simply telling you that this is what you will do: you will work with Mr Apple, you will report to us everything that happens, and you will jump if Mr Apple says jump. Do I make myself perfectly clear?'

'Yes,' said Martin, sullenly.

'Excellent.' Seamus Reilly leaned back, smiling his most bene-volent smile: he was always gratified, if a little surprised, when he managed to bring matters to a satisfactory conclusion. 'One more little thing: naturally, Mr Apple has no inkling of your connection with us and we would like it to remain that way. As far as he is concerned, you were inherited by us with the rest of the fixtures when we took over the shop.'

'Lovely.'

'Yes, I thought you'd like that. Oh, come now, Martin,' Seamus Reilly added, deciding the time was ripe for a spot of largesse, 'it's only for a little while. Then you can get back to your slaughter.'

'When do I have to start this?'

'Oh, not for a couple of weeks. We're having the shop repainted for you – new heaters put in. You'll be very comfortable.'

'Oh, thanks.'

'You're welcome. Very welcome. And who knows, you might end up learning a thing or two from our Mr Apple.'

'No, thanks.'

'It's surprising, really,' Reilly went on, gazing upwards as though summoning his words from on high, 'very surprising, the sources from which one learns. I remember...' Or perhaps he didn't, since he abruptly broke off, finished his drink and stubbed out his half-smoked cigar. 'Well, that takes care of that. I must away. You stay and enjoy your drink. Have another one on me if you like. I'll be in touch next week.'

'Right.'

'Don't look so worried, Martin. You'll love every minute of it.'

'Sure.'

'See you.'

'Bye.'

Martin watched as the waiter glided forward to help Reilly into his coat and bow discreetly as he palmed the remuneration. He suddenly felt very exposed and self-conscious, sitting alone with the potted plants, the cavorting cherubs and whispered conversation for company – and his thoughts, although these were hardly entertaining. All the same, he took them with him along with his drink across the room to one of the enormous windows that boasted panoramic views of the battered city below. He stared out into the darkness, shielding his eyes from the reflection of the room behind. Strange, he thought, how even at night the city failed to conceal its torment, how even the occasional unbroken streetlight seemed to pinpoint some little scene of tragedy. He smiled thinly and studied the rows of abandoned houses, their windows covered with rusting corrugated iron or staring like empty eye-sockets, the barricaded police station, the sandbags and rolls of barbed wire like monstrous hair-curlers protecting the military post at the bottom of the hill, its perimeter lit like a film set by great arclights, and the cars driven recklessly, lights

15

flashing, dipped and flashing again, as people scurried to their firesides and the dubious protection of their homes. To his right, a few yards from the entrance to the hotel, two soldiers, Scots Guards, a sergeant and his inferior, had stopped a woman and were searching her shopping-bag, in a cheerful enough way, it appeared. And it appeared to him then also that all the sacrifices (as he liked to think of them) he had made, all the hardship he had suffered to put an end to just such humiliation as the woman now accepted, had been futile. What had happened to him over the past few years seemed already to belong to a different age, to have been forgotten or, at best, to have sought refuge in some grotesque form of folklore.

And it was from a different age, it seemed, that his mother's face now peered at him from the darkness outside, her features distorted by the thickness of the glass, her grey hair pulled back and curled into her old-fashioned bun, her eyes defiant though not angry: pain dominated her face, and it was this same expression of pain she had worn when she told him, her voice flat, tired, and emotionless:

You're the man of the house now, Martin. Now that your Daddy's gone. It'll be on your shoulders to see to it that somebody pays.

Yes, Mam. I know.

And even if it means the killing of yourself and myself it'll be well worth it in the end.

Yes, Mam.

The evil has got to be driven away, Martin, and you're the one to drive it from this house.

Yes, Mam.

God knows the suffering is only sent to try us, but it wouldn't be right to lie down under it, would it?

No, Mam.

You'll be looking after things, then, Martin?

I will, Mam.

And seeing to it that your Daddy and Steven can lie in peace?

Yes, Mam.

That's my good boy. Ah, sure, God is good to have left me you in His mercy. Are your eggs the way you like them?

16

Martin Deeley left his mother's face to mouth on darkly to itself at the window, and signalled the waiter for his coat. He tipped the man generously (hoping it was more than Reilly had given) and left the hotel, curtly acknowledging the 'Goodnight, sir' of the security guards.

Out on the street, the coldness of the slush already penetrating his shoes, the darkness wrapped itself about him and he relaxed. He walked at a carefully rehearsed pace: not fast enough to appear to be hurrying, not so slowly that he could be accused of loitering, hugging the inside of the footpath, seeking the protection and anonymity of the shadows, his eyes constantly, automatically, darting in all directions, listening for unaccustomed sounds, grateful that the snow, now falling thickly again, offered an extra veil. He had much to think about, but he held his thoughts at bay with a conscious effort, keeping them tucked up warm in his mind until the late hours of the night when he could lie on his bed and summon them one by one from their cosy, secret crevices, dealing with each in turn, being precise and meticulous, using them as a tortuous cure for his insomnia.

— 3 —

Arthur Apple thought hard about the noise his feet made on the frost-hardened snow. It reminded him of something, of some other sensation that for the moment eluded him. At six in the morning it was quiet in Belfast, and the sound of his footsteps cracked loudly, painfully, over the snarling of military vehicles returning from night patrols, the friendly clink of milk-bottles and the slamming of doors as the city dragged itself reluctantly to wakefulness. It could, of course, have been construed as the pleasant enough sound of someone walking without a care on sand, perhaps, but the sight of that tall, stooped figure and the mournful, lined face with its grey, red-streaked eyes distorted by old-fashioned steel-rimmed spectacles would have quickly dispelled any illusions of pleasure.

Three soldiers of indistinguishable regiment stood nursing their rifles on the corner of Cliftonville Road, stomping their feet, their breath as thick as smoke in the crisp, sharp air. They stared with obligatory suspicion at Mr Apple until one of them recognized him and said so to his companions: then the tension lapsed in their eyes and they took to stomping their feet again. They continued to survey his progress, however, thinking perhaps that his mournful air of desolation epitomized the wretchedness of the place. Indeed, the appearance of this gaunt, dispirited figure seemed to lift their spirits perceptibly: the awkward, stilted walk and the agony etched into his face spoke of misery on a scale even greater than their own. For a few moments they seemed to forget the cold, the loneliness and the longing for their wives, forget, even, the possibility of imminent, unsatisfactory death that would probably be remarkable only as a misprint on some official communiqué. One of them (oddly, not the one who recognized him by sight) was moved to try a smile as Arthur Apple drew near, and say huskily, 'Cold.'

Mr Apple stopped as if shot, amazed that anyone should speak to him. 'Yes,' he answered quickly. 'Very cold.' He tried to smile in return but could muster only a tiny twitch, and he felt bad about this. He was genuinely sorry for these young soldiers, their youth haunted by the prospect of death; he was sorry, too, for the strange young men who died trying to drive them out; he felt sorry for everyone, but mostly for himself.

As he plodded along down the Antrim Road he passed a trio of gutted houses, the bricks about the windows blackened by fire and smoke, and he thought for one dreadful moment that he heard the screams of someone trying to escape. Abruptly, he shook his head and ran his cold, bony fingers across his brow, as though this physical gesture would banish such disturbing thoughts, if only temporarily; for Mr Apple was pursued by screams of one sort and another, and he was well, if sadly, aware that no amount of caressing could remove them. Still, he told himself, in a small, futile effort to brighten the day, there was something very noble in the way this city managed to survive and carry on.

He narrowed his eyes as the cold, watery sun glinted on his spectacles: then he paused, rocking on his feet, and chuckled to himself at his error: the sun (if, indeed, there was to be any) would not make an appearance for several hours yet, and he gave a small wave of apology to the streetlight as he passed beneath it and continued on his way. Odd, he thought, that he had been fooled like that, especially since he had the painful momentum of his body to shelter him from illusion: nodding, he alerted his mind against similar mistakes. And perhaps it was this conscious effort to stick with reality that sent the sudden searing pain through his head, as though someone had sneaked up from behind and clubbed him. He stumbled forward, one arm outstretched like one deprived of all vision, while horrific images cartwheeled in his mind, images of appalling humiliation, of faces twisted with derisive laughter, of fingers pointing with filthy nails. A small cry escaped him; then he blinked severely and stretched his eyes wide, grimacing wildly, and abruptly there was only the partially lit street again. It was as if nothing at all had befallen him, and he allowed a little sigh to scold his stupidity, his eyes returning to a fixed stare and adopting their customarily wan, morose cast. Seconds later he was his old self again, indulging in his regular morning speculation about what the day might promise. He lengthened his stride deliberately, determined to put a great distance between the present and his dreams of the night before (although he knew only too well that they had not been dreams but actual experiences, journeys and afflictions undertaken in the arms of darkness – but who would understand this?). It seemed to work, and his spirits rose. The withdrawal of the nocturnal phantoms was only gradual, but it was accomplished with a minimum of fuss. The multiple open sores on his memory began to clot and heal, leaving only scars which were thankfully less painful, though he knew only too well that they were liable to open wide again at any moment.

As he made his way down Duncairn Gardens and reached the corner of Lepper Street, at the far end of which stood his bookmaking shop, he paused, and inflicted on himself a moment's recollection of his troubled sleep. It was a silly ritual that seemed to take place every morning and which he regarded now as a kind of soul-cleansing. In itself, he admitted, it was absurd, since he could never remember with any accuracy what his dreams had been about, although they were certainly unpleasant and seemed to warn him incessantly of some tragedy yet to come. For more years than Mr Apple cared to recall he had suffered the nightly visitations of phantoms and ghouls of a most unfriendly nature, but since he had accepted this new occupation of bookmaker they were becoming more frequent. No, that was not altogether true: not more frequent. But certainly the clamourings had developed a new intensity, as though the nocturnal intruders had invited their more sinister relatives to attend and participate in his torment. Cerebral dry rot, I suppose, he thought, smiling wryly. At my age the brain starts to disintegrate. Pieces drop off and puff away like dust. 'Huh,' he grunted aloud, to disparage these unmedical reflections.

When he finally arrived outside the small, drab premises he could not help wondering what had become of the Frederick Bezant whose name was still painted above the shop. FREDERICK BEZANT. LICENSED BETTING OFFICE. EST. 1935, it proclaimed, in that subdued, slightly guilty way that peeling paintwork has a knack of insinuating. He could never quite rid himself of the idea that old Frederick still hovered over the place (envisioned for no specific or justifiable reason as a small, round Scotsman with a wily brain and a kind heart), peering over Mr Apple's shoulder, tut-tutting, appalled by the transactions he saw taking place, appalled, too, that his long-established and, no doubt, respectable firm should now be a clearing-house for currency of dubious origin. Mr Apple's eyes admitted a wintry twinkle: a small part of him could still enjoy a joke at his own expense. So what if this onetime minor diplomat in Her Majesty's service could now be found offering the odds on Her Majesty's horses? It was a living, and it left him time to pursue his stranger destiny; and it was, when all was said and done, the least humiliating joke that life had played on him.

Fortunately, the joke was not entirely on him, he thought, as he unlocked the door with a gigantic key, switched on the lights and picked up an oblong slip of paper urging him to get his mechanical parts from DOBSONS. Indeed, there was a sardonic twist here that some less self-pitying side of him enjoyed: this frowned-upon profession gave him the one thing he coveted: an emotional isolation that allowed him go about without being expected to like people or be liked by them. Indeed, in an ideal existence Mr Apple would have passed what was left of his life as a sort of spectre, seeing but unseen, thinking but unthought of, and almost everything he did bore witness to this quest for anonymity: his house (modest, terraced, identical to twenty others in an unremarkable road); his clothes (plain, discreet, undemanding of comment); even his voice was normally kept modulated to a level that gave no hint of enthusiasm or emotion. His body, alas, the one thing he most wanted to pass unnoticed, gave him away: that ridiculously long, lean, stooped, unwieldy body sur-mounted by that mournful, grey face with its great beaked nose and baggy eyes, and that awkward walk, stilted, not unlike that of a man recovering from broken legs or polio. Still, his neighbours never intruded: as far as they were concerned, Mr Apple was a quiet gentleman who lived alone now that his mother was dead, lived in comfortable monasticism, alone apart from the whimsical visits of his cat (a white-and-ginger one-eyed creature of erratic loyalty and with a nature as aloof as his own which, perhaps recognizing a kindred tormented spirit, had latched on to him and sometimes answered to the name he had given her: Chloe).

However, unbeknownst to snappy Mr Cahill, who lived on one side and dedicated his life to the culture of Zinnias and cacti, and to the quarrelling Mr and Mrs Bateman, who spent their time dithering about whether or not to quit Belfast and join their son in Australia, Mr Apple had two more lodgers, who dwelt happily enough with him, if only in his mind. They were the perfect tenants, appearing only when he summoned them, always on hand to lend an ear, dole out advice, console him. To Mr Apple they were very real: Mr Divine, a happy-go-lucky little creature, always joking and making him laugh, but capable, too, of penetrating observations; and Sefer, the curiously enigmatic Sefer, rather given to ponderous argument, inclined to pessimism, enjoying forecasts of doom, but entertaining company for all that. They accompanied Mr Apple everywhere, perched as it were on the shoulder of his mind, and he chatted to them quite openly, which presented problems from time to time. Even the unemotional Chloe had looked at him askance on more than one occasion. And just as Chloe depended for food on Mr Apple's weekly visit to the supermarket, so he, Mr Apple, depended for his sustenance on a regular Friday visit from a gentleman known only as Seamus. And Seamus, no doubt, depended on the benevolence of some more senior shadowy Power for his daily bread, for that was how things seemed to work. Not that Mr Apple dwelt for long on the morality of his income. Far from it. He had discussed it once with his friends, and, while Sefer had warned of implications too dreadful to imagine, Mr Divine had chuckled away and told him to go ahead and enjoy it all. Mr Apple had weighed their advice with considerable care, but, as usual, had made up his own mind.

calculations, despite the dire whispered warnings of the morose, despondent Sefer: the immediate present, and, perhaps, on a good day and with the ever-optimistic Mr Divine to bolster him, the second right next to it, were as far as he allowed himself to think.

And that was all there was to it. He was, like Fred Bezant, established. Now, in the small isolated chamber behind the thick glass partition where he spent his days, he began his routine appraisal of the shop. He derived no pleasure from nor felt any sorrow for the patternless conglomeration of characters who wagered their money with him. If they lost, they lost; if they won, they won. It was all the same to him.

He settled himself at his desk, pushed his spectacles more comfortably on to the bridge of his nose, and stared idly at the small pile of betting-slips before him – winning ones that the punters would be in to collect almost as soon as he opened. The lucky ones. The faces that would come in smiling, relieved that they had supplemented their dole. The faces that would be able to confront their wives with a knowing, superior air. Mr Apple was forced to smile wryly to himself: he knew they would give it all back to him, probably that very day. It was, as Sefer had once remarked, not unlike life itself: you think you're ahead and all of a sudden the ground is whipped from under you and you are worse off than you ever were. But, then, Sefer revelled in dismal comparisons.

At the sound of the door slamming Mr Apple looked up, peering over the top of his thick lenses. His assistant – a term of fragile relevance – Martin Deeley trotted across the shop wearing a smile that suggested a truce in their uneasy relationship, suggested that they could, after all, both be on the same side. Mr Apple found himself smiling thinly back, measuring the strength of his smile to match the honesty of the young man's. He sighed inwardly. Perhaps, if it came to it, Martin would be on his side, but he doubted it. He was his watcher. Another shadow hovering over him, put there to keep an eye on things and make sure he fulfilled the obligations of his contract, reporting back with punctilious regularity to Seamus and the mysterious syndicate. Not that Mr Apple was supposed to know all this, and something warned him that it would be prudent to pretend he didn't.

'Morning, Mr Apple. Jesus, it's cold outside. And in here. Forgot the heating again, didn't you?'

'Good morning, Martin. Yes, I'm afraid I did.'

'Not to worry. I'll see to it. I'll see to everything. Just you leave everything to Martin Deeley.'

'Thank you.'

'Oh, that's alright. That's what I'm here for.'

'I'm sure it is.'

' – ?'

' – ?'

'Yes. Well, a cup of tea would go down well, wouldn't it?'

'Thank you, Martin.'

Martin Deeley switched on the heating and busied himself making tea, moving about the place (gathering two mugs and wiping them thoroughly with a cloth, sniffing the milk, selecting teabags) with that strange feline ease that made one wonder if his body was devoid of bone and constructed solely of fine muscle.

'I really don't know what I would do without you to look after me, Martin,' Mr Apple confessed, contriving to modulate his voice and exclude any hint of sarcasm; exclude, too, but from his mind, the uneasy, persistent feeling that his destiny was in some way linked to that of this young man who had been thrust upon him; exclude, also, from whatever region dealt with such things, the feeling of pleasure he experienced when Martin arrived each morning. For Mr Apple found deep and genuine pleasure in anything that was, to his way of thinking, beautiful, and there was little doubt that this nervous, arrogant, boastful, self-assured young watchdog could be seen to be beautiful. No doubt Martin Deeley would have agreed with this assessment, although he would have been the first to admit that his beauty was of an odd, lopsided variety. Each morning as he shaved he regretted – though in a good-humoured, mocking way – that he lacked the perfect features that would have made him outstanding and totally desirable. Still, with a subdued and perverse kind of vanity he was proud that his handsomeness wasn't blatant. He regarded his physical deficiencies as a challenge, and allocated considerable time each morning to making the best of what looks he had. His hair (thick, dark brown and usually unmanageable) was kept brushed in a sort of mini-Afro crown; a small scar from one side of his nose to the right-hand corner of his mouth constrained his upper lip to an almost permanent smile or sneer – which of these depended entirely on the light prevailing in his narrow, green, almost Oriental eyes. His nose, too, had an odd twist to it, and his rare laughter revealed very white but incredibly small teeth, as though nature had made a hash of things or decided, for unkind reasons, that his puppy-teeth would be quite adequate. Taken individually, his features bordered on the monstrous, but collectively they managed to present to a largely disinterested world a lopsided fascination that made his face very dear to him. It had also managed to outwit, or at least sidestep for the moment, the batterings of time's normal dosage of wear and tear, making him appear much younger than twenty-six.

'There you go, Mr Apple. I've even stirred it for you.'

'I don't take sugar, Martin, you – ' Mr Apple began tetchily.

'I know that. I just stirred the milk into the tea for you.'

'Oh. I'm sorry. Thank you, Martin.'

'Service with a smile. That's what I say,' Martin said, smiling extravagantly.

'I'm sure you do.'

'Oh, I do,' Martin insisted, flashing another exotic smile as though offering it as penance for his hypocrisy.

'You don't have to, you know.'

'Don't have to what?'

'Fuss over me. I mean, I can hardly give you the sack.'

Martin Deeley's wide smile froze, hung there for a moment, and was transformed into a grotesque leer as his eyes hardened. A small cruel light like that of a lynx about to make a kill flickered in them.

'I mean, how could I possibly manage without you,' Mr Apple continued, enjoying the discomfort he had created, yet annoyed with himself for having caused it.

'Oh. Well, I don't really fuss over you, Mr Apple. I just try to please,' Martin replied, his smile defrosting, and he made a great business of pouring his own tea.

'I see,' sighed Mr Apple. 'Well, it's very kind of you to take an old man under your wing.'

'My pleasure.'

And he almost meant it. There was, indeed, something very pleasurable and satisfactory in being useful to the Cause (as he still somewhat archaically thought of it), if only as what he glumly regarded as an internal spy, particularly since he was certain his current occupation was only temporary: he was, after all, was he not, far too useful and successful at riskier pursuits that called upon his wits and nerve and reflexes and stunning accuracy? Certainly he was. Oh, yes, they would very certainly need his prowess again. Who could replace him, despite Reilly's catty remark about there being an abundance of 'killers'? For more than three years Martin Deeley had been their most successful assassin, with at least seven unsolved killings to his credit. Yet, oddly, despite his reputation of being passionless and cold-blooded, there was a deep-rooted nervousness in him, a sense of vulnerability and terror. He never dared question this feeling or delve too deeply into its roots, for this would have been to admit its existence. But had he questioned it he would, no doubt, have recognized its growth as being nurtured by the memory of that horrific night when both his father and older brother had been senselessly slaughtered (quite mistakenly as it turned out) as terrorist sympathizers. Martin had been only fourteen then, and as the years passed that bloody scene had clouded in his memory. But a sharp residue remained, a lingering web of cold panic that stretched across his mind, and this was sufficient to leave him with his peculiarly callous outlook. All his actions were performed simply as chores to be fulfilled, albeit to the best of his ability, and this applied equally to creating havoc, making love and inflicting death. On those rare occasions when the strain of his curious existence seemed on the brink of getting the better of him, when he became tense – as he described those moments when he broke into a cold sweat and felt like curling up and hugging himself and sobbing quietly – he would trot along to the nearest Catholic church to kneel before the crucifix, not praying, but indulging in a gruesome daydream. He would imagine the suspended Christ as the man who had murdered his father and brother, and he would smile cruelly, gleening an exotic satisfaction from the thought of the murderer's tearing flesh. And this morbid, imaginary little drama, so precisely enacted in his mind, so vivid and lurid that his own flesh would crawl, would exhaust him to such a degree that it diffused his tenseness, calmed him, satisfied any immediate desire for revenge, and allowed him to leave the church, if not refreshed, at least in that frame of mind that allowed him to continue his existence with apparent equanimity.

And so, when Seamus Reilly had suggested that he 'retire' for the moment from his best work and adopt this new role, he threw himself into it and invested it with an importance it hardly merited. Indeed, once there in that sad, squalid little shop that the new coat of paint had done little to prettify, rubbing shoulders with the gentle, mild, rather insignificant man he had so brashly regarded as a freak, he had become quietly obsessed with his job. For it struck him – and he had several times tried to explain this to himself and failed – that there was some unfathomable mystery attached to Mr Apple which linked their lives inexorably.

'Well, it would please me, Martin,' Mr Apple was saying, his eyes fixed on his mug of tea as though addressing some reflection of Martin in the liquid, 'if you would clean the marker-board and get the betting-sheets ready for the day.'

'Right. No sooner said than done.'

'And pin up the *Sporting Life*.'

'Yessir,' Martin said, saluting.

'Go on, then.'

'I'm going.'

But not yet, apparently: he stood by Mr Apple's shoulder, watching as the bony fingers thumbed through the winning slips. 'One of these days you'll go blind counting all your winnings, Mr Apple,' he remarked innocently.

'Losses, Martin. Losses,' Mr Apple told him with equal innocence, aware that this was the overture to their daily little game of pretending neither knew the other's purpose.

'Oh, sure.'

Mr Apple looked up and peered over the top of his spectacles, smiling mischievously. 'I'll have to explain to you how it all works one day,' he said.

'Yes. I'd like that, Mr Apple. I'd like to get more involved.'

'*More* involved – ?'

'Yes. You know – '

'Oh, I know, Martin,' Mr Apple informed him, staring into his eyes.

For several moments neither of them spoke. Finally, wilting slightly, unable to sustain prolonged contact, Martin asked out of the blue: 'Tell me something – does it ever worry you – taking money from all these suckers? I mean, you know half of them can't afford to lose. Doesn't your conscience bother you?'

'Conscience?' Mr Apple asked, feigning surprise.

'Yes. Conscience.'

'Who's got conscience?' Mr Apple asked, quietly mocking.

' – ? Everyone's got conscience!'

'Oh, do they now? Well, that's very interesting.'

'You know everyone's got conscience.'

Mr Apple removed his spectacles and proceeded to polish the lenses with a large handkerchief he produced from his sleeve. 'I'll tell you something you already know, Martin. A man can jettison his conscience with the greatest ease if the fit takes him,' Mr Apple said sadly. 'Or have it numbed and made useless by others,' he added in a soft, distant voice, as though the afterthought struck him as particularly melancholy. Then he shook his head and replaced his glasses firmly on his nose, indicating that the conversation was over.

But as so often before he was wrong. 'That's a pretty morbid philosophy, Mr Apple,' Martin decided to say in the tight, slightly menacing tone he adopted when he felt people were getting at him.

'Philosophers now, are we?' Mr Apple wanted to know. 'Morbid?'

he asked. 'Mmm. Perhaps it is. True, nevertheless. Anyway, everyone gambles one way or another. You gamble everytime you take a breath.'

'That's different,' Martin said, with a small, frustrated sniff. 'You've *got* to breathe.'

'Some people have *got* to back horses. In this business you've got to work on the psychosomatic theory,' Mr Apple announced pompously, suddenly aware that he was enjoying himself again. 'Betting makes people happy if they think it makes them happy. And there are people who are only happy when they are miserable – don't you ever forget that. Besides – ' Mr Apple took off his long-suffering spectacles again and used them to stab home his next point, 'besides, who thinks about me when I lose? Answer me that. Who cares about my misfortune when they collect their winnings? To hell with him, they say. He's the bookie. *I'm* supposed to have all the ethics and all the pity. Huh. Who wants *them* for a monopoly?'

Martin Deeley shifted his feet and laughed nervously. Somehow the conversation had veered away from the course he had set for it and was escaping his control; worse, there appeared to be a darker side to everything Mr Apple said that for the moment eluded him.

'Oh, you're a wicked man, Mr Apple,' he confided, contriving to make his accusation sound like a little joke.

Alas, Mr Apple decided to see nothing amusing in it. 'Me wicked?' he demanded shrilly. '*Me* wicked?'

'I only meant it as – '

'Oh, never mind,' Mr Apple interrupted wearily, suddenly feeling very tired. Then a strange little glimmer came into his eyes and he continued: 'I'll tell you another thing, Martin,' almost whispering, as though in an odd way he hoped Martin would not hear, his voice sad. 'I think there is something, some demon deep inside you, that has turned you upside down. You make no allowances for humanity. White is white. Black is black. That's the way it is with you, Martin. No shades. No variations. You've got to learn to be flexible or you're doomed.'

'I – '

'And there's a – ' Mr Apple hesitated, mouthing, his fingers moving in strange jerky spasms as though assisting his mind to grope for the word, 'there's a hunger – yes, that's near enough – a hunger in your eyes that frightens me to death.'

In the tense, strained silence that followed this grim observation Mr Apple almost regretted having spoken. True, there was certainly something wild and evil in those green, half-closed eyes, a look of malice and unswerving direction; and yet there was an unnerving quality of pain and sadness there too, and both sadness and pain were old familiars of Mr Apple's. It had struck him before from time to time that the young man who now stood so jauntily and defiantly in front of him, his nostrils flared, the blood slowly draining from his face, seemed to have, tucked away in the shadowy and unused recesses of his soul, a disarming innocence, a strange cleanliness of spirit. Undoubtedly he had committed acts of horrendous outrage – the full atrocity of which Mr Apple knew he had yet to discover – and had done so without so much as turning a hair, had committed them brutally and with probable satisfaction. And yet: somehow Mr Apple could not shake off the impression that there was a strong loyalty in Martin that would prevent him attempting certain horrors. To Mr Apple's mind even one redeeming feature stood for a great deal: in his experience there were very few people who could be credited with any limitation of evil.

'No need for you to be frightened of me, Mr Apple.' Martin's voice slipped amicably into his thoughts.

'I'm glad to hear it.'

'I wouldn't hurt a fly.'

'It's not the flies I'm worried about.'

'Hah.'

And with that Martin was around the partition and into the shop, grinning his head off, skipping about, cleaning the marker-boards and pinning up the racing journals with that feline agility that so amazed Mr Apple. A bemused expression crossed Mr Apple's face as he watched the young man – the boy, as he seemed destined to think of him, perhaps because Sefer in one of his more glib moments had commented that he was not unlike the Minstrel Boy. He was trying in vain to recall the distant sensation of youth: his face softened, and for a moment all impressions of pain and sorrow receded from his features. But then they were back, worse than before, as was always the case after such respites, back like a burning darkness folding over his recollections. The deep, jagged lines on his forehead and cheeks returned to their habitual formations, criss-crossing his flesh like welted scars as he frowned over the betting-slips again and tried, as he usually did, to put faces to the writing on them.

How long he was involved in this harmless pastime before he was quickly brought down to earth by the loud slam of the door he could not tell. He glanced up, and made a determined and fruitful effort to keep a bland face as he watched the two soldiers cross the shop with a fretful swagger, their rubber-soled boots making tiny screeches on the linoleum. It struck him, for no good reason, that they could have been two of the Scots Guards he had seen that morning, but he could not be sure. Not that it mattered. They were all the same despite their differences in uniform: frightened (although they would never have admitted it, regarding fear as synonymous with weakness), lonely (usually hiding this in raucous shouts and ribald tomfoolery whenever the occasion permitted) young men who made slightly frenetic attempts to be friendly with the hostile natives.

Mr Apple switched his gaze for a second to Martin Deeley and was relieved to note that he was assiduously wiping yesterday's betting returns from the boards with a damp rag, just wiping and wiping away with a curiously menacing motion, as though erasing somewhat more than the figures before him. Mr Apple felt certain he could see the hairs bristle on the back of his neck.

'You Mr Bezant?' one of the soldiers wanted to know, politely enough.

Mr Apple rose with what he hoped was dignity and came close to the glass partition. 'Mr Bezant is but a name. A name peeling over our door. He is, alas, no longer with us,' he explained, spreading his hands in a curiously Zionistic gesture. 'I'm Mr Apple. Can I help?

33

You want to place a bet?'

'You the owner?'

'You could say that, yes.'

'I mean, you make the decisions?'

'Oh, I certainly make the decisions,' Mr Apple assured him.

'Ah, well, what we wanted to know...'

But whatever it was they wanted to know was not immediately to be revealed. The soldier turned from Mr Apple (who discreetly contemplated the hidden mysteries of the ceiling) to join his colleague, and indulged in whispered discussion. Mr Apple waited patiently, occupying the lengthening pause with watching Martin Deeley, who had finished wiping and stood motionless by the clean board, the damp rag suspended in mid-air, his eyes unblinking and filled with veiled threats as he, in turn, surveyed the whispering soldiers. Finally a decision was reached, and the spokesman returned to Mr Apple, grinning sheepishly.

'What we wanted to know is if we left some cash with you could we phone in some bets from the barracks? We're not really allowed in here, see?'

Mr Apple felt his breath ease itself from his lungs and pass through his lips in an almost audible hiss, suddenly realizing how tense he had been. With relief he noted from the corner of his eye that Martin, too, had relaxed, and was recleaning the already clean boards. Mr Apple gave a little cough and became businesslike.

'Certainly. We have quite a number of clients who prefer to bet by telephone for one reason or another. And we like to do all we can to help the military, don't we Martin?' he added, on the spur of the moment feeling recklessly mischievous.

'What?' snapped Martin, who had heard well enough.

'Help the military. The good men who are here to protect us from hooligans and suchlike.'

'Oh, sure,' Martin said, and flashed a venomous look across the room.

'I'm glad you think of us like that,' the soldier said innocently.

'But how else should we think of you?' Mr Apple asked, aware that he was perilously close to pushing his luck.

The question seemed to dumbfound the soldier, as though it had never occurred to him that he should be anything but hated. Then: 'Most people don't like us, you know,' he said seriously. 'They seem to think we shouldn't be here at all.'

'Oh, dear, me,' Mr Apple said, shaking his head. 'Did you hear that, Martin?'

'I heard.'

'What strange notions people have, and no mistake. Why, you're only here to keep the peace, to maintain law and order, isn't that all?'

This apparently friendly interpretation of their role seemed to embarrass both soldiers, and they shuffled and grinned to alleviate their discomfort.

'Martin, my very able assistant, will look after you gentlemen,' Mr Apple told them pleasantly. 'Leave that, Martin, and look after these gentlemen, will you?'

Martin Deeley looked as though he could have cheerfully strangled Mr Apple, but he left the board and walked behind the counter to stand facing the soldiers, his face now expressionless.

'How much do you want to leave?' he demanded.

'Twenty – no, make it twenty-five quid.'

'Huh. Big punters. Name?'

' – ?'

'Name?'

'What do you – '

'Shit. I don't want your bloody rank and serial number, just – '

'Martin.' Mr Apple curled the name upwards in mild rebuke.

'We have to have your name so we know who is calling when you pick up the telephone and dial our number and tell us what money you want to put on what horse in what race, don't we?' Martin said, his voice laden with condescension.

'Oh.'

'Yes. Oh. So?'

'Salmon.'

'As in fish?'

'Hah,' the soldier laughed goodnaturedly, though he had heard the remark a thousand times before. 'As in fish,' he confirmed.

'You be making all the bets?'

'Yes. Or him.'

'Great.' Martin sighed with exaggerated exasperation. 'And what's his name?'

'Dukham.'

'As in?'

'Yes. As in.'

'Doesn't he speak?'

'He speaks.'

'But not a lot, eh?'

'Not a lot.'

'Strong silent type, I suppose,' Martin supposed, not bothering to conceal the sarcasm in his voice, nor, indeed, the sneer that crossed his mouth.

'Right. I think we've got that straight. Twenty-five pounds for Salmon and Dukham. Here's your receipt with our phone number on it,' he added, and handed over the slip of paper. 'And, by the way, we don't give credit – when you've lost your twenty-five that's it until you leave some more.'

'*If* we lose.'

'You'll lose.'

'Thanks.'

'Don't mention it. And thank *you* for your business, gents. Now if you'll excuse me I have work to do.' Fucking Scottish bastards.

'Thanks for your help.' Both soldiers, perhaps from force of habit, made as if to salute, but it was a half-hearted effort and fizzled out into something approaching a wave. With that they strode out, trailing another whispered conspiratorial conversation behind them.

'You handled that very well indeed, Martin,' Mr Apple announced without looking up.

'You did that on purpose, didn't you?'

'Did what? Asked you to help by serving the customers? But I thought that was why you were here – to assist?'

'You know I hate the bastards.'

'Really? Good heavens, I had no idea.'

'Like hell you didn't.'

'I didn't even realize you knew them,' Mr Apple said.

'I don't.'

'You don't?' Mr Apple repeated mockingly. 'But how can you possibly hate someone you don't know, Martin?'

'You know what I mean.'

'I wish I did.'

'You know a hell of a lot more than you let on, too.'

'Whatever do you mean by that?' Mr Apple was anxious to know.

But whatever reply might have been forthcoming was forestalled by the door to the shop slamming again. It was eleven o'clock, the hour when the lure of the betting-shop became strongest, and the day's traffic began in the shape of an old, bent man in a flat cap and carrying a plastic shopping-bag, who crept across the shop to the far wall as though pushed from behind by the enormous hand of reluctant optimism. He glued his watery eyes to the prognostications of *Sporting Life*, a rebellious nerve jumping spasmodically below his right jaw. Martin lounged against the counter and watched for a while, then shifted his gaze restlessly, finally allowing it to settle on the small bald patch on the crown of Mr Apple's head, which nodded away, methodically mournful, as he fingered again his accumulating losses.

'Another customer,' Mr Apple said aloud without losing the rhythm of his arithmetic.

' – ?'

'Behind you.'

'Oh.'

Martin turned to the counter and took the yellow slip of paper which the man in the cap offered: a fifty-pence accumulator on nine horses. 'Some bet,' he remarked, trying not to sound patronizing and almost succeeding.

'Jonjo and Francome,' the man pointed out. 'I always back Jonjo and Francome. Don't care what they ride.'

'Good, are they?'

'The best,' the man said with fierce conviction. 'And I've a feeling they'll win for me today,' he added confidentially, as though revealing a dark but profitable secret, as though, too, both jockeys had only his interest at heart.

'Sure to,' Martin said.

'And if not today there's always tomorrow.'

'That's true. Well, good luck.'

'That's all it takes, sonny,' the man told him happily, and shuffled out of the shop. His gait was more confident now that he had sealed his fate.

'Another big punter,' Martin remarked. 'Bahamas this year on the profits, Mr Apple.'

'Don't mock,' Mr Apple scolded gently. 'Every little helps.' There were times when he amazed even himself with the way he treated the business as if it was his own, worrying about losses, cheered by gains – as though any of this mattered to him.

'I nearly told him to take his fifty pence and stuff it – he *can't* win.'

Mr Apple put an elastic band round the counted dockets and patted them flat before turning round. '*I* know that, Martin. *You* know that. So who are we? *He* thinks he *can* win. That's all that matters. Why try and destroy the man's faith in his own judgement?'

'That's a load of crap.'

'Why so? He walked in here and made his choice and had the courage to follow it through despite the odds against him.' Mr Apple peered as usual over his spectacles at Martin, and the solemnity of his tone seemed to suggest there might be something significant in what he had said.

'Some judgement.'

'Yours is better?'

'I don't – '

'Oh, not about horses. You're far too bright a specimen to indulge in that sort of thing. No, I meant about your own preoccupations. You make your own sane judgements and back them up? Of course you do. But you're a very clever chap, aren't you? You want to know

38

something? You're so fierce you can't even see the truth when it stares you in the face.'

'Thanks.'

'The truth is – '

The door slammed again. Mr Apple stopped abruptly and stared at the man in his late twenties who had entered the shop, followed by a woman of approximately the same age. What was remarkable about them was that they were almost identical, even to the haunted look in their eyes; remarkable, too, was the impression they gave of being inseparable, as though the man was doomed to be eternally followed by some transvestite image of himself. As he came closer, Mr Apple put on his glasses and recognized him as a client who had lost considerable money the day before; had indeed lost regularly for several days.

'Mr Apple,' the man said, with a small nod.

Mr Apple came to the counter and waited, sensing unpleasantness.

'You know me,' the man stated in a voice that dared contradiction.

'I've seen you, certainly,' Mr Apple allowed, spreading his hands palms upwards and giving a little shrug.

'I'm Terry Duggan.'

'Mr Duggan.' Mr Apple allowed a whisp of a smile.

'My wife.' Duggan indicated behind him without turning round.

'Mrs Duggan,' Mr Apple said, allowing his wisp of a smile to return momentarily, although this time it seemed to be more sympathetic.

'I was in yesterday,' the man began.

'I remember.'

'And he lost everything we had,' Mrs Duggan interrupted. She pushed past her husband and pressed her gaunt, drawn face against the glass. 'He lost *everything*,' she whispered, but with such intensity it sounded like a roar.

So that was it.

'Shut up,' Duggan ordered his wife. 'Sorry, Mr Apple,' he apologized; more, it seemed for his evasiveness than for having been

39

cut short.

'I understand,' Mr Apple told him, and he did.

'Can you help us?'

'Help you?'

'Oh, boy!' Martin Deeley snorted in the background.

'Quiet, Martin,' Mr Apple said quickly. 'How can I help you?'

'Lend us some of the money back until next Thursday.'

'We have nothing to eat,' Mrs Duggan explained with a wail.

'Shut up, Molly,' Duggan told his wife again.

'And I suppose the next thing is the houseful of kids dying of starvation,' Martin put in. 'Hey, this isn't some bloody moneylender's, you know,' he added, on the one hand fulfilling the duty imposed on him by Seamus Reilly, and on the other protecting Mr Apple, whom he felt would be a sucker for this sort of sob-story.

'I'll deal with this, Martin,' Mr Apple said, half-smiling. 'How much do you need?'

Immediately, a small light of greed flickered in Terry Duggan's eyes. He looked away for a moment; when he faced Mr Apple again all trace of it was gone, replaced by his former misery. 'Twenty?' he suggested optimistically.

'I'll let you have five.'

'Five!' Molly Duggan shrieked, her humiliation making her belligerent. 'What can we hope to get for five pounds?' she demanded.

'Can't you make it fifteen?' Duggan asked, prepared to haggle.

'Five,' insisted Mr Apple, who wasn't.

'Ten?'

'Five.' Mr Apple was getting annoyed as he swivelled his face imperviously between the two supplicants.

'You're *mean*,' Molly Duggan screamed at him, as if this was her most appalling condemnation.

'Yes,' agreed Mr Apple. 'I'm mean.' He turned to walk back to his desk.

'All right. Five,' Duggan said quickly.

'Shit!' Martin exclaimed. 'Don't you give them anything, Mr

Apple. Don't you give them a goddam penny.'

But Mr Apple had made up his mind. He reached into the money-drawer, took out five one-pound notes and shoved them across the counter, quickly withdrawing his hand as Molly Duggan lunged at them.

'What the hell did you give in to them for?' Martin demanded as the door slammed behind them.

Mr Apple blinked and gave a little shrug. 'I don't really know,' he confessed, staring at the empty shop that the Duggans' wretchedness seemed to have left even shabbier. He rubbed his eyes in a gesture of weariness. 'Pity?' he suggested meekly.

'Pity, my arse.'

'I really don't know, Martin.' And that was the truth.

'Well, it's five pounds you can kiss goodbye. You'll never see it or them again.'

Mr Apple brightened perceptibly. 'That could be good enough reason in itself, don't you think, Martin?' he asked, keeping his face impassive.

'Very funny. It's no way to run a business.'

'It will come out of my own pocket. My good deed for the day.'

'Huh.'

It was something of a relief after the Duggans when May van Dyke made her boisterous appearance in the doorway. She was small and fat with hard brown skin like tanned leather, and she had long since abandoned any attempt to control the growth of her dark moustache. Her husband, a floundering Dutch seaman whom she had only too willingly befriended, was Jewish, and through her long years of unstable marriage May had taken on many of his mannerisms. Perhaps by so doing she felt she was getting something out of the relationship. 'Here we go again, Mr Apple. Another small donation towards your Rolls Royce.' She passed over an intricate collection of Yankees and Patents that she had worked out with great precision. She had once made a considerable killing and this had whetted her appetite: if she could do it once she could do it again, couldn't she? She was a steady, reliable client, and a pleasant one despite her tendency to chatter endlessly.

'You'll break me one day, May,' Mr Apple told her in mock anguish.

'Sure I will,' May agreed, and there was an edge to her voice, despite her smiling face, that suggested she meant it.

'You'll have to give *me* a job then. I could be your financial adviser.'

'You've got it, Mr Apple. And you can bring that one along, too,' May told him, indicating Martin, who blushed furiously. 'He could advise me on other things,' she concluded, laughing raucously.

'We needn't worry, then, need we?' Mr Apple smiled, enjoying Martin's embarrassment.

'Hah,' said May, and Mr Apple felt she would have tweaked his cheek if she could have reached him. 'I'll be in tomorrow to collect, you hear?'

'I hear, May.'

'Byeeeee,' May sang, and waddled out of the shop clutching her handbag (in which, it was rumoured, she kept her more valuable trinkets in a small plastic bag: scraps of cheap jewellery, foreign notes and coinage, and a scapula to remind her of her long-forgotten faith) to her bouncing, unsupported breasts.

'Goodbye, May,' Mr Apple called, stapling the bet and placing it on top of the capped man's optimistic accumulator. 'Twelve eleven,' he murmured, glancing at the electric clock on the wall.

'And thirty-eight seconds,' Martin supplied.

Mr Apple stretched. Just under an hour before racing started.

The Extel had just started its waking crackles when three men walked in: Mr Apple had seen two of them before, but it was the third who claimed his attention. He was not particularly well dressed, but he wore his clothes with the air of a man who should have been. He had a cold, aloof bearing that Mr Apple recognized and associated with many men he would have preferred to forget. With his clean white shirt, his Windsor-knotted, striped tie, polished shoes and neatly pressed trousers the man could have been mistaken for an underpayed civil servant with an interest in, say, moths. Until the immobile face caught your eye: that pallid, stoatlike face dominated by pale-blue, opaque eyes filled with restless, wary suspicion. And in the menacing radiance of that face Mr Apple's situation took on its true meaning, and he found himself dizzy and trembling.

The man, flanked at close quarters by his two companions, crossed swiftly to the counter and summoned Mr Apple's attention by pointing one finger in the air. 'Everything all right?' he demanded abruptly in a surprisingly high-pitched voice.

'Yes,' replied Mr Apple, feeling his chin and sighing inwardly with relief that he had remembered to shave.

'Payouts?'

'A few. Nothing very big.'

'How big?'

'Three hundred, give or take.'

'Not much.'

Mr Apple shrugged his shoulders by way of apology for the stupidity of his clients. 'No. Not much.'

The man pursed his lips and thought for a moment. Finally he removed a thick brown envelope from his inside pocket and passed it over the counter. 'Spread this out,' he ordered. 'Eight, maybe ten bets on losing favourites.'

Mr Apple took the envelope. 'I know how to spread it,' he said. The man looked taken aback by this remark, and he frowned again. He allowed a thin smile to bypass his eyes and make its faltering appearance on his lips. 'I'm sure you do.'

'Yes. I do.'

'Good. Well, I want all that gone by today. There'll be plenty more this week and we don't want any of it hanging about.'

'Very well,' Mr Apple said.

'In fact you'll be seeing a lot of me in the future,' the man went on. 'We have had a number of satisfactory transactions.'

'I'm glad to hear it.'

'So, as I say, you'll be seeing a lot more of me.'

'I look forward to that,' Mr Apple lied.

'I'm sure you do. By the way, the usual for yourself is in there – in a separate envelope.'

'Thank you.'

'You've earned it – so far. We always pay well for a job well done.' There was in his politeness that icy quality of condescension that killers seem to possess, as if their superiority were of such standing that they could afford largesse towards their victims. 'Nothing else you need?'

Mr Apple shook his head. 'Not a thing.'

'Good. If you do need anything, let us know.'

'I will.'

'Good,' the man said again. 'Good. I won't keep you any longer,' and true to his word he left the shop, halting only briefly for the door to be opened for him.

When he had gone Mr Apple found himself with a dreadful headache. He tried to rid himself of it and the memory of those lifeless eyes by fussing about, overdoing his interest in some customers (who now came fast and furious into the shop), disputing nothing, ridding himself of others by pretending to be overworked.

The squawking voice of the commentator filled the shop and Mr Apple's consciousness as he took bets, paid out on winners and forged betting-slips to dispose of the contents of the envelope, his eyes watering as the shop filled with cigarette smoke and the distinctive stench of nervous tension. Occasionally he glanced at the faces of his clients: they wore stoicism like armour, refusing to let even the smallest expression reveal that they were losing. All through the long afternoon they came and went, some staying longer than others, the shop groaning under the weight of their frustrations. And through all this Mr Apple could feel the pale-blue eyes boring into him. Watching him, too, but in a different way, he could feel the eyes of Martin Deeley, who as he marked the prices for each race and wrote up the results wondered to himself what really went on behind Mr Apple's bland expression. There was a secret there, he was sure, and something warned him that he would not like it when he discovered what it was. But discover it he would.

As the last despondent customer left the shop, and Martin clattered about tidying up, the telephone rang, and Mr Apple went to answer it.

'Mr Apple?'

'Speaking.'

'Seamus.'

'Yes.'

'Our replacement man was in today.'

'Yes, he came.'

'Everything in order?'

'Yes.'

'No problems?'

'None.'

'No complaints?'

'Complaints?'

'He was respectful?'

Mr Apple suddenly longed to laugh, but he managed to contain himself.

'Yes, he was respectful.'

'Excellent. We don't want anyone to upset you.'

'Thank you. He was respectful,' Mr Apple said again.

'Excellent,' the voice of Reilly repeated, and went on: 'Our syndicate has come into some rather unexpected profits this week, so we will have quite a bit of business.'

'He told me.'

'Oh. Good.' Reilly sounded peeved. 'The syndicate also wish me to express our satisfaction with your – eh – management.'

Mr Apple said nothing.

'Mr Apple?'

'Yes?'

'Oh, I thought you were gone. I was saying – '

'Yes. I heard. Thank you.'

'Right. Well, if everything is going smoothly – '

'It is.'

'Fine. I'll be in touch. By the way, anything you need?'

'Nothing. Thank you.'

'Sure?'

'Quite sure.'

'Well, if ever there is...' Reilly allowed his voice to trail off, suggesting that anything without reservation could be supplied.

'Thank you.'

And with that the phone went dead.

Mr Apple was still holding the receiver in his hand when he noticed Martin standing by his shoulder. 'Martin,' Mr Apple began, but immediately regretted it.

'Yes, Mr Apple?'

Mr Apple replaced the receiver and sighed. 'Nothing.'

'Oh, come on. You were going to say something.'

'Nothing of importance. It doesn't matter.'

'Christ, it really bugs me when you do that: start something and then stop.'

'The story of our lives, Martin.'

'Shit.'

The two of them stood quietly in the deserted shop, and perhaps it was because both of them felt oddly secure in this atmosphere of despair that they felt an intimacy neither of them welcomed.

'All those suckers,' Martin said, to break the silence.

Mr Apple nodded and started tidying his desk.

'Well, I'll be off, then. See you in the morning, Mr Apple. Have a good night and don't do anything I wouldn't do.'

Mr Apple smiled. 'You can count on that, Martin. Good-night.'

Mr Apple, alone, started to put the shop to bed, as he humorously liked to think of it. He put the takings in the safe and switched on the burglar alarm, feeling, as he did every evening, an intense desire to set it off. Instead, he put on his heavy overcoat, his scarf and his hat, and walked lightly across the shop to the door, tip-toeing almost, absurdly scared that he might stand on someone's shattered illusions and dreams of instant wealth. He put out the lights and shut the door behind him, rattling it to make certain it was securely closed.

Well done, my friend, said Mr Divine gaily. Now we can off home and enjoy ourselves.

Same old boring evening, opined Sefer miserably.

46

Life is what you take out of it, Mr Divine said accusingly.

Rubbish, declared Sefer.

'He's right, you know,' said Mr Apple, and coughed hurriedly as a passer-by glanced at him curiously.

He stood for a moment in the doorway breathing in the fresh, bitter night air, and braced himself for the long trudge through the snow. Then, straightening his shoulders in the manner of a man about to take the plunge, he began walking away from the grey little street towards his home and the inevitably ravenous, complaining Chloe.

Of course, as he might have guessed, nothing was to be as simple as that; how could he have expected it to be? Even what should have been a reasonably unhazardous journey from one location to another was to be filled with frustrations, it seemed.

Mr Apple plodded on, bending his body as though shaping it aerodynamically to cut through the wind, the cold, muddy slush making his poor feet ache, making him think of concentration camps and long marches made by the prisoners. Galoshes would be an answer, he advised himself. And it was while his mind pondered those old-fashioned rubber overshoes and conjured up amusing visions of himself wearing them that suddenly, as he rounded the corner of the Antrim Road, he was pounced upon, and, before he fully realized what was happening, he found himself spreadeagled against the hard, cold brick wall, and was being frisked and searched. Nothing was said: the silence and rapid efficiency of the soldiers gave them a dark malevolence out of proportion to their activities. As one searched, two others, one on either side of him, pointed their rifles in the general direction of his knees. Only when the one searching him was satisfied that he was, for the moment at any rate, harmless did one of the others make a gesture of dismissal with his gun. 'You can go,' he said.

It was this casual attitude to his humiliation that made Mr Apple feel suddenly very angry. For a moment he stood staring at the soldiers (who stared back, bemused, unused to this unaccustomed confrontation), contemplating a protest of some description, but life had taught him the folly of protesting against superior odds. He bathed them instead in a knowing, sardonic smile, and strode away with as much dignity as the slippery conditions underfoot would allow.

Perhaps it was the delayed shock of the assault, or perhaps it was because he felt a small celebration was in order, or perhaps just because he simply felt like one; in any case, he yearned unexpectedly for a drink. And it *was* unexpected, for Mr Apple had long since given up alcohol, abandoning its notorious seduction as a source of consolation. Still, one small drink wouldn't do him any harm, the jovial Mr Divine was hinting, and with the idea implanted it didn't take even that persuasion for the desire to become a craving, despite the persistent tut-tutting of the disapproving Sefer. Mr Apple increased his pace and hurried towards the beckoning lights of The White Bird.

'You look like you could use a drink,' the barman said, with sparkling insight.

'I do.'

' – ?'

'Whiskey. A double.'

'Coming up.'

Mr Apple balanced himself precariously on the edge of one of the stools by the bar.

'Anything in it?'

'No.' Mr Apple spoke with uncharacteristic sharpness. He sensed in the publican's unctuous tones the same bland hypocrisy he showed his own clients, and he had no wish to be reminded of that just now. He had only time to take one sip and feel his nerves recover a little before the door burst open and four soldiers, their faces smeared with warpaint, their rifles at the ready, thumped into the pub. Mr Apple watched their progress in the mirror behind the bar. Good God, they seemed to be everywhere tonight. He glanced uneasily at the barman and for a split second the man's face revealed his loyalty: his lips were drawn back slightly, his eyes glazed over and expressionless, his body rigid as though coiled and taut and ready for firing. Fortunately, he was practised in these things and knew how best to handle such intrusions, knew that it was really quite simple to lull these nervous interlopers into a sense of well-being. He produced a smile under his hostile eyes and ventured a touch of jollity in his voice.

'Hello, lads. Not drinking on duty, are we?'

The soldiers gazed about the empty bar, one of them wrinkling his nose as though sniffing out terrorists, another cocked his head as though listening; yet a third tried a tentative smile until he saw the glower on his superior's face. The smile did not fade: it switched off with electric swiftness.

'Come on, have one on the house. You'll freeze your balls off out there tonight.'

The leader of the pack (as Mr Apple found himself thinking of them, wondering giddily if, indeed, they were following him for some demented reasons of their own; perhaps they were renegades up to no good, *bandidos* – ha! –) jerked his head. What looked like a nervous tick turned out to be an order to withdraw. They retreated in unison, actually marching backwards, their precision endowing the moment with a strange overtone of terror.

'Cunts,' the barman said under his breath, and then quickly looked at Mr Apple.

Mr Apple pretended not to have heard. It was better not to hear anything these days; not to notice anything, either, like the nervous twitches that had suddenly come to life on the barman's face. Mr Apple drank slowly and deliberately: the deliriums and horrors of not so long ago never seemed to fade completely.

'No wonder people won't...a man...quiet drink...a little peace...'
The barman's voice floated into his brain and out again, replaced by other voices that gibbered in his consciousness, voices from another time: deceptively friendly voices emanating from flat brown faces:

– *Por qué no?* –

– *Cómo se llama?* –

– *Antichrista* –

– *No se puede vivir sin amar* –

Mr Apple finished his drink with a swift gulp and hurried from the bar, hearing the barman roar for payment, failing to recognize it as such, associating it with those other voices that battered and besieged him. 'Why can't you leave me alone?' he cried.

He was out of breath when he reached home, though he could not remember running, could remember nothing of the short journey: like so many things in his life, it had been conveniently blacked out for the time being by that benign angel who watched over such things. But Mr Apple was well aware that it would be recalled at some future date, recalled and dreaded and used by wild and wilful demons to torment him.

And later, to wash away the thought of future recollections, Mr Apple undressed and took a long, leisurely lukewarm shower. The rattling water drowned the recalcitrant voices that clamoured for attention in his ears. He was sadly aware that the demons and voices would muster during the night to harry him in his fretful sleep, prod him into wakefulness and, by their threats of shattering nightmares, make sleep a dreadful thing. He soaped his body carefully, feeling briefly ashamed at the tenderness he showed himself; feeling, too, like laughing at the preposterous figure he presented. For Mr Apple, undressed, was a sorry sight, the more so as the caressing water from the shower stroked his flesh into unaccustomed contours of relaxation, making him featureless, accentuating the spindly legs that bowed slightly under the weight of his elongated body, which was dominated by a stomach that bulged out and down as though charitably but vainly trying to secrete his wizened little penis. The straight, horizontal, equidistant scars on either side of his chest gave the impression that his ribs had been removed, one by one, with artful surgery. His back, too, was decorated (it was the only word to use) with scars, though these were of more haphazard design, perhaps indicating that the surgeon had made several abortive attempts before finally deciding on the correct location for his incision, or had been drunk, or mad. Across his buttocks a cruel game of surgical noughts and crosses appeared to have been played, the circles like gaping mouths, the crosses like blasphemous crucifixes. Yet when Mr Apple dried himself and, putting on his rather natty spotted pyjamas, concealed his lacerated body, little hint remained of the awful tortures he had undergone except the fear he carried on his face and, if one spotted it, the measured care of his walk.

For several hours Mr Apple lay on his bed writing in an old exercise book. On the shelf above his bed were several more volumes of such writings, stacked neatly between a faded photograph of his mother cuddling a disconcerted Bedlington terrier, and a large stone rubbed smooth and shiny like some dark metal. Indecipherable scribbles covered the pages of these volumes, all written in the same distinctive script, half-crabbed, half-generous, the words sloping steeply downwards, the whole giving the impression of restless movement as if the words had taken on a life of their own and were pacing out some sad and furious misery.

When he had finished his entry Mr Apple glanced back over what he had written, not so much rereading the words as plucking from the pages phrases that conjured up the whole. 'Unusual monotony', 'Mild if inevitable harrassment', 'Oddly disproportionate fear', these were three that disentangled themselves from the blur of writing before him, along with 'Amused at Martin's intrepid practised disinterest', 'Air of chill foreboding as the latest dark avenging angel appeared with instructions', 'Faceless antagonists', 'Plausible and deadly...'

It was, no doubt, this appearance of yet one more sinister angel in his life that made Mr Apple frown and wonder if there was, in fact, anything horribly portentous in his choice of title. And, almost as though he had been waiting patiently in the wings for just this cue, Sefer interrupted with: Verify it, Mr Apple. Always verify. And substantiate, added Mr Divine. Always substantiate.

'Thank you,' Mr Apple found himself saying.

Don't mention it.

Don't mention it.

Mr Apple reached to the shelf above his head and withdrew one of the earliest volumes of his writing, blowing on it gently to remove any dust that might have accumulated. For several moments he held it before him without opening it, staring at the oddly foreign design on the cover. A look of blank, studied trepidation gradually suffused his face: that almost comic, resigned, woeful look beloved of celluloid heroines as they held telegrams from the war office telling them that their loved ones were missing, presumed dead. And, certainly, Mr Apple was aware that something approaching his own death was contained in the book on his lap. With a small sigh of what could have been relief, but was probably resignation, he opened his diary and started reading. The pages he chose were well thumbed, the corners discoloured by constant turning, worn thin and in danger of disintegrating, as if the pages contained some beloved text to be read and reread: the consoling text of a beloved mystic whose wisdom had the power to enlighten the world. Enlightenment, alas, was far from Mr Apple's mind as he dragged himself back over one of the darkest passages of his life.

...and, again, awakening from a fretful snatch of sleep, it seemed still to be night, or if night was still to come I was in a darkness streaked with grey and filled with the sounds associated with daylight and noises that existed in another time; daemonic mariachi bands trumpeting out of key, my name being screamed by instruments of higher pitch, by voices not quite human, screamed in derision, those voices taking shimmering human shapes, floating, and being pointed to by sombre, unsmiling *bandidos* as they dismounted their sweating horses and clamoured to torment me, spectres of the dark; the yelping of pariah dogs, the incessant cacophony of exotic cockerels heralding a never-approaching dawn; the draining heat made all the worse – why, I could not imagine, unless my mind was weighed down under the load of other images – by the stones continually pelted at the walls of that infernal hut wherein they kept me prisoner for what could have been months but was only days. And for all I tried I could not make them understand. How to explain to those flat, hard faces that, yes, I loved them and was sent by princes to save them? How I had reached into the very deepest recesses of my soul and grasped at every branch and root which might assist me in their salvation; how my visions of their redemption brought bright blue summer evenings to my soul, uplifting my flagging spirit, my tormented spirit, and placing it in the wake of a golden scroll of travelling light...

Mr Apple shifted his position and closed his eyes for a moment. Small beads of perspiration gathered on his brow despite the coldness of the room.

...I tried only to make them understand the sadness, the bitter, bitter loneliness of my life before the seven spirits came and raised me; to make them understand that they were the chosen ones on whom I had been told to bestow the everlasting light, to guide them through waterless places, seeking rest which somewhere we must find. I tried to give them dignity, to assure them that every precious stone was their covering, to make them believe they could raise their lives above the stars of God. But when, on what was to be my final visit to that village, that accursed village set in the outrageous glories of the terraced foothills of the Sierra Madre Oriental and protected by those two masters of the earth Popocatepetl and Ixtaccihuatl that rose clear and magnificent though silenced by the power that I was sent to battle above the squalor of their homes, when they welcomed me in the brightness of day and waited only for the shadows of night to attack me (but I, being warned, knew and wept but dried my tears, telling myself, lying again to those factions that lied back, that loneliness and rejection made man stronger, allowing the warm mist that fed on the weeping summits of the great volcanoes to wrap itself about me, conceal me, shelter me from the horror I knew was to come) and drag me through the open street of that village, through the open sewer, and spit on me, curse me, call me pariah and *Antichrista*...

Mr Apple found himself trembling violently, his body damp with sweat. What he read he read for the hundredth time, something urging him to keep the episode alive and vital in his mind. He found himself glancing nervously about the room; strange odours seemed to rise about him, the stench of humid heat and excrement and overwhelming fear that had assailed his senses in the small wooden shed with the corrugated-iron roof into which he had been thrown. Mr Apple continued to read, entranced.

...It was, ominously, the Day of the Dead when they finally pulled me out and manhandled me to the square and dumped my aching body in front of the small church, the bell tolling *Dolente, Dolore* or some such lachrymose incantation, while all I could see, or remember seeing, was the cold, unforgiving eyes of the legless beggar as he squatted outside the cantina, those eyes that mutely accused me of trying to destroy the faith that gave some meaning to his useless life. How wrong he was! I was the saviour! Then, four men grabbed me and held me down: two by the arms and two by the legs. I stared at their faces: faces made darker by the light of the flickering candles behind them, brown, hard eyes, wide, flared nostrils, trickles of saliva running from the corners of their grinning Indian mouths. And then he who appeared to be their guiding spirit (who only days before had welcomed me with open arms, embraced me, said I was his brother, accepted my gifts, swore eternal friendship, insisted his house was mine, shared his bottle of Anis del Mono with me – and refused to wipe the mouth of the bottle after I had drunk lest I be insulted, lest, too, this new found brotherhood be erased by the same gesture) was standing over me, towering in his importance, hatred shining from his eyes as brightly as the candles flashed on the thin, curved knife he held aloft in his hand. I tried, ah, dear spirits of my darkness, how I tried if only with my eyes to tell him he had got it all wrong, that I loved him only as I loved all mankind, and loving him wished to share what I believed to be my salvation with him, that I respected his courage and magnificent dignity in the face of his appalling poverty, but he would see none of this. And just before he started his savage laceration of my flesh do you know what I noticed? I noticed how unbelievably courtly and refined and delicate his hands were despite the grime that lodged so permanently in his skin. And then the pain. Oh, dear and holy ghosts of goodness, the pain! The searing of a million white-hot needles that travelled, not all at once but in procession (like, indeed, these villagers would process later in memory of their dead), slowly, through every fibre of my body to lodge, finally and in agony, in my brain. And through the white-and-scarlet haze of my suffering I saw my erstwhile brother dancing, a sliver of my flesh held high like some heroic trophy, laughing and playing to the cheers and applause of his pathetic audience. He pranced above me like some avenging angel, like the spirit of his ancestors bent on retribution, and I knew that even yet he was not satisfied. His eyes foretold massive mutilation, warned of such disfigurement that I would from then on be regarded with loathing and revulsion. He leaned over me, crouching, the piece of flesh he had already taken dangling from his mouth. Down came the knife again, but this time incising with dainty strokes my chest and through the pain I knew he was using my ribs as guidelines for his attack. Suddenly he stopped and stood erect. Summoning all the saliva he could find in his dry throat he spat at me, whipped my flesh from his mouth and flung it from him. A curious growling and snarling filled my consciousness, a horrible sound that could, I thought, have emanated only from the lowest regions of hell; then it dawned on me that it was only the pariah dogs covetting my body, the smell of blood arousing their instinctive savagery. The true horrific possibilities of this that jittered in my mind were cut short as I was turned on my stomach and the whipping began. It was like a grim satanic party: villagers queued to strike my back and buttocks (as they would queue later to kiss the feet of their protecting saint) as the raw-hide whip was passed from hand to hand, surges of laughter rising each time my body flinched, great roars arising as they sacrificed me on the altar of their hatred...

Mr Apple hurled the book across the room and buried his head in the pillow, clasping it about his ears, his long, scarred body heaving. And it was the best part of an hour before he moved again, dragging himself across the room to retrieve the book, smooth the pages, and replace it on the shelf. Then he climbed into bed and lay there quietly waiting for sleep to release him.

Martin Deeley also lay in his bed, in the small rented room where he lodged, and stared into the darkness, pretending to be endowed with extraordinary night-vision which allowed him to make out the strangely diverse possessions that surrounded him. But each was unidentifiable, anonymous, except for the small wooden crucifix with its white plastic Christ. It was no more than a declaration of his allegiances in the awful struggle that persisted in the province. Yet, lying there, naked but pleasantly warmed by an electric blanket, Martin Deeley seemed at peace with the world, seemed almost an innocent.

As always, however, just when everything held out the promise of a peaceful night, the voices began to gabble in the dark: wholly familiar by now, so familiar that he welcomed their nocturnal intrusion if only because they suspended his isolation...

Mam sat there hugging herself and rocking crazily in her chair, her hair uncombed, her face grey and streaked with tears, his two sisters on the sofa, staring at their fingers that twisted and untwined themselves endlessly, making spires and steeples and churches and all the people in them, everyone longing to comfort the other but none of them knowing how. Only Martin showed no sign of the tragedy that had befallen them. He sat aloof and alone at the table, eating solemnly, chewing each mouthful soberly several times as though recalling some admonition he had been given as a child, each mouthful determinedly swallowed as if the sustenance it gave would strengthen his mind and help him erase or at least accept the grim memories that harrassed him. Curiously, it was not so much the fact that his father and brother had been shot, nor that they had been dumped in a waterlogged ditch, but that their hands had been tied behind their backs before the bullets blew their faces away, giving them, as it were, no reasonable chance of defending themselves, that seared him.

Oh, I knew it would come to this one day, Mam said to nobody in particular, as Cissy and Jo continued to twiddle their fingers with eyes downcast, and Martin forced himself to eat the congealing stew, his thin face close to the plate, shovelling in food in quick darts like a Chinaman plying chopsticks.

Oh, I knew it would come to this, Mam repeated.

So you knew, Martin said between mouthfuls, his voice rough and bitter. The reality of death was easy enough to cope with, but Mam's

56

sing-song lamentations were too much.

And you'll be the next, Mam went on, diving now into the future. Ah, dear Jesus, what a waste. What a waste. All being taken from me. It wasn't worth the pain of having you all.

It wasn't a waste, Martin snapped defiantly. He knew it probably was, but to have admitted it, even to himself, would have left his own apparently inevitable fate perilously open to a similar dismissal, and that was something he had no intention of allowing.

And you could have stopped them, Mam suddenly screamed, her eyes wild and blazing at her son, waiting for some reaction, watching how he ignored her, ignored them all, his thin arrogant face scowling at the empty plate in front of him. They would have listened to you and not gone out, she went on. You know they would have listened to you. They always listened to you and your easy remarks — that was the trouble. Always listening to you and your smooth talk.

I didn't know it was —

You didn't know! Of course you knew. You know everything. Look at you! Mam rattled on, the words possessing her, her voice rising to a shrill whine. Like some wild animal you are. The lot of you. Like wild animals with your fine talk about defending us all and doing it all for the country. Like wild hunted animals, that's what you are, and savage, waiting to kill or be killed. Oh, Jesus, Jesus, Mam concluded, dropping her voice with automatic reverence and retiring into the solace of the holy name.

Shut up, Mam.

And Mam shut up, but only because she could think of nothing more to say. She continued, however, to stare at her remaining son with swollen eyes: sometimes she felt she hated him, hated his cool, unruffled way of dealing with things, hated the way nothing seemed to touch him. She had even taken to believing that some heavenly wrath was punishing her by making her the mother of this monstrous, coldblooded child.

Don't you tell our Mam to shut up, Cissy said out of the blue, more for want of something to say than by way of rebuke.

Martin raised his head slowly and glared sullenly at the two girls, detesting them for taking sides against him. He had the small satisfaction of watching them wilt under his withering gaze. Then he leaned back, clasping his hands behind his head, and closed his eyes with a resigned sigh.

Martin Deeley tossed restlessly in his bed. The memory of that last night at home had become unusually painful. Since then he had suffered the unwelcome intrusion of a loneliness that was both alien and unfathomable. Yet it was this very loneliness, this strange, majestic isolation he continued to impose on himself, that had proved his greatest asset. He could be trusted to speak to no one except in a flippant, shallow way. He would carry out his instructions to the letter, revelling in his attention to detail, and retreat to his room with only the phantoms of his victims for company. He made no friends, though several people thought they had established just such a relationship with him. He carefully limited his sexual activities, imagining on one of his wilder flights of fancy that too much indulgence would bring about some deterioration in his prowess with a gun, and also, perhaps more importantly, because he wanted no intruders trespassing on his private isolation. It seemed a long time since his unerring marksmanship had been spotted at the rifle range of a travelling fair. He had been informed many months later that his craft – as it was put – was needed. He was flattered, his ego bolstered, and he never really thought about his violence, only harboured a vague feeling of power, though sometimes the exquisite sensation created in his loins left him feeling drowsy and peaceful as he dismantled his rifle and vanished into the night. Always the night. Not that he would have hesitated to kill during daylight had he been so ordered; but Martin Deeley was so reliable he was never given instructions as to time or place. So, while his victims determined their own place of execution, he chose his own time, and it was always in darkness. Someone had once told him death should always be inflicted at night so that God would not notice, and he sometimes wondered if, in his case, there was something in this, and that it was to outwit God that he chose darkness. Not that it really mattered, religion had become little more than a sort of tribal definition for him, a symbolism imposed shortly after birth which was mostly a nuisance but, at the same time, created the only identity he knew.

Well, he had been put out to grass (and he grinned in the darkness at the unintentional ambiguity) for a while. But they would need him again, wouldn't they? Certainly they would. Martin Deeley was indispensable, he decided. His mind flickered from image to image, none of them pleasant, and he knew he would be lucky to fall asleep.

Spring was particularly slow in coming to Belfast that year, though there were occasional evenings of balmy warmth that gave promise that it was not too far away. On one of those evenings Mr Apple stayed late in the shop. Even long after Martin had waved him a jovial farewell with a warning to behave himself, he pretended to be busy, as though some invisible colleague still hovered in the smokey air to supervise his actions. And as Mr Apple moved about (shuffling papers, opening and closing drawers, picking tiny scraps of paper from the floor, straightening a long, thin line of paper-clips) some instinct warned him of impending pain: pain of an unusual, as yet unexperienced kind, unlocalized, perhaps unreal, more the threat or promise of suffering. Or perhaps it was just that he felt the shop still hummed with noise, the noise of impish shadows abandoned by their masters, doomed to carry tales of woe, cries of triumph. Mr Apple was very clever at picking up such voices, any voices from the past. Indeed, it had struck him from time to time that certain voices were timeless and, though culled from another time, adapted themselves with such efficiency that they became real, and so audible that they could have been uttered but a moment before. And, though many of these voices terrified him and sent small beads of perspiration coursing down his neck, Mr Apple sensed he would be devastated without them. Now, as he tidied up and tidied again what he had already tidied twice before, he muttered to himself, arguing, quite logically it seemed, the necessity of retaining contact with such voices which, in his mind's eye, he saw as little Lowry men and women, gibbering and bickering, not, perhaps, directly for his benefit but loud enough to be certain he heard. In small fragments of broken sentences he allowed them to penetrate his mind, selecting (as he always did when weariness invaded his body) only such snippets as would not upset him too much.

Outside he paused for a moment to accustom his eyes to the gloom. The unseasonal mildness had brought with it the hazard of fog, which now drifted in over the city, wrapping it in drifts of mystery and giving Lepper Street a murderous look made all the more sinister by the jaundiced yellow complexion of the pedestrians as they passed under the streetlamps. Mr Apple turned up his collar, shivered slightly, shoved his hands deep into his pockets, and set out – but not in the direction of his home. Indeed, he walked in almost exactly the opposite direction, and for company he took with him sad little images of people doomed to isolation: off-cuts from *The Third Man* with musical intrusions seemed to predominate for a while, then in rapid succession but with scant regard for continuity the lonely characters of *Death in Venice*, *A Streetcar Named Desire* and *Brighton Rock* insinuated themselves. *Brighton Rock*! Now there was a thought. Perhaps Martin – hardly...

Colonel Maddox opened the door almost before Mr Apple had finished knocking, looking benign in his civilian clothes but nevertheless commanding respect like a bank manager. 'Ah,' he said, opening the door wider. 'Ah, it's you. I wasn't sure.'

'Yes. It's me,' Mr Apple confirmed although his voice suggested he shared the Colonel's doubt.

'Good. Come in, come in.'

All of a sudden I am in great demand: visitors flitting into my life requesting favours. The latest, a senior representative of Her Majesty's forces no less, keen to have the assistance of my wisdom. Well, hardly. Keen that I let them in on the secret of why I should have been given my lucrative new post; even keener to know who, precisely, offered it to me, and to be kept informed as to what is going on. I should, of course, tell them, but I find their appeals to my patriotism a little obscene. In any case I would be cutting my own throat, so to speak, doing myself out of a cosy little job, doing myself, also, in no uncertain way, out of my livelihood! And, to make a clean breast of it, I rather enjoy being the enemy, or, rather, being on the side of the enemy, which comes to the same thing; being that murky character who funnels cash through murkier channels. All very Raftian, I confess, but fun

61

nonetheless. And somehow I still retain that speck of dignity that prevents me betraying those who have helped me, if only for their own ends. What, I ask myself, would have become of me by now had the dapper little Seamus not visited me and lifted me from my degradation? Anyway, it is all part of the scheme of things, is it not? Those that guide me have arranged it, and it is only by my blind submission to their guidance that I can bring about salvation...

Mr Apple walked past the Colonel, down the narrow hall with walls so dark and featureless they seemed to go on for ever. 'The dampness gets into my bones,' he offered the Colonel for no particular reason as he turned into a small room on the left.

'And mine. Do sit down,' Colonel Maddox invited, lapsing for a moment into his garden-party voice. 'I won't be a moment.'

Alone, Mr Apple took stock of the room, as he did on every occasion he visited it. It was just another harmless little game he liked to play: a game of 'has anything been moved?' As usual, nothing had. Not even the dust, he noted, which after lying undisturbed for a couple of months seemed to have lost interest in accumulating and lay in the same thin film on every surface. Clipped British voices penetrated the wall, but Mr Apple ignored them: he did not want, at this juncture anyway, to know more than he was officially told. He settled himself in an old armchair, easing himself down slowly out of respect for the tired, fragile springs, and hissed thinly through his teeth as he lay back. Strange, he thought, strange that all sense of trepidation had flown from him: now that he was actually in the house, was about to carry out the bi-monthly charade, he felt himself relax and view the forthcoming encounter with considerable amusement.

He must have dropped off for a moment, for the slamming of a door brought him bolt upright, wondering where he was. Almost immediately Colonel Maddox, accompanied by a small man who seemed to prefer to remain in the background but towards whom the Colonel showed considerable deference and respect, came into the room and closed the door carefully behind him.

'Sorry about that,' the Colonel began, with a half-smile of apology.

'Tricky business, all this cloak and dagger. Not really my province, you know. Ah, this is – '

'Asher,' the small man interrupted from the shadows.

'Yes. Quite. Mr Asher.'

Mr Apple nodded. Ashers to Ashers, he thought giddily, and cudgelled his bubbling laughter into a small smile, a replica of the Colonel's.

'Well, Arthur,' Asher said from the shadows, lighting a black cigarette. The flame illuminated his features for a moment, then vanished. 'What has been happening?' he demanded from the darkness.

Perhaps it was the impertinent familiarity of the man, or perhaps Sefer's whispered warning in his ear, that made Mr Apple dislike this man more than he had disliked anyone for a long time.

'Nothing,' he lied promptly, with a facility that amazed him.

'Nothing?' Asher snapped.

'Nothing.'

This negative revelation spurred Asher to move into the light. He shared a dumbfounded look between the Colonel and Mr Apple, a confused expression on his face as though for the moment he had been floored by the absence of intrigue. 'What do you mean, nothing?'

Mr Apple raised his hands in a helpless gesture and looked at the Colonel as though appealing for assistance.

'What can I say?' he asked finally. 'Nothing has happened. Not a single thing. I think you must have been misled.'

'Don't be stupid,' Asher said coldly. 'Our information is always correct.'

'Not, it seems, this time,' Mr Apple told him complacently.

Well done, whispered Sefer.

Brilliant, agreed Mr Divine. You have him all tied up.

Mr Apple smiled to himself mysteriously.

'Perhaps,' the Colonel was suggesting hesitantly, 'perhaps they haven't satisfied themselves about Mr Apple yet.'

Asher dismissed the suggestion with a single economical, rather effeminate, flick of his wrist, and screwed his face into meditative lines, his eyes all the while firmly fixed on Mr Apple, who stared back blandly. Only a tiny twinkle in his eye hinted that he was enjoying the discomfort he was creating.

'Now look,' Asher began. 'We know why this operation was set up. We knew even before it started. And you mean to tell me that you've had no instructions to pass money through the – '

'None,' interrupted Mr Apple bravely.

'I – don't – believe – that.'

Mr Apple shrugged, and in his mind his two conspirators danced with glee, Mr Divine bending double with delight.

'You – are – lying,' Asher announced.

Again Mr Apple shrugged.

A new menace entered Asher's voice. 'I would really hate to think, Arthur, that you were keeping anything from us.'

'Why should I?' Mr Apple asked.

'Oh, I don't think Mr Apple would do that,' the Colonel put in. 'As he says, why should he?'

Asher decided to think again: one could almost discern the movements of his thoughts in the twitching lines on his face as he mulled over the various reasons why Mr Apple should or should not.

Outside a siren wailed balefully. Heavy vehicles thundered past the house, making it shake. A pair of small Goss vases with heraldic designs bounced on the mantelpiece; a print of some forlorn Scottish stag bellowing for intercourse shuddered on the wall.

'...*know* that the Provos did the raid,' Asher was saying, 'and that the money was to go to you to be cleaned.'

Mr Apple kept his silence.

'And you still insist that nothing has been passed on to you?'

'Absolutely nothing,' Mr Apple insisted.

'They could be waiting.' Colonel Maddox tried.

'They never wait *that* long. They need the funds. Tell me, Arthur, what did McIlliver want with you the other day?'

' – ? McIlliver?' It was Mr Apple's turn to be dumbfounded.

'I suppose you don't know him?'

64

'No. I don't,' Mr Apple admitted truthfully.

'I see. You don't, I suppose, remember three men coming into your shop and staying a remarkably short time for anyone wanting to place a bet?'

'Three men. Let me think. Together, were they?'

Asher nodded, somehow making the gesture sarcastic. 'Three men. Together.'

'No. Not offhand. There has been *one* man in whom I had never seen before, but I don't think there was anyone with him.'

'And what did this one man want?' Asher pressed.

Mr Apple raised his eyebrows and peered over his spectacles like a schoolteacher. 'To have a bet, of course. A small bet, I recall. That's right,' Mr Apple agreed, closing his eyes briefly and frowning. 'Yes, that's right,' he said again happily. 'That is quite right,' he said for the third time, determined to keep the objectionable little man waiting. 'He came in and stared up at the prices and then he placed a bet of fifty pounds on the favourite. I would still have his ticket if you want to see it. Lost. The horse, I mean. Fell or brought down early on. But aren't we all?' Mr Apple concluded wistfully.

'Fell or brought down early on,' Asher repeated.

'That's right. He didn't wait for the rest of the race. The man, I mean,' Mr Apple said, smiling at his little joke. 'Just walked out as soon as his horse departed. But then you know he left quickly, if it's the same man you're talking about.'

'Amazing, isn't it, how clearly you remember.'

'I remember the bets. It's my business to remember the bets. . don't remember the faces who put them on. Anonymity is a peculiar requisite of the people I deal with,' Mr Apple explained mischievously, investing his reply with a mild chiding that was rewarded with a light of anger in Asher's eyes. 'Unless they win. Ah, now, that's a different kettle of fish. Now if they *win* they want everyone to know them. They've beaten the system, you see, which is what we're all trying to do one way or another, are we not?'

Asher's eyes continued to flash angrily and, as though his anger was contagious, voices in the street outside adopted its temper, and even the dull thud of running boots pounding on the pavement sounded unreasonably infuriated and ominous. A sudden single sharp crack of gunfire was heard and, without moving their heads, the Colonel and Asher glanced at each other from the corners of their eyes. Mr Apple looked on, for the moment forgotten, while the two men summed up the possible danger of the situation. However, as the shouts and thumping boots grew fainter Asher lit another black cigarette and returned to the matter in hand.

'I'll be perfectly honest with you, Arthur,' he said. 'I don't believe a word of what you've said.'

Mr Apple called upon his neat little hand-spreading gesture to imply that this was, indeed, very sad, most regrettable, that it upset him no end.

'And I don't trust you an inch,' Asher added, as though it might make a difference.

Mr Apple rose laboriously from his chair and stared flatly at his accuser.

'Oh, I do feel Mr Apple would have told us if anything had happened,' the Colonel interjected, feeling it was his duty to ease the tension. 'He really does have nothing to gain,' he added, 'and he has a great deal to lose.'

Asher nodded. 'A very great deal,' he agreed.

'So,' Mr Apple told them, 'I must have been telling the truth.'

'Unless you're a fool,' Asher said.

'Unless I'm a fool,' Mr Apple admitted innocently, and with this solemn observation they were through.

Colonel Maddox ushered him to the front door, herding him protectively past Asher, who had retreated once again to the shadows and had shrouded himself in black cigarette smoke.

'You would tell us if –' the Colonel began when they were alone in the hall, using that conspiratorial tone that suggested he would have wrapped an arm about Mr Apple's shoulder had he not been wary of rebuff.

'What do you think, Colonel? Would I be stupid enough to defy your Mr Asher?'

66

'Oh, he's not my Mr Asher, I assure you,' the Colonel hastened to tell him. 'Between you and me he's a bit pushy, isn't he?'

'You could say that, I think.'

The Colonel seemed to feel that this was a suitably amicable note on which to terminate the proceedings. He gave a quick, sharp, barking laugh as he pictured the gaunt, bent Mr Apple doing battle with the brittle Asher.

'Well, I'll see you in a couple of weeks as usual, unless, of course, you have something to tell me in the mean time.'

'In a couple of weeks, then.'

'And, by the way,' the Colonel went on, leaning closer, 'don't let Mr Asher upset you. He's under a lot of pressure.'

'Aren't we all,' Mr Apple said, but mostly to himself.

Mr Apple thought he heard the Colonel sigh as he closed the door and felt a tinge of sympathy for him. Any man who could sigh couldn't be all bad, he decided. Like people who loved dogs and cats and Beatrix Potter.

Perhaps it was his imagination, or perhaps it was just the effect of leaving the mustiness of the house, but Mr Apple felt it had got suddenly colder. He sucked the chilly air into his lungs and felt it creep into his chest. For a moment, it was as though he felt it travel yet further and enter his brain, freezing for future reference the conversation that had taken place. Then he set off through the tangle of backstreets that led to the Antrim Road and from there to his home: they were unusually quiet and uninquisitive. For some odd reason he felt that people should be rushing up to him demanding to know what had happened, but there was none of that: just silence and darkness. All the curtains were tightly drawn across the small windows, even a couple of cats about to fight merely showed their teeth and screamed their defiance soundlessly.

Onwards he trudged, and with each step the elation he had felt at his deception of the detestable Asher receded a little. His imagination started playing tricks on him, conjuring secret watchers from the gloom. Once Mr Apple was positive he heard someone behind him, following him, trying to match footsteps with his own; but when he

67

stopped suddenly and swung round there was nobody there. By the time he reached home he was thoroughly frightened. Still, Mr Apple had been frightened before, had he not? And he had coped, had he not? And he would cope now, would he not?

'Well, Chloe,' he told the cat that pressed against his ankles, mewling for food. 'It looks as though we have taken sides.'

He put a saucer of food on the floor for Chloe, took off his coat and threw it over the back of a kitchen chair. He stood watching the cat devour the chopped liver, then opened the back door for it to go out, standing aside politely and giving a small bow. 'Happy hunting.'

Now what, Mr Divine wanted to know.

'Now what, indeed,' Mr Apple wondered.

He thought briefly about having just one therapeutic drink, but decided against it. He thought about watching television, but decided against that also. Something to eat? Later. Finally, he seemed to make up his mind and left the kitchen, carefully switching off the light behind him. He walked across the hall to a small cupboard under the stairs, a glory-hole as it would have once been called. He opened the door, straightened his back and walked in, closing the door behind him.

— 6 —

Almost to the minute that Mr Apple vanished mysteriously into the glory-hole, Martin Deeley pushed open the door of the disco and strode arrogantly in. It was his night of sin, as he laughingly liked to think of it, and the companion in his forthcoming fall from grace was already lined up, willing, and hanging on his arm with an intensity that defied anyone to try and take him from her. Martin suffered her smothering possessiveness simply because he knew she would satisfy his needs and make no demands on him apart from gratification.

The cosmetic eroticism of the disco clattered frenetically about them as they pushed their way through the gyrating dancers towards an empty table in the corner, their faces changing shape and colour under the multi-hued lights rotating from a central glass prism in the ceiling.

Martin produced a half-bottle of whiskey from his pocket and placed it on the table beside the two paper mugs that Daphne Cope had produced from her oversized handbag. She always brought special mugs for herself and Martin; for someone of her risk-laden profession she had an abnormal dread of disease, regarding disco glasses and public toilets in the same light, and she felt it her duty to protect Martin from any infection.

Martin released his arm from her clutch and slung it nonchalantly about her shoulder. He stared about him with half-closed eyes, feigning boredom as he felt was expected of a man of his importance, and he was gratified by the glances thrown at him and the whispered, surreptitious comments. Daphne noticed the glances also, and she was none too pleased: she fixed her eyes on his face and pouted, making odd little inclinations with her head like those she had seen employed by Marilyn Monroe in her successful seduction of Robert Mitchum. Though she would have been shocked and hurt by the suggestion, these facial contortions were about the only way left to her to demonstrate her emotions. She wore her 'special' dress of scarlet brocade, a tight-fitting affair cut low to reveal her full breasts, and these she shook gently at Martin from time to time to attract his abstract attention. But Martin sat still, tense and alert, watching for someone he knew would appear before long.

'Cummon, sweetie, let's dance,' Daphne cajoled in her contrived, deep, nicotine-stained voice, taking his hand and tickling the palm with a long, painted fingernail.

'Uh-huh. I'm whacked,' Martin said, without bothering to look at her.

'Aw, my little babby is tired,' Daphne whimpered. 'Okay. I don't really want to dance if you don't,' she consented, clinging to him again, her long, fluttering eyelashes failing to conceal the yearning in her eyes as she longed for his energetic penetration. In her fantasies she saw some future for herself with him: not that her future as a prostitute was bleak. Far from it. She had a good stable of clients, good and generous and usually undemanding clients, and even her dull mind was amazed at the risks some of the military would take for a quick spot of fornication. But that was their affair, and she was happy to cater for them as long as they continued to pay for their appetites without argument. Still, she promised herself, she would give it all up when her father was released from Long Kesh and she no longer had to support her terrified mother, who now refused to leave her house on any pretext and had taken to doodling, which was fair enough except that she used every wall in the house to practise her art. And it was perhaps because of these intermittent longings to become a 'good' girl that Daphne suffered occasionally from severe depression, even contemplating suicide, but always abandoning such an extreme remedy with a laugh as she lustfully anticipated incredible curiosities in the days ahead. Ah, but Martin, her Martin. He was different.

'You got something on your mind, luvvey?' she asked, concerned by the scowl that dominated his face.

' – ? Huh? No. No, nothing.'

70

'But you must have something. I mean, you can't have a blank mind.'

'Can't you?' Martin snapped sarcastically.

'Oh, you're funny!' Daphne exclaimed innocently: it would never have dawned on her that Martin would insult her.

'Jesus, I hate this place.'

'We can go, luvvey, if you want. I don't mind.'

'No, we can't. I'm waiting for someone.'

'Oh. Okay,' Daphne said, and snuggled closer. She had become used to these meetings. After all, Martin was an important man and people wanted to consult him. And they treated him with respect; even much older men, men old enough to be his father, showed how important he was by speaking to him with deference. Still, it hurt her that Martin always sent her away when these meetings took place, never introducing her, smacking her bottom as she left and making her feel cheap. These thoughts had barely reached their sad conclusion when she felt his body stiffen and go rigid in her embrace. She gazed up into his face and saw that he was staring across the room. Following his gaze she spotted a dapper little man, dressed darkly as if for a funeral and incongruous for it, making his way sedately through the dancers, smiling, or possibly wincing at the multicoloured shirts and frocks and blouses that swirled about him offending his impeccably conservative taste. Despite his valiant efforts to look friendly, his eyes remained grim and tired.

'You better go and dance with someone,' Martin ordered as the man came nearer.

'Okay, Martin.'

'Good girl,' he told her, and slapped her bottom.

'Sorry to spoil your evening,' Seamus Reilly said, and sounded as if he meant it. 'But it is important.'

'I gathered that. Anyway, you're spoiling nothing. I hate the bloody place. What's up?'

'Trouble – maybe.'

'Oh? What trouble?'

'Our friend Mr Apple,' Reilly announced, looking down at his polished, manicured nails and up again.

'Mr Apple? Don't be mad. He's no trouble. I'm getting on with him like a house on fire. Even getting to like the old bugger.'

'We've heard whispers.'

'Oh, Christ, not whispers again. Seamus, you and your bloody whispers will be the death of me. And you'll be driven mad if you listen to them all.'

'Just hear me out, Martin. There are whispers that he might be playing both sides.'

Martin's face tightened. 'Doing what?' he demanded in a low, grim whisper.

'We don't know anything for certain yet, but – '

'But what?'

'But we were told that someone who looked like him was seen coming out of the Brits' safe house in – '

'The bastard – '

'Don't fly off into a temper, Martin. It might be nothing. Our man can't be certain. It was foggy and he was too far away. He just said it looked like Mr Apple. He mentioned something about the walk.'

Martin stared at the dancers, shaking his head, unconsciously moving it in time to the music. 'Naw,' he said finally. 'Old Apple would never do something like that. It's not his style, Seamus. He's always on about honour and loyalty and stuff like that.'

'Again, I repeat, it might be nothing. It could have been somebody else,' Seamus admitted.

'It must have been. He wouldn't do anything like that. Anyway, I'd know if he was up to something.'

'Would you?'

'Sure I would.'

'That's really what I wanted to find out.'

'Yeah. I'd know. He'd never be able to hide something like that from me. He'd give himself away for certain.'

'In that case there's nothing for us to worry about, is there?'

'Who says they saw him?' Martin suddenly wanted to know.

'Nobody you know.'

'Reliable?'

Reilly inclined his head and grimaced to indicate moderate reliability.

'Naw,' Martin said again, determined to convince himself, his head continuing to shake for several moments.

'There's been nothing unusual at the shop? No phone calls?'

'No. Nothing out of the way. Clients phone. And you. Anyway, he never minds if I answer the phone, so he can't be hiding anything there.'

'No unusual callers?'

'Uh-uh. But he's not going to invite the Brits in for a chat, is he?'

Reilly ignored the sarcasm. 'Doesn't leave the shop?'

Martin gave a snort. 'Only to go home, and then I follow him most nights.'

'Most?'

'Yes.'

'Not every?'

'No. Not every. Hell, Seamus, some weeks I follow him every night, some weeks just three or four.'

'I see,' Seamus said pensively. 'He doesn't know you follow him?'

Martin shook his head. 'Never even looks behind him.'

A small frown of surprise passed rapidly across Seamus Reilly's brow, but if his thoughts were significant he had no intention, it seemed, of revealing them just yet. 'And he still doesn't suspect you're in the shop to watch him?'

'No,' Martin said, but there was a hesitancy in his voice that prompted Seamus to ask:

'You're certain?'

'Yes. I'm certain, but...well, he's a crafty old sod and you never know what he's thinking.'

'Thinking?'

'Well, he just says things, and you don't know what to make of them. Like he was teasing the whole time.'

'So now you think he might suspect?'

Martin took time off to think about this. He was finding it hard to explain what he wanted to say. 'Not suspect,' he said finally, taking a sip of his drink, swilling it in his mouth, letting it trickle slowly down his throat as though quenching some nagging suspicion that had just struck him. 'Either he definitely knows or he definitely doesn't know. He doesn't do things by halves,' Martin concluded, not quite sure what he meant by the last few words.

'Hmm.'

'Anyway, at this stage, does it matter if he does know?'

Reilly gave a crack of a laugh in which his eyes refused to take part. 'That depends, doesn't it, on what his reactions might be?'

'He wouldn't do anything. I'd stake my life on – '

'You might just have to do that, Martin.'

' – ?'

Reilly smiled. 'So you're happy he's behaving himself?'

Martin nodded. 'He knows what's good for him. He's not a fool.'

'Oh, we know that. He's far from being stupid – '

'He – '

'Let's just leave it at that, shall we?' Seamus interrupted, in a tone that suggested he had settled the matter in his own mind. 'Just be a little more – eh – vigilant, and let me know at once if anything – '

'Of course I will.'

For several minutes the two of them sat without talking, allowing the throb of the music to act as recipient of their thoughts. Seamus Reilly sighed deeply. 'Well, I'll be off and let you get on with your dancing,' he said, rising.

'Huh. I'll see you, Seamus. And don't worry,' Martin insisted, as they shook hands.

'Oh, *I'm* not worried, Martin.'

'Good. Neither am I.'

'I'm pleased to hear it. Good-night.'

''Night, Seamus.'

Martin watched as Reilly squeezed his way through the dancers and left the disco. He poured himself a stiff whiskey and lowered it in one gulp, hoping it would stupefy the nervous twitch in his stomach. Then he closed his eyes and watched jumpy black-and-white images of Mr Apple and himself flicker through his mind like scenes from an ancient silent film, trying, as they jostled each other for screening, to decipher any untoward behaviour by Mr Apple. He was still absorbed with his private viewing when someone tapped him on the shoulder and said: 'Well, if it isn't Martin Deeley. The grand Martin Deeley himself.'

Martin's eyes snapped open and his body froze. He realized the voice was familiar, but he could not for the life of him put a face to it, and it was something approaching terror that prevented him from turning round to see who it was: a gruesome tradition had been established among the many assassins in the province that they would only kill each other face to face.

'And how are you at all?' the voice now wanted to know, its owner moving from behind and presenting himself to Martin's gaze.

'Corrigan! Fuck you, Corrigan, you frightened the shit out of me.'

'Me? Me frighten the great Martin Deeley?'

'Yes, you fucking great shit you. Sneaking up on me like that.'

'Sure I never sneaked up on you, Martin my love. Just came across the room as open as you please to say hello to an old friend.'

Larry Corrigan bestowed the gift of a great toothless grin down and around him, adopting a pose that, in anyone else, would have been seen simply as arrested motion. In Larry Corrigan, though, it acquired a different connotation: with both arms extended and legs wide apart he resembled one of those grotesque figures in early engravings that are only remotely interesting because of their stylized remoteness from life. And Larry Corrigan was a grotesque enough creature: huge and round and flabby and a living denial of the rumour that fat people are jolly and gay. His grey skin told of the many years he had spent in and out of prison. True, he had been free for some time now, and he guarded his freedom with considerable help from his friends: Larry Corrigan was an informer, but an informer of the vagabond breed, reporting to the British such items as he was told to report, always being allowed to deliver sufficient for him to be left at large and in peace.

'And what's all this I hear about you moving into the shady world of gambling, Martin?'

'That's right, Larry,' Martin admitted curtly.

'Bookmaking no less. Dear me, dear me.'

'I'm just helping out.'

Larry Corrigan threw up his hands. 'I'm not prying, Martin. I'm not prying,' he stated hastily, his hands indicating that such a thing would never enter his head. 'Just curious,' he explained. 'Everything going all right for you?'

'Everything's just fine.'

'Oh, good.'

'And you?'

'Me? Surviving.' Larry Corrigan let his eyes rest on Martin's long, delicate hands and seemed hypnotized by the way they clenched and unclenched ceaselessly. 'Relax, Martin,' he said benevolently. 'Just a chance meeting. Nobody wants to know anything. I'm under no pressure. Anyway, you're my friend.'

'Oh, I'm everybody's friend tonight, it seems,' Martin observed wryly.

'You know what I mean. I'd never say anything about you.'

'I know that, Larry,' Martin said, without much conviction. 'I know that. Sorry. Just a bit uptight this evening.'

'It gets that way.'

' – ?'

'Our lives,' Larry said morosely. 'Hadn't you noticed?'

'Never thought about it.'

'It just doesn't make sense, though – '

'I suppose not.'

'You in a bookie's shop.'

'? Oh,' Martin said, finding it increasingly difficult to disentangle the threads of the conversation. 'There's a reason.'

'I'm sure there is.'

Martin stared up at the round, sweating face with a flat, unreadable expression, allowing the pounding music, the shuffling feet and the hands waved in exotic patterns to create some meaning from his blank stare.

'You haven't got into trouble, have you, Martin?'

Martin felt his throat close. 'Shit, no.'

Larry exhaled half a lungful of odorous air and shifted his pyknic body from foot to foot. 'That's all right then.'

Martin was moved by the seeming sincerity. 'You need something?' he asked. 'Money?'

'No, I don't need money,' Larry answered, blushing, his huge body seeming to take offence. 'Even if I did I wouldn't scrounge off you. You know that.'

'I didn't say you were scrounging. I was just asking. Just trying to help. We all need help from time to time. You know that.'

'That's for sure.'

'So you're all right?'

'I'm all right. I'll let you know when I'm not.'

'Good.'

'But thanks for asking.'

'Yeah,' Martin said awkwardly, relieved to see Daphne mincing towards him, her eyes undressing him as she got closer. 'Got to go, Larry,' Martin added, and winked, making this innocent enough gesture brilliantly pornographic. 'Heavy date.'

'Ah. Yes. Well, enjoy yourself, hear?'

'I will.'

'You'll be an awful long time dead,' Larry added. 'A long, long time dead,' he repeated to himself mournfully, as though he had already experienced the hereafter and was none too thrilled by it.

'See you about, Larry.'

'See you,' Larry replied, though sounding somewhat doubtful as he watched Martin and Daphne submerge themselves in the sea of dancers.

Martin had long since dismissed Larry from his thoughts as he allowed Daphne to lead him by the hand up the stairs to her room: one single, pretty dismal room that gave off a corridor with eight doors. Sighs and groans and giggles could be heard through the walls, and Daphne switched on the small bedside radio as if to swamp them. She hummed musically in rhythm with the unmusical voices of some up-and-coming punk group. She had lived in a dozen places since she had left home, but had managed to stamp her presence on each of them in a remarkably short time, putting her mementoes on display, and always managing, somehow, to strategically place, somewhere, a small vase of flowers or a potted plant with extravagant foliage, as though to endorse her femininity and soften any hardness that might have crept into her character.

Martin sat on the edge of the bed and took off his shoes and socks, sniffing the air, hoping his feet did not smell but knowing they probably did. No matter what he did, no matter how often he washed his feet and changed his socks and applied prescribed powders, his feet always seemed to stink. Mam had always been on at him about it. You go straight upstairs and wash your feet and change your socks, you smelly little boy, she'd say.

I'm not smelly.

Your feet are. Like stinky cheese they are. Upstairs this minute with you.

I washed them this morning. And changed my socks.

Well, wash them again now.

That's what's causing the trouble, Martin tried arguing. I'm washing all the natural oils out of them.

Rubbish, Martin, and you know it. No pretty girl will want to marry you if you smell like that. No girl would put up with you.

Then I'll do without.

Well, do without, but get upstairs and wash those feet.

But that had been years ago, and his feet still caused him endless embarrassment. Another of life's afflictions, he thought good-humouredly, lying back on the bed, his head propped on two pillows. He stared about him, his gaze uncritical of the small shabby room with its bulging paintwork. In one corner, on a risky-looking shelf, a small electrified crucifix illuminated a gilt-framed print of Christ, His finger pointing nonchalantly to the blood dripping from his heart, each drop artistically isolated. Other pictures, barely visible in the seductive gloom, hung haphazardly on the walls: a watercolour of a lake, possibly the Bodensee, signed Menzies Jones (whoever he was), two Victorian prints of sugary little girls having animated conversations with, in one, an oversized shaggy dog, and, in the other, with two sharp-snouted terriers, and between these prints, tilting alarmingly, a none-too-clever reproduction of the Goose Girl. Yet despite the overall drabness of the room it was impeccably clean, as though the odour of poverty and aimless love was ruthlessly being kept at bay by the occupant's zealous tidiness. There was a photograph of Daphne's parents on the dressing-table (although dressing-table flattered it somewhat: it was, in fact, a small deal kitchen table, painted a pretty blue with a mirror on top balanced precariously near the back and supported by building-bricks painted white), both of them thin, small people who smiled selfconsciously straight at the camera, obviously embarrassed at being captured in such close proximity and grateful, no doubt, that they were now all but obscured by the conglomeration of perfumes and powders and creams that littered the table about them. Still, Mr Cope gave the impression he was constantly darting little peeps from behind these, a hunted look to his eyes that made a mockery of his smiling mouth, his taut, posed stance filled with a restlessness that gave evidence of his years on the run.

'Come on over here,' Martin said, patting the mattress, putting his arm around her as she snuggled close, her head resting contentedly on his shoulder. Beside them the radio played on, its endless stream of music designed for those who wanted to hear without listening. Martin stared at the ceiling, following the cracks in the plaster, making them into roads down which he had travelled: abandoned, dusty roads upon which he walked alone, wearing sandals, unburdened, a mendicant monk perhaps, and then, as always, inevitably, immediately in front of him, his target appeared, rising spectrelike from nowhere, from within the earth itself, and he was filled with a trembling excitement, not knowing how this particular victim was going to react (and that was always the most interesting aspect – screams or tears? Pleading or disdain? But for the most part they never knew they were targets until the bullet hit them and then it was too late to do anything but die) and he, Martin, aiming, and slowly, slowly squeezing the trigger, and wondering yet again, as he did every time, whether he would feel exalted or, as he knew he should, revolted.

'What you thinking, honey?' Daphne suddenly wanted to know.

Martin jumped. 'Not a lot,' he said finally, closing his eyes. His mind recently had started to stagger at the number of lives he had taken, playing tricks on him, multiplying a hundred times the placid, bewildered faces of death. Too often now he felt terror – the same terror that shot through him that very evening when Larry Corrigan touched him unexpectedly on the shoulder. His whole life, it seemed, was a tenuous, jittery thing linked to the world while he floated, in a wild, disembodied state, in a murky void of uncertainty, forever reaching out and clawing at random for great lumps of reality that glided past always beyond his reach, seeking to get hold of something that would give him an identity, a reason for being alive. Oddly, only Mr Apple with his weak, watery eyes and his gaunt, stooped body seemed to be on offer as a guide to his salvation. It was as though Mr Apple had a monopoly on the knowledge Martin yearned to obtain.

'You've got something on your mind,' Daphne insisted.

'Nothing. Really.'

'You're too good to be mixed up with – '

'Shut up, Daphne. For God's sake, don't go on,' Martin said angrily.

Daphne raised her head and studied him for a moment. 'You're far too good for them,' she repeated solemnly.

'You don't understand.'

'Oh, no. I'm thick. I understand nothing. Huh. What is there to understand? You know, you're just going to end up like all the rest. Locked up or dead. That's what I understand. You think I don't know those creeps you meet with? You think I don't know what they make you do?'

'Shut up.'

Daphne sat bolt upright, her eyes flaring. 'No, I won't shut up, dammit.'

'You don't know the people I deal with.'

'I don't know them? You must be joking, Martin. I've seen everyone of them with their knickers down. I've seen them all trying to be men. So don't tell me I don't know them. You're all I've got to hang on to, Martin. I don't want you to end up on a slab. I care.'

'So you care.'

'What do you do it for? The money?'

Martin snorted.

'Okay. It makes you feel big. I understand that.'

Martin ignored her.

Daphne turned again and stared at him, and her anxiety was not just for his welfare but for the threat to her longed-for, dreamed-of future with him. She looked away as though the sight of him was too sad to bear. Then, 'I love you, Martin,' she announced firmly.

'Sure, sure,' Martin agreed casually, turning to look at her and excluding her love from his life with a tired smile. 'Everybody loves me.'

Perhaps it was the great hurt he spotted in her eyes, or, more likely, perhaps it was his sense of practicality that made him push her back roughly and fondle her thighs, a rage building up in him as he demanded she endorse his masculinity. He crushed her breasts cruelly in his hands and felt that familiar glow of excitement sweep over him as she cried in pain.

'Oh, I love you, Martin,' Daphne sobbed. 'I love you. Love you,' she whispered, biting deeply into his neck as though she wished to devour him and keep him safe within her.

An hour later he lay naked on the bed, smoking a cigarette, frowning, seeing his confidence dissolve like the smoke that drifted away from him in a dim cloud towards the ceiling.

There was always the chance that Dr Solomon was wrong, Mr Apple thought with bitter amusement. That would certainly put the cat among the pigeons. Maybe he had a lot longer to live than old, sad Solomon thought; maybe he was going to go on and on, always on the brink of death but never taking the vital plunge. Immediately he began to fantasize about the activity surrounding his own demise, seeing himself, literally, on the edge of some great precipice, about to place one foot over the edge. Strange, he thought, how death could be so familiar, although one had not experienced it yet. Or perhaps one had. Or perhaps not quite: but one had certainly earned the knowledge to recognize it, to be polite to it, to raise one's hat and wish it good morning, but until it came with all its clamouring fanfare of finality one could not, say, address it on first-name terms. Mr Apple sighed, and Martin Deeley – industriously breaking the paper bands that held the betting-slips in neat numerical bundles – glanced up. 'What's the matter, Mr A.?' he asked.

'Nothing, Mr D.,' Mr Apple replied smiling, allowing this recently evolved familiarity to wash some of the despondency from his soul.

'Oh. Thought you were – '

'I was,' Mr Apple interrupted, bringing that particular speculation to an abrupt halt. Immediately, changing tack, he added, out of the blue and with no warning, 'How long do you plan to waste your time on this job?'

'?' Martin raised his eyebrows, his eyes suspiciously bewildered.

Mr Apple raised his eyebrows also, allowing his spectacles to slither half-way down his nose, leaving the question hanging in the air.

Following what was or should have been, on the face of it, a perfectly innocent enquiry, the silence that followed was inordinately prolonged, broken only by the water grinding in the electric kettle as it started to boil.

'I hadn't thought about it,' Martin confessed finally.

'Oh?' Mr Apple feigned surprise.

'Why "oh"?'

'I would have thought you were more ambitious.'

'I am.'

'Well?'

'I'm not going to do it forever, if that's what you mean,' Martin said, annoyed that he felt himself suddenly on the defensive again. 'There's not much work about at present. Got to take what I can get. There's a lot of unemployment you know.'

'True,' Mr Apple agreed, nodding, moving his glasses back to the bridge of his nose with one finger. 'Still...'

'Still what?'

Mr Apple seemed to be losing a wrestling match with his thoughts. Then: 'Do you ever get feelings, Martin?'

'Feelings? Sure I get feelings.'

'I mean premonitions.'

'Like telling the future?'

'Something like that.'

Martin shrugged, disquieted by the turn the conversation had now taken. He was about to throw out some facetious remark when Mr Apple went on: 'I do, you know. Quite frequently, in fact.'

'Good for you.'

' – and I have this feeling about us – '

'Oh, great.'

' – as though – '

'What?'

Mr Apple shook his head in a series of short little jerks, like a watchful bird.

'For Christ's sake, don't stop now,' Martin insisted, crossing the office and switching off the kettle, jerking his hand away as the steam hit him. 'Shit,' he said as he licked his hand.

' – ?'

83

'Damn kettle.'

'Oh.'

'Anyway, what were you on about?'

'Nothing, Martin. It doesn't matter.'

'Great! Just as I was getting interested.'

'I can't explain it, Martin. Truly I can't. Something, I suppose, to do with destiny.'

'Oh boy,' Martin heard himself saying. It worried him that Mr Apple – yet again! – seemed to be hinting at something significant, something that he himself had sensed from time to time but had preferred to dismiss as soon as it seemed likely to take some sort of shape. And to dismiss it now he busied himself making tea, slopping teabags in and out of the boiling water as though fishing for eels in the mugs, adding milk, and then walking across to Mr Apple holding his mug at arm's length as though avoiding contamination. But Mr Apple appeared to have withdrawn from any thoughts of a common destiny, appeared to have better things to do, and was now busily making dozens of small calculations on a sheet of paper which told him he had another four hundred pounds to lose today. Then he just let the pencil meander, and watched in mild amusement at the amoebic doodles that appeared until he heard Martin's frustrated cough behind him.

'Oh thank you, Martin. Most welcome.'

Martin stared at the back of the old man's head, wishing, absurdly, for one of those sets of scientifically fictitious eyes that could penetrate anything. It seemed to him that many things he wanted to know and understand lay hidden in Mr Apple's brain; things, it struck him now, that were vital to expose; things that were somehow linked with both exaltation and horror. It was as though inside that balding and curiously pointed head were filed precise details of everything he, Martin, had ever done and thought and been afraid of, and from which, now, sallow little one-act plays emanated, depicting moments in his life when he had felt totally bereft and lonely...

...identify the bodies, someone said gruffly in a whirring accent, faintly bored but, at the same time, relieved that two more suspected terrorists could be written out of the records.

I'll go, Mam, Martin said. You two look after Mam and see she doesn't do anything stupid.

Mam doesn't do stupid things, Cissy said.

She's not herself, dammit, Martin snapped. You look after her, that's all.

Let's get going then, the voice commanded without sympathy, though not as strident as before.

I'm coming.

And bouncing over the rutted country lanes (where everything went on as though tragedy mattered not at all, where birds still sang, and bees buzzed and collected pollen, and little insects made a nuisance of themselves, where cattle grazed serenely without bothering to look up) in the back of the military jeep that smelled of oil and sweat and rubber, Martin was shocked to find his stomach heaving with fear. He felt no sorrow, no sense of loss during this drive to identify the bodies of his father and brother, for death seemed to have eradicated all memory of them as people, had in one split second transformed them from loved ones into statistics, into nothing more than another two corpses found by the roadside and reported on the evening news in that same nonchalant voice used to inform the viewers of the prowess of some skateboarding duck or the winner of some Rock and Pop award. If any other emotion found room beside his fear it was simply one that approached resentment that they should have allowed themselves to be killed.

Well? The voice asked.

Martin nodded.

You're sure?

I'm sure.

Right. You can shift them. Come on, jump to it. Get them out of there.

The bodies were hauled from the ditch by young soldiers unused to handling death, placed on large sheets of thick black plastic and lifted into the waiting army ambulance, the muddy water from the ditch oozing from the unfolded ends of the creaking plastic shrouds.

Home?

I'll walk.

Dangerous.

I'm okay.

Up to you.

That's right.

Need you again tomorrow.

Yes.

Still want to walk?

Yes.

Right. Let's get out of here.

They drove off at speed, gears grinding, tyres slithering on the muddy, churned grass verge, the bodies bouncing and flailing on the floor of the ambulance as though they were alive.

Martin crouched by the ditch and stared at the peaty brown water into which Dad and Steven had been dumped. What a hell of a place to die. Nothing noble in that. What was all that shit they talked about the dignity of death? If the ditch had been dry it would have been a little better: the sogginess and slime made it all gruesome and inhuman. One thing was bloody certain: he wouldn't go like that. Not on your life. Oh, no. He'd make bloody certain nobody found his body dumped in a ditch like an animal. Not Martin Deeley.

'...if you're still with us,' Mr Apple's opaque voice was suddenly intruding on the wretched scene.

' – ?'

'Ah, welcome back. A customer. Please.'

'Oh, sorry, Mr Apple. Thinking.'

'A dangerous pastime at the best of times, Martin.'

'You can say that again,' Martin agreed with a small, tight laugh, and turned to the counter to face Peter Taylor, who made the severence from his thoughts complete.

Peter Taylor was a huge man who emphasized his enormity by sporting a sumptuous beard that reached half-way down his chest.

Possibly because of his bulk he suffered spasmodically from quite excruciating cramps, which would attack unannounced and leave him, despite his great size, vulnerable and crying in agony, even writhing on the floor as though in the throes of a particulary virulent epileptic fit; as if to compensate for these lapses of weakness he adopted a fearsome and aggressive brusqueness, though this failed in its duty since his voice was ridiculously high-pitched, and he ended up sounding petulant.

'Must win today,' he announced threateningly. 'Bills to be paid. Gas. Light. Rent.'

'It's a hard life,' Martin commiserated.

'How would you know? Haven't lived yet, you haven't.'

'If you say so.'

'I just did. Why doesn't he come?' Peter Taylor demanded, pointing a stubby finger in the direction of Mr Apple.

'Busy,' Martin said. 'Very busy man.'

'I want him. Get him.'

'He won't like being disturbed.'

'Get him.'

'What's wrong with me, anyway?'

Peter Taylor stared at Martin as if suddenly seeing him for the first time. 'You know the business?'

'Sure I know the business.'

'You're certain?'

'Certainly I'm certain.' Martin leaned forward and signalled surreptitiously for the man to lean closer. 'I'm the real brains here,' he whispered conspiratorially. 'I'm the brains behind the whole operation.'

Taylor was impressed. 'Oooooh,' he soughed, and stepped back a pace for a better view of this newly emerged paragon. The shop seemed to creak under his enormous weight as he leaned forward again and submitted his wager with a subconscious sensation of privilege. 'I'd have asked for you every time if I'd known,' he confided.

'Well, you know now,' Martin told him.

'Yes. And you were right. Life is hard,' Taylor went on, a new quality in his voice that suggested he was now discussing life and its attendant hardships with an equal. 'Nothing but bills. Doesn't seem right, does it, just living to pay bills. Pay one and then another arrives to take its place. Pay that and there's another waiting just around the corner. And he doesn't help any,' he concluded accusingly, pointing again at Mr Apple.

'Well he wouldn't, would he?'

The big man laboriously searched out the logic in this. Then: 'He's not like us, you know.'

'Like us?' asked Martin dubiously.

Taylor nodded. 'Haven't you noticed? You can always tell them.'

'Them?' Martin was intrigued, wondering if despite his air of mild lunacy Peter Taylor had discovered something about Mr Apple that he, Martin, had long suspected.

'Villains,' Taylor announced.

Martin shook his head, grinning. 'Oh, I wouldn't call Mr Apple a villain.'

'I would. They're all villains, people like him. You watch out, young man, or he'll have you turning out like him,' Taylor predicted sombrely, and with this he swung away from the counter and trundled his great bulk from the shop, leaving Martin with his mouth open in amazement.

'Hey, you hear that?'

' – ?'

'You're a villain,' Martin told Mr Apple.

'That's right. I thought you knew.'

'Sure I knew, but I've just had it confirmed by an authority.'

'I'm glad. It must be nice to be proved right once in a while.'

'Very funny.'

Mr Apple glanced up from his desk. 'I wasn't really joking,' he said seriously.

'You never do.'

Mr Apple looked aggrieved. 'Yes I do,' he protested. 'I have a wonderful sense of humour.'

'You could have fooled me.'

'I don't think I could, Martin,' Mr Apple said, his eyes quite still and piercing behind the thick lenses. 'I really don't think I could.'

'Oh, I'm sure you could, Mr A. You're a wily old bird,' Martin said flippantly.

'If you say so.' Mr Apple gave in.

'In fact, I would say you could fool just about anyone,' Martin went on, leading up to something, but not quite sure what this something was.

'I think you believe I really am a villain.'

'No,' Martin said definitely. 'No, I don't think that. Not that. I think, though, that you like to play games with people.'

Mr Apple thought about this for a few moments before admitting: 'Perhaps you're right, Martin.'

'That can be pretty dangerous, you know, Mr A. I mean, you can get into a lot of unexpected trouble if people don't see it as funny,' Martin went on, realizing finally that in a roundabout way, and without fully understanding why, he was trying to warn Mr Apple that one particular little game had been observed and was being taken very badly.

'Hmm,' said Mr Apple, keeping his face impassive. 'I can understand that. Ah, well, being misunderstood is one of the hazards of life, isn't it, Martin?' he asked, looking up. Then, as though he only now appreciated the warning thrown for him to catch, he added 'But don't you worry. I won't play any games with you.'

'I'm glad to hear it,' Martin told him.

'In fact, I can truthfully say that games are the furthest thing from my mind when I think of you.'

' – ?'

Mr Apple tried to summon up a friendly smile. 'You're safe with me, Martin,' he said enigmatically.

Martin thought about pursuing the subject. Once again he felt an inexplicable sensation that, somehow, his destiny was hobbled to whatever befell the old man. But enough was enough. He had done his best to warn Mr Apple that he was under some suspicion and that was as far as he was prepared to go for the moment.

Two women from the factory down the road came into the shop, linking arms, giggling to hide a shared boredom, placed an ill-fated yankee, and scurried out. A young labourer, dressed in jeans and wellington boots turned down at the top and caked with cement, wandered from newspaper to newspaper seeking some certainty, failed to find it, and left to continue rebuilding the city. A pensioner came waddling in, the steel tip on his cane and similar tips on the heels of his shoes making three-legged, staccato taps on the linoleum; he wrote out his bet laboriously, making several changes, altering it every time he consulted the views of another tipster. In the end he despaired of ever getting it right and tick-tocked out again. And so it went. Clients came in with reasonable confidence but left soon afterwards looking bewildered, many not daring to risk a bet. Then, just before noon, a slim young man in an anorak rushed into the shop. He was panting, and he approached the counter with an assurance that indicated he was not the type who took chances on horses. 'Mr Apple?'

Mr Apple rose, his face expressionless, his fingers clenched.

'I've been sent to make sure everything is okay.'

Mr Apple stared at the man blankly, raising just one eyebrow in a difficult theatrical gesture he liked to employ from time to time. He kept his eyes fixed on the man's face, but saw, nonetheless, Martin shaking his head, his finger pressed to his lips.

'You know – ' the man said, fidgeting under Mr Apple's stoically uncomprehending gaze.

'I'm sorry?' Mr Apple offered at last.

'Seamus Reilly.' The man mentioned the name in a reverent whisper, as though this would reveal all.

'Seamus Reilly?' Mr Apple all but shouted the name, making the man wince and glance furtively over his shoulder.

'Yes,' he hissed. 'You know – '

'I'm afraid I don't know. I haven't the remotest idea what you're talking about,' Mr Apple lied convincingly. 'Martin? Come here a minute will you? This young man seems to be somewhat confused.

He says a – what was the name? – Seamus something – '

'Reilly,' the man supplied quickly.

'Ah, yes, Reilly. A man called Seamus Reilly sent him in to see if everything was all right. You don't know any Seamus Reilly, do you?' Martin shook his head slowly, his eyes fixed on the young man on the far side of the counter.

'You see?' Mr Apple said earnestly. 'You must be mistaken. I know an O'Reilly, but he's a David – '

The young man hurried from the shop, keeping his hands in the pockets of his anorak, using his shoulder to push open the door.

'Good heavens,' exclaimed Mr Apple. 'We do get some odd ones in here, don't we, Martin?'

Martin nodded, his silence ominous, his eyes still fixed on the door as if expecting it to open again at any minute. And he was not disappointed: suddenly in came the young man again, almost trotting, followed by Seamus Reilly.

'Good morning, Mr Apple,' Seamus Reilly said politely, scrupulously ignoring Martin.

'Good morning, Mr Reilly,' Mr Apple replied with equal politeness, neatly balancing the proceedings by ignoring the young man.

'Ah,' said Seamus. 'You do know me.'

'Of course.'

'Then – ?' Seamus indicated by a lilt in his voice and a vague gesture that perhaps some explanation was in order.

Mr Apple generously decided to oblige. 'How was I to know you sent him?' he asked reasonably. 'In walks this young man, a complete stranger – even Martin didn't know him – and Martin knows almost everyone, don't you, Martin? – and starts asking me questions. How was I to know – ?' Mr Apple asked again, allowing the question to trail away into silence.

Reilly nodded slowly, glancing quickly at Martin. 'Quite right, Mr Apple,' he said finally. 'Quite right. My mistake. I thought you had met.' Mr Apple overlooked the lie, and bowed his head slightly in recognition of his righteousness.

'A private word, then,' Reilly suggested, waving the confused young man away, watching him as he retreated to the far end of the shop.

'As you wish,' Mr Apple agreed, and, adopting an exact replica of the gesture, waved Martin away, giving him what could have been a little wink.

'Now,' said Seamus, pausing to light one of his little cigars and puff the smoke upwards in his slightly effeminate way, '*is* everything all right?'

'Of course.'

'Excellent.'

Mr Apple waited patiently: he knew that men who hold the whip hand liked their victims to wait patiently.

'No trouble at all?'

'No. None.'

'Excellent,' Reilly said again, continuing to enjoy his cigar, his eyes never leaving Mr Apple's face, using the smoke as an excuse to narrow them slightly. 'You haven't had any – eh – interference?'

'Interference?'

'No questions being asked by strangers?'

'Only him,' Mr Apple said innocently, pointing at the young man.

'Apart from him,' Reilly said with asperity.

'No.'

Reilly gave a small, humourless laugh. 'Sometimes, you know, we make mistakes about the people we trust,' he confessed in an oddly paternal voice.

'To err – ' Mr Apple began, his tone overtly human.

'Sometimes they let us down badly,' Seamus went on. 'It can be very disappointing. Very disappointing,' he said, shaking his head sorrowfully. 'And then, you see – ' He paused briefly to create the proper effect, stubbing out his cigar in the small tin ashtray on the counter. 'And then we have to punish them. Regrettably, of course.'

'Of course.'

Reilly shook his head in wonder. 'It is really amazing, you know, how many people think they can let us down and go unpunished. Even God punishes those who let Him down, doesn't He?' he asked.

'He does indeed,' sighed Mr Apple.

'You would tell us if anyone approached you?' Reilly asked abruptly, his voice suddenly sharp and businesslike.

Mr Apple looked suitably shocked. 'Approached? I don't follow.'

'If, say, the British became interested.'

'Oh. I see.'

'You would inform us?'

'I'm sure I would.'

Reilly smiled. 'Excellent. I knew you would. You know, I like you, Mr Apple. I like you a great deal. It would distress me greatly if anything unpleasant happened to you.'

'You're very kind.'

'Yes,' agreed Seamus in a mildly surprised voice, as if the accolade was foreign to him but deserving nonetheless. 'Yes, I suppose I am. Good. Well, that's that all cleared up. Now, about yourself. Are you all right for cash?'

'Thank you.'

'Excellent. Don't hesitate to shout if you need some.'

'I won't.'

'Just keep up the good work and we'll look after you.'

'Thank you.'

'We always look after our own.'

'I'm sure you do.'

'That's how it should be, don't you think? Always look after your own.'

'Quite.'

A well-dressed, middle-aged man came in and placed a hundred pounds first show on the likely favourite in the first race. Mr Apple dealt with him efficiently and thanked him for his custom, making a mental note to lose a couple of hundred on the same horse if it failed to oblige.

Seamus Reilly waited until the man had left the shop before announcing: 'I must be off. I'll be in touch, Mr Apple.' Mr Apple nodded. 'I'll probably drop in next week.'

'I look forward to that.'

Reilly summoned the young man to open the door for him and swept through it in his elegant, well-polished shoes.

'Very funny people coming to see you this morning, Mr Apple. Funny friends you have. I'm surprised at you,' Martin said.

Mr Apple looked up and seemed on the point of saying something significant. But he changed his mind and said instead, 'Just a business acquaintance with a little problem.'

'Oh, I see.'

'I thought you might know him.'

'Me? No-o-o-o. Never saw him before.'

'I see. Nor the other one, either, I suppose.'

'Other one?'

'The young man in the anorak.'

'Uh-uh. Told you. Never saw either of them.'

'Tell me, why did you – ' Mr Apple began.

'Sharp dresser, wasn't he,' Martin interrupted immediately.

'Who?'

'The man. The one with the cigar. Not the yob in the anorak.'

'Oh. Yes. Very sharp.'

'Must be important.'

'Would you think?'

Martin nodded. 'Very important I would say. Used to having his own way too, I'd say.'

'Would you now.'

Martin nodded again. 'Funny how you can always tell them. They're so polite. You know I'd say if that man stuck a knife in you he'd apologize first.'

Mr Apple smiled.

'And send flowers to your funeral,' Martin went on. 'Oh, I wouldn't have him as a friend if I were you, Mr Apple. And I certainly wouldn't do anything that would upset him.'

'I'll remember, Martin,' Mr Apple said seriously, aware that there was nothing funny in Martin's meaning despite his lighthearted manner.

'Must be nice to have power,' Martin went on. 'You ever want power, Mr Apple? Make people jump when you say jump?'

Mr Apple looked genuinely amazed. 'Why on earth would I want to make people jump, Martin?'

'You know what I mean. Make them do exactly what you want.'

'Most people will do what you want if you just ask them politely. You don't have to have power for that, do you?'

'It helps.'

'Only if you want them to do something unkind,' Mr Apple said quietly, the words retracing their steps to chase some incident in his past, gazing at Martin's face.

'Shit,' Martin was saying, as though kindness and power had nothing whatever to do with each other.

'You would have to say that, Martin,' said Mr Apple.

It proved a boring, uneventful afternoon. Mr Apple managed to lose the remaining money and balance his books nicely. It came as a pleasant surprise when Martin finally announced: 'Another day dead and buried.'

'Yes, indeed.'

'And all of us getting older,' Martin philosophized good-humouredly.

'And all of us getting older,' Mr Apple agreed. 'And not a whit the wiser,' he added.

'I wouldn't say that.'

Mr Apple thought for a moment, frowning as if something was eluding him. Then he brightened. 'You're quite right, Martin. Yes. I forgot. Well, no. I didn't forget. I tucked it away so that I could think more about it tonight.'

' – ? What are you talking about, Mr A.?' Martin asked.

'And thank you,' Mr Apple added. 'Thank you, Martin.'

'I haven't a clue what you're on about,' Martin threw over his shoulder by way of farewell, and by the time Mr Apple looked up he was gone.

Mr Apple took his time about locking up. The incidents of the afternoon had upset him more than he would have thought possible. And Martin's warning would have to be heeded: Seamus Reilly was not a man to be trifled with.

He closed and locked the door and set off down the street, his stilted walk very evident now that his mind was occupied with other things. When he had almost reached the end of the street he noticed two men standing on the corner: pretending not to look he recognized the young man in the anorak and, with him, the tall elegance of the nameless messenger who had given him the latest batch of money to lose. Mr Apple buried his chin in his chest and hurried towards the comfortable bustle of the Antrim Road. He was alarmed to find himself shaking. Yet, when he reached the brighter lights and glanced back, the two men still stood where they had been, appearing quite innocent, like any two men who lived in the area calmly discussing the events of the day. And Mr Apple felt a growing anger within him, as though he had allowed his greatest enemy the chance to invade his body and leave him trembling and a stranger to himself.

When he finally reached home Chloe was waiting at the door, mewling impatiently, implying she was starving to death, and how dare he keep her waiting.

'I'm coming, I'm coming,' Mr Apple told her with uncharacteristic impatience. 'You'd swear I never gave you a bite to eat,' he added, watching the tip of her tail twitch in excited expectancy.

And that night Mr Apple was ravaged by dreams of flesh being torn from his body by gigantic claws that ripped him to shreds. But, fortunately, it seemed that whatever spirit was instructed to watch over him could not stand to see him suffer so, and kept waking him every hour with a strange, nameless alarm.

— 8 —

Colonel Maddox sat at the head of the long mahogany dining-table (beautifully set with glass and silver, an arrangement of imported flowers in the centre), brooding over his wife's futile attempt at *escalope de veau aux champignons*, trying to exclude from his thoughts the chirping of her dinner guests. When he was younger his undeniable good looks, enhanced by his uniform, had been an impressive focus for women's attention, as had the seemingly limitless horizons of his career. But now his lined, exhausted face was just a joke, his career was almost over and he had nothing else to offer. Words left him in regimented barks, and when he tried to join in the inconsequential chit-chat he sounded absurd: his abrupt military intonation creating havoc with all things floral, theatrical and literary. Once he had dreamed of military greatness, of dying at the front, of leading his men over the top with astounding bravery and scant regard for his own safety, of wielding considerable power in Whitehall; but he had long since foresworn such chimeras. His tired, sagging eyes gave the impression of a once great man resigned to mediocrity, and he carried with him the furtive, nervous shadows and tics that service in Northern Ireland seemed to settle upon anyone assigned there. Yet despite the persistent hovering of death Maddox yearned to return there, and wished his leave was at an end. He sat there prodding the diced mushrooms, longing to return to people he understood and, more importantly, who seemed to understand him: men who said everything they had to say in a few words and with a minimum of fuss. He glanced up at his wife and smiled inwardly as she laughed flirtatiously and tried her wiles on an uninterested publisher of soft-porn paperbacks. He wondered what John Asher would make of her: his smile broadened at the thought of the interrogation he would put her through.

97

Leading from there, through Asher and on through the tense, panicky nights of Belfast, Maddox thought about Mr Apple and the game he was certain he was playing. The man must be mad. Shrewd enough, but mad nonetheless: only a madman would try the subterfuge and trickery Mr Apple was attempting. Or was Mr Apple the innocent he pretended to be? Was he, in fact, just quietly doing a job with no sinister undertones whatever? Maddox smiled again: what, indeed, if he and the confident Mr Asher were quite wrong, were barking up the wrong tree entirely, were wasting their time? Suddenly the Colonel hooted out loud with laughter.

'Do *tell* us, darling,' Nancy Maddox purred from the other end of the table, leaning sideways to skirt the flowers and get a better view of the remarkable sight of her husband laughing. 'We would all love to share your little joke.'

Colonel Maddox quickly refolded his features into their normal, mournful contours. 'Sorry. Nothing. Just thought of something.'

'Well, *tell* us,' Nancy persisted, flicking her eyes over her guests to glean support.

'It was nothing.'

'Another secret, I suppose,' Nancy sighed, overplaying her exasperation. 'Matthew collects secrets like butterflies. Really, every time he comes home from that awful place he gets worse.'

'I'm sorry,' the Colonel said, his apology halfhearted as if unsure of his guilt.

'I simply cannot understand why he keeps going back there,' Nancy insisted, addressing herself to her guests, avoiding direct contact with her husband in much the same way as she would were she dealing with a cripple.

'Duty,' Maddox offered, feeling some explanation was needed.

'Duty, indeed,' Nancy snapped scornfully. 'Let someone else have the duty. That's what I say. We should pull out and let those savages kill each other off. Like we did in India and places.'

'Quite right,' the publisher agreed, and then coughed as some morsel went down the wrong way.

'We can't,' Maddox said patiently.

'Whyever not, Matthew?' Nancy wanted to know, deciding to acknowledge her husband's presence. 'Nobody wants us there.'

Colonel Maddox studied the small gold signet ring on his little finger, turning and turning it as though seeking inspiration. He cleared his throat and everyone at the table turned towards him, fixing their eyes on his face in anticipation of wisdom. 'We have a commitment,' he said simply.

'Oh God,' Nancy said, flopping back in her chair and throwing up her arms in mock despair. Inwardly she fumed at her husband's fidelity, faithfulness not being one of her strong points.

'That's the cause of all the trouble, of course,' the publisher, recovered and latching on to Nancy's mild blasphemy, announced. 'God. Protestants and Catholics,' he concluded, placing the sects in the order of superiority as he saw it.

'Not any more,' Maddox contradicted, and wished he had kept his mouth shut.

'Really?' a new voice entering the fray wanted to know.

'I thought it was that simple when I was first sent there,' the Colonel confessed by way of atonement, aware that he was about to be launched on the choppy, treacherous sea of explanation. He searched about for the words that would explain the tragedy of Ulster to the greedy, vacuous faces that stared at him, searched also for something that would orientate his thoughts. He felt himself drowning in the confusion of hopes and distortions, fears, truths, half-truths and lies, political wheelings and religious dealings that created the turmoil of Ireland, and the more his mind thrashed about the more he realized he was sinking. 'The problem *is* – ' He stressed the last word unwittingly, and paused as though some clarification was just beyond his reach but attainable nonetheless. His face twisted in concentration, and the heavy silence of the dinner guests was like the murmur of an expectant crowd. Alas, Colonel Maddox was to let them down: how could he get such complexities across to other people? What took mountains of paper, strategic maps and charts, reports, analyzed reports, analyzed analysis, could hardly be explained over a slowly congealing *escalope de veau*. He stared at their quizzical faces, and his mouth closed over air. Slowly he lowered his eyes to his plate and surrendered.

'Well, that explains everything,' Nancy said brightly, flashing her eyes upwards, and her guests commiserated with knowing smiles and shrugs. 'Now that we have solved that, has anyone here seen *Equus*?'

Mr Apple spooned tomato soup into his mouth and alternated his gaze between Chloe, who was playing with a ping-pong ball, and the television, which was showing pictures of another bombing in Belfast. As he watched the building explode in replay, and the injured being trundled away as though for the second time, he was amazed at his own detachment: it was as though it were all taking place a thousand miles away instead of just down the street. Worse still, it could have been fiction: another episode of some thriller with a cast of heroes who never died, were indestructable. Ah, he thought, that is precisely what the people of this violated city are: indestructable, going about their ways, making love at night, smiling, chatting, ignoring death sitting on their shoulders.

John Asher sat in his office, a tiny green-and-beige painted cell, reading through reports with the avidity of a man possessed, the remains of his supper pushed to one side. He read each word, forcing his cluttered, tired mind to concentrate, mouthing some of the words aloud in case his weary eyes were tempted to skip any. Somewhere on the pages before him might lie the clue to the problem that harrassed him continuously: he knew that the Bezant betting-shop was a clearing-house for dirty money; he knew that Arthur Apple was involved; and, most of all, suspected that there was a great deal more to all this than met the eye. The Provo executives who visited the shop so regularly did not do so because they were ardent gamblers. He could have hauled in half-a-dozen men for questioning, but that would have been a futile exercise: he would merely tip his own hand and, in return, receive nothing but the usual dull, gloating silence. No, he simply had to wait until he had proof, until someone made a mistake, or one of his informers came up with something concrete, or he spotted something in the reports that littered his desk: a casual reference to a person who had been sighted somewhere he had never been seen before, a meeting that at first glance appeared meaningless, but which hid a darker motive.

Asher yawned and stretched. Much as he disliked the Colonel's lenient, conciliatory, somewhat offhand attitudes, he wished he was back from leave. If nothing else, he was a useful testing-ground for ideas. No, that was unfair: the Colonel was a good soldier and a good man: like everyone else he was tired, his mind bogged down by the morass of information, the sense of futility and the unbending realization that they were getting nowhere no matter who they arrested, questioned, imprisoned. Stop the terrorists, they commanded from London. Yes, sir! Easy. Just hold up your hand and they stop. Hah. The trouble was that terrorists appeared in an unending stream, generation upon generation, cut one in half and instead of one dead body you ended up with, it seemed, two live ones – both more dedicated and intense than the one you thought you had destroyed. And they blended into the community to such effect that one never knew who was who, the most innocent-looking often the most guilty, and if Asher had learned one thing through the years he had learned that nobody would ever penetrate the complex, unyielding Irish nationalist mind.

Martin Deeley crouched low in his seat in the darkness of the cinema, his knees resting on the back of the seat in front of him, his eyes fixed, unblinking, on the screen. He chewed his thumbnail, spitting offhandedly into the aisle as a sliver of nail broke off. The cinema was holding a Hitchcock festival for that week, and Martin had patronized it every night: last night *Rear Window*, the night before *Dial M for Murder*, tonight *Psycho*. It was the alternatives of death that drew admiration from him as he watched, safe in the conviction that nobody would spot his enjoyment. The fascination of one person killing another completely overwhelmed him. Just as some people aroused themselves from the monotony of their lives by sharing the romantic and sexual escapades of their screen idols, so Martin felt new energy coursing through his veins as he studied celluloid people in their attitudes of death. Indeed, his interest in how people reacted when dying had nearly been his downfall on more than one occasion, as he lingered that minute too long to study his own victims as they came to terms with the fact that life was irrevocably ebbing from them. And as he focused his full attention on the unfortunate Janet Leigh, her body being systematically punctured and mutilated in the shower, he felt the familiar, glorious throbbing in his loins. He closed his eyes and gasped as the warmth oozed deliciously onto his leg.

Daphne Cope led her client towards her room, scrupulously avoiding any mention of the fact that she recognized him as a soldier despite his natty sports jacket and flannel trousers. It was the shoes that gave them away, of course, always the shoes: too brightly polished, too much spit and polish; no *real* civilian ever went to such lengths. Probably a sergeant, she mused: you could tell that sort of thing both from their bulk and the way they talked to you. Not that it mattered: the money was the same regardless of rank, she thought democratically.

As she waited for him to undress she played her usual little game of make-believe and pretended he was Martin. Then, on the bed, she muttered lustful little catch-phrases to him, getting him going: she had researched this well and knew that some worked better than others; married men, for some reason, needed more goading than others. Through it all she kept her eyes shut tight, feeling in his plump, wide body the hardness and slim outline of Martin. And as he heaved and floundered, determined to assert his tenuous dominance (and calling, between gasps for breath, the name Angela – a girlfriend or wife called on to witness his activity, to share his runting passion and possibly to salve his conscience) she groaned with practised artistry, and drew on the memories of her occasional nights with the young man she worshipped and for whose safety she feared.

Somewhere near the heart of the city a siren wailed, and the eerie tintinnabulation of rattling dustbin-lids shattered the night. Catcalls were launched into the air, shouts as venomous as rockets. Fucking English pigs. Para bastards. Youse fucking animals. Then the growling Saracens moved in. Gunfire cracked. Sidestreets were highlit in the evil blue-green glow of petrol bombs. And all over the city hundreds of doors were slammed tight and bolted, thousands of lights switched off as people settled in for a fretful night, waiting for daylight to reveal the destruction of war.

— 9 —

Mr Apple eased one eyelid open and viewed the dawn with a jaundiced eye. He always regarded Sundays with a mixture of suspicion and joy, since they meant, on the one hand, that he was forced to insulate himself from the particular sorrows which manifested themselves on that day without the comforting distraction of work and the raw collection of characters this brought galloping into his life, but, on the other, that he was free to visit what he liked to consider his private garden, whether Eden or Gethsemane, depending on the humour of the angels he found waiting for him. Such visits were particularly rewarding now that spring had finally come, the great trees bursting with an energy that was, in some way, transmitted to himself, so that he felt a little younger, a little more capable of fulfilling whatever destiny it was that his spirits had in store for him. It was certainly interesting, he thought, levering open his other eye and staring at the ceiling, how one could almost feel the old body rejoice now that it had survived another winter.

Mr Apple swung his feet over the side of the bed and studied his toes, wriggling them for a while, trying to straighten both small ones, which curved painfully under the others. Spring, he thought (reaching into his mind and sardonically pulling out the memory of a song that seemed to be played to death on the radio about this time of year), is in the air; and even a couple of blackbirds shared his perception and sang tentatively, duly fulfilling their obligations to April. Through the open window also (on the sill of which Chloe sat, busily manicuring her nails with her rough pink tongue) came the sounds of Sunday gardeners energetically mowing lawns with that initial burst of fitness and energy that the first real sun of the year seemed to stimulate. It was all so peaceful. Even violence took a day off on the Sabbath, and explosions and expletives were replaced, for the moment at least, by the soulful peeling of church bells as the denominations vied for attention: *Dolente, Dolore*. Mr Apple glanced at the small travelling-clock by his bed: almost ten. He smiled: the churches had long since ceased to push their luck and now offered alternative services at an hour that allowed their flocks the luxury of a lie-in.

'Time to arise and go now, get the sleep from thine eyes and face the world,' Mr Apple said aloud. Then he chuckled to himself, wondering happily if he was, indeed, manifesting the first signs of madness that talking to oneself was supposed to indicate. 'Rubbish,' he almost shouted. 'Utter tomfoolery,' he cried, falling back on the bed and kicking his spindly legs in the air like a child, building up a skittishness within himself, all the while pretending he was just having a little fun with no particular reason for such actions. But Mr Apple knew very well that there was a very particular reason for his foolishness: the first days of spring – came they early or late – were days of atrocious torment that he dreaded. Each year they brought with them the same long procession of appalling memories which seemed to have planned the invasion of his soul with alarming, seasonal precision, coinciding with that one week that had been the darkest in his life. Strangely, once he recognized that the daemonic images were unfolding their seasonal costumes, dusting them off and shaking the occasional sleepy moth from their folds, Mr Apple found that he could face them with a mildness that was quite fatalistic. He no longer grieved over the mutilation of his body that was a constant reminder of his agony; no longer, either, did the harrassment of his nightmares drive him to the brink of suicide: it struck him that, perhaps, some sympathetic angel had cauterized him from the worst things associated with that time. 'Hah,' said Mr Apple, mildly shocking himself by the sudden exclamation, and he found himself suddenly calmed by the realization that now, lying on his bed, he could even cull tiny memories of happiness from that terrifying time. And perhaps, he thought, that was the secret of man's survival: perhaps that was how everyone in this shattered, battered city survived. You've got to see the funny side, Mr Apple now recalled someone saying to him not so long ago, though what the funny side of death was he could not imagine. And yet people all around him seemed to spot it, to hug it tightly to themselves, and carry on as though reality consisted only of the world that revealed itself to the senses, a world of sight and smell and sound, as though tragedy and all such pains that afflicted the soul could be dealt with by a shrug of the shoulders, treated as vague discomforts, something to be put up with as a veteran might recall and dismiss old war wounds in damp weather. Nothing more. The blackness of pain and death came and went, greeted and waved away, and people continued to exist. 'Faustus is dead, long live the Pied Piper,' Mr Apple said, giggling a bit hysterically at his ridiculous joke, springing to his feet and making for the bathroom. He shaved himself carefully, taking inordinate precautions not to nick himself: for some reason he abhorred those specks of dried blood small razor-cuts left behind – lice droppings, he had heard them called – and he shuddered when he saw them on the faces of other men, treating them like evil fetishes that augured much worse bloodshed to come. Then he brushed his teeth, up and down, doused his face in cold water, dried, and returned to the bedroom to dress.

Clad in what, with dry humour, he referred to as his Sunday suit, Mr Apple made his way down the road, albeit without much purpose in his step. He did not walk aimlessly: it was more as though he was heading towards a sound rather than some more definite destination, a sound that played tricks on him, fading occasionally, leaving him temporarily baffled if not quite lost.

'Morning, Mr Apple.'

' – ?' Mr Apple was taken aback by the burring voice at such close proximity. 'Ah,' he finally managed, eyeing suspiciously the small, stooped, sandalled figure, immaculate and balding in khaki shirt and grey flannel trousers, carrying a watering-can, who regarded him with tolerant distaste through thick hornrimmed spectacles from behind the low, trimmed, crew-cut privet hedge. 'Ah,' he said again, composing himself. 'Good morning, Mr Cahill.'

'Churching?' Mr Cahill demanded as if not approving of religion as a pastime.

'Not exactly.'

'Stopped that nonsense a long time ago. Hypocritical, isn't it?'

Mr Apple shrugged. The last thing he wanted was an argument. But Mr Cahill was in fine fettle and, adopting the same scathing tone he used when dismissing from his mind such riff-raff as niggers, coolies, wogs and Pakis (all of whom he claimed to have had dealings with at some time in his life, though in what capacity he kept a closely guarded secret), he declared: 'All of them. Damned hypocrites. Parsons, priests, vicars, all you have to do is listen to them.' Mr Cahill's words sprinkled over Mr Apple as the water from the can now did over the neat row of primulas. 'All they ever do is trot out the old platitudes. Love one another. Huh. Why should I? Can't stand half the people I meet. Anyway, all their sermons are slanted.'

'Oh, not all, I think,' Mr Apple ventured charitably.

'All of them. What did you mean by "not exactly"?'

' – ?'

'When I asked if you were churching,' Mr Cahill explained.

'Oh. Well, I pray – but not exactly in church. I have my own place, you see,' Mr Apple replied vaguely.

'Your own place? You're not a minister?' Mr Cahill sounded shocked.

'No. Indeed no, Mr Cahill. I just like to get away by myself and chat to – '

'You're mad, Mr Apple,' Mr Cahill announced, turning away and striding towards his house (structurally identical to Mr Apple's, but sporting net curtains, looped and tied back at the sides, and pale blue paintwork which stood out garishly), the last drops from the watering-can dripping on the path behind his impatient footsteps like damp exclamation marks.

For several moments Mr Apple stared at the retreating figure, and continued to gaze at the space vacated by it as it now vanished round the side of the house, seemingly leaving some ghostly vestige of itself in the front garden to guard against trespassers. In an odd way he quite liked Mr Cahill, almost admired the old bigot's outrageous forthrightness, and there was always the possibility he had a point. Certainly (and Mr Apple had noted it with some alarm, the more intense when he spotted himself beginning to surrender to its potent inevitability) the tone of the sermons he occasionally saw reported was subtly overladen with politics. And yet, why not? The fine line between religion and politics had become infinitely finer in Ulster, causing frictions of unidentifiable origin. But Mr Apple (he had turned left at the end of the road and now stood patiently by the bus stop almost directly opposite the church of St Enoch) was content to admit that this was a problem for someone else to solve, and he wasn't very sanguine about their chances of finding a solution.

He glanced across the road at the armoured car parked, in a failed gesture of discretion, at the side of the church, its occupants looking embarrassed as the faithful walked by and headed for the open doors of the church. Their dogged determination to confront the Lord with their problems made Mr Apple think about his own efforts at prayer and wonder mildly why they had been so futile. Possibly it was because he had nothing to pray for, or, more truthfully, nothing to pray to. Still, he acknowledged gratefully as the bus came trundling up the road, there had been comfort to be found in the dark corners he always chose, and an odd communal compassion as the congregation struggled to worship a God who seemed to have better things on His mind. Amazingly, he had noted with wonder, this in no way seemed to deter them; their faces relaxed as though the din of their prayers battering His eardrums formed a noisy, impregnable barrier that released their thoughts from the horrors that were committed around them. In truth, Mr Apple had envied them their faith.

Almost before he knew it Mr Apple found himself at his destination, found himself thanking the conductor who helped him alight, found himself walking contentedly and with a spring in his step down the lane to the abandoned farmhouse, found himself moving through the overgrown farmyard with its collapsing outhouses (the rusting corrugated-iron roof of one swaying in the light wind and making baleful whinnies like echoes of the animals it once housed), found himself clambering over the low stone wall with remarkable agility for a man of his advancing years, found himself quickening as he made for the copse in the centre of the field, found, too, a strange serenity descend upon him as he neared it, found, alas, something like terror invade his soul as he entered under the shadow of the trees. He stood quite still, his head cocked to one side, and listened, but not, as one might have thought, for any natural sound: Mr Apple waited for the voices he knew would come to him, the voices that always came to him in this place.

Be patient, Mr Divine told him kindly.

Yes, agreed Sefer, you can't hurry these things, you know.

'I know,' Mr Apple said aloud.

Ah, said Sefer, you're learning.

'Yes, I'm learning.'

Good, said Mr Divine in a pleased voice.

Suddenly Mr Apple felt a terrible, cold chill penetrate his body. His head began to ache as if several headaches had saved up their pain and now heaped it upon him. A strange, pungent smell assailed him, a stench like burning sulphur or putrefying flesh. He felt himself drifting away as though losing consciousness, and the trees about him shimmered and faded. Small blue lights swam in his brain, blinking in a patternless rota. And then he was floating high above the ground, weightless and unfettered, yet the pain in his head grew worse and that part of his forehead directly above his eyes seemed to puff up, and he felt cold, bitterly cold. The awful pain made him close his eyes, but immediately some antagonistic force made him open them again and look down: he was hovering over the little copse, looking down at himself standing there, a forlorn, lost, abandoned figure. It was as if he had somehow inhabited his soul and left his body to fend for itself for the moment. Then the voices came: they drifted in like the sighs of whispering angels who had abandoned their ancient places, yet, although they permeated him, they did not seem to be audible: they were simply there, coming from a great distance and friendly enough. Birds, too, suddenly abounded, long-winged dark furious shapes, each one a strange embodiment of fierce despairs and dreams, each one a vision of his own suppressed memories, floating on warm streams of air, gliding mile upon mile, then dropping through an entanglement of shapes, an incomprehensible entanglement of geometric silhouettes, alighting on invisible timber ghosts, folding their wings, settling like a black conspiracy.

We have been watching you, the voices cried in unison, half-singing, half-wailing.

'Ah,' Mr Apple heard his body sigh.

We are well pleased.

'Ah.'

Your time is not yet come, but shortly. Soon the salvation of one will be required of you. Soon but not so soon as to give you no time to prepare.

'How shall I know?'

You will be given a warning, and then you will know you must sacrifice yourself.

'What warning?'

Your wounds will open. But you will feel no pain. We will carry the pain for you as you have carried ours.

'Ah.'

You need not be afraid. You will find great peace.

The single word 'peace' echoed comfortingly as the voices withdrew, taking with them the awful throbbing in Mr Apple's head, escorted by the birds that rose suddenly, formed columns, and plunged upwards, great wings outspread but unmoving, giving the impression that they were, in fact, diving, that the world had been turned upside-down and that they were plummeting downwards.

Mr Apple came to himself and shivered. There he stood in the middle of the copse, his feet firmly planted on the ground. He shook his head and smiled: as always after these encounters he felt better, felt as though he had been given some energy which would allow him to carry on, but energy in a limited dosage lest he become impertinent and believe he could carry on for ever. Mr Apple smiled again and, with a small wave towards the sky, he bowed to the trees that surrounded him and set off home, walking briskly until his legs complained.

Had the bus taking Mr Apple to his curious rendezvous been a little less punctual, and had he, while waiting, watched the Sunday worshippers enter St Enoch's, he might have been surprised to spot Martin Deeley (dressed respectfully in a dark suit, white shirt and sober tie) among them. Martin Deeley physically fulfilled his obligations of the Sabbath conscientiously every week: it never struck him as incongruous or perverse that he should remain loyal and obedient to this ecclesiastical regulation while cheerfully breaking every other commandment of his faith. Indeed, he would have been both shocked and furious had it been suggested he might as well abandon this one remaining link. Once, many years ago, the ludicrous disparity of his behaviour had crossed his mind, and, with a feeling of wry, guilty amusement, he had likened it to the Mafia allegiance to family and the compulsory weekly visit to the Godfather's table which he had read about or seen in the cinema: almost everything was forgiveable provided that one precept was faithfully observed, and in much the same light Martin faithfully observed his Sunday visit to Mass. But his relationship with God was certainly spurious: he had a healthy respect for the power He would wield over him when he finally died, but as long as there was breath in his body God's influence was easily curtailed. With monstrous profanity Martin Deeley could never quite reconcile himself to the fact that this Being with all that incredible power at his fingertips could get Himself crucified without at least a show of resistance. All that crap about dying for the sins of man! Hang up there, boyo, and save mankind. Well, He must be pretty disillusioned by now. And yet...and yet, Martin Deeley fully realized that in spite of his bold effrontery, in spite of his casual dismissal of all things religious as not applying to him, he still thought in terms of sin rather than crime. When he killed someone a little sign sometimes flickered mischievously in his brain, accusing him of mortal *sin*: and every once in a while, in those brief seconds before he fell asleep and the innocence of his childhood held centre-stage, he found himself mouthing uncharacteristic apologies to the God he had decided it was mature to disown.

Little silvery bells tinkled in the sanctuary. The Host was raised and the heads of the congregation lowered. Martin bowed his head also, but not so low that he could not observe the mass adoration. The weirdness of it all frightened him, and he felt a strange loneliness, as though he was purposely being excluded from the lucid familiarity of something he had sought and received comfort from in another time. Looking about him, wondering at those genuinely adoring faces, he could appreciate the emotions the ceremony induced in others, yet he himself was stirred only, it seemed, to a reminiscence of sadness: he was, he decided, like an archaeologist recreating the dignified solemnity of some ceremony practised by a defunct but interesting civilization. He smiled faintly, his eyes softening and, as the congregation streamed towards the altar to receive communion, he allowed the chill breezes of memory to blow in his mind and toy with the threads of recollection...

The two coffins lay side by side, the floral wreaths shared equally between them, the flowers crippled and twisted into unnatural shapes, cartwheels and crucifixes, the mourners, also, twisted into the odd contours of lament: the women seeming to have shrunk in their misery, the men grown taller in their anger. Martin stood between Cissy and Mam, feeling embarrassed as Mam sniffed and snorted her griefstricken way through the ceremony, feeling irked and jittery as she flicked her way round her rosary, gabbling her Hail Marys at incredible speed, her head bobbing every time she hit upon the name of Jesus. To pass the time he tried to keep up with her, failed, and decided she was only pretending to pray, just going through a familiar ritual, mouthing occasional words from which she had once drawn comfort.

As the coffins were heaved clumsily on to the shoulders of the four bearers the congregation rose and stood stiffly in the pews, glancing furtively at one another, surreptitiously seeking advice on how to behave, wondering, perhaps, what emotions to reveal, how best to demonstrate their feelings, which signs and signals would confirm their reason for being there. In the end they seemed to sort it out, the men leaving the women to shed the tears, the women leaving the silent outrage to the men.

Martin was impressed by the cortège, which (he thought for one gruesome moment, as he noted the flowers bob gaily over the heads of the adults, the carnations and lilies and imported roses still spanking fresh and colourful) could easily have been some happy, festive affair. And for the first time in his life he felt almost proud of his father, proud, too, but strangely envious of his brother. As the procession made its way through the streets the murmur of the mourners (a mixture of prayer and practical conversation) kept step with the rhythmic stomping of the paramilitary boots worn by the masked guard of honour, defiantly armed, that paraded in front of the coffins and lined them on either side, their presence giving the dead a political importance they hardly deserved. They were victims. Nothing more. Not heroes or cowards. Not terrorists or activists or traitors. Not, in any logical sense, the enemy. Not motivated by anything stronger than a desire to live. Just victims in the true and appalling sense, plucked willy-nilly from the community and shot, perhaps in reprisal for some other killing long since forgotten, perhaps as a diabolic warning, or perhaps just as some horrific show of sectarian might.

And even then, barely sixteen though he was, watching the coffins being lowered into the cold, damp, symmetrical graves, and hearing the crackling rifles as they delivered their premonitory salute (the shots seeming to bounce from gravestone to gravestone, multiplying their deadly homage, the echoes taking an inordinately long time to recede and disappear skyward as though launched to placate some angry, warmongering god), Martin knew he would be expected to join the unending cycle of violence and avenge these two hopeless deaths. Oh, yes, Mam would see to that, making it clear she would be ashamed of him if he did nothing about it, she would, in the grim cold tradition of such things, be happy to sacrifice him for vengeance.

And friends would argue knowingly that two deaths in one family were enough, but their arguments would be couched in words that expected rebuttal; neighbours would express their desire that he would not consider any action that might bring 'further misery and sorrow to your poor mother', but their voices would indicate they hoped he would. 'Ashes to ashes,' the priest intoned, trying hard to make his familiarity with the words less apparent, imparting meaning by the fire in his voice, delivering his homily with extravagant praise for the two dead men, investing them with qualities they never possessed...

Before he realized it Mass was over, and the congregation were filing from the church, blinking in the bright sunlight, the turmoil in their souls assuaged for another week perhaps. But perhaps not: their eyes still carried the haunted look with which they had arrived, and their loathing was still apparent when they spotted a gaggle of Paras patrolling further down the street. As Martin watched, trying to decipher the various reactions written on the faces about him, the crowd immediately to his right separated and allowed the dapper figure of Seamus Reilly to pass through: then they seemed to withdraw a few feet, respectfully, as though they suspected sins were about to be confessed, sins it would be better for them not to overhear. Not an altogether idiotic suspicion, since Seamus Reilly in his black overcoat and black hat, carrying his large black missal with its embossed gold crucifix, gave a distinct impression of something clerical, though one could have been forgiven for imagining there was something more of the undertaker about him.

'Lovely morning, Martin.'

Martin nodded, mildly surprised that Seamus should speak to him so openly.

'Makes you think of holidays, doesn't it?' Seamus Reilly continued mysteriously.

'Holidays?'

'Mmm. Feel like one?'

'Not – '

'Good. I'm glad you do,' Seamus Reilly said, looking away for a moment to acknowledge a greeting. 'They tell me Berkshire is at its best this time of year.'

'Berkshire?' Martin repeated, his voice rising in stunned surprise.

'Yes. Know it at all? Lovely spot. Wide, open spaces. Fresh air. Quite lovely.'

'I don't – '

'Be at home about eight, will you? I'll be round to see you.'

'Tonight?'

'Tonight. Eight. Exactly. I'm always on time as you know.'

And with that Seamus Reilly left him, nodding to acquaintances in his friendly way, shaking a hand, squeezing an arm, frowning in concern as some problem was revealed.

Martin stared after him, his heart pumping rapidly, an old and familiar anticipation gripping his stomach.

True to his word, at eight precisely Seamus Reilly put one neatly
manicured finger on the white plastic button and pushed. He had, in
fact, arrived three minutes earlier, but so proud was he of his
meticulous timekeeping that he had waited in the shadows until the
exact time of his appointment before announcing himself.

Martin, coming down the stairs two at a time, raced to the door
and let him in, shouting 'I'll get that' as his landlady poked her head
around the sitting-room door. She withdrew again willingly, closing
the door behind her. 'Upstairs,' Martin said.

Reilly inclined his head in agreement and followed Martin up the
narrow stairs that creaked goodhumouredly under their weight.

'Sorry about the mess,' Martin apologized, smiling. 'I'm not tidy.'

'It's as it should be. Lived in,' Reilly conceded graciously,
although his lips tightened as he viewed the small room with distaste.
'I always say a home should be lived in,' he added, 'although – ' He
waved a small hand in a semi-arc and smiled thinly.

'Yeah. Well, I like it this way,' Martin told him, determined to
make no further apology for the chaos about him: his clothes strewn
everywhere, books in precarious piles, newspapers, shoes, an incongruous tennis-racket.

'To each his own,' Reilly allowed.

'Exactly.'

'I must confess I don't think *I* could live amid such confusion. I
like things to be orderly. A place for everything and everything – '

' – in its place.' Martin concluded the quotation.

'Quite,' Reilly said testily.

'Well, it so happens I think the same,' Martin said, suddenly
realizing that Reilly was meeting him for the first time on his own
territory and was starting to flounder. 'And everything *is* in its place.'

'I see,' Reilly said, looking about him as though seeking somewhere to sit. Carefully he removed a jacket and soiled shirt from a wooden, high-backed chair (using only one finger and his thumb), placed them on the bed and sat down, but not before flicking any possible contamination from the seat with a white handkerchief he produced from his breast pocket. 'Ah,' he sighed comfortably, crossing his legs. Martin sat on the edge of the bed (enjoying the wince his guest gave as the springs protested shrilly) and waited.

'You don't, I suppose, mind if I smoke?'

Martin shook his head, and waited.

Reilly lit one of his small cigars and spoke through the cloud of smoke as if trying to conceal, or at least veil, the frank brutality of his words, words spoken in a calm, gentle voice that in no way lessened their deadliness.

'You'll be glad to hear we have someone who needs to be punished, Martin. We need your special talents. Just a one-off, however. A chance that is too good to miss.'

Martin made no reply: he stared through the smoke in the direction of the voice and suddenly recalled, from what seemed a lifetime ago, a visit he had made with his mother to a relative who had spent all her adult life as a Poor Clare. He remembered the eerie sound of her voice whispering through the black-veiled screen, a disembodied voice that seemed to come from the grave. And he had the same impression now of Reilly's flat, matter-of-fact tones wafting through the smoke which curled and twisted before his breath and seemed, oddly, to give his words their inflections.

'You will, of course, have to take a few days off. Tell Mr Apple you feel ill. Tell him that tomorrow. Tuesday you go. You should be back by Friday, all being well.'

'Go where?'

'Why, Berkshire, of course. Lovely spot – '

'I know: wide, open spaces and fresh air. You told me.'

'So I did.'

'Why?'

With a brisk wave Reilly cleared the smoke from in front of his face like a magician making his appearance, and leaned forward.

'Well, a certain Colonel Maddox – I think you've heard of him? Yes. Well, Colonel Maddox has his home there. He is at his home this minute. He will be returning from leave on Wednesday. We would be grateful if he failed to reach Belfast.'

Martin nodded, his mind already raking up questions he would need answered.

'He's not really of great importance,' Reilly was saying in a voice close to regret, 'but his demise would serve its purpose. Actually, from what we've learned Maddox is decent enough. Doesn't even want to be here. And he's always been – eh – correct, I think is the word.' Reilly sighed as though saddened by Colonel Maddox's upright reputation. 'It distresses me when we have to punish nice people – so much easier when they're blackguards, isn't it? Anyway, it should be straightforward enough. We don't foresee any problems.'

'Protection?'

'No. They don't seem to see Berkshire as a likely place for us to strike. He will have a driver, of course. His wife is there. One house-guest who might have left by Wednesday. A publisher of romantic novels, I hear.' Reilly grinned widely, as if he found romance hugely amusing. 'There's a maid – a *domestic*, we were told.' Reilly allowed his grin to widen for a moment before it disappeared completely. 'And that's all,' he concluded.

'Dogs?'

'Two. A retriever. Old, deaf and friendly. A pug. Hers. The wife's. Dreadful creature. Fat and wheezy. Nothing for you to worry about.'

'Neighbours?'

Reilly shook the ash from his cigar.

'Nobody close.'

'How close?'

'Quarter of a mile? Something like that. Your best bet would be after he leaves the house. There's an isolated lane he has to travel down before he hits the main road. Plenty of cover for you. The hedgerows should be pretty about now,' he added.

'That'll be nice,' Martin said, and, strangely, there was nothing sarcastic in his tone: it was a simple statement of fact, as though the viciousness of killing was in some way lessened when perpetrated from behind a pretty hedgerow.

'Hmm,' Seamus murmured, apparently sharing the sentiment and already sniffing primroses.

'Weapon?'

'There'll be a selection at the usual place. Take the bus from the airport and go straight there. You're expected.'

'Transport?'

'Tommy Walshe will drive you. You get on well with him.'

'He's okay. What time does Maddox leave?'

'Ah. Well. As to that, we're not quite sure.'

'Great.'

'If you fly over Tuesday afternoon Tommy will drive you to Berkshire overnight, so you will be in plenty of time.'

'So I just hang around bloody Berkshire all – '

'No,' Seamus snapped, not about to tolerate impertinence.

'What, then?'

'When I said we weren't quite sure I was referring to the precise time. We do know Maddox flies out from Brize Norton at midday. Whether he decides to arrive early or on time is up to him. Perhaps you would like us to telephone him and enquire as to his precise movements?'

'Very funny.'

'Tommy has friends in Oxford. You can rest up there for a few hours. Leave about midnight.'

'Okay.'

'Anything else?'

'No.'

Reilly reached into his pocket and produced two brown envelopes. He passed the thicker of the two to Martin. 'Rail ticket to Dublin. Plane ticket to Birmingham. Money,' he said.

'Thanks.'

'And here,' he continued, passing over the second envelope, 'is the only photograph we have of Maddox. It's not great, I'm afraid, but it's the best we could do. He refused to pose, you see,' he concluded, grinning again.

Martin Deeley, however, saw nothing amusing in the remark; nothing cheerful, either, in the face that stared up at him from the small, glossy, dog-eared photograph. Doomed was the immediate impression the face gave. No hint of a smile, eyes both sad and confused, turned inwards on his soul and already dead. It was the face, Martin thought, of a man who had failed, or not quite that: it was more a mask that portrayed an incapability to understand. Not that it mattered a damn what he looked like: in Martin's eyes he was already a corpse, and he comforted himself with the thought that he was probably going to put the poor old bastard out of some longstanding misery.

'You're quite happy then?' Reilly asked.

'Yeah. Delirious.'

'Good. Anyway, you're the expert. We know we can leave everything safely in your hands.'

'Sure.'

'Excellent. Well, I'll be on my way.'

'Right.'

'Sorry to have intruded on a Sunday. I always think Sunday is a private day,' Seamus explained. 'I recall my mother would never open the door to anyone on Sundays. But that was some time ago, of course. Still, old habits die hard, don't they?'

'I'm sure they do.'

Martin took Reilly to the front door and opened it for him.

'Oh, by the way,' Seamus said, pausing on the doorstep, turning to show mischievous little lights dancing in his eyes. 'There's an apt little landmark in Berkshire for you to look out for. When you see it you'll know the Maddox house is just down the road.'

'Well, are you going to tell me?'

'Oh – a gibbet, Martin. High on a hill overlooking the Downs. The very last gibbet in England, so they tell me. I thought you'd like that,' he added, grinning wickedly.

'Oh, lovely.'

'Yes. I thought you'd like that,' Seamus said again. 'I know you feel at home in the shadow of death.'

'You really are a charmer, Seamus.'

'So I've been told.'

'No, really. You're so bloody charming you frighten the life out of me.'

'Me? Frighten *you*? Oh, come now, Martin.'

'Yes. You go about all dressed up like a man on his way to a party, smiling and cheerful, ticking off names on your death-list like they were your goddam shopping – '

'Shut it, Martin,' Reilly snapped, his face tightening, any trace of friendliness wiped away. 'Don't you ever talk to me like that again, Deeley,' he hissed. 'Not ever, do you hear? You know nothing about me. Nothing about how I feel or what I think. You imagine I *like* having people killed? Do you? Only shitty little thugs like you enjoy death. Yes, you *do*. You revel in it. It makes you feel important, gives your grotty little life some meaning. Jesus! You are fucking pathetic. You're as bad as those smug-faced bastards who portray us all as psychopathic murderers who wallow in blood and death. I can tell you this: I hate it. I loath it. I – ' Seamus Reilly glanced at the sky in search of a better word, and, finding it, 'I abominate it,' he said in a whisper.

'So you abom— '

'Shut up. And as to the way I dress, what do you want? Jeans? Grubby shirts? Dirty shoes? Oh, yes. That would fit the image, wouldn't it? I wear the best clothes I can out of respect. I mourn the people I've had killed, whoever they are, and I dress out of respect for their passing,' Seamus concluded breathlessly, the weird precious-ness of his remarks making them sinister and frightening.

Martin Deeley decided it would be wiser to say nothing.

'And another thing,' Reilly went on, 'you think it's easy for me to go about ordering punishments, don't you? Just a name on a piece of paper to be struck off. Very clever. You stupid bastard. I *believe* in what we are trying to do, but I am sickened to my stomach at the way we are forced to achieve it. I ordered my own brother killed because he turned informer. I suppose I enjoyed that? I cried for a week. And I still cry when I think of his great pleading eyes. He shouted at me "Not me, Seamus, not your own brother" when they came and took him from the house. Dragged him whimpering and screaming down the garden. But, yes, him, my own brother.' Seamus Reilly paused as if again watching his brother being taken from his home. 'And you say I like it.'

'I didn't know – '

'You know *nothing*,' Seamus informed him. 'Not one damn thing. And maybe,' he added with a sigh, 'maybe it's just as well.' Then his voice changed, returning to its former self. 'Anyway, don't forget to look sick when you see Mr Apple. I'll check with you tomorrow evening,' he concluded, and strode off down the street, his black suit disappearing rapidly in the dark.

'Who was that?' his landlady, Mrs Losey, wanted to know, peering round the sitting-room door, her hair netted and curled for the night.

'Nobody.'

'Oh,' Mrs Losey said, accepting the reply for what it was worth.

'Just a friend.'

'Nice to have friends,' Mrs Losey told him. 'You eaten today?'

'Uh-uh.'

'I have a scrap of shepherd's pie left over you can have.'

'Thanks, Mrs Losey. But no. I'm not hungry.'

'You should eat something. Can't go about all day on an empty stomach and hope not to get sick.'

'I don't want anything,' Martin said sourly, then, seeing the woman's hurt expression, he added: 'Not just now. I have things to do. By the way, I won't be here for a few days. I'm going down to Dublin.'

'Dublin, is it?'

'Just for a few days.'

'I see.'

'You go on back to your telly.'

Obediently Mrs Losey closed the door and went back to her telly.

Alone again in his room Martin counted the money, checked the train and plane tickets, and took another cursory look at Colonel Maddox. Then he lay back on his bed, folding his arms under his head, and stared at the ceiling, thinking:

Hey, someone said, that's pretty good shooting, sonny.

It's nothing.

On the mark every time. I call that something.

It's easy.

Martin bathed in the warmth of the flattery and proceeded to shoot some more, while the stranger stood at his shoulder and murmured continuous praise at his prowess: all about them the noises of the fun-fair continued and gave no hint of the fatefulness of the meeting.

It's just know-how, mister, Martin said.

What's your name, sonny?

Martin.

Martin?

Martin Deeley.

Deeley...Deeley...that rings a bell, the stranger said. Oh, yes, he added, remembering something. Where d'you live, Martin Deeley?

Tiger Bay.

Ah. Brothers and sisters?

Only sisters. Two. My brother was – why all the questions, mister?

No reason, Martin. Just curious.

Oh.

You really can shoot though, the stranger iterated, shaking his head in what seemed to be admiration, though there was something ominous creeping into his voice.

Yeah. You told me that already, Martin said, feeling cocky.

I'll remember you, Martin Deeley. I'll remember you.

And he did, but not until long after Martin Deeley had forgotten him. Eighteen months, perhaps more, perhaps two years later, a man called at the Deeley house in Tiger Bay.

Martin Deeley live here? he asked Mam, who stared at him

suspiciously, squinting her eyes, keeping the thin door on a chain and one foot wedged against it.

Who wants to know?

Me.

And who might you be?

He'll know me.

He will, will he?

He will.

Martin! Mam yelled over her shoulder, keeping her eyes on the stranger. There's someone here who wants to see you.

Who is it?

He says you know him.

What's his name?

Hasn't got one, Mam said.

Coming, Martin called.

Hello, Martin. Remember me?

No – yes. I remember your face but –

The fun-fair. Shooting.

Oh. Yeah. I remember.

I told you I wouldn't forget you.

So?

Some friends of mine want to meet you.

Who?

Friends. They have a job for you.

What sort of job?

A job. It won't take long. Pays well.

I'll think about it.

Nothing to think about, Martin. They want to meet you. Tonight.

Oh.

We'll send a car. Sixish.

Okay.

Good.

Yeah.

Who was that may I ask? Mam demanded.

Just a fella.

I saw that. Who was he?

Someone I know.

From where?

Around.

I see. She didn't, of course, but that hardly mattered. Martin was the man of the house now, and it was neither her place nor was it wise to pry too deeply into his affairs. You'll be careful?

I'm always careful.

I know you are, but still be careful.

I'll be careful.

Don't get yourself used.

I won't.

They can use you without you noticing it.

Not me, they can't.

Don't be too sure.

I'm sure, Mam. I can handle myself.

That's what they all say.

But I know I can.

Oh, you know everything.

That's right.

Well, I hope you know what you're doing this time.

I do.

I hope so.

Don't worry. Like I said, I can handle myself.

I hope so.

I *can*.

And in the months that followed, he showed that he certainly could.

'Jesus, Mr Apple, I feel really terrible this morning,' Martin Deeley announced.

'Yes,' replied Mr Apple.

'No, really. Really I do. I think I'm coming down with something.'

Mr Apple looked up from his desk, and nodded. 'Plague, probably. Or leprosy.'

'I'm serious. I don't think I'll make it through the day.'

'Probably not.'

'You think I'm joking.'

'Well – '

'Well, I'm not.'

'Go home then. See a doctor. Go to bed,' Mr Apple advised offhandedly.

'Jeez, you're full of sympathy, Mr Apple.'

'Yes.'

'But I *am* sick, dammit,' Martin insisted.

'I thought you might be,' Mr Apple announced, suggesting by an odd inflection that he had been waiting for some such calamity. 'And I told you what to do. Go home.'

'I can't just hump off like that. Who'll do the board?'

'I'll manage. There's always someone who'll do the board for a few pounds. It doesn't take genius.'

'Well, I'll tell you what I'll do. I'll set up the board and stay until lunch-time. If I still feel like I do now I'll go home then, okay?'

'Please yourself,' Mr Apple snapped, regretting his sharpness but not bothering to do anything about it.

'You're in a funny – '

But whatever funny Mr Apple was in was to remain a mystery, since Martin's diagnosis was interrupted by the arrival of Ursula

Weeks. She stood in the doorway for several seconds, peeping into the shop like a bird deciding where to perch. 'Good morning, Mr Apple. May I come in?'

Mr Apple glanced up, but only with his eyes: he kept his head bent in that petulant posture he had been using on Martin. 'Come in, come in,' he told her, marvelling at the dexterity she showed in cramming her matronly figure into the Salvation Army uniform, her face (clear and innocent and remarkably young-looking for a sixty-year-old, making one think immediately of a nun) framed by her bonnet.

'I thought I'd come nice and early,' Ursula explained, 'before you got busy,' she added with a smile.

Mr Apple nodded, and fussed with pencils and paper-clips on the counter.

'Anyway, people are always in much better humour first thing in the morning, don't you think?' Ursula asked hopefully. 'Before the day catches up on them.'

'Vulnerable,' Mr Apple muttered to himself, glancing away, catching sight of Martin's raised eyebrows. 'And what is it you wanted, Miss Weeks?' he asked.

'Major, Mr Apple. Major Weeks. I'm a major now.'

'What is it you wanted Major Weeks?'

'Oh, the same old thing, I'm afraid,' Major Weeks explained gaily. 'A donation, if you would be so good.'

'Another?'

'Another,' Major Weeks agreed, sighing. 'There's so little money about we have to keep returning to those fortunate few who have it.'

'Hmm. At the rate you keep returning here I'll soon be one of the have-nots,' Mr Apple told her blandly, his eyes softening.

'Oh, I think not, Mr Apple. I'm afraid your business is far too popular for you ever to be short of money,' Major Weeks told him, somehow making her statement suggest that his forthcoming donation would in some way compensate for his ill-gotten wealth.

Mr Apple peered through his glasses, toying with the idea of telling the Major precisely what he was doing there: that could be interesting; interesting, too, to speculate whether she would still accept the money that came from such shadowy origins.

' – just off on my rounds,' Major Weeks was chirping on. 'We have so many people to comfort. And then I spotted the light in the window and I knew you were open so I said to myself it would be so nice to spend a moment or two with someone who didn't need comforting.'

An odd, melancholy breeze seemed to have accompanied her into the shop (or escaped from the bundle of *War Crys* she carried under her arm) and Mr Apple found himself nodding in uncertain agreement.

'Martin's one who needs your comfort,' he heard himself saying, aware that he was up to mischief, indicating behind him without turning round. 'He's very ill, poor chap. Some horrible, bewildering virus has infected his youthful body.'

'Oh dear – ' Major Weeks began concernedly.

'Don't mind that old fool,' Martin interrupted, passing his face through a number of contortions in an effort to disguise the fierce blush that suffused it. 'He's only kidding you. I just feel rough. Flu probably. There's a lot of it going around. And I didn't sleep well.'

'Who did?' Mr Apple asked vaguely.

'Now it's funny you should say that, young man. I'm not at all a good sleeper,' Major Weeks was offering brightly, as if mutual insomnia was a sort of cure. 'You know it simply does not seem to matter what time I go to bed – the very first hint of dawn and there I am – wide awake. The truth is I used to sleep like a baby before I came to Belfast. The way these poor people have to live!' she exclaimed. 'Oh dear, oh dear me,' she sighed, shaking her bonneted head. 'Oh dear me,' she said again, as though hoping repetition would underline her concern. 'The sheer misery.'

But misery, sheer or otherwise, was something Mr Apple had no intention of getting involved with at the moment. He suspected now, as he had always suspected, that people who expressed horror and indignation at misery and suffering were the very ones who knew nothing about it, who recognized it only as some nastiness that affected others, leaving themselves untouched. People who suffered kept very quiet about it, hugged their misery to them, almost guarding it as if it was an investment in future happiness.

'Here,' Mr Apple said gruffly, surprising himself with such pointed rudeness, and pushing a ten-pound note across the counter, 'take this and relieve the misery.'

'Why, thank you, Mr Apple. You are *such* a generous man,' Major Weeks said, her eyes turning dreamy with gratitude while her brow furrowed under the strain of her rapid calculations as to what benefits ten pounds could bring.

'Yes. I'm generous,' Mr Apple agreed, surprised to find he had spoken aloud. And, as though to cover the mild embarrassment that now came over him, he added 'and so is my assistant, aren't you, Martin? You will donate a little something of your considerable wealth to a worthy cause, won't you? A farthing or two perhaps?'

'Huh? Oh, sure. There you go, miss,' Martin said, pushing a crumpled fiver towards her.

'May God reward you both,' Major Weeks implored, casting her eyes upwards, pocketing her takings and blessing them both with a smile.

Mr Apple and Martin glanced at one another, and for a split second there was an awful understanding between them; yet it was not so much an understanding as an unvoiced bond of fear, some telepathic warning that whatever their reward it would certainly not be from God. But almost as soon as this realization came, it was gone, and they were both smiling at Major Weeks, wishing her well, watching her as she waddled from the shop with that fussy gait which made it seem that some eternal, adolescent virgin inhabited her large womanly body.

Whatever aura Major Weeks had brought into the shop left with her. The door swung closed behind her with its familiar bang like a signal to return to normal: the blower crackled and spat, the voice from the speaker sounding breathless as though it, too, had been waiting for the Major to take her leave before announcing that racing at Ludlow had been abandoned due to waterlogging.

'Only one meeting today, then, Mr Apple,' Martin said, as though vindicating his illness.

'Yes. I heard.'

'You'll be able to manage easily now, won't you?'

'Easily.'

'Hey, I'm sorry, you know. I didn't want to get sick.'

Mr Apple turned from the counter and stared at Martin, his face perplexed, worried. 'Are you really ill, Martin?'

'Sure I am. I wouldn't say I was – '

'No. I'm sorry. It's just – ' Mr Apple shook his head.

'Just what?'

'Nothing.'

'There! You see? You're at it again, Mr Apple. Starting something and then leaving it all up in mid-air. I hate that, and you do it to me all the time.'

'You wouldn't understand. *I* don't really understand.'

'Understand what?'

Mr Apple thought for a moment, frowning, fishing among the swarm of forebodings that danced and shimmered through his brain like transparent smigg, hoping to net some explanation for the feeling of impending tragedy he sensed so emphatically. '"And the whirr of their wayfaring thinned and surceased on the sky, and but left in the gloaming – ",' he quoted, his voice as lost as a wayfaring waif, his eyes about to close: suddenly, surprisingly, Martin finished the quotation: '"– sea-mutterings and me",' he said, and Mr Apple bounced back in astonishment.

'Good Lord!'

'That fooled you, eh, Mr Apple?'

'It certainly did.'

'Oh I'm not as thick as you make me out to be.'

'I never thought you were stupid, Martin. I just didn't think Hardy was in your repertoire.'

'Well, you live and learn.'

'Yes,' Mr Apple agreed. 'Do you believe in premonitions, Martin?' he asked suddenly.

'You mean feeling something is going to happen?'

'Yes, in a way.'

'I suppose I do. I never really thought about it.'

Mr Apple nodded, and his slow, pedantic gesture seemed to indicate he now felt Martin's was the wisest course.

'What about them, anyway?' Martin pressed on.

'I feel that –' Mr Apple hesitated again, and took a moment to sigh a sound filled with bewilderment and sorrow.

'For Christ's sake, Mr Apple, you'll drive me crazy. What do you feel?'

'You really want to know?'

'Yes, dammit, I really want to know.'

Mr Apple turned away and shuddered, but only for a second: he swung round and faced Martin and in that twinkling of an eye his humour had changed. It was as though, inexplicably, some part of him had taken flight, had packed its overnight bag with visions of pain and horror and sadness and run off, smiling gaily, waving a hand and promising to send a postcard. And with its departure Mr Apple found he was smiling too, though none too gaily, wistfully more likely than not, and saying teasingly, 'I don't think it would be good for you to know in your present delicate state of health, Martin.'

'Shit.'

Suddenly the shop was full of customers, and for the next hour they were both busy taking bets, paying out on yesterday's winners, explaining that no runners at Ludlow could go into accumulators since racing there had been called off. They were a strangely matched team engaged in an even stranger pursuit: offering hope with a scrap of blue cardboard, stamping TAX PAID across the frail scribbles of people's dreams.

Only near noon did the shop finally empty, resting before the influx of the regular punters who stood about the shop all afternoon, some seeking warmth, others company, most simply preferring to have their losses audibly confirmed by the Tannoy.

'You're quite sure you'll be able to manage if I go home,' Martin asked during this respite.

'Yes. Quite. I'll manage.'

'I do feel lousy.'

'I'm sure you do.'

'You don't bloody believe me.'

' – ? Of course I believe you, Martin. Why should you lie?'

'Right.'

'Well, then?'

'Okay. I'll go.'

'Martin?'

'Yes?'

'If it takes any longer – ' Mr Apple hesitated, wondering what on earth had made him choose those words. 'If you need longer,' he corrected himself, 'to recover,' he added, 'it won't inconvenience me if you take a few days off. Better to be sure you're fully recovered than to risk a relapse.'

Martin stared at the old man with half-closed eyes, but there was an unusual kindness in his voice when he answered: 'Thanks, Mr A. Maybe you're right. I'll see how I feel in the morning.'

'Do that.'

'Now you look after things, hear?'

Mr Apple smiled tightly. 'I will,' he promised.

'Good.'

'And you look after yourself, Martin.'

'That's one thing you can be sure of, Mr A. Martin Deeley will always look after himself.'

Mr Apple watched Martin walk across the shop towards the door, watched him turn and smile a smile that implored response. Mr Apple raised a hand and returned the smile; and before he could stop himself, before, even, he realized he was saying it, he said 'Martin, if you need a friend, remember I'm here.'

Martin Deeley stopped in his tracks, and the brightness fell from his face, leaving his eyes extraordinarily sad. But only for a moment. 'Hey,' he said, smiling again, 'that's really nice, Mr Apple. That's really nice. I might take you up on that. Thanks.'

Mr Apple nodded. 'Off you go to bed.'

'Right. And – thanks again.'

'Don't thank me,' Mr Apple said quietly, somehow managing to make it sound like a warning.

Martin was about to open the door and leave the shop, but then he froze, turned, and came back to the counter, faced Mr Apple, staring at him through the glass. 'That's a pretty big thing, you know,' he said seriously. 'Offering to be someone's friend.'

'Yes. I know.'

'Hey!' Martin said, with a small wry laugh, 'nobody's ever offered to be my friend before. How about that? That's a first for you, Mr A.'

'I'm happy,' said Mr Apple, although he looked anything but. In fact he looked downright morose about his offer, as though his friendship was like the kiss of death.

'You're a nice old man, Mr Apple,' Martin told him seriously.

'Yes. I'm lovely, Martin. Just lovely. Go on home.'

'Okay. I'll see you when I see you.'

'I hope so.'

'Sure I will. I'm not going to die.'

'No,' agreed Mr Apple, with not much conviction. 'No, you're not going to die.'

'Bye.'

'Bye.'

Already, as he walked through the crowds of pedestrians, Martin found himself panting like a terrier. It was a phenomenon that always took place well in advance of an actual killing, as though he was disposing of his surplus energy, energy which might hinder his exactitude, so as to leave himself calm, unshaking, accurate. Yes, it had always been so, and Martin smiled as he thought of it, even on that very first occasion when he had proudly enhanced his status as a brilliantly accurate marksman.

Bye, said Mam.

Bye, Mam.

Be careful.

I'll be careful.

Come home safe, Mam said. She had scrupulously avoided interfering, though she was well aware what was about to happen, aware, too, that there was a strong possibility that she was about to lose her one remaining son; but she knew, also, that what was taking place within her family was inevitable, and, with that peculiar twisted logic of the oppressed, she was proud of Martin, and in her saddened, lonely mind she endowed the monstrous act he was soon to commit with a sort of glory, making it perversely heroic, seeing her callous, amoral son as an avenging angel whose life she might have to sacrifice.

I'll be home safe. Don't worry.

I won't, Mam promised, steeling herself and drawing on television heroines for her expression.

This is Seamus Reilly, he was told. He will look after you.

Mr Deeley, Seamus Reilly acknowledged, bowing his head slightly.

Mr Reilly, Martin replied. That was nice – and as it should be – being addressed as Mr Deeley. Yes. He liked that. Made him feel good. Grown up. Important.

– simple, Reilly was explaining as the stolen car bounced rapidly along the isolated country lanes. He'll be out at eleven exactly. By himself. Checking. Very regular. Like his cattle. Like clockwork. Simple.

What's he done? Martin asked casually. Not that it made any difference: the man was to be punished and that was that.

Nothing, Reilly replied. Not directly. In fact, not even indirectly, he added his voice trailing upwards slightly as though he was suddenly mildly bemused. He's been selected to repay the death of that child the Paras shot the other night.

Oh.

An eye for an eye, Reilly said quietly. It's all they seem to understand.

Oh.

Stop at the next bend, Reilly ordered the driver, and the driver stopped obediently at the next bend.

134

Reilly rolled down the window and, turning to Martin, placed one hand on his arm: there was something very fatherly about the gesture, and Martin suddenly felt very close to the sinister little man beside him.

You see that clump of trees, Martin? Go through those and you'll have a perfect view of the house. The side door is on the left as you look at it. That's where he'll come from. He'll switch on the outside light before he leaves the house, so you will be warned. Let him walk across the yard. He'll come directly under the light and that is your best chance. He's an easy target, Reilly explained, almost apologetically. You'll have all the time in the world. Come back here when you've done.

Martin settled himself comfortably on the ground, adopting the position he had seen the Paras use, at full stretch with legs splayed behind him, the rifle cocked and pointing towards the dim, shadowy building slightly to the right and below him. It was a very still night, with a watery, half-hearted moon that only revealed itself from time to time. Martin was amazed at how calm he felt: apart from the thumping of his heart and an odd but wholly pleasant sensation in his loins he felt nothing. Then the light was on in the yard below him. A door slammed. A man coughed nicotine from his lungs and spat. Martin aimed the rifle, moving the barrel slowly from left to right, waiting for the man to come under the light. He timed it perfectly: the sights were just in line with the light as the man moved under it. Martin squeezed the trigger. Even, it seemed, before the brittle crack of the rifle reached his ears he saw the man hurtle several feet backwards, saw him attempt to swim, his arms and legs flailing in a grotesque breaststroke, saw him shudder and lie still.

That was nicely done, Reilly told him as the car drove unobtrusively back into the city. Very nicely done.

It was easy.

Easy or not, it was nicely done. Clean. No unnecessary suffering. The committee will be pleased with that.

Good.

Reilly glanced at Martin. You feel all right? he asked paternally.

I feel fine.

No sickness in your stomach?

None.

No – eh – regrets?

Why should I?

Reilly gave what sounded like a chuckle but could have been something else. You sound almost as though you had enjoyed it.

I did. You know that? I really did.

I see, said Reilly.

Don't you? Martin heard himself ask casually, as though discussing something trivial.

I have never killed, Reilly told him tightly.

Never?

Never. It is not my job. I do not have – Reilly paused, searching for the missing requirement, failing to locate it, about to rephrase his words when Martin interrupted generously:

Well, you have me now.

Yes. We have you now, Reilly agreed, a mixture of awe and distaste spreading over the words.

Any time you want a job well done, just call on me.

We will.

Good.

Just one thing –

– ?

Don't become too fond of killing, young man. If you do, your usefulness to us will be over. Good-night.

Good-night.

Mam was waiting up for him, and she hugged him when he came in the door, kissing his cheek and smoothing the hair on his neck with her small, hard hands. You're all right, she remarked gratefully.

Sure, I'm all right. Why wouldn't I be?

Thanks be to God, Mam said fervently.

I'm going to bed. I'm tired.

Have something before you go up. A cup of tea. A glass of milk. I've plenty of milk. I'll warm you some.

No. I just want to sleep.

You should have something to calm you down, Mam persisted, as though she knew all about such things.

I don't need calming down, Martin snapped, feeling oddly insulted. I just want to go to bed and sleep.

All right, son.

Night, Mam.

Good-night, Martin. God protect you.

Yeah.

Do your mother a favour, Martin?

What?

Say a prayer before you go to sleep.

A prayer?

Thank the good God for seeing you safe.

Yeah. Okay. I'll do that, Martin lied.

Thank you, son.

Night.

You're a good boy.

That's right.

Good-night. God watch over you.

Good-night.

And God or some other being had certainly watched over him, for here he was, still going strong, about to add another victim to his impressive list.

As he packed, throwing two changes of underwear, shirts and socks into a small suitcase (take a suitcase, Reilly had told him – not a big one that might be searched, just a small suitcase that one might take for a few days) Martin ticked off in his mind the details of his itinerary. Suddenly Mr Apple loomed up in his thoughts, his long grey face smiling tragically at him, offering him, with hands outstretched, his friendship, but in a way that suggested he was going to need it. Even more extraordinary was the fact that somewhere, somewhere in a dark, unsued cubbyhole of his mind, Martin sensed the truth of this; it was as though the unexpected intrusion of Mr

Apple's generous remark had more to it than met the ear, as though something (perhaps the God that Mam so persistently beleaguered) was on the point of finally linking the destinies of Martin Deeley and Mr Apple together irrevocably. At any other time Martin would have scoffed at such a notion, dismissed it as his understandable nerves playing tricks on him, but now, standing there ready to go, shaved and groomed and polished and scrubbed and nicely dressed, he felt a new and unwelcome element creeping into his life. It was, he thought, puzzled, a sense of foreboding, and he didn't like it one little bit.

That night Mr Apple was assailed by a virulent and terrifying nightmare, the word 'ruination' dominating his fretful sleep. All about him was a scene of utter desolation, dominated by weeds and thorn-bushes: an abandoned orchard, perhaps, filled with terror. To begin with it seemed peaceful enough there, though there was an eerie, hushed and irreverent silence that hinted at unholy places. It was as silent and cold as a grave. No birds, no insects, nothing save himself alone, it appeared, dared enter the dreadful place. All the narrow, crazily paved paths that criss-crossed the enclosure were broken and overgrown. Great thorny tendrils of wild blackberry clawed at the old brick wall over which the spindly nakedness of a dead honeysuckle and dying Wistaria were draped. Currant-bushes, red and black, had capitulated to the systematic onslaught of nettles and cow-parsley and giant thistles. Plum- and pear-trees, once lovingly espaliered, now blossomless and unpollinated, fell forward, their branches buried and rotting in the dank scutch grass. A wooden-framed greenhouse, running the entire length of the far wall, sagged squalidly, saved from total collapse only by the ebbing strength of a tenacious vine, the glass shattered or vanished altogether.

Fearfully he turned his head and stared at the cankerous, gnarled apple tree that grew alone in one corner. At first it appeared to be enveloped in a kind of mist, then he realized that he was crying. He brushed the tears roughly from his eyes, blinking rapidly, and fixed his gaze firmly on the tree. Over the years it had been cruelly mutilated, or (a more optimistic possibility he was pleased to consider) with the passage of time its arthritic limbs had been amputated out of charity, perhaps out of love, so that now its remaining foliage fanned outward only from the top like those thorned acacias of the African veld, leaving its scarred, lichen-covered trunk gaunt and horripilant but for one solitary branch which still protruded at right angles some eight feet from the ground, menacing in its isolation. The tree of death, he thought grimly, forced towards it, hacking his way through the undergrowth with what appeared to be a golfclub, which he wielded like a sickle.

Then it appeared. The instant he saw the apparition he told himself sternly that it was nothing more than another hallucination, and he stood, quite calm, waiting for the object (shaped like a man invisibly suspended by the neck from the sole protruding branch, but faceless, a pale translucent light where the features should have been) to go away. And suddenly it was gone. So he *had* been mistaken once again. Or had he? There it was once more. Or was it? Certainly it seemed to have withdrawn: but no, not quite. There was still something there in some way connected with it, or there on his shoulder, or behind his back, or skipping away and concealing itself as he turned; no...that, too, whatever it was, was going: perhaps, after all, it was only one of those shadows that Blake had so obliquely referred to. Oh, God, he heard himself sigh as he moved closer to the tree, while fully realizing the folly of his supplication: even God seemed unlikely to shed His light in this unhallowed place.

Tentatively he raised one hand as if to touch the branch. At the same time that he realized that the branch was beyond his reach he felt something never before felt with such conviction, with such shocking certainty: it was as though he was surrounded by living, breathing evil. Yet not, it seemed, by a consuming evil, for he immediately became possessed of a curious peace as though the raising of his arm had not, after all, been a wasted gesture, had, rather, become a form of benediction which for some reason protected him. Who are you? he shouted, or thought he shouted, probably did not shout since the words made no sound he could hear. Who are you? he asked again, quietly.

Immediately, suddenly appalled by the realization of what the answer might be, he spun round and hurried from the place, stumbling twice, closing the gate firmly behind him, pressing on it with both hands to make certain it was securely latched, pressing until his fingers ached and small patches of blood appeared on his palms.

Colonel Maddox came down to breakfast in a pleasurable frame of mind. At last the ordeal of leave was behind him and he could look forward to the turmoil and hardship of Belfast. The peace of Berkshire irked him; the twittering birds, the hum of the electric lawnmower, the lowing of cattle on the neighbouring farm got on his nerves. Irrationally. It was the sense of being needed he missed, almost as much as he missed the realization that he might, in some small way, be doing something useful, having a hand in finding the solution to the illness that afflicted Ireland.

Nancy Maddox was already at the table, making a great show of scraping low-calorie margarine on to her slightly burned toast, looking dishevelled in a multicoloured wrap-around khaftan that someone had bought her in Suez when Suez was Suez, her hair brushed but purposely tousled.

'What time are you leaving?' she asked by way of greeting, delicately replacing crumbs of toast in her mouth with her little finger.

'Here?'

'Yes.'

'Elevenish.'

'Oh. I see.'

'Anything wrong?'

' – ? No. Nothing. It just means I won't be here when you leave. Jeff is driving me to London.'

'I see.'

'I've *so* much to do,' Nancy sighed. 'I really cannot see how I'm going to get it all done. What with Ascot and Wimbledon just around the corner – ' her voice trailed off like a weak second serve.

'You'll enjoy yourself.'

'I intend to,' Nancy snapped, waspishly defensive. 'Thank God I have some friends who don't want to see me vegetate.'

Colonel Maddox closed his eyes and watched his good humour scarper like a thief. 'There's no fear of you vegetating, Nancy.'

'I would if I depended on you. You really couldn't care less what happens to me, so long as you are amusing yourself chasing bandits with those uncouth, boozy army friends of yours.'

'It's my job.'

'Hah. They seem to manage very well without you. You don't *have* to go back to Ireland,' Nancy urged, wondering all the while why on earth she tried, albeit half-heartedly, to resurrect the contented marriage they once had. 'You know perfectly well that a word in the right place and you could – '

'I want to go back.'

'Oh, I know *that*. The big brave soldier back to the heart of the battle. It's high time you faced it – you're not even needed. And another thing, as far as any of us can see,' Nancy pointed out, indicating vaguely towards the empty chairs her guests had occupied over the weekend, as though their gossiping spirits had remained behind and were now prepared to bear her out, 'you'll never get the better of those dreadful terrorists. They're far too clever for you, my dear. Wily. That's the word. Wily. They flit about on tiny feet while you clomp about in your great big boots,' she concluded, smiling to herself, pleased she had quoted her publisher friend correctly.

'Perhaps you're right.'

'Of course I'm right. And you know it. You fools in smocks and denim are nothing but target practice for those evil men.'

Maddox discovered he was nodding. There was, of course, some truth in what she said, but there was, also, was there not, a matter of duty? He was about to express this opinion, was prepared, even, to elaborate on it, when Nancy rose from the table. 'Well, I must go and get ready. I have to see my milliner before lunch,' she informed him, and frowned as she spotted him smile at her extraordinarily old-fashioned word.

'I'll see you before you go,' he told her.

142

'Yes.'

Maddox waited until she had left the room (filling the time by wiping imaginary traces of marmalade from his neat, clipped moustache with his napkin) before he settled back in his chair, turning his gold signet-ring round and round on his finger, allowing a varied selection of thoughts to muster their forces and close ranks before marching through his brain, jumbled thoughts of mangled bodies in dingy streets and pretty ladies in the winner's enclosure, the horrendous roar of explosions, the aristocratic applause for a sweating thoroughbred, the flying glass as lethal as any bullet, the clinking of champagne glasses, the wails of anguish as bullets found their target, the oohs of despair as some backhand volley went wide. Dear God, what worlds apart! And who cared? Who really cared?

The Colonel sighed deeply and heaved himself from his chair. In an odd way, he told himself, *he* cared. And it wasn't that he wanted to make a reputation for himself by capturing or killing terrorists – if terrorists, indeed, they were, and he had found himself doubting this occasionally in recent months – in the way the predatory Mr Asher did (I wish I could kill the buggers one by one all by myself, Asher had once said in a moment of conspiratorial frustration, and notch each dead terrorist on the stock of my gun. Better still, herd the bastards into one of their bloody Roman Catholic churches and blow the lot to kingdom come), and if he could have persuaded everyone to sit around a table and make a start on solving the insoluble problem he would have been more than pleased. What he wanted, Maddox now decided, hauling himself wearily up the stairs by the banisters, what he wanted – and at the same time he fully recognized the stupidity and impossibility of his thoughts – what he wanted (and saw in his mind's eye as a sort of dreamy sequence of events somehow linked to daydreams of his childhood, but childish now if only because of his advancing age) what he really wanted –

'We're off,' Nancy brutally broke in upon his reverie, appearing at the top of the stairs, elegantly turned out, beautifully shod, a fawn vicuña coat draped over one arm, her pet publisher draped on the other. 'Tinkle me tomorrow and let me know you got back to war safely.'

'I'll do that. Have a nice time in London.'

'We will. I don't suppose there's any point in hoping you'll make Ascot?'

'I wouldn't think so.'

'No. Not masculine enough for you, is it dear?'

Maddox said nothing, but shifted his gaze to the willowy publisher with the purple neckerchief and back again to Nancy, raising an eyebrow, enjoying his wife's sudden blush, enjoying, too, the odd gesture she made when annoyed or found him tiresome: shaking herself so that her clothes ruffled like a chicken's feathers. 'Is the car full, or do *I* have to get petrol?' she demanded.

'*I'm* taking you,' publishing Jeffrey said. 'We're going in my car.

'Oh, yes. Of course. I forgot,' Nancy admitted, tittering. 'How silly of me. It's just that it's been so long since I've been driven anywhere.'

The Colonel stood to one side and allowed them to pass him on the stairs, wrinkling his nose at the strength of the combined smell of perfume and aftershave, and watched them leave the house, still arm in arm, whispering and giggling, before he went on up the stairs and into his bedroom. He heard the car doors slam and the wheels spin on the gravel, but did not bother to watch from the window: he had seen and heard enough of his wife and her guests during the past two weeks.

Being an orderly man he had almost completed his packing the night before. There had, however, been a few unaccustomed additions to his suitcase this time: a few small items he had never before taken from his home, mementoes of happier times, of less confused, less bitter days, objects of importance only to himself, which he had been prompted to take by some small goblin in his mind hinting that failure to do so would mean their irrevocable loss. There was, for example, an old and tattered, leather-bound biography of Bacon by Dean Church, with an inscription on the flyleaf which had puzzled him since the day he had bought it (along with several other books as a job lot at an auction, longer ago than he cared to remember): 'Ex Libris Denis Redmond (Reverend or, perhaps, not so reverend), suffering banishment of all dimensions', it read. There was also a brown photograph in a circular silver frame, showing a small girl in frilly petticoats and a lace bonnet cuddling a tabby-kitten, and inscribed on the back, perhaps by the man who stood behind the girl and gazed down fondly at her, 'Bishop, Nina and Jo'. Only his shaving-kit and toothbrush remained to be put in the suitcase (an old leather affair with outside straps and brass buckles, plastered with labels of exotic, probably long-since demolished hotels) which lay open on his bed. He now placed these, wrapped in a strip of coloured plastic, beside his shoes, and closed the lid. Then he paced about the room, fingering things, lifting ornaments and other photographs in other silver frames and putting them down again; finally, he took to walking up and down ponderously, killing time, placing his feet in designs on the carpet, his stride awkward, like that of a man trying out new shoes, all the while wondering at the turmoil, the sense of doom that was welling up inside him, trying, too, to recall what he had been thinking before Nancy had shattered his train of thought. To no avail. Alas, it was almost always like that now: memory failed him when he most needed it. He glanced at his watch. In half an hour the car would arrive and that, at least, was a good thing.

Long before the Colonel came down to breakfast in his quiet Berkshire home, Mr Apple was awake and fretting. He had been, yet again, visited by demons with wilful intent who scattered nightmares of the most appalling nature through his sleep, who, worse still, misconstrued just about everything he had written in his diary that night, and threw it back at him, twisting it until the words screamed and crackled as they broke, the shattered letters reforming into meanings and images both lurid and grotesque, making him snap awake, sweating, wondering what could have brought about such an intense affliction. He lay in his bed, quite still, listening, listening for any tiny sound that might explain his awful premonition of disaster. Nothing. Not a sound. Then, suddenly, outside, some distance away, a single bird, a nightingale perhaps, rent the stillness with a stunning cadenza and set its course in search of tetragrammaton.

What was that? a voice seemed to scream in his ear, a voice he recognized as from another time, but to which he could not put a face. Perhaps it never had a face.

Just talking to myself, Mr Apple thought he heard himself reply. Just envying the advantage those small birds have over us – flying off to paradise whenever the fancy takes them.

You think they do? the voice asked, sounding quite like Mr Divine.

I'm sure they do.

Perhaps not so advantageous, Sefer, definitely Sefer was suggesting darkly.

How so?

Striving upwards has its downfalls, Mr Apple was told solemnly.

Ah, was all he managed to get out before 'If thou desirest to mount thou wouldst not be able and in descending thou wilt meet an abyss without any bottom' was being quoted at him.

Yes. I know, Mr Apple heard himself say. I know only too well. But even the abyss can be a source of wisdom.

Or chaos. Don't forget chaos.

Suddenly, as though the elements had been activated by some daemonic force and commanded to assert their ferocious power on his unsuspecting self, all meteorological hell broke loose. Huge purple clouds plunged upwards, thundering against each other. A single ominous shaft of lightning crackled a warning of still worse turmoil to follow. The wind hurled itself across the landscape, bending huge trees, ignoring their awful moans, the screaming of their limbs, and the tragedy that had haunted Mr Apple seemed already to have commenced.

Just as suddenly Mr Apple was awake and all was silent save, incredibly, for the shrill, single note of a lone bird in the garden outside.

Mr Apple eased himself on to one elbow and very deliberately opened the buttons of his pyjama top. There was something comically ceremonious about the way he did this, about the way he folded back the jacket and ran his fingers over the wounds on his chest: he looked carefully at his finger tips and rubbed them gently together. Finally, he lay back with a small sigh of relief, keeping his eyes open lest they turned inwards on his soul and revealed some horrors he could not yet bear to face. But he would, he told himself: he would face them when they came at the appointed time, face them bravely and with confidence in the way he had been preparing himself so to do.

'Oh,' Mr Apple said aloud, his thin voice pitched to almost a cry, and rocked himself on his bed. 'Oh, dear God, help me.'

About the time that Mr Apple (recovered to all outward appearances from the hazards of the night) put the key in the door of the bookmaking establishment, sighing at the prospect of another treacherous day, about the time, also, that Colonel Maddox wiped imaginary traces of marmalade from his neat, clipped moustache with his napkin (sighing at the paucity of his marriage, yet marvelling at Nancy's blatant if petty infidelity), Martin Deeley jogged across the Berkshire skyline and cast a baleful glance at Seamus Reilly's mischievous gibbet. He looked ridiculously small and inoffensive: an isolated little creature in that vast expanse, dressed in a sky-blue tracksuit with natty dark-blue trim and one of those loose-fitting, thin, plastic anoraks with a pocket like a pouch in the front.

Jogger! he had exclaimed, the prospect of such unexpected exercise more surprising, even, than the choice of cover.

Sure, Tommy Walshe told him. Who looks at a jogger? This country is full of them. All ages. All shapes. All running themselves into the ground to stay fit.

Jesus!

And if we do run into trouble there's nothing peculiar about a man in a tracksuit running. You'd look pretty damn stupid galloping across the Berkshire Downs in your Sunday suit, Martin.

Martin guffawed. I suppose you're right.

I'm right.

Martin swung left and headed for the cluster of dead elms, one of which boasted three abandoned rooks' nests. He looked awkward as he ran, swinging only one arm, the other pressed to his side holding the Kalashnikov automatic rifle in place, mistrusting the tapes that secured it to his body. It fitted neatly: tucked under his armpit and resting on his hip; the weapon mechanism and the barrel combined measured barely twenty-one inches. Folded over these, weighing almost nothing, the stock of tubular steel; the magazine in his marsupial anorak, its steady thump against his stomach oddly comforting.

There's a gibbet –

Yeah. Reilly told me.

Hah. He would. He'd like that. Always one for a joke is Seamus Reilly, Tommy Walshe said, shaking his head in wonderment.

Oh, a hell of a joker he is.

Anyway, just below the gibbet there's a bunch of elms. They're all dead. Rot-gut, fluke or something. They're dying all over the place. Soon be no elms at all, Tommy said, giving a little sigh by way of requiem. When you get to the elms you'll see the Maddox cottage. You can't miss it. It's the only house you *can* see from there. Now, count the elms from the left. Under the third there's a hole covered by loose grass and leaves. That's where you bury the rifle before you come back. Easy.

Oh, yes, Martin agreed. Easy.

As soon as I hear the shooting I'll start driving along the road. All you have to do is bury the rifle and your tracksuit and run the fifty yards to the road. You can change into the pullover and trousers in the car, and away we go.

Martin nodded. Like always, it sounded easy.

Any questions?

Martin shook his head. No, except – well, surely I'll be a bit conspicuous running about in my underwear, he said, amused.

Pretend you're a marathon runner. Anyway, who the hell ever shot a British colonel in their underwear?

They both laughed.

Martin reached the trees and immediately counted from the left. Sure enough, the small hole, about two feet deep and packed with leaves and dry grass, was there. Straight ahead, beyond the main road, up a small, winding lane on a rise, was the Colonel's cottage. Some cottage. Bloody great mansion of a place. Down the road he noted Tommy Walshe intently tinkering with the engine of the Vauxhall, his head buried in the gaping bonnet: anyone passing would have dismissed him as yet another lunatic tourist who had overloaded the engine.

Why the bloody boat? Martin had demanded, indicating the dinghy on the trailer.

Aha. Just my little touch of realism, Martin me boy, Tommy Walshe had replied, grinning like a small boy who had just conceived a brilliant idea. Now you tell me: who is going to look for a getaway car pulling a bloody great trailer and boat? We're just a pair of sweethearts on our way to the Lake District for a few days sailing, he explained, giving a camp little flick of his wrist.

Oh, sure. Some sweethearts we are.

It makes it easier for you if I think of details, Tommy said. I have to look after you, you know. Orders from above. You're special.

Yeah. I'm special.

Suddenly Martin froze: a car shot round the side of the house and sped down the lane. Shit. He began ripping the rifle free from his side, wincing as the tape tore at his flesh, his eyes fixed more on the trail of dust in the car's wake than on the car itself. He was still fumbling, trying to assemble the rifle, when the car slowed to a halt before turning on to the main road. Irrelevant details shot through his mind: sports – silver – vintage – Lagonda – or Bristol – top down – powerful – well looked after. Almost by magic the rifle was assembled, loaded, aimed, and the occupants of the car clear in the sights. Martin found himself breathing again, smiling with relief. The driver of the car was certainly not the Colonel and the passenger was a woman, her head thrown back, sitting almost sideways in her seat, her arm across the back of the driver's seat, her hand resting on his shoulder. Martin watched the car as it swung on to the main road, watched it slow as it drew alongside Tommy, saw him wave good-naturedly and shake his head, saw the woman wave back, watched the car gather speed and roar away. Then everything was quiet again. Martin rolled onto his back and gulped in air.

Make sure of this one, Reilly had told him.

I will.

It's important. Let the Brits know we are still in business.

Don't worry.

I always worry, Martin. It's my job to worry.

Well, you needn't.

I admire you, Martin, Reilly confessed, though there seemed to be little admiration in his voice. The way you handle death amazes me.

I don't think about it.

That's what amazes me. I think I would be haunted for ever if I had to kill someone.

Well, you don't, do you? You get someone else to do it for you.

True. And just as well. I would never be able to do it myself. I wouldn't be *afraid* to kill someone, Reilly offered by way of explanation. I just don't have the temperament. As I say, I think they would come back and haunt me. Do they haunt you, Martin?

Who?

Your victims.

Hell, no.

Never?

No. When they're dead they're dead.

Do you feel anything?

Not much. Excited a bit.

A bit excited, Reilly repeated musingly. Marvellous, he said. How you can do something so final and just feel a bit excited?

Well, what do you want me to do? Jump for joy?

No, but I would have thought a little sorrow, perhaps, or –

Shit, Martin snapped.

Yes. Oh, well. We're lucky you're made the way you are.

That's for sure.

But I wonder if you really are –

– ?

Martin stood up and stripped to his underclothes, carefully

placing the anorak and tracksuit in the shallow hole. Then he lay on his stomach, the rifle snug against his shoulder, and waited. He had barely settled into that position when the black Ford saloon appeared on the road below him, braked carefully, swung into the lane and headed for the Colonel's home: Martin followed its progress in his sights and whispered pow, pow, pow to himself like a schoolboy playing cowboys and decimating the Indian ranks.

The Colonel must have been waiting, for he appeared at the door before the car came to a halt. He placed a suitcase a couple of feet from the door and disappeared inside again: Martin trained his sights on the doorway, holding his breath, his finger already tightening on the trigger. It was something that always surprised him, but he was now so proficient at assassination that he could somehow sense the appearance of his victim a split second before he actually came into view. For the moment he had no such sensation and relaxed a little, adjusting the telescopic sights even more finely so that nothing but the doorway was within his vision. He heard Tommy Walshe start the engine of the Vauxhall, gunning it slightly; he heard a skylark take advantage of the silence to demonstrate its vocal prowess. Then, in his sixth sense, the warning came and Martin tensed: the Colonel ambled through the front door and Martin fired. As he fired, however, the driver of the car popped into the picture, standing erect having retrieved the Colonel's suitcase and blocking his superior, taking the bullet in the back of his neck. His head jerked and he collapsed forward into the Colonel's arms, both of them falling to the ground behind the parked car.

'Shit,' Martin whispered. 'You stupid, fucking bastard.'

He leapt to his feet, folded the Kalashnikov and shoved it into the hole, covered it and stomped the leaves and grass down. Then he sprinted down the hill towards the car. He was breathless and panting when he flung himself into the seat beside Tommy Walshe, but immediately started pulling on the pullover and trousers made ready for him.

'See? I told you it would be easy,' Tommy said, grinning.

'Easy shit,' Martin cursed through his teeth. 'I missed the

bastard.'

'You what?' Tommy's voice was suddenly brittle with fear, and for a second he touched the brake pedal with his foot.

'Keep going, for Christ's sake,' Martin shouted. 'I missed the bastard.'

'Oh, Jesus.'

'Oh, Jesus is right. The fucking driver. Up between us. Got *him*. Shit.'

'Why didn't you – '

'I couldn't. Both of them fell behind the car. I had no chance.'

'He would have had to go back in – '

'Yeah, well, I wasn't hanging about to watch for that. How the hell do I know who was in the house? Could have had a phone in the car – he could have reached that without me seeing him. Just you do the driving and let me do the worrying about what I should have done.'

Tommy Walshe obediently drove on in silence, scowling at the road, glancing in his mirror every few seconds, visibly relieved when he saw nothing following. 'They're not going to like it, Martin,' he said finally, obviously concerned.

'That's tough. What the hell do they expect?'

'They expect you to do what you came for.'

'I couldn't.'

'That's all very well – '

'Look, you just get me back to Birmingham and shut up.'

'We're staying in Oxford again tonight.'

'Are we hell. You can dump the boat there if you like but get me to Birmingham.'

'I was told – '

'I don't give a tuppenny shit what you were told. I'm telling you now. Get me to Birmingham so I can get out of here.'

'Okay, Martin. If that's the way you want it.'

'That's the way I want it.'

'You're the boss.'

'That's right.'

They arrived in Birmingham just after five o'clock, amazed that they had not once been challenged on the journey, had not even seen a police car. Martin collected his suitcase.

'Where do you want me to drop you?' Tommy Walshe asked.

'Nowhere. I'll make my own way.'

'You be all right?'

'I'll be fine.'

'Sure?'

'Sure. And by the way – thanks.'

'– ?'

'For being worried about me.'

'Us little guys gotta stick together,' Tommy told him in an extravagant Southern drawl.

'Hah.'

'Watch your step.'

'I will. Don't worry.'

'I do.'

'Don't. Martin Deeley can look after himself.'

'I hope so.'

'See you.'

'See you, Martin.'

Tommy Walshe watched Martin walk away from the car, swinging his suitcase jauntily, but it struck him there was less confidence in the swaggering gait, less spring to the step. It was as though Martin had grown suddenly older, was suddenly unsure, was, perhaps, for the first time in his life, truly afraid.

Mr Apple went to his shop at a ridiculously early hour: it was just after five that he sat at his desk, his hands supporting his head, nursing a headache the likes of which he had never suffered before. He had survived another horrible night which in itself would have been unremarkable but for the subtle changes in the actions of the visiting demons, alterations which gave their invasion an unaccustomed heavy-footedness that left his head throbbing, all of which, he felt sure, had been brought about by the news he had watched with disbelief and increasing outrage the night before. *Police in Berkshire are this evening investigating a shooting in which one man was killed*, the dark-skinned female newsreader announced with practised impartiality, clipping her vowels in an effort to treat this item as just another piece of nastiness in the litany of strife she had been given to read. *It is believed that the intended victim was Colonel Matthew Maddox of the Parachute Regiment, who was preparing to return to duty in Northern Ireland. The dead man has been named as Sergeant Anthony Boone, thirty-three, a married man with two small children, from Aylesbury in Buckinghamshire. Peter Haynes sent us this report.* Obligingly, Peter Haynes took over the screen and launched into his report with gusto, determined to make the most of his few seconds of stardom. *Shortly after eleven-thirty this morning Colonel Matthew Maddox came out of this door and made his way to the car that was waiting to take him to Brize Norton for the journey to Northern Ireland. As he approached the car his driver, Sergeant Anthony Boone, bent down to pick up the Colonel's suitcase. As he stood up, a single shot was fired, hitting the Sergeant in the back of the head and killing him instantly. Police are convinced that the bullet was intended for Colonel Maddox and believe it to be the work of the I.R.A. although they stress that so far no one has claimed responsibility. Colonel Maddox, who was alone in the house at the time, had no comment to make, apart from the fact that he would be returning to Northern Ireland sometime tomorrow.*

Mr Apple absentmindedly cleared a small space on the desk and emptied a single aspirin from the bottle he kept near by for just such emergencies, watched it roll, bump into an unopened brown envelope, and settle down. Then he popped it into his mouth, took a sip of lukewarm tea, threw back his head and swallowed, grimacing at the acrid taste. Perhaps it was the fact that he knew the Colonel (albeit it under pretty tricky circumstances) and quite liked him, recognizing in him a kindred lost wayfarer slogging through the intricacies of life, that made him feel profoundly certain that events had now taken a course the navigation of which promised nothing but sadness, a hopeless floundering on the sharp rocks of despair; or perhaps it was just a warning, not yet fully interpreted, left behind in the recesses of his mind by the hooligans of the night – who even now, despite the recent dosage designed to render them immobile, continued to swim along the perimeter of his consciousness, kicking their legs and hollering to each other – that caused him to recognize the doom and sorrow that were lurking just around the corner. Whatever the cause, there was certainly no doubting the unwelcome shafts of piercing cold he felt penetrating every fibre of his body, nor the sudden pain from his wounds which he knew to be his personal, melancholy overture to fear.

But weren't you afraid?

Yes, Your Excellency, I was afraid.

The ambassador, a kindly man, rejoicing in his appointment to Mexico, spending his free evenings writing a thesis on the tragic Carlotta, the dull Maximilian and their twin Miramar castles, shook his head: I simply cannot understand how you managed to *get* yourself into such a mess. What on earth possessed you?

Possessed me, Your Excellency?

The ambassador continued to shake his head, staring at the gaunt, aesthetic creature sitting before him, telling himself to choose his words with greater care, regretting already the word 'possessed' now that he realized it might have special significance. Why in heaven's name did you go to that godforsaken place?

I was sent, I think, Mr Apple said.

Sent? By whom? the ambassador wanted to know, becoming quite confused.

Mr Apple sighed: I wish I knew. Someone, something – I don't know – urged me to go there. I felt I was saving them.

Saving them? The villagers you mean? From what?

Themselves, Mr Apple said obliquely.

But you simply cannot go about trying to save people from themselves, was all the ambassador could find to say.

Mr Apple shrugged.

You realize, of course, that your actions have caused considerable embarrassment to the embassy – not to mention your personal scandal?

Yes, sir.

In the circumstances I think it might be better if you returned to London.

I will resign, sir.

Resign? The ambassador attempted to look surprised.

I think that would be best. I have other things to do, Mr Apple explained, and, anyway, I'm not really very good at my job.

No, no, Mr Apple, you have been excellent up to now. It is such a pity you allowed – you weren't drunk, I suppose? Sunstruck? Overworked?

Mr Apple smiled: I'm afraid not. Maybe you were right when you said possessed, sir.

'Good morning, Mr Apple.'

Mr Apple jumped. He looked up from his desk, half-expecting to see the nodding head of the kind ambassador peering at him through the glass partition. 'Ah, good morning, Aiden.'

'Good morning, Mr Apple,' Aiden Curren said again, and immediately set about cleaning yesterday's results off the board, hissing slightly through his teeth. He was a man of about fifty, pale and jumpy, with a curiously misshapen face that gave the impression one was regarding him reflected in the back of a spoon. He earned a meagre living as a floating boardmarker, floating from shop to shop, replacing absentees, arousing little interest, neither being liked nor disliked, doing his job, taking his money and going on his way, leaving nothing of himself behind, not even a lingering wonder as to what he might get up to in his leisure hours.

'Three meetings today?' he now asked flatly.

'Yes.'

'Good.'

'Why good, Aiden?' Mr Apple asked, without really caring.

'More for me to do.'

'Oh.'

'More customers. That's good. I like to watch their faces.'

'You do?'

'Oh, yes. Interesting to watch people's faces. Especially their eyes.'

'The windows of their souls, eh?'

' – ?'

'That's what they say, Aiden.'

'I wouldn't know about that. Don't believe in souls myself. Never have done. Mumbo-jumbo, if you ask me. Frighten people into doing what you want.'

'Oh.'

'Tell them the devil will get their soul and you'll have them eating out of your hand before you know it. That's what's wrong with everybody these days. All they think about is what will happen when they're dead. They don't care about what's going on around them while they're alive.'

'I see,' said Mr Apple, trying very hard to see the logic in this pronouncement.

'I can tell you this much, Mr Apple: if you took God out of Ireland you wouldn't have half the trouble you have now,' Aiden Curren said firmly, taking to hissing through his teeth again as though orchestrating his beliefs.

'You might be right, Aiden,' Mr Apple admitted doubtfully.

'Oh I am, I am.'

Mr Apple was relieved to see the door open and the first customer of the day come in, though his relief was short-lived. Nobody knew why, but the lady who made her way purposefully across the shop was known as Our Mary Bradley. She was a small woman, comfortably plump, with a kind face and a not-too-secret liking for sherry. She was also regarded as one of the characters of the area, mildly dotty and usually harmless, and as such got away with utterances for which other people would have been painfully incapacitated. She had a passion for badges, and these she sported festooned across her chest, proclaiming her love for Ian Paisley and the Pope, her enthusiastic support for the hunger-strikers and those who incarcerated them, her desire for a united Ireland and her determination to remain loyal to the Crown. Intermingled with these were others which informed the onlooker that she was a member of such diverse organizations as the Staffordshire Bull Terrier Society, the R.A.C., the Barry Manilow Fan Club, the Merton College Debating Society, the Relief Organization for Palestinian Refugees and the Arthur Scargill Appreciation Society.

'Hello, Mr Apple,' she bellowed enthusiastically.

'Hello, Our Mary,' Mr Apple replied, raising his voice an unaccustomed octave.

'I do believe I have a little something to collect.'

'You have indeed.'

'Ah, glory, every little helps, doesn't it?'

'I'm sure it does.'

'Oh, it does, it does, Mr Apple. How a soul is supposed to manage these days I really don't know – '

'We were just talking about that, weren't we, Aiden?'

'About what?'

'Souls.'

'Oh, dear,' Our Mary said. 'You shouldn't talk about souls in *here*, Mr Apple. God wouldn't like that one little bit. You know He's very fussy where you talk about souls.'

'Huh,' grunted Aiden, holding one finger to the side of his head and twisting it to indicate his low opinion of her sanity.

'Here we are, Our Mary: eleven pounds exactly.' Mr Apple passed the money across the counter.

'Good. That'll buy a titbit for poor Bradley.'

'Ah, yes. And how is Bradley?' Mr Apple asked. It was curious that Our Mary's husband was always referred to by his last name, his Christian name being, it appeared, a dark secret.

'Getting over it.'

'Oh, good.'

'A lot of pain, though.'

'I'm sure.'

'But they're marvellous in that hospital, you know. Putting people back together the way they do.'

'Indeed.'

'I've seen things brought in there that you couldn't really call bodies: bits, just bits and pieces of bodies, carried in and layed out in a line, and the next thing you know those doctors have got everything sorted out and stitched back in place, and those bodies are walking out of there under their own steam.'

'So I've heard,' said Mr Apple, which he had, though not in quite such graphic terms.

'And the lovely thing is, Mr Apple, they don't care who you are or what you are. If the troubles have got at you they'll welcome you in and fix you up like new if they can.'

'But – ' Mr Apple began, about to point out that Bradley had hardly been the victim of the euphemistically-named troubles but changing his mind. A severe scalding by boiling oil from an over-turned chip-pan could not very well be blamed on the warring factions, but his suffering had been real enough, and any pain, however inflicted, seemed to give one the peculiar right to share in the distress of the city. 'But you're coping all right?' Mr Apple managed to switch the question adroitly.

'As well as can be expected. It's not easy, though, is it?'

'No. Life is not easy.'

'Oh, life is easy enough, Mr Apple. I've nothing against life at all. It's the death around us that I find hard. All that killing,' Our Mary said, pursing her lips as though recalling specific instances. 'It means you can't look forward to anything, doesn't it? I mean how can a body look forward to something, if you don't know you'll be alive to enjoy it?'

'Right you are,' Mr Apple decided to agree.

'And what else is there in life besides looking forward?' Our Mary demanded, putting her hands on her hips and resting her case with this extraordinary question.

Try as he might Mr Apple could find no immediate answer. The silence between them grew longer, a silence broken only by the continued hissing of Aiden Curren, who wandered about in the background pinning up the newspapers. Mr Apple found himself becoming mildly frantic, and was on the point of uttering something innocuous and trite when the door opened and Martin Deeley glided into the shop, smiling and giving a comic, exaggerated salute. 'Hiya all.'

'Martin,' Mr Apple heard himself whispering. He cleared his throat and said 'Martin' again, louder.

Our Mary turned and stared at the intruder, eyeing him up and down, while Aiden Curren stopped whistling for a second, glanced across the shop, shrugged, and returned to his papers.

'You look surprised, Mr A.' Martin said.

'I am.'

' – ?'

'I don't know why. I didn't expect – '

'I told you I'd be back as right as rain in a couple of days. It doesn't take me long to shake off the flu. How's everything?'

'Fine. Just fine,' Mr Apple said, eyeing Martin with peculiar intensity.

'Good. You didn't miss me then?'

Mr Apple gave a small smile. 'Yes, I missed you.'

'I must be off,' Our Mary interjected, sensing that the words she was hearing had nothing to do with the sense they made. 'I'll see you later in the week, Mr Apple.'

'Mind how you go, Our Mary,' Mr Apple said, without moving his eyes from Martin's face.

'You do the same,' Our Mary replied, instilling what sounded suspiciously like a warning into her advice as she threw a sideways look at Martin, bathing him in a stare that suggested she knew all there was to know about him.

'Our Mary been winning again?' Martin asked as the door slammed behind her, keeping his voice casual.

'You know Our Mary?'

'Shit, everyone knows Our Mary. Mad as two hatters.'

'Oh,' said Mr Apple. 'You think so?'

'I know so,' Martin affirmed, coming around the counter and setting about making tea as though he had not missed a day. 'So, you missed me.'

'I said I did,' Mr Apple snapped as if he was now regretting the admission.

'Missed the brilliant conversation, huh?'

Mr Apple did not immediately reply: he could not take his eyes off Martin, the pale-blue-lensed stare intensifying by the second. He only spoke when he finally saw Martin starting to wilt under this visual pressure. 'You look remarkably fit.'

'I'm okay.'

'Good.'

'Hey – what did you mean, "remarkably"?'

Suddenly it was Mr Apple's turn to feel uneasy, and he turned away and headed for the confusion of his desk, shuffling papers as he always did when buying time. 'I –' he began, immediately wondering how to continue, searching for words that would rescue him from the tricky position his mildly sarcastic remark had landed him in.

'You want me to stay now that he's back?' Aiden Curren's thin voice filled the silence in the nick of time. 'They could use me over at Graham's.'

Mr Apple felt himself sigh with relief.

'Or maybe he's just visiting?' Aiden Curren suggested, the question implying disapproval that such a thing should happen during working hours.

' – ?' Mr Apple looked across at Martin and raised his eyebrows.

'I'll stay,' Martin said. 'Be good for Mr Apple to have someone efficient here again.'

Aiden Curren came close to the glass partition and stared through it, opening and closing his mouth like some exotic but stranded fish.

'It's only his little joke, Aiden,' Mr Apple said quickly.

'Jokes I can do without,' Aiden snapped.

'Indeed,' agreed Mr Apple. 'Thank you for coming, Aiden. You've been a great help. How much do I owe you?'

'I'll work it out, Mr Apple. I'll drop back in a day or two. No hurry,' Aiden said proudly, enjoying his moment of largesse, hoping it had made a suitable impression.

'Very well, Aiden. Thank you again for your help.'

'My pleasure, Mr Apple. You're a nice man to work for.'

'Thank you Aiden.'

'Jesus, what a bloody groveller,' Martin sneered as Aiden hissed off through the door. '"You're a nice man to work for"' he mimmicked, emphasizing his mockery with a silly, mincing little dance.

Perhaps it was this ridiculous behaviour that roused Mr Apple, or perhaps he was just suddenly tired of all the pretence, or possibly it was the nagging foreboding that had returned that made him ask sharply: 'Martin, where *have* you been the past few days?'

Martin Deeley froze in a posture that at any other time would have been hilarious, but the transformation in his features was frightening. He stood there, rigid and unmoving, one leg bent, his right arm outstretched, his hand hanging limply in a grotesque attitude of high camp, all of which was the more unsightly when one noted the harshness of his face, the eyes now glazed over with cold fury and suspicion.

'You were in England, weren't you?'

Slowly Martin relaxed. He dropped his arm and straightened his leg. Gradually his face softened, his eyes became sad, taking on an appealing, childlike look of guilty bewilderment and mild shame, like that of a small boy caught with his hand in the sweet-jar. He nodded. 'That's right,' he admitted quietly.

'And it was you who tried to kill that Colonel.'

Martin continued to nod. 'And made a right fucking mess of it,' he said with a wry smile. 'I must be slipping.'

'There were others? I mean – '

'Plenty. Well, seven.'

'My God,' Mr Apple said quietly.

'How did you know?'

' – ?'

'That I'd been in England?'

Mr Apple shook his head violently, as if rattling his thoughts into coherency. 'I don't know, Martin. I can't really explain. I have these visions, you know, and somehow – I don't actually remember – somehow I must have seen you.'

'Jesus,' Martin whispered, the creepiness of Mr Apple's explanation making a shiver course through his body.

Mr Apple also shivered but for reasons of his own, and he sat down heavily. 'Aren't you appalled at what you do?' he asked in an oddly matter-of-fact way, taking off his glasses and polishing the lenses.

'No.'

'Doesn't it terrify you?'

'No. It's just a job. It's, well – well, it's exciting. You wouldn't understand.'

'No. I wouldn't understand. How could anyone in their right mind understand such ruthless killing?'

'They got what they deserved,' Martin said defensively.

'Nobody deserves to be killed, Martin.'

'They did.'

'You decided that?'

'No. The Com— ' he stopped abruptly.

'Ah. So that's it.'

'I said nothing.'

'No, you said nothing,' Mr Apple agreed wearily. He looked up: 'This is one you won't get away with, you know,' he said sadly.

Martin narrowed his eyes. There was something so positive in the way Mr Apple made his pronouncement he was alarmed. 'Huh.'

'It's all falling into place,' Mr Apple was saying, almost to himself, frowning and squinting, trying to decipher those visions of recent nights and reconjure their dreadful warnings. 'It must have been you that was hanging,' he said in a whisper. 'That would explain it.'

Martin felt cold sweat breaking out on his spine. 'What the hell are you on about?' he demanded, surprised at the crack in his voice.

Before Mr Apple could reply the door of the shop burst open and two men hurried into the shop, signalling urgently to Martin. Mr Apple watched as the three of them whispered and gesticulated, watched and felt saddened as he saw Martin grow pale and seem to shrink, the cockiness and bravado that was essentially his disintegrating.

As quickly as they had come the two men left, leaving Martin standing in the middle of the shop; he stood there, quite still and expressionless, for several moments.

'What is it, Martin?' Mr Apple asked, trying to make his voice kind and compassionate.

Martin turned slowly and stared at him, shaking his head. Then he came back around the counter, walking slowly, thinking.

'What is it?' Mr Apple insisted. 'I might be able to help.'

'You can't.'

'I might. I'm a very resourceful man, Martin,' Mr Apple assured him, with a sly little smile.

Martin gave a sad, tired laugh.

'Tell me, anyway.'

Martin sighed. 'I'm to be sacrificed,' he said simply, his eyes suddenly hurt and bewildered.

'Sacrificed?' Mr Apple sounded appalled.

'Yeah. That's it, Mr A. Sacrificed. There's more heat than they can handle over the Colonel, so it's been decided to drop my name in the right place. I'll be done, the heat taken off, and everyone'll be happy.'

'Dear God,' was all Mr Apple could muster up.

'Those were friends of mine warning me. They owe me, you see. Quite a few people owe me, Mr Apple,' Martin said, something of his old assurance returning. 'They told me to stay away from my place. To get out of here, too.'

'Then you must go,' Mr Apple said urgently.

'Hah. Go. Go where? This isn't a game, you know. You can't hide from this. I know. I know exactly what goes on.'

'Then you've got a head start,' Mr Apple said, as he fumbled in his pocket and took out a bundle of keys, dropped them, retrieved them, opened the clip, slipped off a single Yale key and held it out to Martin. 'Now, take this. Go round to my house – you know where *that* is, don't you?' Mr Apple said, smiling thinly at this little jibe. 'Go round the back and let yourself in by the kitchen door. Stay there until I get home. Then we'll think of something.'

'I can't go to your place, Mr Apple. They'll know.'

'I don't care what they know. Take it. Do what you're told for once. It will keep you off the streets for a while. We need time. Take it and go.'

'You don't know what you're getting into, Mr A.'

'I know. I know a lot more than you think. Now take this key and go.'

Martin took the key. 'Hey – thanks, Mr Apple.'

'Will you *go*, for heaven's sake. You can thank me tonight when I get home.'

Mr Apple watched Martin hurry from the shop. It was only as the door closed behind him and he found himself alone in the ominous silence that the full significance of what he had done began to dawn on him.

Mr Asher offered Colonel Maddox one of his cigarettes even though he knew it would be refused, accepted one himself, lit it, and stared out at the dark, rainswept streets as the car whisked them into the city from the airport. His face was tense and grey, in total contrast to the Colonel's, which was as usual ruddy, relaxed and calm, if a little mournful. One would have thought (seeing them both, side by side, each, in his own way reliving the events of the past few days) that it was Mr Asher who had so recently escaped the assassin's bullet.

'I still can't believe it,' he said at last, shaking his head.

Colonel Maddox gave a small chuckle. 'Oh, it's true enough, John.'

'God, you were lucky.'

'Yes.'

'The bastards. Right on your own doorstep,' Asher continued, as though the choice of location had been more horrifying than the attempt at murder.

'Anyone claimed responsibility yet?'

'Not yet. They will, though. If only to crow that they can still get at us.'

'Which, of course, they can,' the Colonel pointed out, not without humour.

'Which, of course, they can,' Asher agreed grimly. 'But I'll get someone for this if it's the last thing I do.'

'Not just someone, John. I want no unnecessary reprisals just because it was me they tried to dispose of.'

Asher appeared not to be listening. 'We've pulled in Corrigan for –'

'Corrigan?'

'Hmm. You know him. Larry Corrigan. Big fat lout. No teeth. We use him sometimes. Having him questioned. Knows a thing or two, does Larry Corrigan. I'm going there myself after I drop you off – unless you care to come along. ?'

Maddox frowned. 'Yes. Yes, I think I will. It's a new experience, isn't it? And not without intrigue: attempting to find out who actually tried to shoot one?'

Asher leaned forward and gave instructions to the driver, who responded immediately by swinging the car in a tight U-turn, timing his manoeuvre to perfection, slipping neatly between two oncoming cars without braking.

'Anything exciting over here while I was away?' Maddox asked.

'Not a lot. Routine mostly. You've been the excitement,' Mr Asher said, glancing at the Colonel with an almost envious smile. 'I've had a tighter watch put on Apple's shop, but there's been no activity there. He's got a new assistant, though. I'm checking on that. We'll have to have him in again soon, Mr Apple I mean. I know damn well he's mixed up in something, for all his innocent look.'

Maddox smiled. 'You don't like our Mr Apple much, do you?' he asked.

'No, I don't. Devious little freak.'

'You don't understand him, John.'

'There's nothing to understand. He's just another fool who's been conned or blackmailed into helping – '

'Why do you always call him a fool? I don't think he is, you know. Far from it. And I must say I think you employ the wrong tactics when you question him. I don't think he takes kindly to bullies.'

'I don't have the time for niceties, Colonel. He'll slip up. They all do, eventually. Then we'll have him.' Asher stroked his cheek in satisfaction.

'Unless, of course, they have us first,' the Colonel observed wryly.

'They won't.'

'They might.'

'They won't.'

'They nearly had me.'

Both men swayed as the car pulled sharply to the left to allow a screaming ambulance to pass.

'How did Mrs Maddox take it?'

'Rather well,' Maddox said vaguely. 'I think she was somewhat amused by the episode.'

'Amused?' Asher sounded shocked.

The Colonel gave a wicked little chuckle. 'Yes – in a way. She wasn't there when the actual shooting took place, but they managed to contact her in London. At her milliner's, would you believe,' the Colonel explained, allowing his chuckle to become a small laugh. 'A friend of hers drove her home immediately.' He paused and looked out of the window. He saw again the silver Bristol slither to a stop, sending the neatly raked gravel flying in all directions (and he remembered his annoyance, since he had raked it himself in a pattern of ever decreasing circles), saw Nancy step daintily out on elegant Gucci shoes, noted in her eyes a curious expectancy – but an expectancy of what he could not be sure.

Whatever happened? she demanded, looking about her for signs of carnage. We were told you were shot.

Yes. Someone took a shot at me.

Here? Right here? Nancy stepped quickly to one side as though the possibility of delayed ricochet was imminent.

Yes, dear. Right here. They missed.

I can see that. Why all the police?

Well, they don't really like the idea of someone shooting at me, he told her in his pronouncedly polite way. And I'm afraid my driver was killed.

Here? Nancy demanded again, horrified that her domain had been sullied.

The Colonel nodded.

How dreadful. But you're all right?

I'm fine.

Nancy Maddox shook her head theatrically and tutted. I do wish they wouldn't do it here, she said angrily (and the Colonel recalled her using the same expression and tone when his favourite retriever, now dead, had shat on the lawn). Over there (dismissing Northern

Ireland with a small wave of her gloved hand) you expect it.

I think that's what they had in mind, dear.

What?

That I wouldn't expect it.

Well, all I can say is I wish you wouldn't – Nancy stopped abruptly. Incredibly, she had been about to suggest that he leave his assassins behind him (at the office, so to speak) when the stupidity of this dawned on her.

Wouldn't – ?

Wouldn't get mixed up with such dreadful people, Nancy said lamely.

Colonel Maddox rocked on his heels and laughed until his eyes filled with tears. Even the two uniformed policemen nearest him, who had been unavoidably overhearing the conversation with some amazement, smiled.

Oh, Nancy you are incredible.

Well, you won't be going back there. That's something.

– ? But of course I will. I'll go back tomorrow.

Don't be stupid, Matthew. You can't go back now. They *know* you.

They've *known* me from the first day I set foot in Belfast, my dear.

But they've just tried to kill you.

That's right. So?

You are impossible, Nancy concluded and stormed into the house.

'She made me laugh anyway,' Maddox told Asher. 'I think it was the first time she ever made me laugh,' he confessed. 'The first time for a very long time anyway.'

'Amazing.'

'Yes. She is.'

'They don't understand, do they? Wives,' Mr Asher proclaimed.

'Why should they, John? I don't think we understand it ourselves half the time.'

'Oh, I understand it all right.'

'You do? I didn't think you did.'

Mr Asher rolled down the window a fraction and slipped his finished black cigarette through the gap. Then he rolled the window up again, cutting out the noise of the traffic and wind, and trying to suppress the feeling of resentment that welled up within him whenever the Colonel included him in his inadequacies. He was on the point of making some caustic remark when the car swung left and halted at the gates of Castlereagh police station.

'Anything?' Asher demanded brusquely of the sergeant who met them at the entrance and followed them down the corridor lined with small, anonymous rooms with numbers on the doors, from which issued occasional murmurs.

'Yes and no, sir.'

Asher halted, swung round, and glared. 'What the hell does that mean – yes and no? What the hell sort of an answer is that?'

The sergeant wilted and blushed violently. 'He hasn't exactly said anything – but I think he wants to. He's been insisting on seeing you.'

'Me?'

'Yes, sir.'

'By name?'

'Yes, sir.'

Asher glanced quickly at the Colonel. 'That's odd,' he said, frowning. 'They usually try and avoid me,' he added, his frown broadening and relaxing into a bland smile.

'Yes,' the Colonel agreed non-committally.

'Where is he?'

'Twenty-three, sir.'

'Right. We'd better go and see what he wants, then.'

Asher led the small procession down the corridor and paused briefly at the door of Room 23 to straighten his tie, as though correctness of dress would give him some tactical advantage. 'I'll deal with this. You needn't be here,' he told the sergeant, dismissing him with a curt nod.

'Very good, sir.'

'He has a way of interrupting,' Asher informed the Colonel, as the sergeant retreated up the corridor. 'I dislike being interrupted.'

'Yes,' the Colonel said again, managing to suggest a promise of silence.

'Right. Here we go.' Mr Asher straightened his shoulders and opened the door. He stood to one side and allowed the Colonel to pass into the room first. Then he shut the door firmly.

Larry Corrigan sat on a plain wooden chair which he overflowed, his fat, stubby, nicotine-stained fingers fidgeting nervously on the table before him, his eyes jumping continuously towards and away from the two men.

'You wanted me?' Asher said coldly.

'You Asher?'

'*Mr* Asher. Yes.'

'Who's he?'

'Never you mind, Corrigan. You wanted me and now I'm here. So, what is it you wanted?'

Corrigan shifted his enormous weight painfully in an effort to get his buttocks balanced evenly on either side of the seat of the chair, making it creak. He was breathing sweatily, banging the palms of his hands together silently.

Don't give it to Asher all at once, Seamus Reilly had warned him. Don't seem too anxious to help or he'll know something's up. He's as crafty as they come is Asher, so watch yourself, Corrigan.

I don't like doing this to Deeley, Mr Reilly, Corrigan said. I really don't. He's always been fair to me and didn't laugh at me. He was always willing to help me.

Your affections don't concern us, Corrigan. If you wish to side with Deeley that's your business – and I presume you'll be willing to take the consequences?

Cummon, Mr Reilly, be fair. Can't you get someone else to –

You have always been our source of – how shall I put it – our intermediary with the Brits, Larry. They trust you now. We need them to trust what you have to tell them.

All right, Mr Reilly. But you won't let on to Martin, will you?

Martin will be the least of your worries, I assure you.

Larry Corrigan grinned toothlessly. All right, Mr Reilly, I'll do it. Just leave it to me.

Exactly. We're leaving it to you, Larry. But don't mess it up.

I won't. Hey, why don't you just tell them straight? The Brits *want* to know, don't they?

Reilly sighed. People never appreciated the diplomacy of these negotiations. Because, Larry, he explained, tidying his impeccable clothes, his tone of voice indicating his imminent departure as clearly as if he were donning a hat, because it has been decided that it would be better from everybody's point of view if this information was extracted from you after considerable pressure.

You mean you don't want anyone to know that you set Martin up, is that it, Mr Reilly?

Just do it, Corrigan. Just do it and don't ask so many questions.

'I need a favour,' Larry Corrigan said.

'Well?' Mr Asher asked, and waited.

'I want out. I want to get away.'

'Away?'

'That's right, Mr Asher. Well away. Australia.'

'I see.' Asher seemed to consider this for a moment, glancing once at Maddox. 'An expensive business, Corrigan. Travelling to Australia. Very expensive,' he added, wondering what information Corrigan was about to offer that would warrant such a price. 'It could, of course, be arranged. Anything can be arranged if it's worth my while,' Asher continued speculatively, watching Corrigan's body sag while his eyes brightened in anticipation. 'We would have to learn something very – eh – interesting in return.'

Don't give it to Asher all at once, Reilly warned him.

'I *think* I might be able to find out who tried to hit that Colonel in England – would that be interesting enough?'

'I *think* it might be,' Mr Asher replied, avoiding a look at the Colonel who stood stony-faced and silent by the door. 'When do you *think* you could find out?'

'Do we have a deal?'

'We have a deal.'

Colonel Maddox stared up at the ceiling, trying to concentrate his gaze on the naked sixty-watt bulb, amazed and shocked that the process of treachery and betrayal could be handled with such calm, in such a businesslike way. Despite the fact that it was his own would-be assassin who was being bartered he was appalled by the neatness of the agreements being made.

' – ticket and some cash to keep me going,' Corrigan was now stipulating.

'Agreed.'

'Immediately.'

'As soon as any information you give us has been confirmed.'

'And my name stays out of it.'

'Naturally.'

'Okay.'

Asher sat on the edge of the table and waited. He didn't move a muscle, as if afraid that any movement he might make would distract Corrigan from parting with the information.

'You know Bezant's bookie's?'

'I do.'

'You know the boardmarker there?'

'Apple?'

'No, not Apple,' Corrigan said irritably. 'He's the manager. The boardmarker, I said. Martin Deeley?'

Asher inclined his head, but said nothing.

'He's just back from England. The word is that it wasn't exactly a holiday.'

Asher sucked in air and exhaled it again in a thin, inaudible whistle, controlling his excitement admirably. 'I see. Martin Deeley, you say. And Apple?'

'What about him?'

'He must have had something to do with it?'

By the way, Reilly said just before he left, if they should ask you anything about Mr Apple – it's unlikely, but they might – you know nothing.

Right, Mr Reilly. I'll remember that.

'No,' Corrigan said, shaking his head vehemently. 'Why should he? He's nothing. Just runs the place. Does nothing. Knows nothing. He's not connected with us at all.'

'You're sure of that?' Asher demanded, sounding disappointed and unbelieving.

'Sure, I'm sure.'

'He must have known Deeley was up to something.'

Corrigan shrugged his shoulders, the movement making the chair groan. 'How could he? He's told nothing. Jesus, Mr Asher, he's even a Prod. He just runs his shop, like I told you.'

'Right, Corrigan. You stay here. I'll be back in a while,' Asher said, standing up quickly and making for the door, taking the Colonel with him, an intense, satisfied smile on his face. 'Well, Colonel,' he said as they made their way along the corridor, 'that was nice and neat.'

'Too neat, if you ask me,' Maddox said. 'Can you believe him?' he asked.

'Of course,' Asher replied. 'Come in here a moment,' he added, leading the way into an empty office and closing the door. 'That's the way it works, Colonel,' he whispered, smiling delightedly. 'This Deeley has become a liability, so Corrigan was sent here to unload him.'

'Unload him?'

'That's it, Colonel. They hand over Deeley to us in the hope that we keep the heat off, in case we turn up something more important while we search for your – '

'You mean Corrigan was actually ordered in here to – '

' – to give us the information we want and make a deal for himself? Yes. That's exactly what I mean.'

'Good God.'

'It happens all the time. They're lovely people.'

'How many others have you sent to – Australia?'

Asher laughed, truly amused at the Colonel's naïvety. 'None. And, of course, Corrigan won't be going either.'

' – ?'

'He'll be killed.'

'And you'll allow that, after making an agreement with him?'

'Allow it? Colonel, we'll arrange it. Of course we'll make it look like a punishment for informing, but we'll do it. It's tidier that way, don't you think?'

'But – '

'Just let me handle it, Colonel. I know what I'm doing. You go on. You must be tired after your journey. I've things to do now. As soon as we pick up Deeley I'll let you know.'

'And you call *them* lovely people? John, this is all *wrong*.'

'It's the way we've done things since long before you came here, Colonel. We all have an understanding. Believe me, I know what I'm doing.'

Colonel Maddox shook his head and walked away.

'Jesus,' Asher sighed, watching the retreating figure. 'Jesus, and they expect to beat the terrorists?'

Mr Apple shut the front door of his house simply by leaning his back against it, allowing his long body to rest at an angle, giving his eyes time to focus in the gloom, giving his ears a few seconds to retune themselves to the stillness after the noises outside. Then he switched on the light in the hall and made his way to the kitchen, coughing gently to announce his arrival. Using the shaft of light from the hall for illumination he drew the curtains across the kitchen window before putting on the fluorescent light: it flickered belligerently, and in the intermittent blue-white clarity Mr Apple spotted Martin crouched by the back door, his wave of recognition looking jerky and dislocated in the uncertain light. As the overhead tube settled down to a continuous flow of hard brightness Martin said:

'You frightened the shit out of me, Mr A.'

'I coughed,' Mr Apple told him defensively.

'Yeah, I heard that, but I've never heard you cough before, so I didn't know it was you.'

'Oh. Well, it is.'

'Yep. So I see.' Martin stood up and stretched, then leaned a hip lazily against the table.

Mr Apple ignored him for the moment and, with his eyes, searched the kitchen from top to bottom. 'Have you seen Chloe?' he asked suddenly, his voice ridiculously calm under the circumstances.

'Chloe?'

'My cat.'

'A ginger-and-white thing?'

Mr Apple nodded and pursed his lips, peeved to hear Chloe referred to as a thing.

'Yes. She's been at the window for about an hour. I was going to let her in for company, but she ran off.'

Mr Apple appeared pleased with the cat's discretion. 'She's fussy about the company she keeps,' he said, smiling wickedly.

'Very funny.'

'Animals – cats in particular – can always tell what we mortals are like, you know. I never trust anyone who doesn't get on with animals,' Mr Apple explained obscurely. 'And I wouldn't be without some sort of animal myself. Dear little Chloe. Oh, well, she'll be back when she's hungry I expect,' he remarked. 'You hungry, Martin?'

'I could eat something.'

'Ah. Well, let's see what we can rustle up.'

Mr Apple took off his coat and, donning an apron that extolled the virtues of a particular gravy mixture, busied himself getting something for them to eat, opening a can of condensed chicken soup, and, with customary difficulty, a couple of tins of sardines. 'It won't be very fancy,' he threw over his shoulder, licking the sardine oil from his fingers, 'but it will keep you going.'

'Thanks. Anything's fine.'

'By the way,' Mr Apple went on casually, adding milk to the saucepan and stirring the soup, 'I think the hunt has started for you.'

Martin immediately stood upright, his body rigid. 'What makes you say that?'

'We had visitors in the shop. Two strangers. Never saw either of them before. They weren't dressed right for punters. Too – well, too correct, if that's the word. They didn't say anything, mind you. Just looked around, stayed ten minutes, and left. They pretended to be listening to the race. Of course, I could be imagining things.'

'You don't imagine things, Mr Apple.'

'Oh, but I do, Martin. That's my trouble. Anyway, they went. Here, have this while it's hot.' Mr Apple passed Martin a bowl of steaming chicken soup. 'There's bread in the bin over there if you want some. Butter in the fridge. Salt and pepper on that shelf.' Martin shook his head and started spooning the soup slowly into his mouth, blowing on each spoonful before drinking it.

Mr Apple carried his own soup to the table and sat down. 'Then Seamus Reilly came in,' he said. 'You know him, of course, although you pretended you didn't?'

'I know him. What did *he* want?'

'He said he just dropped in to see how I was – and, casually, why I was without a boardmarker.'

'And?'

'And I told him you were still out sick. That you had come in but had felt weak, and that I'd sent you home.'

'Thanks. What – ?'

'I think he knew I was lying,' Mr Apple said, making a quizzical face as he savoured the soup, getting up to collect the pepper-pot from the shelf and sprinkling its contents liberally into his bowl before adding, 'I have a feeling he'd already been to your home.'

Martin nodded, his eyes reduced to thin slits. 'Probably.'

'I thought you two were on the same side.'

'So did I.'

'Oh.'

'There's no sides here, it seems, Mr Apple. There's only survival. You survive anyway you can.'

'I see.'

'Even if it means trading with the army, you have to arrange your survival,' Martin explained, in a voice that suggested he had just worked this out.

'I see,' said Mr Apple again.

'Still,' Martin said with a small laugh, 'I suppose you could say we're on the same side now.'

'We always were, Martin,' Mr Apple told him darkly. 'Even before we met we were destined to join forces.'

'You don't half say some weird things, Mr A.'

Mr Apple nodded. 'I'm a weird person.'

Martin Deeley pushed his bowl away from him and wiped the thin beige moustache from his upper lip with his handkerchief. 'Not weird. But you're different. You're certainly different, Mr A. Although before I met you I thought you were weird.'

'What changed your mind?'

Martin shrugged. 'Knowing you a bit, I suppose.'

178

'But you don't. You know nothing about me.'

'Yes I do.'

'If you say so,' Mr Apple sighed benignly, scraping the last of the soup from his plate and licking his spoon like a lollipop.

'You don't think I do?'

Mr Apple stared unblinkingly at Martin. 'I know you don't. I don't really exist, you see.'

'Oh.' Martin grinned, but eyed the old man suspiciously all the same.

'I come and go,' Mr Apple went on ponderously. 'Like everyone does, really. We all come and go.'

'Sure.'

'Now you *do* think I'm mad.'

'No.'

'Yes, you do, Martin. You're sitting there saying to yourself that you were right all along. And maybe you're right,' Mr Apple conceded, pausing for a moment before adding: 'But I'll tell you my secret: only my experiences make me exist; when they cease, or even lie for a moment in abeyance, I stop being. Does that make sense?'

Martin laughed nervously. 'Not a lot.'

'It will, Martin. Believe me, it will. The older you get the more you will appreciate that what I say is true.'

'Great. I look forward to that.'

Mr Apple bowed his head and seemed, for the moment, to be lost in unravelling some mystery on the bottom of his soup bowl. Then: 'So what happens to you now, Martin?' he asked suddenly. 'Where do you go from here?'

The abruptness of the question, and perhaps the realization that its simplicity made his predicament all the more alarming, made Martin jump. 'I wish the hell I knew.'

'You're quite certain that you are to be – eh – sacrificed – I think was your word?'

'Yeah. I'm certain. I even know it's Larry Corrigan who's going to drop my name. Poor old bugger. He doesn't know he's as dead as I am. Yeah, I'm certain all right.'

'Well, then,' Mr Apple said, pushing his bowl away and drumming his fingertips on the table after setting his spectacles firmly on his nose, 'we'd better put our heads together and think what we're going to do with you.'

Martin shook his head, a look of amazement spreading over his face. 'You really amaze me, Mr Apple,' he said.

'I don't see why.'

'The way you – never mind. I can't explain it, anyway. I'll just have to disappear, that's all. England for a start, if I can make it. Then God knows.'

'Yes.'

'I can't stay here, that's for sure.'

'Whyever not?'

'And have you dragged into it? Don't be stupid, Mr A. There's a shit called Asher in charge of things – ever heard of him?'

'Oh, yes. Oh, dear me,' Mr Apple was suddenly grinning in delight. 'I know Mr Asher well. Not a nice little man, is he?'

'You've met him?'

'A couple of times. Yes. I was supposed to tell him what was going on in the shop, you see.'

'So they *were* right.'

' – ?'

'You were seen – '

'Yes, I thought I was. I didn't say anything, though. Disliked him a great deal. Mr Asher, I mean.'

'Well, you'll dislike him a hell of a lot more if he finds out you've been hiding me. He'll have you in for harbouring a criminal and *you'll* end up in the slammer.'

'There are worse things, Martin,' Mr Apple said philosophically.

'Oh yeah? Like what?'

'Imprisoning oneself in oneself,' Mr Apple said mysteriously. 'That's far worse, you know, Martin. That really is the most awful thing of all. The constant manacling of the spirit inside oneself.'

'You've lost me.'

'We all lose ourselves...Anyway, you'll have to stay here for a while. I can try and find out what's happening.'

'They'll come here.'

'But they don't have to find you.'

'Hah – you ever seen those bastards do a search?'

'No.'

'Well, I can tell you, Mr Apple, if I'm here they'll find me. They'll tear the place to pieces if they think I'm here.'

Mr Apple smiled cunningly. 'Oh I think we can outwit Mr Asher and his henchmen,' he said cheerfully, as though about to put into operation some enormously amusing game of hity-tity. 'Anyway, they'll only look in places likely to hide a body.'

'Brilliant. So, you going to shrink me? Make me invisible?'

Mr Apple laughed aloud, a strange, cackling, unpractised sound, as though the suggestions tickled his fancy. 'Not quite. Sardines on toast?'

' – ? Oh. No. No, thanks. I've had enough.'

'Certain?'

'Thanks.'

'Right. Come with me, as they say, and I shall show thee things of great import.'

Mr Apple rose from the table with exaggerated dignity and, using his arm like an oar, gestured for Martin to follow in his wake. They left the kitchen and walked down the hall. Mr Apple stopped at the glory-hole and opened the door. 'Now for the wonders of architecture,' he said.

'Jesus, that's the first place they'll look.'

'Yes. I know,' Mr Apple agreed affably. 'It's so obvious, isn't it?'

'And?'

'And, would you believe, the cupboard will be bare. Not a mouse, not a Martin, not a thing.'

' – ?'

'Look,' Mr Apple commanded, switching on the cupboard light. 'Just look,' he repeated.

Martin looked. In the pale forty-watt light he saw only that the cupboard was already as bare as Mother Hubbard's. 'Great,' he said.

'An empty cupboard. So?'

'So they look in here and see nothing,' Mr Apple said, enjoying himself hugely, rubbing his bony hands together.

'You're losing me, Mr Apple. One of us is round the twist – '

Mr Apple indulged himself and enjoyed Martin's confusion for a moment, his eyes glistening behind the thick lenses. 'That is exactly what I intend to do, Martin. Lose you. Behold.'

Mr Apple was suddenly on his knees, fiddling with something on the floor. As he straightened up he lifted part of the floor with him and propped it against the wall. 'Now, then. What do you think of that?'

' – ?'

'Squeeze in and have a peep.'

Martin squeezed in and stared at the opening in the floor. A narrow flight of wooden steps led downwards into darkness. 'What's down there?'

'Your salvation,' Mr Apple told him. 'Your escape, at any rate. Follow me.'

Mr Apple started down the steps, grunting, but manipulating the steep descent with some agility, as though he had practised the exercise frequently. And Martin followed.

'Now, what do you think of that?' Mr Apple wanted to know, switching on a light and waving an arm, as though triumphantly revealing a long lost masterpiece.

'Wow.'

Martin stared about him. It was a tiny room. Immaculately clean. A camp-bed, neatly made and covered by an exotic patchwork quilt stood in one corner. There was a small table and, beside it, one chair with a cushion to match the quilt. A hessian mat covered most of the brick floor, and on the walls hung pictures of beings Martin had never seen before, not even in his wildest dreams. In one, a creature like a black dog, with horns and the face of an ape, straddled a cottage and held a large key in its mouth; in another a succubus reclined, one arm bent back behind her head, her breasts like grinning faces, her stomach and knees portrayed as faces also; there were portraits of

Thomas Darling, Louise Huebner, Aleister Crowley, and a composite of the Monks of Medmenham. Directly over the small table there was a crucifix on which was suspended a negroid Christ, and under it, on a small shelf, lay a scarab, a marble eye of Horus, a bible and a glass bottle containing what looked like dried parsley.

'Christ, Mr Apple,' was all that Martin could find to say.

'Yes,' Mr Apple agreed. 'He has a lot to do with it.'

'It's creepy,' Martin said, shivering suddenly. 'What the hell are all those things?' he asked, pointing at the pictures.

'Ah. Well, aids, I suppose. Symbols of what I must destroy. But don't let them worry you, Martin. They don't effect you.'

'I'm glad to hear that. They're –'

'And, you see, you'll be quite safe here for a while.'

'I'm not so sure about that.'

'Oh, you will. They'll never find you here.'

'That's not what I meant.'

'Oh.'

'Anyway, they'll have dogs with them in case of explosives. You'll be up to your neck in it, Mr A. The dogs will soon sniff me out.'

'Well, now, I had thought of that,' Mr Apple said, tugging at his chin and beginning to look like Merlin. 'That's where the other member of the family comes in. The one you were so rude about. Chloe.'

'The cat?'

'The cat. She has a little tray, you see. To do her nasties in – tee-hee – and I thought if I sprinkled a little of that on the floor upstairs, and, indeed, put poor Chloe in there...?'

'You know, I never would have thought you to be so devious, Mr A.'

'Survival, Martin. That's what you told me. Survival.'

And it wasn't all that long before Mr Apple's survival special was put to the test. He had just settled down in bed to write his diary, and was thinking what words to use concerning the downstairs arrangements, thinking, too, and smiling at the thought, of Martin tucked up under the watchful glare of the daemonic onlookers while Chloe (furious at her restricted liberty and mewling like a mad thing) created feline havoc overhead, when he heard the vehicles skid to a stop outside his house, the muffled orders being given, and the thud of boots running up the path, dividing, some running round the back, the rest thundering up the steps to the front door. Mr Apple leaped out of bed and ran to the top of the stairs, pulling on a threadbare dressing-gown as he ran. He had only managed to negotiate two stairs when the front door splintered and burst open under the onslaught of military footwear. Suddenly, the hall below him was filled with soldiers, all armed. They seemed to freeze for a moment, looking about them uncertainly: then they parted ranks and allowed Asher to make his way to the foot of the stairs and stare up at Mr Apple.

'We have orders to search your house,' he said curtly, somehow making it clear that Mr Apple was privileged to have even this explanation.

'Search my house?'

'Yes.'

'Good heavens,' Mr Apple said, doing his best to look aghast. 'Why on earth would you want to do that?'

'You wouldn't know, of course.'

'I'm afraid I haven't the faintest idea.'

'I warned you some time ago you'd end up in trouble if you tried to cross me,' Asher said complacently. 'And now you're in trouble. Big trouble.'

'Oh dear,' Mr Apple said, switching his expression adroitly to misery. 'Perhaps you'd be so good as to search up here first so that I can get back to bed? I need my beauty sleep, you see.'

Asher narrowed his eyes. 'Right,' he said, and added, sharpening his voice, 'tear this place to pieces if you have to, but make certain you search every inch of it. Get those dogs in here first. And be quick about it.'

Mr Apple sat himself down on the top stair and watched through the banisters as the mayhem proceeded. Two Alsatians were intro-duced to the scene, great pink tongues lolling, tails wagging high in some anticipation: they were sent ahead into each room before their handlers reported the rooms 'clean'. 'Clean, sir,' was exactly what they said, and Mr Apple gave Asher a little wave to acknowledge this passing of his housework, trying to hide his annoyance and anxiety as the soldiers crashed about in the rooms, throwing everything on the floor, emptying drawers, overturning chairs and tables, pots and pans in the kitchen, books and ornaments in the sitting-room, all thrown willy-nilly into piles on the floor. 'Nothing, sir.'

'Upstairs, then,' Asher ordered, standing aside and letting the dogs and soldiers race up the stairs.

'Hello, doggies,' Mr Apple said to the Alsatians, who ignored him, and 'Good evening,' he wished each soldier as he passed, and they ignored him also, though one did look somewhat embarrassed as he passed the skinny, bent figure smiling benignly at him.

And the routine was exactly the same upstairs as down. 'Clean, sir.' Mr Apple's little wave to Asher. 'Nothing, sir.'

Asher came half-way up the stairs and pointed a manicured finger at Mr Apple. 'You are a lucky man,' he said. 'This time. But don't think I've finished with you yet.'

Mr Apple smiled beatifically.

'Right,' Asher ordered. 'Out.'

Down came the soldiers, followed by the dogs, and passed Asher, making for the door. Indeed, all the soldiers had left the house when one of the dogs started sniffing and growling at the glory-hole door, scratching at it. Asher turned his head and grinned triumphantly at Mr Apple. 'And what have we here?'

Mr Apple peered over the top of his spectacles. 'There? Oh, that's my glory-hole, Mr Asher. That's where I hide things,' he said mischievously. 'I wouldn't open the door if I were you.'

'Oh, you wouldn't – ' Asher said, and jerked his head authoritatively at the dog-handler. 'Open it,' he ordered.

The dog-handler, the dark green of his R.U.C. uniform blending with the shadows and making him appear bodiless, reached out and opened the door of the cupboard, standing behind it, leaving his Alsatian to take the brunt of any attack. For a moment there was

185

silence, the men watching the dog, the dog peering into the glory-hole, its head cocked quizzically. Then all hell broke loose: a small, furry, ginger-and-white missile flew from the dark and landed, screaming, on the dog's face, sharp little claws embedding them-selves in the unfortunate animal's eyes. The dog yelped and reared up, shaking itself furiously to rid itself of Chloe, who clung on tenaciously for a few minutes, then jumped nimbly away and dashed out the front door.

'Oh, dear,' said Mr Apple. 'I did say not to open that door, Mr Asher. Chloe does hate her meditation to be disturbed.'

Asher opened and closed his mouth several times, small flecks of spittle forming on the edges of his lips. He cleaned these off repeatedly with his tongue before saying: 'Get that damn dog out and quieten it down.'

'Dear, dear, poor dog,' Mr Apple was saying, coming down the stairs. 'Yet another innocent victim of our times. It's always the innocent who suffer, don't you find, Mr Asher?'

But Mr Asher found nothing, it seemed, but his seat in the car, and by the time Mr Apple reached the front door the invading troops had been loaded up and were pulling out, leaving Mr Apple to gaze into an empty street.

'What on earth have you been up to, Mr Apple?'

' – ?' Mr Apple jumped, taken aback by the unexpected discovery at such close quarters of Mr Cahill, still, it struck him, togged out for gardening despite the lateness of the hour, but at least without his watering-can.

'What brought all this about?' Cahill still wanted to know, standing on tiptoe and attempting to see over Mr Apple's shoulder.

'Sanitary inspectors,' Mr Apple offered by way of explanation, smiling nervously. 'At least, they kept telling each other my house was clean.'

'Not been making bombs, then?' Cahill pursued wittily. 'Can't say I'd have taken you for a bomb maker.'

Mr Apple, perhaps infected by his neighbour's light dismissal of the frightening events, started to laugh. 'You'll never believe it, Mr

Cahill but the combined forces of the R.U.C. and the British Army were driven out, routed you might say, by my cat!'

'By *what*?'

'My cat.'

'That scrawny moggy that steals my milk and – '

'The very same. Who would have thought it? Oh, dear, oh dear,' Mr Apple shook with uncontrollable, jittery laughter.

'You all right?'

'Yes. I'm fine. Thank you.'

'You can stay with me for the night if you like,' Cahill went on, sounding concerned.'

'That's most kind of you, Mr Cahill, but I'm quite all right. They only smashed the lock on the door. Apart from that, no damage.'

'Right. Good-night, then.'

'Good-night, Mr Cahill. And thank you.'

Mr Apple closed the front door and put the little chain across it to hold it closed. He leaned his back against it and started shaking, shaking in sheer terror as the realization of what might have happened sank in. He needed, deserved, a drink. One stiff therapeutic drink was what was called for. He padded into the sitting-room and stared at the mess before him without really seeing it, his eyes seeking out the bottle of brandy he knew should be there somewhere. At last he spotted it, partially concealed by his well-thumbed copy of *The Wind in the Willows*. Mr Apple retrieved the bottle and unscrewed the cap: he was about to take a drink when he changed his mind, screwed on the cap again and went out of the room, making for the glory-hole.

'Was that what I think it was?' Martin demanded as Mr Apple negotiated the steep steps, brandishing the brandy bottle before him.

'That depends what you think it was, Martin,' he said lightly.

'They came, didn't they?'

'We had visitors, yes. Our friend Mr Asher and his entourage dropped in for a moment. But they're gone now, and all's well with the world. Drink?'

Martin accepted the bottle absentmindedly and took a drink,

coughing as the liquid made its way to his stomach. 'I told you they would,' he said, passing the bottle back.

'So you did. Cheers.' Mr Apple drank deeply. 'Aaah,' he said, and belched timidly. 'But they didn't find you, did they?'

'Not this time. They'll be back.'

'Not for a while. By the way, you'll have to show more respect for Chloe in future. She saved your bacon. Attacked like a cat possessed.'

' – ?'

'Drove the invading hordes from our shores,' Mr Apple continued, starting to shake again, taking another mouthful of brandy. 'I thought they had you, though.'

For some time they sat in silence, passing the bottle back and forth.

'Well, that settles it,' Martin said finally. 'I can't stay here.'

'Nonsense,' Mr Apple snapped. 'It's the one place you *can* stay. They've done their search and found nothing.'

'So I just sit down here for the rest of my life?'

'Oh. I see. I wasn't thinking that far ahead. Well – '

Once again they took to sitting in brooding silence, eyeing each other from time to time as though to elicit inspiration.

'Now wait a minute,' Mr Apple said suddenly, brightening. 'I've had a thought.'

' – ?'

'Just let me work this out. You say your name has been given as part of a deal, right?'

Martin nodded. 'That's the way it is.'

'So, what we have to do is to arrange another deal, a sort of counter deal – I'm beginning to enjoy this, you know – to get you off the hook.'

'What – '

'No, don't interrupt me a moment,' Mr Apple said quickly, chewing on his lower lip and frowning. 'Apart from myself, have you anyone else who would help you?'

Martin imitated Mr Apple's frown. 'Yes – well, I think so. Yes.'

188

'Good. Who?'

'Fergal and Billy – the two who warned me in the first place · would, if they haven't been got at.'

'Good. Anyone else?'

'I can't think of – '

'Surely there's someone else. Someone I could contact to – '

'Hang on a minute. Daphne. That's it, Mr Apple. Daphne Cope. A girl I know – '

'*Can* she help?'

'You bet. She knows everyone. Had most of them,' Martin said, with a wicked grin.

'And you can trust her?'

Martin thought for a moment. 'Yeah, I can trust her. She loves me,' he said, starting to blush.

'Poor girl.'

'Lucky.'

'Huh,' grunted Mr Apple, but smiling kindlily enough. 'Where can I get in touch with her?'

'You can phone her. That would be safest.'

'When?'

'Any time. Now.'

'Now?' Mr Apple glanced at his watch. 'At twenty past one?'

'She works late,' Martin said, grinning again.

'Oh.'

'Shit,' said Martin suddenly, 'what am I talking about. *I'll* phone her. You have a phone, I suppose?'

'I have a phone,' Mr Apple said. 'But I'll phone. You stay down here – just in case.'

'In case of – '

'In case – I don't know. Just in case. You know her number?'

'She won't talk to you, Mr A. She doesn't know you. She's careful.'

'Yes. I hadn't thought of that.'

'Let's do it then. I – '

'Wait, wait, wait,' Mr Apple insisted, waving Martin to sit down again. 'What are you going to say to her?'

' – ? Nothing. I just want her to find out what's happening.'

The phone seemed to ring interminably before it clicked and a tired voice filled with the heaviness of sleep said 'Yes?'

'Get me Daphne,' Martin ordered.

'You know what time it is?'

'Yeah, I know. Get me Daphne.'

'Christ, I'm not – '

'Get me Daphne,' Martin repeated, his request becoming a threat. There was silence for a moment, then: 'Hang on.'

Martin covered the mouthpiece with his hand and winked at Mr Apple. 'Gone to get her,' he said. Mr Apple nodded.

'Hello?'

'Daphne?'

'Martin? Is that you?'

'It's me.'

'Oh, dear God, I've been so *worried*. Everyone's talking about you. I've been going out of my mind. Where are you?'

'I'm safe.'

'Oh, God – '

'Listen. What have you heard?'

'They say you tried to kill that Colonel in England – you didn't, though, did you?'

'What else?'

'Oh. Larry Corrigan was sent to grass on you, to make a deal of some sort. Is that true?'

'I'm asking you, dammit. What else?'

'I can't think, Martin. Where *are* you?'

'I'll tell you in a minute. What else have you heard?'

'Just – just that everyone's looking for you. They've been to your place. And they went to your Mam's. They took her in for – '

'They what?'

'She's all right. They let her go again. Martin, where are you? I want to see you.'

'Hang on.' Martin covered the mouthpiece again. 'She wants to see me. It might be better. Can she come here?'

'If you think it's safe – for you and her,' Mr Apple said.

'Daphne? Can you come now?'

'Of course I can.'

'Right. Here's where you come.' Martin gave her Mr Apple's address, repeating it twice and making Daphne say it over to him. 'And be a bit careful,' he advised. 'They've been here already, so we should be safe enough. But you never know.'

'I'll be careful.'

'See you, then. Oh, hang on,' Martin said, suddenly aware that Mr Apple was signalling wildly at him. 'What?'

'Not now,' Mr Apple said. 'Don't have her come here now.'

'Why not?'

'I don't know, Martin. Tomorrow. Have her come over tomorrow. I have a feeling – '

Martin eyed Mr Apple suspiciously. 'Daphne. Leave it till tomorrow evening.'

'But I want – '

'Tomorrow evening, Daphne. You might be able to find out more by then anyway.'

'Yes – but – '

'No buts. Tomorrow.'

'All right, Martin. If you say so. You'll be all right till then, will you?'

'I'll be just fine. I'm being well looked after. Just find out everything you can and I'll see you tomorrow night.'

'Bye then, Martin.'

'Bye.' Martin put down the receiver and turned to Mr Apple. 'Tomorrow night,' he said. Mr Apple nodded. 'You think they're watching the place, don't you?'

Mr Apple shook his head. 'I don't know. I just don't feel right. I have to follow my instincts.'

'Oh, I won't argue with your instincts, Mr Apple.'

Mr Apple gave a bright little smile. 'Mr Apple outwits the army,' he said.

They both laughed wryly until Martin became suddenly serious. 'Hey, have I thanked you, Mr A.? For everything?'

'You've thanked me, Martin.'

'That's all right then. You're really the first one I've had to thank in my whole life.'

'What is worrying me is that I may also be the last,' Mr Apple said grimly. Then he smiled again. 'We'll get through this together. You wait and see. Together we'll conquer the lot of them.'

'I hope you're right.'

'Good heavens. I'm always right. I thought you knew that.'

'Hah. I'm beginning to believe it.'

'Good.'

'You know I still can't believe I've ended up with you as a friend, Mr A.'

'Strange bedfellows – '

'No, don't joke about it,' Martin said seriously. 'It's a funny feeling. I was sitting down there in that dungeon listening to them clobbering about up here, and it dawned on me that you're the only friend I have in the world. It – '

'You've Daphne,' Mr Apple interrupted, feeling inexplicably embarrassed.

'She's different. She wants something. Me. But you – you don't want anything, do you?'

'From you? No. No, Martin, not from you.'

'Can I ask you something?'

' – ?'

'What made you help me?'

Mr Apple thought about this for a while. Then he shrugged. 'It seemed the right thing to do,' he said at last. 'Hah, it seemed the *only* thing to do. It fitted in.'

'Fitted in? With what?'

'Hmm. That, young man, is what I'm still trying to figure out. "There is a tide in the affairs of men" as the bard said, and I'm trying to stop it ebbing away,' Mr Apple said, his voice trailing off, his face puzzled and all at sea.

'You've lost me again.'

'I've lost myself, Martin. That's the problem. Still, we'll muddle through, won't we? We'll come out on top somehow – even if we die in the process.'

'Thanks. Nothing like being cheerful.'

Mr Apple giggled. 'I remember once – oh, a long, long time ago, probably before you were born – I remember someone saying to me – it might even have been my father – no, hardly; he wouldn't, I don't think, have thought along those lines – he worked in the shipyards, you know – a good man, but dull, unimaginative – I think I always held that against him, being unimaginative – anyway, where was I? – oh, yes, someone said to me that the only happy thing about living was knowing you had to die one day. Odd thought, isn't it?'

'Morbid.'

'Only if you're afraid of death.'

'I am. Shit scared of it.'

'Hmm,' hummed Mr Apple. 'I used to be until I died,' he added, closing his eyes.

'Until you *died*?'

Mr Apple opened his eyes again and smiled wistfully. 'In a manner of speaking. Not to worry,' he added brusquely. 'We can talk about that some other time.'

'I don't think I want to.'

'Then we won't.'

Mr Asher sat scowling across the desk from Colonel Maddox, his annoyance intensified by the somewhat mocking smile that played about the Colonel's mouth.

'You look as though you've been up all night,' the Colonel now remarked. 'Don't you ever sleep?'

Asher stretched suddenly and gave a forced, noisy yawn. 'Yes, I sleep,' he said. 'But you're right: I *was* up all night.'

'I hope it was worth it,' the Colonel said, immediately presuming Asher had been having one of his romantic entanglements.

Asher scowled again. 'No, dammit, it wasn't.'

'Oh,' grunted the other sympathetically.

'That damned Apple – '

'Apple?'

'Yes. Apple. Made a fool out of me. Sat there on the stairs gloating. Grinning like a moron.'

'I don't follow – ' the Colonel put in, confused.

Asher stretched again, moving his shoulders in circles to ease his muscles. 'It's a long and boring story,' he said finally, lighting a cigarette, as he always did when about to deliver some explanation that might take time. 'There's something up between those two – Apple and Deeley. I *know* Apple knows where Deeley is. I just *know* it. He was far too smug and self-assured last night. And as for Deeley – he's just vanished from the face of the earth.'

'But what made you go to Mr Apple, John? He's been helping *us*.'

'Has he hell. Colonel, that lunatic has been taking us for a glorious ride.'

'Oh, I don't think so.'

'I tell you he has.'

'But you found nothing at his house?'

'Nothing,' Asher admitted. 'But he knows something.'

'You don't think you're reading more into Mr Apple because you *want* to believe he's involved?'

Asher smiled ruefully and said: 'Maybe I am,' although he was obviously thinking of something else, something that struck even him as rather amusing. 'The damn fool set his cat on us,' he confessed at last, and gave a snorting laugh.

'His cat?' Maddox wondered for a moment if he had heard aright.

'Yes. His cat. Well, he didn't actually set the bloody thing on us, but it leapt from a cupboard and attacked one of the sniffer-dogs. Jesus, you should have seen the chaos,' Mr Asher concluded, laughing snortily again as he remembered the ridiculous scene once more.

'Oh, dear,' Maddox said, joining in the laughter, albeit hesitantly, as though still unsure if a joke was being made or not. Asher could be very touchy about his work, and the Colonel had no wish to offend him at the moment. 'What actually happened?'

'Oh, we searched the place from top to bottom while Apple watched us gleefully. And found nothing. But I still say Apple was just that bit too smug. He let us tramp all over his house as though he knew we wouldn't find anything – no, that's not what I mean. What I mean is, it was more than his knowing there was no one else in the house; it was like he knew we were looking for Deeley and he actually knew where Deeley was.' Asher inhaled his cigarette smoke deeply. 'Does that make any sense, Colonel?'

'I know what you mean, but as to making sense, well – ' the Colonel replied, waving a hand vaguely in the air to disperse the smoke in front of him.

'Hmm,' agreed Asher, somewhat reluctantly.

'You could always ask that chap – what was his name – the one who gave you Deeley's – '

'Corrigan?'

'Yes, Corrigan. You could always ask him again if there was anything between –.'

Asher fidgeted uncomfortably for a second. 'I'm afraid we can't do that, sir.'

' – ?'

'Corrigan has been – eh – removed,' Asher said bluntly.

'Removed? Are you saying what I think you're saying, John?'

'I told you that was the way things were done, Colonel. You didn't seem to object then.'

'I didn't believe – You've had him killed?'

'I – yes, I've had him killed.'

Colonel Maddox shook his head, a mixture of outrage and sadness filling his eyes. 'I don't understand you, John.'

'It was the cleanest thing to do. No questions to be answered. No unpleasant repercussions. I had him shot from behind in the head. I had him kneecapped. It will simply be put down as a punishment killing. And the Provos won't deny it. They'll use it as a warning to others who might feel tempted to talk to us, and it will stop Corrigan telling tales that might embarrass them – you follow?'

'Oh, I follow all right. But it disgusts me. I – '

'You know nothing about it, sir. I have told you nothing. You can read about the – eh – punishment if they ever get around to mentioning it in the papers, and what you read is all you'll ever know.'

Asher contemplated the glowing end of his black cigarette for a moment, and for a moment, also, he allowed himself to recall the pathetic, vicious drama he had orchestrated less than twenty-four hours before.

Where're you taking me? Corrigan had wanted to know.

You want protection, don't you? Well, you can't stay here then, can you? Asher asked in his friendliest voice.

Oh.

We've got a safe house to keep you in until we can arrange the papers you wanted.

Oh. Where?

Not far. A short drive. You'll have an escort no less.

Corrigan beamed. An escort, eh?

Well, we don't want anyone taking pot-shots at you now that

you've done us a good turn. We've got to keep our side of the bargain.

Corrigan continued to beam, and he was still grinning broadly when Asher ordered the driver to stop for a moment.

Just a moment, Larry, Mr Asher said. I just want to check with the car behind. Won't be a tick.

Okay, Mr Asher.

Asher stepped out of his own car and walked to the one following. You can go back now, he told the face at the wheel. We'll deal with it now.

The driver nodded, reversed the vehicle into a gateway, then drove away back down the road.

Asher watched the rear lights fade before returning to his own car. Right, Larry, he said. I'm afraid it's on foot from here.

For the first time Larry Corrigan looked worried, but only slightly: Asher's friendly face reassured him. He heaved himself on to the road and stretched.

You lead the way, Asher told the driver. You needn't worry about the car. We won't be long.

The driver led the way. Corrigan followed. Asher brought up the rear. The procession moved slowly, through a broken gate, up a driveway or small lane, it was difficult to tell which in the dark.

The three of them had only been walking for about three minutes when Asher took a revolver from his pocket, aimed carefully, and shot Corrigan in the back of the head. The great mound of flesh seemed to jump several inches in the air before it crashed to the ground, seemed to bounce like a mass of india-rubber, before it came to a hissing stillness.

Here, help me turn him over, Asher commanded in a harsh whisper.

Together, Asher and the driver heaved the body over onto its stomach and then, without a glance at his victim, Mr Asher fired two more shots, one into the back of each knee of the dead Larry Corrigan.

That's it, Asher said, pocketing the revolver. Let's get home. And you weren't here tonight. Remember that. You saw nothing and know nothing, because you weren't here. Understand?

Yessir.

'So all you're telling me,' Maddox was saying, 'all you're telling me is that you raided Mr Apple, had one man killed, and the man you're supposed to be arresting is still free.'

Asher moved uneasily in his chair. 'Yes, but – '

'That's it, isn't it?' the Colonel persisted.

'Yes.'

'Not what you might call the height of efficiency?'

'Perhaps not, sir.'

'I don't think there's any perhaps about it.'

'No, sir.'

Maddox rose from behind his desk and started pacing up and down the office. He stopped suddenly by Asher's chair and asked in a voice that was unusually cold 'What other surprises have you lined up for me, John? How many more people are you going to have *removed*? I want to know. I simply will not be a party to this – this – this abomination.'

Asher looked up at the long, cold face looming over him. 'But that is exactly what I've been telling you, sir. You are not a party to anything. You don't even know about anything.'

'Will you stop playing games with me, John?' Maddox shouted.

'With respect, Colonel, I am not playing games. I am dealing with a situation in the way that that situation has always been dealt with. To deal with it in any other way would, I suggest, be playing games.'

Maddox continued to stare down at the steely eyes that now seemed to penetrate his soul, hearing, but not really listening.

'And, again with respect, Colonel, I would repeat that you are, after all, the stranger here. You do not – do not – understand how things are done, how arrangements and agreements are made. Of course we are trying to stop what you call "the terrorism" in England, but we have to give as well as take. If we did not turn the occasional blind eye, if we did not overlook certain activities, if we did not ignore the occasional sectarian murder – if we did not do all these things we would be overrun in a matter of weeks, months at the most.'

It was probably the sudden silence that followed Asher's lecture that made the Colonel blink and shake himself back from whatever thoughts had been entertaining him. 'I'm sorry?'

' – ?'

'You were saying?'

'Nothing, Colonel. Just thinking out loud. Nothing that need concern you.'

'Oh.'

'Well, if you'll excuse me,' Mr Asher said, making to rise, 'I'd better be getting a move on.'

'Hmm? Yes. Oh yes, of course. No. Wait a moment, John. Sit down again please.'

Asher sank slowly back into his chair, trying to create the impression that he was at ease.

'John,' the Colonel began, speaking deliberately in a school-masterish voice (indeed, with his grey suit, greying hair and hands folded across his stomach he seemed to be assuming a likeness to suit the voice) 'we have known each other some time now. We are, I suppose, almost friends. I haven't all that much longer to go here, and what you do when I'm gone is entirely your affair. But – ' Maddox paused, unwittingly creating a tension, giving his words an edge of importance. 'But,' he repeated, 'as long as I *am* here I want your word that this brutality will stop. And when – heh – *if*,' the Colonel permitted himself a wry smile, 'you do track down this Deeley character and arrest him, I want to be informed immediately. Immediately, mind you. Not the next day. Or even an hour later. Immediately.'

Asher inclined his head by way of agreement. 'If that's what you want, Colonel.'

'That is what I want. That is what I demand, John.'

'Very well.'

'Good.'

'Is that all, sir?'

'Yes, that's all. I suppose you think I'm an interfering Brit, don't you?'

Asher gave a hint of a smile. 'It had crossed my mind.'

'I thought it might. We really are worlds apart, aren't we, the English and the Irish?'

Asher nodded. 'Worlds.'

'And never the twain, I suppose.'

'Never the twain.'

'Pity.'

Asher shrugged. 'It works both ways.'

'Or doesn't work at all. Ah, well, it's not for the likes of us to philosophize, is it?'

'No.'

'Right. Thank you, John. I won't delay you any longer.'

Asher stood up and placed his dead cigar in an ashtray. 'I'll let you know if anything breaks, Colonel.'

'Thank you. Mind how you go.'

'I will.'

'And remember what I said – I want to be told immediately.'

Asher paused by the door, turned, and gave the Colonel a long, hard stare. 'I'll remember. Colonel, you might think about what *I* said: it would make your life a lot easier all round.'

Maddox raised his head abruptly as though startled from a dream, his mind furiously sifting through the gaggle of words that he thought appropriate by way of reply, but by the time they had sorted themselves into some coherency Asher had gone, leaving the door ajar.

Maddox got up slowly from behind his desk and walked across the office, sucking his teeth. He closed the door firmly and leaned against it while Asher's parting shot ricocheted round his skull. It struck him that there had been some elusive subtlety in the words that still escaped him, some impeachment he could not quite put his finger on. Then, suddenly, at last, though the feeling had been nurtured within him for longer than he would ever care to admit, he was humiliatingly aware of what should have been obvious a long time ago, that he, for all his rank and military power, was there to be manipulated, to put a respectable face on things, to demonstrate to a world for the most part bored with the violence and disinterested in the outcome that something was being done. And being done it certainly was, but by others, sinister men who wheeled and dealed in the business of death while he looked on, like the sole spectator of some tatty tragedy, watching the intricate plot unfold.

Maddox sighed, crossed to the heavily screened window and stared out. Slightly to the right and below him, below and in the shadow of the high granite wall topped by strands of barbed wire, a group of uniformed R.U.C. men smoked and chatted casually, while beyond them, beyond the high granite wall topped with strands of barbed wire, civilians made their way through the day. It all seemed so peaceful. It struck him that it was extraordinary that out there, possibly strolling about with his hands in his pockets, nodding affably to his friends, was the man who had tried to kill him, and for an awful moment Maddox wished he had succeeded. How much easier that would have made things! How much 'cleaner', as Asher always put it. A little heroism, albeit somewhat backhanded, salvaged from a useless life. Maddox shook his head and smiled wryly to himself: at least the wretched Deeleys of the world were doing something positive, however unsuccessfully.

Maddox completed the circle of his office and sat down at his desk again. He leaned back in his chair with a small groan, and clasped his hands behind his head, intertwining his fingers. With his eyes closed he watched as his imagination projected images on to the back of his eyelids, images, he instantly realized, of the man who had been sent to kill him, offering for his selection a variety of bodies supporting faceless heads, heads which, although featureless, seemed to smile at him, smile at him sadly, compassionately and say, 'I am sorry for both our sakes that I missed you.' For some reason the Colonel began to dissect this straightforward repentance, wondering suddenly if it might not have another meaning beyond the obvious; and while he toyed with this possibility his mind's eye saw the faceless bodies take on the weightless quality of spirits, appearing to grow more free, yet at the same time more united, more dependent on each other the higher they ascended into a gleaming light. And, perhaps, he thought, there was something significant in all this. Had not his own life become 'featureless'? Was it not true to say that the more disillusion settled on his shoulders, the farther down he sank? 'Aaah,' the Colonel said aloud, and the loudness of his exclamation brought him back to earth; but not before he had time to wonder if Deeley, too, was harbouring thoughts of wastefulness and disillusion.

Martin Deeley was, in fact, having no such thoughts: he stood in Mr Apple's hallway, the phone pressed to his ear, concentrating on the burring noise it made, impatiently tapping one foot. He had spent the morning in the small room under the glory-hole listening to the activity above him as two workmen fixed the front door under the dour, pernickety supervision of Mr Cahill, who had volunteered to see the job was properly carried out while Mr Apple went to work. About eleven Martin emerged, swinging his arms in wide circles to rid himself of the claustrophobic sensations that had tormented him through the night. He glanced at the front door: just like new. He cocked his head on one side and listened intently: silence. Then he tiptoed across the hall and picked up the phone.

'Hello.'

'Is Fergal there?'

'Who wants him?'

'I do. Is he there?'

A clatter descended down the line as the receiver was dumped heavily on a table, and a voice shouted 'Fergal! It's for you.'

'Who is it?'

'Wouldn't say.'

Martin waited, his foot tapping impatiently once again.

'Yeah?'

'Fergal?'

'Yeah.'

'Martin. Martin Deeley.'

'Shit. How – '

'Can you talk?'

'Just a sec. Shut that door, will you? I can't hear myself think.

Right. Martin? I can talk.'

'First, thanks for warning me – '

'Forget it.'

'I won't. Now, what's happening? Have you heard anything?'

'Quite a bit. They found Corrigan this morning.'

'What d'you mean found him?'

'Dead. Kneecapped and shot in the head.'

'Jesus.'

'Yeah. Well, he's no great loss.'

'Who – '

'Who d'you think? Part of the package deal. He shits on you and that done he's no further use.'

'Christ. Anything new on me?'

'Nothing except they're all out to find you – and they're not fussed whether they bring you in alive or not.'

'That's nice.'

'Lovely. An R.U.C. heavy called Asher is in control.'

'I know.'

'And Reilly has put out the word that – '

'The bastard – '

'Yeah, well, that's the way it's been arranged. Where are you now?'

'I'm safe enough for the time being.'

'Well, stay there then. For Christ's sake, don't show your face anywhere. Every motherfucking sonofabitch is looking for you. You're quite a prize. Anything I can do?'

'Not for the moment, thanks. Fergal?'

'Yeah?'

'Can I count on you if – '

'You can count on me. I don't know what I'll be able to do, but you can count on me.'

'Thanks.'

'Okay. Give me a buzz tonight if you want and I'll try and have more info for you. Make it late, though. About twelve.'

'Right.'

'Hey, take care.'

'I will.'

Martin replaced the receiver and stood staring down at the phone. He thought briefly about Corrigan, feeling a tinge of sympathy for the great fat moron who had been chosen to do Reilly's dirty work and who, finally, had been another sacrificial lamb in the long litany of intrigue; and he wondered what Corrigan had looked like in death, if only because he had been told that fat people lost stones in the seconds before they died. Oddly, it was neither fear nor anger that was uppermost within him: Martin Deeley felt a hurt so deep it all but brought tears to his eyes. It was certainly bad enough that Asher and *his* bastards should be after him, but to have Seamus Reilly instigating a similar hunt, Seamus Reilly whom he had always regarded as a friend – as a father, almost – to have him issue orders that he, Martin, should be hunted out and killed was appalling.

Martin left the hall and wandered into the kitchen. He poured himself a glass of milk and swallowed it in one go. Still, he had Daphne and Fergal and Mr Apple on his side, so all was not lost. Between them they would work something out, and when they did the Ashers and Reillys had better watch out.

Mr Apple had tidied his desk in rather a hurry but had done his accounts carefully enough, and he was walking across the shop when Seamus Reilly appeared in the doorway flanked by two large young men Mr Apple had never seen before.

'Good evening, Mr Apple,' Reilly said, smiling. 'I am sorry to barge in on you like this just as you're setting off home,' he went on apologetically, 'but there's a thing or two I would like to talk over with you.'

Mr Apple decided to say nothing: he stood his ground and peered over his glasses.

'Can we?' Reilly asked, indicating with a wave of his arm his desire that they retreat behind the glass partition.

Mr Apple inclined his head and led the way.

'I would prefer to have no one overhear,' Reilly explained. 'We must have our confidences. Oh, they're good enough boys,' he confessed, glancing at his young bodyguards (both of whom looked strangely lost and awkward without anything close at hand to guard), 'but the less they know, the better. Isn't that how it should be?'

'I wouldn't know,' Mr Apple told him.

For an instant Reilly looked surprised, then he smiled. 'No, I don't suppose you would, Mr Apple,' he agreed. 'Ah, what a wonderfully untrammelled life you lead.'

Mr Apple stared at him.

'Now,' Reilly said, his voice changing as he got down to brass tacks, 'I understand you had visitors last night.'

Mr Apple nodded. 'You might call them that.'

'And?'

'And?'

'And what happened – precisely,' Reilly asked testily.

Mr Apple shrugged. 'Not a lot. They smashed in my front door, ransacked my house, terrified my cat. That's about it,' he said.

'Why?'

'Why what?'

'Why did they come to you in the first place?'

'Oh, they said they were looking for something – what, I cannot for the life of me imagine. They didn't find it, though. At least, I don't think they did. I wasn't told.'

Reilly stared hard at Mr Apple through half-closed eyes. 'And you have no idea what they were looking for?'

'None at all.'

'Did they ask you anything?'

Mr Apple frowned and thought for a moment. 'No, not that I can recall.'

'No questions about this shop?'

'No.'

'You're certain?'

'Quite certain.'

'I think they were looking for some*one* rather than some*thing*,' Mr Apple volunteered innocently.

'What makes you say that?'

'A feeling. The places they looked. Oh, they turned out drawers and overturned chairs but they didn't *look*: they only searched places big enough to hold a person.'

'You're very observant,' Reilly said. 'Any idea who they might have been looking for?'

'No idea at all. Have you?'

Reilly was taken aback by Mr Apple's question, possibly because it was the first time Mr Apple had ever asked him anything. He was on the point of shaking his head, of denying any knowledge of the affair, when suddenly he changed his mind. He smiled thinly at Mr Apple and said: 'As a matter of fact I do.'

'Oh.'

'Of course, there's very little happens in Belfast that I don't know.'

'Of course.'

'They were looking for your boardmarker, Martin Deeley,' Reilly announced, keeping his eyes fixed attentively on Mr Apple's face.

Mr Apple nearly overacted, but stopped himself just in time and played down nicely his imitation of surprise. 'My boardmarker? Martin? Martin Deeley? Good heavens. You do surprise me Mr Reilly. What on earth has Martin been up to?'

Reilly decided he had confided enough. '*That* I don't know. I think they just want to question him about some minor incident that happened the other night.'

'Oh,' Mr Apple sighed, feigning relief. 'I knew it couldn't be anything serious. A nice boy is Martin. Gentle and kind to a fault.'

'Indeed,' agreed Reilly. 'Very gentle and kind. You haven't seen him I suppose?'

'Not since yesterday. As I told you then, he came in but felt sick, so I sent him home again.'

'He's not at home,' Reilly said sharply, but recovered his composure rapidly enough to smile and add, 'If you do see him you might let me know. I think we should assist him if – '

'Indeed,' said Mr Apple.

'Good.'

For several moments they just stood there eyeing each other before Reilly said: 'Well, I'd better be on my way and let you get home. I expect you've a lot of tidying up to do.'

'Yes.'

'Right. Well, good-night, Mr Apple.'

'Good-night Mr Reilly.'

Mr Apple watched Reilly stroll from the shop, followed by his henchmen. When the door closed behind them he rubbed his hands together and did a strange little dance, a sort of jig interspersed with pirouettes, humming to himself and smiling broadly. One up for us, Mr Divine, he thought and Mr Divine seemed to agree; alas, the pessimistic Sefer wasn't at all sure. I'm not at all sure it is one up for us, Mr Apple, he announced solemnly. All you're doing is getting us deeper into trouble. You really are a very silly old man.

Silly or not, Mr Apple was still in an excellent frame of mind and still smiling broadly to himself as he entered his home by the kitchen door. He switched on the fluorescent light and automatically waited for it to settle down. Then he closed and locked the kitchen door behind him and walked into the hall, coughing as he walked.

'Oh, it *is* you,' Martin's voice said from the shadows before he stepped into view.

'Who were you expecting?' Mr Apple asked with what sounded like a chuckle. 'Your friend Mr Asher again?'

Martin smiled: 'I hope to Christ not. Have you seen him today?'

'No. But your other good friend, Mr Reilly, did drop in for a chat. He's very concerned about you –'

'I bet he is.'

' – and would like to know where you are. He wants to warn you there are nasty men looking for you.'

'He's a nice man,' Martin said sardonically. 'Seriously, what did he say?'

'What I told you.'

'Nothing else?'

'Nothing else.'

'Crafty.'

'Very. Have you eaten?'

'I had a glass of milk.'

'I'll fix us something then.'

'No. I'll do it. I want to do *something*. I'm going scatty just hanging about here.'

'Well, make sure the curtains are drawn. I'll go up and change. See what you can find in the fridge – there won't be much. We don't entertain a lot, Chloe and I,' Mr Apple said, making his way upstairs before adding: 'What time is Daphne coming?'

'I'm not sure. Sometime this evening. Whenever she can.'

'Oh.'

'Why?'

'No reason. Just wondering. Eh – do you two want to be alone?'

Martin laughed. 'Hell, no, Mr Apple. You may as well hear everything now.'

'I just thought – ' Mr Apple paused and gave an embarrassed little cough. 'I just thought you two young things might want – ' he let his voice trail off questioningly.

'Jesus, that's the last thing I'm thinking of,' Martin said, 'but thanks for asking.'

'Yes.'

'Maybe you'd like to have a go, Mr A. She's very obliging.'

'Don't be filthy,' Mr Apple snapped, but he smiled to himself all the same, amazed that Martin could carry on this absurd banter while trying to save his own skin.

'Just asking.'

When Mr Apple came down again to the kitchen, dressed in cavalry twill trousers, yellow shirt and neckerchief, Martin had prepared a reasonable meal of eggs and bacon, sausages and fried bread. He had set the kitchen table neatly and placed a single plastic flower in an empty tonic bottle in the centre.

'Very nice,' Mr Apple commented. 'You missed your vocation, Martin.' He took his place at the table and started to eat.

'All right?' Martin asked.

'Very good. Just how I like them – what the Americans call sunny side up.'

'Yeah – keep your sunny side up, up, keep your sunny side up,' Martin started singing. 'That's what we've got to do, Mr A. Keep our bloody sunny side up.'

'Quite.' Mr Apple eyed the young man concernedly, watching him shovel the food into his mouth in quick, nervous actions. 'Relax, Martin. We won't be disturbed tonight.'

'Jesus,' Martin swore and pushed his half-empty plate away from him. 'It's not tonight I'm worried about, Mr Apple. It's tonight and tomorrow night and every fucking night from now on.'

'We'll work something out.'

'Oh, sure.'

'I'm telling you. Finish your meal. Everything will work out for you. I'm telling you we'll work something out.'

'Oh, sure,' Martin repeated, but this time there was something not far adrift of hope in his voice. He pulled his plate towards him and started eating again. He was wiping up egg yolk with a slice of bread when he mentioned: 'I phoned Fergal – one of the men who came to warn me in the shop. He told me Corrigan had been shot.'

'Corrigan?'

'Larry Corrigan – the shit that was sent to drop me in it.'

'Oh. But I don't quite understand – who would shoot *him*?'

'R.U.C., probably. Asher.'

'But he *helped* them.'

'That's right.'

'So why should *they* shoot him?'

'To tidy things up. Tea?'

' – ? Oh, yes. Tidy things up?'

'That's right,' Martin said casually, getting up and pouring out two cups of tea, adding sugar only to his own. 'They probably promised him the usual crap of a new identity abroad and suckered him into feeling he could trust them. It happens all the time.'

'But why kill him, Martin?'

'That's the price Reilly would have demanded for sending him in. Save him the trouble. I mean he – Reilly – wouldn't want Corrigan out and getting pissed and saying he'd been ordered in to land me in the shit, would he? So Corrigan would have had to be killed. Better the R.U.C. do it and clean up the mess than have some half-arsed Brit officer stumble on – '

'Good God,' was all that Mr Apple could think of to say.

'Oh, you've a lot to learn, Mr A. I told you that you were getting into something you couldn't handle.'

This appeared to annoy Mr Apple. 'Of course I can handle it,' he snapped. 'The more I hear about Asher and Reilly the more determined I am that we'll outwit them. You and I. Dammit, they're maniacs.'

Martin threw back his head and laughed. 'They wouldn't like that, Mr Apple. They think they're very nice men.'

'Shhh,' whispered Mr Apple suddenly, and held up a warning hand. 'Quick. Into your room.'

Martin shot out of his chair and made for the glory-hole.

'Wait,' Mr Apple whispered urgently. 'Take these with you,' he ordered, passing Martin his plate and teacup. 'Now. Quick.'

'What's – ' Martin began, just as the front doorbell shrilled.

'Go,' said Mr Apple, pushing Martin in front of him into the glory-hole and closing the door.

'I'm coming,' Mr Apple announced, raising his voice. 'Who is it?'

A muffled cry came from outside.

'Who?' Mr Apple asked again, opening the door a fraction.

'Me,' the voice said enigmatically.

Mr Apple opened the door wider and was confronted by a vision in black: a long, black, cloak-like affair almost reaching the ground, a black floppy hat, a fedora really except that, of all things, it sported a black veil, black gloves and, as far as he could tell, black shoes. For one awful instant Mr Apple wondered if death had popped in to say hello, and was pleased when the gloomy figure spoke again in a high-pitched, nervous little voice. 'I'm Daphne,' was what it said.

'Oh,' said Mr Apple. 'Daphne. Come in, come in. We were expecting you, but not quite this early. I'm Arthur Apple.'

'Yes, I'm sorry I'm early, Mr Apple, but I thought it better to come now as people may want to see me later.'

' – ? Ah, yes,' Mr Apple agreed, and shut the front door. 'Martin,' he called. 'Your friend is here.'

Martin emerged from under the stairs looking almost sheepish about his appearance from such an unlikely place. The great Martin Deeley skulking under the goddam stairs!

'Hello, luvvey,' Daphne said shyly, casting a sidelong glance at Mr Apple, who immediately called upon his training and diplomatically looked the other way.

'Hi, Daphne. Thanks for coming.'

'How are you?'

'Fine. Just fine. Mr Apple's been looking after me and if Mr A. looks after you you're bound to be fine. Right, Mr A.?'

'Huh,' Mr Apple grunted. 'Let's go into the kitchen.'

Mr Apple sat at the head of the table, Martin on his right, Daphne on his left. 'Get the girl a cup of tea, Martin,' he said.

'No – no, thanks, Mr Apple. I really don't want any.'

'Sure?'

'Certain.'

Martin fidgeted under these politenesses and asked abruptly: 'What news?'

'Corrigan's dead. He – '

'I know that,' Martin told her. He was sick and tired of bloody Corrigan. 'Anything else?'

Daphne shook her head. She had taken off her hat and her long hair flapped about her shoulders. 'Nobody's saying anything, but I did hear there's a lot of money on offer for you.'

'Who's offering it?'

'That's the funny thing, luvvey,' Daphne told him. 'Some say from the R.U.C. Others say the army. Others think it might be – '

'Reilly?' Martin immediately wanted to know.

'That's what some say.'

'Maybe they're all right,' Mr Apple put in. 'Maybe you're more valuable than you ever suspected, Martin.'

'You could be right, Mr A. Could that be the case, Daphne? Could they all be chipping in?'

'It sounds like that.'

Martin sighed, letting his breath loose in a long gasp. 'Shit.'

'Why did you *do* it, Martin? Why – '

'Oh, for Christ's sake, shut up. It was my job. That's all.'

'But I told you – '

'Shut *up*,' Martin shouted.

'Shhh,' Mr Apple warned. 'Now for heaven's sake let's not fight among ourselves. Daphne is only concerned, Martin.'

'Concerned be damned. All I need is her nagging the shit out of me when Reilly's chasing me on one side and Asher on the other – '

'Asher?' Daphne suddenly asked. 'John Asher? R.U.C.? Small man, very smooth? Smokes black cigarettes?'

Martin looked first at Daphne then at Mr Apple, then back to Daphne again, his eyes narrowing. 'Sounds like him.'

'Well, isn't that lovely,' Daphne said, smiling brightly.

The two men stared at her.

'What's so effing lovely – '

'Quiet, Martin,' Mr Apple interrupted. 'Daphne?'

Daphne leaned forward and looked shyly at Mr Apple. 'Well,' she said, 'if it *is* the same John Asher, I know him very well,' she confessed. 'I see him every week. Regular. A sort of standing order. Same time every week. Friday evening at half-past nine.'

'You – ' Martin started, but stopped speaking when Mr Apple again raised his hand.

'Let me get this clear, Daphne. And don't be shy. I understand these things better than you imagine. Now, Mr Asher comes to you every week to make love, right?'

'That's right, Mr Apple.'

'And how long does he stay?'

Daphne shrugged. 'Not long. He just does it and goes. About half an hour.'

'And during that time he is quite alone with you?'

'Of course,' Daphne said, sounding shocked.

'No, what I meant was, dear, he has no escort, shall we call it, waiting outside?'

Daphne giggled. 'Oh, no. He wouldn't want anyone to know he comes to me. I'm not really grand enough for him to be seen with.'

'I see. And he comes to your room?'

'That's right.'

'Do you know how he comes to the house, Daphne? Does he walk? Come in a car?'

'That I don't know, Mr Apple, but I know he walks part of the way. I remember he said one night that he had slipped walking in the snow.'

'And it's every Friday?'

'Yes.' Daphne nodded to confirm her answer.

'Then he would be coming tomorrow?'

'I suppose so. I mean, if he sticks to his usual he'll be up tomorrow night.'

'Has he *ever* missed a week?' Mr Apple persisted.

'Oh yes, but not often. About four in the three years I've known him.'

'And tell me, on the nights he didn't come, did he let you know?'

'I don't understand.'

'Did he telephone and say he wouldn't be coming?'

Daphne gave a wistful little laugh. 'Oh, no. He just didn't turn up.' Then, as though she felt she had in some way degraded herself, she added 'But he apologized the following week, telling me he had been busy.'

'One more thing, Daphne. Does he know that you know he's in the R.U.C.?'

Daphne considered this for a moment, pouting her lips and frowning, before saying 'I don't think he *knows* I know. I mean, nearly all my – ' Daphne stopped and blushed. 'Nearly all the men who come and see me are in some sort of uniform, but they don't seem to care.'

Mr Apple reached out and patted Daphne's hand. 'Thank you, my dear,' he said quietly. 'Now, I know you want to see Martin alone, but I'm going to take him away for a minute. I'll send him right back to you though,' he added with a gentle, understanding smile, standing up. 'Martin?'

Martin got to his feet obediently. He had been listening with, if his face could be believed, something approaching awe and respect as Mr Apple put his questions to Daphne, seeing for the first time a Mr Apple he had never suspected, a Mr Apple who was gentle but self-assured, understanding but persistent, a Mr Apple far removed from the doddery creature Martin had once believed him to be. And through it all Martin had been constantly reminded of yet another interrogation he had overheard, but which had not been meant for his ears; or, on reflection, perhaps he had very definitely been meant to overhear:

He's very young, someone said.

Not that young, Seamus Reilly said.

Sixteen?

That's his age, but he's older than that.

I still think it's too important to be assigned to him.

Trust my judgement, Reilly said. He's good – and he's unknown.

And if he fouls it up?

He won't.

If he does? The gruff, doubting voice went on.

I'll see everything goes according to plan – one way or another.

I don't suppose we have much option.

We don't, Reilly said, immediately pushing home his slight advantage. Anyway, he's got to start somewhere if we're going to use him.

And you're certain you can trust him to keep quiet?

Reilly seemed to smile: I am not certain I can trust anyone, but I take precautions. I usually manage to cover myself.

Ha, yes. You do, don't you? All right. I'll leave it up to you. Anything goes wrong, you're answerable – understood?

Understood.

I still don't altogether like it. He – what's his name?

Deeley. Martin Deeley.

Deeley. He's got no background.

His father was shot – and his brother.

I *know* that, the voice said impatiently. That means nothing. That was just another Brit cock-up.

He – Deeley – doesn't think of it that way.

He wants revenge, I suppose.

No, Reilly said, but with something less than certainty in his voice. Avenge rather than revenge, he added.

You were always a one for niceties. I don't want any young kid using us for his personal vendettas.

Of course not.

And no bloody heroics. A clean job.

Of course.

The voice sighed. Jesus, rid me of romantics, it said fervently.

Romantics?

Hmm. Mark my words, Seamus, they're the curse of every

worthwhile cause. Every revolution, every war is started by bloody romantics and then we have to move in and clean things up somehow.

I see, Seamus said, though he didn't sound as though he did.

All right. Let Deeley do it, and we'll see how it goes.

'We won't be long, Daphne,' Mr Apple reassured the girl, and followed Martin out of the kitchen. 'The front room, Martin,' he whispered and padded along the hall. 'Leave the light off, of course.'

In the sitting-room they faced each other, Mr Apple manoeuvring himself so that the dull light coming from the street outside was behind him. 'What do you think, Martin?'

'Think – about what?'

'About what Daphne said.'

Martin shrugged. 'Not a lot.'

'Oh. I rather thought we might suddenly have found ourselves with a means of solving this unpleasantness, of negotiating our own little deal which would allow you to leave Belfast intact.'

'I don't follow, Mr A.'

'Just think about this for a minute. No, first – how far would Daphne go for you? I mean, would she really be prepared to help you in *any* way she could?'

'Yeah. I suppose so. You better ask her. I think she would, though.'

'All right, let's suppose she would. Now, what if someone was waiting for Mr Asher when he arrived to satisfy his lust?' Mr Apple asked, his tone suggesting a broad grin, though it was impossible to tell in the gloom. 'And what if instead of a romantic half-hour Mr Asher was removed from circulation, kept hidden away in the bowels of the earth, so to speak, and used to strengthen our negotiating position?'

'You mean kidnap the bastard?'

'Not to put too fine a point on it: yes.'

'Jeez, Mr Apple. I dunno. Shit, you'd be getting yourself into very deep water that way. Christ almighty, we wouldn't stand a chance.'

'Oh, dear,' Mr Apple sighed. 'I thought it was a beautiful plan.'

This choice of words struck Martin as unreasonably funny, and he could not control an outburst of laughter. 'You mean, you were really considering it?'

'Why not?'

'Why not? For one thing – '

'Desperate situations need desperate solutions – or something like that.'

'For one thing, where would we keep him?'

' – ? Here, of course.'

'Here?'

'In your little hidey-hole.'

'You *are* mad.'

'But why?'

'We can't just kidnap Asher and hope to do a deal. It's – '

'But you told me yourself that's how things are done. We simply have to play the game they understand – and beat them at it.'

'It's no game, Mr A.'

'I *know* that,' Mr Apple snapped.

'Christ – '

'All you have to do is see to it that Mr Asher is brought back here, and leave the rest to me.'

'Me – bring Asher back here? Oh, sure. That's just great. And how do *I* do that?'

'I thought your friend Fergal might help?'

Martin thought for a moment, and in that split second he realized that somehow he was going to be talked into this crazy ploy. 'He might.'

'I'm sure he would.'

'And then?'

'And then, like I said, leave the rest to me. I spent most of my life listening to diplomats lying to one another. I picked up a thing or two. And I think I know the best man to deal with.'

'Who?'

'An acquaintance of yours actually. Colonel Maddox.'

'Maddox?'

'That's right. I've met him once or twice. He's a reasonable man. He'll listen to me anyway.'

Martin walked slowly across the room and slumped into one of the armchairs by the fireplace. Maybe it *would* work. And what had he to lose? Stay here and he would be found eventually. Make a run for it – hah. Maybe the mad old bugger had hit upon the only way out. Maybe he –

'Well?' the mad old bugger was now saying impatiently.

Martin grunted. 'Okay. It's your neck as well as mine.'

For an instant Mr Apple froze as the flickering image of a faceless swinging body to-and-froed across his vision. Then he shook his head and pulled himself together, rubbing his hands. He gave another of his little cackles. 'I'm quite enjoying this, you know. Who would have thought – '

'Yeah, well, I wouldn't start enjoying yourself yet, Mr A. You could very well end up finding yourself dead.'

'Oh, dear. Ah, well. If that's the outcome, who am I to complain?'

' – ?'

'There are worse things, aren't there?' Without waiting for an answer to his enigmatic question Mr Apple became very businesslike again. 'Now, the first thing you do is tell Daphne more or less what we are going to do – if we can arrange it. Tell her nicely, Martin. We don't want the poor child terrified out of her wits. Just tell her enough so that she can rehearse her surprise when Mr Asher is plucked from her,' Mr Apple instructed, now definitely enjoying himself. 'Then, when Daphne's gone, you'll have to get in touch with your friend Fergal and see how he feels. Then we can make plans.'

'I still think it's crazy, Mr A.'

'That's right, Martin. But that's what's good about it. Off you go and chat to Daphne. I've got some thinking to do.'

Daphne rose from her chair and almost ran to him as he came back into the kitchen. She threw her arms about his neck and pressed her body against him. 'Oh, Martin, Martin,' she whispered. 'What are we going to do?' she sobbed, watching her hopes for the future splinter in her mind's eye.

'Shh,' Martin said, at a loss as to how best to console her. 'That's what I want to talk to you about. Mr Apple's come up with a plan. A crazy bloody plan – but it might work. I'll need your help, though.'

'Anything, luvvey. Anything. You just tell me what you want and I'll do it.'

'Okay. Let's sit down and – '

'No, Martin. Please. Tell me what you want like this. I feel better in your arms. Tell me what you want. I'm listening.'

Martin pulled an exasperated face, and twitched his nose as Daphne's long hair began to tickle. 'Well, you know you told us Asher should be coming to you tomorrow night?'

'That's right.'

'Mr Apple suggested we should have someone there when he comes. That we should kidnap him,' Martin concluded abruptly.

Daphne went rigid in his arms. 'Kidnap Asher?'

'Yeah. Great, isn't it?'

She ignored the question. 'And what am I to do?'

' – ? You? Oh, nothing. You just act all surprised and frightened, and when we've gone you can scream a bit if you like,' Martin told her, smiling to himself at the dramatic touch he had added.

For several minutes Daphne said nothing. She ran her fingers delicately up and down Martin's neck, making a strange little purring noise in her throat. 'All right,' she said finally, pushing herself back a few inches and staring into his eyes.

'Just like that. No questions?'

'I don't want to know anything, Martin. You told me what you wanted me to do and I said I'd do it. That's all there is.'

Martin shook his head slowly. 'You're some girl, Daphne.'

'Oh, yes, I'm some girl.'

'You know it might not work?'

'I know.'

'If we're caught you know they'll fix it so we're killed?'

'Yes.'

Suddenly Martin pulled the girl close to him and kissed her with unaccustomed passion. 'Hey, Daphne. Thanks,' he said finally.

Daphne smiled, her face strangely innocent, as if that one kiss had charmed all the hardness and pain from her mind. 'No thanks, Martin. When it's over – '

'When it's over we'll talk,' he told her gently.

'Yes. Well, I better go.'

'Yeah. And don't be afraid – '

'Afraid? Oh, Martin, I'm not afraid. I told you I'd do anything I could to help you.'

'I know, but – '

'No buts, luvvey. You're the only thing I have in my life. If I lose you, then I've nothing. So why should I be afraid?'

'Okay. I'll see you out.'

Martin closed the front door behind Daphne, wondering at her unsettling confession of love. He was, in his own way, still trying to analyse this when Mr Apple peered out from the sitting-room and demanded, 'Well?'

'Oh. Yes. Yes, Daphne will do what I asked. She'll – '

'Excellent,' Mr Apple said. 'Now, Fergal – what about Fergal?'

'It's too early to ring him.'

'Oh. I think you should try anyway. We don't have all that much time.'

'You're the boss, Mr A. I'll try him. Hey – how come you've taken over, anyway?' Martin suddenly asked.

'I have rather, haven't I?' Mr Apple said gleefully. 'Still, I'm going to make a good job of it.'

'I certainly hope so.'

'I will. Ring Fergal.'

Martin went to the table in the hall and rang Fergal.

'Fergal?'

'Yeah. Martin? You just caught me. I was on the way out,' Fergal told him breathlessly.

'I need a few things.'

'Like what?'

'A car, for one.'

'When?'

'Tomorrow evening. About seven.'

'No problem.'

'And a gun.'

'Rifle, hand or submachine?'

'Hand.'

'Same time?'

'Yes.'

'Done.'

'A woollen helmet.'

'Hah. Easy. Anything else?'

'Yeah. A driver.'

'I'll do that.'

'You sure you want to get involved?'

'Will it help you?'

'It's about my only chance.'

'Then I want to get involved.'

'It's a – '

'I don't want to know, Martin. You need me – I'll be there. Shit, what are friends for?'

'Thanks. I was beginning to wonder.'

'Where you want me to pick you up?'

'Ah. Let me think. Best thing is if you drive past the bottom of Lepper Street at exactly seven. I'll be there.'

'Seven I'll be there. You sure that's safe?'

'It'll have to be.'

'Right.'

'And Fergal – '

'Yeah?'

'Don't carry a gun yourself. If we don't pull it off I don't want you to be – '

'You just worry about yourself, boyo.'

'Okay. And thanks.'

'No thanks. I owed you.'

'Sure.'

'See you at seven,' Fergal said, and hung up.

'That's it then,' Martin told Mr Apple. 'All arranged as per your instructions.'

'You see? I told you things would work out. He must be a very good friend, this Fergal?'

'He must be,' Martin agreed.

'I wonder what you've done to deserve such friendship...' murmured Mr Apple, without really expecting an answer.

Which was just as well, for Martin had no intention of trying to explain the obscure loyalty which had formed the bond between himself and the ever-breathless Fergal. Indeed, now that he thought about it, he could hardly explain it to himself, since the incident that had sealed their friendship was nebulous to say the least, and had, apparently, meant considerably more to Fergal than to Martin...

The never-ending abuse rolled off the backs of the Paras as their heavy boots thumped down the mean little street in the Old Park district, the same boots that would shortly splinter and burst open front doors as the military searched for arms and ammunition, the whole operation mounted as the result of a telephone tip-off – possibly placed by one of their own soldiers out for revenge.

Fucking English cocksuckers!

Youse fucking Para cunts!

Six years ago it had happened, but it could have been yesterday or six years hence, so little had the pattern changed. Inevitably a small crowd of men (braver or more foolish than others) gathered at the entrance to the street, among them Martin Deeley and a young weasel-faced, acne-ridden boy of about twelve. At first they just glared at the soldiers, content to curse them and their mothers. They kept their hands in their pockets, some of them jumping up and down to emphasize their expletives, and seemed harmless enough. But the slow, steady progress of the Paras towards them roused their simmering fury and, as if by magic, petrol bombs appeared – already ignited, it seemed – and were hurled. The Paras, instead of retreating, charged, shifting position constantly, their eyes scanning not only the dozen or so bombers but rooftops and windows. Outnumbered (and perhaps not so foolish after all), the crowd took to its heels. Martin found himself running alongside the boy with the weasel face who was already gasping asthmatically. Come *on*, Martin called to him.

I can't go any faster, the boy wheezed.

Shit. Here. Martin reached out and in one gesture scooped the boy off his feet and threw him over his own shoulder, carrying him through the complex of back alleys that separated the rows of shabby two-up, two-down houses, through the stench of outside toilets, to safety.

Now piss off out of here, he told the boy.

Hey, thanks, mister. Youse saved my life.

Shit, Martin told him.

I won't forget you, mister.

And that was all there was to it.

'I helped him out once,' Martin told Mr Apple. 'Did him a favour.'

'Oh.'

'So what do we do now?'

'Now? Now,' Mr Apple said, 'we go and get a good night's sleep. I have to work tomorrow, don't forget. And you have a thing or two on your plate as well.'

And, strangely enough, Mr Apple slept unusually well that night. He woke only once – not lurching as though from a nightmare, but lazily and with a feeling of well-being. He switched on the light and glanced at his bedside clock: four minutes to three. He was about to put the light out again when something told him to look at his sheets; a peculiar instruction, he had to admit. But he did it nonetheless, and was surprised, but in no way alarmed, to see a pattern on the bottom sheet, a skeletal pattern traced in tiny drops of blood. He reached an arm around his back and felt his old scars, stared at his hand and rubbed his thumb and forefinger together. 'Ah,' he said to himself with satisfaction, as he noted the traces of blood on his fingertips. 'Ah.' Then he lay down again, reached up a long bony arm to switch out the light, pulled the blankets over his head and drifted off into a bright, untroubled sleep.

'In there,' Martin said. 'That's as good a spot as we're likely to find.'

'Right.' Fergal pulled over and reversed the inconspicuous Morris into the parking space. 'Which is the house?'

Martin pointed. 'That one. With the light over the door.'

'Oh. What do we do now?'

'Wait.'

'I hate waiting,' Fergal said. 'Always have done.'

'Yeah,' Martin said vaguely. 'You'll remember what I told you?'

'Sure, Martin.'

'As soon as I come out that door with Asher, get this heap moving.'

'I will. I suppose Asher will turn up?'

'He fucking better,' Martin said, and laughed shortly. 'Shit, I've got myself all geared up for this.'

'So've I.'

They slid down in the seats and fixed their eyes on the door with the light over it.

'And don't say anything once Asher is in the car,' Martin warned.

'I won't.'

'I don't want him remembering your voice when all this is over.'

'I won't say a word,' Fergal promised.

'Good.'

A taxi passed them and pulled up a few yards past the house they were watching. Fergal raised his head. 'Is that him?'

Martin said nothing. He stared at the taxi, waiting for the passenger to get out. 'Naw,' he said finally, as a tall figure emerged from the taxi and made for another house, heaving a suitcase from one hand to the other every few paces. 'But that fucking is,' Martin announced suddenly. 'That there is our man.'

'That's Asher?' Fergal asked, surprised that the huge reputation of their victim should be so let down by his insignificant stature. 'Jesus, he's smaller than I am.'

'What did you expect? A bloody giant?'

'No. But I thought he'd be bigger, that's all. I mean, you wouldn't think a little fart like that could be so important, would you?'

They watched John Asher stroll up the street like a man without a care in the world. He went up the steps to the house two at a time, pushed open the door, and went inside.

Martin looked at his watch, holding his wrist sideways so that the streetlamp lit the dial. 'Right,' he said, his voice suddenly hoarse. 'Ten minutes and I go in. He should have his knickers off by then.'

Fergal giggled. 'He'll shit himself,' he said happily.

'That's what I want,' Martin said with a wicked grin. 'I hope to Christ she remembers to leave her door on the latch,' he added, suddenly serious.

'She knows she's supposed to?'

'Of course she knows she's supposed to.'

'Sorry.'

'Shit, I'm dying for a fag.'

'Better not,' Fergal said sympathetically. 'Anyway, you'll enjoy one all the more later.'

'I hope so.'

'Don't worry. It'll all go like clockwork.'

'I hope you're right.'

'Sure I am.'

The ten minutes seemed like an hour in passing, but finally it was time for him to go. 'Don't forget: as soon as we come through that door, get this car moving,' Martin said, and got out of the car.

'Don't worry about that, Martin. I'll do my end.'

'Okay. Well, here goes.'

'Mind yourself.'

Martin crossed the road like a shadow and entered the house, his right hand already holding the gun in his inside pocket. Inside he stood rigid, listening, his eyes constantly moving. When he crossed the hall he seemed to glide rather than walk, his black plimsolls silent as a breath on the worn linoleum. And it was as though he walked on air as he raced up the stairs, his toes barely touching the metal strips on the front of each step. He hugged the wall as he crept down the corridor, stopping every few paces to listen. Suddenly, in a room some way behind him, a radio came alive, making him jump and freeze in an oddly contorted posture which he held for several seconds as he listened to the measured tones fill the wavelength with tales of an air disaster, almost gloating as it told of debris littering a hillside, of bodies scattered in the darkness. It was all too much, it seemed, for the owner of the radio, and the dial was turned back and forth, finally settling for some music that could have been Django Reinhardt or Eddie Lang, but was probably neither.

Martin relaxed and took several deep breaths: four more strides and he was outside Daphne's door. The immediate temptation was to burst in and confront Asher, but Martin resisted this, determined to follow the scenario he had worked out so meticulously in his mind the night before. He gripped the doorhandle and eased it round, using his knee to push the door inwards a fraction. He smiled (although nothing of this showed on his face) as he heard a muffled grunting, and then he was in the room with the door shut behind him, all without a sound. In the dull red glow of the little electric crucifix he could make out Mr Asher runting merrily on the bed, his face buried in Daphne's neck, his naked, round, white bottom bouncing up and down like a distorted balloon. He had not, it seemed, yet reached his climax, and Martin took his time crossing to the bed, gun in hand, his head cocked, listening for the first gasp that would indicate John Asher was about to come: and when he heard it a wide grin spread across his face and he pushed the barrel of the gun into the nape of Mr Asher's neck. 'Well, well, well, and what do we have here?' he said. 'No. Oh, no, *Mister* Asher don't get up. Just stay right where you are. You can even finish off if you want.'

'Oh, dear God,' Daphne started, raising her head slightly and smiling up at Martin. 'Oh, don't shoot us, mister. I haven't done anything. Oh, mister, don't – '

'Shut up, you slag,' Martin told her through his teeth, giving her a wink and sardonically applauding her performance with a thumbs-up sign. 'Shut up, or I *will* blow your stupid head off.'

Daphne shut up.

'Had enough, Mr Asher?' Martin asked.

'What do you want?' Asher asked, attempting to raise his head but finding it pushed down by the gun.

'Not a lot,' Martin told him. 'You, in fact. That's all I want. We're about to take a little trip, you and I.'

'Who the hell are you?'

'Me? Oh, I'm sorry. I thought you knew that. I'm Martin Deeley.'

Asher felt his whole body wince. 'You're mad, Deeley. Coming here. Everybody in the country is looking for you.'

'I still have you where I want you, though, don't I, Mr Asher? And if they find me now – well, that's just tough on you. You won't even have time to get your prick out let alone use it again.'

'What do you want?' Asher asked again, slowly reaching the stage when his embarrassing nakedness was troubling him more than his deadly predicament.

'I told you. We're going to have a little chat.'

'About what?'

'Oh, this and that. About you. About me. About Corrigan. About the prospects of life. About the dangers of death. You know, general things that affect us all. And you can get up now. Nice and slowly, though. I wouldn't want you to injure your little cock,' Martin told him, giving his white bottom a hearty slap with his free hand.

Asher eased himself out of Daphne and knelt over her for a second before gingerly placing one foot on the floor, organizing his balance, all the while feeling the coldness of the gun at his neck.

'Right,' Martin told him. 'You can get dressed. I thought about making you come with me naked,' he went on, moving back a few paces but keeping the gun aimed at Asher's head, 'but you're so fucking ugly I think you better dress.'

'You haven't a hope in hell of getting away with this, Deeley,' Mr Asher said, ignoring his underclothes and pulling on his trousers. 'You're as good as dead,' he added, buttoning his shirt.

'I die, you die,' Martin said reasonably. 'And I don't really care what happens to me.'

'Another bloody martyr,' Mr Asher said, feeling he could afford a sneer now that he was dressed.

'That's right. Me and St Stephen,' Martin said, without really knowing why he had chosen the saint who set the ball rolling. 'Put this on now,' he ordered, tossing a woollen helmet across the room. 'And pull it down over your ugly face.'

Asher caught the helmet and pulled it on, giving one quick glance about him before covering his face.

Martin stepped quickly behind him. 'Now move,' he said, giving him a nudge in the back.

'I can't see,' Asher said, his voice its old petulant self.

'You don't have to,' Martin said, pushing him towards the door, turning briefly to mouth 'I'll phone you tomorrow' to Daphne and make a dialling gesture with his hand. 'And you stay there and keep your mouth shut,' he ordered her roughly, blowing her a kiss.

'Oh, I will, mister. You'll never hear a word from me.'

'I better fucking not.'

Fergal had the car by the pavement and the back door open as they reached the last step, and Martin bundled Asher in and climbed in himself. 'Go,' he said.

Fergal suddenly turned and gaped at him 'Where?' he mouthed, remembering not to speak.

Martin pointed furiously straight ahead. 'On the floor, you,' he said as the car sped away. He leaned forward, cautioning Fergal to slow down by waving the palm of his hand downwards, putting his mouth close to Fergal's ear. 'Make for St Enoch's,' he whispered. 'I'll tell you after that.'

Fergal nodded.

'And for Christ's sake take it easy. All we need is to be pulled in for speeding.'

Fergal glanced in the rear-view mirror and grinned.

For a kidnapping, the journey to Mr Apple's house was ridiculously mundane. Asher remained on the floor, grunting occasionally;

Martin gave directions in a cool, calm whisper; and Fergal drove confidently at a sedate pace, once pulling to the side of the road like a good citizen to allow three armoured cars to pass.

'That's it, there,' Martin whispered finally. 'Just pull in and nip up and knock on the door. Then get back here sharpish.'

Fergal nodded.

Mr Apple must have been waiting within feet of the door, since he opened it almost before Fergal had stopped knocking. He had dressed himself for the occasion: smart suit, white shirt, deep-red tie that contrasted nicely with the grey flannel. He had, however, forgotten his shoes, and he wriggled his toes as he waited for Martin to bring Asher in. 'Welcome, welcome,' he said gaily as the helmeted Asher was pushed past him. 'Your room is all ready. This way,' he added, closing the front door and leading the way down the stairs off the glory-hole. He had been busy: the walls were stripped of their strange pictures and prints and were now quite bare save for the crucifix, which he saw fit to leave. The table and chair had been removed also, leaving only the iron cot. 'You'll be very comfortable here,' he told Asher politely. 'Do take that helmet off him, Martin. We really don't want the good man to suffocate.'

Martin whipped off the woollen helmet and stood back to watch Asher blink, focus his eyes in the light, smooth down his tousled hair and round on Mr Apple. 'I *knew* you were behind this,' he exploded.

'Did you?' Mr Apple asked. 'That was clever of you.'

'You're a fool to have got mixed up with that scum,' Asher went on, licking the saliva from the corners of his mouth. 'You're as dead as he is.'

'Oh, dear,' said Mr Apple, who seemed to be enjoying himself no end. 'I don't think he cares much for you, Martin.'

Martin sniggered. 'That breaks my heart.'

'You'll have more than your heart broken,' Asher told him. 'And as for you – you degenerate,' he spat at the inoffensive Mr Apple, 'as for you, I'll see you wiped off the face of the earth.'

'Oh, dear,' Mr Apple said again, shaking his head. 'I'm afraid you've been beaten to it. I haven't been of this earth for a long time now, you know,' he confided mysteriously.

Martin pushed Asher in the chest, sending him reeling back on to the cot. 'You just sit down and keep your mouth shut,' he ordered. 'We've had enough old shit out of you. Cummon, Mr Apple, let's get upstairs – he stinks this place.'

Together they left the room, Mr Apple giving Asher a little wave before he closed and bolted the door. 'No problems?' he asked Martin, when they finally reached the kitchen.

'None.'

'I knew there wouldn't be.'

Martin stared at Mr Apple for a moment, frowning: Mr Apple stared back, smiling.

'Look, Mr A. I'm worried. You're taking this so – well, you're treating it a bit like a joke.'

Mr Apple drew himself up, appalled at the monstrous accusation. 'I most certainly am not,' he said. 'I am treating it most seriously.'

'But you don't seem to give a damn what happens to you –'

'What's that got to do with it? As a matter of fact, I don't. My fate was decided a long time ago, Martin. The only thing that does matter is that we negotiate a deal that gets you out of trouble.'

'You see? There you go again. Talking bloody rubbish about your fate. We've got to get you out of this too.'

'Oh, Martin, Martin, will you just leave everything to me? I know what I'm doing.'

'I wish to hell I did – know what you are doing, I mean.'

'Well, I'll tell you. I'm seeing Colonel Maddox tonight, to start with.'

'You're what?'

'Seeing your friend Colonel Maddox tonight. At midnight, actually. I thought that would be a good time.'

'How the hell did you arrange that?'

' – ? Why, by telephone of course.'

'You just rang him up and said, "Hey there Colonel Maddox, how about a chat at midnight to make a deal?"'

'Not exactly. I rang him up, yes. Then I told him I had something very important to tell him, and asked him nicely if he would meet me at midnight.'

'And he said yes?'

'And he said yes.'

Martin shook his head in disbelief. 'And why should he agree to meet you?'

'Ah, well. You see, I'm supposed to be spying on you and Mr Reilly. I'm supposed to have been doing it since I came to the shop.'

'And have you?'

'Funnily enough, no. Mr Asher was always there and somehow I never took to him. So I pleaded ignorance on all counts. But the Colonel quite likes me, you know. We understand each other.'

'I bet you bloody do.'

'I'll ignore that, Martin. Actually, Colonel Maddox is a very civilized man. I was very annoyed with you when I learned it was you who tried to kill him.'

'He's a fucking Bri – '

'He's a good man, Martin. I don't care where he comes from or what absurd opinion you have formed of him. He's a good man. An honest man – and there's precious few of those left '

Mr Apple filled a glass with water from the tap in the sink and drank deeply. 'Anyway, he's the only hope *you* have of getting out of this mess.'

'Some hope.'

'Water?' Mr Apple asked.

Martin shook his head.

'Would you like to come with me?'

' – ?'

'I just thought you might like to see the man you tried to murder.'

Martin felt himself growing pale. Perhaps it was this, or perhaps it was the mild challenge in Mr Apple's remark that made him reply, 'Yeah. I'll come. I want to hear what you two get up to, anyway.'

Mr Apple smiled. 'Good. It should be an interesting evening.'

'What about him?' Martin wanted to know, jerking his head in a direction that could have indicated anywhere.

'Oh, yes. You know, I'd forgotten about poor Mr Asher.'

'Well, you better remember him, Mr A. He's a bloody liability now.'

'Hmm,' sighed Mr Apple. 'I suppose we'll have to tie him up,' he said regretfully.

'And gag the bastard.'

'Maybe you're right. I dislike mistreating people, but I suppose in this case – '

'Too damn right. And we better get a shift on if you want to meet Maddox by twelve.'

Together they tied the protesting Mr Asher's hands behind his back and secured the nylon clothesline to the head of the cot. They then tied his feet, looping the rope securely round and round one of the cot's legs. While Mr Apple muttered his apologies for such ungracious treatment, Martin swore under his breath and tied a teacloth around Mr Asher's head, forcing it between his teeth. 'That should shut you up,' he said.

'You're still sure you want to come with me?' Mr Apple asked Martin as they climbed the stairs.

'Yeah, I'll come.'

'I mean, do you think you can face the Colonel?'

'Of course I can face him – if we ever get there. The way you're quizzing me, Mr A., he'll be fed up waiting.'

Mr Apple struggled into his coat and donned his hat at a jaunty angle. 'Are you warm enough? I can let you have a pullover.'

'I'm fine. I'm a hot-blooded creature, you know.'

Mr Apple gave a small chuckle. 'I see.'

Outside, the wind had risen and the forecast of rain seemed to be coming true. Already it was spitting as they hurried along, Mr Apple clinging to Martin's arm, muttering to himself from time to time. As they turned the corner into the street where the safe house was located Mr Apple came to a halt and turned to face Martin. 'Now, I want you to let *me* do the talking, Martin,' he said. 'None of your smart-alec nonsense.'

'I won't say a word,' Martin promised.

'Huh.'

'Honest.'

'Good. I have it all worked out, you see. Up here,' Mr Apple explained pointing to his head. 'And if you start interrupting I'll only lose track.'

'I told you, I won't say a word.'

'Right. Let's get to it,' Mr Apple said, and bustled down the street, leaving Martin standing. 'Come along,' he called over his shoulder.

By the time Martin had caught up, Mr Apple had come to a halt again, and was standing outside a lightless house, his hand already raised to the knocker. 'Not a word,' he whispered.

'Not one,' Martin whispered back, smiling helplessly.

'Right.'

Mr Apple knocked three times, an action that seemed to amuse Martin, who gave a barely stifled laugh.

'What's so funny?' Mr Apple demanded.

'Knock three times and ask for Joe,' Martin said.

'Rubbish,' Mr Apple said, but he smiled nonetheless.

He was still smiling when Colonel Maddox opened the door and reciprocated with a smile of his own.

'I'm sorry to be late,' Mr Apple began.

'Oh, no,' the Colonel said waving the apology aside and ushering them in with a single, sweeping gesture. 'In fact, I'm afraid we may have to wait a while. Mr Asher hasn't arrived yet. I've been trying to contact him since I got your call. I had to leave a message for him in the end. And this is?'

'Oh. A friend of mine. Nameless for the moment, Colonel.'

'Ah. I understand,' Maddox said, and held out his hand politely.

For a moment Martin hesitated, but wilted under Mr Apple's baleful gaze. He took the Colonel's hand and shook it. 'Colonel,' he said.

'Getting up like rain again,' the Colonel said, ushering them into the small, dank, dust-laden front room.

'Yes,' Mr Apple agreed. 'Inclement, isn't that the word?'

'I believe it is, Mr Apple. I believe it is. Do sit down. Both of you.

Do sit down.'

Mr Apple settled himself in the armchair he had always used, while Martin retreated across the room and sat on the arm of the sofa, taking with him an ashtray he spotted on a small table. Mr Apple's eyes followed him intently. 'I'm sure the Colonel won't mind if you smoke.'

'Hmm? Oh, no. Not at all. Please do. You have an ashtray. Good. I do hope Mr Asher comes soon. I dislike keeping you waiting like this.'

Mr Apple rotated his hat on his knee and cleared his throat. 'Colonel,' he said, 'I'm afraid Mr Asher won't be joining us.'

'Won't be – what – how do you know that?'

'Well, we have detained him.'

'You've detained Mr Asher? I'm sorry, I – '

'Yes, Colonel,' Mr Apple said. 'We've detained Mr Asher. I think if I tell you that that young man over there is Martin Deeley you'll begin to understand.'

'Martin Deeley?' The Colonel frowned, confused, repeating the name once more before its significance dawned on him. 'Martin Deeley – the man who tried – '

'To kill you, Colonel,' Mr Apple explained.

'Good God,' was all Colonel Maddox could summon up. He attempted to conceal his loss for words by looking about him for a chair. He spotted one by the door and moved to it, sitting down heavily.

Mr Apple cleared his throat again. 'We have a problem, Colonel,' he said.

If Colonel Maddox heard he gave no sign of it. He stared at Martin as though transfixed, as though he was mesmerized by the cool green eyes that stared arrogantly back at him.

'Colonel?' Mr Apple tried to break the spell.

'Hmm? Sorry. You – '

'I was explaining that we have a problem. But we have a solution to that problem – if you'll agree to it.'

Maddox turned his head. For a while, he said nothing. There was, in truth, nothing he could think of to say. He was aware that matters were getting out of hand, that they had been taken from his control, that what he had expected to be a simple passing of information was rapidly developing into something far too complex for him. And it was probably this frustration that made him ask in a strained, tired voice, a voice that accepted defeat, 'What am I to agree to?'

'I had better explain the problem first, I think,' Mr Apple said. 'As you know, Mr Asher is anxious to arrest Martin – as, indeed, I am sure you are. Well, Martin is just as anxious that such an arrest should not take place. He wants, quite simply, safe passage, I believe the term is, out of Ireland.'

'But – '

'Let me finish, Colonel. In order to ensure that such a passage might be obtainable we have kidnapped Mr Asher, and – '

'You've kidnapped Mr Asher,' the Colonel repeated dully, accepting it simply as a statement of fact, devoid of drama or intrigue.

'We've kidnapped Mr Asher,' Mr Apple repeated, 'and we are willing to trade his safety for Martin's. I think that would be a fair swap, don't you?'

'But why come to me? *I* can't arrange any such – '

'Oh, come now, Colonel,' Mr Apple said. 'You belittle your powers. I am quite sure you could arrange things most satisfactorily.'

'I can't do deals,' the Colonel said firmly.

'You can, you know. Everything is done by making deals – some of which are not carried out. One Larry Corrigan, for example.'

Maddox winced. 'I had nothing whatever to do with that.'

'You knew about it.'

'Yes,' the Colonel confessed. 'But I had nothing to do with it.'

'You could have prevented Corrigan's execution.'

'I don't think – '

'And all I'm asking you to do is prevent another: Mr Asher's,' Mr Apple pointed out frankly. '*I* certainly don't want Mr Asher killed. Neither does Martin. But I'm afraid he will have to be if you and I cannot come to some arrangement.'

Something seemed to strike the Colonel as odd: he perked up

suddenly and frowned. 'What about you, Mr Apple. What deal do I have to agree to for you?'

'Me? Why?'

'Do you want free passage?'

'Good heavens, no, Colonel,' Mr Apple chortled happily at the idea. 'I want nothing for myself. I'll be perfectly all right.'

Maddox found himself forced to smile at Mr Apple's bright and shining optimism.

'Anyway,' Mr Apple went on, 'I am my own concern. What you have to consider is Mr Asher's safe return and Martin's healthy exit.'

Maddox fumbled in his jacket pockets for a cigarette before remembering he had forgotten to buy any, and he was taken aback when Martin offered him one. He was on the point of refusing, but some strange, old-fashioned sense of politeness made him change his mind. He reached out and accepted the cigarette, accepted, too, the light which followed it. He inhaled deeply and allowed the smoke to leave his lungs in company with, 'It would have been so much easier if you hadn't missed.'

'It sure would,' Martin agreed, a touch of sadness in his voice, though sadness for what only he could tell.

'Supposing,' the Colonel said, turning his attention to Mr Apple once again, 'supposing I *could* arrange an exchange,' he said. 'How would it be carried out?'

'Quite simply. I have one or two details still to work out, but basically you would see to it that Martin was escorted to the airport and put aboard a plane to a destination of our choosing. Martin would telephone me when he arrived safely. Within twenty-four hours I would see to it that Mr Asher was returned to the fold.'

'I could, of course, have *you* arrested.'

Mr Apple spread his hands. 'You could. But then, alas, Mr Asher would die. Of starvation, if exposure didn't finish him off first. Poor chap, he's probably feeling wet through already,' Mr Apple lied.

'And how long do I have to agree to all this?'

Mr Apple spread his hands again. 'As long as you like, Colonel. Or rather, as long as you think Mr Asher can survive this – eh –

inclement weather.'

'I need time to think.'

'Of course you do.'

The Colonel rose suddenly to his feet. 'I'll contact you tomorrow,' he said. Then, smiling sheepishly, he asked 'Where do I do that?'

'All day I'll be at my little betting-shop. In the evening I'll be at home. Both numbers are in the book.'

'I'll phone you tomorrow.'

'Thank you,' Mr Apple said politely, and got up from his chair. 'Colonel, I want you to believe me that I regret having been forced to make you the intermediary. I do respect you.'

Maddox nodded.

'Come along, Martin,' Mr Apple said. 'We'll see ourselves out, Colonel.'

' – ? Oh. Yes. Right.'

'I'll hear from you tomorrow?'

'Yes.'

'Good-night, then, Colonel.'

'Good-night.'

'You were bloody marvellous, Mr Apple,' Martin said as they made their way home through the dark, silent streets. 'Bloody marvellous, you were.'

'I'm not so sure, Martin,' Mr Apple replied, his voice troubled. 'There's something not quite right. I have a feeling I underestimated the Colonel's conscience.'

'Conscience?'

'Hmm,' Mr Apple said. 'Some people do still have them. And the Colonel certainly does. And a sense of duty. Queen and country before anything else. Oh, we're not out of the woods yet.'

'He'll arrange it.'

'I wonder if he will. He might, but it will be difficult for him to convince himself he should.'

'He's got no choice.'

'Oh, but he does, Martin. That's the trouble. He *has* a choice. It's a question of balance. Mr Asher's life against his duty as a soldier.

He might very well choose duty.'

'So we've been wasting out bloody time?'

Mr Apple shook his head. 'I didn't say that. I said he had a choice – and he might choose in our favour.'

'And if he doesn't?'

'If he doesn't – well, we'll have to think again. Anyway, look on the bright side – you'll be no worse off than you are now.'

'Like shit I won't! Fucking kidnap round my neck.'

'You know, I don't think that will ever be mentioned. Mr Asher likes to be thought of as a proper man. I don't somehow think he would take kindly to it being broadcast that he was caught – eh – with his pants down!'

Even Martin was forced to laugh at that. 'Christ, it *was* bloody funny, you know, Mr Apple.'

'That's what I meant. Anyway, let's wait and see what tomorrow brings. Tomorrow is, as they say, another day.'

'Yeah, another bloody day.'

'Meanwhile, what we need is a nightcap, and then bed. We'll let the unfortunate Colonel do the worrying tonight.'

'Huh. I wonder what he's thinking now.'

The Colonel was, in fact, thinking about the unholy mess that had suddenly engulfed him. He had switched out the light (trying to conceal, perhaps, even from himself, the aching loneliness, the brooding, cold horror he felt at the intrigue he was now being sucked into), and the darkness murmured and was palpable. It struck him that for the first time he had been made aware of the brutal reality of the terrorism he had been sent to wipe out, a reality drained of compassion and fuelled by hatred and generations of fomented revenge. And now he was part of it: the aloofness of his position wiped away by a few words from a strange old man. Colonel Maddox was not a man given to anger, but he felt a virulent, consuming anger now. It was as though some reckless, murderous power was drawing him on, taunting him, forcing him (while he tried to remain passionless, aware of the all-too-possible consequences) through a bombardment of solutions, only one of which he was to be allowed to accept. Slowly it became clear to him that the only course he could follow was the very one that would necessitate his being as devious as John Asher, as cruel and calculating as John Asher, as conscienceless as John Asher.

Maddox dragged himself to his feet and away from the uncharacteristic thoughts that had so appalled him. He stretched, feeling the twinges of rheumatism in his shoulder, switched on the light and glanced about the room with a look almost of affection: the sort of bewildered, loving–hating look bestowed by celluloid war-heroes on, say, an empty and abandoned hangar that brought back memories of scrambles, and dead friends, and wartime love-affairs. His eye fell on the ashtray Martin had used, and he gave a small sigh. Yes, he thought, perhaps it would have been better if he, instead of his driver, had been killed. A heroic death of sorts. Nancy would have appreciated that, would have made a great show at his funeral, would have adored the military honours, the pomp, would probably have enjoyed even the grief. Oh, military funerals are the most exciting things in the world, she had once proclaimed, as usual displaying a curious choice of words. That trumpet, she exclaimed, when it wails! My God, it makes my flesh creep! Maddox smiled wistfully, and astonished himself for an instant by regretting he had let her down. 'The sick hearts that honour could not move,' he quoted aloud sadly. Then he said the words again, vexed that he could not recall what came next. 'And all the little emptiness of love,' he concluded, and immediately frowned, asking himself why on earth he had thought of the poem in the first place.

As he left the house and made his way back to the barracks on foot he wondered what his friends would have thought, comfortable in their solid English homes, if they could have seen him walking quite unmolested through the streets of what they liked to call 'that demented city'. Probably they would have castigated him, called him a fool – and, he admitted, perhaps he was. Oddly, since the attempt to kill him, he had become unconcerned about his personal safety; it was as though his survival had made him inviolate, untouchable; or perhaps he just felt that precautions were futile. Again (and why should Rupert Brooke suddenly be so dominant in his thoughts tonight?) words that had struck him as being, when he read them for the first time, wholly directed to himself strolled into his mind: 'Unbroken glory, a gathered radiance. A width, a shining peace, under the night.'

Whatever peace under the night, there was, alas, no glory of any sort for him. Inglorious dealings were, it seemed, to be his lot.

As soon as he turned the corner into Lepper Street Mr Apple knew that something was wrong. Although the street was empty – as it always was at that hour of the morning – he sensed shunting echoes of movement. He paused, contemplating the foolhardiness of walking into a trap, before straightening his shoulders and making his way with an air of unperturbed determination down the street. He passed no one, yet it was as though the very windows of the houses were eyes watching his progress, glinting at him suspiciously, noting every movement he made.

Still, he arrived at the betting-shop safely, and was quietly scolding himself for imagining things, when he heard a car being started up, it's engine being gunned slightly. He tried to be casual as he glanced up and down the street: nothing, just the continued throb of the invisible engine. Mr Apple frowned and put the key in the door: he was vexed rather than surprised when it would not turn. He fiddled with it, bending down and peering at the lock, pulling the key out and reinserting it several times. He stood back and gazed at the door. He was about to make one final effort, using, as he thought of it, considerable force to gain entry, when the black Ford Escort slid around the corner and came to a sudden halt behind him.

'Mr Apple?'

Mr Apple turned, taking his time, giving himself a few seconds to gather his wits. 'Why, Mr Reilly!' he exclaimed, giving a fair impression of surprise.

'A word, Mr Apple,' Seamus Reilly said.

The back door of the car swung open and one of the young men who had escorted Reilly on his most recent visit to the shop stepped out and gestured for Mr Apple to get in with a sweep of one hand, holding the car door open with the other in the manner of a well-trained commissionaire. Mr Apple raised his hat politely and stepped into the car, immediately followed by the bodyguard, who squeezed in with difficulty, pressing Mr Apple against another man sitting on the back seat (perhaps his brother bodyguard, Mr Apple thought, although it was difficult to be certain without actually taking a good look, and Mr Apple had no intention of doing that for the moment), and slammed the door.

Reilly, sitting beside the driver, gave a flick of his wrist and the car sped down the street, slowed for a moment, turned left, and gathered speed again. For the time being nothing was said, and nobody seemed keen to look at anyone else: Mr Apple found himself counting the gear changes. ' – disappointed,' suddenly filtered into his mind.

'I'm sorry?'

'I am very disappointed,' Reilly repeated.

'Oh,' said Mr Apple, sounding concerned.

'Yes,' Reilly went on. 'Very, very disappointed,' he said in a desolate voice.

'Oh, dear.'

'I had so hoped ours would be a fruitful relationship,' Reilly continued, addressing himself to the windscreen, but allowing himself a fleeting look in the rear-view mirror that he had twisted to his advantage. 'Without complications.'

Mr Apple decided it was wisest to say nothing. He stared glumly ahead as the car continued through the city, taking a circuitous route out to the countryside.

Reilly turned, rested his arms on the back of the seat, and took a long, cold look at Mr Apple before saying, 'I understand you've been meeting with a Colonel Maddox?'

'Oh,' was all that Mr Apple could muster, genuinely taken aback by the abruptness of the question.

'You sound surprised,' Reilly told him. 'Did you really think we wouldn't learn about it?' he asked with a tight little laugh. '*Nothing* happens in Belfast that we don't know about,' he added pompously. 'What we can't find out one way, we find out another.'

'Yes. I'm sure you do.'

'Oh, we do. We certainly do. In fact, you would be amazed how we learn things. Amazed the people who come to us for help when they find they can't solve their problems without us.'

'I'm sure.'

'And you have now created one of those problems, Mr Apple. And you have placed us in a very embarrassing situation.'

'Oh, dear. I really don't – '

Reilly barely raised a hand from the back of the seat, but this tiny gesture was sufficient to make Mr Apple be silent. 'I will explain it all to you, Mr Apple. I always believe that an explanation is due when one's life is at stake, don't you?'

Reilly took a minute to light one of his little cigars, blowing the smoke from the corner of his mouth so that it would not obstruct his view of Mr Apple. 'I was summoned from my bed in the early hours of this morning. I do *not* like being summoned from my bed, Mr Apple. I like to rise when I feel the time has come for me to rise. But, as I say, I was summoned and made to present myself to your friend Colonel Maddox.' Which was not altogether true: Reilly had been awakened by someone breaking the front door of his house down, was hauled from his bed by what appeared to be a battalion of Paras, was, it had to be admitted, allowed to dress, was jolted through the dawn in the back of an army jeep, was all but carried and dumped across the desk from an aesthetic-looking Colonel in full uniform who was told, curtly, that this is Reilly, sir.

The Colonel nodded. 'Right, sergeant. You can wait outside,' he said.

'So you are Seamus Reilly,' he went on, when they were alone. 'You may sit down.'

Reilly sat down, immediately alert, aware now that there was more to this than he had first suspected. 'And you?' he asked tentatively, already in his mind trying to establish some advantage.

'My name is Maddox,' the Colonel informed him.

Reilly's face was stony.

'You've heard of me no doubt.'

'Yes.'

'I'm sure you have.' Maddox gave a small smile. 'And I of you, Reilly. And I of you.'

Reilly blinked coldly, but said nothing.

'You have,' the Colonel told him, 'quite a reputation to live up to. I've been told – correct me if my information was wrong – I've been told that you are the one to deal with if one wishes to make a – negotiation.'

Reilly smiled thinly. 'And who, I wonder, could have told you that, Colonel?'

'Someone who knows quite a lot about you. A Mr Asher.'

'Ah. May I?' Reilly held aloft his packet of small cigars.

The Colonel nodded.

'Thank you. So Mr Asher has been talking to you about me. I suppose I could be of some help in an emergency. Depending, of course, on how the – eh – negotiations were conducted.'

'Strictly between yourself and myself.'

Reilly nodded. 'That would be satisfactory.'

Maddox stood up and paced about the office, his hands clasped behind his back.

'It would also depend – to a lesser degree, of course – on how I would be recompensed.'

'Of course,' Maddox agreed, keeping up his tour of the office.

'And what you wanted me to do for you.'

Maddox returned to his desk and sat down, staring at the man opposite him, aware that he was about to implicate himself inextricably in the shadowy world of intrigue he detested. He put his elbows on the desk and folded his hands under his chin.

'Mr Asher has been kidnapped,' he said simply.

Reilly exhaled slowly, his eyes narrowing. 'I see.'

'He has been kidnapped by two people. I believe you know them both.'

'Indeed?'

'A young killer called Martin Deeley and a bookmaker named Mr Apple.'

Reilly found himself spluttering with laughter. 'Mr Apple? Kidnapped Asher? I can't believe that, Colonel.'

'Oh, I assure you it's true. He told me so himself not an hour ago.'

'Mr Apple told *you* he had *kidnapped* Asher?' Reilly asked incredulously.

'He and Deeley.'

Reilly shook his head, lost for words.

'They asked to meet me – or rather Mr Apple did – and they both arrived and told me. They're holding him somewhere – Mr Apple mentioned something about Asher being in danger of exposure, although I think he may have been trying to fool me – and they want to do a deal.'

'A deal. Yes. Yes, that is understandable.'

'You see, they know that a man called Corrigan was sent to give Deeley's name to us – '

'Why was that?' Seamus Reilly asked innocently.

'Because, as you well know, Reilly, he tried to shoot me when I was in England.'

Reilly looked hurt. 'Why should I know that, Colonel?'

'Because,' the Colonel told him, forced to smile at his effrontery, 'because you know everything that goes on.'

Reilly accepted this. He smiled.

'I suspect you even organized my assassination,' the Colonel said.

Reilly stopped smiling. He stared at the Colonel, saying nothing, his eyes blank.

'Anyway,' Maddox went on, 'they know Corrigan gave us Deeley's name. They know that we are now hunting for Deeley. They want to trade Deeley's safety for Asher's.'

Reilly nodded. 'And is that not reasonable?'

'No. It is *not* reasonable.'

'An eye for an eye? I always understood that was acceptable.'

'Not in this case.'

'Oh. This is special? No. Don't answer that,' Reilly said, holding up one hand. 'So where do I come in?'

'I want Asher found and released unharmed,' Maddox said.

'I see. You mean you want *me* to find Asher and release him unharmed?'

Maddox nodded.

'And in return?'

'You can have Deeley.'

Reilly grinned. 'We will have Deeley in any case, Colonel. We really don't have to negotiate with you to have Deeley. Martin Deeley is ours to do what we like with. However –' he paused to stub out his cigar in the ashtray on the desk, 'however, if Deeley *and* Mr Apple can be disposed of by us and we have your guarantee that no unnecessary – '

'No,' the Colonel said. 'Not Apple.'

'Then – ' Reilly raised his arms to indicate that, alas, he could see no further point in these discussions.

'But why – why on earth would you want Apple?' Maddox wanted to know.

Reilly leaned back in his chair, relaxing for the first time since he had been brought into the office. 'Colonel, you have your way of dealing with things, and we have ours. We have a – a passion for cleanliness. Some people call us the punishment squad, some call us the cleaners. Both have their truth, but the latter more so. We dislike leaving any loose ends, any threads that may unravel and lead to complications. One can't be squeamish, Colonel. Either a job is properly done or not at all, and if any operation is undertaken and not completed satisfactorily, then someone else has to pay. I don't intend to pay, Colonel.'

'And that's why Deeley – '

'Deeley, Deeley. Deeley is a nothing. A thug. A little killer. A good one – usually – ' Reilly presented the Colonel with the glimpse of a smile, 'but we have so many young men only too anxious to prove they can kill. The Deeleys of this land grow in every dung-heap in the city. Look in any house and you'll find one waiting to be discovered.'

'Dear God.'

'Which, incidentally, Colonel, is one of the reasons we will survive long after you have all given up in despair.'

'And if I give you Mr Apple?'

'I will give you Mr Asher – provided, of course, he is still alive.'

'I'm sure he is.'

'I meant by the time we find him.'

'Oh.'

'Do I take it we have reached an understanding, Colonel?'

Maddox bowed his head. 'Yes,' he said.

'We deliver Asher and keep Deeley and Apple?'

'Yes.'

'Excellent,' Reilly said contentedly, rising and straightening his jacket. 'I'd better go and see to things, then. Maybe we will meet again, Colonel.'

'I doubt it, Reilly.'

'Oh, you never know when we might need each other. After all, this is *my* country, Colonel. You are the outsider, and outsiders do tend to find themselves in hot water from time to time.'

'You have it all worked out, don't you?'

'Yes. Yes, I think we do. We have a lot of experience, you know. You can hardly expect to overcome us with a handful of uniformed schoolboys, can you? In a way I feel sorry for you all,' Reilly told the Colonel, and he sounded as if he meant it. 'It must be soul-destroying to be sent over here with no hope of achieving anything and every possibility that you will have to die. Oh, not you, Colonel. Not you. The unfortunate youngsters under your command are the ones I sometimes feel sorry for. We watch them all the time. If only they knew how easily we could kill them if we wanted to – why, you would have mutiny on your hands, if that is the word. Does it apply to the army?'

Maddox did not seem to hear the question: he just sat at his desk and stared unseeing at Reilly, watching him straighten his jacket again and smooth his hair with the palms of his hands.

'In fact,' Reilly went on, 'I suspect you would rather like to die, Colonel. And I understand that. You are not alone, of course. Life is so complicated these days, don't you think? It would be so much easier to shuffle out of it with a little glory than to live on admitting that one had made a shambles of it.'

'Glory.' Maddox heard himself say aloud sadly, and for one frightening second he wondered absurdly if Reilly had managed to penetrate the thoughts he had conceived a few hours ago.

'Unbroken glory,' Reilly went on, his choice of adjective making the Colonel even more uneasy. 'It's what we all seek, one way or another. We settle, most of us, for the reflected variety, but it's not quite the same, is it? It's the personal kind we want, that strange, unattainable something that will make people remember us. How awful it is that most of us will just die, be buried with a modicum of ceremony, and be quite forgotten. In a week it will be as though we never existed,' Reilly said thoughtfully. 'And maybe we never did exist. Maybe it's just the great illusion. It makes one wonder —' Reilly decided to wonder in silence. He stopped talking and looked down at the Colonel. There was something bizarre, something almost pitiable about the pair of them, facing each other, both locked in their cages of wishfulness, both feeling a curious sympathy for the other, both aware that this understanding was fleeting, was already dissembling, would, in the twinkling of an eye, appear (if Reilly was right), like themselves, never to have existed.

And perhaps Reilly sensed this; perhaps, too, he realized the danger in such thoughts, and how easily such compassion could be construed as weakness, for he now coughed abruptly and said: 'I will be in touch, Colonel.'

Maddox looked up. 'Yes,' he said. He cleared his throat. 'Yes,' he said again, and watched Reilly to the door. 'I'll have the sergeant see you home.'

Reilly smiled. 'Just out of here, Colonel. Once outside these walls I'll be perfectly safe. Outside here, I'm in my own territory.'

'Of course.'

So much for Reilly being 'made to present himself' to Mr Apple's friend, Colonel Maddox.

'Ah,' Mr Apple said, wondering what was coming next, wondering, too, where on earth he was being taken now that the car had been driven to the outskirts of the city and was making its way back again by a different route towards their point of departure. 'Ah, Colonel Maddox.'

'You *do* know him?'

'Oh, yes. I know the Colonel. A civilized man.'

'Quite,' Reilly interrupted, not, it seemed, anxious to discuss the Colonel's possible merits. 'And you have seen him recently I understand?'

'Yes,' Mr Apple agreed.

'Very recently.'

'Very recently.'

'And attempted to make – to come to an arrangement with him?'

'None too successfully, it would appear.'

'None too successfully, as you say.'

'Ah, well,' Mr Apple sighed, not, apparently, greatly perturbed.

Reilly made a clicking noise with his tongue. 'Why didn't you come to *me*?' he wanted to know, sounding offended, hurt. 'I've always tried to be your friend. You're supposed to call on friends in time of trouble.'

Mr Apple smiled. 'I could hardly have done that under the circumstances. I don't think Martin has a great deal of faith in you, Mr Reilly.'

'Martin? Oh, Deeley. Martin Deeley is not your concern, Mr Apple. You should never have concerned yourself with him. As it is, you have only succeeded in – '

'But Martin *is* my concern, Mr Reilly. He always was. He was my concern long before I met him. Before I met you. Before I was born.'

' – ?' Reilly scowled at this curious pronouncement. But he decided to ignore it, to let it follow his momentary compassion for the Colonel into oblivion. 'As it is, you have placed me in a most difficult, a most regrettable position.'

'I'm sorry,' Mr Apple apologized politely.

'Sorry? Huh. Your sorrow doesn't help *me*, Mr Apple. Your stupidity has forced me to give way to demands from Colonel Ma— '

'Oh, I'm sure you didn't give way too much, Mr Reilly. I'm sure you came out of it very nicely,' Mr Apple heard himself say, heard, too, an angry note in his voice. 'People like you always come out of things nicely. Somehow you manage to exploit the weaknesses and distress of others. You treat people like pawns. You shift their souls about in an evil game, crying brotherhood and patriotism and freedom and every other mindless cliché that fanatics have cried for centuries. And all the time you know what you are doing? I'll tell you what you are doing *Mister* Reilly: you are committing fratricide, you are crippling your country, you are chaining your people to the skeleton of horror and terror and hatred. That's what you're doing.'

If Reilly was taken aback by this unexpected onslaught he gave no sign of it. He seemed, indeed, to be mildly bored by it; he had heard it all before, and the more he heard it the less truth there seemed to be in it. 'Have you quite finished?' he asked coldly.

'Yes. I've finished.'

'Good. I hope you consider those words a fitting epitaph,' he said, and turned away to stare out of the windscreen. 'Pick up Deeley,' he ordered curtly after a moment.

The driver seemed to settle more comfortably into his seat following this order, and even the engine seemed to purr more sweetly now there was some definite destination. Only the men on either side of Mr Apple failed to change their attitudes: they sat stiff, tense and uncomfortable, an uneasy look almost of distaste on their hard, grim faces, as though they sensed that the man between them was doomed, was already dead.

The black Ford slid to a stop outside Mr Apple's house. Reilly gave the driver a wordless command, jerking his head in the direction of the house, making no attempt to move. Mr Apple watched the driver climb out of the car and walk smartly, openly and officiously round the side of the house. He appeared again almost immediately, gave a curt nod, and stood his ground, waiting.

'Bring him in,' Reilly said, without turning round. Getting out of the car, he walked briskly to the house.

The man nearest the pavement opened the rear door and got out, holding the door open, extending his other hand to assist Mr Apple.

Mr Apple took the hand and eased himself out, feeling a sudden dampness down his back. He smiled at this, or perhaps he was smiling his thanks to the man who helped him steady himself: whichever, he smiled and followed Reilly.

The first thing that struck him as he came in the kitchen door was that the kitchen table had been overturned. Afraid at what more ominous sights might await him, Mr Apple began to pick out trivial disasters: a cup and saucer, the former broken, on the floor. A pool of milk. Cornflakes, like giant sawdust, scattered near the sink. Slowly Mr Apple raised his eyes, trying, and almost succeeding, to blur his vision as he bypassed the forlorn figure seated on the chair and focusing on the three strangers who stood behind it. Yet, he noted, they were not all strangers: one of them, the tallest – and perhaps for this reason the most sinister – Mr Apple recognized as the man who had delivered occasional brown envelopes to the shop: he had one hand outstretched, holding the hair of the person in the chair. Mr Apple followed the line from the man's shoulder, came to the hand, lowered his eyes another fraction and came to rest on Martin Deeley's face. Immediately he flicked his eyes away (but not before he noticed the red weal running down Martin's jaw) and concentrated on John Asher, seated in the corner, a look of mixed apprehension, fear and defiance on his face, shifting constantly in his chair as though these slight movements would defend him from any attack from the man who stood behind him. Mr Apple turned his head and stared pointedly at Martin. He was touched to receive an exaggerated wink.

Reilly also looked about him and was displeased at what he saw. He snapped his fingers. 'Pick that up,' he snapped fiercely without indicating anything. Immediately one of the men behind Martin moved forward, looked about for aid, got it from the driver, and between them they lifted the table and set it upright. Then they retreated, looking absurdly humiliated.

Reilly balanced himself against one corner of the table, thinking. As usual, to help himself concentrate he lit a cigar, taking an inordinately long time about it, and it was not until he had inhaled and exhaled the smoke several times, had left the table and crossed the kitchen to the refrigerator, had leaned against this and satisfied himself that he had a clear view of the entire room that he said, shaking his head like a disillusioned father about to scold recalcitrant children, 'Why, oh, why do you fools *put* me in a position like this?'

In the silence that followed Mr Apple removed his hat and placed it on the table. This done, he paused, perhaps waiting to see if anything more was to be said; but as the silence continued he took off his overcoat, folded it, and put it on the table beside his hat, patting it a couple of times as though it were a friendly, nervous animal. 'Jesus!' he heard someone behind him exclaim. 'He's covered in blood!'

Reilly was immediately alert. He sprang forward, touched Mr Apple's blood-sodden jacket, rubbed his fingertips together and peered at them. 'Which of you – ' he began, looking furiously at the two men who had sat either side of Mr Apple in the car, both of whom glanced at each other, both shaking their heads in terrified bewilderment. 'Mr Apple – ' Reilly tried again.

Mr Apple turned to him and bathed him in a strange, contented smile. 'It is nothing,' he said. 'Just some old wounds. I had been expecting them to bleed soon,' he added enigmatically.

'Expecting them to?'

Mr Apple nodded 'Hmm. A small sign I've been promised,' he confided.

'A sign?'

'A sign.'

'A sign of what?'

'Ah, as to that, I'm not altogether sure. Death I think, but it hardly matters.'

Reilly took a couple of paces backwards, recoiled almost, a look of suspicious discomfort showing momentarily in his eyes. 'If this is one of your tricks – '

'Tricks?' Mr Apple swung round in amazement. 'Oh, no. It's no trick, Mr Reilly. As I said, it's my old wounds. Sefer always warned me they would bleed when – ' he stopped as Reilly demanded:

'Sefer?'

Mr Apple heard himself chuckle. 'A friend of mine. You wouldn't know him, Mr Reilly. He comes and goes. He's always on hand when I need him, though, aren't you, Sefer? Of course you are. Always there when I need you.' Mr Apple dropped his voice to a whisper. 'Thank you for the warning,' he said, gazing upwards.

Automatically, everyone looked upwards, and they were still gaping at the kitchen ceiling when Reilly shouted furiously: 'Shut up, Apple!' His whole body was shaking.

'Oh, I'm sorry,' Mr Apple apologized. 'I thought you asked – '

'Shut *up*,' Reilly said again more quietly, making a considerable effort to compose himself.

'Certainly,' Mr Apple told him, turning away, belatedly returning Martin's encouraging wink.

'You,' Reilly said gruffly to John Asher. 'Are you all right?'

'Yes,' Mr Asher replied.

'Take him out,' Reilly ordered. 'Is there a front room? Take him there,' he said, 'and keep him there. Don't let him out of your sight.'

Asher was lifted by his collar from the chair and frog-marched from the kitchen. As the door closed behind them Reilly crossed the room and took up a position in front of Martin, legs spread, hands clasped behind his back. Bending slightly, he said, 'Martin, Martin, dear, oh, dear, we had such high hopes for you.'

'Yeah,' Martin said, sneering. 'Real high.'

Reilly didn't like that, didn't like it one little bit, and a glint of bitterness entered his eyes. 'You know we cannot allow this random activity. We can't have people taking actions on their own without consulting us first.'

Martin shrugged.

'It disrupts the balance of things, Martin,' he went on. 'Makes everything so untidy.'

'Shame,' Martin volunteered.

'Yes. Yes, Martin. You're right about that. It is a shame. As you know, it always grieves me when I am forced to inflict punishment,' Reilly told him, shaking his head mournfully. 'But, as you also know,

I have my job to do.'

'Some job, Seamus.'

Reilly blinked several times. 'Yes,' he said. 'Painful, but quite necessary, as you well know. I had hoped you would be more understanding, would help me – '

Martin gave a huge guffaw. 'Jesus, Seamus, you really are something else. Look, I know fucking well you're going to kill me, so just get on with it. You don't have to give me all that old shit about how sorry you are. I've heard all that crap from you before.'

Reilly gave something approaching a smile and nodded his head several times. 'Yes,' he said finally. 'Yes.'

'Good,' Martin said, his voice defiant but the blood already beginning to drain from his cheeks. 'You all right, Mr A.?' he asked suddenly.

Mr Apple turned and stared at him, stared and nodded before coming over to him. 'Yes, Martin,' he said. 'Yes, I'm fine. I'm sorry – '

'Sorry? Why the hell should you be sorry, Mr A.? You said everything would work out. Well, it has, hasn't it?'

'Yes, I suppose – '

'No supposing, Mr A. It's worked out fine. I think this is what I wanted to happen. And I'll tell you something else, you mad old bugger. I bet you knew this was what I wanted all along.'

Mr Apple thought about a denial, but changed his mind: he smiled at Martin, bent down and took hold of one of his hands. 'Maybe,' he said, an odd crack in his voice.

'Hey, cummon, Mr A.,' Martin said gruffly, squeezing the bony fingers, 'I don't want any shit out of *you*.'

'No.'

Martin laughed. 'Jesus, I don't half choose my friends,' he said. Then he suddenly leaned forward and impulsively kissed Mr Apple lightly on the cheek. 'And thanks for being my friend,' he whispered.

Mr Apple knew he was crying, and he was content to let the tears course down his cheeks.

'Hey, quit that, you old fool,' Martin told him kindly. 'I feel terrific. You know, it's the best thing that ever happened to me in my life!'

'Oh, Martin –' Mr Apple began. There was so much he wanted to say, but as he searched for the words he noticed one of the men behind Martin start to screw a silencer on to the barrel of a revolver. He saw him point the gun at Martin's head and glance at Reilly.

' – and free,' he heard Martin say happily.

Mr Apple had just time to kneel down and extend his arms as the man fired. *Pfffft*, and Martin collapsed forward, the wooden chair slithering sideways and cracking against the wall.

Mr Apple cradled the warm body in his arms, pressing it against him, rocking it gently as though sending it into a comfortable and untrammelled sleep, muttering to it, only occasional words decipherable. 'Peace', was certainly one of them. And 'joy'. Then, strangely, 'with you soon'. And 'unafraid'.

Reilly turned away: he believed in grief, believed, too, that it merited respect and privacy. Grief, he thought, was a noble emotion, far surpassing such jaded ideals as love or honour. It was, he now told himself, grief that made people and countries great, set them apart, made them worthwhile, and he admired it all the more, he knew, because it was an emotion of which he himself was incapable. Mild sorrow was as far as he went: anything deeper had long since been gouged from his soul. Mildly he wondered about this, and was no nearer discovering a reason for it when he heard 'Christ!' exclaimed behind him. He swung round, half-expecting to see Martin Deeley standing upright, grinning at him defiantly. For a second he was relieved to see this was not so, yet what he did see was, for some inexplicable reason, more frightening, more – he could not find a word – more sinister. Mr Apple had keeled over, still clutching Martin Deeley's body in his arms, and now lay staring into space, unmoving.

'Jesus, he's dead,' the man who had killed Martin said in awe.

And he was almost right. Mr Apple was not dead, not quite, but he was certainly dying. Or perhaps he was, indeed, dead, and it was his gentle spirit that lingered for a moment, taking, as it were, a last, sad, baleful look over its shoulder. We have been watching you, voices said. We are well pleased, they added, as great black birds swooped in and seemed to raise him up, flapping their gigantic wings, causing the gathering mist to swirl about him. Ah, Mr Apple thought he heard himself sigh. He thought, too, that he could make out shapes, familiar shapes, hovering over him. Faces loomed, dark Mexican faces, pale Irish faces all appearing together, disintegrating, withdrawing. Hey, I feel terrific, was whispered to him suddenly, and he smiled, the smile freezing on his lips, remaining behind.

Reilly leaned down and felt Mr Apple's wrist. Rising, he nodded. 'Yes,' he said quietly. 'He is dead.'

'What do we do with them now?'

'Leave them be,' Reilly said, and walked to the window, gazing out, fixing his attention on a ginger-and-white cat that stalked an unsuspecting sparrow. 'Wipe the gun and put it in his hand,' he ordered without turning round, watching the cat crouch lower and cover the ground almost on its belly.

'Whose hand? Apple's?'

Reilly swung round, his face livid. '*Mister* Apple's,' he spat. 'It's *Mister* Apple to you, you thug,' he said vehemently, and turned back to the window.

He heard the shuffling behind him as one of Mr Apple's hands was released and the gun placed carefully in it; he heard, too, and winced at the small, helpless cries the sparrow sent up as the cat grabbed it, secured it in its mouth and loped off into the bushes.

'It won't fool anyone,' Reilly said quietly, glad that he had been able to compose himself. 'But that hardly matters.'

'We've done that, Mr Reilly. Anything else?'

Reilly turned and looked down at the two bodies, almost envying them their peaceful attitudes.

'You two take Asher and leave him outside St Enoch's.'

'Do we –'

'Just do what I said. Take him and leave him outside St Enoch's. Nothing else. And you,' he added, turning to his driver, 'you wait in the car.'

Alone, Reilly crossed the room until he stood directly over the bodies. For a while he seemed content just to stare down at them, unable to see Martin's face, which was buried in Mr Apple's shoulder, but seeing clearly and wondering at the smile on the old man's face. And there was something in that smile that made him feel it was directed at himself, not in any cruel, taunting way, but with a friendliness that moved him. It was as though Mr Apple was smiling in gratitude at an old friend, an old and trusted friend who had done him a great and wonderful favour. Reilly bent down and smoothed Mr Apple's hair and fixed his spectacles at a correct angle on his nose, making him, as he thought of it, respectable. Then he stood upright again and a smile came to his lips, perhaps in satisfaction at the neatness of his handiwork, perhaps just returning Mr Apple's. Then he turned on his heel and hurried from the house.

Mr Asher sipped his neat whiskey and eyed Colonel Maddox balefully: he was worried about the Colonel, worried that he seemed so morose, so distant, not at all what he had expected from one whom, he felt, should be in jubilant mood and celebrating his, John Asher's release. But it was not so. Maddox had welcomed him well enough and offered him a drink, but there was something about his manner that Asher could not quite put his finger on, and he thought about this as he waited for the Colonel to speak again.

'You say Mr Apple was *not* shot?'

'No, Colonel. Just Deeley. Apple seems to have died of a heart attack. I'll know more definitely in the morning.'

'And Mr Apple had the gun in his hand?'

'Yes. Put there, obviously. Made to look like *he* killed Deeley. Quite neat, really. Trust Reilly to give us a way out.'

'A way out?'

'Of course. We can write it off as a lovers' tiff. A pretty serious tiff I grant you. But – '

'Lover's tiff? Good God, John, they weren't – '

'No, of course they weren't, Colonel. But that's not what matters. We will simply *say* they were. Who's going to deny it?' Asher asked, pleased that things had worked out so well.

'But you can't go about saying that. It's so unfair,' Maddox said, sounding ridiculously petulant and proper.

'Would you prefer the truth to come out, Colonel? No, I thought not,' said Asher, noting the look of sudden consternation in the Colonel's eyes. 'Don't worry, Colonel. Leave it all to me. You won't be involved in any way. I owe you that much.'

'Yes,' the Colonel said, indifferently. 'And he was smiling?'

' – ?'

'Mr Apple was smiling?'

'Yes. Yes, he was,' Asher confirmed, smiling himself in surprise as he remembered the strange look of peace on the face. 'Beatifically, I suppose is the word.'

'Ah.'

'Holding Deeley in his arms – but I suppose that was another Reilly touch.'

'But you said something about blood? A lot of blood on his back, you said.'

'Hmm. Odd, that. We had a look at that in the mortuary. Very odd. He had a lot of little criss-cross scars on his back, and they all seemed to have opened for some reason.'

'Criss-cross scars?'

'Yes. As if he'd been whipped.'

'Reilly didn't – '

'Oh, no. They were old wounds. They had just split open. No obvious reason for it. Maybe it happens when you die suddenly. Like ejaculating when you hang?'

'Do you?'

'Do I what, Colonel?'

'Do you ejaculate when – '

'So they say.'

'And you think – '

'I don't know. A possibility, I suppose.' Asher sipped his whiskey again.

'And this is all you found of interest?' Maddox asked after a while, indicating a collection of exercise-books bound with tape that lay on his desk.

'Hmm. That's all. Seems to be a diary of some sort. I just glanced through it. Mad ramblings, if you ask me. Talks about his dreams and that sort of drivel.'

Maddox nodded, and stared at the exercise-books.

'I wouldn't bother with them, Colonel, if I was you.'

'No?'

'No. The best thing you can do is put the entire incident out of your mind. It's over and done with. I'll tidy up what needs to be done.'

'And that's all there is to it?'

'That's all there is to it.'

'Dear God. Two men die and are dismissed without a second thought.'

'That's the way life goes here, Colonel. Anyway, it's two we don't have to worry about any more. No more potshots at yourself,' he said airily.

'And now?'

'Now? Like I said, I'll tidy up.'

'You'll tidy up,' the Colonel repeated, but mostly to himself.

'Yes. I must say you arranged things very nicely, Colonel. It's very satisfactory to have someone like Seamus Reilly where we want him.'

'Seamus Reilly where we want him?' Maddox asked. He knew that he was repeating almost everything Asher said, but he succumbed to this willingly since it saved him a lot of thinking.

'That's right.'

'But I gave him my word there would be no repercu— '

'Ah, yes. You gave him *your* word, Colonel. But that hardly affects me, does it? I mean, I can't be held responsible for what you promise,' Asher said smugly. 'You don't really believe we could let that shifty little bastard get away so easily, do you?'

'Yes, John, I'm afraid I did.'

'Oh, dear,' Asher said. 'You are an innocent, Colonel. Anyway, not to worry, you'll probably be long gone from here before we have occasion to benefit from Reilly's situation.'

Maddox stared at the man across the desk. He suddenly felt very sick and very tired. His weariness outweighed his feeling of sickness, though, and in an odd way this consoled him. It numbed his thoughts, leaving only traces of sorrow – sorrow for what, he was not sure. 'I think I'd like to be alone, John, if you don't mind,' he said quietly.

' – ? Yes. Yes, of course, Colonel,' Asher said, finishing his drink and standing up. 'I've a lot of things to see to anyway.'

'Tidying up, I suppose,' Maddox said, immediately regretting his mild sarcasm.

Asher grinned. 'Yes, tidying up. I spend my life tidying up.'

'That's what Seamus Reilly told me. Cleaning up *he* called it, though.'

'Indeed?'

'Yes. You two seem to have something in common.'

'We do, don't we?'

'Yes, you do.'

Asher gave a short, sharp laugh that was really a snort. 'That's quite amusing when you think of it,' he said.

Maddox looked up at him with a long, mournful gaze. 'That must be what's wrong with me, John. I can see nothing remotely amusing about it. The two of you revel in deceit and corruption. I have never held either in very high regard.'

'Only because you've never before had to resort to them, Colonel,' Asher told him. 'Your nice, comfortable, Berkshire lifestyle doesn't lend itself to devious ways. We, however, have extraordinary lifestyles that demand extraordinary measures. You call it corruption and deceit, we call it merely wheeling and dealing. Wheels within wheels and deals within deals. It leads to only one thing – survival. Survival, if you want, of the fittest. The fittest in this case being the one who can deal the better hand, deal himself the aces. Seamus Reilly is now one ace in *my* hand, and I would be fool if I failed to use it,' Asher concluded.

Maddox closed his eyes and sighed, hoping that when he opened them again Asher might have gone. But: 'In a sense we play games,' Asher continued. 'Rather vicious, dangerous games, I agree, but games nonetheless. Games,' he added, 'that we know we really cannot win. That nobody can win.'

Maddox opened his eyes slowly and nodded.

'Yes. Well. I must be off,' Asher said. 'I'll let you know the results of those tests on Apple tomorrow.'

'Thank you.'

'Good-night, sir.'

'Good-night, John.'

And that was that: an official report would be on his desk in the morning, neatly typed, objective, inhuman, uncaring. As inhuman and uncaring as he himself had been when he agreed to Seamus Reilly's terms. But that had been done in the name of duty, had it not? Had been done for reasons beyond reproach, had it not? Certainly. Colonel Maddox leaned forward and stared again at the bundle of exercise-books before him. Poor old Arthur Apple, he thought. And poor old Matthew Maddox. Fools, the pair of them. Dreamers. Believers in ideals long since extinct.

Maddox pulled what John Asher had scathingly described as a 'diary of some sort' towards him, and flicked it open at random. He gazed at the words, letting them float up to him, it seemed, rather than actually reading them.

'...gloating in the grim and terrible slaughter, exulting in the destruction of those who only yesterday were children.' Immediately he closed the manuscript and pushed it from him roughly, feeling an unwelcome chill travel down his spine. He rose and walked to the window, to stare out at his reflection staring back: a gaunt face, grey and haggard. Death, he thought, death staring me in the face. He shuddered, shaken by his morbid thoughts.

Away across the city a milk churn, standing unobserved in the back of a parked lorry, exploded, sending shards of jagged metal screaming in all directions, ripping into flesh, rendering limbs useless, flicking life away with elegant precision.

'Sir?'

Maddox jumped and swung around.

'Sir. Another explosion, sir. A bad one. Some of our lads were caught in the middle of it.'

'Dear God.'

'At least five dead, sir. A lot injured.'

'The destruction of those who only yesterday were children,' Maddox heard himself say.

'Sir?'

'Nothing, sergeant. Nothing. Nothing at all. Just thinking what a useless, useless mess this all is.'

'Yes, sir.'

'You think so too, sergeant?'

'Sir?'

Maddox smiled sadly. 'Never mind. Never mind,' he said quietly, almost as though he were offering comfort to himself. 'It doesn't seem to matter.'

'No, sir.'

'I'll be down directly.'

'Sir!'

The Colonel indeed made as if to follow the sergeant down directly, but then he hesitated. He reached out and laid a hand on Mr Apple's strange manuscript, stranger now that he had read a few of the words. Those few words, though, had suggested that it contained nothing but a horrible truth, and for a time he seemed to be praying. Then he pulled himself together, straightened his shoulders, and marched smartly out of the office: out and away from the white shadows that haunted him, that tormented him and would, he knew, be there waiting for his return; out and away into the shrieking, frightened city.

LONELY THE MAN
WITHOUT HEROES

For Timothy Lynott

. . . and I despair as I watch them trudge aimlessly through their short days of youth. They are offered nothing, not even the hope of anything that is noble and good. Yet worse, there seems to be no one to guide them towards human dignity, no one for them to admire, no one worthy of emulation. A strange and terrible figure has risen from the ashes of discontent, a remorseless demon that beckons them down the road of violence that leads only to degradation and sorrow, but mostly sorrow. And those who should shine out and be admired are really creatures of the night, hugging the shadows, fearful of recognition. Alas, there are no heroes now, and I weep as I see the awful, lonely plight of these young men without heroes.

'The Visions and Visitations of Arthur Apple'

· ONE ·

COLONEL MATTHEW MADDOX crossed the narrow gravel path, wincing as the small, sharp stones penetrated the flimsy soles of his carpet slippers, and walked very slowly towards the huge chestnut tree under which his wife insisted on breakfasting now that summer was officially here. He intensely disliked eating out of doors, detested the tiny opaque insects that lay in wait for him and committed suicide in his coffee. Still, he admitted to himself, it was easier to put up with their intrusion than to face an argument with Nancy.

'Good morning, dear,' he said quietly, easing himself into the deeply-cushioned garden chair and closing his eyes for a second as though the effort of the short walk across the lawn had strained him considerably. His long, lean body had grown still gaunter since his return from Belfast, and involuntary retirement had aged him. True, he had been sleeping badly of late – the nightmares and persistent spectral visits from the dead Arthur Apple doing little to help – but that was only partly to blame for his rapid physical deterioration. Curiously, the peacefulness of his Berkshire home made him nervous, and he had developed irritating little spasms and jerks that seemed to occur with embarrassing regularity just as a cup or glass was halfway to his mouth.

Nancy Maddox lowered the *Telegraph* a couple of inches and peered at her husband over the rim of her tinted glasses. 'You haven't shaved,' she scolded by way of greeting.

'No,' he confessed.

'I do wish you would. You really are letting yourself go to seed, Matthew. And those clothes – you look like a country bumpkin.'

Maddox diplomatically kept his eyes closed and contented himself with a tiny, inaudible sigh. She was right, of course. Still, he liked his scruffy old tweed trousers, his Viyella shirt, and his fawn, multi-darned old cardigan – perhaps because they were some of the few remaining garments he had actually purchased himself. Without warning he gave a chuckle, and immediately regretted doing so as Nancy pounced.

'And what is so funny?' she demanded.

'Oh nothing.'

'Don't be so infuriating, Matthew. There must be something. Only a total idiot could laugh at nothing.'

He hesitated before answering. 'I was just thinking that all the time I was stationed in Belfast you were trying to persuade me to get transferred nearer home. And now that I am home – permanently – I seem to do nothing but get on your nerves.'

'And that's supposed to be funny?' Very deliberately Nancy Maddox put down her newspaper, folding it carefully, and removed her spectacles.

'The truth is – and you well know it – the truth is you have never come back from that damned Belfast. You're absolutely besotted with that dreadful place. Dear God – even in your sleep you mutter about that disgraceful Arthur Apple and those other shifty little horrors you had to deal with. Look at last night. You fell asleep in front of the television and immediately you were ranting about that wretched monster who tried to kill you.'

'I –' he tried to interrupt.

'Well, if you had stayed awake you would really have had

2

something to prattle about. You can read all about it in here,' Nancy told him bitterly, tossing the paper on to her husband's lap.

Maddox watched her go, allowing the enormity of her accusation to find anchor in his soul. She was probably right. What was it Asher had said to him? Or was it Seamus Reilly? Just set foot on the soil of Ireland and you'll be crucified to it for ever? Whichever, he had had a point. Without doubt, there was something about the futility, the sorrow, the shame, even the bravery of the place that made it cling to one's mind – dismissed from time to time, of course, but always managing to claw its way back, leaving one guilty, not so much for having missed the chance of doing something, but for being willing to do nothing at all.

He fumbled about in the pockets of his cardigan for his spectacles, and swore mildly as he realized he had left them on the table by his bed. He held the newspaper awkwardly at arm's length and squinted: BIZARRE DOUBLE KILLING IN BELFAST. An old familiar feeling of dread scuttled down his spine. Then his hands started to tremble uncontrollably. It was as though he was about to read something he already knew, something he had seen in his constant nightmares, something whispered ghost-like in his ear by old Arthur Apple.

In a city where sectarian killings are almost commonplace, police disclosed last night the discovery of what is being described as a ritual murder. The victims have been named as Colonel Guy Sharmann, 44, of Army Intelligence, and Fergal Duffy, 22, a suspected IRA sympathizer.

Maddox groaned quietly to himself, seeing again the horror of the night, imagining the bodies being dumped on the steps of the cathedral. So they had finally reported it!

Both bodies were found shot on the steps of St Patrick's Roman Catholic cathedral, their arms linked. The Colonel had been killed by a single bullet. Duffy had been shot several times in the head and chest. What is particularly confusing about this latest atrocity is how the bodies came to be placed in such a public place without anyone noticing it. . . .

He smiled sadly at the naïveté of the reporter. Without anyone noticing indeed! He hurled the paper from him on to the grass. 'Dear God,' he whispered, holding his head in his hands. He saw in his mind's eye the cold-eyed Sharmann, so confident and smug that he would wipe out terrorism once and for all. Sent, indeed, as Maddox's replacement, sent to 'pick up the pieces', no doubt. Precious few pieces he'd be picking up now. He lay back in his chair, allowing the flickering images of his brief meeting with Sharmann to hold his attention.

– Sharmann, sir, he had introduced himself, standing stiffly to attention and looking ridiculously pompous and absurdly young.

– Ah, said Maddox. They told me you'd be coming.

– I'm to replace you in Belfast, sir.

– I see.

– They felt it might be beneficial if we had a talk.

– Did they, indeed? And you?

– Me, sir?

– Do you think it would be beneficial?

– I'm sure it will, sir.

– Well, in that case you better sit down – and don't be so damned formal, for heaven's sake.

– Thank you.

– A drink?

– No. Thank you. I don't.

– Very admirable, Maddox said dubiously. Your first tour in Northern Ireland, is it?

– Yes.

– Oh dear.

– Why 'oh dear', sir?

4

– I've no idea. I just wonder what you'll make of it.

– There's nothing for me to make of it, is there? I'm going there as part of my duty. To do a job, that's all. I'll have my orders and I'll simply carry them out.

Maddox smiled, helping himself to a large Scotch. That's just what I thought, he admitted. But it doesn't seem to work out that way over there, you know. I had a colleague – dead now, I'm afraid – who served for years in the Congo. He loved to say, 'the thing you've got to remember, Matty –' he always called me Matty, Maddox explained in a slightly surprised tone – 'the thing you've got to remember is they're not like us white folk'. You *could* apply that philosophy to Northern Ireland. They're definitely *not* like us, but that is something we've never wanted to recognize. Proselytize, make unto your own image and conquer – how does that strike you?

Colonel Sharmann sniffed.

– You see, Maddox went on, we're told here that we are just a peace-keeping force, but once you get into Belfast you find you're – ah, well, over there you are an invasion force. And they have a point, you know.

Sharmann generously overlooked this mild treason. – Whatever you say, sir. However, to be more specific. I'm told you worked closely with a man called Asher. An RUC Inspector.

– Not as closely as I thought, it seems, Maddox said quietly. Yes. Yes I did. As I suppose you will. You two might get on very well together. You both have –

– How would you see the man, sir?

– See him?

– Yes. How does his mind work. I wondered –

Maddox opened his eyes. He wondered if Sharmann had found the time to discover how Asher's mind worked. Hardly. Old Arthur Apple must be laughing his head off if, indeed, spirits had heads to laugh off. He heaved himself out of the chair and stretched, grimacing as the pain of arthritis scorched his shoulder. For a while he gazed about him, his eyes

5

finally settling on the newspaper, its pages flapping in the light summer breeze. I won't take it in to the house, he thought. Better to let sleeping dogs lie.

· TWO ·

ALMOST THREE MONTHS to the day after Martin Deeley, the young man suspected of attempting to assassinate Colonel Maddox, had been buried, two men sat watching a video-recording of the funeral. They looked at the screen intently and listened carefully as the reporter interpreted what was happening; the running, brick-hurling battle (euphemistically described as the 'disturbances') had broken out only when the assembled RUC forces had demanded the removal of the black beret and gloves from the coffin, refusing to allow the cortège to proceed until this was done. In his practised, modulated voice the reporter succeeded in making this provocative demand sound perfectly reasonable, almost scolding the deceased for daring to flaunt his preferred allegiance. Even as the coffin swayed alarmingly on the shoulders of the jostled bearers he seemed to suggest that this Provo ritual displayed petulance and naughtiness while the RUC intervention was something mildly heroic and certainly quite proper.

Brigadier Brazier stopped the tape with his remote-control device.

'Right. I think we can stop it there. We'll go through it again in a minute. I just wanted to set the scene. I think,' he went on, wagging a conspiratorial finger, 'we could both use a drink. I have your tipple, Guy, never fear,' he added, clearly pleased with himself, launching himself upright and making for the circular oak table between the two long windows of the enormous room. 'Perrier water and a slice of lime, isn't that it?'

Colonel Guy Sharmann inclined his head. 'Thank you, sir,' he said quite pleasantly although a small flicker in his eyes showed he was irked. Why he should feel guilty for not drinking alcohol he could not imagine, but he did, as, indeed, he did about so many things in his life.

'I wish I had your powers of abstinence,' the Brigadier said, none too convincingly. 'You don't smoke either?'

'No, sir.'

'Good, clean living, eh?'

'Something like that. Yes.'

The Brigadier busied himself pouring drinks, allowing himself a large gin.

'You've been to see Colonel Maddox?'

Sharmann nodded, pleased to get down to the matter in hand. 'Yes. I went up to his home to Berkshire the day before yesterday as instructed.'

'And?'

'And nothing really. The man's a wreck.'

'Yes. Well. He's had his problems. He wasn't really the right man for Belfast although we weren't to know that. Too . . . too . . . well, sensitive, I suppose. Got too involved. It happens. Still, he must have told you something about what lies ahead for you?'

Sharmann shook his head impatiently. 'Not much. He rambled on a bit about Deeley,' he admitted, waving a hand that dismissed as unimportant the occupant of the coffin frozen on the television screen. 'And about the other one – Arthur Apple who was found dead with Deeley.'

'Ah, yes. Yes, he would. And Reilly? Nothing about Seamus Reilly?'

'The Provo? Yes. He mentioned him. Seemed to quite like

8

the bastard. Kept insisting that Reilly had a point of view, that he was true to his ideals. Huh. Ideals!'

'And Asher?' the Brigadier prompted.

'Yes. He –' Sharmann seemed to sneer as he paused to take a sip of his Perrier. 'He said that he had only met two men in his life whom he mistrusted totally. Eichmann was one – apparently he met him briefly in Israel before his trial – and Asher was the other.'

What Colonel Maddox had actually said was that, until he had met Colonel Sharmann, he had only met two men he totally mistrusted. But Guy Sharmann was not about to disclose any such reflection. Indeed, Colonel Guy Sharmann, son of the late Brigadier General Sir Anthony Wedgewood Sharmann, educated at Harrow and Sandhurst, and with the music of Mozart the only passion in his life, went to some pains to keep secret almost everything about himself. He was obsessed by anonymity. Nothing about his appearance was remarkable: no distinguishing features, no scars, no moustache, no rings. His blond hair was cut short and brushed straight. He was of average height and unremarkable build. He was forty-four but looked a little younger. Although he did not know it, when his name was put forward for the operation about to be discussed his main asset was the fact that he 'blended' so completely as to be almost obscure. In fact the assembled brass had tested this quality by taking it in turns to try and give an accurate, recognizable description of him, and each had failed.

'You know you'll be expected to work closely with Asher?'

'So I understand.'

'But not too closely – you also understand.' The Brigadier smiled wickedly.

'Yes.'

'You are, in fact, an experiment that might or might not work. God knows we've tried just about everything else.' Brigadier Brazier sighed. 'Mind you,' he went on immediately, 'I want you to know that I was one of those opposed to this entire operation. In my view it's quite wrong for us to

9

engage in such tactics, but the powers that be are starting their annual panic. If only the Provos would keep their bombs and bullets on their side of the Irish Sea it would make our lives so much easier. It's when they get too close that the politicians feel they have to get in on the act and tell us what should be done. So, ostensibly you are simply replacing Colonel Maddox, with Captain Little as your two IC.'

'And Barton?'

'Sergeant Barton won't join you for about ten days. He's – eh – practising.'

Sharmann seemed to enjoy the turn of phrase and smiled. 'I see.'

'We don't seem to have had a lot of use for his particular talents recently and he wanted – as he put it – to get his eye back in.'

'Yes.'

'You see,' Brigadier Brazier went on, picking up his drink again and staring at it, aware that he was explaining himself and the situation badly, probably because his military conscience found the whole scheme totally distasteful, 'if we just put you into Belfast without an official posting you would be spotted immediately. Anyway, we tried that with the SAS and they didn't achieve a great deal, did they?' Rivalry, or was it jealousy, crept into his voice. 'Our hope for this operation is that the IRA intelligence – something, by the way that never ceases to amaze and terrify me – will think us incapable of conceiving such –'

'I *do* understand, sir,' Sharmann interrupted, peeved that his superior should think these explanations necessary.

'Yes,' the Brigadier said, obviously relieved. 'Good. Anyway, as far as anyone is concerned your special activities have nothing whatsoever to do with the Army and we don't want to read in our Sunday newspapers that they do. Of course, in the eventuality of your being exposed, any authorization from this side will be most strongly denied at the highest possible level. No doubt if you succeed you'll all get medals – possibly posthumously but that rather depends on yourself.'

Once again Colonel Sharmann allowed himself a tight smile.

'Dear God, how I hate these undercover operations,' Brigadier Brazier said, meaning the hatred to be only a thought and covering his alarm at having spoken aloud by drinking deeply from his glass.

Sharmann pretended not to notice, dismissing the reaction as typical of the Brigadier's generation. 'Who actually knows about the operation, sir?' he asked.

'You and me. It will be up to you to tell Little and Barton as much as you think is necessary.'

'Nobody else?'

'Nobody you need know or worry about.'

'And in Belfast?'

'Absolutely nobody.'

'Asher?'

'Good God no. Not even the Chief Constable has been told – against my judgment, I might add.'

'Good.'

'But don't you underestimate Asher. Maddox is probably right – the man is evil. But he's nobody's fool, and like the IRA he has his own alarming network for gathering information – and from the most unlikely sources. One slip and Asher will have you. And another thing that Maddox seems not to have mentioned: Asher and Reilly are not above collaborating in schemes for reasons of their own. Our friends in Whitehall and those bog-trotters in Dublin scoff at the idea and refuse categorically to believe that the security forces and the IRA collaborate. But we know quite positively that they do on occasion. And why not if it pays dividends to both sides. We've done the same on occasion, I remember. Cyprus for one. War of any kind breeds strange bedfellows, I can tell you.'

'I'll remember.'

'Right. Let's look at this tape again and you can see a couple of the characters in motion. They're in your file but the more images you take with you the better.'

The video-tape went skidding back to the beginning of the report and the two men settled down to watch.

The coffin was carried from the drab terraced house. It was draped in the tricolour, the black beret and gloves carefully placed in the centre, and below these, Seamus Reilly's tribute: a tiny posy of violets. Six masked men in paramilitary uniform followed the coffin from the house, three on either side. Immediately the hearse, laden with flowers, their stems twisted into the shapes of crucifixes and hearts and circles, each arrangement with its own black-rimmed card to identify the sender, eased into position. Then the mourners formed up in ranks, hundreds of them, only a few looking mournful, the majority seeming more harassed than sad, more like the observers of some pageant in imminent danger of going wrong.

The Brigadier stopped the tape again, getting up and walking closer to the television. 'That's Reilly,' he announced, stabbing his finger at the screen.

Colonel Sharmann leaned forward, squinting at the frozen frame. '*That's* Reilly?' he asked, his voice rising incredulously. 'That little runt?'

'Oh yes. That's Seamus Reilly. Small he may be but he's godfather of all he surveys. Strange how small men are often the most powerful – and the most dangerous.'

'Oh, I think we will cope with Seamus Reilly all right.'

The Brigadier returned to his chair. 'I wouldn't get over-confident. He's very well protected. It might seem that he wanders as he pleases through the streets but I can assure you he is watched and covered every inch of the way, as we know to our cost.'

'We'll get him,' the Colonel insisted, staring almost vindictively at the dapper little man in the long black overcoat and the Anthony Eden hat, the gloved hands folded reverently in front of him.

'I'm sure you will. Unless, of course, he gets you first, Colonel.'

Sharmann started as if such a possibility had never crossed

his mind. Indeed, Seamus Reilly looked as harmless as Rip van Winkle, his lean face radiating understanding and benevolence. It was only when one concentrated on the eyes that one got some idea of the man. They were icy, conveying no emotion whatsoever; eyes that never joined in when his lips smiled. 'I'll put him top of the list,' Colonel Sharmann decided firmly.

'I would have thought it wiser to start with one of the more vulnerable targets. You might have a very long wait before you catch Seamus Reilly off guard, and I'm sure you won't want to wait too long before you swing into action,' he added, shocked at the words he had used and at the anger in his tone.

'We'll see.'

'Yes. We will, won't we?'

'Anyone else of interest on that frame? Who's that – the one beside Reilly?'

'That is Clement Donovan. He's on file. We're not altogether clear about his importance. Maybe he's of no consequence.'

'But he's there. At the funeral. He must be.'

'So are two or three hundred other people. We can't just decide they're all important and wipe out the entire Catholic population.'

'He's front rank,' Sharmann pointed out defensively.

The Brigadier shrugged. 'Someone has to be,' he said patiently.

For a moment it seemed as though Sharmann was going to argue the point, but something made him think better of it, and he relaxed back in his chair.

'Further on we have someone else,' the Brigadier said quietly, watching the Colonel's eyes and waging a small mental bet with himself that they would light up at his statement. He almost laughed aloud when he won. He set the tape in motion again and watched the unmourning mourners plodding along in silence for a few seconds. 'There,' he announced suddenly. And then: 'Good heavens. I never noticed that before. The lad seems to be crying.'

13

'The one in the red anorak?'

'Yes. Extraordinary.'

'What –'

'Oh, sorry. Just that I hadn't noticed it before. Yes. Fergal Duffy. Close friend of Deeley. Our information is that he was involved when Deeley kidnapped Asher. Nothing proven, of course, but our source is usually reliable.'

'So why's he in the file?'

The Brigadier looked surprised and uncomfortable. He pointed to the ceiling. 'They,' he said, visibly relaxing as he passed on the blame, 'say it is expedient. Duffy is, in their words, potentially dangerous. They want what they see as his threat nipped in the bud. Besides, his – eh – removal would close, once and for all, the Deeley matter.'

'I see. Good.'

Sharmann's acceptance of the explanation pleased the Brigadier. 'And that's it, I'm afraid. The others on file didn't attend the funeral for one reason or another.'

'No matter.'

'I didn't think it would – matter, I mean.'

'Well, sir, if there's nothing else, I'd better get going,' Sharmann announced as he stood up.

The Brigadier gave a wry smile. 'You do amaze me, Guy, if you'll permit an old man to say so.'

'Sir?'

'You're so casual about the whole thing. No. I'm sorry. Not casual. That's quite the wrong word. So unruffled, more like. So calm and matter-of-fact.'

'I don't –'

'What I mean is – quite between ourselves, you understand – doesn't it worry you at all?'

'Why should it, sir?'

The Brigadier sighed and shook his head. 'Maybe I'm just old-fashioned. That's probably why I'm stuck here instead of on active service. I just find it so very difficult to come to terms with all the intrigue and double dealing that you youngsters take in your stride. I was thinking about it while I was waiting for you to arrive this evening. I thought to myself how horrified I would be if someone asked me to get involved in the sort of skulduggery we're asking you to get mixed up in.'

'You're beginning to sound like Maddox, sir.'

'Am I? Well, maybe he and I are of the same breed. Maybe we were brought up too rigidly on things like honour and –'

'Honour is fine, sir, when you're dealing with honourable men,' Sharmann interrupted. 'But this lot –' he tapped the blue file tucked under his arm – 'this lot wouldn't know the meaning of the word.'

'You think not? Maybe you're right. Anyway, I'm glad it's you and not me who makes that decision.'

'Yes, sir,' Sharmann heartily agreed.

There seemed nothing more to be said. 'Well, good luck and do be careful.'

'Thank you, sir.'

Alone, Brigadier Brazier finished his drink and decided his mood was depressed enough to warrant another. Halfway across the room, however, he changed his mind, moved to the telephone and stared at it thoughtfully. Finally he picked up the receiver and dialled.

'Brazier,' he announced brusquely. 'That's in order. It's now in the lap of the gods,' he added and replaced the receiver.

With no hesitation this time he made his way to the drinks table and poured himself another gin and tonic. 'To the gods,' he said aloud, toasting the air. Outside, a car door slammed, an engine was gunned and wheels spun on the gravel. He waited until the noise of the car had disappeared. 'And may God help us,' he added to himself with some feeling. He finished his drink and left the room, carefully switching off the television and the light, and closing the door behind him.

· THREE ·

T IM PAT DUFFY was a small, thin, overlookable little man in his late forties. Almost bald on top, he had taken to growing what hair he had very long and combing it across his head with uncharacteristic vanity, plastering it into place with a green, sweet-smelling jelly that came in a fancy, ribbed pot. It was a petty enough deception that worked quite well in making him appear more like an older brother to his only remaining son until the wind blew. Then the strands were prised from his scalp and flopped greasily about his neck and shoulders, giving him the look of a rather pathetic, ageing hippy. He needed glasses but never wore them, admitting, but only to himself, that to do so would be acknowledging the middle-age deterioration in his body.

At 7.30 in the morning, some two months after Brigadier Brazier had toasted the gods, Tim Pat sat at the scrubbed deal table in the kitchen of his terraced house in Clare Street taking sips of strong black tea, and puffing on one of the under-stuffed cigarettes he rolled himself. Every so often he would cough raucously, scolding himself after each attack by shaking his head and muttering 'You're killing yourself, you fool.'

Across the table, still in her dressing-gown but with her hair combed and her make-up already neatly applied, his wife sat watching him, her arms folded, her hands cupping her elbows. It was a little ritual that had developed over the last few years, quite unintentionally. By any standards, Rose Duffy was a plain woman, about five years younger than her husband, yet from time to time with a look or a smile or a girlish toss of her head she could give the impression of someone about to be beautiful. People tended to describe her as a 'lovely' woman while recognizing that this attribute had more to do with her serenity than her physical looks. She was deeply religious, believing unswervingly in her Catholic God. For Rose, God, or Jesus as she preferred to call Him, was there to be spoken to, to be consulted and asked the occasional favour, and to be revered, certainly. He was not to be fawned upon or treated like a poltergeist that shimmied His way through her life, meddling and obstructing and threatening. Rose Duffy was one of those fortunate creatures who enjoyed their prayers, seeing them as simple conversations with a friend who was prepared to listen, and it mattered not one whit that Jesus seldom seemed to lift a finger to help her with her troubles.

'Isn't Fergal up yet?' Tim Pat asked suddenly, setting off another rasping cough.

'He's awake but not up, I don't think,' Rose replied. 'I heard the radio in his room as I was coming down.'

'Oh.'

'Why?'

'Just wondered.'

'You're worried –'

'No. No I'm not worried,' Tim Pat insisted quickly but there was little conviction in his voice.

'Yes you are, Tim. So am I. He's changed so.'

'He'll get over it soon enough.'

Rose shook her head dismally. 'That's just the trouble. I don't think he will. Ever since that friend of his was found shot he's been – I don't know – so morose. So cold and unlike himself.'

'Well, it's always a shock when someone you know gets killed. And he's still young. Death is bound to make a bigger impression on him than it would on us.'

'I didn't even know he *knew* that Martin Deeley, let alone was friendly with him. Dear God, I wouldn't have had a night's sleep if I'd known he was mixed up with that sort of person.'

'He only knew him, Rose,' Tim Pat said patiently. 'You can't grow up here in Belfast and not know –'

'But he was a killer –'

'So they say.'

'You don't think so?' Rose asked hopefully as though the answer would restore her peace of mind.

'I didn't say that.'

'They say he was the one who tried to kill that army officer in England. He –'

'They say. They say. Rose, would you ever grow up? It's easy to blame killings on those who are already dead.'

Rose Duffy stood up, thought for a moment and then sat down again, resuming her exact position. 'You know what Fergal told me?' she asked in a whisper.

'Not until you tell me.'

'He told me that Martin Deeley saved his life once.'

Tim Pat looked only mildly surprised. He shook his head and smiled reassuringly. 'He imagines things. Exaggerates.'

'He was very positive about it.'

'You know him – always was a convincing story teller. You said so yourself. Makes a story really live, you said. Anyway, you've got to make allowances. He's naturally upset. We all say crazy things when we're upset.'

'He was so serious about it. It didn't strike me he was ranting at all.'

'Look –' Tim Pat said, adopting a pleading, logical tone – 'don't you think we'd have heard about it if Fergal's life had ever been in any danger?'

18

Fleetingly Rose looked relieved. 'Yes. Yes I suppose we would.'

'Of course we would. Don't you worry. He'll be back to his old self soon enough. He'll be right as rain before you know it. You know what kids are like. They're like animals – they forget their pain quickly.'

'If only he'd smile. You know, I haven't seen him smile since the funeral.' She sighed. 'It's like he became a tired little old man overnight. I wouldn't mind if that Deeley was worth it. But –'

Suddenly and with surprising agility Tim Pat was on his feet, his wooden chair skidding backwards on the linoleum and crashing into the fridge. He rested his hands on the table and leaned across, glaring down at his wife, a strange and frightening fury in his eyes. 'Everyone is worth it,' he screamed in a whisper. 'Everyone. I don't ever want to hear you make a stupid remark like that again.'

Rose gaped at her husband's furious face. She was shocked, even a little frightened, yet at the same time she had an almost uncontrollable desire to giggle: anger somehow made poor Tim Pat seem preposterously comic, as though small men and clowns had no claim to rage. Only once before had she seen him so furious and that had been over some trivial, albeit uncharitable remark against hunger strikers.

'I only meant –'

'I know what you meant,' Tim Pat interrupted, flicking his tongue over his dry, thin lips. 'Let's drop it.'

'I'm sorry –'

'Yes. Forget it.' Tim Pat pushed himself upright, his face relaxing into its familiar creases, his eyes into their glazed, watery regard. Still standing, he finished his tea in one gulp and spent several seconds extinguishing his cigarette. Then he stretched himself as luxuriously as a cat, groaning pleasurably as his muscles tensed, walked to the window and peered out. 'Looks like more sodding rain,' he announced, his voice flat and composed again.

'Yes. They said last night there'd be more.'

'I'll just nip down to the shop before it starts.' In the hall he spent a few seconds flattening his hair with the palms of his hands, grimacing into the mirror that was the centrepiece of an ornate imitation Chinese coat-stand, a wedding present from an aunt long since dead. 'Rose?' he called. 'Where's my coat?'

'Oh Lord. I forgot. I left it in to be cleaned. It was filthy and I want you to look smart tomorrow.'

For an instant Tim Pat stood stock still, a curious look of fear and suspicion in his eyes; but almost immediately he relaxed and smiled knowingly at his reflection, scolding it by shaking his head and pulling an absurd face. 'Hah,' he said aloud. 'I don't think they'll care too much what my coat looks like at the milk depot.'

'Maybe they won't, but I do. You were lucky to get the job and there's no need to turn up on your first day looking scruffy. They'd think I didn't look after you.'

'I suppose if I'm nifty I can get to the shop and back before the rain starts.'

'Take Fergal's coat. There's no point in your risking getting drenched. That's all I need – you down with pneumonia. And wear a hat. That wind is still bitter enough.'

'Right. I was going to anyway.'

Dressed, then, in his son's distinctive red anorak and wearing his Tyrolean hat, he closed the front door behind him, pressing against it with his back to make sure it was firmly shut. He hesitated for a moment to zip the anorak closer about his neck, and smiled to himself: the fact that Rose still accepted his new-found job as a stroke of luck took a weight off his shoulders and helped put a spring in his step. Then he frowned: the thought of the repercussions there would have been had she known that the job at the milk depot had been as carefully chosen for him as he for the job made the nerves in his stomach jitter. He shook his head abruptly, dismissing the thought, and set off down the garden path, stopping to admire the red and yellow tulips that were doing their utmost to open in the pale, grey light. As he opened the wrought-iron gate he noticed the dark green car parked on the opposite side of the street, its engine running. For a moment he faltered, immediately averting his eyes as the stranger stepped from it: it was safer, he knew, to act normally and notice nothing untoward if one could manage it.

Thirty seconds later Tim Pat Duffy was dead, his body almost severed in two by the ferocity of the bullets that ripped through it with such force that they carried particles of his flesh with them as they embedded themselves in the front door.

For what seemed a very long time (certainly until well after the assassin had returned to the car and been driven off at high speed), the street remained eerily quiet. An old tabby tomcat in the process of cleaning a front paw froze in an attitude of stone; small birds, sparrows mostly, that had been foraging for fat spring grubs flew on to the rooftops. Even the wind that had been building up seemed to hold its breath, the echo of the gunfire lingering threateningly in the air. At last, a dog barked: immediately another, taking courage, joined in. It was only then, very slowly, like timid nocturnal animals caught in a trapper's brilliant light, that people appeared in doorways, stiff and wide-eyed, but none of them venturing beyond the imagined safety of their porches, where possible clinging to one another, holding hands or linking arms as if this contact with the living, however slight, would ward off any evil attached to this sudden intrusion of death.

Remarkably, Rose Duffy was one of the last to come out on to the street. She did not rush to her husband's body screaming her anguish as might have been expected: she walked very calmly towards it, her arms folded across her thin, almost breastless chest, her eyes unblinking and vacant, her lips clamped in a thin, tight, expressionless line. There was something about her stark, precise, emotionless approach that carried with it an air of acceptance, of inevitability almost, that made the killing seem more than usually appalling.

It was only after she had been standing over the body for several minutes, wondering at the look of mild surprise on Tim Pat's face and amazed, in a curiously detached way, how lifelessness made him shrink and seem so small and vulnerable, that Fergal dashed from the house wearing nothing but his trousers. Perhaps it was genuinely the shock, or perhaps the despairing bewilderment he felt that made him seek refuge and consolation in his mother's arid attitude. Whichever, he stood quietly beside her, staring as vacantly as she at the body, showing no sign of grief or outrage or even disbelief, feeling incongruously only a mild irritation that his anorak had been ruined. He sensed but ignored the slowly converging neighbours. He heard them mutter to each other, whispering their religiously tainted phrases culled from the stock reserved for such occasions, repeating them willy-nilly as though rehearsing their future words of condolence.

'Dear God,' someone said.

'Oh Holy Mother,' came the response.

'Dear God above,' the first voice intoned as if the Almighty's location lent strength and potency to the invocation.

'Sweet Jesus.'

Rose Duffy sniffed quietly to herself and straightened her shoulders. She glanced up at the sky, blinked, and ran her fingers through her hair, tucking some loose strands behind her ear. It struck her as strange, as outrageous, that this, the third such killing in the district in as many weeks, seemed to move her less than the other two. She had wept freely and unashamedly as she had comforted the two other widows, moaned with them and shared their terrible plight. But now, standing here over her own murdered husband, she felt detached, somehow uninvolved. It was as though, the thought struck her and in a way frightened her, her dead husband was no longer hers precisely because he was dead; it was almost as though any expression of grief or anguish would be seen as gross, unwarranted and impertinent. To rid herself of these confusing thoughts she glanced at her son and saw him shiver.

'Run along inside and put some clothes on,' she told him automatically, her voice absurdly calm and friendly.

Fergal stared blankly at his mother.

'Go in and get dressed like a good boy. You'll catch your death of cold.'

'But —' Fergal tried to protest.

'Fergal, don't but me,' Rose snapped sharply. 'Your father is dead and you standing there half naked and gaping at him isn't going to bring him back. There's simply nothing we can do for the moment. Now will you please go in and put some clothes on?'

Possibly it was the brutal truth of the statement or possibly the sudden realization of the sadly ridiculous figure he presented that made Fergal obey. 'You'll be all right?' he asked.

Rose smiled at him, and touched him gently on the cheek. 'Yes. I'll be all right,' she said kindly, and watched him pad back up the garden path, watched, too, the neighbours fall back and let him pass, averting their gaze in the way that people do who feel that staring at sorrow is akin to gawking at cripples.

'Better get her inside and fix her a cup of tea,' Rose heard someone suggest finally, smiling inwardly at the way they had of talking as if she could not hear. 'The shock can't have reached her yet and she'd be better off sitting down when it does.'

'What about —' a man's voice started to ask.

'Betty's gone to call the ambulance.'

'Oh.'

'Someone better stay.'

'I'll stay,' the man volunteered. 'You get her inside. I'll stay out here.'

'And send those children away.'

'They've seen it all before —'

'They don't have to see it again.'

Rose found herself being manoeuvred away, a neighbour either side of her holding her firmly by the elbows, shepherding her into the house. Oddly, through it all, she realized that a cup of tea was exactly what she needed, remembering suddenly that she had been on the point of having her breakfast. Indeed, she would probably have been munching contentedly

23

on her slice of toast had she not, for some reason that now took on a tragic melancholy, wandered through into the sitting-room to watch her husband set off for the shop. Meekly she allowed herself to be steered away from the body, away from the scene that cried out for sorrow – an emotion she could not yet bring herself to evoke. As she climbed the four steps that led to the front door she allowed each step to underline an incident in the sequence of events: the shooting, her first sight of the body, her instructions to Fergal, the advancing, inevitable cup of tea. Suddenly, imperceptibly at first, she felt herself getting giddy. She wanted to scream out that she didn't want tea, dammit. She wanted no part of this neighbourly kindness. She wanted no consolation, no holding of hands, no sympathy – nothing that might make her cry. Least of all did she want the barren, lonely, aching days and nights that stretched out so bleakly ahead of her. What she wanted was simply to go back to bed again and wake up before all this had happened, to prevent Tim Pat from going out. She felt herself about to cry and immediately, firmly and consciously, she controlled herself and bowed to the regulations in hand, accepting the ritual of the tea as though to disrupt the order of the ceremony would be intolerably unkind, even cruel.

And so, as she sat in the armchair (that creaking, overstuf-fed, uncomfortable armchair always regarded as Dad's chair from the day they bought it together at auction) staring at the single bar of the electric fire that someone had thoughtfully switched on, perhaps in the hope that it would remove some of the chill from the awful event, Rose Duffy became painfully aware of how little she actually knew about her husband. It struck her as nothing short of amazing that she had lived for more than twenty-five years with him, had borne and reared his three sons, seen two of them emigrate only to die in a gruesome, freak boating accident in Manitoba even before their first cheery letter had reached Belfast, had watched him grow older and become a little more secretive in the way age seems to make people, watched him adopt new foibles and irksome, petty little habits as he slowed down, and still

24

managed to know nothing intimate about the man she had married.

'I've called the police,' a woman announced breathlessly, possibly the reliable Betty.

'For all the damned good *they'll* be.'

'They've got to be called.'

'Huh.'

'Anyone see them?'

'Who?'

'The killers.'

'Probably UDR bastards.'

'You saw them?'

'Me? No. But –'

The tight, snapping conversation swirled about over Rose's head, jabbing at her brain. 'I don't think it was,' she heard herself say, glancing quickly about her as though startled by the sound of her voice, intending the words only as a thought. 'I don't think it was,' she repeated if only to cover her confusion, the rattle of her teacup on her saucer heightening the silence that immediately surrounded her remark.

'What makes you say that, Rose?' someone who sounded like Vera Quilly asked.

'He *looked* different. He –'

'*You* saw who did it?'

'Yes. Oh yes. I saw him. I just happened to come in here and watch Tim Pat go out. I don't know why. I just did,' she concluded apologetically with a tiny embarrassed smile.

'And you actually saw who fired the shots?'

Rose nodded.

'And?'

'Leave her be,' someone protested.

'Yes. Can't you see she's –' someone else started to agree.

'No. It's all right,' Rose said. She closed her eyes and sat silently for a little while. 'There were two of them,' she explained eventually. 'One who did the shooting and one who stayed in the car. Driving, I suppose. The car was dark green. Ordinary. Squarish. The man who got out was nicely dressed.

In a suit. He wore a tie and –' Rose paused as though a new thought had struck her. She shook her head, frowning, keeping her eyes tightly shut. 'There was something different about him, something –' Again she floundered as she tried to enlarge the flickering negatives in her mind, gently banging one knee with her fist. 'Something *different*. No – not really different. Something just not right,' she decided finally, sealing her judgment by nodding, opening her eyes and finishing her tea. She put the cup and saucer carefully on the floor beside her.

'Something not right?' a voice behind her prompted.

'That's right. Something out of place.'

'Out of place?'

'Yes.'

'What was –'

'I don't know. No. I think I *do* know but I can't identify it for the minute. Just a little something. I remember thinking to myself that it was unusual. Maybe I imagined it. Maybe it was nothing. I don't know. It might come to me later.'

And it did, but much later. Before it came to her another month had passed and three more men were murdered.

· FOUR ·

IT WAS LATE in the evening before Clare Street returned to normal. All day long people came and went: the ambulance keening its way through the small mean houses, jolting into and out of the potholes, swerving to avoid the rubble left after some long since forgotten battle, collecting the body and gliding away; the RUC in droves, questioning, photographing, questioning again, alert to being lulled into a gruesomely baited trap, watched and covered all the while by the Mobile Unit; the soldiers, from 3 Para this time, their growling armoured vehicles playing havoc with the traffic, 'assisting' the RUC, it was claimed, but clearly they were combing the area for reasons of their own, ready to report back anything suspicious to TAC HQ; the press preparing their nightly news report, joyful that they had something to send to London, scurrying for eyewitnesses; and civilians, drawn inexorably by the fascination of death, eyeing and pointing to the bloodstains on the footpath. Only when darkness came was the street left deserted, returned to its residents.

In his room Fergal Duffy lay naked on his bed, staring at the cracks in the ceiling. No matter how hard he tried he could summon up no sorrow at the death of his father: he was so drained of sadness by the killing of Martin Deeley, it was as though there was simply no remorse left in him for anyone else. His friendship with Martin had been brief, but, as far as Fergal was concerned, intense. It had started with what he saw as an heroic gesture, although Martin had always dismissed this notion as ridiculous. Nevertheless, if not exactly heroic it had certainly been brave and generous. It had happened when Fergal was twelve. . . . The never-ending abuse rolled off the backs of the Paras as their heavy boots thumped down the mean little street in the Old Park district. At first the small crowd of men and women, among them Fergal and Martin, jeered and swore. But the slow, steady progress of the Paras towards them roused their simmering fury and, as if by magic, petrol-bombs appeared – already ignited, it seemed – and were hurled. Instead of retreating the Paras charged, shifting direction constantly, their eyes scanning not only the handful of bombers but the rooftops and windows. Outnumbered, the crowd took to its heels. Fergal found himself running alongside Martin, his breathing already rasping asthmatically from his lungs.

'Come ON,' Martin had shouted at him.

'I can't go any faster,' Fergal had gasped.

'Shit. Here –' Martin Deeley had reached out and in one gesture scooped Fergal off his feet and threw him over his shoulder, carrying him through the complex of back alleys that separated the rows of shabby two-up, two-down houses, through the stench of outside toilets, to safety.

'Now piss off out of here,' he told Fergal.

'Hey thanks, mister. You saved my life.'

'Shit,' Martin told him.

'I won't forget you, mister.'

. . . And that was the start, but the friendship was to be shattered before it could thrive. Yet still Fergal loved Martin Deeley, perhaps more so now that he was dead and unable to mock in his arrogant, bluff way, unable to scoff at this affection. And Fergal had made an uneasy, ghostly hero of Martin, imagining all the awesome deeds they could have achieved together had he not been killed. He talked to this understanding spectre, and convinced himself Martin was beside him as he fell asleep, his comforting arm thrown over his shoulder.

Fergal swung his legs off the bed, and sat there, his head in his hands, his thin, white body looking undernourished in the ungenerous light. He rocked himself back and forth as though to alleviate the persistent shame of feeling no grief for his father. The small transistor radio by the bed crackled as some vehicle on the road outside interfered with the air-waves, then settled down again to allow Billie Holiday to continue her plaintive song – 'I hold out my hand but my heart will be in it . . .' Fergal listened to the radio until the song ended. Then, abruptly, he stood up, stretched and gazed about him, seeking solace from the eyes of the pop-stars on the posters that covered one wall. Billy Bragg. Status Quo. Boomtown Rats. He turned and eyed the white plastic Christ on the crucifix above his bed. Martin hadn't had much time for God and, in a scared way, feeling disloyal, Fergal hoped that God had shown more time for Martin.

– You don't really pray, do you? Martin had asked him.
– Sure I pray.
– You're crazy.
– Don't you?
– Me? Not on your life. You know what I do? I go in there and I look up at that crucifix and I think what a waste of time it all was, going through all that rigmarole to save the souls of men! Well, a pretty lousy job He made of it is all I can say.
– You shouldn't talk like that.
– I'll go to hell?
Fergal nodded.
– You know something, Fergal? I've been in hell all my life. Any change would be a change for the better.
– But you go to Mass.
– Of course I go to Mass. Everyone goes to Mass, you fool.

That doesn't mean much. Half the people who go to Mass go because they're afraid not to. Afraid what the neighbours will say. Anyway, going to Mass shows which side you're on, doesn't it? Seamus Reilly goes to Mass and don't try telling me he's a bloody saint. To tell the truth, I've enough trouble getting on with this life to start worrying about another. You don't even know if there is another one.

– Of course there is.

– Oh yeah? Great. I hope you enjoy it.

While Fergal was debating with his conscience, in a room over a sweet-shop in the Old Park district of the city, an emergency meeting of the Intelligence Council of the Provisional IRA was being called to order. At such short notice only five members of the Council had been able to attend, but the presence of the Chief of Staff underlined the meeting's importance. A short, stubby man with spectacles, he sat slightly apart from the others, his forefinger occasionally stroking the scar that ran the length of his right cheek. When he spoke his voice was soft and gentle, 'fatherly' it had once been called.

'Well, Seamus,' he began, mellowing the intensity of his gaze with a benevolent gesture of one hand.

'I don't understand it,' Reilly confessed. 'I simply don't understand it. Nobody can have known about Duffy. Even he didn't know until the day before yesterday.'

'Somebody knew,' the Chief of Staff pointed out. 'Somebody was told,' he added, a note of menace vying with the tolerance in his voice.

'That can't *be*,' Reilly insisted, longing for the support of one of his small cigars but abstaining, aware of the Chief of Staff's abhorrence of smoking.

'I'm afraid it can, and it has jeopardized our intended operation in no small way. You realize we will have to suspend our –' the Chief of Staff paused long enough to allow his eyes to flick about the room – 'our activities in a certain field until you come up with some answers?'

'Yes. Of course.'

'And that failure to find out who killed Duffy and how they knew about him in the first place could have unpleasant consequences closer to home?'

Reilly winced. 'I'll find out. You can be sure of that. If it's the last thing I do.'

'There's an answer to that, Seamus.'

Reilly tried a half-hearted smile, and while he digested the words the Chief of Staff took the time to polish the lenses of his spectacles.

'It should be easy enough to find out,' Michael Condon said somewhat brashly. 'I mean, all you have to do is question the people who knew about Duffy's appointment.'

The Chief of Staff replaced his spectacles carefully on the bridge of his nose, easing them into place with one finger, and smiled thinly. 'The only problem about that is the fact that only two people knew about Duffy – apart from Duffy himself, of course. Seamus here, and myself. So either it was one of us who shot Duffy, or we told someone about him and arranged to have him killed.' He turned to Seamus Reilly again. 'You say you only told him what we wanted him to do the day before yesterday?'

'Yes. The day before yesterday. I told him myself.'

'What exactly did you tell him?'

'Simply what we – you and I – had agreed to tell him, that he would be employed by the milk depot and that he would deliver the –' Seamus stopped uneasily.

The Chief of Staff waved his hand. 'No, that's all right.'

'– he would deliver the weapons at the stops with the milk.'

'Had *we* delivered anything to *him*?'

'No. Nothing. That was to take place tomorrow.'

'Well, that's something. And there was nobody who could have overheard?'

Seamus Reilly looked aghast. 'Of course not.'

'His wife?' the Chief of Staff persisted. 'And he has a son, doesn't he? Could he have –'

'No. There was nobody else in the house when I told him.'

The Chief of Staff shook his head and took to tracing his scar again. 'Has *anybody* any suggestions?' he asked.

'SAS?' someone suggested.

This really seemed to annoy Seamus Reilly. 'Of course not,' he snapped. 'They could *not* have known. Besides,' he was emphatic, 'we know exactly what the SAS are up to at all times.'

'Would there be any link between Duffy's death and the killing of Brennan and Fogarty?' Michael Condon lobbed into the air.

'Well?' the Chief of Staff asked, turning to Seamus. 'Could there?'

Reilly shrugged. 'I suppose it's just possible. Unlikely, though. I mean, Brennan and Fogarty were well known and active. Duffy was different. He'd been sleeping for five years, dammit. And it still doesn't explain how someone knew about Duffy so quickly.'

'It's strange though, isn't it,' the man who had suggested the SAS as a possibility put in, 'that nobody has claimed responsibility for Brennan and Fogarty. It leaves us, really, with three unexplained killings.'

The Chief of Staff raised his eyebrows at Reilly.

'It does,' Seamus felt bound to agree.

'Could there be some new group in?' Michael Condon tried.

'You mean some sort of assassination squad?'

'Something like that.'

Seamus Reilly shook his head. 'They've tried that. Anyway, we'd have spotted them by now.'

'Well, somebody's having a whale of a time at our expense,' the Chief of Staff remarked. Despite the levity of his words, he was obviously not amused. He glanced at his wristwatch. 'I have to get back to Clones tonight so I think we may as well sum up what little we have. Firstly, there may be a link between all three killings. Secondly, someone must have found out we were about to use Tim Pat Duffy. Third, they can only have found that out within the past forty-eight hours. On the other hand there may be no connection between the killings, which would indicate that Duffy was a separate, special target. Agreed?'

Only Seamus Reilly said 'Yes.' The others nodded.

'Well, Seamus, it's up to you then.'

'Yes. It usually is.'

'And we need a result on this one. And quickly.'

'I'll do my best.'

'I'm sure that will be good enough.'

Across the city another meeting was taking place. Colonel Sharmann sat in his office in TAC HQ, furious. Across his desk stood Captain Little and Sergeant Barton, waiting for him to speak. 'Well,' he said eventually. 'Say something.'

Captain Little coughed. 'I'm sorry, sir. We –'

'Sorry! Christ Almighty! Only our third bloody target, the simplest one of the lot and you two have to go and cock it up.'

'We didn't know –'

'You're *supposed* to bloody well know. Jesus God!'

'He looked like his son –'

'Oh sure. He's twenty fucking years older than his son and he looks just like him,' Colonel Sharmann stormed, small flecks of spittle gathering in the corners of his mouth.

'He had the son's anorak on and he wore a hat.'

'Great. So if there were fifty people in red anoraks wearing hats you'd have shot the bloody lot, would you? Christ, you're marvellous.'

'And he was the same height. We couldn't see his face.'

'You couldn't see a damned thing, if you ask me.'

'It was a genuine mistake, sir.'

'There's no such thing.'

'We could hardly ask him for identification, sir.'

Suddenly the Colonel burst out laughing, throwing back his head, swaying wildly in his chair, guffawing as though the Captain's remark was the funniest thing he had ever heard. 'No, I don't suppose you could,' he managed to say at last, wiping his eyes. 'I don't suppose you could.' He leaned his elbows on his desk, gasping, taking time to compose himself once more. 'Shit. It doesn't matter a damn anyway. He was probably a Provo. Just tough on him if he wasn't. Still, it'll make getting the son that much harder.'

'We'll get him, sir.'

'I know we will. But he'll have to wait. Jesus, what a way for the little bugger to get a reprieve!'

'There are others?'

'Others? I'll say there are. Plenty. No news of that damned Reilly though.'

'He'll surface.'

'I want that bastard *now*,' Sharmann shouted, thumping his desk.

'Yes, sir.'

'Right. Barton you can turn in.'

'Yes, sir. 'Night, sir.'

'And next time for God's sake try and get the right person.'

'Yes, sir. Thank you, sir.'

'Good night.'

''Night, sir.'

Colonel Sharmann waited until the Sergeant's footsteps had well receded before asking: 'How was he?'

Captain Little looked momentarily surprised. 'Fine.'

'Good. Didn't seem – bothered?'

'No. Asked no questions. Just did as you told him.'

'Almost,' Sharmann could not resist the jibe.

Little smiled. 'Almost.'

'Excellent. I just wondered. He's been at it a longish time. Cyprus. Aden. Sometimes people like that develop a conscience. I've seen it happen. Anyway, we'll just have to be a *bit* more careful in future. Dammit, we'll have the whole bloody population wiped out if we're not careful. Not that that would be such a bad thing.'

Captain Little said nothing.

'And nobody spotted you?'

'Not that I know of. Someone might have seen us from one of the windows, but out of uniform we look rather different.

34

And probably someone did see the car but we've dumped that.'

'Good. By the way, Asher's been in touch with me about it, you know. Seems to be a bit concerned for some reason. He's coming to see me in the morning. Eleven-thirty. No doubt he'll tell me all his troubles then.'

'No doubt.'

'Well, I'm for bed.'

'Yes, sir. I better make for bed too. Good night, sir.'

Inspector John Asher tossed restlessly. He was a man who liked to have things neat and tidy and pigeon-holed, and there was something going on in the city that worried him. Three killings in as many weeks. And the shooting today . . . strange. Nobody had admitted to seeing or hearing anything, but that was inevitable. They would have him believe that they came out of their little homes and, hey presto, the body was just lying there. It was par for the course. What disturbed him especially was the reason behind these killings. Even in Belfast, despite what the know-alls in Dublin and London liked to believe, there was always a reason. Yet for this latest in particular there seemed to be none. Duffy had no record. No known connections with any organization. On the face of it he was just an out-of-work, harmless nobody. And yet . . . and yet. John Asher's methodical mind could not accept this. 'There's always a reason,' he said aloud, thumping the feathers in his pillow into shape and settling down again.

Rose Duffy tiptoed from her bedroom and down the landing, pausing to listen for a second outside Fergal's door before going downstairs to the telephone. She checked the code for London and dialled, primping herself nervously in the mirror as she waited for her call to be answered.

'Hello?'

'Hello? Declan? It's Rose. I –'

'Hello? I can't hear you. Who –'

'It's me, Declan. Rose,' Rose Duffy said, speaking louder, glancing up the stairs hurriedly.

'Rose? Hey, how are you? It's a bit late for you to be calling. How are you?'

'I'm fine. Declan, listen. Can you come over? Tim Pat's been killed.'

'Tim Pat what? Killed? How?'

'I don't want to go into all that now. He was shot. Can you come over?'

'Oh Jesus. Sure I'll come over. Is Fergal all right?'

'Fergal's grand. Upset of course, but he's fine.'

'I'll catch the first plane in the morning.'

'No. No, Declan, don't do that. Come the day after tomorrow, will you?'

'If that's what you want. Why not tomorrow?'

'I want tomorrow alone with Fergal. You understand?'

'Sure. Sure, I understand. Okay. The day after tomorrow. I'll come straight to the house.'

'I'll have your room ready. And thanks. Thanks, Declan.'

'Don't be silly. You're sure you're all right.'

'Yes.'

'Good.'

'I'll see you then. 'Bye.'

Declan Tuohy leaned back against the wall and stayed there for quite a while after Rose had rung off, his eyes closed, the receiver still in his hand, growling at him. The call had come. His failure to escape would be completed by this voluntary return. Declan laughed to himself and replaced the receiver. He was still in the clutches of Belfast and he could no longer pretend that his literary career had taken off. Still, he had achieved some small fame as a reporter and he was held in some esteem by Fleet Street and in particular by *Insight* magazine to which he was contracted. Nevertheless it was all a far cry from the young man who had written a little poetry and won a little award and whose name had been mentioned with reverence in literary circles for a short while. That Declan

Tuohy, they said, will be another Yeats, you mark my words. Hah.

He glanced at his watch, then picked up the phone and dialled quickly. 'Hello? Ken? Sorry to disturb you so late. It's Declan. I've got a problem. I've got to go away for a few days. Maybe longer. My brother-in-law has been shot in Belfast.'

'Jesus, I'm sorry. Is it serious?'

'He's dead.'

'Oh Christ!' the editor of *Insight* exclaimed. 'Christ, I'm sorry, Declan. Of course. Stay as long as you want, but you just mind yourself over there. They're crazy bastards.'

Declan gave a wry chuckle. 'Not that crazy, Ken. But I will mind myself. And thanks.' He walked quickly into his bedroom and pulled his suitcase from the top of the wardrobe. He was an expert packer, and had almost finished when the phone rang.

'Hello, Declan, it's me again. Ken. A thought struck me.'

'Yes?'

'Since you're going over there anyway I wondered if you might have the time to –'

Declan had almost expected this. 'You're a callous sod.'

'No, really. It doesn't matter. I just thought that since you're going to be there anyway, and if you have some time on your hands –'

'Ken, what is it you want?'

'You remember that diplomat chappie who was found dead with a gun in his hands and an IRA thug in his arms, about three months ago? We thought at the time there might be more to it . . .' the editor's voice trailed off hopefully.

'We decided there wasn't.'

'We could have been wrong.'

'We weren't.'

'I'm not so sure. I mean, in conjunction with the rumours we've been hearing . . .' Again his voice soughed upwards, insinuating unforeseen possibilities.

Declan took a deep breath. 'If I've time,' he said flatly.

'Of course. Only if you've time. Good man. Now that

Colonel who was retired pretty damned quick after the incident – Maddox, wasn't it?'

'Yes. Maddox. What about him?'

'I've found out that he's a friend of a friend of a friend. If – well, I could arrange for you to see him before you went, I think.'

'Oh could you. Jesus, you *are* a scheming bugger, Ken. Where is he?'

'At his home. Berkshire. It'd be a nice drive,' Ken cajoled. 'I still have a feeling there is something in it. They hushed it up so damned quickly.'

'They hush everything up quickly when it's to do with Belfast. Haven't you noticed? The Home Office likes to keep the peasants in the dark. What they don't know won't worry them. Anyway, we'll see now.'

Rose Duffy curled herself up in bed, staring wide-eyed into the darkness, willing it to wrap itself round her. It was only now, alone and without Tim Pat beside her, without the smell of his body, without the snorts and coughs he gave before he finally slept, without, too, the annoyance that he would sprawl across the bed and accidentally thump her into wakefulness, that the full extent of her loss and loneliness dawned on her. What was most curious was that the love she had for him when they were first married, the love that had swept her off her feet and made her float into her first pregnancy, the love that had gradually dried up and become more a kind of affable tolerance, now came sweeping back over her. Isolation – that was the word. She was the widow of a murdered man – not at all the same thing as just a widow. Not in Belfast at any rate. She was now, she thought, one of the untouchables: on the one hand oddly respected, on the other shied away from as though in fear of contamination. She knew other women who had gone through what lay ahead of her, had seen them age and withdraw into the isolation of their souls. It was the horror of this that now, quite unexpectedly, made her cry.

· FIVE ·

I T WAS, IN FACT, five minutes past eleven when Mr Asher arrived at Colonel Sharmann's office. He was dressed in grey flannel trousers and grey herringbone sports jacket, a navy raincoat over his arm. He looked tired. 'Good morning, Colonel,' he said politely.

'Good morning, Inspector.'

Asher grimaced and sucked in his breath audibly. 'I do –'

'Oh yes,' Sharmann interrupted impatiently. 'I forgot. *Mister* Asher.'

'Just Asher will do.'

'Very well. Asher. Take a seat.'

Mr Asher chose a chair and pulled it closer to the desk, setting it at an angle so that the light from the window did not shine directly in his face. It was all a far cry from the days when Colonel Maddox had been in charge: the small office had been repainted, the furnishings renewed, the dust and clutter that had given the room the beguiling security of a solicitor's office had been swept away. Still, mysteriously, despite the efforts to evict his spirit, something of Maddox lingered, and for a moment, squinting, Asher imagined him, tall and gaunt, and utterly confused, staring paternally across the room at him.

You frighten me to death, John, he seemed to be saying. You frighten me to death . . . Mr Asher blinked. 'May I?' he asked, holding up his box of black cigarettes that Maddox had called his 'smelly little trademark'.

Sharmann scowled but shrugged. 'If you must.'

Asher took his time and lit his cigarette carefully, blowing his first lungful of smoke towards the ceiling. He felt he had won a round against the Colonel, and relished the victory, however humble. He disliked the new Colonel. He objected to his attitudes. He resented his lofty unwillingness to listen to suggestions. Most of all he detested his snide remarks that hinted at the RUC's ineptitude. Without meaning to he yawned widely. 'I'm so sorry,' he apologized, trying to cover his embarrassment with a little laugh, and making a great show of patting his mouth. 'I slept very badly last night,' he explained. 'For some reason I kept thinking about that shooting in the Shankhill yesterday.'

'I would have thought you'd be used to such things.'

'Yes. We're used to them, Colonel. But it doesn't stop us thinking about them. We don't just dismiss murder with a wave of our hand. And this one – you've heard about it, of course?'

'Of course,' Sharmann snapped petulantly as though suspecting the question had been intended as a reflection on his intelligence. 'Well?'

Mr Asher raised his eyebrows. 'Well?'

'Why should this particular shooting stop you sleeping?'

'Oh. Because there's something odd about it. You see, Colonel, there was no reason for it.'

'No reason?' Colonel Sharmann loaded the two words with derision. 'No reason? Since when did that lot need a reason to kill each other?'

When he replied there was no mistaking the cold anger in Mr Asher's voice. 'Always. There is always a reason for any killing that takes place in the province.'

'What a load of rubbish. I –'

'You'll forgive me if I contradict you, Colonel,' Mr Asher

interrupted, keeping his voice icily calm, refusing to allow his fury to get the better of him. 'It is not rubbish. And, if I may say so, you are hardly in any position to judge – yet. You have been here – what is it? – three weeks? A month? Hardly time enough for you to understand the rules.'

'Rules!' Sharmann scoffed. 'You're not trying to tell me –'

'Oh, but I am, Colonel. There are very strict rules,' Mr Asher pointed out, 'and all the players accept them and adhere to them – whichever side they are on. And in a sense it is a game we play. A deadly and senseless game, if you will, but a game nonetheless. And really *you* should be grateful that it is, Colonel. You should be particularly grateful that we have rules. You see, if there were *no* rules, if killings were allowed at random, then, I'm afraid, that lot, as you call them, would make short change of both you and us.'

Colonel Sharmann looked as though he was about to explode. 'You –' he began.

Mr Asher interrupted. 'You simply don't understand,' he said very slowly, giving a small despairing gesture with his hands. 'Why do you think, with all your military power and know-how, with all your intelligence and all your patrols, why do you think the Provos are still alive and well and thriving? They know everything about you – you being the British Army,' he explained, and was momentarily puzzled by the flick of what looked like fear in the Colonel's eyes. 'And they usually know every move you make long before you make it. You can come here with your Paras and your SAS and your God knows what – and you know what the Provos do? They laugh. That's what they do. They laugh. And when you pat yourselves on the back because some tawdry little informer gives you a scrap of information – that he's usually been told to give you anyway – and you make some arrest or find a little cache of bomb-making equipment, they laugh. They laugh their bloody heads off because for every informer you have they have two, and for every Provo you kill they – well, Colonel, read the statistics.'

41

Colonel Sharmann stood up and walked to the window. He stared down and around him, seething. The worst thing, he realized, was that Asher was probably speaking the truth, although he was certainly not about to admit it. He swung round. 'You mean to sit there and tell me that –'

Mr Asher held up one hand as if he were stopping traffic and was amazed at how effectively his little gesture worked: Sharmann stopped talking immediately, leaving his mouth partially open. 'I'm simply pointing out the facts, Colonel. And that is what has me worried about yesterday's shooting. All the rules seem to have been broken. In the first place Duffy has no form. He's on no file – not ours, not the Army's and, I'm reliably informed, not the IRA's. Also, more than twenty-four hours have elapsed and nobody has claimed responsibility. And *that* is most odd,' Asher stated, shaking his head and frowning. 'You see, in order to protect ourselves if we do have occasion to kill someone both we and the IRA will claim the responsibility almost immediately. There are variations, of course. It is sometimes expedient that the Provos admit to one of our activities and we have occasionally reciprocated, but responsibility is *always* claimed. By someone.'

'Jesus!' the Colonel exclaimed, returning to his chair. 'You make it sound as though you were hand-in-glove with the bloody terrorists.'

Mr Asher smiled indulgently. 'In a sense we are, Colonel. How else do you think we could have avoided wholesale slaughter? That is precisely what I meant when I said you had no idea of the rules. Anyway, that's why Duffy's murder is so intriguing. It's almost as though – ' Mr Asher paused to light another cigarette, using the cloud of smoke as a screen through which to watch the Colonel. He decided to back-track. 'It makes the third unclaimed killing recently, and that is unheard of. It is as though,' he went on, swinging back to his original idea, 'it is as though someone or some group unknown to us as yet had decided to move in and destroy the equilibrium we have established.'

Colonel Sharmann felt a small ticking in his stomach: he

concentrated his gaze on Asher's face, making it as cold as possible, but said nothing.

'Anyway,' Asher went on, 'it's a police matter. It need not concern you. And my sleepless nights are my own.'

Sharmann decided silence was still the best option.

'Still,' Asher continued, brightening a little, 'they won't last for long,' he said almost cheerfully. 'We always get to the truth in the end, you know. Sometimes it takes us a while, but we get there, plodding along in imitation of your good British bobbies. And I happen to know the Provos are as bewildered by these killings as we are. Especially Reilly – Seamus Reilly, I mean. You'll know about him, of course?'

'Of course.'

'It's his job to see his boys don't step out of line and he gets most perturbed when they do. He's most anxious to exonerate his side, so if we can't find out the answers Reilly will, you can be very sure of that.'

For an instant, in a small, uncontrollable action, the Colonel's eyes flicked to the bundle of files on his desk: immediately he looked away again, an almost undetectible flash of annoyance crossing his brow. But Mr Asher saw the look and noted the Colonel's uncharacteristic reluctance to meet his eyes. He stared at the files, unblinking, like some music-hall telepathist hard at work, as if he was soaking up their contents with intense psychic powers. Momentarily, and without any foundation he could yet imagine, he felt within himself that peculiar, particular warning that twenty-five years of police work had taught him to recognize and respect. But he controlled the urge to confront Sharmann, and waited.

'I don't like it. I don't like it one little bit. All this *we* this and *we* that. Christ Almighty, Asher –'

Mr Asher widened his smile generously. 'Yes. It must be confusing. Of course you're never told *that* side of things before you're sent over to – eh – keep the peace, are you?' he asked. 'Perhaps even the great and wonderful bodies in Whitehall don't know,' he added, savouring the thought with mild satisfaction. 'Anyway, you've nothing to worry about.

We'll –' Asher paused wickedly to let the word take effect, '– get the answers. We'll even give you the credit if you like.'

Colonel Sharmann seemed on the point of apoplexy. 'I don't need any damned credit for your –'

'Just an offer, Colonel,' Asher said kindly, clearly enjoying himself and the reaction his little taunts were getting, and alert to the fact that he was uncovering interesting weaknesses in the Colonel's rather thin armour. 'We're a very friendly, hospitable people we Irish, you understand. We do our best to make all our foreign visitors feel happy.'

Sharmann glared across the desk, slowly beginning to appreciate why Maddox had said Asher was evil.

Realizing that the Colonel was not going to say anything further, Mr Asher stubbed out his cigarette. 'Good heavens! Is that really the time?' he asked, cocking his elbow and holding his wristwatch to his ear as if to make sure it was still working. 'I had no idea I'd been here that long. I really must be off. I'll keep you fully in the picture, Colonel, never fear. Any developments and you'll be the first to know – well, almost the first to know.'

Mr Asher closed the office door behind him and made his way down the corridor. He walked slowly, his head bowed, one hand tugging at his lower lip, thinking. By the time he had reached his car he had decided that this was one of those occasions when a meeting with Seamus Reilly might be beneficial – but to whom he could not yet be sure As his car was driven rapidly through the streets he was already organizing the complex intricacies of setting up the meeting, and he grinned to himself as he thought of the outrage and protest his decision would have created in Whitehall.

'Colonel Maddox?'

'Ah. You must be Mr Tu . . .'

'Tuohy, Colonel. Declan Tuohy.'

'Ah yes. Mr Tuohy. I was told you might call. Do come in. These warm spring days can be very deceptive, can't they? Treacherous, in fact, especially when you reach my age.'

Maddox led the way across the hall and into what he liked to call his study: a pleasant, square room with a high ceiling, the walls lined with books, a welcoming log fire burning in the wide, stone fireplace. 'Do sit down,' he invited, indicating a high-backed, buttoned chair like a sedan. 'As soon as I saw you drive up I asked Penny to organize some coffee. Unless you'd prefer something stronger –'

'Coffee will be fine. Thank you.'

'To tell you the truth, young man, I can't for the life of me imagine why you would want to talk to me. I'm very uninteresting. Still, you must know what you're up to if you've come all this way.'

'It's about Belfast, and –'

'Oh dear,' Colonel Maddox moaned sadly but his eyes twinkled.

Declan Tuohy smiled kindly. 'Yes: oh dear.'

'You know what I mean, then?'

'I have a good idea, Colonel. I was born there.'

'Were you, indeed?' Maddox asked in a tone that somehow suggested he was truly surprised that anyone would admit to being born in such a place. 'Ah, Penny, thank you,' he went on, rescued, as he saw it, in the nick of time as the maid brought in the coffee. 'So what was it about Belfast that you think I might know?' Maddox asked, sitting down again gingerly, his coffee cup and saucer balanced precariously in one hand.

'About the time you served there. And specifically about Arthur Apple and the circumstances of his death.'

For a moment it looked as though Colonel Maddox was about to be annoyed: he pursed his lips and frowned extravagantly. But he must have changed his mind. 'Ah. Dear old Arthur Apple,' he remarked quietly. 'Extraordinary man,' he added, his face assuming a particularly friendly look.

'I understand you knew him.'

'I met him,' Maddox admitted. 'Several times. But I wouldn't say I knew him. I wouldn't say anyone actually knew him.'

'He ran a betting shop for the IRA,' Declan Tuohy pressed on, aware that he was making statements rather than asking questions, but it seemed the thing to do.

'As I understand it, yes. Among other things.'

'And the man who tried to kill you – Deeley – he worked in the betting shop as well.'

The Colonel nodded. 'Yes. And I met him too, you know. In fact Mr Apple brought him along to meet me. A strange experience. Very strange. I suppose I must be one of the few people who have ever actually shaken hands with their would-be assassin. He was only a boy, really,' Maddox continued in an unhappy voice. 'Very unsure of himself. Of the two of us I do believe he was the more distressed by the meeting. There wasn't much light in the room, and I remember he kept shifting himself back into the shadows. It's a terrible thing, you know, when the pleasure of killing gets a hold of you. I've seen it happen quite a few times in my life, but you don't want to hear about that. You were saying?'

'Tell me, Colonel, was Mr Apple involved in the plot to murder you?'

Colonel Maddox looked thoroughly shocked. 'Good God, no. Mr Apple was a most gentle man. I'm certain he was as horrified as anyone when he found out.' Suddenly he laughed. 'You know, I never really thought of it as attempted *murder* until you mentioned it. I don't quite know what I thought of it. But not murder. That seems far too vicious a word.'

'How did he die?' Declan Tuohy lobbed the question in out of the blue, hoping to catch his host off guard but nonetheless feeling a little guilty at his tactics.

'Who? Mr Apple? Oh. A heart attack, I understand. That's what the official report said, isn't it?'

Declan nodded. 'That's what it said. Do you believe it?'

The Colonel employed some tactics of his own: he sipped his coffee and took his time about it. 'I have no reason not to,' he said at last.

'I see.'

'I doubt that you do,' came the unexpected reply. 'Anyway,

46

why are you so interested in how Mr Apple died? After all, it was some time ago now.'

It was Declan's turn to finish his coffee and, like the Colonel, he took his time about it. Curiously enough, he was beginning to feel he had no right to quiz the old man, as though asking him about Mr Apple was like asking him to reveal darkly personal secrets of his own. 'At the time of his death we were interested, but everything – all the normal details – were . . . well, they *seemed* to be covered up. There seemed little point in pursuing it. Clearly we weren't going to get anywhere.' He was expecting some kind of reaction but was disappointed. The Colonel just fixed him with his vague, noncommittal stare and kept silent. 'But now I've been . . . My brother-in-law has been shot so I have to go over and –' —

Maddox jumped. 'I'm so sorry. I was . . . Senile decay. Your brother-in-law. Oh dear. How dreadful it all is,' he said sadly, shaking his head and falling silent for a moment. 'Might I ask his name?' he enquired unexpectedly, as if dreading the answer.

'His name? Tim. Tim Pat he was always called. Tim Pat Duffy.'

The Colonel's reaction was quite extraordinary. In one surprisingly agile movement he was on his feet, his face ashen, his long stooped body shaking violently. And perhaps it was to disguise this trembling that he took to pacing the room, clasping and unclasping his hands, finally gathering them behind his back, his fingers flexing all the while. 'Duffy,' he said aloud, staring balefully out of the window at the green lawn that stretched away from him. 'Duffy,' he repeated. 'Tim Pat?' he asked abruptly, rounding on Declan and making the question sound more like an accusation. 'That's not the –' Maddox stopped, and smiled a small, fragile, apologetic smile. 'I'm sorry. It's just – do you place any credence on dreams, Mr Tuohy?' he asked, his voice quite steady now but filled with foreboding.

The question caught Declan off guard. He was on the verge

47

of making some flippant, dismissive retort when he noticed the very real distress that filled the Colonel's eyes. 'No,' he said simply.

'Or premonitions?'

'I've never had any.'

'Ah,' Colonel Maddox sighed, filling the exclamation with sympathy. 'Then you will think me quite mad,' he said. 'Quite, quite mad. You see, every night for the past few weeks,' Maddox continued, his voice now oddly flat and impersonal as though it was coming from a recording. 'Three men. Irrevocably linked. And that is very strange since they clearly detest each other. But they are definitely linked. In death. And one of them is called Duffy.' He closed his eyes. 'I knew it would happen,' he went on blithely, but now there was a brittle edge to his voice that hinted at madness. 'He always told me he would be at hand to warn me of things that – well, you understand.'

Declan didn't. 'He?'

'Mr Apple, of course. Didn't I say? We were talking about Mr Apple, weren't we? He used to say he was already dead, you know. I knew what he meant. So many of us are, don't you think – already dead. But I sometimes think he really was.' Suddenly the Colonel laughed. 'No wonder you thought there was some sort of cover-up! Can you imagine the pandemonium as they tried to explain the death of . . . A ghost! That's really what he was, you know. A wandering spectre. Outwitted us all. Inoffensively meandering through our machinations. Watching us tie ourselves up in our webs of deceit. Probably laughing at us – although kindly. He was very kind, you know. Very kind. I used to think – just to myself, you understand – that in a sense he tried to show us how even goodness can be swamped by evil. And now – now he is very concerned. Although what he expects me to do about it I cannot imagine . . .' The Colonel allowed his voice to trail off. 'Such a pity you never read his diary.'

By now Declan was totally confused by Maddox's ramblings. He wavered between laughing out loud and simply getting up and leaving. In the event he did neither: he sat there, unmoving, as the Colonel went on.

'I wasn't allowed to keep them although I did so want to,' he confessed sadly. 'They were whisked away. Burned, I believe. A small sacrifice. Unless he planned it that way. . . . I wouldn't put it past him. Yes,' the Colonel decided emphatically, brightening considerably. 'Of course. It was the only way he could take them with him, don't you see?'

Declan saw no such thing but he nodded his agreement.

'However,' Maddox said, lowering his voice conspiratorially, 'I did manage to photocopy certain passages that appealed to me particularly. I read them frequently. Almost every night. "The Visions and Visitations of Arthur Apple." That's what he called them. There is one paragraph – I'll just get it for you,' Maddox decided, and was on his feet and gone from the room.

Alone, Declan felt an awful chill as though some unfriendly spirit had occupied the Colonel's chair: instinctively he picked up the poker and prodded at the logs to encourage a better blaze. He smiled ruefully at his success. Maddox returned, a sheaf of papers in his hand.

'Here it is,' he announced, handing Declan a single sheet. 'The second paragraph. Read it and see what you think.'

Declan Tuohy took the paper and stared at the writing. At first glance it seemed to spread itself helter-skelter across the page, the curious Gaelic d's, the t's crossed midway up the stem like wayside crucifixes. Yet, as he focused his eyes, he saw the writing was anything but haphazard. Each word was joined to the next by a loop that faded just before it reached the following word so that he was left with the impression that the writer's mind was one word ahead at all times, and somehow created the compulsion to read.

. . . and yet there is hope or the promise of hope. For this unholy trinity, drawn as they are from the ranks of Satan and imbued with an evilness that must surely be rejected, will be exterminated by the wrath of their sinister god, their merciless and unforgiving, unloving god. And this is the significant factor: it is their own god who brings about their downfall, their hatred his weapon of death, their blindness his ruthless snare. There is a soul perched high above the awful tragedy that continues to unfold, a soul coming to God in the extreme and painful tradition of kenosis, an unlikely soul experiencing the Golgotha of the absolute spirit in all its starkness. And, wonderfully, man can become divine, can learn to love, and love is the only bridge between above and below, the only bridge that spans the abyss of eternal despair. Only love is as strong as death, and with this love each man consumes Christ. But to attain this love one is forced, it seems, to live a life of apparent depravity among whores and murderers and evil schemers, taking their sins upon his own shoulders. And I repeat: such a one exists, unknown to all. Unknown even to himself. And in him rests the hope I speak of.

Declan Tuohy handed the sheet of paper back to the Colonel, trying desperately to think of something to say. Maddox saved him. 'Tell me, did Mr Duffy have any children?'

'Yes. He left one son, Fergal.'

'I wonder,' the Colonel was clearly toying with some new idea but eventually seemed to abandon it. 'How old is he? Fergal, I mean,' Maddox wanted to know.

'I don't quite know. Twenty. Twenty-one. Twenty-two – something like that.'

'I wonder,' Maddox was now wondering again, perhaps regurgitating the idea he had jettisoned earlier. 'You don't suppose it was this Fergal that Mr Apple was so concerned about, do you?'

'Colonel, maybe I'm just being –'

'Sceptical? I've come to expect that reaction,' Maddox told him. 'If I didn't like you I wouldn't persist, but I do most sincerely beg you to think a little more about what I've been saying. There is evilness in Belfast and, despite what the churchmen say, evilness is not man-made. But it's up to you, isn't it? I can only – well, pass on the message, so to speak.'

'I appreciate –'

'Promise me one thing: promise you will at least keep an eye on your nephew, just in case.'

'Of course I'll do that. I would have done that anyway.'

'Yes, I know you would. But a special eye.'

'I will. I promise,' Declan Tuohy promised if only to extract himself from what he felt was something quite beyond his ken, something he wanted nothing to do with.

'And one last thing: promise me you will call on me, without hesitation, if you feel I can help in any way.'

'I promise.'

His promises obtained, Maddox seemed to lose interest. Declan got up quietly and left the room, not looking back, overwhelmed by the sensation that he was walking on tiptoe away from death.

Late that night two black cars drove slowly, almost silently, up Clare Street, their lights dimmed. They came to a halt outside the Duffy house. From the first, three young men jumped out and immediately seemed to disappear as if by magic, vanishing into the shadows; a few seconds later Seamus Reilly stepped from the second car and walked swiftly up the short path to the front door. He had thought carefully about this visit, and had meticulously devised the pattern the conversation would take.

'Mrs Duffy?'

'Yes.'

'My name is Reilly. Seamus Reilly. I was a friend of your husband. May I come in?'

Rose Duffy eyed the neat and elegant little man for a few seconds. Of course she recognized the name: everyone in the Shankhill would have recognized the name, but to connect it with this small, dapper figure was difficult. His stature did not match his reputation. Still, his power was indisputable, and she opened the door wider and stood to one side.

'Thank you.' Reilly's manners were impeccable and he removed his hat as he stepped in and followed Rose into the sitting-room. From force of habit, no doubt, he glanced about the room somewhat suspiciously, finally selecting a straight-backed chair against the wall, and sat down, crossing his legs. Immediately, as though the action was reflex, he produced a flat tin of small cigars. 'May I?' he asked.

Rose nodded and handed him an ashtray, settling herself in Tim's armchair as he lit his cigar.

'I've called to express my deepest sympathy on your very great loss,' Seamus said, waving the smoke from in front of his face.

Rose bowed her head slightly by way of acknowledgment and thanks. Words, she decided, were inappropriate.

'And to ask of there is anything we can do for you?'

Inexplicably Rose felt her muscles tighten: the plural struck her as singularly sinister. 'We?'

Seamus Reilly switched on his most dazzling smile, deflecting the question by its brilliance. 'As you can imagine, Mrs Duffy, we are always deeply concerned when one of our friends is –' he paused for a second, the ludicrous phrase 'sinned against' jumping into his mind – 'is attacked,' he settled for. 'And, alas, it falls to me to visit the relatives to see if anything can be done to alleviate their sorrow, and by way of retribution.'

'I don't –'

'Now you may very well say, Mrs Duffy,' Reilly went on as though uninterrupted, 'that you would prefer we do nothing. It is an understandable attitude. An attitude frequently adopted by the bereaved. An attitude which in other circumstances would be highly commendable. However, you have to appreciate our position. It is imperative that we discover who is responsible for your husband's most brutal killing, and that a suitable punishment is administered if only to maintain the status quo. So, regretfully, there are some questions I must ask,' Reilly concluded, uncrossing his legs, and giving a little cough. 'Firstly, have you any idea at all who shot Tim Pat?'

Rose shook her head.

'No idea at all?'

Again Rose shook her head.

'I see. Well, did you see anything?'

Rose thought about shaking her head yet again but something about Reilly's tone, or perhaps it was just the way he straightened his shoulders, warned her he already knew the answer. 'Yes,' she said.

'Ah.' Reilly sighed the word as if he had satisfactorily negotiated the first hurdle. 'Now in your own words and in your own time I would appreciate it if you could tell me exactly what it is you saw.'

'Two men –'

'I'm sorry, Mrs Duffy. In exact order. I assure you it is much easier to remember details – and it is often the details that are most important – if you try and remember everything in its exact order. Now, before the two men –?'

Rose frowned for a moment. 'I watched Tim Pat walk down the garden path. He stopped once, to look at the flowers, I think. He went out of the gate. There was a car parked across the street, and a man –'

'Excellent,' Seamus Reilly interrupted. 'Let us take it step by step. The car. What can you tell me about the car. What make was it?'

'I've no idea. I know nothing about cars. I'm sorry,' Rose apologized, for some reason feeling quite stupid.

'You're like myself, then, Mrs Duffy,' Reilly told her, smiling nicely. 'I know nothing about cars myself. I don't even know how to drive. And they all look the same to me. Perhaps you remember the colour?' he suggested hopefully.

'Green. Dark green, I think. I've thought about it and maybe it was black, but at the time I thought it was dark green.'

'Dark green or black,' Reilly repeated, and one could imagine some little gnome scribbling the information down in his brain. 'Large or small?'

'Medium sized. Squarish, I remember. It looked old although I don't know what made it look old.'

'Fine. Then what?'

'A man got out.'

'Can you describe him?'

'Not really.'

'Try, Mrs Duffy. How tall was he, for example?'

'It's so difficult. He was taller than Tim Pat. Maybe about six feet. Quite heavy – he didn't seem to get out of the car all that easily.'

'Excellent,' Reilly said again, and sounded as though he meant it.

'I do remember thinking how nicely dressed he was.'

'Why was that? Why did you think he was nicely dressed?'

'I liked his suit. It was plain grey. I'd always wanted Tim Pat to get a plain grey suit but he never would,' Rose explained.

'A plain grey suit,' Reilly repeated, giving the gnome something to do.

'And a red tie. I thought the red tie contrasted well with the suit without being flashy.'

'I see.'

'Black hair. Neatly trimmed. Very black and straight. Shiny. As though he brushed it a lot.' Suddenly Rose smiled. 'I think I was so taken by the shine on his hair that I forgot to look at his face. His face didn't seem to matter.'

'You said there were two men?'

'Oh. Yes. But the other one stayed in the car. I didn't see him at all. He never got out.'

'But it was a man?'

'Yes – I suppose so. I don't know. It never occurred to me that it wasn't.'

'So it could have been a woman?'

Rose nodded thoughtfully. 'Yes. It could have been.'

'Good. And then?'

'The man – the one in the grey suit – he got out of the car, reached back in . . . when he stood up there was a gun in his hands –' Rose broke off and buried her face in her hands.

Seamus Reilly watched her carefully, not looking for anything specific, trying to eavesdrop on her mind, listening for that tiny, indefinable something that would give her away, that would indicate to him that she was holding something back, that she was lying. And he knew that if Rose was, in fact, lying he would spot it as he had spotted it on so many other occasions when interrogating people, people who thought they could deceive him but who had themselves been deceived by his bland and friendly manner. 'Can I –' he started to say at last, intending to offer to fetch her a glass of water.

'I'm sorry. I'm all right. I'm fine.'

'You're quite sure?'

'Quite sure.'

'Then, may we continue?'

'There's nothing else. The man shot Tim Pat, got back in the car and was driven away.'

'You saw that?'

'Of course I –'

'I mean you saw the man get back into the car?'

'Yes.'

'You weren't watching your husband?'

'No. I –'

'You didn't leave the window and run to him?'

'No.'

'I see. And there's nothing else you can tell me?'

'Nothing else.'

But there was a slight skipping hesitation in her reply that made Seamus Reilly insist: 'You're quite sure? No small thing that might –'

'Just –' Rose said and stopped dead.

'Just?'

'Just – it was only a feeling. A feeling that something was out of place. I remember I actually said to myself "That's funny".'

Reilly sucked in his breath in expectation. 'Tell me about it.'

Rose gave a half-hearted smile. 'There's nothing to tell.

Something struck me as – well, something just struck me. I don't know what it was. I can't remember. I've been trying to think what it was but it just won't come to me.'

'I see,' Reilly said, clearly disappointed. 'You said you felt something was out of place.'

'I know I did. But that's not quite what I meant. There was something different. Something I wouldn't have expected. Do you understand?'

Reilly wasn't too sure that he did, but he nodded anyway. 'No doubt it will come to you in time. Don't try forcing yourself to think. That's a certain way of not remembering. When it comes to you be sure and let us know.'

Rose nodded.

'Now, Mrs Duffy – and this is most important – can you think of any reason why someone would want to kill your husband? Any reason at all?'

Rose shook her head. 'No. None.'

'Did he have any personal enemies?'

'Not that I know of. None that would want to kill him anyway.'

'He wasn't involved in any –'

Rose gave what amounted to a snort as Reilly hesitated delicately. 'Huh. Poor Tim Pat. He was far too timid to be involved in anything. He'd just got himself a job and was looking forward to going to work again.'

'Oh. A job?'

'At the milk depot.'

'Ah. Doing what?'

Rose looked surprised. 'Delivering milk.'

'I see. And how did he get that job?'

'What do you mean, how did he get it?'

'What I mean,' Reilly said, keeping his voice admirably flat and impersonal as though it had not been he who had arranged Tim Pat's job, 'what I mean is was it offered to him, did he see it advertised in a paper? How did he get it?'

'He just went down and asked for it. He went out every day looking for work. I think he said someone mentioned there was a job going at the depot so he went down and asked for it and got it.'

Seamus Reilly presented himself with another small cigar by way of celebration: clearly, he had now decided, Rose Duffy knew nothing of her late husband's involvement, nothing of his hoped-for usefulness. 'Tragic,' he murmured. 'So tragic. But that's often the way in life, isn't it? Just when one's problems seem to be on the point of energetic solution –' he stopped and shrugged his shoulders. 'You have a son, Mrs Duffy?'

Rose felt herself go rigid again. 'Yes.'

'Fergal, I believe?'

'Yes. Fergal. Why?'

'I wondered if I might have a word with him since I'm here? Just a quick friendly word, you understand. Nothing to be alarmed about. A question or two in case he saw something.'

'He's in bed.'

'Not ill, I hope?'

'No. Asleep.'

'Ah,' Reilly sighed and nodded approvingly. 'If only more young people went to bed at a reasonable hour we would have far less trouble on our streets, don't you think?'

Rose felt obliged to nod.

'It concerns me no end the way youngsters are allowed to roam the streets at night,' Reilly went on, sounding absurdly pious, and yet obviously meaning every word he uttered. 'It can lead to untold difficulty, can't it?' he asked, as though it was important to get Rose Duffy on his side. 'That family closeness gets eroded and when that happens, well –' he concluded, allowing the hazards of erosion to speak for themselves.

'And now Fergal?' he added abruptly.

'I'll get him.'

'Thank you. I won't keep him from his bed a minute longer than is necessary.'

Alone, Seamus Reilly stood up and moved to the centre of the room, staring rapaciously about him, feeding his curiosity with the details he rapidly assimilated, trying to remember how the room had looked on his one previous visit, and unable to find any change.

– We are alone? Seamus had demanded, making it evident that this was a prerequisite of any conversation.

– Yes, Tim Pat Duffy assured him. Rose and Fergal are both out.

– We're calling you in.

– I thought that might be it.

– Yes. You're to take up a job we've arranged. Nothing too glamorous, I'm afraid. Delivering milk, in fact.

– That'll be nice.

– Yes. Very nice. You will also be delivering a quantity of small fire-arms with the milk to special customers whose names you will be given.

– I see.

– The fire-arms will be concealed in pint cartons of orange juice – or rather, pint cartons that are supposed to contain orange juice.

– Right.

– The cartons in question will be placed on your van each morning.

– Right.

– If you should be caught you know nothing about them.

– Of course. Tim Pat smiled: It's good to be back.

– I'm sure it is. It must have been difficult to spend so long on the sidelines, but it will pay off now.

– Yes.

– Enjoy your new job. And be careful.

– Thanks. I will.

'You wanted me?'

Seamus Reilly swung round, furious with himself for not having heard Fergal come into the room, but he concealed it admirably. 'You must be Fergal,' he said.

'That's right.'

'I'm Mr Reilly. Seamus Reilly.'

'I know.'

'Oh?'

'My mother told me.'

'Ah. Yes.'

'So?' Fergal demanded, blatantly impertinent.

Seamus Reilly studied the young man thoughtfully: accustomed as he was to dealing with every conceivable type of young hoodlum he was unable, for the moment, to fathom the reason behind the hostility and loathing in Fergal's eyes.

'So,' he said with unparalleled tolerance, 'I wanted to ask you a few questions.'

'You shot Martin Deeley, didn't you?'

If this unexpected question surprised Seamus Reilly he did not show it. Slowly, casually almost, he smoked his cigar, his eyes half-closed, only the slight flaring of his nostrils giving any indication of emotion. So that was it! Dear God, back ever again to that damned Apple and his raving predictions. What was it he had said – something about the living haunting the dead more than the dead haunting the living? Something along those lines. 'No. As a matter of fact I did not.'

'Perhaps not yourself, but you had him shot.'

Again Reilly inhaled deeply, the smoke billowing from his mouth as he spoke. 'Yes. I had him shot. He stepped out of line. It is my job to see to it that people stay in line. I had him shot.'

'He only tried to save himself.'

'That's all any of us do,' Reilly heard himself say and was relieved to discover he had spoken it only to himself. 'You seem to know a lot about Deeley,' he said aloud.

'He was my friend.'

'I see. That, young man, makes your question legitimate but does nothing to excuse your downright impertinence. Indeed, if you had not given me that explanation I can assure you we would have done considerably more than just talk. Sit down.'

Fergal Duffy sat down as though shot, choosing the chair Reilly had vacated. 'You didn't have to kill him,' he said, looking forlorn, his eyes no longer filled with hatred, but now brimming with tears.

Seamus Reilly perched himself on the arm of Dad's chair, his mood severe. 'I want you to listen to me very, very carefully. What I say to you now I will say only the once. I am not accustomed to explaining my actions to young fools like you. I am not accustomed to having my actions questioned. That is something I simply will not tolerate. However, I do admire friendship,' he said in a wistful voice that suggested it was something he had not himself experienced often. 'Even more than friendship I admire loyalty, and it takes great loyalty to stand by and defend the dead – how much easier it is to wipe them from our minds, erase them completely, pretend they never existed. And so I will explain to you why your friend Martin Deeley had to be killed. I will explain, that is, if you want to listen –'

Fergal bowed his head but said nothing.

'Do you?' Reilly snapped.

Fergal nodded. 'Yes.'

Reilly relaxed, and took to smoking again in silence for a few moments. Then with something approaching compassion in his voice, he asked, 'Do you know what a rogue is? I'm sure you do. A bright young man like you is sure to know that. Well, your good friend Martin Deeley was a rogue, and alas for him rogues are something we cannot tolerate within the organization. He made the mistake of setting himself above our rules. He was obsessed with his sense of indestructibility, and with this obsession he had a lust for killing that terrified even me. And as if that was not enough he jeopardized an operation it had taken us a great deal of time and effort to put together. That is why Martin Deeley had to die. Do you understand?' Reilly insisted on knowing.

Fergal only nodded.

'And don't you think for one minute it was a spur-of-the-moment decision on anyone's part. I had warned him on several occasions that he was getting out of line, but he would not listen. I pleaded with him to come to me with his problems, but he ignored me. By a vain belief in his power to survive outside the system, his sense of immortality, I sometimes thought of it, he demanded to be killed if only as a lesson to others,' Seamus Reilly concluded, almost sadly. He was not a cruel man by the standards inflicted on him by his strange, twilight society. He abhorred violence even though his own life was regulated and dominated by little else. He grieved sincerely for those he had ordered killed; he had prayers said for them, aware that perhaps his own were none too acceptable in the sight of God. He was, put at its simplest, a man of his times, a man of his environment, a man who had grown to near middle-age without a childhood, without even experiencing the painful pleasures of adolescence. He was not a person who made friends and for this he had always been thankful since those who had got within reach of his friendship had nearly all died by atrocity, or hunger, or simply in spirit: that was the worst death of all – the slow, ineluctable death of the spirit, the end that Seamus Reilly feared most of all.

He stood up and walked to the window, staring out, imagining briefly that out there in the cold wet night was the promise of death, perhaps his own, perhaps –

Rose Duffy came back into the room, coughing warningly as she did so. 'Have you finished talking?' she wanted to know.

Seamus swung round. 'Yes, I think we've finished. That's a nice boy you have there, Mrs Duffy. An honourable boy. He mourns his friend.'

'Yes,' Rose said.

'Now,' Seamus said abruptly. 'Are you quite sure you're going to be all right?'

'Quite sure. Thank you.'

'You need have no fear of any – eh – unwelcome visits. We have taken care of that. But financially –'

'No. We'll be fine. Thank you.'

'If ever you do find –'

'Thank you.'

'I'll take my leave, then.'

Back in his car Seamus Reilly lit another cigar. He was smoking far more than his self-imposed allowance. But he was worried. His problem was increasing: if Tim Pat had not mentioned his activities to Rose (and Seamus was convinced that he had not) then only he and the Chief of Staff had known about them, and the implications that held out were something he did not wish to speculate on for the moment. 'You did as arranged?' he asked the man who sat beside the driver.

'Yes.'

'Three?'

'Three. Two in back. One in that empty garage opposite.'

'Good. Replace them at six-hour intervals but make certain there are at least three for the next four or five days.'

· SIX ·

'HELLO, ROSE.'

'Declan!' Rose Duffy threw her arms about her brother. 'Oh, Declan, thanks ever so much for coming.' She stood back a little for a better look. 'Come in, come in.'

Declan carried his suitcase into the house, and was immediately assailed by the familiar smells. Although it was the best part of fifteen years since his last visit, the particular odours made it seem like just the other day, and he was astounded that it looked exactly the same. 'It hasn't changed,' he remarked.

'Hasn't it? No, I don't suppose it has,' Rose said self-consciously as though blaming herself for lack of initiative. 'Tim Pat never liked anything changed,' she explained, absolving herself adroitly. 'We used to spend hours talking about the alterations and decorations we would have done when we won the pools,' she added wistfully. 'I'm sorry.'

'Sorry? Don't be daft. I like it that nothing has changed. It makes me feel I haven't been away so long.' He looked at her carefully. 'Rose, how are you?'

'Coping.'

Declan nodded. Rose would always cope. Even when their

father had been blown to kingdom come by a bomb he was time-setting in a culvert, and their mother had died (of a broken heart, some said), Rose had coped. When the two eldest boys had been drowned in Manitoba, Rose had coped. And now, with that enviable stoicism, she was coping with the latest tragedy in her life. Indeed, at first glance it appeared she was only slightly bothered by it as though violent and unexpected death was an old familiar to be treated with sombre and sober seriousness but in no way kowtowed to.

'And Fergal?'

Rose shrugged. 'You know Fergal. Never the one to let you know what he's thinking. He doesn't attach himself to people very often but when he does –' Rose shrugged again. 'A friend of his was shot a few months ago and it really seemed to shatter him. I don't think he had room in him to mourn his father. Funny, now that you mention it, he seemed a bit better today. More like his old self. Perhaps the visit –' Rose broke off and leaned forward to switch on the electric fire.

Declan waited, sensing his sister had something to add.

'Seamus Reilly came to see us last night – to see if we needed anything, he said.'

'Seamus came here? Poor old Seamus. God, I haven't seen him since –'

'There's nothing poor nor old about Seamus Reilly, I can tell you, Declan. Here, give me your coat and I'll go and make us a cup of tea.'

– Since . . . Alone, Declan Tuohy smiled grimly to himself. Already, it seemed, having barely set foot in the city, the cold and avaricious fingers of Belfast were clutching at him. And he thought he had escaped! Without thinking he gave a loud, mocking laugh.

'What's so funny?' Rose called from the kitchen.

'Just thinking of something. Nothing important. Just something I remembered.' He leaned back in his chair, clasping his hands in front of his face, making steeples of his fingers from time to time, remembering.

– I really did like those poems you sent me, Seamus Reilly

had said and sounded genuine enough. Very moving. People seem to think you're going to be big in the literary world.

– Do they?

– You know they do. Modesty doesn't become you. What did you mean by a 'man with a mission'? The inscription: For Seamus Reilly, a man with a mission.

– I just thought it was appropriate. But Jesus, Seamus, I wish to God you'd get out before it's too late.

– Do you believe what you write?

– Yes. I hope I do.

– Well, Declan, I know I believe in what I'm doing. I absolutely believe in the fight –

– Ah, the cause. I know you do, Seamus. I know you do. And maybe you're right.

– Then why won't you join us? We need you, Declan. We need someone who can use words, someone who can speak for us.

Declan shook his head. – I'm simply not that someone, Seamus.

– You are, dammit. People listen to you. And if we don't start talking soon I shudder to think what will happen.

– No, Seamus, you're wrong. Some people hear the words I write but they don't listen to them: nobody listens to something they don't want to hear. And nobody, believe me, wants to hear about the unification of this country, about –

– If we don't start talking now – and I do mean now, Declan, the violence is going to take over. Everyone has a hunger for death in their eyes. Hundreds of people are going to be senselessly killed. . . .

He had been right: twenty years ago he had been right, was probably still right only now it was too late. In his mind's eye Declan saw himself and Seamus quite clearly as those two young, intense men who had shared the same classroom, the same pew at Mass, had gone to the altar side by side to receive Holy Communion, shared the same jagged dreams, shared, too, the last day before Declan had taken off for London. Indeed, it had been Seamus who had come to the station with him, had held his hand, had, at the very last moment, embraced him, begging him to reconsider. And it had taken some years for their closeness to dissipate: they had written to each other, regularly and at considerable length at first, but less and less as the years passed, each letter underlining how their views had diverged, until finally their correspondence had dwindled to a few lines in a card at Christmas. And it was curious, Declan now thought, how Seamus had slowly and with apparent reluctance changed his attitudes: gradually the pleadings for Declan to return home and join the 'cause' lost their tremor of conviction, became like small, forlorn cries, until, about three years ago, his message had been a gentle, concerned warning to 'stay away from all the grim and detestable turmoil that shatters our hearts' – strange words, indeed, for Seamus Reilly, although he had always tended to uplift his vocabulary in homage to 'you, the poet' as he put it, tongue in cheek. Well –

'Here we are,' Rose said, carrying in the tray. 'I've made you a little sandwich as well.'

'Thanks, Rose.'

'You look tired. Been writing too much?' she asked, trying to veer away from the subject she knew would have to be broached before long.

'I wish I was.'

Almost in unison they stirred their tea, each waiting for the other to speak, their familiarity impoverished by the sadness that hung over the house.

'Rose, have any arrangements been made?' Declan asked bluntly.

'Arrangements? Oh. No. No not yet. They won't release Tim Pat for a few days. They never do when someone's been –'

'I forgot.'

Again a silence. Declan, out of politeness, took a bite of the sandwich, chewing monotonously, swallowing. 'Why, Rose? Why?' he suddenly asked.

'Why? I wish I knew, Declan. That's what everyone is

asking. Why Tim Pat? Nobody seems to have an answer. Not even the almighty Seamus Reilly seems to have a clue. I thought – I thought you might be able to find out.'

'Me?' Declan Tuohy was completely taken aback. 'Me? How on earth –'

'You know people. You –'

'I don't know people, Rose. For heaven's sake, I've been away for –'

'You know Reilly.'

'Seamus Reilly is different. Anyway, you just said he didn't have a clue.'

'He doesn't know who did it, but I think he knows why. He knows something. He –'

'Hah. Seamus always knows something.'

'Well then –?'

'He's not going to confide in me, Rose.'

'Yes he will. He worships you.'

'Ach, don't be so damned stupid. We were friends a long time ago, that's all. Things have changed. We've changed.'

'You write to each other.'

'A card at Christmas is not writing to each other.'

'So you won't even try? I need to know, Declan,' Rose persisted. 'I desperately need to know. If there was a reason – any reason – it wouldn't seem so bad.'

Declan sighed his agreement.

'Promise?'

He could not resist the grin. 'I promise.'

Just then, the front door slammed, making them both jump, and Fergal came into the room.

'Hey, Fergal!' Declan exclaimed. 'My God, how you've grown. You know, the last time I saw you you were knee high to a grasshopper.'

'Hello, Uncle Declan.'

'Just Declan. Drop the "uncle" for goodness' sake. You're a grown man now. It makes me feel too damned old to have you calling me uncle.'

'Where've you been, Fergal?' Rose said, raising her voice.

'When did you arrive?' Fergal asked, ignoring his mother.

'Just now. About an hour ago. I still can't get over how you've grown.'

'It happens,' Fergal said.

'Fergal, I want to know where you've been,' Rose tried again, now sounding slightly hysterical.

Fergal eyed her. 'Just out. Nowhere particular. Just out and about.'

Oddly, this seemed to satisfy Rose. 'Oh,' she said, and left it at that.

'How long are you staying?'

'A few days. A week at the most, I should think. That's all right, is it?' Declan asked, a hint of good-natured sarcasm in his voice.

'Hmm? Sure. Sure, that's fine.'

Suddenly Declan felt uncomfortable: the mournful face of Colonel Maddox seemed to loom behind Fergal, and Declan could almost hear him pleading for a special eye to be kept on the young man. So he really looked at Fergal now, studied him, as though seeking the truth behind the Colonel's dire prognostications. But he could find nothing in Fergal's face to suggest that death was stalking him: for the first time in months he looked almost cheerful, his eyes bright, his rather tentative overtures friendly enough. On that day a stranger would have described him as a nice young chap, a little shy, perhaps, but amicable and easy-going.

'Seen enough?'

Declan jumped, almost upsetting his tea. 'I'm sorry,' he apologized. 'It's just so long since I've seen you,' he explained lamely.

'Well,' Rose unwittingly came to the rescue, 'you two will have ample time to get to know each other. You said you were tired, Declan. If you want to go on up –?'

Declan nodded. 'Yes. I think I will.'

'Early to bed and early to rise,' Fergal quoted, smiling.

'Alas, it doesn't always work,' Declan said, getting up.

'Shame. Well, I'll be off to bye-byes too. See you in the morning.'

'Yes. Good night, Fergal.'

'Good night. 'Night, Mum.'

'Good night, love. Don't forget to say your prayers,' Rose added automatically: she had issued the admonishment for as long as she could remember although now it was done with only a slim hope that he would return to his childhood ways.

'He seems to have taken it well,' Declan observed, glancing at the ceiling as the sound of Fergal's radio penetrated from above.

'I think your coming over has done him good. It's the first time I've seen him smile in months, although –' Rose broke off, frowning. 'Perhaps something Seamus Reilly said to him made a difference.'

'Seamus spoke to Fergal?'

'For a long time. Last night. When he was here. Oh, Declan, I don't want him getting mixed up with Reilly. I –'

'Shhshh.' Declan hissed the warning as the radio upstairs suddenly went quiet for a moment, only to blare out again, louder than before.

'Will you be seeing Reilly?'

'I should think so. I bet he knows already that I'm here.'

'Tell him to keep away from Fergal, will you? He's all I have now.'

Declan gave an ironic snort. 'You don't tell Seamus what to do, Rose. But I'll ask him. And while I'm here I'll keep an eye on him.'

Their conversation ended and together they got up, smiling at each other for their simultaneous decision. For the first time Declan noticed there was a politeness between them, a reserve that weakened the closeness they once shared.

Suddenly Rose ran to her brother and threw her arms about him. 'It's so good to have you here, Declan. I don't know what I would have done if you hadn't come.'

Declan patted her gently on the shoulders. 'It's good to be back,' he told her, glad she could not see his face as he lied, wincing as he admitted to himself that the very last thing he really wanted was to be back in Belfast, aware that the city was closing in on him, seeking him out, still determined to involve him in the intrigues and treacheries that were part and parcel of everyday life.

Even the cold, crisp comfort of the linen sheets tucked about him did little to lessen Declan's misgivings. He tossed sleeplessly in his bed, dozing fitfully for a few minutes at a time but always awakened by gloomy images that padded about the hem of his consciousness: Colonel Maddox and Seamus Reilly, as unlikely a twosome as ever was, performing an outrageous duet, holding hands and skipping about while chanting their discordant warnings; Rose, wailing now, mouthing inaudible accusations he could neither hear nor attempt to comprehend; Fergal, emerging from the shadows of his brain – nothing timid or shy about Fergal, it seemed, as he stood there brazenly berating him, looking cold and arrogant, a thundering, rumbling sound drowning his words.

Outside, two men, hidden behind the old, broken-down shed at the bottom of the Duffys' back garden, heard the heavy Army vehicles lumber down the street, grinding out their threats of retribution. The two men tensed, their guns cocked. As the armoured cars passed they relaxed, smiled nervously at each other in relief, and settled back to watch, listening for the slightest sound.

The mechanics of organizing the meeting had been set in motion, and the negotiations had gone on all day, messengers scurrying back and forth without, as yet, the two main parties being involved. Now John Asher waited. As though in recognition of the secrecy such dealings demanded he sat in the dark, waiting impatiently for the telephone to ring, the ashtray on the arm of his chair filled with the stubs of his black cigarettes. At intervals – usually when denying himself the pleasure of smoking yet again – he took to chewing his thumbnail. He made a lunge for the phone as it rang shrilly. 'Yes.'

'And a very good evening to you too, Inspector,' Reilly's voice came sardonically down the line.

Asher could not withhold his chuckle. 'Good evening.'

'I take it this is urgent.'

'Very.'

'Oh. Right. Tomorrow?'

'Yes.'

'Evening?'

'As you wish.'

'Right,' Seamus Reilly made up his mind after a very brief pause. 'Right. Tomorrow evening at nine-thirty. Usual procedures, I imagine?'

'No,' Asher said.

'No?'

'I'll dispense with mine,' Asher added surprisingly.

'Dear me, it must be urgent.'

'I said it was.'

'So you did. Same house, I thought.'

'Yes.'

'Good. I'll see to your security then.'

'That should please the Chief Constable,' Asher said, pleased with his little joke.

Reilly hooted with laughter. 'I bet it would. I'll be expecting you.'

'I'll be there,' Asher promised, barely getting the words out before the line went dead.

Seamus Reilly pursed his lips, staring at the phone for a considerable time after he had hung up, wondering what on earth had put Asher into such a state of excitement. It was clearly no small matter since he had waived his right to cover himself with his own men – something that on previous occasions had caused delays before agreement on strategy and deployment could be worked out. 'Clem!' Reilly called, taking a small silver flask from his pocket and treating himself to a little drink.

'Mr Reilly?' Clem Donovan asked.

'Shut the door.'

Clem Donovan shut the door and leaned against it.

'Tomorrow evening at nine-thirty I'm having a meeting in our house at the back of St Patrick's. You will be in charge of security – and I mean security. Inspector Asher will be joining me. He will leave his car near the playground as usual. You will see to it that he is met and brought safely to the house. Nobody is to come anywhere near us. Nobody. You can have as many men as you need for the job.'

'Yes, Mr Reilly.'

'You can put Regan outside the door of the house. He can then escort the Inspector back to his car when we've finished.'

'Yes, Mr Reilly.'

'And no slip-ups.'

'No, Mr Reilly.'

'Right. Get to it.'

Seamus Reilly listened to Clem Donovan clattering down the stairs. He heard the front door slam, and a car start up and drive away. He moved across the room, his elegant Italian shoes making no noise on the uncarpeted floor, and perched on the wooden table, swinging a leg. Too many things were happening that needed his immediate attention. Was he getting too old for the job? It was not exactly the sort of occupation one could retire from, at least not voluntarily; and certainly there would be neither golden watch nor handshake at the end, no pension either. Reilly sighed. Oddly, the thing that was upsetting him most was something he had been sure he would look forward to with great pleasure. But Seamus Reilly was a great believer in premonitions of tragedy, and when he was told that Declan had been spotted at the airport he had felt a coldness in his bones, and a great sadness, as when he had ordered his own brother shot for informing to the RUC, a sadness so intense he could all but feel the weight of it pressing inside his chest.

He got to his feet and dusted off the seat of his trousers with one hand. Would that one could dust off the promise of doom so easily! He laughed grimly as the thought wandered through his mind. Would that everything could be dismissed with the

flick of one hand. He strode to the window, shaking his head as
though to banish his thoughts. If only he could dismiss his
Catholicism, that curious, taunting faith, part myth, part
truth, part pure human fabrication but mostly faith, branded
on his soul without his being given a say in the matter, with its
promise of everlasting peace or damnation, its promise of
judgment. He saw his own reflection in the window and then
he saw the gaunt, jaded face of that old fool Arthur Apple
peering at him and he remembered him saying: But you
cannot kill me, my dear Mr Reilly, for I am already dead!

Reilly shuddered and signalled for his car by quickly
drawing the curtains.

Sharmann put all the files from his desk into a drawer and
locked it carefully. 'You're clear about everything?' he asked
Captain Little. 'I don't want another cock-up.'

'No, sir.'

'This Clement Donovan won't be any push-over. He's got
no regular habits. You'll have to get him blind. As for
transport –'

'Barton's getting that tonight, sir.'

The Colonel nodded his approval. 'The one thing in our
favour is that the Provos always feel secure in their own
homes. They tend to think they're inviolable. They seem to
relax a little. But for Christ's sake be careful. In and out as fast
as the hell you can.'

'Yes, sir. That's why Barton is switching to explosives for
this one. We can be well gone by the time it detonates.'

'Just make damned sure it does.' Sharmann smiled. 'If
nothing else it should wake the bastards up a bit earlier than
usual.'

John Asher made himself a cup of cocoa. He thought about the
enormity of the suspicion he was going to place before Seamus
Reilly. Fortunately it was only a suspicion. But if it proved
justified . . . dear God, the horror of the repercussions frightened him to death. The politicians would go berserk, and the

Provos . . . Instantly Asher had a vision of Reilly on the rampage, seeking vengeance, quite literally pillaging as only he knew how.

· SEVEN ·

CLEMENT DONOVAN PEERED sleepily at the luminous dial of the bedside clock: 4.55. He wondered, but none too seriously, what had woken him up at such an ungodly hour, and he listened for any clue. But everything was quiet apart from his wife, heavily pregnant, who snored gently and rhythmically beside him. He leaned over and kissed her fondly on the shoulder, his nose wrinkling pleasurably at the scent she was wearing. He longed to place his hand on her stomach to feel their first child kick, but refrained for fear of waking her. She needed her sleep: three miscarriages in as many years had left her fearful of sleep lest, while sleeping, this new infant would be whipped away from her, leaving her barren and demented again. Clement settled down, the joy of the impending birth lulling him. He had barely closed his eyes when the bomb went off. The small, semi-detached house seemed to rise in its entirety several feet from the ground before sinking again as a pile of flaming, groaning rubble, the houses either side of it folding inwards over it as though in an effort to conceal the horror of the shattered bodies underneath. Then a fearful silence, until a flock of starlings, outraged at being woken in such a manner, lifted themselves from the trees and circled the devastation, screaming their fury. As the dust settled so did the birds, fluffing their shiny feathers and cackling as though it had only been a dreadful nightmare.

Seamus Reilly was brought the news at 5.20 by a runner. For several minutes he simply could not bring himself to believe it. Standing there in his silk pyjamas, he felt his scalp tighten as the blood rushed from his head. He closed his eyes to steady himself. 'Tell me that again,' he whispered.

'Just like I said, Mr Reilly. Someone put a bomb in Clem Donovan's house and blew him and his missus to smithereens.'

Seamus Reilly shook his head and sat down heavily. 'I don't believe this,' he said, mostly to himself. 'I just don't believe it,' he repeated aloud.

'It really did happen, Mr –'

'I know it happened,' Reilly snapped. 'I just don't believe anyone would – Jesus God, what the hell is going on?' he demanded of himself.

If the runner knew the answer he wasn't giving it: he stayed with his back to the door, watching carefully as Reilly flexed his fingers ceaselessly, his eyes livid with anger, the blood seeping back into his face giving it an unhealthy, mottled hue. Suddenly he was on his feet. 'Get me Regan and Dowling and O'Neill. Tell them I want to see them in –' he glanced at his watch – 'in forty minutes.'

'Yes, Mr Reilly. Where?'

'Where what?' Reilly demanded impatiently.

'Where do you want to see them?'

'Oh. Our house in the Falls. And tell them I don't want any excuses: they're to be there.'

'Yes, Mr Reilly.'

Reilly ran up the stairs, stripping off his pyjamas as he went. He dressed hurriedly, surprised and angered at the problem he had doing up the buttons of his shirt, finally abandoning it and donning a polo-necked sweater. His hands shook violently as he zipped up his trousers. 'Jesus holy God,' he swore. 'I still don't believe this is happening.'

Forty minutes later to the second he was at the safe house in the Falls. He had, it seemed, mostly recovered his calm: his astonishment and disbelief replaced by a deadly, whispering composure. 'You've all heard?' he asked, and watched the three men nod. 'Regan, as of now you take over Donovan's duties,' he said, the use of the dead man's surname sounding harsh and cruel. 'Dowling, you replace Regan. You, O'Neill, replace Dowling. Regan,' Reilly went on, hurrying his words in the manner of a man in fear of forgetting them, 'your first priority is to organize the security for my meeting tonight, and you, Dowling, will be responsible for the protection of the immediate location. You, or someone reliable and answerable to you, will be stationed outside the door for as long as the meeting lasts; you and only you will be on hand to escort Mr Asher safely back to his car.'

'Yes, Mr Reilly.'

'O'Neill, I want you to start asking questions about this – this appalling outrage. Get as many of the boys as you need together and scour the neighbourhood. Stick at it all day. Find out everything and anything you can. Someone somewhere must have seen something. I want every detail of information, down to the name and address and sex of every goddam insect that so much as farted last night. And I want that information before I meet Asher.'

'Yes, Mr Reilly.'

'And don't just ask. I want the answers and it's up to you to get them any bloody way you can.'

'Yes, Mr Reilly.'

'Get to it then,' Reilly said curtly, managing to dismiss all three men with a single jerk of his head. He watched from the window as the men got into their cars and drove off. Then he hurried downstairs himself and dived into the back seat of his own car, ordering his driver to get him home as quickly as possible. As the car swung crazily through the narrow streets, deliberately avoiding those most likely to be used by the ambulances and the security forces on their way to or from the scene of the explosion, Reilly felt a terrible rage building up inside him. This, he told himself, was the fourth unprovoked, inexplicable killing in his territory, and what enraged him most was his apparent impotence to do anything about it.

John Asher was up and dressed and enjoying his breakfast when the phone rang. He listened to the information without changing his expression. 'How many dead?'

'Two that we know of.'

'Injured?'

'At least eight.'

'Dear Christ! Can you handle it?'

'Yes, sir.'

'Good man. Have a preliminary report on my desk by nine-thirty, will you?'

'Yes, sir.'

'By the way, either of the dead been named?'

'Yes. Donovan. Clement Donovan and his wife, Angela.'

Asher clucked to himself for a second. 'Clement Donovan – he's on file, isn't he?'

'Yes he is. Been arrested four times. Served time twice. Possession with intent. He's a known Provo. Seems to have been lying pretty low these last few years, although there's a note that indicates he's been moving up the ranks.'

'Has he indeed. I see.'

'It's been rumoured – you remember, sir – that he's Seamus Reilly's chief sweeper.'

'Reilly's – *that* Donovan. I see,' Asher saw again. 'Right. With your report I want the complete file on Donovan.'

'Yes, sir.'

Asher went back to his muesli, instantly aware that this latest murder would add a new and terrible dimension to things.

For once Sharmann looked quite pleased, bestowing a generous smile on Captain Little and Sergeant Barton.

'No trouble?'

'None.'

'And then there were two,' Sharmann quoted. 'Just two. Fergal Duffy and Seamus Reilly.'

'Yes, sir.'

'We'll give it a week and then have another go at Duffy.'

Captain Little nodded and glanced at Sergeant Barton, who remained stony-faced, staring straight in front of him.

'Reilly's the one we really want,' Sharmann went on. 'It won't be easy. But we have time – all the time in the whole wide world.'

Little nodded again.

'Besides, it wouldn't be any fun if it was easy,' Sharmann said.

Barton broke in.

'Yes, Sergeant?'

'Nothing, sir.'

'You were going to make a comment. Make it.'

'I was going to say, sir, that fun is not the word I would –'

'Not the word you'd use, eh?'

'Something like that, sir.'

Colonel Sharmann seethed under the rebuke, but he realized there was precious little he could do about it. He could hardly antagonize Barton at this stage – after all, it was he who actually carried out the killings, was it not? 'Quite right, Barton. Quite right,' Sharmann conceded. 'Thoughtless of me. It must be difficult for you.'

'That's not what I meant, sir.'

Sharmann frowned: he sensed problems developing. 'Well, what did you mean, pray tell?'

'I don't quite know how to say it, sir. It's not at all difficult for me to kill, sir. I've been trained to do that. But –' Barton stopped. 'Have you ever killed someone, sir?'

'No. No, Barton, I haven't.'

'Well, sir, when you kill someone – I mean when you actually set out to kill someone, plan it, maybe stalk your victim for weeks or months – when you plan it all and finally kill him, you learn to respect him, sir. And somehow when he's dead you respect him even more since by killing him without warning you take away his chance to die with dignity. That's what I meant, sir,' Sergeant Barton concluded, his voice very faint for such a large man, a voice tinged with awe.

'I see,' Sharmann said, although he certainly did not sound as if he did. 'That's very noble and high-minded, I'm sure. But these bastards –'

Sergeant Barton shrugged. 'They're people, sir. I don't think we should call it fun –' Barton blushed, the thick veins in his neck pumping furiously, an uncharacteristic look of contempt filling his eyes.

Suddenly the Colonel switched on his smile, defusing the tension. 'Don't you worry about it, Barton. A couple of weeks, a month at most, and we'll have you out of here. Back in the bosom of your family.'

The redness in the Sergeant's face deepened.

Sharmann would have been wise to let matters rest there, but he could not resist what he saw as a satisfactory humiliation. It was the first in a string of minor errors he was about to make. 'See if you can organize a cup of tea for the Captain and myself, will you, like a good chap?' he asked, his smile collapsing into what looked like a sneer.

Sharmann stared at the closed door long after Barton had gone. 'What the hell's the matter with him?' he demanded. 'Do you think he's cracking?' he asked.

Captain Little shook his head. 'Barton's all right, sir. He's touchy, that's all. I got the same thing myself from him when I said there was something of the Clint Eastwoods about him. He's very professional. They seem to have their own code of ethics, these professionals. He's all right though, sir.'

'I hope so. Anyway, like I said, we'll leave things for a week or so – that'll give him time to get on with his mournings.'

'Yes.'

'I hope you're not undergoing any peculiar changes I should know about, are you?'

Little grinned. 'No, sir. But then I'm just the driver. I'm like yourself. I don't actually take life, do I?'

It was early evening when Rose called Declan to the telephone. 'It's him,' she said tartly.

'Him?'

'Reilly.'

'Oh.'

Declan took the phone and waited until Rose had gone back into the kitchen and closed the door. 'Hello, Seamus.'

'Hello, Declan. I heard you were home.'

'I thought you would.'

'Welcome back. It's been a long time.'

'Well, you know what they say about time, Seamus – it's relative to expectations.'

Reilly chortled. 'So much philosophy in one so young,' he chided. 'I'm very sorry about Tim Pat. Truly sorry.'

'Thanks.'

'How long are you staying? I'd like to see you.'

'Of course. Why not?'

'I thought under the circumstances you might –'

'Might have disowned you? I've known you too long for that, Seamus.'

'When is the funeral?'

'I'm not sure. We hope in three days.'

'I see. Well, could we meet tomorrow? Would you be able to find your way to Clancy's pub after all this time?'

'Yes.'

'Good. He still keeps his little room at the back for special visitors. His snug, you remember?'

They arranged to meet at seven.

'I look forward to seeing you, Declan,' Reilly said, sounding very tired, as if all the intervening years had caught up with him in one fell swoop.

81

· EIGHT ·

B Y A QUARTER to nine that evening the area around St
Patrick's cathedral was almost deserted. The comings
and goings throughout the day of men seldom seen in daylight
were sufficient to warn the inhabitants that it would be wise to
stay indoors. Bolts were shot and lights dim behind curtains,
the volume of radios and television sets was lowered, giving
the place an eerie, doomed aspect. Here and there a curtain
moved fractionally, but the movement was so slight you could
well have imagined it. The school playground (usually the
nightly scene of adolescent flirtation was quiet, its grey, cold
concrete and high wire fence suggesting anything but love.
From time to time a car was driven slowly around its perimeter, lights dipped, its engine almost silent.

At five minutes past nine the radio in the circling car
crackled, and a voice half strangled by the airwaves passed a
message. Immediately the driver swung his car to the pavement and stopped, switching off both lights and engine. 'He's
just left,' was all he whispered.

Others, too, it appeared, had heard the communication, for
now the lights of other cars parked in darkness were flicked on
and off, and men, or the shadows of men, appeared and

filtered away again, taking up positions, running, half-crouched, acolytes at some demonic ceremony.

Before John Asher had driven fifty yards he knew he was being followed, that between his house and the meeting place, cars would criss-cross through the streets of the city, interchanging their routes, always keeping him in view. It was one of the things Asher most admired about the IRA: this thickly-woven pattern of intelligence that allowed meticulous planning of whatever they did whether, as now, a relatively simple matter of security or a more deadly escapade. Their information was extraordinarily accurate, gleaned from every possible source, even, he suspected, from fellow officers in the RUC, by what they euphemistically called 'persuasion', and certainly from members of Her Majesty's forces.

He signalled and turned left, smiling as the car behind him carried straight on only to be replaced by another that emerged from a side street with precise efficiency. Another thing he admired, albeit reluctantly, was Reilly's intrepid honesty. The man never lied. While capable of the most appalling intrigue and abominable horrors, dispensing death with the largesse of Maundy money, Reilly was fanatical about the truth. Indeed, he clung to the truth as if recognizing it as the last vestige of honour left within him. In all the years they had known each other Asher had never known him even to bend the truth, and Asher had reciprocated. A strange mockery of friendship had developed, each recognizing the threat the other represented, yet each prepared to set aside their antagonism when the uneasy equilibrium of their territories was unbalanced by some interloper. And, curiously, both men, for very different reasons, regarded the British presence as a threat. For all his hatred of the IRA, for all his deep-rooted if somewhat flimsy Protestantism, for all his allegiance to the Crown, Asher was first and foremost an Irishman, and there was something in his Irish blood that abhorred the pounding of British boots on Irish soil. And yet he felt nothing but sympathy for the soldiers, who understood nothing of the internal conflict and who woke each morning with little but the promise of death staring them in the face. This was something he shared with Reilly, a shared sympathy that had come to light at a previous meeting and astounded him. What was it Reilly had said? 'I loathe the uniform they wear but I weep for the bodies I order killed.' Asher had understood, for Reilly had often referred to life as 'that most precious commodity' and there had been no doubting his sincerity. 'All my life, it seems, all my life,' Reilly had gone on sadly, 'I have dealt in death. A pedlar of death, I've been called. If they only knew! I have seen a whole generation of young men grow up around me, young men who revel and glory in taking life, in wiping away that most precious commodity. And that is what terrifies me: this lust for death.'

Asher touched the brakes as another car swung into position in front of him, its hazard lights flicking for a few seconds. Then it indicated left, slowed down, and pulled to the side of the road. Asher pulled in behind, watching as a man got out and approached him. Obligingly Asher rolled down his window.

'If you would leave your car here and come with us,' the man asked politely, though leaving no room for argument.

Asher stepped out, and set about locking the door.

'That won't be necessary. Leave your keys in the car, please,' he requested quietly. 'It will be quite safe.' He ushered Asher to his own car, jumped in beside the driver, gave a curt nod of his head, and they were driven off at speed.

Seamus Reilly, smartly dressed for the meeting, left his house.

'Good evening, Mr Reilly.' His driver managed to incorporate a salute into the words.

Seamus smiled. 'I hope it will be.'

Sitting, cocooned and protected in the back seat, pampered and respected like a monarch, dreaded and feared like Beelzebub himself, Reilly was trying to trace the moment when the seed of weariness, as he thought of it, had been sown. It certainly had nothing to do with the mellowing that is said to accompany advancing age, and even less with the more fractious elements within his organization. Rather, it was the feeling that no matter what he did or said, the turmoil and the mistrust and the atrocities would continue. Most of all it was caused by the quiet but determined warning from God. He shuddered at the thought, as he lit one of his little cigars, holding the match upwards and watching the flame flicker and die just before it singed his fingers. And so, he thought morbidly, shall my soul be extinguished just before I reach the sight of God. Still, there was a path through Hell as Blake well knew, and perhaps when he died . . . 'But you are already dead!' Seamus Reilly started as the benevolent, warning voice of old Mr Apple whispered in his ear. It dawned on him that perhaps, just possibly, his so-called seed of weariness had germinated at the moment of Mr Apple's death. Reilly closed his eyes, hoping the darkness would erase all memory of the man. Alas, it was not to be: in the gloom behind his eyelids Reilly saw himself standing over the bodies of Martin Deeley and Arthur Apple, staring down at them, unable to see Martin's face which was buried in Mr Apple's shoulder, but seeing clearly and wondering at the smile on the old man's face, feeling that the smile was directed at him, not in any cruel, taunting way, but with a friendliness that moved him. It was a smile that said you, too, Seamus Reilly, will come to know the peace and generosity of death, and will welcome it, as I have done; you, too, will feel it consume you long before you die and will be happy to be consumed; you, too, are, in fact, already dead.

Reilly opened his eyes. He rolled down the window an inch and held the remains of the cigar in the breeze for a couple of seconds, watching the sparks sheer off it before releasing it on to the road. He leaned forward and peered at the illuminated clock on the dashboard: good. He would be there in a couple of minutes and in excellent time. He would be there first. That was important. It meant he held the position, the tactical advantage claimed by possession.

The room was small and uncarpeted. The walls were bare of

pictures, the fading wallpaper showing patches of damp and mould near the skirting board. A small fire had been lit in the grate, and someone had put four daffodils in a chipped vase and placed them on the mantelpiece. In the centre of the room was a table, dust free and nicely polished (the smell of the synthetic spray still permeating the air), with two glass ashtrays strategically placed upon it, and on either side an executive-style swivel chair. Low over the table hung a light, its sixty watts concentrated downwards by a cheap enamel shade, green outside and white within. The curtains, thick and red and plush, and tightly drawn across the only window, looked as though they might have been rescued from a recently demolished cinema.

In one of the chairs, rocking himself back and forth, his hands clasped, tweeking his nose with both forefingers, sat Seamus Reilly. As John Asher was ushered in he rose, bowed slightly in his odd, old-fashioned way, smiled tentatively, and waved his guest to the other chair. It was part of the unspoken, unexplained protocol of these meetings that they did not shake hands: they did, however, use Christian names as a reminder of their mutual trust. They were also pedantically polite.

'Good evening, John,' Reilly said.

'Good evening, Seamus. Thank you for meeting me.'

'It was an offer I could hardly refuse,' Reilly countered, his eyes twinkling.

Asher settled himself in his chair, all the while with an eye on Reilly who sat down also, crossing his legs, gently swinging an elegantly-shod foot. It was clear that Asher would need a little time to get down to brass tacks, so Reilly gave him the time, consoling himself with the thought that there was, after all, no great rush, and lit another of his small cigars, blowing out the match with a single sharp puff, and adroitly tossing it over his shoulder and into the grate in the style of a regent disposing of chicken bones. Finally, John Asher leaned forward, elbows on the table, cupping his face in his hands. 'These recent killings,' he said, and left it at that for the moment.

Reilly said nothing. He turned the palm of one hand upwards and raised his shoulders slightly, indicating he was prepared to listen without expressing any opinion of his own for now.

'I'm worried about them,' Asher announced, and frowned to enhance his statement. 'Very worried.'

'As am I,' Reilly allowed.

'Perhaps I shouldn't be, since it seems to be your lot at the receiving end for a change.'

'Yes. We do, don't we?' Reilly's face remained impassive.

'Let me ask you this: have you any idea who is behind them?'

Reilly kept his face blank, but the methodic computer in his brain was rattling out alternative answers. Then: 'To be perfectly honest we have no idea. One thing I can assure you: the culprits are not from within our organization.'

Asher sucked through his teeth.

'That doesn't please you?'

Asher smiled tightly and shook his head. 'It's not what I wanted to hear. You see, I don't believe it was any of the other local paramilitary units either.'

It was Reilly's turn to smile, and he did so, a little smugly. 'I know it wasn't,' he announced emphatically. 'Like your own, our intelligence is pretty good and we would certainly have known by now if anyone local – as you put it – had been responsible.'

'So what does that leave us?'

Reilly's smile widened. 'That's what I hope you are about to tell me.'

Asher stood up and walked to the fire. He stood there in silence for some minutes, using the toe of his sensible brogues to toy with a small remnant of kindling wood that protruded from the grate, staring at the glowing coals as if for inspiration. 'Before I tell you anything, Seamus,' he said almost inaudibly and without looking round, 'I want your word that you will not act until both of us are satisfied beyond all shadow of doubt that my suspicions are correct.'

'You have my word.'

Asher returned to the table at once, drumming his fingers on the polished surface. 'Right,' he said aloud, making up his mind. 'I believe the Army is behind this spate of killings.'

If he expected some reaction he was disappointed. Reilly took the information without a blink, but there was no doubt he was assimilating it and turning the possibility over in his mind. 'I see,' he said at last.

'You don't seem surprised.'

Reilly gave a little hoot. 'My dear John, nothing ever surprises me when it comes to this city. The most implausible things are plausible. The most unlikely most likely.'

Asher sighed. 'Yes,' he agreed. 'Anyway, my suspicion is based on tenuous evidence, to say the least. Mostly on a feeling. Nothing more.'

'I see.'

'You remember Maddox – Colonel Maddox –'

'I'm not likely to forget him.'

'No. Of course. Well, his replacement is a Colonel Sharmann.'

Reilly nodded. 'Guy Sharmann. Forty-four. Single. An arrogant pup.'

'Yes. I was in his office the other day and I just mentioned Duffy's murder. His reaction was – well, that's the trouble. His reaction wasn't quite right. There was a small pile of files on his desk. As soon as I mentioned Duffy he glanced at them. I probably would not even have noticed that if he hadn't looked away again too quickly. Then he looked at me as if to find out whether I'd noticed, and looked away again. Something that wasn't right.'

Reilly nodded. 'As you say, pretty tenuous.'

'So I did a little checking. Nothing much on Sharmann. Nothing much on Captain Little who arrived with him,' Asher said, and paused briefly for effect. 'However,' he went on, speaking much more slowly, 'ten days after Sharmann and Little joined our community a Sergeant Barton was

88

sent to join them – and Sergeant Barton is really very, very interesting.'

Seamus Reilly raised one eyebrow theatrically, and waited in silence: years of experience in the questioning of informants had taught him how disruptive it could be to interrupt a man on the point of imparting information, how easily a misplaced word could distract him, make him latch unwittingly on to that word and overlook those minute details that were so often the essence of good intelligence, make him swerve away from his own line of thought. Of course, he had already known about Sergeant Barton: there were few British soldiers above the rank of Corporal serving in Northern Ireland that he had not heard about. But thus far his knowledge of Barton was based on rumour and innuendo. There were a few facts, for example, that he was married and had one son whom he worshipped; that he was taciturn and very much a loner; that, remarkably, he spent most of his free time reading, particularly Malcolm Lowry, Edward Lewis Wallant and William Blake; and that, equally remarkably, he sought comfort for his omissions, whatever they might be, from his own particular Christ, attending services regularly but, it seemed, with no particular preference for one denomination, spreading the salvation of his soul equally, and remaining for some time after such services were concluded to confide, it must be presumed, in God. Seamus Reilly had stored away all this potentially useful information: one never knew when such snippets could be satisfactorily utilized.

'He is what the Army call a legitimate transporter – you must admire their terminology – a legalized killer in other words,' Asher explained, and paused again for a reaction.

This time Reilly obliged: he raised both eyebrows and said 'I see,' making the words sound darkly conspiratorial.

'Naturally there's not too much detail in his file but –' Asher shrugged, and smiled bitterly, clearly indicating that all one had to do was read between the lines – 'but he seems to surface in all the trouble spots – and this is what is most interesting – always with Sharmann or Little.'

'Now that is intriguing,' Reilly admitted.

It was Reilly's turn to stretch his legs. He re-lit his cigar and stood up, aimed and flicked his match into the fire, waited for it to flare, and then started to pace about the room, placing one foot directly in front of the other like a tightrope-walker, puffing heavily on his cigar, sending out clouds of smoke. 'If you're convinced – as you certainly seem to be – why don't you do something about it? Why tell me?'

Asher looked genuinely taken aback by the question. 'Me? Come now, Seamus, you know quite well I can't do anything about it. If, as I suspect, Sharmann and company have been sent here precisely for this mission, any questions I might ask would be very quickly dealt with. I would be told I was imagining things. I would be told it was outside my sphere of activity, as they say. I would be told to concern myself with –'

'But why tell me at all?' Reilly interrupted, conceding Asher's explanations. 'I would have thought it would give you some satisfaction to see my men being eliminated,' he added, smiling.

'It's the way they are doing it – that and, of course, who is. We can't have –' he stopped. He had nearly said 'foreigners' and the slip amused him. 'We can't have the British Army moving in here simply disregarding the law.' Any trace of a smile now vanished, lines of worry furrowing his brow. It was as though for the very first time he had identified his dilemma. He was an RUC officer, and an Irishman, and like every other policeman he was incensed each time the Army usurped his power, at the continued suggestion that the RUC were incapable, and it infuriated him each time the Army was allowed to make a mockery of what law there was and to indulge in flagrant injustices in the name of eliminating terrorism. Most of all John Asher could never quite rid himself of the belief that the British Army was an invading force, an English force, a force that had no right whatever to be there. While he was prepared to tolerate its presence if only because he could do nothing about it, he was certainly not about to allow it to abuse the law into which he genuinely put his faith. If dirty tricks were the only way to put a stop to such abuse then he would use them and to such effect as to confound all and sundry.

It was Reilly's turn to smile. 'Indeed, we must always uphold the law,' he said.

Asher recognized the ambiguity of the statement and grinned. 'You know what I mean.'

'Yes. I do.'

'I've told you before, Seamus, the only way this whole bloody mess is going to be solved is for the Army to be taken out, the politicians to shut up, and people like you and me to sit down and talk it out. We could do it, you know.'

'Perhaps we could, John. Perhaps we could. But I doubt it. The trouble with us is we're getting old and tired. Young people dream of the future, while we dream of the past. And that's what we're doing, you know. Dreaming.'

'I'm thinking of the future,' Asher protested. 'I –'

'Yes. I know. But we'd like the future to resemble the past, and that's where we fall down, I'm afraid,' Reilly told him thoughtfully, sitting down again and stubbing out his cigar. 'Anyway, to the matter in hand. What are you suggesting?'

Asher widened his eyes in mock innocence. 'Suggesting? Me? Why, I'm not suggesting anything.'

Reilly shook his head. 'What an evil old bastard you are. Right. Leave it with me. I'll see what I can find out. Meanwhile, you do your own digging. Then we'd better have another meeting.'

Asher nodded.

'If it's true what you suspect you know what we're letting ourselves in for?'

Asher nodded again. 'Yes.'

'So long as you know.' Reilly walked Asher to the door. He had his hand on the knob and was about to twist it when he turned. 'This Barton – you know he has a son?'

'Yes. Dotes on him.'

'In England, is he?'

'Yes. With his mother.'

'I see. Thank you.'

Asher looked as if he was about to say something but changed his mind. Then he left the room and was escorted downstairs.

Twenty minutes later the grapevine gave the all-clear. Lights shone brightly in the windows again. Radios and televisions were turned up, and somewhere the mournful tones of someone playing the saxophone could be heard. Two mongrel dogs scampered past the safe house, growling at each other on their way to scavenge. And the nameless men, the strangers who had silently guarded the house, packed up their shadows and vanished into the desert of the night like Bedouins.

· NINE ·

Fergal Duffy woke slowly. He kept his eyes closed, drowsy and comfortable in the warmth of his bed. He heard the starlings outside and smiled inwardly at their rapacious persistence: he knew they were hated for their brazen impertinence, shot at as acceptable targets. In an odd way, he sympathized with this rejection. He rolled over on his back and opened one eye.

– Good morning, Martin, he said quietly.

– Good morning, Fergal, Martin replied, and smiled at him.

So the singular, bizarre ritual of Fergal's day had begun. It was the same every morning: this eerie exchange of salutations with his dead friend. While their relationship had been tentative in life, after Martin's death Fergal had transformed it into an intense love that bound them ever closer together. It was a process beyond Fergal's control: the bewildered spirit of Martin Deeley had simply set up house within him, but Fergal welcomed his ghostly squatter with open arms, using this spectral tenant to overcome what he thought of as his own weaknesses, so that now, many months after Martin's death, Fergal could be, and often was, two people, though this he would have denied most vehemently.

– Did I tell you I had Seamus Reilly to see me yesterday? He wanted to explain why he had you killed. He said you were a rogue, and he could not and would not tolerate rogues in the organization.

– And did you believe him?

– I told him you were my friend.

– I bet he liked that!

– He did, as a matter of fact. He said he admired loyalty – particularly to the dead.

– Jesus!

Fergal grinned again. I thought that would please you. He ended up by saying if I ever needed help or advice all I had to do was get in touch with him.

– Great. He said the same to me. He's a great one for helping people is Seamus Reilly.

– I'm not a fool, Martin. I didn't believe him. You needn't worry – he won't catch me the way he caught you. I can play his game. I promised you I'd pay him back for killing you, and I will. Between us we'll fix Seamus goddam Reilly. We're bloody invincible. Fergal laughed aloud. I want Reilly to think I'm a little lost soul. I want to wheedle my way into his confidence. And when the time is right I want to give him exactly what he gave you.

Seamus Reilly stood under the shower, letting the warm water soothe away his aches, wash away the tiredness that weighed upon him. It was almost half-past eight, and he had not been to bed. He was getting far too old for these sleepless nights. At least the night had not been wasted. He had managed to set things in motion, managed, too, to get phase one (as he now thought of it) of his plan off the ground. After his meeting with Asher he had been driven across the border, and spent the best part of two hours on the phone to London, safe in the knowledge that in the Republic his calls would not be monitored. It was a credit to his organization that within those two hours he had been able to locate the whereabouts of Mrs and Master Barton, had been able to ensure that they would receive a surprise and unwelcome visit within seconds of his giving the word. Already, he knew, two men, two seemingly respectable and respected gentlemen, a graphic designer and a television lighting engineer, would have called in sick, and would be travelling – separately but aware they were not alone – to Aylesbury, would be settling into the designated hotel, possibly having a tipple in the bar, and waiting there, within a few minutes' drive of the village where the Bartons lived, for orders.

Seamus switched off the water and stepped from the shower, wrapping himself in an enormous, fluffy towel. All he had to do now was to arrange for a little chat with Sergeant Barton, in the hope that no undue pressure would have to be brought to bear. The chances of that were remote, alas. Still, people were so unpredictable, particularly under stress. The very ones you expected to summon heroic resistance acceded timidly; those you were certain would make facile prey fought with a tenacity that had at times astounded him.

Dressed impeccably if somewhat more casually than was his wont, he had just finished his coffee when his car arrived at the door. He smiled to himself, pleased with its punctuality. It augured well: if nothing else the day had started on the right note. He left the house, stopping briefly on the lawn to turn up his collar against the chill wind.

'Where the hell is Barton?' Sharmann demanded. There was no particular reason for his vile temper: he had simply got out the wrong side of his bed.

Captain Little looked surprised. 'I've no idea, sir. He's off duty. You did say you wouldn't want him – want either of us today.'

'I've decided it's high time we got Duffy.'

'I thought we were going to wait a week or so.'

'I've changed my mind. I'm tired of pussyfooting around. I want Duffy and I want him tonight.'

Captain Little, probably wisely, decided to say nothing.

'With him out of the way we can concentrate on Reilly,'

Colonel Sharmann offered by way of explaining his change of mind.

'I see,' Captain Little said, giving the Colonel a sideways look that suggested suspected madness. 'That doesn't give us much time.'

'It gives you all day. Go find Barton and get things moving, for God's sake. We've got the bastards on the run and I intend to keep it that way. If we hit Duffy you can bet your life it will bring Reilly out and that's when we'll get him. And it's Seamus bloody Reilly I want.'

'I understand that, sir, but –'

'For Christ's sake don't argue with me, Little,' Sharmann snapped.

'I'm sorry, sir.'

'Just go find Barton and get things moving.'

'Yes, sir.'

Sergeant Barton was nowhere to be found. Not that he was deliberately hiding. Dressed soberly and inconspicuously in civilian clothes, he was sitting in the corner furthermost from the altar in the chapel of the Poor Clare convent, a retreat he used from time to time. There was nothing significant in the fact that this was a Catholic chapel: Sergeant Barton avowed allegiance to no particular denomination, was not swayed by the attributes of any particular God. Indeed, he would have been hard pressed to expound his exact regard for religion, and religion had precious little to do with his presence in the chapel. He simply liked the place, liked the smell of beeswax, incense; the perpetual quiet appealed to him.

Like most men who deal in the business of death he was mesmerized by men of peace. God, like Mahatma Gandhi, like Raoul Wallenberg, like Mother Teresa, fell into that category. Yet it was the suffering of Christ that comforted him, for the possibility of forgiveness of the soul which it gave him. Barton pined for forgiveness. This was a relatively recent and unexpected hunger which had grown since the birth of his son. He had developed an illogical and morbid fear that whatever evil there was within him would be transmitted to his child. He killed and there was never much sign of remorse. There had been instances when he had even enjoyed killing, doting on his rifle, caressing it, praising its accuracy aloud and extravagantly. But there had never been malice in his actions: he had done what he had been ordered to do, unquestioningly. He had been content to allow the stigma of guilt to dwell on the parched consciences of his superiors. Military life demanded this. Obey, don't question, and succeed. This was the motto he had lived by until recently. Until only, it seemed, the other day. Perhaps it was the arrogant disregard for the dignity of death displayed by Colonel Sharmann that had made the difference; perhaps it was just the jaded weariness he sometimes felt; perhaps it was the realization that his own death could only be a stone's throw away; but probably it was the fact that his beloved son was growing up, was asking questions, was looking admiringly up at him, that made him recoil now when ordered to administer death. It was as if the crimes of the father would assuredly be visited on the child.

Barton knelt down, holding his head in his hands. He did not pray. He did not know how to pray, the formalized language as strange and incomprehensible as the Latin now being sung by the nuns behind the black, forbidding screen. Instead he thought of the trickery he was currently involved in, pretending to be one of the peacekeepers yet all the while creating mistrust, panic, pain. And this led him to ponder on the trickery he was playing on himself. What was that phrase that stuck in his mind? 'Death and truth could rhyme at a pinch'?

The nuns completed their requisite, plaintive chant, and fell into silent meditation. Suddenly he felt a hand on his shoulder, and for the first time in his life he knew what it was to be utterly paralysed with terror. He discovered he could not move from fear. Only his brain, it seemed, would function, and that ran riot, striking images he could barely fathom, quagswaying them, jumbling them up, always

97

with the horrible, humanized figure of death in the background.

'I'm afraid we must ask you to leave now, son.'

'—?' Sergeant Barton managed to look round.

'I'm afraid we must ask you to leave now. We have to lock the chapel,' the young priest said apologetically once more. 'The nuns depend on donations, and twice in the last month vandals have come in and stolen the offertory box. We open the doors again at five for benediction.'

Sergeant Barton nodded, relieved, but disillusionment filling his heart. How like a cinema it was! Doors open at 5 pm. *Jesus Christ Superstar*. First showing 5.15. Each performance divided by cartoons: grotesque caricatures hurtling across the screen dressed in army uniforms. He shuddered. 'I see. Thank you.'

The priest smiled, and looked as if he was about to say something but changed his mind, perhaps deciding his sad and wistful smile said it all.

Barton left the chapel, feeling he had been expelled, and made his way back to the barracks, hands now clasped behind his back, head bowed, unaware of the middle-aged man carrying a plastic shopping bag, a man who looked for all the world as though he had just nipped out to collect a few much needed groceries, a man who followed him.

'Ah. Mr Asher. I had given you up. I was just off for a spot of lunch,' Sharmann said, slipping adroitly into the casual tone he adopted when confronted by people he was wary of.

Asher summoned up an appropriate smile of apology. 'I am sorry. I got held up.'

Sharmann waited for a few seconds, hoping Mr Asher would suggest he continue on his way for a spot of lunch, the hope quickly receding as Asher stared back, before saying: 'You'd better come in, then, and close the door.'

'Thank you.'

Asher selected a chair and sat down, taking his time to make himself comfortable, and produced his packet of black cigarettes, this time lighting one without requesting permission. He pretended not to notice the Colonel's displeasure.

'Was it anything important?' Sharmann asked, waving away a wisp of smoke that had bravely strayed his way.

'No, nothing specific, Colonel. We're supposed to – to liaise, I believe.'

'Yes,' Sharmann agreed sharply.

'Your predecessor, Colonel Maddox, and I –'

'I'm sure we don't want to discuss Colonel Maddox,' the Colonel interrupted.

'No.'

Again Sharmann waited.

Mr Asher sucked on his cigarette, and waited also.

'It doesn't seem that we have anything to discuss,' Sharmann said finally, getting up and looking as though he was about to go for lunch after all.

'Well, there was one thing, Colonel.'

'Yes?'

'You'll be glad to hear we have made significant headway in our investigations into the recent spate of killings.'

The Colonel acted brilliantly: only for a split second was he caught off balance. Then with elegant composure he sat down again, and beamed innocently across at Asher. 'That is good news,' he said.

'I thought you'd be pleased.'

'And what is this significant headway?'

It was Asher's turn to smile, oozing charm and friendliness and total confidence. 'I never like to count my chickens, Colonel, but we now have several leads. Information is simply pouring in from a number of very reliable sources. Nothing conclusive yet, mind you, but it's all falling into place nicely. What we have to do is to sieve through it all and jettison the rubbish. And dear me,' Mr Asher chuckled, 'dear me, some of it is the most frightful rubbish, you know. Dear Lord, Colonel, if you only knew some of the things we've been told.'

'Like?'

Asher kept up his relaxed mien, trying all the while to detect the slightest hint of duplicity in the Colonel's eyes. 'Like – well – dear me.' Mr Asher skilfully brought his chuckle to the boil, as if what he was about to say was quite the funniest thing he had ever heard. 'Someone has suggested that it was the British Army itself that was responsible.'

Try as he might, Sharmann could do nothing about the rush of blood that suffused his cheeks, but he did manage to stare Asher squarely in the face. 'Hah,' he scoffed at last.

'That was exactly my reaction, Colonel. There were no names mentioned, of course. Names are always slow to come. Something to do with that old Irish abhorrence of informing. But they do come eventually. Still, can you imagine anyone expecting us to believe such a scatterbrained idea?'

The Colonel shook his head.

'Still, even the ludicrous suggestion will have to be looked into, won't it? We're a little paranoid over here about justice being seen to be done and all that nonsense. We waste more time checking out absurd accusations which we know are red-herrings before we start. I wondered if maybe you, Colonel . . . ?'

'I'm sorry?' Sharmann yanked his mind back to the matter in hand, furious at himself for allowing it to wander. For the very first time, he was entertaining the possibility that he might be uncovered.

'I was merely suggesting –'

'What was that?'

Asher sighed tolerantly. 'You seem distracted, Colonel. I was about to suggest that you might like to carry out any investigation that involved the Army – once we have the facts, of course, and provided those facts merit investigation.'

'You think –'

'Of course not. But as I say, we like to be thorough.'

'Yes. Yes, of course. Yes indeed. I'd be glad to investigate.'

'Excellent,' Mr Asher announced and stood up. 'I won't keep you from your lunch any longer then.'

'There can't possibly be any truth –' Sharmann started to say.

'Of course not, Colonel. Good heavens. What a thought! The Army would never be so foolish as to meddle in such an appalling way. The repercussions would be too awful to imagine.'

'No, of course not.'

'I'll be off. Have a nice lunch, Colonel. Me, I just have a sandwich. A full meal in the middle of the day sends me to sleep, I fear. And I have to keep my wits about me, eh?'

'Yes,' Sharmann agreed vaguely.

'I'll keep you fully informed,' Mr Asher promised.

'Yes. Thank you.'

Even before Asher had left the office and closed the door behind him, Sharmann had abandoned any thought of lunch. His stomach was churning. His palms sweated. As he now saw it there was only one answer: both Duffy and Reilly would have to be eliminated immediately, the entire operation completed without any delay. After that he and Captain Little and Barton could be recalled with a minimum of fuss. After that – well, after that hardly seemed to matter a jot.

By lunchtime and all through the afternoon a curious unease had settled over the Duffy household. Fergal had been out most of the morning but even in his absence had managed to leave something of his simmering unrest behind, and on his return, refusing anything to eat and making his way up to his bedroom, his unease hovered downstairs; Rose was tetchy, answering questions curtly, thinking constantly about Tim Pat's funeral. Declan wandered aimlessly and gloomily about the house, touching things in lamentation for what he had lost, and, indeed, for what he had never found: the perfect existence he had sought when he'd left home, success as a writer, success in love. He was suddenly overwhelmed by the thought that life was passing him by, leaving him like a mendicant with no home, no roots.

The trouble, he told himself as he dressed for his meeting with Seamus Reilly – a meeting that required a certain formality of dress – was that any love he had in him was for Belfast and he was haunted by a continuous, probing guilt for having abandoned it. He had been given the chance to stay and do something about the turmoil, by Seamus Reilly no less, to try, no matter how unsuccessfully, to spearhead a movement towards talks of peace and away from the horror of violence. He had scorned that chance; he envied those who had a cause to follow, be they Protestant or Catholic, envied those who could, at the end of the day, at the end of their life even, know that they had at least tried.

Declan looked at the old-fashioned alarm clock on the table by his bed. Christ: eight o'clock. He started to bustle about, seeing in his mind's eye Seamus Reilly's scolding look if he arrived late, his beringed finger wagging in admonition. Even Seamus Reilly – hated by many, feared, wanted for monstrous crimes – even he would be able to gasp out a last cry of 'I tried', to face unashamed the Celtic spirits that hovered perpetually in the skies. And yet, the thought struck him, Seamus Reilly admired him. Or maybe, the thought continued less kindly, maybe he just pitied him now. He would soon find out.

Ready, and suitably attired to attend Reilly's court, Declan left his room and went downstairs. Rose was ironing in the kitchen.

'I'm just off,' he told her.

'Mind how you go. You'd better make sure you've enough petrol. I haven't used the car since Tim Pat – since Tim Pat died.'

'I'll check.'

Rose stood the iron on its end and stared hard at her brother. 'Be careful, Declan.'

'Don't worry. I will. I promise.'

Rose smiled at him rather wistfully.

'See you in the morning.'

'Yes. Please God.'

Declan was backing the old Austin on to the road when he spotted Fergal running towards him, waving frantically for him to stop.

'What's up, Fergal?' he asked.

'Do me a favour?'

'If I can.'

'You're going to see Mr Reilly, aren't you?'

'How did you –'

Fergal grinned boyishly. 'I heard you on the phone. You're going to see him, aren't you?' he asked again.

'Yes. Yes, I am.'

'Tell him I'd like to see him, will you?'

Declan felt his mouth go dry, no words willing to scrape their way through his parched chords.

'Look,' Fergal was suddenly explaining generously. 'It's no big deal. The man was really nice to me. He took the trouble to speak to me about things. He made me feel better – well, about Dad being killed and stuff. I just want to see him and thank him.'

'You can write.'

'No. That's not the same. I want to see him in person. I'll get to see him anyway. I just thought it would be better if you asked.'

'All right, Fergal, if that's what you want. I'll mention it to him.' Declan narrowed his eyes. 'You're not –?'

'Not what?'

'Not –'

'No, of course I'm not. I simply want to thank him. Honest.'

'All right. Have a nice evening,' Declan said in an affected American drawl.

'I'll try.'

Declan drove slowly down the street, trying to get the feel of the erratic engine, images of Fergal in paramilitary uniform fixed in his mind. As he slowed at the intersection the car backfired. Immediately everything went quiet. Two women, gossiping by their front doors, froze; a lone man on his way home recoiled to the shelter of a privet hedge: only the starlings voiced their fear. They rose screaming from the trees, flying high into the clear night.

· TEN ·

CLANCY'S PUB WAS not, in fact, Clancy's at all. G. P. Clancy was long since dead and buried, but his name lingered on giving the crabby old man a permanency he could hardly have expected. It was a small, crumbling, ramshackle affair with a thatched roof and two weed-ridden hanging baskets by the door, but it was strategic-ally situated, close to the border, and approachable only by a narrow dirt track which was clearly visible from the windows.

It was up this track that Declan now eased and coaxed his car, pandering to the soughing and snarling of the rickety engine, hanging on for dear life to the steering wheel as the deep, muddy ruts played havoc with the suspension. He parked by the side of the pub under a sign with an arrow and the word GENTS painted in white, the arrow pointing, it seemed, to a spinney. Purposely he slammed the car door, and walked round to the entrance, smiling as he spotted the glowing end of a cigarette under the gaunt, windswept elm tree at the top of the lane: although his was the only car in view he was positive it was one of Seamus Reilly's protectors keeping an eye on things.

'And a very good evening to you, sir,' the publican greeted him. 'And what can I get you?'

Declan glanced about the bar. 'I'm expected,' he said, and only then did he notice the man sitting alone at the table in one corner. He also saw him nod to the publican, and jerk his head towards the glass-panelled door behind the counter.

The barman smiled obsequiously. 'This way, sir, if you please,' he invited, lifting the wooden flap with a flourish. 'This way, please,' he said again, closing the flap after Declan had passed through, and throwing open the door. 'Your visitor, Mr Reilly.'

Seamus Reilly cocked an eyebrow at Declan, but said nothing.

'Oh – eh, a Scotch.'

'And Scotch it is for you, too, Mr Reilly, isn't it?'

Reilly nodded, his eyes still focused unblinkingly on Declan's face. 'In that case I'll bring you the bottle and you can help yourselves. It'll save me running in and out and disturbing you,' the publican rationalized, and went off humming to himself.

They were left alone. For a few seconds neither of them spoke, as though each was deciding how the other had changed. It was Reilly who finally broke the ice. 'How are you, Declan?'

'I can't complain, Seamus. How are you?'

'Come and sit down, for goodness' sake. I'm fine. I'm alive.'

They looked a pretty quaint couple sitting either side of the turf fire, two men old beyond their years. The room was tiny, the walls mellowed by smoke to the colour of the pale turf. Here and there sepia photographs of young men in 1916 uniforms were on display, ghostly and ethereal behind the grime on the glass, their names, written in gothic script, half-hidden by the dark brown frames, as if their identity was sinking away from them. The two small armchairs either side of the fire and a stained wooden table provided the furnishings. A converted oil-lamp hung from the ceiling but it had not been switched on, and the blue-gold flames from the fire saved the room from total darkness.

Again the two men were silent, both staring into the fire, Declan determined to let Seamus lead the conversation, Seamus deciding to wait until the drinks had been brought before saying anything more. He had not long to wait: the publican flounced in and placed a bottle of Scotch, two glasses and a jug of water on the table. He left quickly without a word.

'Cheers,' Seamus toasted when they were alone. 'Welcome home,' he added, passing Declan a drink and settling back in his chair.

'Cheers.'

'What does it feel like to be back after all this time?'

'Depressing.'

Seamus seemed surprised. 'Depressing?'

Declan nodded. 'Very depressing,' he stressed. 'And it hasn't anything to do with Tim Pat's death. I hardly knew him. It's the whole atmosphere of decay and mistrust that depresses me, Seamus. It's like a city waiting to disintegrate.'

Reilly thought about this for a moment. 'Yes,' he finally agreed but without much conviction. 'I suppose it could seem like that.'

Declan smiled grimly. 'It's amazing, you know. I was so certain I knew what to expect. I'd seen the film reports, seen the replays of the explosions, seen the haunted, agonized faces – but it has only dawned on me these past few days how little they mean on celluloid. It's when you actually come here that the atmosphere closes in on you, that you can feel the fear.'

'But you must have known –'

Declan smiled sadly. 'Yes, I must have known.'

'Why did you come back then?'

'Rose asked me to.'

Seamus gave a small snort. 'Knowing you, Declan, that's never a good enough reason,' he declared. Another silence filled the room as before: 'Tell me, how's the writing progressing?' Seamus was pretty sure he already knew the answer.

'It's not, I'm afraid.'

'Oh dear,' Reilly sighed as he trotted out his favourite expression of sympathy again. 'I thought –'

'So did I. Actually,' Declan decided to explain, 'there's another reason I came over. My editor thought there might be a story.'

Seamus Reilly, on the point of lighting another of his little cigars, almost choked, blending his coughing with uproarious laughter. 'A story! Dear God, Declan, what a marvellous word! A story! Long live Beatrix Potter. A story! Oh, you'll find any number of stories over here. And if you don't – well, you can always make one up. A nice, gory fairytale – the media do it all the time.'

'About the diplomat who died. Arthur Apple.'

Reilly's laughter, like Mr Apple, keeled over and died. He started coughing again, violently, doubling up in his chair: still choking and spluttering he reached for his glass and swallowed the contents in one gulp. 'Ah,' he wheezed and leaned back, closing his eyes briefly. 'Dear Lord, will no man rid me of this meddlesome ghost?' he misquoted. 'You know,' he added, cheering up, 'that misguided little man has been more trouble to me dead than he ever was alive – and he was quite enough trouble to me then.'

Declan raised his eyebrows, waiting.

'Up he looms, day after day. If ever there was an unlayable ghost it is our friend Arthur Apple. I swear to God he's haunting me,' Seamus confessed finally, but in a mocking, good-humoured way.

'You're not the only one who thinks that.'

'Really?'

'I had a word with Colonel Maddox before I came over. He goes a step further. He says he talks to Apple.'

Reilly chuckled. 'He would. He probably does too. I liked him – Maddox, I mean. I don't believe I've ever seen a man more out of his depth. Honourable. That was his trouble. He was too damned honourable to be over here.'

'Did you kill him – Apple?'

'Me? Kill Apple?' Seamus Reilly was clearly shocked by the

suggestion, but he managed to keep the remnant of a smile on his lips that lent him an unpleasant, menacing air. 'No. No I did not. I have never killed anyone in my life,' he said truthfully.

'Who did?'

'No one. He died of a heart attack. Or –' Reilly stopped, and lapsed into thought.

'Or?'

'The official report – the official *British* report,' Reilly stressed as though it might be significant, 'said he died of a heart attack, but a few hours before he actually died he told me he was already dead. The odd thing was I really felt I had to believe him. He also told me I was already dead, which wasn't encouraging,' he added, gloomily. 'But there's no story there for you, Declan. It was just a slightly remarkable episode. A bizarre little flash in the fire of life,' he concluded, smiling widely at his dreadful simile, and flicking his finished cigar into the grate.

Declan could not resist returning the smile. 'I wonder if Apple would have agreed.'

'With?'

'With his life, or rather his death, being – what did you call it – a bizarre little flash in the fire of life?'

'I think he probably would.'

'I wonder.'

'I think he probably would,' Seamus Reilly said again, rather more emphatically. 'He was a rare bird, you know. A creature bred in some demonic paradise. Into strange dabblings. Black magic, I believe. He was a wreck when I first came across him. An abandoned alcoholic. Got into all sorts of trouble and was slung out of the diplomatic corps. Mexico, someone told me. Anyway, we saved him. Gave him a job running one of our businesses. A betting shop to be exact. Mind you he was useful to us,' Reilly explained.

'I'll bet he was.'

'Oh he was – well, you wouldn't expect us to employ someone who wasn't, would you? We put Martin Deeley in to keep an eye on things. That was our first mistake. Too easily influenced was Martin. Too vulnerable. Still things went very well for a while, then Martin decided to take matters into his own hands. He stepped outside his designated role, you see. Actually tried to kidnap – indeed, succeeded in kidnapping an RUC Inspector. Well, we couldn't have that, could we? Alas, Mr Apple decided to assist him in avoiding retribution. The result,' Reilly paused and shrugged, 'was inevitable. But nobody killed Mr Apple, Declan. He timed his own death. I'm sure of that,' Reilly concluded, or rather, Declan thought he had finished and was about to speak when Seamus went on in a sedate, pedantic tone as if he was once again quoting: 'It's not life or death that is important, anyway. It's the way one lives and the reason one dies. And that, come to think of it, is possibly why our city depresses you. There is a stench of wasted life and futile death. Things have changed so. There seems very little glory left to us. There are no heroes. The hoodlums are trying to take over – have taken over in some areas: youngsters suckled on blood and with that terrible lust for power, a power only satisfied, it strikes me, by killing and mutilation. And I'm supposed to control them!' Seamus Reilly shook his head at the apparent impossibility of his task.

'You did help create them, Seamus. The monster is partially yours.'

'Only as a last resort.'

'Nevertheless, you did help create these monsters. You encouraged the violence to begin with, knowing better than anyone that violence breeds violence. You can't whimper now that it's got out of control.'

Seamus Reilly straightened up in his chair, looking both puzzled and annoyed. 'I can assure you I'm not whimpering, Declan. I abhor the fact that violence appears to be our only weapon. And as to encouraging it – what else could we have done? Sat back and allowed ourselves to be abused and humiliated? We could not all pack our bags and trot away with our tails between our legs, could we?' he demanded, aware that his question was brutally cruel and probably unjust.

Declan accepted the jibe meekly. 'Thank you.'

'Oh I'm sorry, Declan,' Seamus apologized swiftly, leaning forward as if to touch his friend and sounding genuinely contrite. 'That was uncalled for. You struck a rather raw nerve, I'm afraid,' he explained with a cajoling, winsome smile that could be, and was now, very affective. 'Things really have changed here, you know. Fifteen years ago we were still fired with – with a sense of destiny, I suppose. At the very least a sense of purpose. I certainly was – you know that. I dreamed I was following in the footsteps of our glorious patriots. I dreamed they watched over me. I dreamed I was emulating their sacrifice and courage and love for this poor old country.' He allowed his voice to drift away. 'But,' he went on after a few moments, now sounding tired and wistful, 'my heroic patriots receded as these new and wanton tactics were forced upon us. They withdrew as though ashamed, some-how managing to take with them all the glory from our fight.'

Declan heard the sincerity in Reilly's voice and it saddened him deeply. Here was a man who had, quite literally, been swamped and bludgeoned by events, a far cry from the eager young man with the bright, keen eyes and the infectious nervous energy who had, so to speak, taken Declan Tuohy (orphan, dreamer and closet Marxman) under his wing, and, unwittingly, inspired at least one of the poems that had generated Declan's rapturous if transient acclaim.

'– city of Moloch,' Seamus Reilly was suddenly saying.

Declan shivered. 'What was that?'

Seamus grinned. 'I was quoting you. You see? I still remem-ber.' He gave a short laugh. 'Don't you remember how furious I was when you called Belfast "The city of Moloch, the hieratic legend, the land that split when Christ was crucified"? I thought you had taken leave of your senses!'

'Maybe I had.'

Reilly shook his head. 'You were inspired,' he said with a kind of awe. 'How sad it is that we have so little to say to each other now,' he added out of the blue but quietly, as though talking to himself. 'We are strangers – to ourselves as well as to each other,' he stated sadly. 'It might have been better if we had never met.'

Declan found himself nodding, but not in any agreement it seemed. 'I'm glad we met again, Seamus.'

'If only to say goodbye,' Reilly murmured.

'If only to say goodbye.'

A sod of peat collapsed and fell apart in the grate, shedding sudden light into the room for a few seconds: then it flickered out and settled down to smoulder.

Seamus stood up and put on his overcoat. He spread his hands in that gesture beloved of priests as they command their flock to go in peace, and said: 'Well, goodbye, Declan.'

For a moment Declan hesitated, thinking that surely there was more to be said. Then, heaving himself from his chair, he walked to Seamus and embraced him. 'Goodbye, Seamus.'

Seamus seemed somewhat taken aback, but he smiled and held Declan at arm's length. 'You look after yourself.'

'I will. I'm more concerned about you.'

'Me? Hah,' Seamus scoffed. 'You forget I have it on good authority that I am already dead. What can anyone do to me?'

'Just be careful.'

'I will. Oh I certainly will.'

Reilly moved across the room and grasped the handle of the door. Then he turned. 'And keep an eye on that nephew of yours,' he warned, a flicker of anxiety in his eyes.

'Ah – I forgot. He wants to see you.'

'Fergal? See me?'

'That's what he said. He wants to thank you for something.'

Reilly frowned, but nodded his head as though he understood. 'You have my number,' he said at last. 'Have him phone me. No. No, don't do that. You phone me. Better still, leave it be. I'll get in touch with him in a day or two.'

Declan eyed him quizzically.

'Just precautions, Declan. Just precautions. Just for a second or two when I was speaking to him, your Fergal had a light in his eye I recognized only too well.'

'Meaning?'

Reilly shrugged. 'Nothing.'

'Tell me, Seamus.'

'It was probably my imagination but when people want to kill you they have a certain way of staring at you – as though they were already visualizing you dead.'

'Fergal would never –'

Seamus Reilly held up one hand. 'I'm sure he wouldn't. But I was sure a number of other people wouldn't but they tried. Revenge, alas, is far stronger than forgiveness, you know. And something in here,' Seamus thumped his chest, 'tells me – warns me that –' Suddenly he laughed. 'I'm a suspicious old bastard, aren't I?'

Declan found nothing funny in this. 'No,' he said. Then: 'Yes,' and despite his misgivings the about-face made him grin.

'That's that settled. Tell him I'll call him anon.'

'Seamus: you ARE afraid of what he might –'

'Might do to me? No, Declan. That's not what scares me. What frightens me to death is what I might have to do to him.'

And the ominous, tragic quality of Reilly's parting remark filled Declan's mind all the way home, and was still gnawing at him as he crept into the house and tip-toed up the stairs.

'That you, Declan?' Rose called drowsily from her room.

'Yes, it's me.'

'Good night.' She sounded relieved.

'Good night.'

City of Moloch! Undressed to his underclothes, Declan stood at his bedroom window and stared out across the city. City of Moloch! The things one wrote; the things one thought! Although who or what represented the awful Jahveh he could not, even now, for the life of him imagine. Still, the sacrificial children were real enough, their little souls burned on the pyre of prejudice and hate. He watched the car move slowly up the street and wondered, sleepily and without much interest, if the driver would even have heard of Moloch. Then he turned from the window intending to go to bed.

It was highly unlikely that the driver of the car had ever heard of Moloch. Captain Little would not have cluttered his mind with such useless information. He liked to keep it open, he would say, the better to receive his instructions and carry them out unquestioningly.

'Captain, the Colonel is wrong, you know,' Sergeant Barton said.

'Maybe,' Little allowed, but damned if he'd side with the Sergeant against his superior.

'No maybe about it, Captain. It's way too soon. We should have waited another week at least.'

'It's not our place to question –'

'I'm not questioning anything, Captain. I just know my trade. I know it's far too soon.'

'You can take it up with the Colonel tomorrow.'

Sergeant Barton gave the Captain a sideways sardonic glance. 'Sure.'

'Jesus, look! That's him at the window,' the Captain screamed in a whisper, already smelling of excitement.

Barton shook his head. 'Uh-huh. Far too tall.'

'It's got to be him. There's only him and his mother in the goddam house.'

'It's not him,' Barton insisted, nonetheless cocking his rifle and aiming at the figure stretching in the window, outlined by the light behind him.

'It fucking well is him, Barton. For Christ's sake take him.'

'That's an order?'

'That's an order. Jesus, he's going.'

Barton shrugged, pressed his eye to the sights, deliberately aimed six inches to the right of the turning figure, and fired. Pfffft: the silencer deadened any noise from the rifle but the crash of shattering glass sounded incredibly loud. For a second the man in the window stood stock still: then he seemed to topple over lifelessly.

'Nice work, Sergeant,' Captain Little commended, gunning the engine and speeding down the street.

Sergeant Barton did not reply. Quietly, methodically, he

dismantled his rifle. For the very first time in his life he felt sick after a shooting. He also wanted to laugh: sick on the only occasion he had deliberately missed a target.

· ELEVEN ·

'I FAIL TO see anything amusing about this,' Seamus Reilly
said, cold with anger, his voice slightly raised with the first
tremulous note of fear.

He had been in bed no more than ten minutes, had cuddled
the blankets warmly about him, and was slowly drifting off
into the sleep of the exhausted when the phone rang shrilly
beside his bed. It was Declan calmly announcing down the
crackling line: 'You'll never believe this, Seamus. Someone
just tried to shoot me.'

Seamus summoned his car, dressed and was at the Duffy
house within minutes. Now, at one o'clock in the morning
Declan stood in front of him, still in his underclothes,
laughing, a few minor cuts on his right cheek the only
evidence that anything untoward had happened.

'Will you please stop that laughing?' Reilly demanded,
conjuring a small cigar from his pocket and lighting it. 'You
could have been killed,' he added fatuously from behind the
smoke.

'That was the idea, I think,' Declan pointed out, controlling
the hysteria which was vying for supremacy.

'You haven't called –'

116

'The police? No. Only you.'

Reilly nodded his approval. 'Good. The fewer people who know about this for the moment the better. I'll take care of everything.'

'I'm sure you will.'

'And you might mention to your sister that the less said the better.'

'I'll do that.'

'How is she?'

'How do you think? Frightened.'

'Yes. And the boy?'

'Fergal? Hah. You never know with Fergal.'

'Where is he?'

'Upstairs. Why?'

Reilly dismissed the question with a shake of his head. 'Just asking. No reason.'

'You always have a reason, Seamus. You want to see him?'

'No,' Reilly answered after a meditative pause. 'Not now. I've too many other things to deal with.'

Suddenly Declan was very serious. 'You know something about this, don't you, Seamus?'

Reilly pretended not to hear, pretended to be deep in thought. He puffed energetically on his cigar until the tip glowed.

'You do, don't you?' Declan persisted. He smiled. 'I know you too well. For such a devious little man you're remarkably easy to read. You haven't bothered to ask me a single question since you arrived. What exactly happened? Did I see anything? Not one single question. It's like you don't have to because you know the answers already.'

For several seconds Reilly studied the tip of his cigar and then, slowly, transferred his gaze to Declan, eyeing him up and down, but saying nothing.

'Come on, Seamus. For Christ's sake don't fart about with me. It was my goddam life that nearly went out the window.'

Reilly took one last lungful of his cigar before tapping it out delicately in the ashtray. 'I can't tell you everything, Declan, because, quite truthfully, I don't know everything yet. I can tell you that we suspect some sort of conspiracy is going on. And if we're right, we'll have to deal with it ourselves. Quietly.'

'And while you deal quietly with your conspiracy we just sit here and get shot, is that it?'

'No. That is not it,' Reilly snapped. 'You'll be perfectly safe here from now on. I can promise you that,' he added with such force as to make it irrefutable.

'Oh. I see. You're going to protect us. That's really very encouraging,' Declan said with some sarcasm.

Reilly ignored the remark. 'Meanwhile I want both you and the boy to stay indoors. Under no circumstances are either of you to leave the house. Keep away from the windows. I want the killers to believe they've succeeded in –'

'Jesus! And how long are we supposed to stay –'

'Not for long, Declan. I can promise you that, too. Not for long.'

And, it seemed, this was one promise Seamus Reilly was most determined to keep. Twenty minutes later, as the car slowed down approaching his home, he leaned forward and told his driver: 'When you drop me get Dermot Regan and have him come here as fast as he can. And you'd better pick up Dowling and bring him along as well.'

'Yes, Mr Reilly.'

'And I'm afraid you'll have to be on stand-by. There won't be much sleep for you tonight.'

'That's all right, Mr Reilly.'

'As soon as you can, then.'

Reilly stepped from the car and slammed the door behind him. His driver watched him go safely into his house before putting the car into gear and driving smoothly, swiftly away.

– Heard the latest? Fergal asked Martin Deeley. Someone tried to bump off my Uncle Declan. Missed, though. Your friend Reilly was round here in a flash. Christ, he was hopping mad.

Livid as a pregnant contortionist. I heard him say he was going to protect us from now on.

— Who's going to protect you from him?

Fergal grinned in the darkness, winking at his spectral friend. — Why, you are, of course. Like I keep telling you: between us we can outwit Reilly any time.

Martin seemed to agree.

— I also heard him tell Declan there was a conspiracy of some sort. And with that on his mind I'll have a better chance of getting close to him. Fergal chuckled.

'Put this on before you catch pneumonia,' Rose ordered, handing Declan his dressing-gown. 'I've made some tea. You want a cup?'

'Yes. Please. Thanks, Rose.'

Now that the initial jittery amazement had passed Declan found himself shivering violently. The proximity of death, measurable in inches, finally began to dawn on him, and for a second he thought he was going to faint. He could hear Rose rattling the cups in the kitchen and the very friendliness of the sound heightened his sensation of dread. He wanted to rush upstairs, pack his bags and run. Yet he wanted to know who had tried to kill him even more. And WHY. For every killing, no matter how mindless it appeared, there was a reason, wasn't there?

'Here you are,' Rose said interrupting his thoughts. 'Drink that.'

Declan reached up and took the cup, gazing into his sister's eyes. 'You amaze me, Rose. I never thought you could be so calm.'

'I'm not. I'm frightened to death, Declan. There's a lot of things women don't show. Anyway, what would be the point in my getting hysterical?'

'None, I suppose.'

'There you are, then.' Rose sat down with amiable self-righteousness, and started to sip her tea.

For some time they sat in silence, listening to the occasional sounds from the street, glancing furtively at each other, neither wishing to display their fear. They heard a car arrive: but within seconds its door slammed and it was driven away again. There was the rattle of metal from across the street as some garage doors were opened or shut. Then silence.

'What did Reilly have to say?' Rose asked at last.

'Hmm? Oh, not a lot.'

'Not a lot you can tell me, you mean?'

Declan smiled. 'No. Just not a lot. You know Seamus. He likes to be dramatic. He said something about a conspiracy, but it was probably his imagination. He also said he would be protecting us from now on.'

'Him protecting us?'

'Yes.'

'And that's supposed to be a comfort?'

Declan smiled again. 'Yes.'

Rose flicked her eyes towards heaven in a gesture of ridicule. Then: 'What baffles me is why anyone would want to shoot *you*. It's crazy. You're not –'

'I don't know. Maybe because I met Reilly earlier.'

'You think –'

'I don't know. It's the only thing I can think of that makes any sense. Unless –' Declan stopped.

'Unless what, Declan?'

'Rose: Tim Pat wasn't mixed up in anything, was he?'

Rose shook her head firmly. 'No. I'm sure he wasn't. I thought about that myself. I've gone over and over it in my head, and I'm certain he wasn't. He couldn't have been. He hardly ever went out. Just down to the shop. Now and again for a drink. Nothing else.'

'There must be a connection,' Declan said quietly, mainly to himself. 'It seems too much of a coincidence – the two of us from the same house. What about Fergal?'

'What about Fergal?' Rose asked sharply, immediately defending her son.

'He's not –'

'No, he's not, Declan.'

Declan Tuohy shook his head. 'I just can't see why. Oh, shit!'

And that, as they say, was what hit the fan when Regan and Dowling arrived at Seamus Reilly's home.

'I thought I ordered a twenty-four-hour watch on the Duffy house,' he said quietly, the very civility of his observation making it particularly menacing. He felt alert now, all trace of fatigue driven from him by the decisions he had made. And he had, in his peculiar, respectful way, washed and shaved, and donned a dark blue suit and sober tie: he knew he would have to order punishment and it was fitting to dress for such a verdict.

'We did have three men there,' Regan explained. 'Two in the back and one in the garage opposite, just as you ordered.'

'You don't say! And what were they doing? Sleeping? Masturbating? Playing tiddly-winks?'

Regan and Dowling looked at each other and took to shuffling their feet.

'Who was in the garage?' Reilly demanded.

The men were silent.

'I asked you a question,' Reilly snapped.

'O'Callaghan.'

'O'Callaghan?'

'Luke O'Callaghan. He's quite new.'

Reilly frowned and sat down, composing himself before making a judgment. 'I want him replaced,' he announced quietly. 'Immediately. Now. And I want an extra man put into that garage.'

'Yes, Mr Reilly.'

'And as for O'Callaghan –' Reilly paused, running his fingers through his hair, and then smoothing it down again. 'O'Callaghan will have an accident,' he said. 'You, Dowling, will take care of that personally and tonight.'

'Yes, Mr Reilly.'

'Regrettably it will have to be fatal. But it must look like an accident. I want no room for enquiries afterwards.'

'No, Mr Reilly.'

Seamus closed his eyes for a few seconds, planning his course of action. 'Regan,' he said at last, not opening his eyes and speaking in measured tones as though reading the words, 'I want you to get in touch with Intelligence and learn everything you can about a Sergeant Barton. He's posted here with TAC HQ. I want to talk to him within the next few days. You will select as many men as you need to ensure I can have that talk.'

'Yes, Mr Reilly.'

'I understand he's a bit of a loner who gets out and about by himself quite a bit, so it shouldn't be all that difficult for you. If you absolutely have to you can tell him we have his wife and son under observation – but I would prefer to keep that as a surprise.'

'I understand.'

'Most importantly I want you to get a message to Mr Asher asking him to contact me here as soon as possible. Tonight – today, if possible. You can mention it is extremely urgent.'

'Yes, Mr Reilly.'

Reilly now lit a cigar, mulling things over in his mind. 'This O'Callaghan – is he married?' he asked finally.

'Yes.'

'Children?'

'No.'

'Ah. Good. See to it that the usual arrangements are made for the widow, will you? That's it, then, for the moment. Make sure you have Mr Asher contact me as soon as possible.'

'I'll see to that immediately,' Regan promised.

'Thank you,' Reilly said politely.

Within the hour, much to Reilly's surprise, Mr Asher was knocking on the front door.

'I didn't mean for you to call round, John.'

'I thought I'd better,' Asher said, unbuttoning his overcoat but making no attempt to take it off. 'I was told it was extremely urgent.'

'Yes. Eh – a drink?'

'Thanks. A small Scotch, if you please.'

Seamus Reilly poured two drinks and passed one to Mr Asher, waving him to a chair at the same time. 'There's been another incident.'

'Indeed? Cheers.'

'Cheers. Yes. At the Duffy house again. Someone tried to shoot Mrs Duffy's brother. He's staying there for a few days. Over from England for the funeral.'

'And?'

'They missed.' He paused. 'You won't be hearing about it through official channels. We've decided to keep this one to ourselves.'

'I see.'

'However, I told you I'd let you know before we made any move. Well, we are going to have to make a move now.'

'What sort of move would that be?'

Reilly smiled at the suspicion in Asher's question. 'Nothing too drastic – yet.'

'What sort of move?' Asher persisted.

'We're going to bring in that Sergeant Barton for questioning.'

'I see. You think you'll be able to?'

'I believe so.'

'But will he talk?'

'I think we can make him see reason.'

Mr Asher pursed his lips. 'How?'

'We have a card or two up our sleeve.'

'I'm sure you have, Seamus, but all the same I'd like to know a –'

'Let's just say that his wife and son should be able to persuade him it would be in everyone's best interest for him to talk to us.' Seamus Reilly sipped his drink and waited, giving Asher the chance to make up his mind.

'I will want your word that nothing will happen to either the wife or the son.'

'Nothing will happen to them. They will have visitors while

we question the Sergeant. Nothing more. You have my word.'

'It's one thing you abducting people over here, but the mainland is quite another kettle of fish.'

'I realize that, John.'

'How long will you hold Barton?'

Reilly shrugged. 'That rather depends on how co-operative he is, doesn't it? But not too long, I hope.'

'You know all hell is going to break loose?'

'I don't think it will, you know. What can anyone do without involving a lot of very unwelcome questions? No, I think – if your suspicions are correct – I think they'll keep very quiet about it, certainly for a day or two, and I doubt we'll need longer than that. It's a slight gamble, but only slight.'

'A day or two?'

'A day or two.'

'And after that – what about Barton?'

'Oh, I think he can safely be returned to the bosom of the Army.'

'You think?'

Reilly grinned. 'I'm certain. We will return him intact, John.'

'Within forty-eight hours?'

'Within forty-eight hours.'

Asher put his drink on the table beside him and tapped his fingertips together, thinking. 'Right,' he decided. 'I can let you have forty-eight hours. After that –' He stopped and spread his hands apologetically.

'Quite,' Reilly acknowledged.

'And you'll let me know exactly what transpires?'

'Of course.'

'I –'

'Damn. Excuse me,' Seamus Reilly interrupted and went to answer the phone in the hall.

John Asher leaned his head against the back of the chair and closed his eyes, half listening to Reilly's chopped conversation, again wondering what the Chief Constable would say if he knew what was taking place under his nose. Life would be so much easier if the British would simply leave Northern Ireland to look after itself – with a little financial help, to be sure. That, of course, was the rub. If –

'Sorry about that,' Reilly apologized, coming briskly back into the room. 'Sad, really,' he went on, sounding anything but sad, 'one of my men, a young lad named O'Callaghan, has met with an accident. Seems he was fiddling with some wires in his garage when he electrocuted himself. Dreadful.'

'You don't seem too put out.'

'Of course I am, John. I'm shocked – if you'll excuse the word.'

'Well, we'll be called to look into it no doubt.'

Reilly glowered. 'I don't think that would be a good idea. I'm sure you have better things to do.'

'You'd prefer that I had better things to do.'

'Something like that.'

'What did he do – this O'Callaghan?'

'It was just something he didn't do.'

'Oh?'

'Truly, nothing that need concern you.'

'Everything you're mixed up in concerns me, Seamus.'

'Not this. Believe me. It's strictly an internal matter of discipline.'

'No repercussions?'

'None.'

'Very well.'

Reilly gave a little sigh. 'Good.'

Mr Asher stood up and started buttoning his overcoat. 'Now listen: no messing me about. I want to be kept fully informed on this Barton matter. If I find out that –'

'I've told you I'll keep you informed. Don't worry, it only leads to an early grave.'

'I can think of worse ways to go.'

'So can I, John. So can I.'

'I can expect to hear from you soon?'

'You will. Safe home.'

Asher walked to his car. He was about to get in, hesitated, and walked back to the door of the house.

'Forgotten something?' Reilly asked.

'No. Thought of something in fact.'

Reilly raised his eyebrows.

'You're quite certain nobody knows about this shooting?'

'At Duffy's? Quite certain. Only Declan, his sister, his nephew, you and me.'

Mr Asher was amused. 'And that's nobody?'

'I'm sorry. I thought you meant –'

'I did. Well, in that case I think I might pay Colonel Sharmann another visit. He might just slip up.'

'Ye-e-es. He might at that.'

'Well, good night, Seamus.'

'Good night, John.'

· TWELVE ·

COLONEL SHARMANN sat waiting in his office, his tie loosened, his top shirt-button undone, looking very tired. He had been up all night, pacing about and sitting down again, cursing Captain Little for taking so long to report on the night's exercise. Now, at seven-thirty, haggard though he was, he seemed mightily pleased, occasionally smacking his thin lips as though tasting success, rocking back his chair on its two back legs. 'You're quite certain you got him?'

'Quite certain, sir,' Captain Little reassured him.

'Excellent. Well done, Barton,' he continued, turning to the Sergeant.

'Thank you, sir,' Barton acknowledged. There was not a flicker of emotion on his face.

'Then all that's left is Reilly,' Sharmann said deliberately and with clear satisfaction.

'Yes,' Little agreed. 'That's all. But it won't be easy. Reilly's not like the others. He's always protected.'

'Just serve to test your metal, Captain.'

'Yes, sir.'

Colonel Sharmann got to his feet. 'I can tell you one thing:

I'm off for a few hours' kip. We'll meet again later – say about four. I'll be here from two if you want me.' He waved a hand at the chaos on his desk. 'I've all this damned paper-work to get out of the way.'

'Very good, sir.'

'And well done again, Barton.'

'Thank you, sir.'

Declan tossed incessantly in his sleep, waking frequently, then dozing off, hounded by cries of 'city of Moloch'. They were not even human cries, but emanated from a smouldering grey mass over which, like a menacing hand, writhed whisps of smoke. Then from this the mournful face of Colonel Maddox appeared, or rather, the face of Colonel Maddox partially concealed behind a mask of yet another face, a face which Declan could never quite recognize but which he clearly ought to know and which recognized him, a smiling face, the smile toothless and frozen, trying to mouth words but gurgling horribly instead. 'What time is the next bus?' some voice asked. 'To where?' 'To anywhere.' 'Jesus!' Declan heard himself scream seconds before he woke. He looked about the room. Nothing: nothing but the strange darkness as the morning seeped through and round the blanket which had been pinned across the broken window. 'Jesus,' Declan said again. 'Dear Jesus.'

'May I come in?' Mr Asher poked his head round the door of the Colonel's office. Colonel Sharmann stared at his unwelcome visitor. 'Mr Asher! Yes. Yes, come in.'

Mr Asher closed the door carefully behind him. 'I'm sorry to barge in on you like this, Colonel,' he apologized as he walked across the office to the nearest chair and perched himself on the edge of the seat, perhaps hoping to offset the offence the fumes of his cigarette generated. 'I did ring earlier but I was told you wouldn't be back until two,' he decided to explain, puffing happily away. 'Then, as I was passing, I took a chance that you'd have made it back by now.'

'Paper-work. Nothing but damned paper-work,' Sharmann said.

'Ah yes. I know the feeling.'

'You do?'

Mr Asher nodded. 'We're all civil servants, aren't we?'

Sharmann parried the question with one of his own. 'To
what do I owe this visit, Mr Asher?'

'May I? Thank you.' Mr Asher reached across and delicately
tapped the ash from his cigarette into the waste-paper bucket.
'As I said I was just passing so I thought I'd drop in and
bring you up to date. Not that we've made a great deal of
progress, I'm afraid. People simply will not talk to us these
days.'

Colonel Sharmann tapped his teeth with the end of his biro
and waited for Asher to continue.

And Mr Asher obliged. 'One thing has emerged, however.'

'Yes?'

'Yes. Those ridiculous suggestions that the Army might
be involved in our recent unpleasantness have proved quite
unfounded.'

'Did you expect otherwise?' Sharmann remained cool.

Asher allowed himself a little chuckle. 'No. No I did not,
Colonel, but –' he spread his hands as though begging tolerance of his inferior mind – 'we do have to consider every
possibility.'

'I suppose you do.'

'Oh we do, Colonel. After all it wouldn't be the first time
we – well, we had a few problems when the SAS first arrived. I
think they thought we Irish were Arabs, so we had to – how
shall I put it – calm things down for them.'

'Quite.'

Mr Asher decided to light another cigarette from the butt of
the first, and used the silence to plan his strategy. 'Still, there is
light at the end of the tunnel. All things come to those who
wait, don't you think? The more of these unexplained
incidents there are the more likely it is that a mistake will

be made, and the better our chance of catching the culprits.'

'I hope so.'

'Yes. It's all a question of patience. Along we plod, picking up a snippet here and a snippet there, then bingo! Everything falls into place. Wonderful.'

'I'm sure it is.'

'You take last night's shooting, for example –'

'Duffy's? What about it?' the Colonel wanted to know, getting bored and paying rather more attention to the papers on his desk than to the drone of Mr Asher's voice.

'Oh, you've heard about it?' Asher asked, keeping his voice as bland and casual as he could.

It was only then that the Colonel realized his mistake. For an instant, he froze, while his mind raced through a gamut of alternatives. He could feel himself blushing, could feel his ears tingling, could feel Mr Asher's eyes boring into him. He decided to play for time. 'Hmm?' he hummed, keeping his head bent over his papers.

'You've heard about it?' Mr Asher repeated.

'Heard what?' Sharmann asked, composed enough now to look at Asher.

'About the shooting last night.'

'*Last* night? No. I have no report on any shooting last night. I thought you were talking about –'

'The late Tim Pat?' Mr Asher smiled pleasantly, as though indicating his appreciation of how one could be led to such a misunderstanding. 'No, we had another shooting in the same house last night. Rather too much of a coincidence, don't you think? What I was about to say was that, luckily for us, whoever did the shooting made a bad mistake, and if it's the same people responsible for the other incidents . . . well, like I said, bingo!'

Colonel Sharmann waved away some of the acrid cigarette smoke that was blowing his way, and he used this apparent threat to his health as an excuse to go to the window and open it an inch or two. For a short while he stood there, staring out without really seeing, conscious that Asher was watching his every move, interpreting it in his solid policeman's way. 'You were saying?' he asked, but without inflection, without, too, bothering to turn round.

'Only that they made a mistake last night, Colonel,' Asher repeated, trying not to enjoy the moment too much, but his excitement apparent in the way he sucked hard and often on his cigarette, barely waiting for his lungs to empty before inhaling deeply again.

'And what mistake was that?'

'The most basic. They failed to kill their target,' Asher told him, a wicked light dancing in his eyes as he watched the Colonel all but gasp, a small nerve in his neck pulsating rapidly.

Sharmann turned slowly from the window and faced Mr Asher. 'They missed, you say?'

Asher nodded almost sympathetically. 'By the proverbial mile.'

'So Duffy's still alive?' the Colonel continued, trying to inveigle relief into his voice, almost succeeding.

Mr Asher produced an expression of exaggerated puzzlement. 'Why do you keep saying Duffy, Colonel?'

'I presumed –'

'Ah, yes,' Asher cut him short. 'Because it was Tim Pat Duffy's house you presumed everyone there would be called Duffy. Quite logical. I can see your point. No. The man they shot at wasn't a Duffy. It was a visitor. Over for the funeral. A newspaper reporter, I believe. I imagine he'll have quite a field day with this – you know what these reporters are like. They sensationalize things so.'

'Yes,' was all the Colonel trusted himself to say, and this he all but whispered.

'Well, I must be on my way,' Asher said, standing up. 'I'll leave you to all that wretched paper-work, Colonel. I've a mountain of the stuff waiting for my attention but it will have to wait. First things first, I always say. Any further developments and I'll let you know.'

'Thank you.'

'Don't mention it, Colonel,' Asher said, the Colonel's title almost beheaded as he closed the door behind him.

Colonel Sharmann moved quickly to his desk, wondering what the hell he was gong to do, listening to Asher's footsteps recede down the corridor, searching mentally for a possible escape route. Kill Asher was the first thought. Then: kill Captain Little. Kill Barton. He shook his head sharply and jettisoned these panicky ideas. He had to remain calm, in control of the situation, of himself. He had to try to bluff his way through the inevitable. Clearly Asher had stumbled on what was going on, but he certainly had nothing definite to go on or he would never have raised the matter. Damn him! And the reporter had seen nothing. Even if he had – what could he have seen? A car? Long since abandoned. Two men? Some help that would be! Already the Colonel had conned himself into feeling better. Asher could suspect whom he bloody well liked as long as he could not prove it. Sharmann managed a smile: and given a few more minutes he might have been able to wheedle himself into a satisfactory state of optimism. It was unfortunate for Captain Little, therefore, that he chose that precise moment to enter the office, knocking and opening the door. To make matters worse, he was smiling broadly. 'Good afternoon, Colonel.'

'You can wipe that stupid bloody grin off your face to start with, Little,' Sharmann said viciously.

The Captain looked amazed.

'I've just had Inspector Asher here. You know you missed Duffy last night?'

'What?'

'Not only did you not kill him, you never even took a shot at him. It was some other bastard. Some damned reporter friend from London.'

'Christ!'

'Christ is right. Where's Barton?'

'I've no idea, sir. I thought he'd be here.'

The Colonel was now working himself up into quite a rage,

stamping about the office. 'Good God! Can't I trust you two to do anything right?'

'I'm sorry, sir. It was –'

'Sorry!' the Colonel exploded. 'Damn your sorry, Captain. Where the hell is Barton?' he demanded again. 'Sorry!' he mimicked, rounding on the Captain, tell-tale flecks of spittle oozing from the corners of his mouth. 'You know what you've done, don't you? You've just about ruined this entire operation.'

Captain Little opened his mouth as though to apologize again, but stopped himself in the nick of time. He hung his head and stood, meekly accepting the abuse heaped upon him, not really listening. Soon, he recognized the tail-end of one of the Colonel's tirades washing over him. Silence followed, and Little realized that Sharmann was waiting for an answer to a question he had not heard. What was he to say? He raised his head, stared the Colonel in the eyes, and did his best to look penitent.

'I asked you a question, Captain.'

Little decided the safest thing to do was to shake his head slowly, as if to indicate his inferiority and bewilderment.

This seemed to appease the Colonel: he gave a scoffing, self-congratulatory grunt and went back to staring out of the window, the cynical words of Brigadier Brazier now rattling in his brain and doing nothing to console him. 'As far as anyone is concerned your special activities have nothing what-ever to do with the Army and we don't want to read in our Sunday newspapers that they do.' And, of course, that was exactly what Sharmann now saw reflected in the window. RUC ARREST ARMY COLONEL. CONSPIRACY IN HIGH PLACES: These were two of the kinder ones. COLONEL VIGILANTE, was another, while the least scrupulous tabloid promised the SECRETS OF THE MURDERING COLONEL. And there were photographs too, show-ing Guy Sharmann at various stages of his career. In each one he appeared narrow-eyed, shifty. Sharmann shut his eyes. 'Where the hell *is* Barton?' he asked, his frustration and venom almost boiling over.

Little was quick to spot his chance of escape. 'I'll go and find him for you, Colonel.'

'Hmm?' The Colonel turned from the window and stared at Little as though he had never asked a question.

'Barton, sir. I'll go and see if I can find him.'

'You go and do just that. You find Barton and have him back here on the bloody double.'

By the time Captain Little had volunteered to locate the Sergeant and escort him at the bloody double to Colonel Sharmann's office, Barton was across the border and being driven rapidly towards the town of Clones. He was in the back of a small blue van that purported to belong to a firm of plumbers, lying on his stomach, his head resting, comfortably enough, on some folded sacks that smelled of layers' mash. On either side of him squatted a young man, each holding a Kalashnikov rifle. Oddly, the Sergeant was unafraid. Lying there, trussed up like one of the chickens that had gorged itself on the contents of the empty sacks, he felt at peace, an unexpected and pleasant calm filling his consciousness. It was as if through all the years of assassinations, through shades of grief and remorse and guilt, he had been longing to get caught, then captured and tortured, as if only this would expiate his sins. From time to time (and more frequently in the last few years), he had day-dreamed about just such an eventuality, searing his mind with images of the most horrendous cruelty inflicted on him as he writhed and vomited and agonized in his own excrement, screaming that Christ would redeem him, yet all the while aware that it was not his own redemption he sought, but his son's.

When they came for him, he had been sitting quietly in the park for almost an hour, indistinguishable from the men of Belfast. As usual he had chosen a bench remote from the others, facing a bed of primulas and pansies. He liked flowers, their intricate patterns of colour that never clashed. He was contemplating the delicate shades of the massed pansies when an old man joined him, a tramp it appeared, in a ragged overcoat, who was throwing crusts to the flowers. Barton eyed him, faintly amused.

'You think I'm mad, don't you?' the tramp asked mildly. 'Everyone thinks I'm mad just because I feed the flowers. Very partial to a bit of bread they are. Only brown bread, mind you. None of that white pappy stuff. Roughage. They like the roughage. Good for their bowels.'

'I see.'

'You don't believe that.'

'Yes, I do.'

The tramp burst into a high-pitched cackle. 'You're a bigger fool than I am then.'

Not a man given much to laughter, Barton found himself shaking his head and rocking himself back and forth. 'Why do you do it?' The tramp leaned closer conspiratorially. 'A tip,' he confided, touching the end of his nose with his forefinger. 'Always pretend to be mad in Belfast. You can get away with murder here if they think you're mad.'

All trace of the Sergeant's good humour vanished; a familiar, warning tingle tickled the back of his neck. Yet, it seemed, there was nothing to fear from the tramp, nothing ominous in his secret: he calmly finished his dispersal of crusts, blew up the bag and burst it with a bang, grinning gleefully, winked at Barton and shuffled away without a backward glance.

Sergeant Barton watched him go. He knew he was feeling vulnerable, but he saw in the tramp some part of himself, a part that merged madness with innocence, half crazed, half credulous. He felt a prod in his back and froze.

'Don't look round,' the voice said. 'Just sit there nice and quietly for a bit and listen.'

Barton did as he was bid.

'Someone wants to talk to you and we've been sent to take you to him. If you do as you're told you'll be all right. Mess us about and you're dead. Understand?'

Sergeant Barton nodded.

'Good. Now look to your right – slowly.'

Sergeant Barton turned his head slowly.

'You see that blue van?'

Barton nodded.

'That's where we're headed. Just get up and walk nice and easily to the van. When we reach it open the back door, climb in and lie face down on the floor with your hands behind your back. Clear?'

Again, Barton nodded.

'Good. Let's go then.'

Mr Asher made his decision and decided to phone Seamus Reilly on his private number. He knew there was an element of risk, but there was an element of risk in everything he did these days, was there not? He heard Seamus grunt on the end of the line, and said: 'It's the boy they're after.'

'The boy? Fergal?'

'Yes.'

'Right. Thanks. I'll deal with it. And – we've moved.'

'I understand.'

The evening editions carried a small item under the sinister heading BLACK BOX DEATH. All it said was that a man named Luke O' Callaghan had been found electrocuted in his garage. After exhaustive enquiries the police concluded that he had been accidentally killed while trying to defraud the electricity board by fitting a black box to his meter, and they hoped this tragic event would act as a warning and deterrent to any other potential users.

On his way to Clones Reilly had his driver stop at a call box.

'Declan?'

'Yes.'

'Seamus. I can't say too much. Don't let Fergal out of your sight. Make sure he stays in the house.'

'Why? What's happened?'

'Nothing yet. Just do as I say, will you? I'll be away all night but I'll get in touch in the morning. Just make sure Fergal stays in the house.'

'Can't you tell –'

'I'll explain it all tomorrow.'

'He's in trouble?'

'He could be.'

'You –'

'Not with us. I'll explain tomorrow. 'Bye.'

· THIRTEEN ·

THE COMMANDER IN CHIEF of the IRA arrived first, and was waiting patiently for Seamus Reilly, sitting, as was his way, very upright in his chair, his hands folded almost primly on his lap, his spectacles polished and set just below the bridge of his nose. Despite the importance of the meeting he was quite relaxed. He and Reilly knew each other far too well for any affectation to be warranted. They liked and trusted one another. Indeed, the Commander, a solitary, isolated man whose position forbade the outward display of real friendship, looked forward to these private sessions with his long-standing colleague. They were the only occasions on which he could unbend a little, 'be himself', even jocular, for an hour or so. Given the chance, he was an amusing, entertaining man. 'Who's been a busy little chap, then?' he asked Seamus, holding out his hand, his eyes twinkling.

'Busy isn't the word.'

'We all have our trials.'

'Hah. You can have mine any day.'

'I doubt if I or anyone else for that matter could cope as well as you, Seamus. It can't be easy for you.'

Reilly acknowledged the compliment with a grateful smile. 'Practice,' he said, embarrassed by the praise.

The Commander ran his forefinger the length of the scar on his cheek, eyeing Reilly through half-closed lids. 'You sound tired.'

Seamus nodded. 'I am, to tell the truth.'

'And almost disillusioned.'

Reilly frowned. 'A little, perhaps.'

Now the Commander nodded, folding his hands on his lap once again, looking concerned in a fatherly way. 'I can understand that,' he said sympathetically.

'Frustrated I think would be a better word.'

The Commander continued to nod, encouraging Reilly to talk by keeping quiet himself.

'It strikes me we take two steps back for every one we take forward.'

Again the Commander waited.

'This endless violence,' Reilly murmured as though he was just thinking, this time shaking his head.

'It is forced on us, Seamus.'

'Oh, I know it is. I know it is. That's the tragedy of all of it. It seems there can never be an end to it.'

The Commander unfolded his hands and crossed his legs. 'Not in our lifetime I wouldn't think,' he agreed quietly in a tone that signified he was well aware of the appalling implications of his statement.

'So we achieve nothing.'

'You know we are doing everything we can to move away from the violence, Seamus, despite internal opposition. We try to arrange talks, and what happens? We are snubbed. Dismissed. Any politician, British or otherwise, who tries to seek an end to the situation by including us in talks is vilified. We move into what they call – without, I think, realizing the significance of the term – the political arena, and we are mocked as terrorist front men gaining votes at the point of a gun.' He looked up. 'You know, I truly believe that some leading politicians want the agony to continue. God alone knows what purpose they think it will serve apart from securing their own positions. And on top of everything else we have to contend with this latest business. I take your assessment to be correct? The Army is definitely involved?'

'Asher is positive, and he doesn't make many mistakes. When I leave you I have to go and question Barton. When I've spoken to him I'll know for certain one way or the other.'

'And if it is confirmed how do you propose to deal with it?'

Reilly gave a tired smile. 'I haven't honestly thought that far ahead.'

'We could certainly exploit it.'

'Yes. We could do that. I wonder, though, if it would be the wisest course for us to take?'

'It must be your decision, Seamus.'

'Oh, I know. I'm just wondering if it wouldn't be better to try and keep it under wraps and do a deal?'

'You think you could – do a deal?'

'I believe so. The Brits will be only too happy to keep this one quiet. What we get, though, will depend on how much we want.'

The Commander grinned. 'I can think of a number of things.'

'So can I. Whether we get them or not is another matter.'

'It surprises me Asher has been so co-operative.'

'Asher's all right. He's a bit like myself really.'

'Is he, now?' the Commander asked, feigning shock.

'A bit. He wants a quiet life. He wants law and order. He just has a problem of choosing between duty and his mistrust of us. Still, he needs me like I need him.'

'Fortunately.'

'Fortunately,' Seamus agreed.

'Ah, well, I'm sure you'll bring things to a satisfactory conclusion. Let me know how things go tonight.'

'I will, of course.'

'And keep the faith.'

'There's not much else left, is there?'

'Not much.'

Suddenly Seamus Reilly gave a long-drawn bitter laugh. 'Tell me, do you ever feel like saying to hell with it all? Feel like packing your bags and high-tailing it away from here as fast as you can?'

The Commander smiled thinly. 'Often,' he confessed. 'But where would I go? America? Australia? What good would that do, Seamus? I couldn't run away from myself, could I? I'm afraid, my friend, you and I are a crucified breed, nailed well and truly to this unfortunate land.'

Reilly nodded.

'Between ourselves – you know the most awful thing about it all? Neither side can win as things stand. Oh, I know the tally of dead is heavily in our favour and we could increase that without any bother –' the Commander snapped his fingers – 'but that is no solution. I'm afraid we are all – we and the Unionists and the RUC – we are all hamstrung by the whims and greed and power-mania of the politicians: and not only in London. Dublin too, and Belfast. We are all useful hooks on which they can hang their avaricious hats. All we can do is to be sure we make our presence felt until such time as someone in power recognizes the futility of it all, puts the country above their personal ambition, and –' The Commander stopped and sighed. 'You know all this already. Well, there seems no such person on the horizon, does there?' he concluded sadly.

Seamus Reilly tried to think of someone, but failed. 'No,' he admitted. 'There doesn't.'

'Still, who knows, someone might turn up.'

Declan pretended to read the paper, holding it high in front of his face, listening to the rhythmic clickety click of Rose's knitting needles as they plained-and-purled their way through another row in a pullover for Fergal. He had been deeply troubled since Seamus' warning, feeling himself being sucked into a simmering intrigue the exact elements of which were deliberately being withheld from him, leaving him wondering what the hell was going on, wondering, too, what possible role Fergal could be playing in it all. He wanted to talk to Rose about it, but up to now he had decided against this: she was bearing up remarkably well, but he sensed she was nearing breaking point. Like so many other women in Belfast she had developed a curious mechanism which switched off any recognition of tragedy, allowing it to be activated only when alone, her stoicism and meek acceptance anchored in her faith in the often incomprehensible justice of God.

'Anything in the paper?' Rose asked suddenly.

'Not a damned thing.'

'I see. You all right?'

'I'm fine.'

'Sure?'

'Sure I'm sure. What about you?'

'I wasn't shot at.'

'No. Rose . . .' Again Declan was on the point of telling his sister about Reilly's phone-call; and again he rejected the idea.

'Yes?'

'Nothing.'

Rose let it pass and contentedly went on with her knitting.

'Where's Fergal?' Declan asked, trying to sound casual.

'Upstairs. Why?'

'Just wondered. He spends so much time alone.'

'Yes. He's like me. Alone, he can keep the hurt to himself,' Rose explained, putting down her knitting and gazing into the electric fire. 'It's a very strange thing, you know, Declan. I like being alone. I can create my own little world. I can go anywhere. Into the future. Back to the past. Just anywhere.'

And that was no word of a lie. Rose Duffy found herself peopling her fantastic world with old friends now that Tim Pat was gone. Often she would start the process by seeing herself in her mind as a small, pretty child with long ringlets and big, blue bows, even smelling the smells of childhood: baby powder, the lavender her mother packed in muslin bags and stashed in drawers and under pillows, the special soap, and hay – although where the scent of hay came from she had long since forgotten. Often, too, alone and pottering about the house, cooking or cleaning, she would chat to herself, playing dual roles, even having heated arguments, creating a life wherein everything was normal. She delighted, most of all, in altering the actors in her playful dramas (some superficially: her mother from the round, short, rather dowdy little woman she had been to something lithe and elegant with a touch of Veronica Lake; some more profoundly: her father from the conniving, drunken bully to a man of wit and charm and full of love) and, perhaps significantly, they all had one thing in common: they all worshipped Rose, and showered her with the affection she had always craved but never received.

'– upstairs,' Declan was saying.

'I'm sorry?'

'I'm just going upstairs,' Declan repeated.

'Oh. Yes,' Rose said, taking hold of her knitting again. 'Don't be long. It's nice just sitting here with you.'

'I'll be right down. Nature.'

Rose smiled. 'I haven't heard that for years. Do you remember Dad always said that?'

'Did he?'

Rose nodded. 'Nature calls, he used to say. Do you remember what Mammy used to answer?' she asked, her voice softening at the mention of her mother.

'No. What?'

'Open the window when you're finished. And when he came down she would be up those stairs like a shot to make sure the window was open.'

'The things you remember! I'll be sure to open the window.'

'Don't be silly.'

Fergal had his bedroom window open. Indeed, it was always kept open except on those days when the wind blew the rain directly into his room. It had nothing to do with a passion for fresh air, however: it was kept open to allow Martin (or Martin's spirit as he sometimes thought of it if only for convenience) to spread his wings, so to speak, and exercise his muscles. And Fergal would sit there as he was doing now, watching, amazed and a little envious at the ease with which his friend could move, gliding, loop-the-looping, skimming the rooftops, stopping and hovering, motionless. And when Martin returned, blowing from his exertions, Fergal, too, would feel his heart thumping, would feel exhausted and collapse on to the bed, the sweat pouring from his face.

'A penny for them.'

Fergal jumped, and swung round sharply, fear in his eyes. 'Jesus, you frightened me,' he said, clearly annoyed.

'I just wondered if you were okay,' Declan explained.

'Of course I am. Or I was till you scared me half to death.'

'I'm sorry. Can I come in?'

'Sure, if you want,' Fergal permitted, but without much enthusiasm.

Declan Tuohy came into the room and closed the door behind him. He looked about for a place to sit: apart from the chair which Fergal occupied there was only one other, and that was piled high with magazines, clothes, and a broken tennis-racket in its press. Declan chose the bed and sat on the edge.

'Anything special?' Fergal wanted to know. 'You've never come to my room before.'

'Well, I thought it was time we had a chat.'

'About what?'

'You?'

'Me? What's there to chat about me?'

Plenty. Fergal's underhand involvement for one thing; Reilly's admonition for another – although discussing that was something Declan wanted to postpone for the moment. Fergal would, of course, ultimately have to be told, would have to be warned to stay in the house, but how on earth to do it? To order him to stay indoors would be tantamount to inviting instant rebellion. Clearly, what he would have to do, Declan decided, was to inveigle him to remain in the house by making it sound far more exciting than anything he could hope to encounter outside. 'Well, for a start, I spoke to Seamus Reilly like you asked.'

That certainly got Fergal's attention. 'And?' he asked.

'And he's agreed to see you. Indeed, he wants to see you.'

'Oh?'

'You must have impressed him. He seems to think you're a pretty bright young man.'

Fergal smiled, pleased with the flattery.

'In fact, I believe he wants you to do something for him.'

'What?'

'He didn't say. He wouldn't tell me anyway. If he does want you to do something it would be between you and him.'

Fergal nodded, seeing the logic in this. 'When?'

'I don't know. He just said to tell you he'd be in touch soon,' Declan said, gratified and relieved he had received the reaction he wanted. 'However, he did make one stipulation.'

Immediately Fergal looked suspicious. Careful, Martin warned him. Don't commit yourself. Careful. 'What's that?'

'He doesn't want you to be seen about for a day or two. He wants you to promise you'll stay in the house until he contacts you.'

– That seems fair enough, Martin said.

'That seems fair enough,' Fergal said. 'I suppose it's something to do with last night.'

'I suppose it is.'

'Well you can tell him I'll do that. I'm quite happy in my room anyway. I've lots of things I can be doing.'

Declan stared at Fergal's face as though trying to fathom what was going on in his brain. 'Tell me –' he began but stopped when he saw Fergal's eyes narrow. 'I know you'll think it's none of my business,' he started again, 'but it is in a way. You and Rose are the only family I have now. You're not . . . you're not mixed up in any of Reilly's –'

'No,' Fergal interrupted quickly.

Declan continued to stare.

Fergal looked away and back again. He smiled innocently but his eyes remained cold. 'You don't believe me?'

'Yes, I believe you,' Declan confirmed none too convincingly. 'You will be careful, won't you, Fergal?'

'Careful? I'm always careful.'

'You won't let yourself be talked into doing anything stupid?'

'I'm not stupid, Declan.'

'I know you're not.'

'Well, then?'

'I just want you to be careful.'

'I'll be careful.'

'That's all I ask. I've known Seamus a long, long time and he could try and take advantage of you. You won't let that happen?'

– Like hell we will, Martin put in.

'Like hell I will.'

Declan looked sad and worried, looked as though he wanted to pursue the conversation yet further, but Fergal had turned away again and was staring out of the window, effectively putting an end to the discussion.

'Right. I'll leave you to it.'

'Yes. Oh – and Declan: thanks for arranging things.'

'As long as you know what you're doing,' Declan said.

'We know.'

'We?'

For a second Fergal looked uneasy. Then: 'Me and my shadow,' he sang. 'You know what they say – keep friends with your shadow and you'll never be alone.'

Seamus Reilly was driven from his meeting with the Chief of Staff to a remote slate-roofed farmhouse about eight miles from Clones. Set in sixty acres of arable land, it had been purchased with IRA funds some ten years earlier and farmed, quite legitimately and with considerable productivity, by a Provo of unquestionable loyalty. About the house were a number of out-buildings – a milking parlour, a couple of stables, a chicken shed and such like – grouped to form a courtyard, cobbled and weedy. Seamus made his way on foot to the far building of the quadrangle, threading like a dancer through the weeds and puddles and blotches of muck, wincing occasionally as a stone all but penetrated the thin soles of his elegant Italian shoes. As he reached the building the door was opened and he stepped in. The stench of slaughter was appalling. Traces of blood from the hundreds, perhaps thousands, of pigs that had been killed and disembowelled there, were splattered on the stones floor and walls. On a low, oak slaughter-and-scrubbing bench looking uncomfortable, perhaps sensing the indelicacy of perching oneself on a table whereon so many beasts had screamed as their throats were cut, sat two men, both in paramilitary fatigues, each with a rifle. A single unshaded light dangled from the roof and, under it, on a stool probably once used for milking, was Sergeant Barton, his hands tied behind his back, his feet bound together and to the legs of the stool. Reilly did not, yet, look directly at him; instead he glanced about the shed and, as if by telepathy, a chair was produced. Reilly indicated the exact spot he wished it placed: two feet in front of the Sergeant. He dismissed all three guards and sat down, crossed his legs and lit a small cigar. He blew the first lungful of smoke upwards from the corner of his mouth, watching it rise, his eye catching the long line of vicious meat hooks that hung from a metal rail which ran the length of the shed. Involuntarily he shuddered. 'I'm sorry about this,' he said, using his cigar like a baton to indicate the gruesome interior.

Sergeant Barton closed his eyes slowly and opened them again, saying nothing.

'There is nothing, I assure you, significant in bringing you here.'

Barton remained silent.

'And if you co-operate and tell me what I want to know I can also assure you that you will be returned, safe and sound to –' Reilly paused to give a little smile – 'to the bosom of your family.'

Still the Sergeant said nothing.

'On the other hand –' Reilly sighed and shrugged – 'well, let me just advise you that at this very moment two of my men are visiting your wife and son, and –'

Immediately Sergeant Barton came to life, straining at the ropes, his face contorted in fury. 'You bas –'

Reilly's hand shot into the air, demanding silence. 'You have my word that they are merely visiting. Nothing untoward will befall your loved ones if you answer my questions. And you can telephone your wife as soon as we have concluded our – eh – business and reassure yourself as to their well-being.'

'If anything happens to them –'

'That, Sergeant, depends entirely on yourself. We are not – as you may have been led to believe – savages. We fully realize that you are but an instrument in the scheme of things. We have no desire whatever to punish you or your family. But there are certain things we have got to know – and, believe me, we will, if forced, use every means in our power to get the answers.'

'What do you want to know?'

'Now we're getting somewhere. I am pleased,' Reilly said, genuinely sounding it. 'Let me tell you what we already know, and then you can help me fill in the details. We know that Colonel Sharmann, Captain Little and yourself were sent over here to assassinate certain members of my organization. We know that you have been successful in most cases. Most of them I can understand, but the first thing I want to know is why did you kill Tim Pat Duffy?'

Sergeant Barton looked away from the penetrating eyes, looked across the shed and then down at his feet. Somewhere in that short journey he saw his son, terrified and screaming, having, like the wretched pigs, his throat slit, his blood pumping from the great gaping wound. 'It was a mistake,' he said almost to himself.

Reilly looked bewildered. 'A mistake?'

'We were meant to kill somebody else.'

'I don't understand. Who were you supposed to kill?'

'His son.'

'His son?' Reilly asked incredulously.

'Yes.'

148

'Why his son?'

'I don't know.'

'I presume Sharmann gives the orders?'

Barton nodded. 'He has a list.'

'Ah. He has a list of people who are to be killed?'

'Yes.'

'I see,' Reilly said thoughtfully. 'We'll come back to that in a minute. Just let me get this straight. Your orders were to kill Duffy's son and you killed Duffy himself by mistake?'

'Yes.'

'That was – careless.'

'The description fitted.'

'Now, last night's shooting. Was that meant for young Duffy as well?'

'Yes.'

'What on earth is so important about Duffy?'

Barton shook his head. 'I don't know.'

'So, you thought it was Duffy last night and –'

'No.'

'No?'

'I knew it wasn't. Captain Little said it was but I knew it wasn't.'

'But you shot anyway?'

'I missed.'

Reilly gave a choked, angry snort. 'I know you missed but –'

'On purpose.'

Reilly, about to launch into a tirade, stopped, leaving his mouth open. Imperceptibly his eyes softened as he stared at the Sergeant's face, seeing, fleetingly, that look he had so often spotted in his own eyes, a look, almost but not quite, of remorse, a look of pain and torment and fear, a look that seemed not to belong to the killer but to the victim, a look that foretold that the executioner died while the executed lived . . .

'You are already dead' . . . the lachrymose words of Mr Apple weaved their way into Reilly's brain and, for a moment, Reilly thought he had grasped what the old man had meant. But only for a moment. 'You missed on purpose?'

'Yes.'

'And why, pray, would you do a thing like that?' Reilly wanted to know, erasing his thoughts of Mr Apple with the heavy sarcasm.

It took what seemed a very long time for the Sergeant to speak. 'Have you ever killed?' he asked.

Reilly shook his head. 'It is not my job to kill.'

'You have never killed?' Sergeant Barton asked, but in the tone of someone drawing a conclusion.

'No.'

'Then you couldn't understand.'

'Try me,' Reilly said, immediately frowning at his choice of words. 'Just a moment, though.'

He went to the door and returned with one of the guards, who untied the Sergeant and left the shed, swinging the ropes behind him, making them whistle eerily.

Reilly watched Barton as he flexed his fingers and rubbed his wrists. Then he sat down again, waiting for his prisoner to speak.

'Thank you,' Barton said.

Reilly inclined his head.

'I don't know if I can explain what I wanted to say.'

Reilly waited, while Barton sat, tormented by the memory of the men and women he had killed: in Biafra, Cyprus, Aden and, finally Ireland. In those split seconds as one face was whisked away and before another could be substituted Sergeant Barton caught glimpses of his son's face, grown old and hard, his own face, in fact, placed on his son's shoulders.

Reilly decided he had waited long enough, recognizing the torment Barton was enduring. 'This list you mentioned,' he said. 'Apart from young Duffy – who else is on it, do you know?'

Sergeant Barton opened his eyes with a start. 'Apart from – only one other, I think. A man called Reilly. Seamus Reilly.'

Seamus blinked, astounded, yet he hid his reaction by staring ahead. 'Seamus Reilly,' he repeated, fascinated.

'Yes. He's special. Colonel Sharmann has kept him until last.'

'I see.'

'He's important.'

'I'm sure he is,' Reilly said, allowing himself a thin smile. 'And tell me – should we let you go from here, and should the good Colonel order you to kill this important Seamus Reilly – will you kill him?'

Sergeant Barton shook his head. 'I don't know.' Then: 'No.' Then: 'I don't know.'

'I see.' Reilly said again. 'Why the doubt?'

Barton knew he was about to break every rule, but continued nonetheless. 'I don't know that either. Perhaps –' he began, but faltered.

'Perhaps?' Reilly prompted.

'It comes back to what I was trying to say earlier. If you have never killed anyone I don't think you would understand,' the Sergeant explained and seemed about to leave it at that. Suddenly, though, he shook himself and sat up straight on the stool. 'When you are young and are ordered to kill someone it seems – it seems –' The Sergeant floundered as the word eluded him.

'Acceptable?' Reilly suggested.

'I suppose,' Barton agreed. 'Not even that. You just don't question it. If it is an order it *must* be the right thing. But as you get older you become afraid – not of being caught – that's the risk you take – of –' The Sergeant broke off again.

'Of dying?' Reilly asked. His own secret dread.

'No. Not of dying exactly. I mean I have no fear of actually dying.' The Sergeant gave a forced, bitter, jittery laugh. 'You know what I'm afraid of?' he asked, clearly intent on making a clean breast of it but already embarrassed and moving about on the stool, squirming almost. 'It's after death I'm afraid of. Afraid of being face to face with the people I have killed. Afraid of finding out they were innocent.' He paused for a moment before adding: 'Most of all I'm afraid they will want to forgive me.'

Seamus Reilly felt an unpleasant chill working its way up his spine as though what Barton feared most was an aspect of eternity he, Reilly, had managed to keep out of his thoughts. But there it was now, flaunting its peculiar horror, and he was forced to recognize it as indeed a fearful and melancholy prospect. Yet it was something he would have to think about later: right now all he wanted was to get away from the Sergeant, get away, too, from all talk of death. Involuntarily he raised his hands in a gesture of absolution. 'I have decided to let you go,' he said. 'But on certain conditions.'

Oddly, and contrary to what Reilly had anticipated, Sergeant Barton's face took on an even gloomier aspect. 'Why?' he asked, and immediately frowned as though bewildered by his question.

Reilly waved away the question, petulantly flicking his wrist. 'I want you to keep this meeting a secret. Mention it to no one. Imagine it never took place.'

Barton nodded.

'If Sharmann gives you any further orders to kill, you will go ahead and obey them.'

'I –'

'You will obey them.'

Again Barton nodded.

'And I beg you to remember that, if necessary, we can show our displeasure in a very unpleasant way – on your family.'

Sergeant Barton nodded his agreement for the third time.

Seamus Reilly stood up, delicately flicking some ash from his trouser leg. 'Incidentally, I don't think Sharmann will be issuing many more orders,' he declared, sounding a little smug. 'And I think you'll find yourself transferred back to England pretty soon.'

Sergeant Barton stood up also. 'Who are you?' he asked as if Reilly's absence of identity had just dawned on him.

Reilly grinned wickedly. 'Me? I'm the important Seamus

Reilly,' he said, tempted to wink but just closing both his eyes briefly instead.

Barton suddenly laughed, at the irony of it all.

'Yes,' Reilly admitted. 'It is quite funny, don't you think?' he asked and tidily carried his chair from the centre of the room and placed it against the wall. 'Just remember, Sergeant, this meeting never took place. And when you get back to England you just look after that boy of yours. Don't let him follow your – our – footsteps.'

And with that Reilly walked briskly from the shed. Outside he leaned his back against the wall and drew in several deep breaths, forcing the stink of porky carnage from his lungs.

'Everything all right, Mr Reilly?'

'Everything is fine. Just fine. Get him back to Belfast.'

'But –'

'Just get him back to Belfast,' Reilly snapped. 'Unharmed. I want him alive and well – for the moment.'

'Yes, Mr Reilly.'

'If you're stopped – well, then shoot him. Otherwise –'

'I understand.'

'Good.'

'Hello, love,' Sergeant Barton said.

'David! I've been so worried.'

'Are you all right?'

'Yes. Yes, I'm all right. It was you I was worried about. When those men came I thought something dreadful had happened.'

Sergeant Barton let his breath out slowly. 'They didn't – upset you?'

His wife gave a small laugh. 'They were lovely, really. They played with Simon when they'd finished checking the house. One of them even read him a story when he went to bed.'

'They've gone now?'

'Oh yes. They had a phone call here about an hour ago. They really were very nice, David. They explained they did this for all the men serving in Northern Ireland.'

'That's right.'

'When will you be home?'

'Soon, love.'

'Really?'

'Really. I must go. Give Simon a kiss for me.'

'I will. I love you.'

'I love you, too.'

'Take care of yourself.'

'I will.'

''Bye.'

''Bye.'

The first thing Seamus Reilly did on his return home was to write a note to Mr Asher and send it round to him, instructing his driver that any reply should be returned to him without delay. Then he took a shower (tossing all the clothes he had worn into a corner of his bedroom), using a rather highly perfumed soap, sniffing himself from time to time as though for reassurance that all smell of the slaughterhouse had been washed away. Satisfied, he dried himself thoroughly, slipped on his dressing-gown and went downstairs. In his sitting-room he injected a tape of Mahler's Third Symphony into the cassette-player, and sank gratefully into an armchair. Folding his hands on his lap and putting his slippered feet on to an upholstered stool, he closed his eyes, waiting.

Mr Asher smiled at the curious wording of Reilly's note. The pigeon has been returned to its roost, indeed! Asher laughed aloud. YOUR SUSPICIONS CORRECT. THE PIGEON HAS BEEN RETURNED TO ROOST. SUGGEST A MEETING BEFORE WE PROCEED.

'You say Mr Reilly wants a reply?'

'He said if there was one I should bring it back to him immediately.'

'Tell him yes. Same time, same place, tomorrow.'

· FOURTEEN ·

IN THE EARLY hours a violent, crashing storm hammered the city, the jagged forks of lightning reaching down to the ground, the claps of thunder seeming to batter on and on as they shunted their echoes. Rain, light and tentative at first, gathered strength and fell in a steady sheet at times so dense the lightning seemed reflected in glass. Soldiers on night patrol huddled in doorways for shelter, cursing their luck, cursing, too, the bloody Irish who had caused them to be there. Children cried, and dogs whined and panted, terrified by the noise. In the trees, their heads packed under their wings, the starlings sat out the deluge, remaining motionless, hoping, perhaps, that whatever demon was on the rampage would pass them by.

By morning the storm had passed leaving behind a sodden, steaming city on which a fine drizzle fell from heavy black clouds that presaged nothing but misery.

Colonel Sharmann shook his topcoat before hanging it on the peg behind the door, and stamped his feet on the small mat. The nightmare of the previous day had left him drained and frightened. He had been stranded on that menacing grey sea of panic, threatened by the warrant of exposure. At one stage, just as dusk was falling, he was surprised and shocked to find himself crying, something he could not remember ever doing since childhood. Only the thought of a confrontation with Barton had succeeded in raising his battered spirits. Now he felt that the violence of the storm was but a foretaste of the furore that was about to be unleashed. It was something of a relief when Captain Little and Sergeant Barton reported as ordered.

'Good morning, sir,' Little tried tentatively.

The Colonel nodded.

The Captain, encouraged, ventured: 'That was quite a storm.'

The Colonel's reaction was extraordinary. 'Jesus how I hate and detest this bloody place,' he shouted, almost running to the window and pointing out on to the city but with his fist clenched and arm held high in what was instantly recognizable as a Fascist salute.

Captain Little looked at the Sergeant, raising his eyebrows in disbelief and grimacing in a manner used by schoolboys when silently enquiring if their teacher had gone raving mad. But Little noticed that Barton was gazing straight ahead, paying him not the slightest heed, mesmerized, it seemed, by some invisible object in the corner. Perhaps it was retaliation for such lack of support that prompted Captain Little to announce: 'I've brought Barton, sir. You said you wanted to see him.'

'I CAN see him,' Colonel Sharmann said angrily.

'Yes, sir.'

Sharmann turned from the window and made his way back to his desk. 'You know,' he said as he lowered himself into his chair, 'that we've made a right botch-up of this mission?'

For a moment it looked as if Captain Little was going to be foolhardy enough to protest. But only for a moment: he soon changed his mind.

'I thought you were supposed to be a marksman.' The Colonel addressed his statement to Barton who continued to gaze ahead. 'A simple target like that and twice you make a mess of it.'

'There were –'

'Oh, do shut up, Little,' Sharmann said, sounding jaded. 'Anyway,' he went on with rather more energy, 'I've spent the night thinking about it. There's only one way we can hope to redeem the situation. We'll forget about Duffy and go all out to get Reilly.'

Captain Little brightened. 'That seems like the best thing, sir.'

'Thank you,' Sharmann said, loading his thanks with sarcasm. 'However, due to your ineptitude we have an additional problem. Inspector Asher suspects what we're here for. I'm sure of that. So –' The Colonel leaned back, clasping his hands behind his head and pursing his lips, apparently thinking. 'So,' he went on after a second or two, 'we will have to add Inspector Asher to our list. It will work out quite well. We can use one to flush out the other and kill two birds with the one stone, as they say.'

Captain Little was appalled at this outrageous suggestion but experience had taught him to control his feelings in front of Sharmann. 'Yes, sir,' he said, managing to keep his voice steady.

'There are one or two details I want to finalize, but I want you both on standby. Timing will be imperative,' the Colonel insisted, sounding like a master strategist. 'And I don't want you wandering off again, Barton. Where were you, anyway?'

Sergeant Barton moved his gaze from the wall to the Colonel's face. For an instant he thought about revealing all that had happened to him but immediately rejected it. Fear for the safety of his family was the first reason. But, in the brief time he had to consider his reply, he found himself loathing the Colonel's uncaring attitude to death, his complete lack of a morality. He recognized the contrast with Seamus Reilly who had kept his word and whose men had shown tenderness to his son. He knew those same men would have cut his son's throat

157

and murdered his wife had he failed to co-operate. Nevertheless Reilly had kept his promises, had shown an understanding of Barton's predicament, appreciated that orders were orders and made remarkable allowances for that. Further: in the blinkered, shaded world wherein lives are traded, Reilly had shown a compassion and respect which the Colonel would certainly have scoffed at. 'Nowhere in particular, sir,' Sergeant Barton answered.

The Colonel grunted, and started to gather up the papers on his desk into neat piles. 'Well, that's it for now. Remember. I want you both where I can find you at a moment's notice.'

'Yes, sir,' Little said obligingly.

'Sir,' Barton said quietly.

Declan was surprised when Seamus Reilly called at the house, even more startled at the way he looked and sounded. It was a Seamus Reilly Declan had never witnessed before: his eyes sunken, the pupils dilated – that was the only word appropriate; his voice, also, had undergone some transformation, an octave lower, it sounded hoarse and gruff, a voice, in fact, adapted to giving commands rather than indulging in polite conversation.

'I need to talk to you, Declan.'

'Come in. In there,' Declan said, indicating the sitting-room.

'Thank you. Perhaps you'd close the door?'

Declan shut the door and elected to wait by it, observing Reilly who paced about the room, tapping his jacket pocket as though to make sure his cigars were there should he need the calming benefit of one.

'You'd better sit down,' Reilly said, trying a tentative, reassuring smile.

Declan was curious but accepted the advice, deciding to say nothing. Reilly stood staring into the mirror over the mantelpiece, and it was to his reflection he seemed to speak when he said: 'What I'm going to tell you is strictly between you and me. I'm only telling you because I am going to need your help.

158

And I'm going to ask your help because there is nobody else I can trust.'

'I'm listening,' Declan said, the words 'curiouser and curiouser' coming to mind.

Reilly turned from the mirror and sat down opposite Declan, sitting well forward in his chair, knees apart, his hands clasped and thumping the air as he accentuated his words. He did not look Declan in the eye as he spoke: frowning, he seemed to concentrate on something far away, a glazed, ecstatic shadow hovering before his vision. 'Let me start by saying that Tim Pat was killed by accident. The shot taken at you was also a mistake.'

'A mistake? Huh. How do you know that?'

'I've spoken to the man who killed Tim Pat and shot at you. He assured me – and I believe him – that he could have killed you if he had wanted to. It was Fergal they were after.'

'Fergal! What in Christ's name would anyone want to kill Fergal for?'

'He was on their list.'

'Their list?'

'Yes. Their list. Along with Donovan, Brennan and Fogarty, who were killed just before Tim Pat – and myself.'

'You?'

Reilly found time to withdraw himself from his distant gaze and smile wistfully. 'Me. Now let me explain what has been happening,' he said, closing his eyes now, then opening them again and adopting his strange glazed expression once more. 'We have learned that three men – a Colonel, a Captain and a Sergeant – were sent over here by the British Army to eliminate certain members of our organization. How they compiled their list of victims I have no idea – yet. With a little persuasion – very little, I assure you – we managed to get the Sergeant to talk to us.'

'Was it him who shot at me?'

'Yes.'

'What –'

'Please –' Seamus Reilly unclasped his hands and held one

over his heart, somehow conveying a plea for Declan to refrain from interrupting. 'Now, it would be possible for us simply to get our revenge by removing all three men permanently. Not easy, but possible. However, by so doing it would be used as another example of what they love to call wanton IRA violence. That would merely give them the propaganda advantage and we have no intention of allowing that to happen. So, we intend to do a little bargaining. And for that, Declan, we need an intermediary. Someone unconnected with either party. And that is where you come in. Who better to handle the negotiations than a journalist of your considerable standing?'

'Oh no, Seamus. Not on your life. I'm not getting involved in any of your schemes.'

'But you *are* involved, my friend. From the moment we offered protection to this house you were involved. We will make it quite clear that you are in no way interested in our activities here. In any case, it will be a very, very quiet affair. The last thing the British will want is to have their nasty undercover schemes exposed. They will negotiate, I promise you. All we want from you is that you get our message to the right quarter.'

'And how do you propose I do that, for heaven's sake.'

'I thought, perhaps, through Colonel Maddox.'

'Maddox? But he's retired,' Declan said, immediately realizing how fatuous the remark was.

'True. But he would know the right people. And it is only with him that I – we – will be prepared to negotiate.'

'Maddox will never agree.'

'He'll have no option. Don't you worry about that. We will see to it that he has no option. We can be quite persuasive when we put our minds to it.'

'I'm sorry, Seamus. You'll have to get somebody else.'

'There is nobody else. If it helps you can think you'll be preventing a bloodbath.' Reilly tried to help, purposely being dramatic. 'Anyway, I would have thought you owe this much to poor Tim Pat.'

Declan sneered cynically. 'Come off it, Seamus.'

Graciously Seamus acknowledged the rebuke. 'Just trying to persuade you kindly,' he said. And then his attitude changed. Gone, now, was any hint of vagueness, gone, too, was any suggestion that he would brook rejection of his plan. 'Declan,' he said in a cold, menacing tone that obliterated their years of friendship, 'I regret that, like Maddox, you have no option now. As they say in the films, you already know too much. Besides,' he added, brightening, certain that his warning had been received, 'it's not as if we were asking you to do anything unpleasant. Quite the contrary.'

Declan stared at Reilly for several seconds with what looked like hatred. 'What precisely do you want me to do?'

Reilly exhaled slowly, trying to keep the relief from showing on his face. He smiled almost compassionately, the benevolent conqueror. 'Just what I told you, Declan. Act as an intermediary when the time comes.'

'And when will that be?'

'Shortly. Within a day or two.'

'Tim Pat's funeral is tomorrow.'

'Oh. They've released the body?' Reilly asked.

Declan nodded.

'Well, we wouldn't ask you to miss that. Anyway, I have a number of things to see to before we are ready to – eh – start negotiations.'

'I'm sure you have.'

'Don't worry, Declan,' Reilly said, standing up and reaching out to place a consoling hand on Declan's shoulder. 'You know I wouldn't ask you to do anything that would lead to your being harmed.'

'Wouldn't you?'

Reilly was offended. 'Of course not.'

Declan let the remark pass. Before he had time to say anything Reilly was apologizing: 'I won't be able to make the funeral myself. I hope you'll forgive me. And even if I could I don't think it would be the wisest thing for me to do. It might give the wrong impression. Might suggest that Tim Pat had been – well, you understand how minds work. There could be repercussions on Mrs Duffy.'

'You're very considerate,' Declan said tightly.

'I try to be,' Reilly agreed, oblivious to or simply ignoring the sarcasm.

Alone, standing at the window, watching Seamus Reilly bustle down the path and into his waiting car, Declan Tuohy felt nothing but rage. Reilly had manipulated him into this dreadful situation. Worse, he'd been so weak and pliable. Yet even as he fumed a couple of things filtered into his mind that to some degree assuaged his anger. He recalled, vividly, the aberrant and fantastic words of Mr Apple that Colonel Maddox had given him to read; no, it was more than that he recalled them: he could hear them – hear them being whispered in his ear by a trembling voice, aged yet filled with life, close by, yet far, far away, a voice he could not recognize, yet seemed to know extremely well. 'And there is a soul perched high above the awful tragedy that continues to unfold . . . an unlikely soul,' the voice recounted. 'And I repeat,' it continued, seeming to move away, 'such a one exists, unknown to all. Unknown even to himself. And in him rests the hope I speak of,' the voice concluded, now so distant that Declan found himself straining to catch the dying phrase. Suddenly another voice, this one booming so loudly that Declan winced and swung round, loomed into his consciousness. 'The thing you have to remember is that with Mr Apple there are no buts. He deals only in facts. A trifle obscurely, I grant you, but facts nevertheless,' Colonel Maddox was telling him in a friendly enough way, although making it clear there was no room for contradiction. Then: 'Destiny,' someone else put in, and Declan Tuohy smiled grimly as he recognized his own voice.

Fergal was dreaming. Although they were filled with turmoil and consumed by death he never thought of his dreams as nightmares. Even now, awakening from a fretful sleep wherein he had witnessed his own demise. He was even a little disappointed to find himself alive. Death had seemed so peaceful. How it had come about he could not recall, but he had seen his own spirit rise. It was beautiful to behold, a spirit welcomed by the open arms of his only friend, a smiling Martin Deeley. They had held hands, Fergal's soul drawing strength and peace from Martin's. Together they had gazed down and seen the crumpled body of Seamus Reilly lying, curled and motionless, on the ground.

– I promised you I would release you, Fergal said.

Then they watched as Reilly's soul dragged itself upwards, only to fall back, pleading for their help. They laughed as Reilly cried again: help me, someone help me. Slowly, like burning tissue-paper, Reilly's spirit began to crumble, breaking up, becoming tiny particles of ash, and blowing away in the wind . . .

The rain continued all day, easing about midday for an hour but returning again to a steady, relentless downpour. By evening there were reports of severe flooding, of three people being killed as a lorry aqua-planed and jacknifed into a passing car, of the sewer overflowing in one area of the city. The thundery mugginess was gone and it had turned quite cool, making Seamus Reilly shiver more than once as he waited for Mr Asher to arrive, making him fret, too, lest something unforeseen had happened to prevent the meeting taking place. Finally, twenty minutes late, Mr Asher was escorted into the room, puffing and shaking his raincoat before tossing it over the back of a chair.

'It's like the end of the world,' he said, blowing into his cupped hands and then rubbing them together.

'I hope not,' Seamus hoped.

'I didn't think I was going to make it. All the traffic has been diverted – even *your* escort couldn't circumvent that.'

Reilly smiled. 'We are only human,' he said wryly.

'That's reassuring,' Asher told him, returning the smile. 'So,' he went on, sitting down at the table, moving the ashtray closer and widening his smile, 'the pigeon has returned to the roost?'

Seamus Reilly chuckled loudly and joined Asher at the table, he, too, placing his ashtray strategically by his elbow. 'I thought you might enjoy that.'

'I did.'

'And did you get its significance?'

'Oh, yes. Yes, indeed. The Sergeant, I take it, co-operated?'

Reilly nodded. 'He was most helpful. I felt quite sorry for him, really. He's a tired man, you know. Tired, I suppose, of doing other people's dirty work,' he said wistfully, kindly. He sighed. 'But we now have one hell of a problem.'

'That,' said Asher curtly, 'is nothing new.'

'No, but this – this is somewhat more delicate. Sensitive, I believe they say.'

'But you have something in mind?'

Reilly scratched his temple, and took the time to light a cigar before answering. 'Yes. I have something in mind, but I'm not altogether certain if I can make it work.'

Mr Asher, tempted beyond all reasonable resistance by the smell of Reilly's cigar smoke, and noting the satisfaction the nicotine brought to his face, lit one of his black cigarettes, inhaling deeply. 'Are you going to tell me about it?'

'Oh yes,' Reilly said emphatically.

'I don't know that I like the sound of that.'

Reilly made a little cajoling face. 'I am going to need your help to make it work.'

'Sorry,' Asher said sternly, clearly adamant. 'There's no way I can help you further on this, Seamus. Dear God, if I get involved any deeper –'

Reilly leaned forward and put his elbows on the table, cupping his chin in his hands, his cigar dangerously close to his ear. 'Will you just listen to me for a minute, John? I have no intention of involving you. All I want is for you to set up something for me. It can be made to look very innocent. Indeed, I'm hoping our – eh – quarry will suggest it himself.'

Mr Asher looked very doubtful but nonetheless intrigued. 'Go on.'

Seamus Reilly gave a small wriggle on his seat. 'I want you to get this Colonel Sharmann into the open for us. That's all.'

'That's all? Christ, Seamus, you must be going mad. There's no way I can get publicly involved.'

'Oh there is, you know. Use me as bait.'

'You as bait? I don't –'

'I'm a special item on his list. Barton kindly told me, before he knew who I was. It seems that the Colonel is more than anxious to – let me be dramatic – to liquidate me. I think if you were to casually mention that you were going somewhere to, say, observe my behaviour, our Colonel Sharmann would be only too willing to come along. They're burying Tim Pat Duffy tomorrow afternoon. I thought his funeral would be appropriate. Ironic and appropriate.'

'Just supposing I agreed. What do you intend to do?'

Reilly wagged a forefinger at Asher. 'That is something you need not concern yourself with. Just get him to the funeral and, well, withdraw a little. Turn a blind eye, as they say. There will be no fuss. No disruption.'

Mr Asher was shaking his head. 'It's far, far too risky.'

'Only for us, and we are well used to taking risks. Once we have the Colonel,' Reilly went on persuasively, 'things will sort themselves out. I have already arranged our intermediary and I will insist on having Colonel Maddox – you remember Colonel Maddox?' he asked, grinning wickedly.

'Of course I remember him.'

'Well, I will insist on having him act for the Army.'

'Maddox?'

'Maddox.'

'Now I know you're mad.'

Reilly shook his head, serious again. 'He's perfect. He knows us. He's as honest as the day is long. He understands how we have to operate. The Brits would trust him. More importantly I would trust him.'

'You may be right,' Asher conceded.

'I am right. It's the only way we can clear this mess up without a bloody riot. You know that.'

'I don't know it, Seamus. But it seems to make sense. Then, you always seem to make sense – that's what's so damned dangerous about you.'

'I've always kept my word to you.'

'True.'

'So?'

Mr Asher finished his cigarette and crushed it out in the ashtray. 'You just want me to get Sharmann to the funeral?'

'That's it,' Reilly agreed reasonably.

'Nothing else?'

'Not a thing. We will look after everything else.'

'All right.'

Reilly fell back in his chair and wiped his brow in an exaggerated, theatrical movement. 'Phew. You make me work hard, John.'

'Don't get too happy yet. I haven't got him to the funeral. He might not come.'

Reilly smiled again. 'Just you tell him I'll be there and he'll come. I told you – I'm his Number One priority.'

'You think he might try –'

'To kill me? *He* won't but I suspect he'll try and arrange it.'

Rose Duffy knelt on the floor of the bedroom she had shared with her husband. About her, strewn haphazardly, were all that she had to remember him by: his clothes. She reached out and picked up a pullover, dark green with a design of brown deer prancing across the chest, and held it close to her, biting it, rocking herself, weeping. She was still crying, making small pained noises in her throat, keening in fact, when Declan knocked on the door and came in.

'Hey, Rose. Rose – what's the matter?' he asked, crouching down on his hunkers beside her.

Rose shook her head and looked away.

'Come on,' Declan whispered, putting his arm about her shoulder and pulling her gently towards him.

Rose wanted no sympathy. She wrenched herself away, scrambling to her feet and moving to the bed, sitting down. The last thing she wanted was to be consoled. For, loath as she was to admit it, she felt little sorrow: anger and loneliness, but no sorrow. How could she mourn a man who left so few memories: nothing but a bundle of old clothes? She couldn't.

'Leave me be, Declan,' she said.

'I don't like to see you like this.'

'I'm fine. I need to be by myself.'

'You're sure?'

'I'm sure.'

Declan got to his feet and left the room with a troubled backward glance. Rose, regretting her abruptness, smiled at him encouragingly, and she kept smiling until he closed the door behind him. Alone, she sat very still, hugging the pullover. Then, in one sudden and violent action, she hurled the garment from her, leaped to her feet, and started kicking the other clothes that were scattered about the floor. Finally, exhausted, she collapsed on to the floor, and curled herself up, rolling from side to side, sobbing.

· FIFTEEN ·

MR ASHER MADE his way down the corridor to Colonel Sharmann's office with trepidation. Yet he felt excited too, the sort of tingling, nervy excitement his English colleagues had mentioned they felt when on the brink of solving some seemingly impossible case. And, miraculously, it was a bright and sunny morning, more suited, he thought, to picnics than funerals, so this, too, probably lent the spring to his step and his jaunty, familiar tap on the door. 'Good morning to you, Colonel Sharmann. Thank you for seeing me.'

'We are supposed to be working together.'

'Ah. Yes. Quite. Still, it can't be – what's the word? – it must be annoying for you to have me dropping in like this. We do have rather different methods. I mean the theory of policing and the theory of soldiering are very different. I imagine it frustrates a soldier like you to have to come over here and "keep the peace" as it's put. It would be a bit like sending me to soldier in the Falklands, don't you think?'

Colonel Sharmann gave a half-hearted smile of agreement.

'Action,' Mr Asher went on. 'That's what I tell myself I need: action. This slow, ponderous sorting through piles of information is not my cup of tea at all. I like to be out and about. I feel I'm getting somewhere when I'm out and about – even if I'm not. Getting anywhere, I mean. That's why my spirits have risen today, Colonel. I've abandoned the desk. I'm off to do a little spying.'

The Colonel showed a glimmer of interest. 'Spying?'

'That's right. Spying. Well, observing really. But I like to think of it as spying. Silly. It's a silly game I play.'

'Really?' The Colonel sounded bored again.

'We like to keep an eye on the boyos, you know. Funerals are by far the best place to see them. Better even than political rallies. They all turn up at funerals. Like the Mafia, I suppose. Great respect for the dead our terrorists have. Probably they hope they've got another martyr on their hands.'

'I don't quite follow –'

'I'm sorry, Colonel. I'm rambling, aren't I? I have to go to – no, I have to observe a funeral today. They're burying that Duffy man. I've learned that quite a few of the big boys will be there. I want to keep an eye on them – from a distance, you understand.'

Apparently the Colonel didn't quite. 'For what exact purpose?'

'New faces turn up. Ranks change. By their position in the cortège we can see who's been promoted. By the absentees we can learn who's out of favour – or disappeared. Take that Donovan who was blown up. Now he was pretty big. I might just learn who has taken his place as Reilly's confidant.'

For one split second a flicker distorted the Colonel's gaze. 'And who is Reilly?' he asked coolly.

'Haven't we spoken about him? I am surprised. Seamus Reilly is just about the most evil bastard you could ever wish to see, Colonel. They regard him as something of a godfather. Any atrocity that takes place you can be sure Reilly is behind it.'

'And this Reilly will be at the funeral?'

'Without a doubt I should say.' Asher could feel Sharmann's mind nibbling at the bait.

'Mr Asher, since we are working together, I wonder if it

might not be a good idea if I went with you today. To observe, as you put it.'

Asher looked doubtful. 'I don't really think it would be of much interest to you, Colonel. You wouldn't know any of them. You –'

'It would get me away from this,' Colonel Sharmann said, indicating the papers on his desk, smiling appealingly. 'It would get me out and about,' he added.

Mr Asher succumbed. 'Why not, Colonel? Why not? But civilian clothes, I'm afraid. If you went like that I fear yours would be the next funeral I would have to attend.'

The Colonel beamed at Mr Asher's morbid little joke. 'Of course.'

'I'll pick you up here at about one-thirty then.'

'Excellent. And thank you, Mr Asher.'

'A pleasure, Colonel. Who knows, you might spot something that is so familiar to us we've overlooked it.'

Mr Asher had barely closed the door when the Colonel was on the phone. 'Find both Captain Little and Sergeant Barton and get them to report to me immediately. Immediately,' he stressed before hanging up.

Seamus Reilly was mustering his forces. Seated at the table in the meeting-room of the safe house, he had surrounded himself with a conglomeration of matchboxes and matchsticks, an old-fashioned inkwell, two pens and a pencil, and adopted the poise of a generalissimo (he always preferred El Caude's title), moving the diverse objects in patterns, explaining each move to the four men grouped about him. 'We will have one chance and one chance only,' he was saying. He looked up from his battlefield. 'Regan: you and your men will follow Mr Asher from the moment he leaves his house. He tells me he will be setting out to pick up Sharmann at one o'clock. He knows you will be following him. As soon as he has selected his point of observation you will inform Dowling, MacLeish and Foley by radio.'

'Yes, Mr Reilly.'

'Then, when Asher manoeuvres himself away from Sharmann I want all of you and your men to move in and surround Sharmann.'

'Won't –' Regan started.

Reilly gave him a testy look. 'Mr Asher will have chosen a spot where such a move will be unobserved. Or, anyway, not out of place. You'll be following a funeral, don't forget, so movement for a better viewpoint will seem natural enough.'

'Yes, Mr Reilly.'

'We are deliberately forgoing any military honours for Tim Pat. RUC presence will be at a minimum, and, anyway, Mr Asher will steer well clear of them. Once you surround Sharmann I want him on the ground and unconscious immediately. Into the van and away to Clones.'

'Yes, Mr Reilly.'

'I'll go through it again. Mr Asher,' Reilly said moving the inkwell to one side. 'Sharmann.' A matchbox joined the inkwell. 'The cortège.' The pens and pencil were placed end to end. 'All of you.' The matchsticks surrounded the matchbox, isolating it from the inkwell. 'Clear?'

'Yes, Mr Reilly,' the four men chorused.

'But everything is dependent on you, Regan. We can't do a damned thing until we know Mr Asher's position.'

'I understand that, Mr Reilly.'

'I certainly hope you do. Now, I want you all to make your move as the cortège actually passes Sharmann. Everyone will be watching the coffin, so it's by far the best time.'

'Yes, Mr Reilly.'

'Dowling, I'll leave it to you to alert everyone that Mr Asher is under our protection. In fact, he will be your responsibility. As soon as you've got Sharmann you will see to it that he is escorted safely from the area. O'Neill has organized the transport?'

Dowling nodded.

'Good. That seems to be all. Any questions?'

All four men shook their heads.

'Good,' Reilly said again. 'I need hardly impress on you that this is a very, very, very important operation. I want no slip-ups,' he concluded, his tone leaving little doubt what would happen if there was. 'One final point. IF anything should go wrong under no circumstances is Sharmann to be killed. Is that clear?'

The men nodded.

'You're to let him go and get the hell out of the area as best you can. If you're caught it'll be your tough luck. You'll deserve whatever befalls you.'

Again the men nodded, not, it seemed, daring to look at one another.

'Right. You better go and get yourselves organized. You won't see me again until I come to Clones.'

Reilly watched his men troop from the room, the adrenalin subsiding, leaving him tired. He was quite aware of the things that could go terribly wrong in the next few hours.

Fergal dressed himself with extra care, preening himself in front of the mirror, reknotting several times the black tie his mother had bought him, even going to the extreme of wetting his fingers with spittle and flattening down his eyebrows.

— Big day today, Martin. But I don't feel like it's a funeral at all. I should, I suppose. My Dad and all that. But I don't. Do you think they'll volley over the grave?

— I doubt it.

— They shot over yours.

— Of course they did. I was important, wasn't I? Hell, you couldn't get much more important than me.

— Shit. That was only for show — so nobody would know Reilly had you killed.

— I was important.

—Yes — but not *that* important.

— That important.

— There's hope for me yet, then.

— Hah. They'll probably shoot you *before* you go into your grave.

172

Fergal took a last look at himself, twisting sideways, almost turning his back to the mirror and looking over his shoulder. He removed a hair from his jacket. He wished he could feel something for his old man. It didn't seem right to bury him without feeling anything.

He left the room and went downstairs. 'I'm ready, Mum,' he called.

Rose opened her bedroom door an inch. 'I won't be a minute,' she called back, but she was nowhere near ready. She was terrified to put on the black suit she had purchased for the occasion. It was like finally admitting her widowhood. As she put on the jacket she realized it also seemed an admission of age: drying-up, an aridness of body and soul, a searing yearning for love stifled, a slowly disintegrating individual seen as being beyond the desires of love, beyond, even, affection.

Rose glared at the plastic bag filled with Tim Pat's old clothes. 'Damn you, Tim Pat Duffy. Damn you!' she whispered vehemently. 'Don't for one minute think I'm going to mourn you.' Abruptly she recoiled, clasping her clenched fists to her mouth, biting on them, a look of horrified bewilderment on her face. Defiantly, however, if only to satisfy her determination to be 'sensible', she brought herself under control, stiffening her body, clamping her teeth, gouging the tears from her eyes. Carefully, she placed the small black hat on her head and folded the veil up over the brim and away from her face. She took her handbag and her prayerbook from the dressing-table and marched out of the room.

'We've flushed him!' As Colonel Sharmann took the credit, his eyes gleamed.

'Sir?' Little enquired.

'Reilly, Captain. Damned Seamus Reilly. I know where he's going to be this afternoon.' Sharmann could not hide his glee.

Little and Barton exchanged puzzled glances.

'Don't you understand what I'm telling you? Seamus Reilly will be there for the taking this afternoon. At a funeral, no less,' the Colonel went on, finding the location of the proposed murder quite hilarious and laughing maniacally to himself. 'That stupid misjudgment you both made when you shot old Duffy has worked out well for us in the end. This afternoon as they set about burying Duffy, Reilly will be there in the congregation.'

The Captain gave a short cough. 'You want us to shoot Reilly this afternoon at Duffy's funeral?' he asked in amazement.

'Of course! We might never get another chance like this.'

'Colonel, you don't think that it would be taking a terrible risk to try and assassinate a Provo leader at a Provo funeral in Provo territory?' Little asked, speaking with exaggerated deliberation as though trying to impress the foolishness of some prank on a child.

'No more of a risk than usual. Less, I would say. Who will ever expect us to be so audacious? All you have to do is get yourselves a good vantage point near the church, and as soon as Reilly appears in the procession shoot him.'

'There will be too many people there, Colonel.'

'All the better for you to escape, Captain,' Sharmann pointed out, his eyes narrowing as he privately considered Little's warning.

The Captain continued: 'I'm sorry, sir. I can't agree.'

Colonel Sharmann stopped dead in his tracks and gaped as though he could not believe his ears.

'You can't agree?' he burst out. 'YOU can't agree? And who do you think you are, Captain? Just who do you think you are?' Sharmann was almost screaming, spitting out the words with speckles of saliva, as he saw what he thought of as his last and only chance of escape being whittled away by Little's logic. 'I give the orders. YOU do what I tell you. And I'm telling you that this afternoon is our chance to get Reilly.'

Captain Little blushed like a schoolboy being scolded and ridiculed before his classmates, and looked away.

'The funeral is at two o'clock,' Sharmann told them in a

174

more moderate tone, running his fingers through his dishevelled hair, mollified that he had, it seemed, brought the impertinent insubordination to a healthy conclusion. 'That gives you –' he glanced at his watch – 'forty minutes to get your – eh – goods together and get into position. You better get a move on.'

'Colonel –' Captain Little said again, an odd, mocking tone to his voice.

Sharmann swung round, glaring.

Little switched to mild sarcasm. 'Perhaps you'd tell us how we recognize Reilly?'

For a second it looked as if the Colonel was about to explode, but he thought better of it. He opened one of the drawers in his desk, rummaged a while, and produced a file. Then he sat down, leafing through the papers. Finally he ripped a photograph from its stapling and tossed it across the desk. 'There,' he said sharply. 'You can't mistake him.'

Captain Little took the photograph and studied it for a minute before passing it to Barton. 'When was that taken, sir?'

'Recently. Very recently. All right?'

Little nodded, collected the picture from Barton, and passed it back politely to Sharmann. 'Thank you.'

'Anything else?'

'No, sir.'

'Then, move.'

Mr Asher was surprised to pass Captain Little and Sergeant Barton in the corridor outside the Colonel's office; he was even more surprised that he had been convinced he had heard the Captain say something like 'he's stark raving mad'. He paused before knocking on the door and pursed his lips, looking back down the corridor at the receding soldiers, wondering. Finally he shrugged, and tapped on the door.

'Ah. Mr Asher.'

'Colonel.'

'Punctual as usual.'

'A little early, actually.'

The Colonel ignored the correction, and stood up, doing a slow about turn.

'Civilian enough?' he asked.

'Perfect.'

'Good. Shall we go?'

'If you're ready.'

'I'm quite ready. I can't wait to see –' He decided against finishing the sentence.

Mr Asher overlooked the Colonel's decision. 'Right. You will remember to stay close to me, Colonel. We will be well protected but it will make the job that much easier if we stay close.'

'Anything you say, Mr Asher. You are in charge.'

Mr Asher smiled. 'Yes,' he admitted. 'I suppose I am.'

Seamus Reilly came downstairs at one-thirty-five. In the hall he put on his overcoat and hat, and looped an umbrella over his arm. Just before he opened the front door he dipped his finger into a small mother-of-pearl font hanging on the wall and pressed down on the little sponge, soaking his finger in holy water. Carefully he blessed himself. 'Jesus protect me. Holy Mother pray for me,' he said, and stood for a moment in silence. Then he stepped briskly out of the house and slammed the door behind him.

· SIXTEEN ·

HAVING LIVED IN the one area all her life Rose Duffy had expected a reasonable number of people to come and pay their last respects to the luckless Tim Pat: she had certainly not expected the crowd that turned up, filling the church, lining the path between the pollarded chestnut trees, spilling out on to the road. She was deeply touched. She did not know that Seamus Reilly's men had done their job well, organizing whole communities into neat parties of respectful mourners, careful not to let the men outnumber the women by more than two to one. And while they might have wondered at this unprecedented duty no one had questioned it, but their curiosity lent a strange intensity to the occasion as they pretended to mourn, all the while keeping their eyes peeled lest they miss the reason for their being there. Some of the women (possibly those who had lost husbands or children of their own) openly wept, adding authenticity to their presence; and the ceremony itself was conducted sympathetically by Father Tierney, who was good at funerals, and gave a eulogy that endowed Tim Pat with attributes unrecognizable even to Rose.

Four strapping henchmen, supplied with the coffin, formed up either side of the trestle, and arranged the wreaths. One, outrageously, was designed to represent a winning post in red and white carnations presumably in tribute to Tim Pat's addiction to a small punt on the horses each Saturday. In one united movement, the men heaved the coffin on to their shoulders. Down the aisle they processed, their faces reddening under the strain but solemn and mournful nonetheless, past Rose and Declan and Fergal, past the genuine mourners who craned their necks to try to catch a glimpse of their wreaths, past the anticipating frauds, and out into the bright, clear sunshine, blinking in the light, readjusting the coffin as if the brilliance of the day had added mysteriously to its weight.

Rose, her veil now down over her strained face and with Fergal and Declan just behind her, followed the coffin out, smiling wanly her gratitude to the strangers who lined the route. She stood quietly on the footpath as her husband's body was loaded into the hearse, her only sign of tension the whiteness of her knuckles as she gripped her prayerbook, her nails digging deep into the leather cover. She nodded and smiled thankfully to Declan who bent and whispered something to her although she had no idea what he had said; and meekly she allowed him to place her arm in his as they set off towards the graveyard on foot, aware only of the puffs of blue smoke from the exhaust of the Bentley and the rumble of walking feet and murmured conversation behind her.

A hundred yards from the church the road swung sharply to the left, passing between what was really a car park but looked more like a dump for burnt-out vehicles, and an old cinema, now a bingo hall, its walls daubed with graffiti and murals berating the presence of the British. And it was on this corner, opposite the bingo hall, that Colonel Sharmann and Mr Asher waited, mingling with the crowd but staying well back from the road.

The Colonel nudged Mr Asher. 'They're coming now,' he whispered.

Mr Asher disliked being nudged. 'I can see they are,' he whispered back snappily.

'Where's Reilly?'

Mr Asher craned his neck. 'I can't see him yet.'

'You're sure he's here?'

'No. I'm not sure. I suspect he will be, though.'

'I thought you said he would be here?'

Mr Asher turned his head and glared coldly at the Colonel. 'I said I thought he would be here. I'm not all that interested in Reilly. I came to see everyone that was here, Colonel.'

As the cortège moved closer the Colonel stood on tiptoe, weaving his head from side to side, determined to spot Reilly if he could, hoping he would see him suddenly lurch and die. He moved back a step, looking about him, seeking something on which to stand: behind him, about five feet away to the right, the ground rose slightly. The Colonel jerked his head at Mr Asher to follow and moved to his new vantage point. It was perfect timing. Asher spotted the men moving in on the Colonel, all with their backs to Sharmann, to all intents and purposes all concentrating on the funeral procession, desiring only a last glimpse of Tim Pat Duffy. He recognized one of them as the escort Seamus Reilly had once provided, now giving him the slightest warning with his eyes. Asher turned away and looked back to the funeral. A minute later he thought he heard a cry behind him. He was certain he heard a car door slam and an engine start up. And he was about to investigate this when a voice said quietly in his ear, 'You can go home now, Mr Asher. Cut through the car park behind you and work your way round that way to your car. You'll be quite safe.'

Asher looked over his shoulder, only intending to express his thanks. All he saw was a line of faces staring away from him, all looking grieved as they moved further down the road towards the cemetery. He could not resist a smile, and shaking his head in grudging admiration, he made his way past the spot where he had last noted Colonel Sharmann, through the car park and away, a bounce in his step.

At that moment Sergeant Barton was smiling also. Lying on

his stomach on the roof of the bingo hall with Captain Little kneeling beside him, he had watched with considerable amusement the drama that had taken place almost directly beneath him, watched it intimately through the telescopic lens of his rifle. And to think the horrified Captain had nearly succeeded in talking him out of coming!

'For Christ's sake, we better go somewhere, Barton, and talk this thing out,' Captain Little had said as they walked down the corridor, away from the manic insanity of Colonel Sharmann's office, passing a man whom the Captain recognized but, for the moment, whose name he could not recall.

'Sir,' Barton had acquiesced.

'The man's gone stark, staring raving mad,' Captain Little had diagnosed, striding along, almost kicking open the door of the toilet.

Barton allowed one corner of his mouth to droop into a grin, and joined the Captain at the urinal, giving him a sideways glance as if surprised the Captain had only now spotted the Colonel's affliction.

'There's no way we're going anywhere near that funeral. Reilly or not,' Little had said. 'No bloody way. We'd never get out.'

'We have our orders, sir,' Barton said.

Captain Little was already rinsing his fingers in the basin. 'Fuck our orders.'

Sergeant Barton shook his head. 'I'm sorry, sir. You needn't come, but I have to go,' he said, the dire and menacing instructions of Seamus Reilly echoing in his brain.

'I'm ordering you not to,' Little said, but with light conviction.

'Sorry, Captain, I've already got my orders.'

Then the Captain had taken to shaking his head. 'It's suicide,' he said.

'Maybe.'

'There's no maybe about it.'

'There's always a maybe, sir. Anyway, I've got to go and change. I can't go like this.'

'You're really determined to go?'

'I've got to.'

'Shit. Come on.'

And so Sergeant Barton found himself on the roof of the bingo hall with the Captain kneeling beside him.

'What's happening?' Captain Little asked.

'They're coming out of the church.'

'Can you spot Reilly?'

'Not yet.'

A few seconds later: 'What's happening?'

'Not a thing,' Barton said, watching fascinated as he saw Colonel Sharmann move to slightly higher ground, saw a group of men sidle innocently enough towards him, pretending to be concentrating on the sad procession.

'Any sign of Reilly?'

'No –' The men had now encircled the Colonel who, his eyes fixed on the mourners, seemed totally unaware of what was happening to him.

'Maybe the bastard never came,' Captain Little said hopefully.

'I told you there was always a maybe,' Barton said, watching, mesmerized, as Colonel Sharmann suddenly vanished, swallowed up, it seemed, by the earth itself.

'What's happening?'

'I've told you, Captain, not a damned thing.' Eight men, walking slowly, one of them supported by his friends, probably overcome with grief, moved away from the onlookers and made their way to a small, blue van. Caringly the stricken man was placed in the van, the door slammed, and away it went at a steady, unhurried speed, bouncing in and out of the potholes, until it reached the road: then it gathered speed, cornered and was gone from sight. Barton took his eye from the lens and squinted up at the Captain. 'Reilly's not here, sir.'

Captain Little sighed heavily with relief. 'Thank Christ for that. Let's get the hell out of here.'

'Not yet, sir. Relax. Wait until the stragglers have gone,' Barton advised coolly, starting to dismantle his rifle.

'Yes. Yes, of course,' he agreed, sitting back on his haunches. He'll have it in for us again. Sharmann's going to have a fit.'

'I wouldn't worry too much about the Colonel, sir. He'll get over it.'

Little turned to Barton, intrigued. 'Barton, if Reilly had been here, would you have shot him.'

'Yes.'

'Even if it meant the both of us getting killed?'

'Yes.'

'Just like that?' Captain Little snapped his fingers.

'No. Not just like that.'

'Then why?'

'Because I was told to.'

Seamus Reilly was, in fact, there, but not in the procession. He had, as was his duty, attended the service, choosing a seat near the back of the church, near the confessionals, a shadowy place, a place coloured blue and vermilion and green by the sunlight through the stained-glass window, coloured, too, he had once remarked (possibly to Declan, now he came to think of it) by the sins muttered close by. And after the church had emptied he stayed there quietly by himself, sitting, his head bowed, his hands folded piously on his lap, his eyes almost closed, his feet resting comfortably on the kneeler, grateful for the silence, thinking. He went to church often, every Sunday without fail, on the holy days of obligation, to attend weddings and baptisms and funerals, more funerals, he admitted, than weddings or baptisms. He found them gloomy, relentlessly depressing, more like places of the night than sanctuaries of joy and hope and light. To think he had once contemplated becoming a priest himself! No. To think that his mother had once planned for him to become a priest. That was certainly more like it. 'Seamus is going to be a priest, aren't you, pet?' she liked to say to anyone foolish enough to listen. 'He's going to be a priest and see to it that we all get into heaven. Oh it will be lovely to have my pet saying Mass up there at the altar.' And

Seamus had nearly fallen for it, had, indeed, gone so far as to apply for admission to a seminary in Waterford, had even been accepted. . . .

Then they had arrested his father, and his mother's priorities had swiftly altered course. Priesthood, it seemed, would have to wait. Perhaps a God who had allowed her poor darling man to be arrested and thrown into some stinking prison was not, all He had been made out to be. And when her poor darling man hung himself she all but severed her relationship with the Almighty, and spent her days urging Seamus and his brother to satisfy her lust for revenge. No sons of mine will sit back and let them Brits kill their father, she used to boast – Jesus meek and mild put well and truly in His place. Even as she died, croaking and heaving with bronchitis, she could only think of retribution, her last hard rattle filled with hate.

Seamus shuddered. It was just as well she had gone when she had, for two days later Seamus had discovered his brother had informed the RUC of an impending murder, and he, Seamus, now, if not the High Priest, at least the Archdeacon of the Punishment Squad, had been forced to order his execution. Curiously, in the nightmares that predominated his sleep, the screaming outrage of his mother was always drowned by the terrified wails of his brother, begging forgiveness.

'It's all clear, Mr Reilly. I have the car ready.'

'Oh. Thank you.'

'Everything went nicely.'

'Good. I'll be out directly.'

Seamus Reilly knelt down and held his head in his hands. He tried to pray but his thoughts were constantly shattered by his brother's agonized pleas for mercy. Help me, Seamus, he cried. I'm sorry. I'm sorry. Help me!

'I'm sorry,' Seamus Reilly managed to pray. 'Help me,' he added, wondering if anyone was there to hear. He blessed himself and stood up. For a minute he stared about the church, the whiff of stale incense filling his nostrils, his eyes returning again and again to the crucifix over the altar. He shook his head sadly. Then he genuflected and hurried to his car.

· SEVENTEEN ·

WITHIN A FEW hours of the Colonel's kidnapping, IRA intelligence informed its British counterpart of the incident. The messsage was detailed, indicating the reason for the action, listing the names of the victims involved, giving just sufficient evidence to establish the veracity of the claim, and stipulating the precise conditions under which any negotiation would be tolerated not only for the Colonel's safe return, but also for keeping the matter under wraps and for the fringe benefits the IRA would expect. The communiqué caused considerable consternation.

Brigadier Brazier was appalled. This was not the outcome he had expected: it was not an outcome he had even considered, and now he could barely believe it had happened. Oddly enough, what irked him most was not, as one might reasonably have expected, that his plan had been outmanoeuvred, not that his own career and the careers of certain eminent politicians were on the verge of lying in tatters, not even that exposure of military complicity could bring down the government and bolster the terrorist cause. No, what rankled was that the IRA had demanded that all negotiations be carried out by Colonel Maddox, the very man the Brigadier had been instrumental in retiring. To make matters worse, his superiors had acceded to the demand without the slightest hesitation.

'Colonel Maddox is here, sir.'

Brigadier Brazier turned from the window and nodded curtly. He had already decided there was only one way to play this. 'Show him in.'

Colonel Maddox ambled into the huge room looking bewildered, as though the initial surprise of the summons had not yet quite left him. Indeed, alarm might have been a better word, probably would have been since that was how Nancy had seen it.

'Who was that?' she wanted to know as her husband returned to the table from the phone. 'You look alarmed.'

'I am a bit, to tell the truth. I've been summoned to London,' Maddox had said, shaking his head.

'London? You? By whom?'

Colonel Maddox gave a little cackle. 'I don't quite know.'

'What do you mean, you don't quite know? You must know who you were speaking to.'

'I don't, actually. I was simply given an address and told to be there this afternoon.'

Nancy raised her pencilled eyebrows. 'You can't just go wandering off to London on the demand of someone you don't know and to a place you don't –'

'Oh, I know the address. I've been there before.'

'I thought you said – what is it?'

'The address? I can't tell you, I'm afraid.'

Nancy narrowed her eyes. 'Have you been up to –'

The Colonel interrupted her with a good-humoured laugh. 'I don't think so. You never can tell, though. Whoever it was on the phone was most courteous. *Very* polite. I suspect –' Maddox stopped and took to sipping his coffee.

'You suspect?'

'I suspect they want me to do something for them.'

And he knew his suspicions were correct the moment the

Brigadier strode across the room, his hand outheld in welcome, saying: 'Matthew, Matthew, my dear chap. How good it is to see you again. And how well you look.'

Colonel Maddox accepted the hand and shook it. 'Brigadier.'

'George, Matthew. The name is George. We can't stand on ceremony, we two. We've known each other too long for that, don't you think? Come and sit down. I was just about to have a cup of tea. Join me?'

'Thank you.'

Promptly the Brigadier stuck his head out of the door and organized tea for two. 'Tea for two! That goes back some way, eh, Matthew. Doris Day, I think.'

'I believe so – George.'

'Dear me, they don't write songs like that any more, do they? I don't know about you, but I can't make head or tail of the rubbish they play nowadays.'

Colonel Maddox stared kindly at the Brigadier.

'Things have certainly changed,' the Brigadier went on. He was trying to find an opening through which he could launch this interview. 'And how's retirement treating you?'

Colonel Maddox shrugged. 'Kindly.'

'Good. Excellent. We miss you, of course, Matthew. Can't say I approve of the youngsters they're sending to replace us. Too brash for my liking. No sense of diplomacy. Head down and charge in without thinking of the consequences. . . . Ah, tea. Tea for two,' he added, smiling away and wagging his head. 'Thank you – just on the table. We'll look after ourselves.'

The Brigadier strode across to the table and started setting two cups in their saucers. 'Milk?'

'Please.'

'Sugar?'

'No. Thank you. Just milk.'

'Snap,' the Brigadier said, coming back and passing the Colonel his tea before settling himself into a chair, sighing. 'I imagine you're wondering why we sent for you.'

Colonel Maddox smiled. 'Yes.'

'We need your help, Matthew. Your help in a very delicate matter.'

'I'll help, of course, if I can.'

'I knew you would. I told everyone we could rely on you.'

Colonel Maddox seemed not to hear the flattery. 'What's the problem?'

The Brigadier cleared his throat, his usual prelude to coming to the point. 'We've got ourselves into a bit of a scrape in Northern Ireland, Matthew. To be frank it's one hell of a mess. The chap we sent over to replace you has gone and got himself kidnapped.'

'Oh dear.'

'The trouble is – and this is between ourselves, you understand? – he was involved in a special operation.'

'Oh dear,' Colonel Maddox said again. 'Am I allowed to know the nature of this special operation?'

The Brigadier winced.

'Ah. Dirty tricks.'

'Yes,' Brigadier Brazier admitted gratefully, 'which, if they came to light, could be very embarrassing.'

'I can imagine. But how can I help?'

'Well – tell me, do you remember an IRA chappie called Reilly?'

'Seamus Reilly?'

The Brigadier nodded.

'Yes. Yes, I remember Seamus Reilly. I met him.'

'Well, the IRA are prepared to negotiate and from what we can gather Reilly is in charge of the operation.'

'Yes,' Maddox said, smiling thinly. 'He would be.'

'Although they have nominated an independent intermediary.'

'Oh?'

'A reporter from London. Tuohy. Declan Tuohy.'

Maddox smiled sadly. 'Poor Mr Tuohy,' he said, wondering how on earth his visitor had managed to get himself mixed up in all this. 'I still don't see how I can be of any help.'

'The only one they will talk to is yourself, Matthew.'

'Me? Good heavens. Why me?'

'I've no idea. There was something – hang on a minute.'

Brigadier Brazier got up and walked to his desk in the corner, and started to riffle through some papers. 'Ah,' he said, and proceeded to read something to himself. 'A copy of the demands,' he announced, looking up briefly before absorbing himself in the paper again. 'Yes. Here it is. Quote: "Be clearly understood that the only representative of the British forces and government acceptable to us will be Colonel Matthew Maddox whom we consider to be a man of honour." That's what they had to say about you.'

'Good heavens,' Maddox said again.

'So you see . . .' The Brigadier allowed his voice to trail off.

Colonel Maddox answered by shaking his head.

'There's no alternative, Matthew. It's you they want.'

Almost despairingly, Colonel Maddox pleaded: 'I wouldn't know how to negotiate –'

'Oh come now. You underestimate yourself. You dealt admirably with this Reilly fellow before. And he trusts you apparently – that's half the battle won. We have every confidence in you, Matthew. And anyway we have no choice.'

Maddox's sigh seemed to indicate to the Brigadier that he had agreed. 'Just one thing: whatever deal you are able to make, Matthew, you must insist that the matter is not made public. You can let the terrorists have what they want – within reason, of course – as long as they agree to keep the matter quiet.'

It took a few seconds for the full significance of the Brigadier's words to sink in. 'And my replacement – Sharmann – what sort of deal am I to make for him?'

Brigadier Brazier looked away. 'If you *can* save him so much the better. The important thing – the *only* thing you have to remember is, as I said, that the operation in which Sharmann was involved is not made public.'

'So, Sharmann can be sacrificed, is that it?'

'It's not a question of sacrifice. It's a question of priority. Sharmann knew the risks if he was caught. I told him myself in this very room,' the Brigadier said, waving an arm to indicate the vastness of his foresight. 'They could have shot him out of hand. It's a bonus for him that you might be able to get him out of this.'

'I see.'

'Well, will you go and talk to these men on our behalf?'

'I will try to save Sharmann – yes.'

'Damn Sharmann. Oh I'm sorry, Matthew. You have no idea the pressure I'm under. God, how I hate politicians. Of course try to save Sharmann, if you can. But will you please try to do whatever you can to keep his operation under wraps?'

'I will try to do that too.'

The Brigadier sighed with relief. 'Thank you.'

'On one condition –'

'What?' the Brigadier demanded sharply, not so relieved.

'That whatever deal I do make will be honoured to the letter.'

'Of course. I'm surprised you need my reassurance for that.'

Maddox smiled unhappily. 'I wish I didn't. I've been a long time in the Army. I've seen the changes. I also know how we tend to forget our promises. I'm pretty sure I can get Seamus Reilly to agree to a deal with me – but I know for certain he will take a terrible revenge if we break our word.'

'Any deal you make will be honoured, Matthew. You have my word on that.'

'I hope so. I hope so.'

The matter of honour and trust neatly dealt with, the Brigadier moved on to more immediate things. 'Can you go over there right away?'

'Now?' Maddox asked with some alarm.

'Tonight.'

'Tonight? Yes. Yes, I can go tonight.'

'Excellent. Once there you can work from your old office.'

'Temporarily vacated –?'

'Eh, yes.'

'One thing: who else was – I mean, I presume Sharmann wasn't alone.'

'No.'

'Who else was involved.'

'Only two others. Captain Little and Sergeant Barton. They're both still there.'

'I presume I can question them?'

'Certainly. You can question the whole damned Army if you think it will help you.'

Maddox raised his eyebrows. 'I doubt if it would. Before I do anything – eh – George, you'd better tell me what exactly you put the unfortunate Sharmann up to.'

Oddly for him the Brigadier blushed. 'Yes. Of course. I'll do that. I always said it was a mad scheme.'

'But you went ahead?'

The Brigadier nodded, looking rather ashamed. 'Had to. Overruled. Outvoted. That's part of the trouble, you know, Matthew. These young hotheads coming in – no patience – rush in and be damned.'

'Usually they are – damned, I mean,' Maddox said vaguely.

'We'll all be damned if you can't do something.'

'Well, you'd better tell me about this fiasco.'

'You may as well tell all.' Seamus Reilly sounded like a confessor.

Colonel Sharmann glared straight ahead.

'Not that it makes any difference if you don't. We already know almost everything. It would be nice to have it confirmed – from the horse's mouth, as it were.'

Still Sharmann kept his mouth firmly shut, trying to concentrate on the numbness seeping into his fingers, doggedly wriggling his wrists against the ropes that bound them together.

'Ah, well,' Reilly sighed. 'So be it,' he added solemnly, standing up and walking slowly down the line of hooks that hung from the rail in the piggery, glancing at them, looking

190

back at Sharmann, glancing at the hooks again. He gave a wicked laugh. 'You really did make a mess of things, didn't you? They must be wetting their knickers in London. It's a wonder they haven't sent the SAS back again – this time to deal with you, Colonel.' He sauntered back to the centre of the slaughterhouse and stood directly in front of Sharmann, staring down at him. 'Did you really think you could simply come over here and murder us? What a silly, misguided little man you are. I suppose they said just pop over to Belfast like a good chap and remove some of those IRA nasties, did they? Poor Colonel Sharmann – you're pathetic. We've been watching you from the day you arrived, you and that poncy Captain, and Sergeant Barton. I feel quite sorry for him – Barton, I mean,' Reilly went on, closing his eyes briefly. 'Poor sod got all the dirty work to do. He'll get all the blame, too, I suppose. What did you do, Colonel? Sit behind your desk and issue the instructions? Arrange the strategy?'

For a moment it looked as though Sharmann was, at last, about to retaliate. He opened his mouth, but all that emerged was a strangled, croaking sound.

'Hah,' Reilly scoffed, and spat on the floor. 'If only you knew how much I detest men like you, Colonel. You've no courage. You hide behind your desks. You want glory, and you think the easiest place to find it is over here.'

Suddenly the Colonel launched himself from his stool. For a moment it looked as if he might land on top of Seamus Reilly: for a moment, too, he seemed suspended in the air, parallel to the ground. Then he fell, crashing down, his face smashing on the concrete floor. Groaning, he rolled over, staring up at Reilly, blinking as blood oozed over his face. 'I'll have you, Reilly,' he screamed, before rolling on his side and lying still.

'You'll have me in hell,' Reilly told him, swinging away and making for the door. 'Get him cleaned up,' he said to the man who had called him. 'And keep him handy. I might want him before the night is out.'

'Yes, Mr Reilly.'

'They'll never learn, will they?' Reilly asked. 'Dear God, they'll never learn.' Then he stepped into his car and settled back for the trip to Belfast.

It wasn't difficult for Mr Asher to arrange for himself to meet Colonel Maddox at the airport.

'We meet again, Mr Asher,' Colonel Maddox said.

'Indeed we do, Colonel. I must confess I never thought we would.'

'You hoped we never would, Mr Asher,' Maddox suggested wryly.

Mr Asher smiled. 'You did cause us a few problems.'

'You cause your own problems. Other people find themselves stuck with them,' Colonel Maddox said, getting into the unmarked military car and moving across to allow Mr Asher to join him.

'It's a circle,' Asher said, lowering the window an inch preparatory to lighting a cigarette. 'You cause us problems, we solve yours and create our own, you come to sort out ours and – well, on and on it goes.'

'You really believe that?'

'Of course.'

'You may have a point – and a cigarette if it will stop you fidgeting there.'

Mr Asher laughed. 'Thank you.'

'Tell me, what do you know about this business?'

Asher allowed the match to burn half its length before applying the flame, and he puffed for several seconds before tossing it out of the window. He took the cigarette from his lips. 'Truthfully?'

'Truthfully.'

'More than I want to know.'

'You'll tell me about it?'

'Yes. Later.'

'Thank you. Later will do.'

'Were you surprised they – Reilly asked for you?'

'Certainly.'

'So was I to begin with. I never thought . . . Reilly thinks a lot of you, you know, Colonel.'

'I can't imagine why.'

'You kept your word. That's very important to Reilly. One's word.'

'So it would be. It's about the only thing left to us, isn't it?'

'Hah. You could say that.'

'How is he?'

'Reilly? The same. A little older. No, actually, he's changed somehow. Don't ask me how. Somehow.'

'You know, I'm quite looking forward to seeing him again.'

Colonel Maddox stared out of the window. Nothing had changed. Everything couched in terms of normality, everything anything but normal. Even his conversation with Asher had been some sort of deadly banter: politeness leading to heartache and destruction. Fortunately, before he had a chance to pursue his morbid theme, the car slowed down, turned left at St Enoch's, and pulled into the gates of the barracks.

'Welcome home,' Asher said.

Had it not been mentioned Maddox might never have thought of it that way. Yet Asher was right: surrounded by soldiers, the smell of denim and leather and sweat filling the air, Maddox felt very much at home, even if this home meant betrayal, incessant wheeling and dealing. 'You tired, Mr Asher?'

'No.'

'Care to share a nightcap? I brought a little something –'

'I had a bottle sent to your office, Colonel. A token of – let me call it esteem.'

Maddox was touched. He gripped Mr Asher by the arm. 'That was very kind of you. I appreciate it, Mr Asher.'

'It's nothing. Anyway, I'd be pleased to share a nightcap.'

Later, together, they sat in Sharmann's office sharing a nightcap.

'I see all trace of me has been removed,' Maddox said, eyeing the new furniture and repainted walls.

'A feeble attempt. You haunt the place.'

Maddox laughed. 'I hope not . . . this is a very good whiskey.'

'I like it. They don't make it any more, unfortunately.'

Colonel Maddox twisted the bottle and studied the label. 'Bluebird,' he read aloud. 'An odd name for a whiskey. Bluebird of happiness,' he added, happiness furthermost from his voice as he asked: 'Will you tell me what you know about this business now?'

'You probably know as much —'

Maddox held up his hand. 'Never mind what I know, Mr Asher. I really want to hear what you know.'

'All right. Put simply your successor, Colonel Sharmann, was sent over as head of a small assassination squad. They succeeded a few times, messed up twice, got caught, and now Reilly has Sharmann. That's about it.'

'Just like that?'

'More or less.'

'You played no part in any of it?'

Mr Asher sipped his Bluebird.

'I need to know, Mr Asher.'

'Colonel, you know Reilly and I co-operate from time to time. This was something we had to stop. Yes, I played a small part.'

'How small?'

'Very small.'

'How small?' Colonel Maddox persisted.

'I was the first to be suspicious.'

'And you conveyed those suspicions to Seamus Reilly?'

'Yes. I had to, Colonel. I didn't want my men getting blasted off the face of the earth for something they knew nothing about.'

'I'm not blaming you, Mr Asher. Yet. Go on.'

'Reilly got Barton — Sergeant Barton, the actual gunman — and persuaded him to talk.'

'Persuaded him?'

Mr Asher nodded. 'Sent a couple of his men to visit Barton's family. Anyway, no harm came to anyone.'

'Barton?'

'Barton was allowed to go provided he kept his mouth shut.'

'And he did?'

Mr Asher grinned. 'So it seems. Reilly got Sharmann, didn't he?'

Colonel Maddox nodded slowly, watching Mr Asher carefully. 'How did he get Sharmann?'

'At a funeral.'

'Sharmann was at a funeral? Unprotected?'

'Yes he was at a funeral. I took him.'

'*You* took him.'

'Yes. He wanted to go.'

'Why would he want to go to a funeral, Mr Asher?'

'You won't believe it.'

'I might.'

'He had it set up for Reilly to be shot at the funeral and he wanted to watch.'

'You knew that?'

'Of course.'

'You warned Reilly?'

'No. I didn't need to. Reilly's no fool. He knew he was next on the list.'

'So Reilly didn't show?'

'Oh, he was there all right. Somewhere. I felt him there. I didn't see him, but he was there all right. Anyway, I was distracted for a moment and when I looked for Sharmann he was gone.'

'You reported this?'

'No. I wasn't supposed to know anything about it.'

Colonel Maddox quite calmly (much to his own surprise) poured himself another drink, offering one to Mr Asher, who refused. 'And what, do you suppose, the Chief Constable will say when I tell him this?'

Mr Asher smiled coldly. 'You won't tell him, Colonel.'

'I might.'

'Oh, you won't. If you want to make a deal with Reilly you

195

won't. Reilly owes me a favour, you see. Your silence about me will be part of any deal he makes.'

'Truly nothing changes, does it?'

'Why should it, Colonel? We have to live here while you – the peacekeepers – I mean,' although Mr Asher didn't exactly sound as if he meant peacekeepers, 'come and go. So we learn to protect ourselves in whatever way we can.'

'But you and Reilly are poles apart – or should be. You – you're the police, he's a terrorist.'

Mr Asher pursed his lips. 'We're both Irish, Colonel,' he said in what amounted to a whisper. 'That's the mistake you made when you were here and you're making the same mistake again. *You* are the outsider. With the best will in the world you can be nothing but an outsider. Reilly will tell you the same thing if you ask him.'

Only too pleased to tack away from Asher's theory, Colonel Maddox asked: 'Yes. When do I see Reilly?'

'Tomorrow morning, I understand. But that's unofficial. Actually, you'll be meeting an intermediary first.'

'Mr Tuohy?'

Mr Asher looked surprised until it dawned on him that he had no reason to be. 'Yes.'

'How did that poor man get mixed up in all this?'

'He's not "mixed up in it" as you say, Colonel. He's known Reilly for years. They went to school together, I think. Reilly trusts him like he trusts you.'

'Ah.'

'You sound as though you know him – Tuohy.'

'I met him once.'

'You know us all then, Colonel.'

'Yes. I know you all. . . . You – are you to be part of the –'

Mr Asher threw up his hands in exaggerated horror. 'Certainly not. My participation is over, Colonel. It's all down to you and Reilly. And I wish you luck,' he said, finishing his drink and standing up. 'I'll leave you now, Colonel. I expect you'll want to get some sleep.'

'Yes.'

'Mind yourself, Colonel.'

'I'm sorry?' Maddox sighed. 'You know, Mr Asher, I feel safer with Seamus Reilly than I do with you. You frighten me. Your strange, lopsided logic is dangerous and evil. You really frighten me.'

For a second Mr Asher looked annoyed. Then he smiled. 'I don't believe you're a man who's easily frightened, Colonel. You just don't understand us. If ever you do you'll realize we're just ordinary people trying to survive against the odds. That's all. Put yourself in our shoes. What would you do?' he asked, putting his glass on the desk.

Maddox sighed. 'Thank you for meeting me.'

'My pleasure. It's nice seeing you again. You know, come to think of it, you've made your own little niche in Irish history. Not many men could claim that.'

'I'm not too sure it's a compliment.'

'Believe me, it is. I'll say good night, Colonel.'

After Mr Asher had gone, Colonel Maddox swung himself round and round on the fancy swivel chair, using his feet as paddles. He stopped the chair and walked to the window, peering through the protective mesh. Nothing but blackness, he brooded. From far across the city the mournful sound of a ship's siren loomed towards him, and for an instant he saw himself as the unfortunate von Aschenbach sailing to his untimely death in Venice on board the *Esmeralda*. Again the hooter sounded, sharp and short and far less melancholy, breaking into the Colonel's preposterous ravings. He stretched himself. A niche in history: that made him laugh. And still chuckling he made his way to bed.

When Declan opened the door Seamus Reilly's first reaction was shock. 'What happened to you?' he asked, very concerned.

Declan shrugged it off. 'It's nothing,' he said, waving his heavily bandaged hand in the air. 'I caught my fingers in the car door, that's all. Bloody painful but nothing broken.'

197

'I thought something – you know what I thought.'

'That's all you ever think, Seamus. Come on in.'

Reilly followed Declan into the sitting-room, giving Rose Duffy a friendly if reserved wave as she popped her head out of the kitchen door. 'Your friend Colonel Maddox has arrived,' he said, accepting the chair Declan pointed to.

'He's hardly my friend, Seamus.'

'Well, he's arrived.'

'Are you trying to tell me something?'

Reilly summoned up a charming, boyish grin. 'Yes. I'm afraid I am.'

Declan showed his annoyance. The pain in his hand was worsening progressively, his head ached, the sombreness of the funeral still clouded about him: he was definitely in no humour for any twisted diplomacy. 'What is it, Seamus?' he demanded brusquely.

'I need you to come with me when I start negotiations with Maddox tomorrow.'

'I'm sorry, Seamus. No. I told you before. This has gone too far and I'm not getting mixed in it anymore. I'm going back to London tomorrow night.'

Seamus Reilly stared at his friend. 'I *do* need you, Declan.' He was persuasive.

'I'm sorry.'

'I'm afraid – let me put it this way: we have already put forward your name as our intermediary in negotiations and it has been accepted.'

'You what?' Declan gasped.

'All I want is that you accompany me. You need not say anything. Just observe. A silent witness,' Reilly explained.

'You gave me as an intermediary?' Declan demanded furiously, still stranded with the shock of this imposed role.

Reilly nodded. 'We needed an independent witness. Somebody not involved, somebody we could trust to tell the truth if anything were to go amiss. Who better than you, Declan?'

'You're a bastard, Seamus.'

'So I've been told,' Reilly admitted. 'You remember our last talk – when I told you about the conspiracy? Well, that has been proven. We now hold a Colonel Sharmann in safe-keeping. He was in charge of the – of the fiasco. He will be the mainstay of our negotiations. You could think of it as saving his life. Without you no talking can take place.'

'Don't give me –'

'I assure you it's true. Maddox has been sent over to represent one side, you have been accepted as representing ours. Only – well, to be honest – we feel it would be better if you just sit quietly in the background and listen. There's no danger in it, Declan,' Reilly assured him. 'It will all be very civilized.'

'No.'

'The Brits are very anxious that the whole affair is kept quiet,' Reilly went on, keeping his voice calm and even and coldly persuasive. 'It will simply be a matter of choosing the conditions of such a silence. Nothing more.'

'No, Seamus. No.'

'If the talks do not take place,' Reilly went on in the same tone, 'and we are forced to expose the matter, then I will not be able to answer for the repercussions. Undoubtedly many soldiers will be killed and that, in turn, will lead to many innocent civilians being murdered. I shudder to think who they might be,' he concluded, his gaze casually but deliberately coming to rest on a photograph of Fergal all dressed up for his First Communion.

Declan followed Reilly's gaze. 'If anything –'

'Nothing will happen to any of them if I can help it,' Seamus promised. 'But I might not be able to help it, Declan. That,' he said simply, 'is why I need your help.'

Declan took the photograph in his hands and stared at the boy. He knew, now, he was going to accede to Reilly's demands. For Rose, if for no one else. And for Fergal. 'You just want me to listen?'

Reilly inclined his head.

'Nothing more?'

'Nothing more.'

'And I have your word that after the talks that will be it?'

'Yes.'

After a pause: 'All right.'

Immediately Seamus Reilly was on his feet, brushing the creases from his jacket. 'Excellent. I knew I could count on you, Declan. All being well you can still be on your plane back to London tomorrow night as planned.'

'Thanks,' Declan said sourly.

'Now, tomorrow morning, we'll send a car for you. About nine. We've scheduled the meeting for nine-thirty. All right?'

Declan nodded. 'Where?'

Reilly hesitated. Then he grinned. 'A little place specially chosen for the occasion.'

'Tell me.'

'It's better you don't know yet. Just a house. You'll see tomorrow. You'd better get some sleep – we need you bright eyed in the morning.'

Declan closed the front door and pressed his forehead against the cold wood. Oddly enough, now committed, he felt a previously unexperienced excitement. He could hear his heart thumping. Then, without warning, he felt sick, violently sick. His stomach heaving, he raced upstairs to the bathroom.

· EIGHTEEN ·

REILLY HAD SPENT until the small hours with the Army Council of the Provisional IRA preparing demands, gleefully proposing some that were utterly outrageous, but finally whittling them down to a few unalterable, unnegotiable essentials. Apart from the one or two light-hearted moments it had been tedious work as the demands were reworded again and again, honed to exact specifications. Now, tired though he was, it was up to Seamus Reilly to see to it that they were met. Unfortunately, as Reilly well knew, things seldom went according to plan. Past experience told him that someone was bound to suffer. 'But not I,' he told himself, as he finished dressing. 'Not I.'

He was the first to arrive at the house. Purposely. It allowed him some twenty minutes to look around before the others were due. But, while he had deliberately chosen this particular house as a joke, however warped, Seamus began to wonder, now, if the symbolism wasn't fetid and the joke on him. Staring down the hallway towards the closed door of the kitchen he suddenly felt scared and cold. The house had been uninhabited and boarded up since Mr Apple's death. Half expecting to be attacked by some spectral watchman, he made his way slowly down the hall, almost creeping, sliding his feet along the carpet, the slightest protestation from the floor-boards making him stop instantly and listen. Yet, when he finally reached the kitchen he indulged his mind in wicked trickery, making him see the bodies of Mr Apple and Martin Deeley lying, clasping each other, on the floor. Worse: neither was yet dead. They seemed to be rocking each other and singing away in grossly high-pitched tones a nursery-rhyme about little piggies going to market, or staying at home, or having bread and milk, or having none, or crying weeeeee – the scream from the two phantoms piercing Reilly's brain, transfixing him, forcing him to watch them as they turned and gazed eyelessly at him, distintegrated and vanished, one final jibe, however, lingering, a mocking wail that cried 'You too are already dead.'

Seamus Reilly was on the point of fleeing from the kitchen, when a small, ginger and white cat appeared at the window, mewling and rubbing its cheek against the glass. Reilly was brought back to his senses and let the cat in through the kitchen door, trying to recall the animal's name until it dawned on him he had never known it. 'Hello, puss,' he said as the cat purred about his feet. He picked it up, quietly scratching it behind the ears, as he stared out of the window. He recalled how he had watched it stalk a sparrow as he listened to the shot that toppled Deeley into the outstretched arms of old Mr Apple, hearing the crash of the chair as it scudded backwards and crashed against the wall. He swung round: the chair stood upright, and he remembered now how he had ordered it to be set tidily in place.

Seamus Reilly sighed with relief as he heard someone arrive at the front door. He dropped the cat and brushed its hairs from his coat as he left the kitchen, closing the door behind him. 'Ah, Declan. We'll go in here,' he said, opening the door that led to the sitting-room.

'Only us?' Declan asked.

Reilly looked at his watch, made for the window, opened

one of the shutters, and looked at his watch again. 'We're a little early.'

'Oh.'

'No problems, I hope?'

'Getting here? No. None.'

'Good.'

'Did you expect any?'

Reilly smiled. 'No. No, I didn't. But you never know. You never know what surprises lie in store.'

Declan gazed about the room, wondering at the chaos: the cushions on the chairs upturned, the two small tables upended, the books strewn all over the floor, a picture lying in the grate, its frame smashed. 'Trust you to find a place like this,' he said, intending it as a joke.

Reilly turned his head and stared at him balefully.

The jest failing, Declan pressed on: 'Don't tell me someone actually lives here?'

Reilly shook his head. 'Not any more. You've heard of Mr Apple? It was his house.'

Quite literally Declan gasped. 'Mr Apple?'

Reilly nodded.

'Jesus. You're meeting Maddox in Apple's house?'

Again Reilly nodded.

'Christ you're evil, Seamus.'

'It seemed amusing at the time,' Reilly said, clearly any amusement long since dissipated.

'It's cruel.'

'I didn't really intend it to be, Declan. I thought it might be to my advantage, certainly,' Reilly admitted. 'I'm not so sure about that now,' he added sadly.

Declan stooped and picked up a book from the floor. *The Wind in the Willows*. He let the pages whir from his fingers, picking out occasional lines that seemed to leap at him. 'There was no more talk of play-acting once . . .' 'Then a change began slowly to declare itself . . . the mystery began to drop away from them.' ' "What sort of games are you up to," said the Water Rat severely.' He looked quickly across at Reilly.

'What sort of games are you up to?' he asked, trying to sound severe.

The particular game Reilly was up to was, it seemed, private. He was on his knees, holding in his hands a piece of crumpled paper he had just unscrewed from a ball. He appeared none too happy. He was staring at a picture of a man, a bald man with a serpent slithering across his shiny pate. His name was Aleister Crowley, if the name on the bottom was to be believed. Just for a split second, he took on the appearance of Reilly himself before receding back to his own sinister evilness. Seamus screwed the paper back into a ball and hurled it towards the fireplace, just as the last few words of Declan's question penetrated his consciousness. 'What was that?'

'It was nothing. . . . That sounds like Maddox.'

Before Reilly could answer, Colonel Maddox came into the room. He looked about him disapprovingly, his sense of order appalled, before letting his eyes meet Reilly's. 'Still surviving, I see, Mr Reilly,' he said, pleased that his remark brought some puzzlement to Reilly's face.

'I'm sorry, Colonel?'

'The last time we met, you assured me that you would survive long after we had given up in despair.'

'Ah. That.'

'Yes. It was quite a little speech you made, I remember. Glory was your theme. Or one of them. Death was another.'

'You've met Declan, I believe,' Reilly said, somewhat unbalanced by the Colonel's recollections.

'Yes. Yes, indeed. Mr Tuohy.'

'Colonel.'

Colonel Maddox took a couple of steps into the room, threading his way carefully between the books. 'You do choose the strangest places for your meetings, Mr Reilly,' he said, looking about him and frowning. 'I don't believe I've ever been here but . . .'

'No. I don't think you have, Colonel,' Reilly put in sharply.

'Strange,' Maddox went on, still frowning, moving about now, touching things. 'It seems somehow familiar. Very odd.

204

Very odd indeed. Anyway, down to business, I suppose,' he concluded, setting a cushion back on one of the chairs and sitting down. He crossed his legs and leaned back, waiting for Reilly to speak.

Reilly chose to perch himself on the arm of a chair. 'You received our demands?'

Colonel Maddox nodded slowly.

'And?'

'Before we discuss those, what about Colonel Sharmann?'

'What about him?'

'Where is he?'

Reilly grinned. 'In safe-keeping. He's fit and well. Rather peeved, I'm afraid, but fit and well.'

'You make no mention of him in these – these demands.'

Reilly shrugged. 'No need to, Colonel. Sharmann is of no interest to us, as long as you and I can reach a satisfactory arrangement. That done, you can have him back with pleasure.' Reilly gave a quick laugh. 'He's actually more of a problem to you than we are.'

Maddox scowled. 'Yes,' he admitted. 'Then you will see to it that he is returned unharmed?'

'Of course.'

'Right. Now, your demands – you didn't really expect London to agree to them, did you?'

Reilly smiled, saying nothing.

'I mean, they're outrageous.'

Still Reilly waited.

'You know quite well the government would never agree to release –' The colonel stopped and glanced at Declan Tuohy.

'You were saying?' Reilly interrupted, ignoring the Colonel's clear discomfort.

'I was saying you know quite well the government would never agree to release convicted terrorists.'

Reilly stood up and smiled almost kindly down at the Colonel. 'My dear Colonel Maddox,' he said, his voice oozing tolerance. 'Why do you think I asked specifically for you to come? You of all people should appreciate our methods. You know the demands that must be met just as you recognize the red herrings. You also know that had we listed only our priorities no negotiation could have taken place. So,' he said, giving a small gesture of largesse, 'we tossed in a couple of things we knew you could not agree to. We felt it would be a kindness to let you think there was some give and take.'

Colonel Maddox tried hard to forestall the grin that was shaping on his lips, and nearly succeeded. 'So the release of the prisoners is not a priority?'

'Of course not.'

'The re-trials?'

'Those, yes. You can see our point. This supergrass system is hardly what you could call justice.'

'The government does not like to be seen tampering with the judicial system.'

Reilly gave a small bow. 'It need not be seen, Colonel. We won't say anything, if you don't,' he said, grinning wickedly. 'A simple word from the Home Secretary in the right ears could work wonders. Anyway, I can tell from your voice they've acceded.'

'They have, actually,' the Colonel confessed, sounding surprised. And as though to compensate for the agreement he went on: 'The barring of the peace-keeping forces from certain areas is out of the question.'

'Naturally. We can easily arrange that they won't want to come in.'

Colonel Maddox sighed as though a great weight had been lifted from him. 'Your other two demands were considered, believe it or not, reasonable, although what difference it will make if the media stop calling your political front men terrorists I cannot imagine.'

'I don't expect you can, Colonel.'

'No, I can't. Still, I suppose you have your reasons.'

'Indeed we do. And the new concessions for the prisoners?'

'Yes. They, as I said, were considered reasonable.'

'Excellent.'

'You realize, of course, that we are going out on a limb. We only have your word that our agreement will guarantee your – your silence about this unfortunate affair?'

Reilly looked hurt. 'I have never broken my word, Colonel,' he said solemnly.

'I shudder to think what would happen if you do.'

'To me?'

'To all of us. To all of us. . . . Now – Sharmann.'

'Ah, the poor Sharmann.'

'When do we get him back?'

'When would you like him back, Colonel?'

'When will you give him back, Mr Reilly?'

Reilly thought for a moment. 'What about midnight tonight? It's a propitious time, I always think. Midnight. You can pick him up yourself on the stroke of twelve,' Reilly announced dramatically. 'Outside St Patrick's. How about that?'

Colonel Maddox nodded.

'I think it better that we supply your transport, Colonel. My men – well, you know how it is: the sight of – yes. Well. Declan here will pick you up and bring you to the cathedral,' Reilly said, turning his head and raising his eyebrows to Declan.

Declan was astonished. 'Me?'

'Yes. As our neutral observer I would have thought you were the obvious choice. We don't want the good Colonel getting jittery, do we?'

Colonel Maddox pushed himself out of his chair and stood quietly staring across the room at Declan. 'Poor Mr Tuohy. You're like myself, aren't you? Caught up in this savage conflict. You know, I thought when I was recalled and retired that I would be freed of all – all this,' Maddox said inadequately. 'It's not like that, though. I'm afraid, Mr Tuohy, once this accursed city gets its fingers into you there is no escape. Don't let him bully you. Stay clear of all this intrigue. Get yourself back to your work in London. That's my advice.'

'Declan is going back to London tomorrow,' Reilly put in, his voice hard.

'Tonight,' Declan said. 'I'm going back tonight.'

'We'll discuss that in a minute,' Reilly said affably.

'I'm going back tonight.'

'We'll discuss it,' Seamus insisted, still prepared to sound reasonable. 'Well,' he went on, still reasonably, 'that seems to have taken care of that.'

'Yes . . . Mr Reilly, let Mr Tuohy go back tonight,' Colonel Maddox requested.

'We'll see. Anyway, someone will pick you up tonight.'

'Very well.'

'Thank you for your help. I expect you'll want to be getting back to your office now and report to Big Brother?'

Colonel Maddox gave a tired smile. 'Yes.'

'Seamus, I don't give a damn what you say, I am not staying in Belfast one minute longer than I have to. I'm catching tonight's plane and that's final.'

Seamus Reilly pursed his lips, and sat down again on the arm of the chair. 'Sit down, Declan,' he said.

'I'll stand.'

'Sit down,' Reilly said firmly.

Reluctantly Declan went and sat in the chair the Colonel had used.

Reilly cleared his throat. 'Do you believe in fate?' he asked.

Declan looked as if he thought the man had gone mad. 'Fate?'

'Destiny.'

'Destiny?'

Reilly flicked his hands nervously. 'Don't keep repeating my words. Do you believe in destiny?'

'No,' Declan lied.

'Do you believe in premonitions?'

Declan shrugged. 'Yes and no.'

'Normally I don't. But –' Seamus Reilly was on his feet, his hands clasped behind his back, staring at the ceiling. 'I have this feeling inside me, Declan. . . . I can't explain it. Some-thing tells me you have got to be there when Sharmann is handed over tonight.'

'Come off it, Seamus. You know damned well it doesn't make a toss of difference who's there when you hand him over.'

'Will you listen to me?' Reilly shouted, rounding on Declan, moving towards him, peering into his face. 'I *know* you have to be there tonight. I *know* it. There's no rational explanation. I just *know* it.' Suddenly he straightened up. 'I *know* I will die if you're not.'

'Oh, for Christ's sake, Seamus.' Declan began to protest at the absurdity, but immediately stopped. It was nothing about Reilly that caused him to stop: Seamus Reilly was quietly gazing away into the distance, looking as if he was trying to conjure up some new method of persuasion. And for some little time even Declan could not diagnose the reason he had bitten off his words so abruptly. Then, slowly, floating into his mind came that same sad voice he knew but could not recognize, still persisting, '. . . unknown even to himself. And in him rests the hope I speak of.'

'Declan?'

'What?'

'You look as if you've seen a ghost,' Reilly declared.

'Rubbish.' Declan dismissed the supposition. 'Anyway. Even if I wanted to I couldn't drive Maddox,' he said, sound-ing strangely disappointed now, holding up his heavily ban-daged hand.

Reilly was not to be put off his stride by this. He accepted it calmly, consoling Declan with a hand on the shoulder.

'Well, you'll just have to accompany him, then. Someone else can do the actual driving.'

'You're determined to have me there, aren't you?' Declan asked, no longer bitter.

'I *have* to have you there.'

'All right, Seamus. You arrange a driver and I'll go. But don't you ever ask me to do anything for you again.'

Reilly smiled. 'No,' he said kindly. 'I won't. I won't have to,' he concluded.

Barely waiting for the car taking Declan home to disappear, Seamus Reilly gave instructions that he be driven to the nearest phone box. He leapt from the car, coins ready in his fist, and dialled, tapping his foot impatiently, praying that Fergal and not his mother would answer the phone.

'Hello?'

'Fergal?'

'Yes. Who's that?'

'It's Seamus Reilly.'

'Hey, Mr Reilly! I've been –'

'Just listen, Fergal. This is very important. I want you to do something for me.'

'Sure. Anything.'

'I want you to drive your uncle and another man to a meeting tonight.'

'Sure, I'll do that.'

'Now, your Uncle Declan won't like it. You'll have to persuade him.'

Fergal chuckled down the line. 'I can persuade him, don't worry.'

'And your mother?'

'She won't even know, Mr Reilly.'

'Good man. I knew I could count on you.'

'Oh, you can count on me all right, Mr Reilly.'

'Good man. I want you to leave your house about a quarter past eleven tonight with your uncle. Pick up this other man. Declan, your uncle, will tell you where, and drive them both to arrive at St Patrick's just on midnight.'

'I've got that.'

'Can you do it?'

'Sure. No bother. Will you be there?'

'I'll be there.'

'I'll deliver them safe and sound to you.'

Reilly came out of the phone box and stood for a second on

the footpath, frowning. Something bothered him. Perhaps he was imagining it. Cracking up, he thought to himself, smiling. Still, there had, he was sure, been a warning change of inflection in Fergal's voice when he had asked 'Will you be there?' Reilly shook his head. 'Cracking up,' he muttered to himself but he did not altogether dismiss his worry: he tucked it away, keeping it handy, just in case.

At a quarter past ten that morning a Major in British Intelligence flew into Aldergrove airport. He was met by an unmarked car and driven directly to meet the Commander in Chief of British Forces, Northern Ireland. Shortly afterwards Sergeant Barton was summoned. As soon as he arrived the Commander in Chief excused himself and withdrew.

'Barton.'

'Sir.'

'I'll come straight to the point. I've been sent over to salvage what I can from this mess.'

'Sir.'

'Your career is virtually finished, but you have one chance to leave with credit.'

Barton waited.

'Colonel Sharmann is to be handed over tonight. Midnight. At St Patrick's cathedral. You know it?'

'Yes, sir.'

'See to it that the Colonel is dead before we get him.'

'Sir.'

'Check with armoury. I've made special requisitions available. Any extras you want, just ask.'

'Sir.'

'That's all.'

'Sir —'

'That's all, Sergeant. Just do it and I'll see to it that you come out of this clean.'

'Sir.'

'Reilly phoned you?' Declan demanded, furious.

'That's right. Why not?'

'You're not going to do it, Fergal. I can tell you that straight away. There is no way I'm going to let you drive –'

'I'm going to do it,' Fergal said, eyeing Declan sullenly.

'No.'

'I'm going to do it.'

'Look –' Declan began, hoping to make his nephew see reason.

'There's nothing to look at. Mr Reilly simply asked me to drive the car and keep an eye on you,' Fergal lied convincingly. 'He's worried about you. He thought if the two of us were together we'd be safer. He's just thinking of us.'

'Reilly never thinks of anyone but –'

'He does. I thought you were his friend? He told me he was worried about us. Anyway, there's no danger. Just driving you and some other man to a meeting. Christ, Declan, you'd imagine he'd asked me to kill someone.'

Declan shook his head. 'You don't understand.'

'I do. I'm not a child.'

'You promise to stay in the car?'

'Okay. If that's what you want.'

'That's what I want.'

'Okay. I'll stay in the car.'

'And for God's sake don't say anything to your mother.'

'Why should I? We'll just be toddling out for a little farewell drink. Men together, like.'

'I still don't like it, Fergal.'

'You don't have to. Come on, nothing's going to happen. Anyway, I figure I owe Mr Reilly one.'

'You owe him nothing.'

'I say I do.'

After that, Fergal could hardly wait to tell Martin. He ran to his room, locking the door behind him.

– Hey, Martin, he whispered. It's tonight. We'll get Reilly tonight.

– You think so, do you?

– I know so. Jesus. After all these months. Tonight.

· NINETEEN ·

IT WAS AS though the city simmered, as though the awful
midnight secrets had been roared from the rooftops. By
sundown the streets around St Patrick's were deserted; even
the line of mean, suffocating trees had been forsaken by the
starlings, their spindly, gaunt branches etched like claws
against a glowering unfriendly sky. From time to time a light
wind blew in from the docks sending newspapers scudding
across the playground, some pages blown against and clinging
to the wire perimeter fence, others, caught in a sudden uplift,
rising high and then falling on the steps of the cathedral, lying
there, twitching like vulgar sacrifices to a caged, unheeding
God.

Just after lunch Sergeant Barton went to the armoury.
'Barton,' he said.
　'Ah. Yes. Been expecting you. You know how to use one of
these?'
　Barton took the Heckler-Koch G3, and examined it closely,
fitting the butt into his shoulder and peering along the barrel.
'Yes,' he said.
　'Anything else?'

'A scope. Schmit and Bender.'

'Schmit and Bender? Why all this –'

'Have you got one?'

'Sure. Sure. We've got everything.'

'Get it then. And . . . got a starlight scope?'

'I said we've got everything.'

'Great. Just get what I asked for,' Barton said, already dismantling the rifle and stowing the pieces inside his raincoat.

'Here you go.'

Barton took the two scopes.

'That all?'

'Yes.'

'I thought maybe you'd like a couple of rockets, a few bombs, a tank. . . .'

'Very funny,' Barton said, not amused.

'Have it your own way. Happy hunting.'

Barton was driven in the back of a laundry van to the Opera House. From there he took a taxi to St Patrick's cathedral. It was eight minutes past two as he climbed the steps and went in. For a moment he stood just inside the doors, blinking, focusing his eyes in the gloom, listening, picking up the rattle of rosary beads, the murmur of someone praying. Slowly he walked up the aisle; he bowed his head to the altar and moved sideways into a pew, sitting down, his eyes constantly moving, searching. Yet, despite his alertness Barton felt amazingly calm; he felt, he decided, at peace for the first time in his life; he felt resigned, and he believed the decision he had taken to be right and noble. It was fitting, therefore, to his way of thinking, that this final act of killing should be carried out from a church, and by a sad and misguided quirk he saw nothing pathetic in identifying himself with the Christ he had tried to know, sharing, if nothing else, the humiliation of self-sacrifice.

The click of the rotating rosary beads behind him stopped abruptly, and the woman, still murmuring her adorations, got to her feet and shuffled from the church, the door wheezing behind her on its air-compressed hinge. Immediately Barton left the pew and moved towards the nave. He pushed open the small gilt gate and entered the sanctuary. Swiftly, he headed for a door, one of two that led from the sanctuary, a plaster archangel on a marble plinth guarding them, sword raised. In one rapid, lithe movement Barton opened the door, stepped inside, and shut the door quietly again behind him, cutting off all sound, cutting off, too, he thought, all hope of retraction. All the while looking upwards, he started to climb the stone steps that led to the roof: ascending – the word struck him as particularly poignant. Round and round, ever higher the spiral stretched as, giddily, he recalled a film he had seen in which someone had climbed a stairway to Paradise, each step lighting brilliantly as he ascended. 'I'll build a stairway to Paradise,' he sang softly to himself. 'With a new step every day.' Which was all one ever tried to do, some more successfully than others, it seemed.

Barton was surprised at how breathless he was when he finally reached the top, and rested, leaning back against the wall, for a few seconds. Then, using both hands, he pulled back the two bolts that secured the door, breathing deeply as the high fresh air blew in his face. He stepped gingerly on to the roof and moved on hands and knees along the parapet, raising his head every few yards to peer down and about him. Finally satisfied, he settled back and started to unpack the parts of his weapon, placing each section carefully on the leaded gutter. That done, from his inside pocket, he took a small handgun and, fondling it, he closed his eyes and waited.

Fergal was dressed and ready hours before time. He had tried desperately to be nonchalant about the whole thing, dawdling over his toilet, deciding to go casual in jeans and leather jacket. But his heart was thumping and there was a wild, excited light in his eyes. Martin was no help either: he seemed to have taken off for the day. Fergal stared at the clock, willing the hands to move faster, then walked to the window, staring out, half-expecting Martin to come swooping in, smiling with his tiny

215

teeth, sharing the suspense and excitement. All he could see, however, was the caravan of starlings, covering the barren apple tree like poisonous fruit. He slammed the window shut and pulled the curtains, groping in the darkness until he found the light.

All at once the room seemed terribly cold and Fergal shivered. Someone, perhaps Martin although it didn't sound like him, was screaming in his head, warning him. He frowned, trying to decipher the words. He went to the mirror and turned it to the wall; moving round the room he placed each photograph face down where it stood. He ripped the posters from the walls, crumpled them, and hurled them into one corner, his movements jerky. Then, as though his exertions had exorcized his mania, he walked to his chest-of-drawers and took out the gun. Holding it in both hands he raised it above his head, offering it up, but to whom he had no idea. That done, he slipped it into the pocket of his jacket and left the room, seemingly his old self, clattering downstairs, shouting: 'Come on, Declan. I'm ready, and dying for a drink.'

Colonel Maddox waited in his office in darkness. He had let the night creep in undisturbed. And he had watched it come, rolling in on soundless, padded feet. Perhaps like dying, he thought. How rapidly and stealthily it overtakes one! Yet not as rapidly, it seemed, as the memory of Mr Apple's anguished words reappeared to sear his mind. Although the feeling had been haunting him for longer than he would have cared to admit, Maddox was seized by the cruel, irrevocable knowledge, which only animals seem able to accept with equanimity, that one will soon be dead – that, indeed, one had already been measured for shroud and coffin, that one was already dead. He snapped his eyes open, surprised to find himself shaking. For an instant he felt he was on the point of identifying something momentous and appalling. But try as he might to recall it, the premonition, if that was what it had been, was gone: like his dreams, gone.

Since leaving Colonel Maddox, Seamus Reilly had been on the go, reporting to the Commander in Chief, organizing, ensuring as best he could that everything went according to plan. Now, he was putting the finishing touches to his instructions, speaking quietly, calming the jangled nerves of his men.

'You're satisfied with security?'

'Yes, Mr Reilly,' Regan said.

'You're certain the area is fully protected?'

'Oh yes. We moved our men in at four this afternoon.'

'And their positions?'

'Twelve men on the ground, Mr Reilly. Nine in buildings surrounding St Patrick's.'

Reilly nodded. 'Good. Now,' he said, turning to Dowling, 'the escort – you've seen to that?'

'Yes, Mr Reilly. Tuohy's –'

'Mr Tuohy's,' Reilly snapped, displaying the only sign of nerves.

'*Mr* Tuohy's car will be followed from the moment it leaves the Duffy house.'

'And Sharmann?'

'That's all taken care of. He'll be brought to the cathedral at midnight exactly. Eh – Mr Reilly?'

Seamus Reilly stiffened, sensing trouble.

'Mr Tuohy. When he picks up the Colonel. What about –'

Reilly waved away the question with a small, relieved gesture. He even smiled. 'That's taken care of. Colonel Maddox has seen to it that no – eh – problems will arise at his end.'

'Oh.'

'Anything else?'

There was, it appeared, nothing else.

'Good,' Reilly said. 'You'd best get going.'

'Right,' Regan said. 'Good luck, Mr Reilly,' he was fool-hardy enough to add.

'Luck, Regan, has nothing to with us,' Reilly said coldly. 'Unless anything goes wrong. Then it will be all bad. For you.'

Alone, Seamus Reilly removed the small tin of cigars from his pocket, and placed them in a drawer of his desk. It was a small superstition he had, an offering, a token of good intent as he saw it, promising St Jude a couple of candles and a prayer if he brought about the impossible.

· TWENTY ·

As Reilly's car approached the cathedral the driver flicked the lights on and off twice. Then he pulled to the side of the road and stopped a few feet behind the Duffys' battered Austin. Seamus lowered the window and waited until two men appeared as if from the air and came to the car.

'No problems?' Reilly asked, ever pessimistic.

'Everything's nice and quiet, Mr Reilly. We're just waiting for the car from Clones. The others are here.'

Reilly nodded. 'Ask Colonel Maddox to join me,' he said, opening the door and stepping out, glancing briefly upwards. 'Ah, Colonel,' he said as Maddox came up to him. 'You seem taller in the dark.'

'An illusion,' Maddox said fatuously.

'Yes. I know.' Reilly gave the Colonel a shrewd, questioning look. 'You seem nervous.'

'Of course I'm nervous.'

'There's no need to be, I assure you. Everything will go like clockwork. It – you see?' Reilly pointed out with satisfaction as the car from Clones veered into view, dipped its lights and came to a halt. 'We are very well organized, you know.'

'Let's just get this over with,' Maddox said, surprising even himself with his brusqueness.

'Certainly,' Reilly replied. 'Follow me,' he said, already making his way towards the cathedral steps, signalling with two curling fingers for Declan Tuohy to join them.

'You stay here,' Declan warned.

'Sure I will,' Fergal agreed. 'I said I would,' he pointed out.

'Well, just be sure you do.'

Hurrying to catch up, Declan joined Reilly and Maddox, and together the three of them approached the steps. It was one minute to twelve.

True to form Seamus Reilly waited for one minute, following the second hand of his watch as it moved, amused that the light from the streetlamps created a minuscule, blurred shadow behind the hand, making it appear to retreat even as it swept on. At midnight precisely, Reilly signalled for Colonel Sharmann to be brought out.

Sergeant Barton watched, focusing his sights on the car. As the front passenger door opened he cocked his rifle. A man stepped out, glanced about him, glanced, too, at Seamus Reilly for confirmation, then opened the back door. Colonel Sharmann got out, brushing aside the hand extended to help him, looking puzzled and annoyed. Dispassionately Barton studied the face through his scope, surprised that any man in the Colonel's predicament could manage still to look arrogant. Then he tightened his finger on the trigger and fired, watching Sharmann lurch backwards, collapse almost back into the car, and slip limply to the ground. Immediately, as though purposely denying himself the time to think, Sergeant Barton threw down the rifle and, taking the handgun, placed the barrel in his mouth and shot himself, his last image that of a small boy smiling admiringly at him.

Below, for what seemed an age, nobody moved. Then bedlam broke loose. The area was filled with armed men, instinctively racing towards Reilly, surrounding him, pulling him, pulling

Declan and Maddox too, towards the cars. Curiously nobody shouted, giving the running feet a frightening menace of their own. Instinctively everyone was looking upwards, scanning the rooftops, paying no attention to Fergal as he calmly got out of the car and, steadying his hands on the roof, aimed at Reilly, and fired. The crack of the revolver brought the fleeing men to a skidding halt. Declan was the first to realize what had happened. 'Jesus,' he screamed. 'Fergal!'

Instantly everyone looked at the car, at Fergal still standing there, the gun still pointing at Reilly. He seemed to be smiling, and the smile stayed on his lips as the bullets ripped into him, spinning him round, lifting him from his feet, sending him crashing to the footpath. He felt no pain, no hurt, no warmth. He was cold, and he was crying for the warmth he had been promised. 'Martin,' he tried to call, but the name was garbled in blood. And there was no sign of Martin. He was alone. Slowly, achingly he stretched out one hand, raised it upwards, his fingers trying, it seemed, to grasp something. Then, bewildered, he withdrew his arm. His head fell sideways.

'I'm all right, dammit,' Reilly shouted. 'Declan, Colonel. With me. My car,' he ordered, feeling only now the pain in his shoulder. 'Regan – where's Regan?'

'Here, Mr Reilly.'

'Get those cars out of here.'

'Yes – the –'

'Dump them. Dump them on the steps over there. Then get everyone out of here.'

'Right.'

'Move, dammit,' Reilly ordered his driver. 'Drop me off and get these men back safely.'

Numbed, Declan sat beside the driver, staring out at the road in front of him, watching it being eaten up under the car. 'You bastard, Seamus.'

Reilly winced.

'You fucking bastard.'

'I'm sorry, Declan –'

'You couldn't leave us alone, could you? You –'

Colonel Maddox leaned forward and placed a consoling hand on Declan's shoulder. 'Shh,' he whispered. Then, strangely, leaning back into his seat, he placed his hand on Reilly's knee and patted it.

Three days later a couple of items were given a small mention in the newspapers. One reported the tragic death of a Sergeant Barton who had been accidentally killed while cleaning his rifle. The second announced that a Captain Little had been found murdered: the IRA were suspected although no one had as yet claimed responsibility.

The discovery of the bodies of Colonel Sharmann and Fergal Duffy was not made public for ten days.

A DARKNESS IN THE EYE

For Martin and
Alison Deeley

. . . Still, as we well know, 'the fault, dear Brutus, is not in our stars but in ourselves'; and yet with what facility and sleight of mind we ascribe our foulest deeds to that great charlatan, destiny. How sad that in reaching for those stars, those bright and burning emblems of man's most noble and holy aspirations, we dim their radiance by treachery, and eclipse their brilliance by furtive acts of duplicity and shame. Oh, tragedy proclaimed! We yearn and cry for dignity in death, but death merits only scorn if the life it extinguishes has been useless, futile, and a sham. Surely it is the giving of life that is glorious, and the living of life that merits dignity. Is it not life, with all its sufferings and tribulations, that elevates us to the region of the stars, makes us worthy of our place in the presence of God? Death is a grim and inevitable defrayment, nothing more. I do not believe that any man dies bravely: he dies in peace – reward enough; or, with an awful darkness in the eye, he dies screaming for the power of Shekinah to protect him. Alas, by then it is too late for mercy, too late, even, for pity . . . . But reach for those stars, reach and strive to clasp their wondrous splendour, remembering always that they are, however, cold. The warmth for which we hunger is in man's glowing spirit, attainable, and so very close at hand.

'The Visions and Visitations of Arthur Apple'

· ONE ·

THE KILLING OF Seamus Reilly would unquestionably have made the headlines in every morning newspaper in Belfast had not, on the same evening, and at approximately the same time, a young man from Clones decided it was his turn to be featherweight champion of the world, and bring about the miracle of uniting a battered community if only for a few hours. Consequently, Seamus Reilly's untimely mishap was relegated to page 2 and allotted only a dozen or so cryptic lines: even in death, it seemed, Reilly was capable of shrouding himself in shadows, and of advancing his soul as collateral for further intrigue.

Indeed, even the London dailies, intoxicated by the euphoria surrounding the young boxer's outstanding and surprising victory, were reticent to intrude on Northern delight with a terrorist's murder. The *Telegraph* headed its single, terse paragraph with TERRORIST LEADER SHOT, explaining that police had identified the man shot dead by Security Forces the night before as Seamus Reilly, 44, the 'self-styled Godfather of the Provisional IRA', ruthless, callous and vicious.

The reporter might have been correct about his name and

age. However, the claim that the Security Forces had terminated Reilly's life was pure, if unwitting, fabrication: *that* information was a piece of trickery the likes of which would have done credit to Reilly himself, and of which he would surely have been proud.

Colonel Matthew Maddox stared out of the bedroom window of his Berkshire home, a cup of black, sugarless coffee in his hand, an open copy of the *Telegraph* on the floor, a small, moustachioed triumphant boxer smiling up at him. For some months now he had taken to having breakfast upstairs, away from his nattering wife and her recent addiction, morning television. So Seamus Reilly was finally dead. Hoist on his own petard, Maddox mused. He stood up and opened the window wide, breathing deeply: he had given the huge expanse of lawn its first mowing of the season the evening before (perched on the seat of his newly acquired rotary machine, and playing a gloriously childish game, imagining he was Fangio no less as he twirled the mower round the base of the enormous copper beech, pretending it was a particularly tricky chicane, leaning extravagantly sideways, and shouting wheeeee), and he relished the scent of the freshly cut grass under the dew.

The thought returned: Seamus Reilly was dead. Perhaps it was the weight of this knowledge that made Maddox feel suddenly giddy. He sat down, resting his slippered feet on the window-sill . . . He had probably been cheerfully wheeeeeing his way round the tree at the moment Reilly had been crying for mercy. But no. Reilly would certainly not have made any fuss about dying: it would not have been his style at all. He would have accepted death with dignity, welcomed it as an inevitability. The fact that it came violently might, even, have appealed to his cruel, warped sense of justice.

Maddox smiled wryly. The awful irony of it! Just when Reilly was trying his utmost to bring about an end to the violence that crippled the province, he had fallen victim to that violence. The Colonel sighed, a sincere sympathy for the murdered terrorist welling up inside him. At least Reilly had tried! But there were, alas, no rewards for trying, unless one considered death as a reward – which, come to think of it, was not too flamboyant an hypothesis. What was it Reilly had told him? 'Colonel, I am long since dead. That old fool Mr Apple was quite right, you know. We are all dead in this blighted land. The innocent and the guilty – we all died a long, long time ago.'

– You know that what you propose to do will – , Colonel Maddox had said before Reilly interrupted him by holding up his hand. As long as you know, the Colonel concluded.

– I know.

– 'It is a far, far better thing,' Maddox began. Reilly winced at the quotation.

– Nothing so dramatic, I fear, Colonel. Nor for such noble reasons.

– Sacrifice is always noble, Maddox countered, as though longing that the opportunity for sacrifice would step his way. Reilly was cynical.

– You're still missing the point, Colonel. It has nothing to do with sacrifice. Years and years and years ago I swore I would do everything in my power to see to it that Ireland was united. And, from time to time, violence was the only option.

– I don't –

Again Reilly had held up his hand.

– You know it's true, Colonel. You won't admit it, but you know it's a fact. You saw for yourself how things worked when you were stationed here in Belfast.

The Colonel nodded.

– Yes. Yes, indeed I did.

– Well, Reilly shrugged, things have now changed. There is just a glimmer of hope that we can achieve our ends by political means so the violence has got to stop. Unfortunately, there are some, even within our own ranks, who disagree with this policy. They see negotiation as weakness, terror as strength. Some of our most loyal followers have broken away from us and have sworn to continue the killings and bombings. Someone – finally – has to take a stand against violence. Someone from within our

3

organization. So . . . Reilly smiled thinly and raised his eyebrows.

So – Seamus Reilly was dead.

'I see you've heard.' The senior editor of the BBC's current affairs programme 'The Right To Speak' eyed Declan Tuohy's grim face with some apprehension.

Tuohy nodded. 'Yes. I've heard.'

'I'm sorry, Declan.'

'We killed him, you know. As surely as if we held that gun to his head and pulled the trigger we killed him.'

'Come off it, Declan. We – '

'Oh yes we did. We made a deal with Reilly. He kept his side of the bargain. What did we do? What – '

'It was taken out of our hands.'

'Ah – that's to be the excuse, is it? That's how we make everything all right? Christ above! Reilly was supposed to be the conniving bastard. What we did to him was worse than anything he would ever do. He trusted us, dammit. He trusted us.'

'I know he did, Declan. But it had nothing to do with us that – '

'Oh, piss off.'

Inspector John Asher of the RUC learned of Reilly's death about an hour after it had happened. He was appalled. On the face of it, he should have been delighted, of course. But for all his innate Protestantism, his suspicion of everything Catholic, and for all his fundamental adherence to law and order and his loathing of terrorism, Asher felt an inexplicable loneliness at the death of Seamus Reilly. For the first time in his life, he knew what it was to be saddened. He knew that he could never be seen to grieve and would have to smile and rejoice and pretend he fully endorsed the myth that Belfast would be a better place now that another IRA bastard was killed.

It was some consolation that he had tried to warn Reilly: what he proposed to do was folly. Reilly had agreed that perhaps he was being foolhardy, but he had then gone ahead and done precisely what he had intended to do in the first place. Asher sighed again. That was the bloody IRA for you: let them get an idea in their heads and it became a damned obsession that nothing, not even their Holy Roman Pope, could remove. His years of wheeling and dealing with Seamus Reilly had taught him one thing: the IRA were just ordinary men doing what they saw as fit and proper for their cause, resorting to violence because otherwise nobody would pay them any heed, prepared to take life if it enhanced the chances of realizing their dream, yet equally prepared to sacrifice their own lives for the same end. And, or so it seemed, that was exactly what Reilly had done. He might, at least, have hoped for a more dignified execution. It would have been the betrayal that would have hurt him most. Asher poured himself a large whisky. He raised his glass. 'Here we go, Seamus, you devious old bugger. I'll miss you.'

Apart from those actually involved in the murder, the Commander in Chief of the Provisional IRA was probably the first man to know that Seamus Reilly was dead. For several seconds he stared at the messenger before dismissing him with a vague, preoccupied wave of his hand (a gesture he had unconsciously picked up from Reilly himself) and slumping into the leather armchair. He stayed like that for some twenty minutes: unmoving apart from an occasional twitch of the scar that ran the length of his bearded jowl. It wasn't until his youngest child yowled upstairs that he sat up. He removed his horn-rimmed spectacles and, taking a handkerchief from his breast pocket, wiped his eyes, smiling sadly to himself, thinking that anyone seeing him do this might have suspected him of crying. They would have been tears of frustration, not loss or remorse. He was angry at himself for not speaking out, for washing his hands of what had become known internally as the 'Reilly affair', for having allowed himself to get into a situation from which there was but one, inevitable, tragic escape; and afraid because now the precariousness of his own position, despite his treacherously diplomatic neutrality, was clearly evident. That, of course, was always the trouble when one chose sides, particularly when the strife was within the ranks: and for the best part of a year the internal wrangling had been going on, gathering force and becoming more aggressive and spiteful with each passing month, the two factions (the hawks and doves as they were classified by the tabloids) entrenching themselves ever deeper in their opposing beliefs, the menace of outright rebellion only just held at bay, mostly through the efforts of Seamus Reilly who had somehow become ensconced in the role of mediator, while the Commander in Chief had sat quietly in the background, smoking his pipe, watching coldly, summing up the arguments, preparing the decision that would ultimately be his, allowing Reilly to take the flak, allowing him to make himself vulnerable.

– Damn you, Reilly, the Commander now thought, getting up and walking to the window. No, not damn you. God love you. God love and protect you.

Upstairs the child screamed again, and was immediately comforted by its mother who crooned. 'Slower and slower and slower the wheel spins,' she sang, the words lulling the child, and sweeping over the Commander who found them distinctly mournful. Slower the wheel spins . . . and when it finally, irrevocably stopped? Involuntarily he shuddered, as if someone had walked on his grave. A vengeful spirit in search of retribution perhaps. He pressed his forehead against the cold glass of the window. Away to his left, only just visible in the yellow light of the moon, the mist surrounding its peak like a gently falling shower of pollen, rose the Sugar Loaf Mountain. The feeling had been growing within him for longer than he cared to remember, but now he knew and recognized that the real and true calamity of Seamus Reilly's death was the almost certain evaporation of any hope of peace within the IRA. The chance, slim though it might have been, had been there. But he had abandoned it; abandoned, too, far worse, his friend Seamus Reilly. If only . . . ah, if only.

He turned from the window, stretched and yawned, and made his way to bed. If only. . . .

A neighbour mentioned to Rose Duffy that Seamus Reilly had been killed.

'Oh, dear. Poor man,' Rose said, hawing on the glass she was polishing.

'He's probably better off, though,' she added, smiling brightly. 'Still, I think I'll set his little place at the table just the same – in case he feels like coming back. He's a terrible man for that – popping in when you least expect him. Always better to be nice and prepared for the unexpected. That's what I say,' she concluded, holding the glass at arm's length away from her, and admiring the glitter with bright, crazy eyes.

· TWO ·

COINCIDENTALLY, AND NOT without a certain irony, four separate meetings were scheduled to take place in the first week of May 1984. All, in their various ways, were to lead to tragedy.

The first meeting to take place was informal. It was in Seamus Reilly's sitting room, and was attended only by Reilly himself and the Commander in Chief of the Provisional IRA. The atmosphere was very relaxed, both men sipping their drinks, smoking, talking quietly, giving no indication of the turmoil and bitterness that had taken place the night before. True, the Commander was a little edgy to begin with, his sharp bespectacled eyes darting restlessly about the room, but this was attributable to his natural nervousness, a sort of fidgety discomfort he always felt outside his familiar territories.

'You handled that very nicely, Seamus,' the Commander said, reaching out and tapping the bowl of his briar pipe in the glass ashtray.

Seamus Reilly spread his hands demurely, as if to suggest it had been quite a simple task and that such praise was

8

unwarranted. But he was clearly pleased.

'No. I think you handled it very well indeed. It's never pleasant having to expel old colleagues from the Organization.'

Reilly shrugged. 'It had to be done.'

The Commander nodded, accidentally blowing into his pipe and sending up a cloud of blue smoke which he waved away apologetically, a hint of a grin on his face like a schoolboy attempting to forestall chastisement.

'I know,' he said finally. 'But it's never pleasant.'

'True,' Reilly agreed, adopting an appropriately mournful look. 'But they gave us no option.'

'I suppose not.'

'There's no supposing about it, Commander. They were given every chance. The whole success of our campaign depends on discipline. This willy-nilly killing can no longer be tolerated. It does us nothing but harm.'

'And you think they will stop?'

Reilly shook his head after a moment's thought. 'No,' he said grimly.

'Even though we have warned them they risk being shot?'

'Even so. They'll fight us. They think we're getting weak. Or jaded. Or both. They believe our move into the political arena is a sign of submission. No, they won't stop. They'll fight us all right. And they'll have their supporters both here and in Dublin. We're the doves now, don't forget, and the symbolism of dovery makes them puke.'

The Commander allowed himself a wry smile. 'I would never have considered you as a dove, Seamus.'

Unexpectedly, Reilly took the observation seriously. He frowned. 'Things change. People change. Continuous, useless killing is bound to affect us, don't you think?'

The Commander nodded in tentative agreement, and set about refuelling his pipe. 'Of course.'

Seamus Reilly watched the operation with interest, wondering why on earth anyone would bother to smoke a pipe if it required such elaborate preparation. He lit one of his small, thin cigars, and closed his eyes as he enjoyed the first lungful.

9

'They'll blame you, you know,' the Commander went on, still stoking his pipe. 'Not me. You.'

'That's nothing new,' Reilly answered, keeping his eyes closed.

'They might – ' the Commander began, but stopped abruptly.

Reilly opened his eyes immediately. 'Indeed they might, Commander. But it wouldn't be the first time someone tried.'

'You'll be careful?'

Reilly feigned shock. 'I'm always careful,' he said.

While he might have appeared to lead a pretty normal existence, nothing that Seamus Reilly did was on the spur of the moment. Everything was most meticulously planned. Every journey he made, be it to another country or just across the city, was monitored, his car escorted by a constantly changing, interweaving selection of bodyguards in fast, if innocuous-looking vehicles; every visitor he received was given inconspicuous security the likes of which would have been deemed excessive by many. His home was under twenty-four hour observation, his car bulletproof. Seamus Reilly was careful all right.

The Commander had managed to get his pipe going, and puffed contentedly for a few minutes, holding the bowl in his fingers and tapping the stem from time to time on his teeth. 'It's that woman I worry about,' he then said. 'She's the one that will most resent the power being taken from her. They always do. Women.'

'I wouldn't know.'

'Just you keep an eye on her, Seamus.'

'I will.'

'You see that you do.'

The second meeting was rather more sinister. It took place in the evening and in some secrecy in the Andersonstown district of Belfast, in a small bare room over a sweet shop, and it was attended by two men and a woman. Although all three knew each other well, there was a tense furtiveness about them as if they were, in fact, strangers.

'Well?' Patrick Moran asked, arching his eyebrows but managing to keep his eyes impassive. He was a small man, running to fat and balding, and he had an air about him that suggested he was suspicious of everyone including himself. 'Where do we go from here?'

Eddie McCluskey coughed into his clenched fist before answering. He was younger than Moran, about twenty-eight, a handsome, swarthy man with the drooping moustache of a Spanish pirate and wide-set, intense eyes enhanced by thick brows that met over the bridge of his nose. 'We carry on as before,' he said, in a tone that implied he had found the question spurious.

Moran gave a thin hissing laugh. 'Oh, really?'

'Yeah. Sure. Why not?'

Moran raised his eyes to the ceiling as though seeking deliverance from some imbecility. 'Why not? Didn't you listen to anything that was said last night?'

'I listened,' McCluskey said, turning sullen.

'Then you heard what Reilly said?'

'Sure I heard. So what? Fuck Reilly. Who the hell does he think he is anyway?'

The obscenity, about par for McCluskey, brought tiny beads of sweat oozing onto Moran's face. Thus far his clashes with Reilly had been wholly verbal and he had always come off second best: the suggestion, albeit only by implication, that he should physically oppose Seamus Reilly was more than he cared to think about. It was a measure of his very real dread that 'Watch it,' was all he could bring himself to say, and that in an awed, frightened whisper.

McCluskey, ever brash, gave a scoffing snort. 'Shit. Reilly's a nothing,' he sneered.

Not that he meant it. McCluskey, too, was scared of Reilly's awesome powers, but he had an aptitude and penchant for tiresome bravura, a cockiness found in mindless men, displayed, like a peacock's tail, only when secure in the knowledge

11

it will neither be challenged nor, indeed, overheard by the subject.

'If you believe that, it's the biggest mistake you'll ever make,' Moran warned. 'It's a mistake a lot of fools have made only you won't find any of them about to tell you. Reilly has more power than you could ever imagine. Believe me, what he says goes.'

'Big deal. So what do we do? Sit on our arses and do nothing?'

'I didn't say that. We just have to be careful. Very bloody careful. When Reilly said he would have us shot if we didn't keep in line he meant it. Reilly doesn't joke. I don't want to find myself dead in a ditch some night if you do.'

'So what do we do?' McCluskey demanded, running the tip of his tongue over the ends of his moustache as he always tended to when frustration was getting the better of him.

'We carry on our campaign as before only we concentrate on England. And we make damn sure those bloody doves know nothing about it until we're good and ready.'

It was the woman who spoke: her voice calm and cold and certainly educated, almost English. She was a most unlikely-looking terrorist: tall and blonde and beautiful, her slim and graceful body a far cry from the squat, butch, cropped females beloved of television plays about the Troubles. Only her curiously oriental, almond eyes gave any hint of the fanaticism that made her dangerous. Sometimes, behind her back, men called her Pussy Galore but she had little in common with the Bonded lady: it was a nickname that simply did not apply, but caused chauvinistic amusement none the less. 'What we have to do is to give Reilly and his lackies enough to think about over here, plan and execute a proper campaign in England, and then, if need be, take out Reilly himself.'

McCluskey really liked the sound of such an approach but Moran objected. 'We can't. We'd never get away with it.'

'We will if we're careful,' the woman insisted, her voice subtly patronizing now that she had one of the men on her side. 'Of course, if you want out, Moran, there's nothing to stop you going,' she added. 'One good coup in England is all we need, then we'll get enough support from here and Dublin to get rid of the shits and appoint leaders who see things our way.'

Poor Moran was still not convinced. He shook his head dejectedly. 'Reilly will find out. I know he will. Jesus, he'll have us as mincemeat before we – '

'Not if we're careful,' the woman insisted.

Still Moran was unhappy, and it was a sign of his intense dissatisfaction that he continued to protest, something which, as a general rule, he was terrified to do. He was, in a sense, a battered man, perpetually nagged by his far younger, far more intelligent wife, his slow mind plundered of any calmness by the continuous screaming and crying of his children. 'It doesn't matter how damn careful we are,' he argued, flinching at his boldness. 'Reilly will know. He knows everything that goes on. He knows most things before they even happen.'

'Then we'll have to make certain this is the first time he doesn't know, won't we?'

Moran found this simple logic irrefutable. He stood up and started to pace about the small room, measuring his strides with some precision in the manner of a man used to taking what exercise he could in a prison cell, and continually glancing towards the window as if reckoning it as a possible, if inadequate means of escape. Finally he stopped and faced his two colleagues. 'I'll have to think about it,' he told them hesitantly, relieved when the woman smiled pleasantly enough and nodded: 'Fine,' she agreed. 'Take all the time you want, Patrick.'

Sensing his winning streak might end abruptly, Moran said: 'I better be off. It'll be the wife who murders me if I don't get home soon.'

'Sure,' the woman agreed again. 'You get on home. We'll be in touch.'

'He's trouble,' McCluskey diagnosed as soon as Moran had gone. 'As sure as hell he'll be trouble.'

The woman shook her head and pursed her lips. 'No. No, I don't believe he will. In fact, Eddie, I think he'll be very useful.' She smiled. 'If things go as I hope Reilly will suspect us for sure.

Well, we might just throw him off the scent for a while if Moran happened to turn up dead.'

'Jesus, you don't – '

'It's up to him, isn't it? If he sticks with us he'll be useful – if he doesn't, well – ' she shrugged, ' – we'll simply have to make use of him. That's all.'

McCluskey shook his head in wonderment. 'Christ above, you think of everything.'

'Someone has to.'

'I'd hate to get the wrong side of you.'

'Then don't.'

Brigadier Brazier drummed his fingers on his desk, approximating the rhythm of the Sousa march. From time to time he stopped and sat quietly, cocking his head to one side, listening, waiting for Major Fisher. The Brigadier gave a noisy, vulgar belch, and glanced at the clock on the wall: three minutes to go. In about two minutes the thump of the Major's steel-tipped shoes across the landing would announce his arrival; Fisher's slow, methodical walk, the dogged strides of this obstinate Yorkshire miner's son, his measured, labouring walk, approximated his cumbersome way of thinking, his complete acceptance of the stultifying military code. He had achieved a rank far above his expectations, was fearful that any novel idea might be seen as some intolerable impertinence.

'Come in, come in,' the Brigadier now called, smiling to himself as he noted the knock had come dead on time.

Major Crispin Fisher came in. 'Sir.'

'Come in, come in,' the Brigadier said again, waiting for Fisher to walk across the room, eyeing him somewhat warily as he stood smartly to attention in front of the desk. 'Relax, man,' he added, somewhat testily. 'This is quite informal. Do sit down like a good chap.' Fisher sat very erect, his hands resting primly on his knees.

'I take it you've been briefed?'

'Yes, sir.'

'Good, And?'

'Sir?'

The Brigadier swallowed his annoyance. 'You think you can handle it?'

'Yes, sir.'

'Hmm. Excellent. You – you've been made aware of the risks?'

'Yes, sir.'

'And that you are not being ordered to undertake this?'

'Yes, sir.'

Brigadier Brazier looked away, for the moment feeling a rare twinge of guilt. The Major's unequivocal subordination irked him: was he simply a moron or had he been brainwashed? It was, he now thought, not impossible that he had been chosen precisely for his simple unquestioning loyalty, 'I don't want to appear rude,' the Brigadier went on, genuinely not wanting to, 'but you have thought this thing through carefully, haven't you? I mean, it is a very risky undertaking, you know. And if anything should go wrong you will be entirely on your own.'

Perhaps sensing his superior's tetchiness, Fisher slightly altered his response, preceding it with a steady, positive nod. 'Oh, yes, sir. I've thought it through carefully.'

Which was more or less true. He had certainly thought about it, if never in the light of refusal: he saw this unexpected mandate as the ultimate recognition of his obedience and submission to military discipline. Indeed, he was flattered that he had been volunteered, and managed, in the days that followed, to enhance the possible sacrifice of his life with a certain nobility, thus giving his dull, lonely, secretive existence a meaning and purpose it had never before achieved. Somehow, although forbidden to mention it to his colleagues, the option of probable death set him apart, and, had he thought about it further, he might have admitted that he would be almost disappointed if he were to come out of this affair alive.

'I'm glad to hear that,' the Brigadier said, and he was, immediately shifting responsibility onto the Major's shoulders. 'You're a brave young man, Fisher.'

Fisher blushed and moved uneasily in his chair.

'No, I mean it,' the Brigadier continued. 'It isn't everyone who could be entrusted with such a mission. Those IRA boys don't mess about, you know. If they find out – well, let's just hope they don't.'

Fisher smiled again, his smile enhanced by a curious lopsided charm, or perhaps it was cunning. 'Yes, sir.'

'One great thing in your favour is that they're pretty desperate just now, and this rift in their ranks is just the break we've been looking for. And God knows, we need a break.'

'Yes, sir.'

'The fact that they've helped two – eh – genuine – ' the Brigadier underlined the final word with aggrieved distaste, ' – deserters in the past month will have made them less suspicious, I suppose.'

'Yes, sir.'

'Although that won't mean they'll relax their vigilance.'

'No, sir.'

The Brigadier stopped for the moment. He sensed, even now, before the covert operation had properly got under way, that it was all going to go disastrously wrong. 'You're quite certain you can cope?' he asked in a quiet voice, his tone coaxing as if hoping the Major would retract his assurances. 'No second thoughts?'

'None, sir.'

Lest he should change his mind the Brigadier stood up abruptly and held out his hand. 'Well, good luck to you Fisher.'

'Thank you, sir,' Fisher said, shaking hands, managing to make even this gesture deferential, and then made for the door. As he reached it he turned. 'One thing, sir – '

'Yes, Major?'

'If – if by some chance something *does* go wrong and I don't – I don't get back – will you explain everything to my father?'

The Brigadier nodded, his eyes unsteady. 'Of course,' he lied.

'It's just that he's very proud of me, sir. I'm the only one he has left and it would kill him if he thought I really deserted.'

'You need have no worries on that score. I'll see to it

16

personally that he is told the truth,' the Brigadier confirmed, shocked that he could lie so glibly. 'In any case I have no doubt you'll be back to tell him all about it yourself.'

'Thank you, sir.'

For some time after the Major had gone the Brigadier kept his grey, watery eyes fixed on the closed door, the pathetic, time-worn phrase 'lamb to the slaughter' bleating in his mind. Then he reached for the telephone. Carefully he dialled, using a pencil, and then tapping it like a drum-stick on the desk as he waited for his connection. Then:

'I've just seen Fisher.'

'And?'

'He seems all right.'

'He is. He's perfect.'

'He's a bit – '

'Dumb? That's just what we want. The bright sparks are no damn good. They tend to have consciences. And they ask too many questions.'

'I was going to say helpless.'

'So much the better. Far less chance of our – helpless – Major being suspected.'

'I – '

'Don't worry, sir. We know what we're doing.'

'I hope so. I certainly hope so.'

A cackle reverberated down the line. 'We do.'

'You said that about Colonel Sharmann, and I need hardly remind you what a fiasco that turned into.'

The voice coughed. 'We all make the occasional mistake. Anyway, this is quite different. This will work.'

'You really think so?'

'We know so, sir.'

'I wish I had your confidence.'

'Just leave it all to us. You'll see.'

'You'll keep me fully informed?'

The voice sounded surprised. 'Of course.'

'I mean *fully* informed.'

'Of course.'

Myles Cravan popped his head round the door of Declan Tuohy's cramped office. 'Sorry I'm late. Got held up.'

'Traffic or politics?'

Cravan grinned. 'A bit of both.' He sat on the corner of the desk, swinging one leg. 'Had a chance to read that report?'

Tuohy nodded. 'Yes. I've read it.'

'You think it's true?'

Tuohy shrugged. 'Probably. There have been rumours of a split for some time now. You know – the bullet versus the ballot box and all that crap.'

'So what'll happen?'

'Christ knows.'

'You must have some idea – as our resident expert on Irish affairs,' Cravan said, hoping the mild flattery would work as it so often did with what he liked to think of as his little band of temperamental reporters.

'It depends on what support the hawks can muster in Dublin. If they can't get enough I wouldn't give much for their chances. Seamus Reilly and Co. won't take kindly to being opposed.'

'And if they can get support?'

'Then one side will have to back down, and I don't see either doing that without a fight. Reilly certainly won't.'

Myles Cravan used his middle finger to move his rimless spectacles more comfortably up onto the bridge of his nose. Despite his friendly, almost nonchalant behaviour he was a shrewd man, aware of his limitations, recognizing the fact that his genius lay in organizing rather than actual reporting. If this disappointed him he never showed it, seldom interfered, and had the enviable reputation for fighting the ditherers within the system when he believed his reporters were in the right. With these attributes it was not difficult for him to gather together a team of the highest quality, always willing to draft in new talent from outside television as, indeed, he had done with Declan Tuohy. 'You seem very sure of that.'

Declan leaned back and rocked himself sideways in his

swivel-chair, his hands clasped behind his neck, a slightly mocking look in his eyes. Of course he was sure of it! 'Oh, I'm sure of that all right,' he asserted, somehow giving the words a sinister connotation as though his surety was culled from some inside, secret knowledge. Which, in fact, it was – well, up to a point. 'I've known Seamus Reilly all my life. Even at school he would fight like a demon to get what he wanted,' he went on, his voice softening, perhaps the memory of childhood something he liked to recall, something that held pleasant episodes he had a special fondness for. He laughed. 'Seamus Reilly is probably the most honest, most dangerous man I've ever met, or am ever likely to meet,' he said.

'An odd combination,' Cravan said, letting the statement hang like a question.

'Yes,' Tuohy agreed. 'He's an odd man. An orphan of terror – that's what he once called himself: he has a penchant for enigmatic phrases. He'll quote Blake to you by the hour – very into Blake is Seamus. You can never really tell what he's up to. One minute he's being transported to another world – another of his phrases – by Bartok, and the next he's ordering the murder of someone who has stepped out of line. Of course,' Tuohy added, smiling sardonically, 'maybe Bartok does that to you.'

'Maybe,' Cravan agreed, the word tossed in like a goad.

'One thing you can be sure of – if Reilly says he'll do something, he'll do it and damn the consequences. If he gives you his word you can truly believe him – that's what I meant by his honesty. If you give him your word and break it he'll deal with you as ruthlessly as only he can, no matter who you are or how much he cares for you: that's being dangerous. You know, he even had his own brother shot for informing?'

'You told me.'

'Anyway, I can also tell you that he's sick and tired of all the violence. He sees the future of the IRA in politics, and, believe you me, he won't let the hawks have the last say if he can prevent it.'

'So?'

'So – there are rough days ahead, Myles. You can bet your life there'll be an escalation of the killings. Whoever is the better organized will come out on top.'

'Tell me, Declan – how well do you know Reilly? I mean, apart from knowing him all your life – how *well* do you know him?'

Declan Tuohy smiled ruefully. 'Very well. I might even know him better than anyone else. We were very close – still are, I suppose.' Declan paused and thought for a moment. 'Put it this way: if I ever had a problem, any problem, I would probably think of talking it over with Seamus first.'

'And you're certain he wants to see an end to the violence?'

Declan shrugged. 'He wants a stop on what he calls "useless violence" but I wouldn't wager that he means all violence by that.'

'Do you think he'd talk about it? Openly – on television?'

Declan Tuohy hooted with derisive laughter. 'You're joking of course. Seamus Reilly on telly? Not in a million years.'

'Why not? He'd have a chance to – '

'Come off it, Myles. There's a thing called Reilly's law, and the first commandment is self-preservation. If Reilly even hinted he was about to give an interview he'd be dead meat within minutes – regardless of his power. Anyway, it's not his style. He operates from the shadows. That's why he has the power he has. Nobody can ever quite pin anything on him. You'd never get a man like Reilly to expose himself. You'll have to think up some other ruse to boost the old ratings.'

'You wouldn't even ask him?'

'It'd be a complete waste of time. I can just see him. Jesus! He'd probably die from apoplexy. He wouldn't do it, Myles. I'm telling you. He'd think I'd gone mad.'

'You don't know until you try.'

Declan Tuohy shook his head in amazement at the editor's persistence. Yet, of course, there was something fascinating about the possibility. 'Okay,' he said. 'Okay. I'll try.'

Craven beamed. 'Good man.'

'We'll give it a week or two and see if anything breaks over there – if the rift is as serious as we're making out. Then if there is a story I'll see how Seamus feels about it.'

'That's all I ever ask. Try.'

'Yea . . . by the way – if by some miracle Seamus does agree he'll want guarantees.'

'Promise him anything you like.'

'But will you back those promises?'

'All the way.'

'I have your word on that?'

'Yes. You have my word. Just get him in front of a camera.'

'I'll try.'

'Like I said – that's all I ever ask.'

Word of the split in the leadership of the IRA spread rapidly throughout the Catholic areas of the city, spearheading a renewed fearfulness. Immediately neighbours were less open, less friendly towards each other. They spoke less, more reluctant than ever to take sides, speculation of the outcome only discussed in secret with immediate relatives, and even then with caution. The tension was almost tangible. Everyone just waited.

· THREE ·

THE STOLEN DARK-BROWN Volvo moved at a respectable pace through the darkened streets. Patrick Moran drove: when there was a job to be done that involved transport he always drove. Surprisingly, for a man who jittered and twitched like someone in the last stages of Parkinson's disease, he became nerveless and calm when behind the steering wheel. Beside him Eddie McCluskey chewed on his finger nails, tearing off jagged shards with his teeth and spitting them out. 'Why not cut through there to the left?' he asked now, between titbits.

'Too quiet. The more traffic you have about you the less likely you are to be noticed,' Moran told him, sounding superior. 'That's the first principle of this job, Eddie. Don't be noticed. Keep in the thickest traffic and remember the rules of the road.'

'Huh,' McCluskey grunted. Oddly, for the moment, it was he who showed the most uneasiness, yet he knew that once the car stopped and he had the gun in his hand, the cold metal would transmit an awful peace to his mind, and he would kill without the slightest qualm. That was the first principle of his trade, he thought: no feelings.

The car slowed down at the intersection, allowing the armoured trucks to pass, their engines growling. Moran voiced his own resentment. 'I don't like taking orders from a woman,' he said, but tentatively, as if testing his companion's feelings.

McCluskey looked sideways at him, but said nothing.

'You think she knows what she's doing?'

'She knows,' McCluskey confirmed. 'Anyway, who else is there? You?'

Moran shook his head and started the car moving again. 'There's you, Eddie. I'd sooner take my orders from you,' he said, knowing that this would appeal.

Eddie McCluskey smiled pleasurably. 'Yea. Well, she's the boss for the moment.'

'But she didn't even consult us about tonight. She should have at least asked us what we thought,' Moran insisted, suddenly democratic.

'Just standing there and telling us we *have* to do it. I don't like it, Eddie. Another thing: why didn't she come with us?'

'She's got other things to do. Anyway, three's a crowd.'

'Like what, for Christ's sake? I bet she's just sitting on her arse waiting to see if we come back safe.'

'She's all right.'

Moran took his eye off the road for a moment and glanced at McCluskey. 'Hey – you fancy her, don't you?'

McCluskey glowered and kept silent.

Taking this as confirmation Moran went on: 'You really do fancy her. Been having it off then?'

'Fuck off.'

'Come on. Tell us. What's she like in the sack?'

McCluskey blushed furiously and, ignoring the question, stared out of the window.

'Jesus – it must be like shagging a bloody Amazon. I suppose she tells you what to do in bed too?'

'Just drive and shut up.'

'Touchy, are we?'

Yes. Eddie McCluskey was, indeed, touchy on this particular subject. It was an understatement to say he fancied the

23

woman: he lusted after her. Each night, alone and frustrated, he stripped her roughly, threw her on his bed and raped her, ignoring her cries of pain, smiling exultantly to himself as she succumbed, finally, to his sexual prowess, pleading for more. It was one of the contradictions in Eddie McCluskey: these wild erotic chimeras were hobbled by an equally fierce determination to adhere to the narrow sexual precepts of his religion, the archaic doctrines of which (hammered into his brain by family and the Christian Brothers) stultified his manhood and, in a terrible sense, made him afraid of women. 'Jesus, Eddie,' he heard Moran saying, ' 'tis a brave little lad you are putting your dickie-dock at risk like that. Christ above, she'd devour you for breakfast.'

'Very bloody funny.'

Having taken a long, circuitous route through the city, Moran now drove the car along a pleasant, tree-lined avenue in what he always enviously regarded as one of the 'nobby' parts of Belfast. He longed for a house with a garden but was unlikely ever to achieve it, lumbered as he was by a wife and seven children, a crippling rent, and his lack of ambition. Conveniently, he was a great believer in fate. It was at all times handy and there to be blamed for his continuous failure. Fate, he told himself, was either with you or against you. It was responsible for his ugliness, for his sweaty hands and feet. It was fate that had made Mary pregnant at seventeen and thus forced him to marry her, pinning him irrevocably to a domestic drudgery from which he was all too glad to escape. So, he had decided, it was fate that had driven him from the house and into his involvement with the Provisionals. For this he was thankful, feeling important for the first time in his life. He responded with a willingness to please that soon came to the notice of the hierarchy. He was given assignments of considerable trust and these he executed with dedicated efficiency; so much so that within a couple of years he was voted onto the Council: fate had done him a good turn. Then he blew it.

'Slow down,' McCluskey whispered. 'That's the house over there. You don't want to park right outside.'

'I can see it,' Moran answered gruffly, irked by the slight.

'Well pull over then. I'm not just calling in for tea.'

Patrick Moran eased the car to the side of the road, and switched off the lights. He took his time about killing the engine, but finally reached forward and turned the key. Immediately he began to shake.

'For Christ's sake will you stop that jittering about,' McCluskey told him.

'It's nerves.'

'I don't give a shit what it is – just stop it.'

'I can't.'

Nor could he. His entire fat body twitched and perspiration oozed onto his face.

McCluskey swore silently to himself.

'I'll be all right,' Moran assured him. 'Just you go in and get it over. Once I can get the car started again I'll be fine.'

'You bloody well better be. When I come out I want this heap moving before I close the door.'

'I'll be okay,' Moran insisted.

'Shit.'

McCluskey left the car and, for a second, stood beside it, breathing deeply, suffocating the dancing nerves that now attacked his stomach. There's nothing to it, he told himself. Just walk up to the door and press the bell. Kelly would answer the door himself and – bang. Then back to the car and away. Nothing to it. Only there was a lot more to it. This was special. He knew if he messed this one up he was certain to be killed himself. One didn't execute one of Seamus Reilly's men and live very long after it. For an instant, the horror of Reilly's absolute retribution struck him, and he hesitated before resolutely crossing the street, his stride swift and soundless. This was it, then. The declaration of war, he thought. No turning back after this. He moved quickly along the length of the cropped privet hedge, and slid sideways through the wrought-iron gate that someone had left half-open. The house was in darkness apart from an eerie, flickering light in a downstairs room. Television. McCluskey crept up the short driveway, crouching, one hand outstretched, using the side of the silver Austin Ambassador to keep his balance. He felt his feet sink into the soft earth of the flowerbed under the lighted window, and instinctively he scuffed his shoe-marks, making them unidentifiable. Then, raising himself slowly, he peered in, smiling with relief as he noted Tom Kelly alone, slumped lazily in an armchair, watching what was almost certainly a cowboy film. Easy.

McCluskey moved quickly now, jumping back across the flowerbed and onto the concrete driveway, running to the front door. He shoved his right hand under his khaki jacket and grasped the gun, pressing the doorbell with his left. Licking his lips and moving from foot to foot he waited. He pressed the bell again impatiently. A door inside the house slammed and an outline appeared on the frosted-glass panel of the hall door. He tightened his grip on the gun. As always in situations like this he controlled his breathing, inhaling deeply, purposely relaxing himself, widening his huge eyes to an expression of innocence, and steadfastly maintaining these attitudes as the lock clicked and the door opened. An amber light streamed from the hall onto McCluskey.

'Eddie!' Tom Kelly exclaimed, surprised, but pleasantly so.

'I need a word, Tom.'

'Sure. Sure – come in,' Kelly stood to one side.

McCluskey smiled and nodded and stepped into the house.

'In there,' Kelly went on, indicating the room he had just come from with his newspaper.

'A private word,' Eddie told him, standing his ground.

For a moment Kelly looked puzzled. 'Oh. Yea. That's okay. In there. I'm alone.'

'Ah. Good,' McCluskey said, cleverly, he thought, making himself appear nervous, giving the impression by cowering slightly that Kelly was the only one who could solve some immense problem. 'Nice room, Tom.'

'Thanks. Grab a chair,' Tom Kelly invited, making his way to his own chair and flopping into it comfortably. When he looked up he saw the gun pointing at him.

Perhaps significantly, as though acknowledging that the inevitable outcome of terrorism was sudden and unexpected and violent death, Kelly showed little surprise. Indeed, if anything, his eyes showed only a mocking defiance tinged with curiosity; possibly, also, a hint of annoyance with himself for being so gullible and stupid and unprepared. 'You bastard,' he said flatly.

McCluskey shrugged. 'It comes to us all.'

'You little bastard,' Kelly repeated.

Since repetition seemed to be in order, McCluskey gave another shrug. 'It's nothing personal, Tom. It could have been any one of Reilly's men. You just happened to be handiest.'

'Jesus! You're more of a moron than I thought you were, McCluskey. Setting yourself up against Seamus Reilly, are you?' Kelly asked before bursting into a great roar of laughter. 'Christ, even you could surely have picked an easier way to commit suicide. I'll give you twenty-four hours before Seamus finds out and cuts your goddam balls off for starters.'

McCluskey smiled thinly. A tiny jumping nerve in his temple showed that the remark had hit home. He tightened his finger on the trigger and fired. Pfffft.

Rapidly now McCluskey unscrewed the silencer and slipped it into his jacket pocket. He tucked the revolver into his belt, blowing on it first, perhaps in homage to the rampaging cowboys who thundered and yoo-hahed across the small screen behind him, all the while watching Tom Kelly twitch away from life.

'Tommy?' a shrill woman's voice called from upstairs.

McCluskey froze.

'Tommy? In heaven's name will you turn down that telly. I can't get a wink of sleep.'

McCluskey moved across the room in three strides and turned down the volume.

'And come to bed yourself,' the voice went on.

McCluskey waited.

'Did you hear me?'

McCluskey produced a loud, meaningless grunt from the back of his throat.

'Well, come on then.'

The sound of footsteps in the room overhead and a door closing made McCluskey release his breath in a long, hissing sigh. He gave Tom Kelly a final, uncaring glance, and left the house, taking pains to close the front door silently behind him.

True to his word, Patrick Moran had the engine ticking over. 'What the hell kept you?' he demanded.

'We had a chat,' McCluskey told him, injecting a swagger into his voice.

'Oh lovely. I'm out here sweating like a pig and you're in there having a little chat.'

'Get this thing moving.'

Moran put the car into gear and drove sedately down the road. 'What did he say?'

'Not a lot.'

'Some chat.'

McCluskey chuckled. 'There wasn't a lot he could say. He *did* say Reilly would have our balls off within twenty-four hours.'

The Volvo lunged as Moran's foot slipped on the accelerator. 'Oh shit,' he whispered, and changed down a gear, glancing sideways at McCluskey. 'You think he will?'

'Sure to,' Eddie said, nodding, clearly enjoying the very real terror his news had inspired. 'Do you no harm. All those bloody kids you have. High time you were gelded.'

Moran was not amused. He was sensitive about the size of his family, feeling, he knew not why, that there was something a bit dirty about fathering what amounted to a litter. In fact, he had gone to some lengths to prevent his last two children being conceived, but, as usual, things had gone wrong. Apprehensive of the sinfulness of contraceptives they had stuck to the rhythm method, but his wife had missed the beat and together they had waltzed into another pregnancy; dismayed, he had stared sin in the face, and tried a Durex: alas, it had burst, and one more little Moran was soon on the way. 'At least I can bloody well do it,' he said.

'Fuck you,' McCluskey muttered, and immediately regretted the words, aware that he had left himself open for Moran's scathing: 'I doubt if you could.'

They headed back into the city in silence, Moran suddenly feeling quite cocky, McCluskey fuming. As they neared St Enoch's 'Where you going to dump this?' was all he wanted to know.

Moran thought for a second, screwing up his face. 'The docks probably.'

'Well, you can let me out here then.'

Obligingly, Moran pulled over to the side of the road. 'Eddie,' he said. 'About what I – well, shit, there's no point in us squabbling.'

'Forget it.'

'I'll see you tomorrow?'

'Yea. Ten as arranged.'

'Sleep well.'

Moran watched Eddie McCluskey saunter away from the car, his stride nonchalant, for all the world a man without a care in his head: certainly not one who had just committed murder. Briefly Moran felt a twinge of pity for him: some day, he thought, some day the awful ghosts of those he had killed would rise up against him. Moran shuddered, his eyes still following the slight figure as it swaggered away into the gloom.

· FOUR ·

Seamus Reilly was seething with fury. Not, it must be said, so much that one of his most reliable and long-standing henchmen had actually been murdered, but that he had clearly been killed by someone he knew, someone Kelly had permitted to enter the sanctuary of his own home, someone familiar enough to be able to lull him into such a state of unreadiness that he could be shot between the eyes without any trace of a struggle: all of which ruled out any 'acceptable' protagonist, and pointed to someone within their own ranks. Of course, Reilly had been expecting some brutal retaliation (one didn't expel members from the Organization without some ill-feeling, did one?), but the speed with which the revenge had been levied certainly surprised him. This, coupled with his awareness that Kelly's death was but a foretaste of yet more violence to follow – a vile aperitif, he was to call it later – filled him with disgust and deepened the foulness of his humour. Therefore, instead of his usual pleasant greetings to his driver, he grunted sourly, slamming the car door behind himself, and puffed vigorously on one of his short cigars. As the driver carefully twiddled the rearview mirror, Reilly's patience snapped. 'For heaven's sake move. I'm late enough as it is.'

'Yes, Mr Reilly. Sorry.'

'Well move then.'

In fact he was not late. He was almost never late. His manic fastidiousness about punctuality was all but proverbial, so much so that on the exceptional occasion when he was not dead on time those waiting tended to regard their watches as somewhat less than reliable.

As he was driven through the streets along a predetermined route and monitored throughout by his own security, Seamus Reilly began to relax to the extent of mildly upbraiding himself for allowing his vexation to become obvious: he abhorred emotional demonstrations of any kind, particularly in himself. But like most things in Seamus Reilly this abhorrence was contrived: over the years his position as head of the IRA Punishment Squad, and the sinister title of Godfather that went with it, had forced him to suffocate any generous feelings he might once have had, so that now he could issue orders for the assassination of what he termed 'troublemakers' and arrange for the support and care of their wives and children with equal equanimity and objectiveness. Or, at least, up until recently he had been able to. He sighed deeply. The strain of it all must be getting to him, he conceded. Small wonder. Drastic change could hardly be expected to take place without leaving its mark, and the changes in Seamus Reilly's life, slow and unnoticed by anyone but himself, had undeniably been drastic. As the Organization splintered and bickered within itself, as successive British governments had vowed to wipe them from the face of the earth, what had started in early manhood as the dramatic and patriotic continuance of an unfortunately violent bequest with clear-cut ultimatums and a clear goal had deteriorated into a struggle for personal survival, and the passionate hope of peace receded.

Reilly lowered the car window an inch and dropped out his finished cigar, opening his fingers slowly and watching the smouldering butt being whisked away. Just when things seemed to be on the point of solution, all hope would be whisked away by an inopportune remark, some stupid harassment, or a

31

wanton killing. He rolled the window up again, carefully, with one hand, replacing the few strands of his hair that had been ruffled by the breeze. He gave a small shudder. That, of course, was the rub: despite his reputation for cold-bloodedness, despite the easy, dispassionate way he had administered death and the brutality and fear that he had used to keep his more recalcitrant men in line, Seamus Reilly had, finally, grown tired of violence. The steady pounding of bombs, the sheer and utter wastefulness of death had come, strangely and quite un-expectedly, to sicken him. That did not mean to say he would not, still, order the extermination of anyone foolish enough to oppose him: he most decidedly would, and ruthlessly: but he would prefer it if the occasion did not arise. The visions of heroic battle leading to the freedom he desired for his country no longer lured him inexorably, no longer either did the prospect of dying for one's beliefs seem all that attractive, perhaps because he now realized how little time was left at his disposal at any rate. The thought brought a wry smile to his lips. Whereas not so long ago he had fancied himself as being remembered for having died – by the bullet, by hunger strike, by bomb it mattered not – now he dreamed of being a sort of elder statesman, negotiating wisely at the table, impartially be-stowing the fruits of his vast experience. And to some extent he was on the road to achieving this, for he had gently been leading the Executive round to his way of thinking, by a word here and a phrase there coaxing them towards a political solution, cajoling them into standing for office in elections, gleefully watching them win seats.

Alas something always happened to upset the apple-cart. Some politician, bereft of attention and craving promotion, would issue some ludicrous statement to the effect that the IRA were being soundly trounced, were on the point of abject surrender, and lo and behold, the bombing and killings would start again just to deprive the idiotic pronouncement of veracity; or, more deadly still, the brainless element within the ranks who saw power as emanating only from the barrel of a gun would rebel, as some had only recently done, would be expelled, would slide away and set up their own little covens, creeping out in the darkness to shatter the uneasy stillness with yet more violence.

'We're here, Mr Reilly.'

Reilly jumped. Slamming the door behind him, he walked briskly across the footpath and into the safe house, noting, from the corner of his eye, that he was well and discreetly protected.

The quiet murmur of voices ceased immediately as Reilly appeared in the doorway. For a moment he paused, staring about him as if displeased, wrinkling his nose. The room was almost bare, with only a long, scrubbed, kitchen table and seven chairs as furniture. It was uncarpeted and unadorned, although someone had put a red rose (an Enid Harkness by the look of it) in a jamjar and placed it on the mantelpiece. He turned his attention to the three men waiting for him to speak, all of them standing respectfully. With almost ceremonious decorum Reilly nodded a greeting to each of them in turn, and waved a hand by way of invitation for them to be seated, now ready to preside over this emergency meeting of his nefarious executive. It was responsible for the day to day running of the Belfast branch of the Organization as well as the enforcement of the banning of drugs from the Catholic areas of the city, the collection and distribution of donations, and the sometimes dire punishment of those who stepped beyond the proscribed lines of conduct. Most importantly Reilly's executive was also charged with the investigation of the deaths of any of the Organization's members other, of course, than those they had instigated themselves, although even these were later scrutinized in some detail since there was always something to be learned.

Nobody seemed anxious to begin so Seamus Reilly coughed again and said: 'I presume you've all heard about Tom Kelly?'

All three men nodded, keeping their eyes fixed on Reilly's face, one of them going so far as to open his mouth as if to speak. Reilly spotted this. 'Yes, Regan?' he asked sharply almost as if demanding an interruption.

'I was just going to say, Mr Reilly, we – me and Jim here, have been over to his house this morning.'

33

'Ah. Good. And?'

Regan looked uncomfortable, glancing at Jim Dowling for help. Not getting any he was forced to admit: 'Nothing, Mr Reilly.'

'What do you mean nothing?'

'Just that, Mr Reilly. Nobody saw anyone. His wife called down to him to tell him to turn down the telly. He turned it down and his wife went back to bed and fell asleep. She found him dead in his chair in the morning,' Regan explained. 'With the telly still going,' he added as if it might be important.

'She didn't hear the shot?'

Regan shook his head. 'She heard nothing.'

'And there was no sign of a struggle?'

'No. Nothing. It must have been someone he knew.'

Reilly nodded.

'I think that it was done to get at you, Mr Reilly.'

Reilly raised his eyebrows, more in surprise at this astuteness than in mockery. 'Do you now? And what would make you think that?'

'Well,' Dowling frowned as he sought to explain his thoughts, 'there's a lot of people have it in for you, Mr Reilly, and they know they can't get at you yourself, so they have a go at those – well, those close to you.'

Reilly conceded this with another nod.

'Or it could be,' Dowling went on, uncharacteristically emboldened by the success of his first explanation, 'it could be that someone wants to take your attention away from something else that's being planned. Using Kelly as a sort of diversion, if you know what I mean.'

Reilly knew exactly what he meant: the diversionary tactic was one he had employed himself several times. A bomb in the city would occupy the minds of the Security Forces while an ambush on the outskirts could go unhindered and leave several soldiers dead or maimed – the mutilated unfortunate shekels of war as one over-zealous magazine had called them. 'And from what,' Reilly now wanted to know, 'do you think they might be trying to divert our attention?'

Dowling shrugged. 'You know there've been rumours, Mr Reilly.'

Reilly gave a tight smile. 'There are always rumours.'

'Yea. But this time it's a bit different.'

'Indeed?'

'He's right, Mr Reilly.'

For an instant Reilly showed a flicker of annoyance. 'I seem to be the only one who hasn't heard them,' he said. 'Maybe one of you would enlighten me?'

The three men took it in turns to look at one another, none of them keen to enlighten. Not surprisingly. It was definitely tricky, for in recent months Seamus Reilly could be easily roused to anger, and only a fool would offer himself to bear the brunt of his rage.

'Well?' Reilly persisted impatiently.

Perhaps because he was feeling left out of things, or perhaps because he was just the most foolhardy, Sean O'Neill decided to speak. 'The rumour is that some of the boys you had expelled are planning something big in England,' he said bluntly.

Reilly froze, the blood draining from his face. 'I see,' he whispered hoarsely. He pointed the two fingers holding his small cigar at Regan, wagging them up and down, ignoring the ash that dropped onto the table. 'I want you,' he said very deliberately, 'to follow this up. Find out more about it. Find out every damn thing you can. I want to know who's involved, who's setting it – whatever it is – up. And I want to know soon.'

'Yes, Mr Reilly,' Regan agreed. 'But I –'

'There's nothing more I want to say about it for the moment,' Reilly interrupted. 'Just you find out what exactly is going on – if anything is. Then we'll talk some more.'

'Yes, Mr Reilly.'

'And be discreet, for God's sake. If something is planned I don't want them to know I suspect anything.'

'Right, Mr Reilly.'

Seamus relaxed. Carefully he wiped the ash from the table with one hand, catching it deftly in the other and tipping it into his ashtray; then blowing on his palm to remove any traces.

This done he pushed the ashtray a little further from him, folded his hands, interlacing his fingers and studying his neatly manicured nails for a few seconds. 'Now,' he said finally. 'Any other business?'

'I did get a bit of information that could be useful,' Regan told him.

'Not, I hope, another rumour?'

Regan smiled apologetically. 'No. A little more solid than that.'

'Ah.' Reilly sounded relieved.

'It seems the Brits are about to try the old defection trick again. I'm told they have – or are about to – move someone in with orders to desert and have us help him.'

'Your source?'

'London. My own contact. Usually very reliable.'

'So you alone are aware of this?'

'I would think so.'

'Hmmm. No names, I suppose?'

Regan shook his head. 'Not yet.'

'Pity.'

'Yes. Still, I'll get it later.'

'And you don't know if this – this deserter is actually here yet or not?'

'No.'

'But you say your contact will be able to let you know?'

'I hope so.'

Reilly frowned. 'Well, that's something. Not to worry. Better keep this strictly to yourself, Regan. I've a feeling we'll be able to use it to our advantage in more ways than one. And you two haven't heard it.'

Reilly stood up and put his chair back against the wall tidily. 'If anything comes up either about those rumours or about the deserter let me know at once,' he said to all three as he made his way to the door. 'Fine. Well, take care,' this was said as a sort of benediction. 'By the way,' he added, turning and pursing his lips. 'Did you deal with that pusher from Derry?'

'Brannigan? Oh yes, Mr Reilly. We dealt with him all right.'

'He won't be peddling his drugs here any more then?'

Regan beamed wickedly. 'Not unless he does it from his wheelchair.'

'Ah. Good. Excellent. It's the one thing I cannot stand and will not tolerate,' Reilly announced self-righteously, and left the room.

Major Crispin Fisher sat on the edge of his bunk, his elbows resting on his knees, his head in his hands, thinking under the watchful eye of Christ crucified nailed defiantly to the wall. Or rather, remembering, and wishing he could go back in time. He was aware, if not fully, of the hazards that lay ahead of him though strangely, three weeks in Belfast, three peaceful enough, uneventful weeks made it rather more difficult to admit the dangers of his mission, and, more than once, he had found himself being lulled into a perilous state of well-being, even finding himself wondering if his superiors had not exaggerated the power and evilness of the enemy.

Now, sitting there, among the familiar and comforting stink of stale sweat, and denim and leather, the grunts and groans and restless shiftings of his sleeping colleagues assailing his ears, he quietly mourned his past: the day his brother – hopeless, demanding, moronic – finally died. He died at eight o'clock in the morning. On Sunday. He was fourteen. There was no breakfast. Nothing but mugs of tea that Dad made while Mam drifted aimlessly about the house, like a lost spectre, closing the curtains (to keep the devil from setting eyes on the dead, she had once explained). It was probably at that point that Chris, already seventeen and about to join the army, wondered if death was the only way to attract the affection and respect he longed for. It was a ridiculous notion: a macabre, perverted fantasy, but it had stayed with him, shimmering in his mind, making death curiously desirable.

He stood up and automatically smoothed the blanket on his bed. Well, perhaps he would find out: perhaps fate, whatever that was, or Christ or some not too preoccupied guardian angel would provide the answer.

'What do you mean she's not coming?' Moran demanded angrily.

McCluskey stared at him complacently. 'She's not coming,' he repeated.

'Shit. She said we were to meet here this morning.'

'Yes. Well, she phoned me last night. She's gone to Glasgow.'

'Glasgow? What in the name of hell has she gone to Glasgow for?'

'I didn't ask.'

'When's she coming back?'

'She didn't say.'

'Christ,' Moran swore, eyeing distastefully McCluskey's persistent chewing of his nails. 'Didn't she ask about Kelly?'

McCluskey shrugged, taking the time to nibble a tricky sliver before saying: 'Just asked how it had gone.'

'That's all?'

'That's all. Stop worrying. She'll be back soon enough.'

'I bloody well hope so.'

The Security Officer at Glasgow airport smiled indulgently at the six young children being ushered along by the tall, attractive woman. 'Quite a handful,' he said pleasantly.

The woman returned the smile. 'Yes.'

'Not all yours?'

The woman widened her smile. 'Oh no. None of them, in fact. Just bringing them over for a few days break. Away from – well, you know.'

'Ah,' the officer sighed sympathetically, patting one of the children on the head, only to be rewarded by a sideways, suspicious look. 'Of course.'

· FIVE ·

IT WAS GETTING on for midnight when Seamus Reilly heard the car door slam outside his house. He had been sitting in the dark, listening contentedly to *Das Lied von der Erde*, but now he reached out and switched on the lamp beside his chair, looking about the room, making sure everything was neat and tidy, frowning like a nervous hostess. He heard his driver insert the key in the front door, the murmur of voices. He was on his feet and moving forward with perfect timing, one hand outstretched, when Inspector Asher was shown into the room. 'Ah, John,' he said. 'You're welcome. It must be mighty important.'

'Seamus,' John Asher acknowledged with a curt nod of his head, shaking hands.

One might have supposed from the civilized greeting that the two men were friends, and in an obtuse way they were, bound by a steely, unwavering patriotism. True, their views were different, but both were totally Irish; both found the military presence insulting and provocative; both smarted under the dismissive arrogance of successive British governments; and while one warred constantly against the invading forces, using violence and intimidation as his weapons, the other waged his battles rather more subtly – but none the less effectively – by upholding law and order by any means, even, on more than one occasion, calling upon the co-operation of the IRA, through the auspices of Seamus Reilly, to further his ends. Both admitted now, after years of struggle, and only to each other, that their prospects of ever reaching a satisfactory outcome to their dreams were slim. It was probably this almost inevitable sense of pending failure that threw them together, attempting to maintain an uneasy peace, yet always bearing in mind that the other was, to use Asher's phrase, a 'ravenous ally'. The dubious friendship was emphasized by the use of Christian names when they met privately, while the distrust remained clearly displayed in the cold weariness of their eyes.

'A drink?' Seamus offered, already making his way to the small table.

'Thank you. I could use one.'

'Ah. That sort of day.' Seamus Reilly sounded as if he understood, and generously added an extra measure to the tumbler.

'That sort of day,' Asher agreed, taking the drink, raising his glass by way of thanks and toast, and swallowing a mouthful of Teachers.

Reilly returned the toast and sat down, waiting. The fact that Asher had asked to see him, had come to his home in the dead of night, had scorned the use of normal security, meant, clearly, that he had something urgent to discuss and for that he liked to be given time to feel his way and select his words. So, Reilly waited, sipping his drink, comfortable in the knowledge that when he was good and ready his visitor would come straight to the point.

Asher had all but emptied his glass before he spoke. 'Seamus, I need your help.'

Reilly inclined his head graciously. 'Of course. If I can.'

'Our intelligence says something big is brewing. Ever since you expelled certain members from your Organization, there

40

have been reports of – well, of activity the likes of which we haven't seen for many a year.'

Reilly raised his eyebrows, but maintained an interested silence.

'The trouble is,' Asher went on thoughtfully, 'the trouble is, Seamus, that our information is that another campaign against mainland Britain is being plotted,' he said, allowing his voice to rise half an octave over the last few words to form a question.

Reilly said nothing, purposely not reacting.

'Are you involved?' Asher demanded bluntly.

'No.'

'Do you know who *is* involved?'

Reilly shook his head, frowning.

'Have you heard anything about it?'

Reilly continued to shake his head. 'Nothing directly.'

'Indirectly?'

Reilly placed his glass on the table beside him, and spread his hands in his curious little Jewish gesture of humility. 'We've had rumours circulating. Nothing definite.'

'I see.' Asher indicated he was not convinced. 'You know what repercussions such mindlessness will have on us here?'

'Of course I do, John.'

'You would tell me if you knew anything?'

Reilly retrieved his glass and took a long, steady drink, keeping his eyes on the bottom of the glass, using the exercise to consider if (if, indeed, there was anything definite to reveal) he would confide in Asher. It was a moot point. Jaded and sickened he might be by the continuous violence, but the good of the Organization would, he knew, always come first. On the other hand, if some plot was being hatched that was detrimental to, and without the sanction of the Council, a plot which would nullify his own efforts to 'calm things down' as he was fond of saying, he would certainly join forces with Asher in an effort to scupper it. 'Of course, John,' he said at last.

'And if you hear anything – definite – in the near future you will let me know?'

Reilly smiled. 'Probably.'

Asher seemed satisfied with that: he relaxed, and settled more comfortably into his chair, sipping contentedly at his drink. In the silence he grinned wryly to himself as it dawned on him that here, in the heart of what should have been hostile territory, he was safer than anywhere else in the city. Reilly's security, usually invisible, was better even than his own, better, probably, than any security in the province. Which brought another thought to mind: 'That Kelly – one of your lot wasn't he?'

'Yes.'

'Careless, don't you think? Not like your disciples to get themselves killed so easily.'

'You've had a report?'

'Yes.'

'Anything I should know?'

'I only glanced at it. Nothing significant in it. Nothing in it at all, in fact. Just that he was shot. It *did* strike me that it could be internal . . . ?'

'Perhaps it was, John. We are almost certain it was – well, let's just say it could tie in with what you were asking me earlier.'

'Oooh,' Asher said as if he appreciated the significance.

'We'll find out, though, never fear.'

'And then you'll tell me, of course.'

Reilly found himself forced to grin. 'Of course. Now you tell me something: you're not party to any army skullduggery, are you?'

Asher looked genuinely surprised. 'Like?'

'Only another rumour.'

'About?'

'Something to do with a plant being sent to desert.'

Asher grimaced. 'No. I've heard nothing. Not, mind you, that I would be all that likely to. The army don't confide their dirty tricks in us. Don't confide much at all.' Suddenly Asher snorted. 'We have as much trouble with the army as we do with you.'

Seamus Reilly liked that. 'Poor you,' he chuckled with mock sympathy.

'Yes. Poor me.'

The woman, wearing a long tweed overcoat and a floppy hat, the brim of which she held in one hand, keeping it low over her face, walked briskly along the road, making for a flat in James Gray Street, Glasgow. It was dusk, and the street lights had not quite reached their maximum, glowing an orange-red, giving the high, dour buildings a warmness and comfort they scarcely merited. From time to time she slowed her pace and listened, never stopping but altering her speed as if testing anyone who might secretly be keeping step with her.

When she reached the flats she took off her hat and shook her hair free in a prolonged, circular gesture, using this extravagant action to scan the road down which she had come. Satisfied, she went in and made her way upstairs, wrinkling her nose at the stench of urine, boiling vegetables and rotting woodwork that assailed her. Then slowly, all the while looking upwards, she mounted the stairs. At a door on the third floor she stopped, glanced back down, then knocked. There was a scuffling sound from inside before someone came close to the door and asked in a low, gruff voice: 'Who is it?'

'Me.'

The door opened a fraction, and an eye peered out suspiciously. Then it was thrown wide. 'You're late.'

'You try getting six kids to go to bed.'

'Come in.'

The woman entered, and instinctively started to size up the room. It seemed perfectly ordinary: a glorified bed-sitter: one large room with a tiny kitchenette off it, and a bathroom the size of a cupboard. Along one wall a divan doubled as bed and sofa. There were a couple of armchairs and a table with a red formica top. A light with a paper shade dangled from the low ceiling. The centre upright of the gas fire spluttered. A pale green fitted carpet, stained and balding, covered the floor. Most noticeable, however, despite the attempted cosiness of the fire, was the atmosphere of disuse: it was as though the room, confused perhaps by an ever-changing occupancy, had long since abandoned any attempt to acquire a character.

'Want a drink?' the man asked, already opening a can of beer.

She shook her head.

'Well, sit down. Sit down. How are things?'

She shrugged. 'Rough.'

The man nodded understandingly. 'Yea. Bound to be, I suppose.'

For a while they were silent, the woman seeming to think, the man sucking noisily on his beer, standing, swaying from foot to foot. He was in his late twenties, tall, with sandy neatly-cut wavy hair, and curiously bulbous eyes. He looked tired.

'Well, Dermot, what did you think of my idea?' she asked finally.

'Terrific – if it works.'

'Can you make it work?'

'I think so. I'll need the right equipment.'

'Can you get it?'

Dermot grinned. 'I can get anything if I have the money.'

'You'll have the money.'

'Joe and Peggy have already been down to Brighton. They stayed one night in the hotel. They say there's no problem as long as we can plant our explosives soon enough.'

'How soon?'

'Six, eight weeks before the Convention.'

'That gives them too much time to find them.'

Dermot shook his head. 'They won't find them. I know my job. They won't find them.'

The woman stared at him as if trying to detect a chink in his assurance. 'You'll have the necessary money within the week.'

'Good. That's what I like. No messing.'

'You know what will happen if it goes wrong?'

Dermot laughed. 'The same as will happen if it goes right.'

Two steets away, also in Shawlands, in a flat even smaller than

44

the one where the woman had been speaking to Dermot, Joe Mulcahy and Peggy Dunne lay naked together in bed. They had just made love, although anything amorous had been purely incidental: it had been a dispassionate, mechanical exercise, each seeking comfort rather than satisfaction from their act. Now, still in each other's arms, Joe smoking, they had an air of desolation about them, a sense of inevitable abandonment. As 'sleepers' they were under constant pressure, but pressure of a strange, haunting kind. It was one thing to be hunted for actually doing something: it was quite different to know that one would be the subject of intense investigation if one, for a single moment, ceased to remain faceless. To preserve their anonymity they seldom went out except at night when the darkness blurred their features and hid their anxiety. And there was something else that weighed upon them: the frightening loneliness of waiting. Away from everyone they knew and cared about. Just waiting to be useful. Wondering, from time to time, if they had simply been forgotten.

'Why do you think Dermot wanted all those details about the Grand?' Peggy asked, pulling Joe's hand towards her and sucking a lungful of cigarette smoke.

'God knows.'

'It seems funny he's interested in Brighton.'

'He'll tell us if he wants us to know.'

'What do you think?' Peggy insisted.

'I don't. It's better not to. All I want is to get out of this place. Christ – I hate fucking Glasgow.'

Peggy sighed but did not reply. Although none too keen on Glasgow herself, for her it had its compensations. Plain and dumpy, shy and easily embarrassed, she had, at least, the companionship of a man – something she knew she would have found difficult to procure at home. Aware though she was that any attention he paid her was because of the restrictions of their occupation she managed, in the way lonely women have, to make of him considerably more than he was. 'I'm sure they'll move us soon,' she whispered by way of comfort.

'I hope to Christ they do.'

'They will. They never leave anyone in one place too long.'
'We've been here too bloody long already.'

Declan Tuohy could not sleep. He was exhausted, but sleep simply would not come. He tossed in his bed, sitting up and thumping his pillows every so often, seeming to wreak revenge for his insomnia on the feathers. Of course it was that damned Seamus Reilly who kept him awake; or rather the possibility of getting him to speak. He threw back the blankets and got out of bed, groped about for a cigarette, lit one and puffed for a few minutes. He made his way into the kitchen and poured himself a glass of milk, dolefully eyeing the emptiness of his fridge. One never knew with Reilly. It was not that he was in any way unpredictable: far from it. Anything Seamus did or said had a definite if circuitous logic.

Declan finished his milk and padded back to his bedroom. Somewhere outside a clock struck, and he glanced at the glowing dial of his radio-alarm: one o'clock. Regardless of the hour he stood up and stretched, stubbed out his cigarette, and made determinedly for the telephone in the next room. It would do Reilly good, he thought wickedly, to be woken up. He checked the number in a small book, dialled it with the code for Belfast, and waited.

Only a second. After one ring the phone was snatched from its cradle. 'Yes?'

'Seamus? It's Declan. Declan Tuohy.'

There was, Declan imagined, a small gasp. 'Just a minute,' Seamus said.

It was difficult to surprise Seamus Reilly, but the sound of Declan's voice left him little short of amazed. He put the receiver on the table beside his bed and set about making himself comfortable, folding his old-fashioned bolster double and propping his pillow against it. He reached out and took his dressing-gown from a chair and wrapped it about his shoulders, instinctively letting his fingers feel the old bullet wound in his arm not because of any pain but probably since it

46

was Declan's nephew who had put it there. 'Sorry. This is a surprise.'

– Yes: without doubt it is, Delcan thought. To get a phone call out of the blue at one o'clock in the morning from someone who had not been in touch for the best part of two years was bound to be a surprise. Oddly, despite the bloody and tragic outcome of their last encounter, Declan felt guilty about his long silence, the more so since Seamus had made several efforts to contact him, presumably to heal the rift.

Their relationship had always been touch and go. Childhood had been equitable enough: two small, Catholic boys, bright and romantic, laughing and conning their way through school, snickering at how innocent the priests thought them to be. Adolescence had been tricky: both young men finding themselves inevitably caught up in the horror of sectarianism and the rampant seduction of patriotism, and both with disparate views as to what should be done: Seamus, heir to the military tradition of Collins, raging about fighting to the death; Declan coyly insisting that the pen was indeed mightier than the sword. But it was adulthood that brought about the real trouble: Reilly firmly ensconced as Godfather glorious of the Provisional IRA, constantly wheeling and dealing, plotting and planning, gleefully thwarting the efforts of the Security Forces to subdue his activities; while Declan, rejecting Reilly's pleas to join him, and after a somewhat overblown success with a book of poetry (dedicated to Reilly) that had the pundits scrabbling for superlatives, had turned his back on Belfast, gone to London and receded into dispassionate journalism. Yet they had always written to each other, frequently at first, then less so, until finally it had dwindled to a Christmas card.

'I'm sure it is. How are you?'

Seamus chuckled. 'Never my best at one in the morning. Apart from that I'm fine. And you?'

'Can't complain. Working hard.'

'So I hear.'

'Oh?'

Reilly chuckled again. 'Been keeping an eye on you.'

47

'I see,' Declan said, sounding none too pleased.

'I like to know what my friends are up to,' Reilly explained. 'Just in case I can help,' he added.

Declan knew that was perfectly true. Whatever else, Seamus was fiercely loyal to his few friends, often aiding them without their knowledge, clearly embarrassed when they found out and thanked him. Indeed, this same man who had ordered the execution of his own brother for informing, could perform acts of extraordinary generosity when he considered them appropriate.

'I'm managing,' Declan told him.

'Yes. Television, no less.'

'You are well informed.'

'Of course.'

'Anyway – the reason I rang: I might be over soon. I'd like to see you.'

Reilly did not reply immediately, and when he did there was a cautious tone in his voice. 'You make it sound ominous.'

Declan laughed. 'I didn't mean to. Just something I want to discuss with you.'

'When are you coming?'

'First week of August?'

'I'll be here. I'm not planning on going anywhere. Ring me when you arrive. I look forward to seeing you again. Declan – is everything all right?'

'Yes. Why?'

'You sound – I don't know – upset.'

'No. Everything's fine. You're imagining things.'

'Perhaps. I'll hear from you then?'

'You will.'

· SIX ·

THE SUMMER OF 1984 thus far had been remarkably sunny. Belfast simmered in the unaccustomed heat. Nerves were unusually taut, tempers controlled on short wires. Towards the end of June, Major Fisher, in casual civilian clothes, made his way on foot past nameless doors and faceless windows into the Old Park district of the city. Although it was still reasonably bright outside, there can have been little light inside the dingy, squalid houses. It was uncannily quiet.

At the end of the street he turned left, crossed the road, and headed for the pub. This was his fourth visit and he winced as he thought of what to expect: the stench of stale beer and acrid, lingering cigarette smoke; the stench, too, of his own fear as he tried to ignore the cold, suspicious stares. Still, the antagonism seemed to be lessening, although this, he conceded, could have been wishful thinking. But the landlord's nod of welcome was real enough. 'Guinness?' he asked, remembering.

'Thanks.'

Fisher took his pint and moved to the end of the bar, propping himself comfortably in the corner. He looked about the room as inconspicuously as he could. It was considerably larger than one would have imagined from outside. There were eight or nine tables, and benches all the way round the walls. At the far end was a stage, a Sinn Fein banner the backdrop. On the walls were photographs of men, some very young, with the legends of their deaths typed beneath their staring faces. Framed slogans proclaimed the need for and the inevitability of a United Ireland. From two rattly speakers on either side of the stage the thin, wailing sound of a ceilidh band emerged, and the twenty or so men already seated nodded away to the rhythm, some of them even as they carried on whispered conversations. Two strips of neon light gave everyone's face a yellow, sickly look, and an underpowered extractor sucked uselessly at the smoke.

Fisher knew he was being watched. Nobody looked at him directly: eyes would flick across him, absorbing him in transit. He knew, too, that some of the men were discussing his presence. Not that he minded. Indeed, it was what he wanted. On previous visits, feigning drunkenness, he had let it slip that he was, to put it mildly, disenchanted with army life; that he, as a Catholic, was ashamed of what he was being forced to do; that he had been misled by biased propoganda. But he had been careful, never being specific, never suggesting that he intended or wished to desert, just dropping hints and leaving the door open for a move to be made.

Suddenly the music stopped: immediately all conversation died. As if on cue the door burst open and four Paratroopers strode in, their faces blackened, their guns at the ready. Despite their harsh training they were all clearly afraid and sublimated this by adopting an almost arrogant strut as they moved about the room, saying nothing, staring at faces, their rubber-soled boots screeching on the linoleum making the only noise. Whatever the exercise was in aid of it was soon over and they left, backing out.

Fisher found himself trembling. That was all he needed: to be arrested for drinking in a Republican pub. Jesus! He stared hard at his drink, trying to control himself by shaking his head.

Perhaps misinterpreting this action the landlord came along

the bar towards him, wiping a glass as he came. 'Bastards,' he said.

Fisher looked up, sensing that some precise retort was now expected. Tricky. He had to be careful. Nothing too derogatory. Nothing out of style. He nodded. 'They're made do it,' he replied.

'Fuck them,' the landlord said, still, it seemed, probing.

'Half of them don't want to. Half of them don't even want to be here,' Fisher replied quietly.

The landlord busied himself stacking the wiped glass on top of several others, forming a precarious pyramid. He stood back and admired his handiwork.

'That's nice,' Fisher volunteered.

The landlord looked at him. 'You could always get out.'

Fisher decided to look puzzled.

'Of the army.'

'Oh. It's not that easy.'

'You've tried?'

'Well – no – '

'Well then?'

'It's not that easy,' Fisher said again, dropping a hint of frustration into his words.

'If there's the will there's the way,' the landlord informed him, and left him to ponder the wisdom, moving back down the bar to pull a pint.

Fisher finished his drink and stood up. It was a good time to leave. No point in forcing things. Perhaps the landlord had meant nothing significant. He buttoned his jacket and made to leave, waving in a friendly way to the landlord who looked as if he was about to return the gesture but at the last minute transformed it into a beckoning for Fisher to come closer. 'I meant it,' he said. 'If you want to get out there's always a way.'

Fisher gave a tiny, wistful smile. 'I'll remember that.' Outside he breathed in deeply, the night air, chilly now, rasping in his lungs and making him cough. Frowning, he set off back to the barracks.

51

Seamus Reilly made a steeple of his forefingers and tapped them against his lips. Across from him Thomas Regan waited, looking pleased with himself. 'And you're certain he's the one?' Reilly asked.

'Positive. The name came through this morning from London. The description is him to a tee.'

Reilly nodded. 'Good. How often did you say he's been there?'

'Tonight was his fourth visit. I was told after his first and I had him followed there twice more.'

'How's he playing it?'

'Cool, as they say. Not pushing himself at all. Pretending to get pissed and just saying enough to make us interested.'

'A Major no less . . .' Reilly reflected.

'Yep. Hardly looks old enough though.'

'And Sandy has put out a feeler?'

'Yep – '

'Don't say that,' Reilly snapped irritably.

'Sorry, Mr Reilly. Yes. His usual line. Where there's a will there's a way. You know.'

'And?'

'Fisher didn't really react. But he will. He will.'

'We *know* that, Thomas. The thing is how do we get Moran or McCluskey to do the lifting?'

Regan frowned, confused. 'Why would you want them to lift him, Mr Reilly?'

Seamus Reilly appeared to ignore the question, tapping his lips again, already the embryo of a plan forming in his mind. He started to explain. 'I want someone in with Moran, McCluskey and that woman. I want to know if they *did* kill Kelly. I want to know what the hell they're up to. That's why I want them to lift Fisher when the time is right. Get him in there and give him the time to find out what is happening. Then we can take him.' Clearly Reilly liked this and smiled contentedly to himself. 'You go and see Sandy in the morning. Tell him that when he thinks Fisher is ready to get in touch with McCluskey and tip him off to the desertion. Nothing else. He's just to say he has this Brit who wants out.'

'Right, Mr Reilly.'

'And keep an eye on Fisher himself. I want to know every move he makes between now and the time he's lifted.'

'Yes, Mr Reilly.'

'You did well, Thomas.'

'Thank you, Mr Reilly.'

Alone, Reilly poured himself a nightcap, put on a tape of Handel's *Jephtha*, and settled back in his chair, allowing the drink and the music to lull his brain. More and more he treasured these rare moments of tranquillity, more, too, he liked to be alone. – 'Such mighty blessings bring us peace – '. Reilly heard the words of the aria and grunted: there would be precious little peace in the immediate future as far as he could see.

'He's ripe, I tell you,' McCluskey said, almost shouting as if to defy contradiction.

'I don't like it,' Moran said.

'You don't have to,' McCluskey announced, looking towards the woman.

'How can you tell, Eddie?' the woman asked.

McCluskey made a face. 'I can tell. I've seen plenty of them.'

'He could be a plant,' the woman went on.

'Not this one. I've seen him three times in Sandy's place. He's no plant. He's too scared.'

'You can't be sure.'

'I am sure.'

'I still don't like it,' Moran insisted.

McCluskey gave him a scathing look, and turned back to the woman, saying: 'It's too good a chance to lose. You know damn well we could use someone like him if – '

'It's too bloody risky,' Moran insisted, refusing to be put down.

The woman stood up and went to the window. For several

53

minutes she stared out, seeming to consider the possibilities. 'I suppose he could be useful – '

'Of course he bloody well could,' McCluskey interrupted. 'Jesus, without Reilly it's our best chance of getting info from inside.'

'Have you spoken to him?' the woman asked, coming back from the window and sitting down again.

McCluskey shook his head. 'No.'

'Has Sandy said anything?'

Again McCluskey shook his head. 'No.'

Moran gave a scoffing noise. 'Oh great.'

'Fuck you.'

'Stop it you two,' the woman snapped, vexed. 'Eddie's right. This Brit could be useful.'

'We'll have to move sharpish. We don't want Reilly and his boys beating us to it,' Eddie McCluskey said, pushing his advantage.

The woman frowned. 'I'm not going to be rushed. Just you go on watching him. And keep your ears peeled. When you're certain he's ripe we'll have another meet.'

'We'll lose – '

'Just watch him another while,' the woman insisted.

'By the way.' Brigadier Brazier said as an afterthought, 'What news of Major Fisher?'

There was a moment's silence at the other end of the line. Then: 'Progressing nicely, sir.'

'What does that mean?'

The voice gave a small hollow laugh. 'Just that. Progressing nicely.'

'That's all you have to tell me?'

'That's all there *is* to tell, sir.'

'Well, as long as we don't have another débâcle.'

'We won't, sir.'

'For all our sakes I hope not.'

Dermot Drumm walked the short distance between the two

54

Glasgow flats, chain-smoking. He looked about him for several minutes before hurriedly crossing the street. He raced up the stairs two at a time. When he reached the flat Joe Mulcahy already had the door open, letting him in without a word, without even a nod of welcome.

'We've got a job on,' Dermot announced, looking about for an ashtray, seeing none and tossing his butt into the empty grate.

Joe Mulcahy and Peggy Dunne looked at each other but said nothing, waiting for Dermot to explain.

'Next Friday I want you both to go to Brighton again. You've been booked into the Grand in the name of Mr and Mrs Clark.' Dermot reached into his inside pocket and took out a brown envelope which he tossed across to them. 'Go out and buy yourselves new clothes. Everything. Shoes, socks, knickers — the lot. Get your hair done. You're newly-weds, you'll be glad to hear, so act a bit dumb when you get there, and look as if you're madly in love. I'll contact you there on Saturday — okay?'

'Okay.'

'They have lots of honeymooners who stay there so they probably won't pay too much attention to you. Just don't attract any unnecessary attention. In fact the less they see of you the better. It'll only seem natural if you stay closetted in your bedroom anyway,' Dermot told them grinning. 'On Thursday I'll bring you a small overnight bag. That goes with you. Treat it carefully.'

The manager of the Grand Hotel, Brighton ushered his assistant into a chair and sat down behind his desk. 'It's been confirmed,' he said. 'She'll be staying here during the Party Convention. Plus most of the Cabinet.'

'Oh boy!'

'Quite. Still, we've plenty of time to prepare. It's not till October.'

'Three months isn't all that long.'

'No, but it's enough.'

'Who'll be handling security?'

'Special Branch, I imagine.'

'They'll want plans of the suites, I suppose?'

'I would think so. I haven't been told, but I'm sure they will.'

'I'll see to that right away.'

'Good.'

'And you'd better see to it that no bookings are taken for the PM's suite from, say, the middle of September.'

'Right . . . . Should we give it a lick of paint?'

The manager smiled mischievously. 'Our rooms are impeccable at all times.'

'Of course.'

· SEVEN ·

ON THE FIRST Saturday in August, Declan Tuohy arrived in Belfast and went directly to his sister's house. He would have preferred to stay in an hotel but knew it was his duty to spend a few days in his old home. Since the death of her husband and son, Rose had deteriorated rapidly, unable to cope with the horror. Now she cocooned herself in a shadowy, haunted world wherein the dead were as real and alive as the living. Neighbours, he knew, dropped in frequently to keep an eye on her, but their visits appeared superfluous: Rose managed remarkably well, keeping her house in sparkling condition, often holding tea-parties for guests that existed only in her mind. And although she had aged she took care of her appearance, always dressed neatly, her hair tidy and nails manicured, just as if she was permanently on the point of setting out for Mass.

He was upset more than shocked when she opened the door to him. True she invited him to enter graciously and smiled a genuine, warm welcome, but there was a wounded wildness in her eyes, and he suspected she did not know who he was: a suspicion confirmed when she asked him politely: 'And you're – ?'

'It's me, Rose. Declan.'

For a second Rose looked puzzled. Then she smiled. 'Of course. How silly of me. Declan. How nice to see you again.'

'I'm sorry to barge in like this, but I had to come over for a few days. I thought you might put me up.'

Rose's eyes twinkled. 'Of course you can stay. Your old room is still where it was,' she said, tittering at her little witticism.

'Thanks, Rose.'

'You just go up and unpack and have a wash, and I'll make us both a nice cup of tea. Have you eaten?'

'I had a bite on the plane. I'm not hungry.'

Declan put his small suitcase by the foot of the bed and threw his jacket on top of it, staring about the room, a curious sense of timelessness sweeping over him. It was as if he had never been away, as if what he had done in the last few years was of so little account the gods had decided to erase it. And perhaps they were right. Of course the window had been mended, and he walked to it and ran his fingers over the new panes. Outside on the street everything was peaceful. A cat preened itself pretending not to notice the party of sparrows near the gutter. Four women chatted, laughing occasionally; three small girls played hopscotch, giggling delightedly as they wobbled on one hopping leg. Declan sighed. It had been just as peaceful the night the bullet had shattered the window, missing him by inches, a bullet, as it turned out, meant for his nephew, Fergal. Everywhere you turned in Belfast reminded you of some tragedy, it seemed. Even the small front garden, so lovingly tended by Rose's husband, was like a horrible memorial to death, its unkempt flowerbeds and overgrown grass, the thistles and nettles, the paper bags, the beer can and two plastic mugs seeming to jeer at the unfortunate man who had been shot in error by the gate. Declan turned away from the window. City of Moloch, he had called it once, much to Seamus Reilly's annoyance – but city of Moloch it certainly was.

When he came downstairs Rose was already in the front room with tea nicely laid out on a tray. 'All settled?' she asked, and without waiting for an answer, went on: 'Now yours is milk but no sugar, isn't it?'

It wasn't, but Declan could not muster an argument. 'That's right.'

'I thought that was it. I remember because it's the opposite to the way Mr Reilly likes his. His is sugar but no milk,' Rose explained.

Declan was astounded. 'Seamus Reilly comes here for tea?' he asked.

'Oh yes. Every week. He manages my money, you know. Some pension fund Tim Pat subscribed to. Mr Reilly collects it for me and brings it round. Then he has a cup of tea and a chat, and off he goes until the following week. Such a nice man. Always cheerful and happy. He *does* make me laugh,' Rose explained, giving a little laugh as if to demonstrate Seamus Reilly's effect.

Declan managed a smile: the thought of Reilly being cheerful and happy was enough to make anyone smile. His smile widened as he recognized the tactful hand of Reilly in Tim Pat's 'pension fund'. Some pension. It was typical of Reilly's delicate humour to disguise the inevitable IRA donation to a member's widow in such innocuous terms. Not that he could have told Rose any different: she would, in all probability, have been appalled to learn that Tim Pat had been in any way involved. True, his participation had been limited: he had been on the quiet list for several years, and the fact that he had just been asked to become active when he was shot (he, too, mistakenly taken as Fergal) was purely coincidental.

'He's a very funny man,' Declan agreed, barely masking his sarcasm.

'And kind,' Rose went on. 'He always brings a little present for me. A few flowers. A pot of honey. Some chocolates. Always some little thing to keep the colour in my cheeks as he says.'

Declan found it difficult not to laugh outright. Although surprised and touched by this new side of Seamus Reilly, the vision of him producing pots of honey by way of offering was somehow hilarious. And the only flowers Declan could reasonably associate with him were the posies he always sent to funerals. 'That is kind,' he admitted.

Rose sighed gratefully. 'Everyone is kind to me,' she told him, for the first time looking at him directly, making him feel uncomfortable, perhaps accusing him.

'I'm sorry I haven't kept in touch more often, Rose.'

'But you have. I remember getting hundreds of letters from you.'

'Hardly hundreds.'

'Oh yes. All those lovely little poems you used to send me – what was it we said? – by the fairy post? Don't you remember?' Rose sounded disappointed. 'When you came home from school you'd slip them under my pillow and tell me they came by fairy post.'

Declan felt suddenly very sad; annoyed, too, that the innocence of childhood should now make him feel so embarrassed; and, stupidly, guilty as if anything so delightful as fairy postmistresses had no place in the hard reality he had so often been accused of avoiding.

'Anyway,' Rose was saying, 'Mr Reilly's been telling me all about you. He always brings me a little snippet of news about what you're doing. It is you who has gone into television, isn't it?'

Declan nodded. 'It is.'

'I thought so. That must be nice.'

For a while they sat in silence, at least Declan did. Rose, on the other hand, although not actually speaking, gave the impression she was fully occupied as hostess, smiling quietly to herself from time to time, mouthing silently, shifting the milkjug and sugarbowl and teapot about the tray as in some elaborate boardgame, or perhaps just needing to touch things to reassure herself of their reality.

At length Declan stood up and put his cup and saucer on the tray. Looking down at his sister he reached out and lightly touched her hair. 'You're a wonderful girl, Rose,' he told her softly.

'Rubbish,' Rose said shortly.

When Declan's flight was some twenty minutes from landing Seamus Reilly was talking to Inspector John Asher. The meeting was at Reilly's suggestion, and took place in a safe house frequently used for such get-togethers.

'There's been a development?' Asher was asking hopefully.

Reilly made a denying grimace. 'I'm not sure,' he told him guardedly.

'Oh.'

'We *have* located the so-called deserter.'

Asher waited in silence.

Reilly, too, remained silent, smiling mischievously.

'He does have a name?' Asher weakened first.

'He does.'

'But I'm not to be told?'

Reilly took a moment to think about this. 'That depends, John,' he said finally.

'On what?'

'On whether we can come to an agreement as to what should be done.'

'We usually do.'

'Yes. We do,' Reilly conceded. 'But . . .'

'But?'

'But like myself you have your loyalties.'

And that was certainly true. Like Reilly, Asher was getting old and tired. Like Reilly he had become sickened by the lawlessness that masqueraded under the guise of 'defending rights'. And like Reilly he wished to God that the fanatics and the politicians and the do-gooders and the meddlers would just vanish and leave the people of the province to sort out their own problems. Not that God had much to do with it as far as Asher was concerned: His ministers – the 'citrus' clergy (as Reilly had once called them) and the tarmac-kissing Polack (as Asher had responded) – were equally laughable, using their religions to pile yet more misery on the community. Yet, while feeling wholly Irish, Asher was sometimes even pompously loyal, in general terms, to the monarch in whose service he was. And

61

while he could and did wheel and deal with the best of them, ultimately, he knew, it was his duty to uphold what remained of law and order.

'So what agreement are we talking about?'

'Let's say a temporary small conspiracy of silence.'

Asher raised his eyebrows.

'We want him left alone, you see. We *want* him to desert – but not to us.'

Asher looked confused. 'No?'

'No. You remember I promised to tell you if I heard of anything big coming down in mainland Britain?'

Asher nodded.

'Well, we are almost certain something of the kind is being planned – without our sanction. We don't know what – yet. We think we know who. And it is to those people we want this man to desert.'

'And then?'

Reilly smiled benevolently. 'And then, when we feel he's learned enough, we lift him, and persuade him to tell us what he knows.'

Asher gave this some thought. 'You know, of course, Seamus, that I should report this?'

'Of course, but then we wouldn't have as good a chance of solving the riddle of what's going on. Besides, you know as well as I do that the army wouldn't thank you for it.'

There was logic in that, certainly. Although supposedly working together to maintain a troubled peace, the army and the RUC were often at loggerheads, the army resenting their role of policing, the RUC resenting the army's usurpation of that role. Indeed, very little information passed between them, each guarding their secrets jealously, each hoping to outdo the other. All of which suited Seamus Reilly.

'I'll tell you what I'll do, Seamus,' Asher decided. 'You give me the name of this soldier, and promise me you'll let me know instantly you have some knowledge of what is being planned, and I'll keep it to myself. How's that?'

Reilly laughed pleasantly. 'Good enough as far as it goes. But I'll need a little more than that, John.'

'Like?'

'Like I'll want all you can get me on our – our soldier friend. There are details you can get at that I can't, and I need to know everything.'

Asher nodded. 'If I can I will. What else?'

'If we find out what is being planned for England I want you to let us handle it. We can always fix it so that you get the credit, but we must handle it.'

'Will you be able to?'

Reilly grinned. 'Oh yes. You see, John, if something is going on we are, like I said, pretty certain who is behind it.'

'Can you tell me?'

Reilly shrugged. 'Why not. You can probably guess anyway.'

Asher decided to guess. 'Moran?'

'And McCluskey and – '

Asher wagged a finger at Reilly. 'You shouldn't have been so lenient with them.'

'Oh they were warned what would happen if they tried anything off their own bat. If we can prove they are involved in something they know what to expect.'

'It might be too late then.'

'It might indeed.'

'And the soldier?'

'Fisher. Chris Fisher. Major.'

Asher looked surprised. 'A Major no less.'

'Quite.'

'I'll see what I can find out. But don't you forget – not a move unless I'm warned.'

Reilly put his hand on his heart. 'Not a move.'

As Declan was drinking tea with his sister, Seamus Reilly was drinking something stronger with the Commander in Chief of the Provisional IRA. He had driven there directly from his meeting with Asher, crossing the border without any problem, arriving in Clones only minutes behind the Commander.

'You look harassed, Seamus,' the Commander observed.

'I am harassed.'

'Ah. That's the first time I've ever heard you admit that.'

'The way things are going it won't be the last,' Seamus told him with a wry smile. 'I hate having to deal with unknown quantities. Give me facts and I can cope, but this "is there isn't there something going on?" business is unbearable.'

'Well – is there or isn't there?' the Commander enquired, swilling his drink in his glass, his eyes dancing good-humouredly behind his spectacles.

'Very probably. Everyone seems to think there is. But we don't *know*. And it's taking too long to find out. *If* something is about to happen I can tell you who's behind it.'

The Commander gave a short laugh. 'You don't have to, Seamus. I warned you that woman would be nothing but trouble. You should have let me have her dealt with there and then.'

Seamus looked gloomy. 'I know. But the repercussions could have been worse. She has support, you know, both here and in Dublin.'

'It wouldn't be doing her much good if she was dead.'

'I'm afraid it's a case of the devil you know.'

The Commander took a long drink, and coughed as the liquid burned his throat. When he next spoke his tone had changed: far less genial, it had a hardness that Reilly recognized all too well. 'It is imperative, Seamus, that nothing happens that will upset the balance of things. The elections are coming soon and we need to win seats if we are ever to deliver this unfortunate country from the horror it suffers. The last thing we need now is some stupidity in England. We've tried too long and too hard to show ourselves as reasonable men to have all our efforts destroyed by these hotheads.'

'I know. I know.'

'Well do something about it for God's sake.'

Seamus held out his hands in a gesture of appeal. 'What?'

64

The Commander ignored the question, warning instead: 'If you don't find out what they're up to and put a stop to it you will be blamed, Seamus, and even I won't be able to save you.'

'Dammit, I don't even know for sure if *anything* is going on.'

'I presume, at least, you've had that woman watched.'

'Of course.'

'And she's done nothing that might arouse your suspicions?'

Reilly made a little face. 'Not really. She took a party of children to Glasgow for a few days, but she's done that before.'

'Glasgow?'

'Yes.'

'Who have we got there?'

'Eight sleepers.'

'Any who might support her?'

'A couple of hard-liners who might. Dermot Drumm for one. If he supported her then Joe Mulcahy would.'

'Did she meet with Drumm?'

Reilly looked suddenly uncomfortable. 'Not that we know of. She did give our man the slip one evening for a couple of hours,' he confessed.

'So she could have seen him?'

'She *could* have.'

The Commander frowned his displeasure. 'Could they, then, be planning something in Glasgow?' he asked, sounding impatient.

'What in the name of heaven could they be planning in Glasgow?' Seamus asked in return. 'It'd be crazy.' .

'Crazy people do crazy things. And crazy people seeking revenge do even crazier things.'

Reilly sighed deeply and shook his head. 'Just leave it with me and I'll sort everything out.'

'I hope so, Seamus.'

'I will. I'm working on it night and day. I've even had Asher agree to help in a way.'

The Commander was forced to laugh. 'You and Asher. The terrible twins. Dear God. If the Brits ever found out about you two being hand in glove all hell would break loose.'

'All hell would have broken loose long ago on many occasions if we weren't.'

'You use whoever you want, but just sort this mess out.

Seamus Reilly was exhausted by the time he got home. He had stripped and was making his way to the shower, a woolly monogrammed towel wrapped about his groin, when the phone rang. 'Damn,' he swore, and tut-tutted his way back to the bedside table. 'Yes?'

'Seamus? It's me. Declan.'

'Oh, Declan,' Reilly said abruptly, trying to orientate himself. 'Where are you?'

'Here. In Belfast. At Rose's.'

'Oh.'

'What's the matter with you? You sound – '

'I'm sorry, Declan. I've had a rough day. I've only just got in. I was on my way to the shower when you called.'

'I'll call back later. I – '

'No it's all right. I'm glad you're here. I look forward to seeing you again. It's been a while.'

'Yes. Can I see you tomorrow?'

'Of course. What time? After Mass?'

'What Mass do you go to?'

'Twelve o'clock, I'm afraid. The flesh and all that. Why don't we have a bite of lunch together?'

'Fine.'

'Right. I'll pick you up at one.'

'I look forward to that.'

'Me too.'

Chris Fisher leaned on the bar, propped in his favourite corner. From the moment he had entered he had sensed that something significant was going to happen. Perhaps it was the more than usual friendliness of the landlord, Sandy: or perhaps it was the fact that not everyone stopped talking when he came in.

'That's a muggy class of a night,' the landlord greeted him, smiling. 'A Guinness as usual?'

'Please.'

'And this one's on the house. You're a regular now.'

Fisher drank slowly, and wiped the line of froth from his upper lip with one finger. Without actually meaning to he found himself watching the landlord. He saw him nod to someone in the bar and then jerk his head towards the end of the bar. In the mirror behind the bottles he saw a small man with a moustache get up, place a hand on his companion's shoulder, lean down to him and whisper, and then come across the room towards the corner where he stood. He found himself stiffen in the way (if such was true) that people do when they are about to die.

'You're Chris, aren't you?'

Chris Fisher turned his head slowly and stared the man in the face, noting the wide smile and the cold non-participating eyes. 'Yes,' he admitted.

'I'm Eddie,' the man told him and held out his hand.

When they had shaken hands, Eddie McCluskey said bluntly, 'Sandy tells me you want out.'

Fisher looked about him hurriedly, as if terrified that someone would overhear.

'You don't have to worry,' Eddie consoled him. 'You're safe enough here. Is it true?'

'I don't know,' Fisher said, trying to sound bewildered.

'What d'you mean you don't know?'

'Yes. I want out. But – '

Eddie beamed. 'That's better. We knew you did. We can always tell. You bring your drink and come over to the table and meet a pal of mine.'

Fisher followed McCluskey across the room to the table, aware that every eye in the place was on him.

'Come on. Sit down,' Eddie insisted. 'This is Pat. Pat – Chris.'

Moran looked up and nodded imperceptibly. He was still not happy. Stupid they might think he was but he had instincts about things, and instinct now told him there was something not right about this. Oddly enough it was not so much that he

67

suspected this Fisher of being a plant, more that he sensed, without any conceivable reason, that the hand of Seamus Reilly was behind it, ludicrous though that might be. He had come across Reilly a couple of times since he had been expelled, both times after Sunday Mass, and Reilly's reactions then had been strangely sinister. He had been too disinterested, too nonchalant, dismissing the presence of Moran and what was mobile of his huge family with a bland flick of his eyes as though they did not exist. That was not Reilly. Everything was of importance to him, and he would certainly have been keen to observe what reaction the meeting of their eyes would create.

The three men sat in silence for a while, sipping their drinks, listening to the music, McCluskey keeping time to the rhythm by drumming his fingers on the formica-topped table and occaionally mouthing the words. When the song finished McCluskey said: 'It'll take a bit of time, you know.'

Fisher accepted this. 'Sure.'

'Just you go about your business as usual for the next week or so. When we're ready we'll let you know.'

'Okay.'

'You'll be coming here in the meantime?'

'Should I?'

McCluskey grinned. 'Why not?'

'I thought – '

Moran interrupted. 'We'll do the thinking. Anyway, there are some people you'll have to meet before we do anything.'

'Of course.'

Moran finished his drink, all the while keeping his watery eyes on Fisher.

'I'm off,' he announced putting down his glass. 'You coming?' he asked McCluskey.

Eddie looked a little surprised and peeved, but he said yes.

'You better hang on here for a while after we've gone,' Moran said.

'Right,' Fisher agreed.

'And by the way, don't you ever approach us. If you see

either of us in here or anywhere else don't even acknowledge that you know us.'

Outside Moran turned up the collar of his jacket, and stood staring back at the bar, shaking his head.

'What's up with you?' Eddie demanded, determined not to let Moran dampen his expectations.

'I still don't like it, Eddie. We don't need to help the bastard. He can't do us a damn bit of good.'

Feeling suddenly sleepy and not, for the moment, prepared to argue, Eddie said: 'Well, he can't do us any harm,' and started to walk away.

Moran followed morosely in his footsteps, already visions of the harm that the Brit could do clamouring in his mind. 'You're wrong, Eddie,' he said, not caring that McCluskey was too far ahead to hear. 'You're wrong. He'll do us nothing but bloody harm.'

The desk clerk at the Grand Hotel watched Joe Mulcahy sign the register in the name of Mr and Mrs Clark. He gave them the friendly, slightly naughty smile he reserved for newly-weds, and tapped the small brass bell, signalling with his forefinger for the porter to take their luggage upstairs.

His conversation with Declan over, Seamus Reilly made for the shower again. He had almost reached it this time when the phone rang for the second time. Reilly threw up his hands in despair and the towel slipped to the floor. He kicked it angrily out of his way and went naked back to the bedroom. 'Yes?'

'Mr Reilly. It's Regan.'

'Yes, Regan.'

'Sandy just called me. They've made contact. McCluskey and Moran had a drink with him. They stayed together about five minutes then McCluskey and Moran left. Fisher stayed on for a quarter of an hour, then he left too. I thought you'd want to know.'

Reilly sat down on the edge of his bed. 'Yes. Thank you, Thomas. Where did they go?'

'Moran went home. McCluskey went to another bar, stayed twenty minutes and then he went home. Fisher went back to the barracks.'

'Right. I'll have a think about it and talk to you on Monday.'

'Very good, Mr Reilly.'

· EIGHT ·

SUNDAY. THE SABBATH. The day, it is said, that God took a well-deserved rest after His labours. Seamus Reilly frowned at the thought. The way things were going with the world it might have been better if He had spent His Sunday destroying what He had created and starting from scratch again. At least people seemed to act more kindly towards each other on Sundays, like, say, at Christmas, and that, surely, was commendable even if their goodwill was brought about only by their terror of what Christ might make of them when they appeared at His altar for communion.

Reilly clambered out of bed, scattering the newspapers he had been reading onto the floor. Balanced precariously on the small table by his bed was a tray with the remnants of his breakfast: the peel of a grapefruit, crusts of toast, an eggshell. He stretched himself luxuriously, glancing at the clock: 10.45. Just time to shave and dress, have one more cup of coffee before Mass.

At ten minutes to midday he was kneeling respectfully in his pew, waiting for the parish priest to make his entrance. The church was packed, whole families rallying to the latest

71

possible Mass, many left without a place to kneel and cluttering the doorway. Yet in Reilly's pew there was plenty of room. At least four more worshippers could have squeezed in, but no one presumed to infringe Seamus Reilly's right to space. He liked it at the back; for as long as he could remember he had used the same place so that now it was known as Mr Reilly's place, and spoken of with respect. He could see everyone without turning round, and, of course, everyone could see him as they came in. For Seamus it was important to set an example. To be seen. It made him mortal, belying the rumours of his cruel inhumanity. As they came in now people smiled at him timidly, and he smiled back, sometimes giving a tiny wave like a blessing. There was nothing arrogant in this gesture. They were, after all, his people. He protected them and their interests, and he genuinely loved them. Most of all he admired their tenacity to live out their lives in the face of the appalling brutality that surrounded them, content in the assurance that their God was always close at hand.

Reilly bowed his head reverently at the consecration, trying to pray. As ever he failed. His mind would not adapt to prayer: the hypocrisy of appearing to worship a Christ to whom he could not pray disturbed him. He had even spoken of it once to a priest, long since dead, and had been told rather enigmatically ' 'tis your vanity that stands in your way, Seamus. You should follow the admonition of old Ezra Pound and "pull down your vanity" '. His failure irked him, and made him envy the simple, uncomplicated faith of his family, or what was left of it. Even his brother whom he had ordered to be executed had managed a liaison with God denied himself. And his mother . . . Seamus Reilly stared up at the ceiling of the church as though for succour. His mother with incredible blindness had accepted the fratricide as the will of God, had never reproached him, had mentioned it only once, and that when she was dying and too weak to argue. 'That's something between you and Jesus,' she had said. 'If you deserve it, He'll forgive you.' But would He?

Mass over, Reilly blessed himself, sidled from his pew,

genuflected, and walked from the church, nodding appreciatively as a group of men by the door stepped to one side, allowing him to exit unhindered. Outside he set his hat at precisely the right angle on his head, and tucked his missal under his arm. He acknowledged with a single blink the appearance of two men on either side of him and walked towards his car, stopping a couple of times for a word with someone, his hand resting sympathetically on their arm as he spoke, and the faces that had been worried were more cheerful when he left them. Reilly himself felt better that his words had solved their problems. It was what he was there for. He settled back in his seat, and lit one of his little cigars. 'Home first,' he told his driver. As the car moved away he glanced out of the window, and tensed. Patrick Moran, his wife and four of his brood were waiting to cross the road. For an instant Moran's eyes met Reilly's, and a sense of warm satisfaction swept over Seamus as he noted the fear.

Within walking distance of the church that Reilly had just left, in a small house with a pleasant garden, a house neatly and tastefully furnished that smelled of wax and with flowers in nearly every room, the woman, dressed in a scarlet cat-suit, sat in an armchair, one leg curled underneath her. She held a drink in her hand, and each time she moved the ice in the glass clinked. Across the room, in another chair, Eddie McCluskey, wearing what would once have been called his 'Sunday suit', sat smoking, nervously tapping the ash into an ashtray after every drag. Clearly he had just said something that had given the woman something to think about: she had thrown her head back, frowning. McCluskey took to eating his nails. 'Don't do that,' the woman said irritably, glaring at him in disgust.

McCluskey stopped instantly, blushing like a child.

'And you don't agree with Moran? You think he's all right?'

'I'm sure of it,' McCluskey said. 'Sandy thinks so too, and he doesn't make mistakes.'

'We *all* make mistakes,' the woman said, sitting up and sipping her drink.

'Not this time,' McCluskey insisted.

'You think not?'

'I'm certain.'

The woman shook her head slowly, not convinced. 'They've conned us before now.'

McCluskey made a curiously old-fashioned sound. 'Pshaw! That was when Reilly's men handled it.'

'But you know better?'

'Sure.'

The woman thought again for a minute. 'We could use him,' she conceded finally.

'You're damn right we could. He's a Major for Christ's sake.'

'Yes,' the woman agreed but vaguely as though rank was the furthest thing from her mind. 'I won't take any chances, though. He'll have to prove himself first.'

'I can arrange that.'

The woman finished her drink and put her glass down hard on the table, clearly coming to a decision. 'All right. If he proves himself we'll lift him. If he doesn't – ' She shrugged.

McCluskey grinned. 'I know.'

'Pick someone from his own regiment. Someone he's bound to know. If your Major shoots him, okay. If not you shoot him.'

'Right,' McCluskey said, obviously pleased.

'And arrange it soon. I don't want this thing hanging on. I've enough to think about as it is.'

'Do you want to meet him?'

The woman shook her head. 'No. There's no point. Time enough if he's genuine.' She stood up. 'You better clear off. My sister and her husband are coming for lunch. I've the mint sauce to make.'

It had started to drizzle as Reilly and Declan went up the steps into the hotel. As they neared the main door one of the security guards moved forward, one hand outstretched as if to stop them. Reilly removed his hat and fixed him with a furious glare. Instantly the guard froze, and then transformed his act of restraint into a small salute that hinted of respect and brotherhood. 'Morning, sir. Sorry. I didn't recognize you.'

Inside Declan followed Seamus across the open foyer, through the lounge and into the restaurant: as they entered the headwaiter's eyes flickered a warning to an underling and moved forward to greet them. 'Ah, good morning, Mr Reilly. Nice to see you again. I have your table all ready. This way please.'

He led the way across the room to a table isolated from the others in the bay of the window. He snapped his fingers and a waiter glided towards them, his hand already out to accept Reilly's coat and hat.

When they were seated the headwaiter handed them each a menu. 'I'll leave you to decide, Mr Reilly. A drink, perhaps, while you make up your mind?'

Seamus looked across at Declan, cocking an eyebrow by way of invitation.

'Are we having wine?' Declan asked.

'Of course.'

'Then I'll wait.'

'We can have the wine brought now,' Reilly said.

'Fine. I'll have wine, then.'

'Red or white?'

'Whichever.'

Reilly smiled tightly. 'White, I think. Pouilly Fuisse.' He looked up.

'So,' Seamus said, unfolding his napkin and spreading it across his knees. 'You're back.'

Declan nodded. 'I'm back. For two days.'

'A short enough visit. May I ask why?'

'I wanted to talk to you.'

Reilly stared across the table and remained silent.

'Something I wanted to ask you.'

Reilly spread his hands. 'Feel free.'

'We've heard things in London. Something – '

Declan stopped and leaned back as the waiter brought the wine. He poured a mouthful into Reilly's glass and waited for him to taste it. Seamus made a great show of this: sniffing the

75

bouquet, swilling the wine under and over his tongue, a light in his eyes answering Declan's mischievous smirk. 'Excellent,' he said at last.

'You were saying?' Reilly went on as the waiter moved away.

'The grapevine has it that something big is to come down soon in England.'

Reilly sipped his wine.

'Is it true?'

Seamus Reilly put his glass carefully on the table, holding it by the stem, twisting it in small circles. Then he looked up, his face bearing an impish quality, his eyes serious. 'Come now, Declan, you don't expect me to answer that.'

'I hoped you would. You see, the grapevine also says that it's some breakaways who are planning it and that you are – well, none too pleased.'

Reilly gave a small laugh. 'Well I wouldn't be, would I, if it was true?'

Before Declan could answer the headwaiter hovered over them, his little pad at the ready.

'Ah,' Seamus said. 'What do you think, Des?'

'The Dover sole, Mr Reilly. I know you're fond of fish and the sole is very good.'

'Sole for me, then, Des. Declan?'

'The same for me would be fine.'

'Nothing to start with, Mr Reilly?'

'No. And just coffee afterwards. A little spinach with the fish though. And a jacket potato.'

'And you, sir?' the waiter asked Declan, almost as an afterthought.

'The same for me. Thank you.'

The waiter topped up their glasses, whipped the menus away and withdrew.

Declan leaned forward. 'That's my point, Seamus. We hear that you *are* very displeased.'

'You have an imaginative grapevine, Declan.'

'I'm not so sure. Let me put it this way. Off the record as they say. Suppose – just suppose, that the rumours were true. And suppose that you were determined to put a stop to it as I presume you would. And suppose I told you my editor wanted to make a programme giving your point of view which could enable you to put the IRA in a better light. Suppose all that for a minute: would you talk on film?'

Seamus Reilly's eyes narrowed to two penetrating slits. He looked out of the window, looked back again, studied his nails, and finally took to drumming what sounded like a tango beat on the tablecloth with his fingers. Then he looked Declan in the eye. 'Are you really being serious?'

Declan nodded.

The fish arrived, neatly off the bone. The vegetables were spooned onto their plates. The glasses were again topped up. Then they were by themselves again.

Seamus Reilly attacked his meal. He knew he ate too fast, 'gulping' his food his mother had said as if it was the last solid meal he was expecting to have for a long time. It was only when one side of the fish was gone that he spoke, wagging a forefinger at Declan. 'It's certainly an intriguing idea. But tell me: how long do you think I'd live if I did something like that?'

'That's not what I meant, Seamus. There would be nothing underhand about it. You could clear it with your executive. Look, you're trying to become political. If you want to succeed you need the media. You need to drum up sympathy. Let's face it you and I know that everyone in England believes the IRA look like thugs with cabbage ears and broken noses. If you went on and spoke reasonably, perhaps even – '

Reilly was shaking his head. 'It's not me you want, Declan. I'm no politician, nor have I any ambition to be. I can put you in touch with plenty of our men who might consider your proposition, although whether they'd ever be allowed to talk is another matter.'

Now Declan was shaking his head. 'That wouldn't be the same. It's you or nobody.'

Reilly chewed a morsel of sole. 'In that case it's nobody.'

Declan grimaced his disappointment. 'That's a shame.'

Seamus smiled benignly. 'You'll live,' he said enigmatically, making Declan blush slightly, admonished.

They finished their meal almost in silence, once or twice chit-chatting for a couple of seconds, and it was not until the coffee had been left on the table that Reilly spoke seriously again, surprisingly returning to the subject he had dismissed. 'I'll promise you one thing, Declan,' he promised in a voice that suggested his words had already been carefully weighed. 'If ever I feel that your suggestion would be beneficial I'll contact you without delay.'

Declan studied his host's face quizzically. 'That almost sounds as if you think it might be – eh – beneficial one day.'

Reilly beamed. 'Who knows?' Then he leaned forward, his elbows on the table, his eyes suddenly troubled. 'And I'll tell you this as a friend: there *is* considerable friction right now, and we *do* believe something is being planned to discredit those of us who believe in political rather than violent solutions. But you can believe me when I say that I will do anything – anything – to prevent a disruption of a possible chance for peace.'

Declan stared at his friend. How he had changed! Or rather, how he had changed and yet remained the same. Despite his declaration that a peaceful solution was now his desire, his old ruthlessness remained, and he saw nothing ironic in the insinuation that he would cheerfully use violence to ensure that peace.

'Why don't you say that publicly, Seamus?'

'Because it's not for me to speak publicly. I'm only a small cog in the wheel. We have our spokesmen.'

'You? A small cog?' Declan was derisive.

Reilly grinned like a little boy. 'Well – maybe not so small. But nevertheless it's not my place to make announcements.'

'Not even if you got the all-clear? You could ask.'

'No.' Seamus Reilly was adamant.

Later, as Declan was being driven home, Seamus put a hand on his arm. 'I'm sorry you've had a wasted visit,' he said.

'It wasn't a waste. It was good to see you again.'

'We'll talk again before you leave, I hope?'

78

Declan shook his head. 'I'm afraid not, Seamus. I'm off back to London first thing in the morning.'

'Oh,' Reilly said, clearly disappointed, as the car slid to a stop outside Rose Duffy's house. 'Well, at least try and keep in touch a bit more.'

'I will.'

'I know it was hard for you to forgive the things that happened last time you came. But it's the way things are here. Friends and relations die, and they are forgotten almost before we have the time to mourn. You won't believe it but I would sooner have died myself than have your nephew shot.'

'I understand. By the way – thanks for looking after Rose.'

Reilly dismissed this gratitude with a shrug. 'It's the least I can do. Anyway, I'd do the same for anyone.'

Declan laughed. 'You're a terrible liar, Seamus.'

Reilly looked unaccountably sad. 'Yes. I am, aren't I?'

Brigadier Brazier felt replete after his excellent lunch, and glowed in the haze of brandy. He sat, cross-legged and relaxed opposite Colonel Maddox, cupping his glass in both hands. 'That was a most excellent lunch, Matthew. When I asked to see you I didn't expect such royal treatment.'

'It was a pleasure, I assure you. I have so few visitors now, you know. Ancient officers are easily forgotten.'

'You should come down to London more often. Berkshire is all very well but I've always thought the country was strictly for vegetables,' the Brigadier remarked, giving a curious, snuffling laugh.

'Perhaps that's what I've become. Well, perhaps not quite. I read a lot now. Far more than I used to. It's amazing what you can learn from books, you know,' the Colonel observed, smiling inwardly, aware that his little joke would be lost on his superior.

The Brigadier agreed anyway. 'I'm sure it is. May I?' he then asked, producing a pipe.

'Please feel at home.'

The Brigadier went through the mysterious operation of

loading and lighting his briar, puffing a lot, using several matches before getting his bonfire (as Maddox saw it) under way. Finally, he took the pipe from his mouth and, holding the matchbox over the bowl, said: 'No doubt you're wondering why I wanted to see you.'

'It had crossed my mind.'

'Well I'll come straight to the point.'

But he didn't. He decided to take a more circuitous route, thinking of it as 'softening' Maddox. He had, after all, been warned that the Colonel could be tricky, could, indeed, be downright weird, and that the proverbial kid gloves should be worn. 'The trouble with you, Matthew, is that you've always underestimated yourself. We were talking in the club the other night, and all of us agreed that you were the very man to help us with a little problem we have.' He stopped and peered at Maddox through a cloud of smoke.

'Ah,' was all that the Colonel had to offer, but he did lean sideways for a better view of the Brigadier, encouraging him to go on.

'Now there's no one with a better knowledge of Northern Ireland than yourself – '

Colonel Maddox had a fit of coughing. The unexpectedness of the Brigadier's statement took him completely unawares, not least since he knew it to be quite untrue. Admittedly he had done a tour of duty in Belfast, but so had many others, and few tours had ended in such acrimonious circumstances as his. Indeed, his present retirement had been 'suggested'; and Colonel Maddox had been only too willing to comply. Baffled and pained by the duplicity and treachery he had encountered he had withdrawn to his home in Berkshire, only to find himself haunted by the people he had dealt with in Belfast. It could, however, truthfully be said that he had got closer to an understanding with IRA leaders than any of his predecessors, had, in fact, established a crude understanding with Seamus Reilly. But the manipulation of lives had left him scarred and repulsed.

'I'm sorry,' the Brigadier was saying, waving a hand to clear the area of smoke, and continuing blithely, ' – so we want to recall you to duty, temporarily, and would like you to go back to Belfast – just 'till the end of the year.'

Maddox looked aghast. He opened his mouth as if to reply, but nothing emerged, and he hid his discomfort by taking a long drink of his brandy.

Conveniently taking the silence as acceptance, Brigadier Brazier went on, warming to the subject, suddenly becoming quite military, clipping his words and editing his sentences, dropping verbs and adjectives at will. 'Put you in the picture. Trouble brewing, intelligence says. Big. Here. England, dammit. Got a man in, though. Fisher. Major. About to infiltrate. Need you there to liaise.'

The staccato information pinged off the Colonel's brain, making him shudder. He felt, suddenly, as if he was drowning, wave upon wave of remembered intrigue washing over him, and through it all something someone had said to him bellowed: 'if you once put foot in Ireland you will be crucified to it for the rest of your natural days'. But the Colonel was going to have none of that, was he? Certainly not. He was going to protest. 'I – ' That was as far as he got. The Brigadier held up his hand. 'Let me finish. You've dealt with Reilly. And Asher. Handled them well. Bound to be involved. Get them in. Find out.'

Colonel Maddox gave the Brigadier his most doleful look. Already small, menacing *doppelgänger*s of Reilly and Asher were stamping their feet on his mind. He wanted nothing whatever to do with them, nothing to do with their conniving or their treachery. He had almost succeeded in putting the whole bewildering mess behind him and yet here it was, regurgitated again, beckoning him with horny fingers. Dear God, that mad, mad Mr Apple, that crazy mystic, that lampoon who had ultimately been responsible for his downfall, had been right when he said he would be called back from afar.

'I don't think – ' Maddox began.

'You're not going to refuse, I hope,' Brigadier Brazier said, sounding as if a court martial was in the offing. 'We *need* you to handle it. Dammit man, your country needs you,' he added patriotically.

The Colonel wanted to laugh, but, as always, he quietly acquiesced, nodding gently and saying in a whisper: 'Very well.'

'Good man!' the Brigadier exclaimed. 'I knew we could count on you. There's not many of us old-timers left. We have to show the whizz-kids that we still know a thing or two.'

'When do – '

'As soon as possible. The sooner the better. The quicker you can get installed the better for all of us.'

Colonel Maddox smiled wryly.

'You just tell me when you *can* go and I'll make all the arrangements. The end of the week?' the Brigadier suggested, typically usurping the right of choice. 'Can I tell Belfast you'll be there next weekend?'

'Very well. The weekend.'

'Excellent.'

In his bathroom at the Grand Hotel Joe Mulcahy worked quickly and precisely, whistling through his teeth: a cheerful little tune in the manner of a man enjoying himself. Deftly he unscrewed the panelling about the bathtub, laying the screws in a neat, straight line on the floor beside him, making a little pattern by placing them head to tail. Lifting away the panel he leaned it against the wall; then he lay on his back and wriggled his way under the bath, using a torch to see. 'Hey, Peg, bring me in that case, will you?' he called.

Peggy Dunne reluctantly stopped admiring her reflection in the mirror: the new nightdress was, without doubt, the nicest garment she had ever owned: that it had been purchased on the promise of death probably never occurred to her. She primped herself one more time and then collected the case and carried it in to Mulcahy, who, now, was sitting cross-legged on the bathroom floor. 'Very nice,' he said.

'Thank you,' Peggy said, curtsying.

'And very seductive,' Mulcahy added, taking the bag and unzipping it, keeping his eyes on Peggy.

'You just keep your mind on your work,' Peggy told him primly.

Joe grunted. Carefully he lifted out the bomb. Then, methodically, he wrapped it in layer after layer of heavy-duty plastic.

'It doesn't look very big,' Peggy observed.

Joe looked up and grinned. 'Plenty big enough for what's wanted.'

An hour later, the explosive secured to the bath by tape and further kept rigid by being wedged between the bath and the wall, the panelling safely restored, and all trace of interference having been removed, Joe and Peggy lay in bed, both of them perspiring. Their intercourse had been violent and prolonged, Joe's unusually hectic rutting possibly stimulated by the proximity of destruction to his act of creation. Not that he would have thought of it like that: he had one of those opaque minds that could treat sex and killing with equal indifference.

'It's a shame we have to leave here tomorrow,' Peggy whispered, in her naiveté wistfully imagining the whole episode as a true honeymoon, clinging to the illusion of romance for all she was worth.

'Yea. Back to sodding Glasgow.'

'Maybe they'll call us home now.'

'Maybe.'

'Or send us somewhere else.'

'I don't care,' Joe told her. 'Anywhere but bloody Glasgow,' he added and, perhaps to dispel recurring images of the city he loathed, he rolled on top of her again.

It was after midnight when John Asher telephoned Seamus Reilly, awakening him from a deep, untramelled sleep. 'Have I got a surprise for you,' he announced.

Reilly groaned. The last thing he wanted right now was a surprise: to his mind, like telegrams, they meant only disaster and woe. 'God, John, I hate damn surprises – especially at this hour of the night – morning.'

'Guess who's coming to Belfast?'

Reilly groaned to himself again and winced. 'Superman.'

Asher chortled. 'Close. Maddox actually. Colonel Matthew Maddox.'

That made Reilly sit up. He switched on the light by his bed and groped for a cigar with his free hand. 'What for?'

'A message just came through. He's back for six months. Temporary replacement they call it. I've been told to meet him.'

Reilly lit his cigar and gave a short cough. 'It'll be like old times. I thought he was retired.'

'He was. They must have something special in mind to take him out of mothballs. My orders are to co-operate fully with him.'

'When does he get in?'

'The end of the week.'

'I wonder . . . .'

'Wonder what?'

Reilly did not immediately reply.

'Wonder what?' Asher insisted.

'Nothing. Let me think about it. I'll speak to you later. And John – thanks for calling.'

'I thought you'd be pleased.'

And, in a sense, Reilly was pleased. He liked Maddox – 'old Maddox' he always thought of him. He respected the man's integrity, and he was one of the only Brits he had been able to isolate from his Englishness.

Reilly blew a thin stream of smoke towards the ceiling, frowning and looking puzzled. Why on earth would they take the old man out of retirement and send him back? They had been only too glad to be shut of him in the first place. Perhaps they had got wind of . . . perhaps, as usual, they suspected that he, Reilly was involved . . . perhaps Maddox . . . . Oh, dammit, Reilly thought, stubbing out his cigar. He would work it out in the morning. He switched out the light, and settled down to sleep.

· NINE ·

THE SELECTION WAS almost inevitable. Corporal Sammy Wilson, a coward at heart but a bully when surrounded by troops and dealing with unarmed civilians, had long been on the list. For all of the following week McCluskey and Moran watched him themselves whenever possible. There would have been easier victims but they both wanted Wilson, their hatred of him increasing the longer it took to kidnap him. By Friday, the stocky, bull-necked, strutting Corporal had all but driven McCluskey to a frenzy. 'Jeez I want that bastard,' he told Moran.

'We'll get him. They all make mistakes some time.'

Moran was right. At two-thirty on Friday afternoon Wilson made his mistake. Disobeying all the rules, he left the barracks alone to buy a birthday card for his girlfriend in Liverpool. Moran spotted him, despite the anonymity his civilian clothes almost provided, and nudged McCluskey, pointing. 'There's your boyo.'

'Jesus!' McCluskey exclaimed. 'He's thicker than I thought.'

Moran drove the van slowly, keeping well behind the strolling figure, his face breaking into a wide grin as they saw him go into Gerry Carson's newsagents. He indicated and guided the van across the road, parking outside the shop.

'Let's do it,' McCluskey said urgently.

'No. Wait. Let that woman and kid come out first.'

The wait seemed interminable. The woman was dithering, pointing at something then changing her mind. They could see the activity clearly through the shop window, and both men sucked in their breath as they noted Wilson move to the counter, a card in his hand. For a second it looked as though he was going to be served first, but in the nick of time the woman made up her mind and made her purchase.

She had barely put foot on the pavement, dragging the child behind her, when McCluskey and Moran were out of the van and into the shop. With no hesitation McCluskey walked up behind the Corporal and gave him a viscious swipe on the head with a short, leather-covered cosh, catching him as he fell and immediately dragging him behind the counter.

'You didn't see that,' Moran told Gerry Carson.

'See what?'

Moran grinned.

'A Brit?' Carson asked.

'Yea. And a right bastard.'

'Aren't they all?'

'We'll need to leave him here for a few hours,' McCluskey put in.

Carson shrugged. 'There's a shed out the back.'

'Got any rope?'

Gerry Carson stared at them blearily. 'That's what I admire about you boys. So professional. Always prepared.'

'Fuck the crap,' McCluskey shouted. 'Got some rope?'

'There's a ball of strong plastic string in the shed.'

McCluskey and Moran manhandled the unconscious Wilson out through the back door and into the shed. They trussed him up like an oven-prepared chicken, and shoved an oily rag into his mouth, securing it there with a buckleless belt that hung from a nail.

86

The shop was still without a customer when they returned. Gerry Carson looked up from his paper. 'All done?'

McCluskey nodded. 'That back gate. Does it open?'

'It opens.'

'Leave it unlocked for us then. We'll be back later.'

'What's later?

'Later. He'll be gone by the morning.'

'Who will?' Carson asked, and went back to his paper.

McCluskey clasped his hands behind his head and lolled in his seat as the van moved across the city. Now for the bit he liked. Now they'd see if the famous Major was genuine or not. His eyes glazed over with cold, sadistic pleasure.

'You're quiet,' Moran observed.

McCluskey chuckled. 'You ever watch "the A Team"?'

'The kids do.'

'Well, I love it when a plan comes together,' McCluskey told him, finding his quotation hilarious, and bursting into laughter.

At eight o'clock Chris Fisher left the barracks and made his way on foot to what he always now thought of as Sandy's pub. He sensed, as he usually did, that he was being watched, but he knew he was safe enough: he would be safe as long as he was potentially useful. Nothing seemed untoward when he entered the pub: he got the same smile from Sandy; the usual pint was placed before him; none of the regulars gave him a second glance. It was not until twenty minutes later, when Sandy sidled along the bar towards him, that the feeling seemed about to be proven.

'You're wanted outside,' Sandy told him, comically using the side of his mouth.

'Outside?'

'Eddie.'

When he got outside he found Eddie waiting beside the open door of a small, dark-blue car, all smiles and friendliness. 'In you get,' he said, holding the door, and slamming it behind Fisher. Then he hopped into the car himself, sitting beside

Moran in the front. As the car moved off he turned in his seat, resting his arms on the back and his chin on his arms, staring pleasantly at Fisher.

'Where are we going?' Fisher asked reasonably enough.

'You'll see,' McCluskey told him. 'All in good time.'

As they reached the outskirts of the city Moran drove faster, leaning forward over the steering wheel. In ten minutes they were in the country and speeding down narrow lanes with high hedgerows either side, once sending a flock of furious starlings screaming into the sky, their slumber shattered. Then the car turned into a gateway, over some bumpy, muddy ground, and skidded to a halt outside a stone, windowless barn with a corrugated iron roof.

'Right,' McCluskey said. 'Out we get.'

Moran led the way to the barn door. He spent several seconds unlocking it, cursing to himself as the padlock refused to yield. When he finally got it open he signalled McCluskey and Fisher to wait by pushing the flat of one hand in their direction, and slipped in the barn alone. There was a clattering noise from inside as if someone had walked into and overturned a metal bucket; then a glimmer of light appeared. Gradually the light strengthened, and Moran's head appeared in the doorway. 'Come on,' he called.

It took a while for Fisher to accustom his eyes to the light; when he did, he was appalled by what he saw. The floor of the barn was of stamped earth. Four rafters supported the roof and from these three oil lamps, now lit, were suspended, giving the place an eerie, fearful look of sickness. A wooden box had been placed against the wall at the end, and on it sat a man, gagged and tied.

'Ungag the bastard,' McCluskey ordered, and Moran did as he was told.

Instantly the bound man tried to speak, but only an unintelligible squawk emerged. Swallowing hard the man tried to induce saliva into his throat. 'Major,' he cried finally.

Chris Fisher made to move closer, squinting to try and

88

identify the man. McCluskey grabbed him by the arm. 'You're fine right where you are,' he said.

'It's me, Major. Wilson,' the man called, sounding as though on the verge of panicky tears.

'Wilson! What – ' He rounded on McCluskey. 'What the hell is this all about?'

'It's about trust, Chris,' McCluskey informed him coldly, his familiarity sounded oddly out of place. 'We have to be sure that we can trust you, don't we? So, we want you to do a little job for us. Call it an initiation if you like,' he went on, taking a gun from his inside pocket. He held it out to Fisher, using both hands as if he were a second at some ceremonial duel. 'There's just one little bullet in it. We want you to use that bullet and kill him.'

Fisher felt rooted to the ground. He was certain he was going to vomit.

'I – ' he began.

'Now,' McCluskey went on in a steady matter-of-fact voice, 'in the gun that Pat has there are six bullets. If you happen to miss with your single bullet three of Pat's will go into that bastard, and the other three will go into you.'

Wilson rolled on his box, moaning.

Fisher shook his head. 'I can't shoot a man in cold blood. I – '

'It's up to you. He'll die anyway. We just want to know who's side you're on. I mean, we're not going to take the risk of lifting you if you're not with us all the way, are we? Here, take it.'

Chris Fisher took the gun in his hands, and stared at it.

'Don't kill me, Major. Please, Major. Oh, please, please, Major don't – '

'Shut that fucker up, will you,' McCluskey shouted.

Moran stood his ground. 'Get your man to shoot him – that'll soon shut him up.'

'You've got ten seconds,' McCluskey told Fisher, and pulled his shirt up on his wrist, studying his watch. 'Nine, eight, seven – '

Major Fisher felt himself starting to tremble. A horrible logic screamed at him that Wilson was doomed anyway. Fear screamed that he would die also. The word 'duty' loomed into his consciousness and he grabbed at it, using it to suffocate his fear. He had a mission to accomplish. He raised the gun and pointed it.

'Jesus don't, Major. For Christ's sake, Major. It's me. Wilson. Don't kill me. Please.'

' – three, two – '

Fisher fired. The mingled roar of the gun and Wilson's terrified scream created an appalling crashing wail. Wilson keeled over off his box and lay kicking and shaking pathetically on the ground. Fisher watched, mesmerised. He saw the kicks become little jerks and twitches, heard the gurgling, hollow cry of death. With one final heave, Wilson lay still.

'Just in time,' McCluskey said, tapping his watch, and using a tone that suggested a schoolmaster admonishing a recalcitrant pupil. 'You could have joined him in fairyland in another second,' he added, taking the gun from the Major. Then, sternly, he said: 'Let's get the hell out of here. It gives me the creeps.'

'What about him?' Moran wanted to know.

'What about him? Leave him there. Come on, for Christ's sake.'

In the back of the car, rushing back through the countryside, Fisher fought back the tears. Already shame was penetrating his soul; already the agony of sin was pummelling his mind.

The car came to an abrupt halt, and McCluskey turned his head. 'Here you are, Chris. Back home safe and sound. We'll meet in Sandy's tomorrow. Now that you're with us there's someone you have to meet.'

He clambered blindly out of the car, and trudged away down the street. He had no idea where he was. He did not care where he was. An ambulance raced by, keening, and, immediately the awful wails of Wilson hammered his brain.

'Funny boyo,' McCluskey said, watching the receding, hunched figure. 'He never even said goodnight,' he added, grinning.

'You're fucking evil,' Moran told him, driving on.

McCluskey lay back comfortably in the seat and smiled and smiled. Nice to see a plan come together.

Seamus Reilly listened attentively as Thomas Regan relayed the news. '. . .Waited in the van,' he was saying, 'until a woman and child came out. Then they both went into Carson's shop. Twenty minutes later they both came out. I left Dowling to follow them and checked out the shop myself. Carson was there reading his paper, but the man who went in before them was gone.'

'You're sure?'

'Certain. When Carson saw who I was he got jumpy but I didn't push him. I thought I better check with you first.'

Reilly nodded appreciatively. 'Go on.'

'Dowling followed them back to Moran's house. They stayed there until just after five. Then they drove back to Carson's. They went round the back though, and loaded what Dowling says was a sack of something into the back of the van. He couldn't get close enough to see properly without being spotted himself. Then they took off. That's when Dowling lost them. Evening traffic. It's hell, Mr Reilly.'

Accepting the traffic problems, Seamus Reilly asked: 'This man – the one you think they followed into Carson's – any idea who he was?'

'None. Possibly a Brit. Not from round here, that's for sure.'

'It wasn't that Fisher?'

'Oh no. O'Neill spotted him going into Sandy's this evening. He followed him in. Fisher just had a drink as usual,' Regan said, and then started to shuffle his feet and look uneasy.

Reilly knew the signs. 'Go on, Thomas. Tell me. What happened?' he asked his voice filled with resignation.

'O'Neill went for a pee. When he came out Fisher was gone. His drink was still on the bar. O'Neill went outside and searched up and down the street. Nothing. He must have gone off in a car.'

Reilly nodded. 'That's what I was afraid of.' He stood up and

91

started pacing the room, thinking. He came to a halt by the window, and, staring out he said: 'Right, Thomas. Nine o'clock tomorrow morning I want you to pick up Carson and bring him to the piggery. At ten o'clock tell Dowling to get Sandy and bring *him* to the piggery. I want to find out what's happening.'

'Right, Mr Reilly.'

'And no excuses this time. No traffic problems and no kidney problems.'

'No, Mr Reilly.'

'Good.'

John Asher saw the report minutes after it was passed to the RUC. The unexplained disappearance of any British soldier was a matter of concern and, despite the hostility that existed between them the army always informed the RUC on such matters. Asher's first reaction was to wonder if this Wilson could be the deserter Reilly had mentioned, until he remembered the name given had been Fisher, and that he had been a Major and no mere Corporal. Still, no harm would be done by a word with Reilly: it was always possible (barely but possible) that Reilly had got it wrong: despite his reputation of infallibility he had been known to make the odd mistake.

So, immediately he got home he phoned Seamus Reilly, carefully rehearsing his words as he waited for him to answer. As soon as he heard Reilly's customary monosyllabic 'Yes?' he asked: 'Seamus – you're sure the name was Fisher?'

'Certain.'

'Oh.'

'Why?'

'And you haven't been up to any skullduggery that I don't know about?'

'Probably,' Reilly said. 'Why?' he asked again.

'Soldier gone missing this afternoon.'

'Oh, dear,' Reilly sighed, but not overly concerned.

'Left his barracks at two-thirty and not been seen since.'

'More than likely he's drunk and shacked up somewhere.'

'No,' Asher said. 'At least it's most unlikely. The report says

92

that just before he left he told someone he was just nipping out to get a birthday card for his girlfriend. There's a newsagents just up the road from the barracks. That's where he said he was going.'

Reilly felt a tingle running down his spine. 'You wouldn't know the name of the shop?'

'No. Not off-hand. Why? Seamus – you *do* know something. I can tell.'

'No, John. I don't *know* anything. But – look, can we meet tomorrow afternoon?'

'Yes – no. Not in the afternoon. I've got to pick up Maddox at the airport. The evening?'

'About seven?'

'Yes.'

'The usual place, then. Leave your house at six-forty and I'll arrange security.'

'Right. And I expect you to tell me everything. Don't start buggering me about.'

Reilly laughed. 'Not everything, John. You know we never tell each other *everything*.'

'You know what I mean.'

'Oh I know what you mean all right. See you tomorrow evening.'

' 'Till this evening.'

'Hang on a tick. You couldn't give me a rough description of this missing soldier, could you?'

John Asher thought for a moment, trying to see the report in his mind's eye, trying to recall the image on the small photograph stapled to one corner. 'Mid-twenties. Five foot ten – I think. Clean shaven. Mousey hair. Heavy build. One thing: from the photo it looked like he had no neck.

'Right. Thanks. I'll see what I can have for you by tomorrow night. But don't expect miracles.'

'I never do.'

Seamus Reilly kept the telephone receiver in his hand, using one finger to disconnect the line. Then he dialled another number, nimbly lighting a cigar while he waited. 'Thomas? Seamus Reilly.'

93

'Yes, Mr Reilly?' Thomas Regan answered, sounding apprehensive.

'The man McCluskey and Moran followed into Carson's papershop – mid-twenties, five foot ten, brownish hair, short-necked – could that be him?'

'It could be, Mr Reilly. I only saw the back of him and he was sort of hunched up. He had one of those zip-up jackets on with his hands in the pockets.'

'I see. But it *could* have been him.'

'It could have been.'

'Right. Now one more thing. Mr Asher is meeting me tomorrow evening. He'll be leaving his home at six-forty. See to it that he arrives at the safe house in one piece.'

'Certainly, Mr Reilly.'

'I'll see you in the morning at the piggery. It's more important than ever now that I speak to Carson.'

'I'll have him there.'

'Good. Goodnight.'

Colonel Matthew Maddox mournfully eyed the suitcase on his bed. It was already packed: only his shaving gear and toothbrush remained to be added in the morning. Beside it was a framed photograph, a book, and a sheaf of papers. Reaching down he picked up the photograph and studied it. How young and resplendent he looked in his ceremonial uniform, how full of hope and promise he seemed, smiling broadly as if the whole world stretched out before him and the young woman on his arm. And how soon it had all collapsed! The childless marriage had been little more than a supreme act of tolerance, and his career – well, the less said about that the better. The trouble was that he had been born into the wrong age. He belonged, he assured himself, to an age of chivalry. And here he was heading for the one place where honour was a dirty word, where intrigue and double-dealing were the norm. Yet he had found a curious contentment in that sorrowful place. It was as though lost souls had congregated there, using each other and the battered streets to play out the desolation of their lives, always hoping that from somewhere peace and happiness would come. That, of course, was what kept everyone sane: the hope. And there was hope was there not? As long as man breathed there was hope.

Carefully he put the papers and the book (a shabby, leather-bound volume, gold-embossed, but with the gilt so wasted the title was illegible) into the case. Then he stood up again and returned the photograph to its perch on the chest of drawers, as though by deliberately leaving the picture behind he was ridding himself of some oppressive obligation.

'How did it go?' the woman asked.

'He did it,' McCluskey told her. 'I told you he was all right.'

'You gave him the gun and he did it. Just like that? No hesitation? No argument?' the woman wanted to know.

'Hell, of course he didn't *want* to do it. I thought he was going to puke all over the place. But he did it. Shit, you should have heard that sod screaming for mercy.'

The information on Fisher's reluctance seemed to put the woman's mind at rest. 'What about the body?'

'We left it there.'

The woman frowned. 'I suppose that's all right.'

'Sure,' McCluskey assured her. 'Nobody'll find it for weeks. Months.'

'When have you arranged to see Fisher again?'

'Tomorrow evening.'

'Good. What time?'

'No particular time. I just said at Sandy's. He's usually there at about eight.'

'I'd better meet him. When he arrives give me a ring at home. Then we can meet here.'

'Right. Hey, what if something happens and he can't make it?'

'That's your problem. He's your baby.'

Chris Fisher awoke from a nightmare wherein he was being clawed to death by a flock of furious starlings, their screams of anger identical to that awful noise the gun and Wilson's cries of terror had made. The light from the corridor outside, permanently ablaze, shone through the small glass rectangle above the door, covering the wall opposite in a dull, yellow glow. Christ on His crucifix cast a shadow twice His size, the shadowy arms no longer seeming to be nailed to the cross but reaching out and down. A heavy vehicle, a Saracen probably, lumbered to a halt outside, its threatening weight shaking the wall, and the shadow moved. Instinctively Fisher recoiled. 'Oh, Jesus,' he moaned. 'Oh Jesus, forgive me.'

· TEN ·

ON SATURDAY MORNING Seamus Reilly was up with the birds. Indeed, their half-hearted, September-time dawn chorus had only just started by the time he had reached the bathroom and begun to shave. He loathed shaving, mostly because he usually nicked himself but he had to go through the routine, sometimes twice a day: his black beard satanic if not shorn to the roots regularly. He chose his clothes carefully: the piggery was not the most pleasant of places, and he dressed accordingly: a roll-neck sweater, a pair of tweed-like trousers, stout shoes. Then he went downstairs, ticking off in his mind the items on the day's agenda. It had all the prospects of being an interesting day.

In the kitchen he went through his morning ceremony: percolating his coffee (a mixture of Kenya and Brazil in equal parts) and toasting his bread, setting a tray and carrying the lot into the sitting room. He was just finishing when he heard his car arrive. By the time his driver inserted his key in the door Seamus Reilly was in the hall, his overcoat already on, his hat in his hand.

'Good morning, Mr Reilly. I didn't keep you waiting?'

97

'Morning, Danny. No. Timed it to perfection, you did.'

The trip to the piggery did not take long: it could have taken less but Reilly did not enjoy fast driving. He used the isolation of his car as a sanctuary for quiet thoughts, and he illogically felt that the speeding engine would hustle him into making errors. There was, of course, another reason: he liked to be seen by his people as he was driven along. He believed this was important. So many upheavals had taken place within the community over the years, so many people had been arrested, or been killed, or simply disappeared, that his constant visible presence gave a continuum to the Organization. He was seen to be there; there to be spoken to, to be consulted, to give advice, to solve problems. Nobody had ever dared actually stop his car to avail themself of his largesse, but they all felt they could if needs be.

The piggery was about eight miles from Clones, across the border: sixty acres of arable land purchased with IRA funds, and farmed legitimately and profitably by a Provo of unquestionable loyalty. Behind the farmhouse itself, and forming part of a quadrangle of out-buildings, was a long, low building. It was the old slaughter house, no longer used. Inside it stank. Traces of blood from the hundreds, perhaps thousands of pigs that had been killed and disembowelled there were splattered on the floor and walls. A single naked bulb hung from the ceiling, and a long line of vicious meat hooks dangled from a metal rail that ran the length of the shed. The sheer gruesomeness of the place had its advantages: it terrified the people who were summoned there, and it was for this reason that Reilly used it when he wanted answers quickly. One such person, already scared out of his wits, was there by the time Seamus arrived.

'Ah,' Reilly said, wrinkling his nose at the stench, 'Mr Carson,' he added politely. 'Thank you for coming.'

Gerry Carson held his tongue, his wide eyes rolling.

'I'm sure you'll want to get back to your business as soon as possible so I'll be brief. Mr Regan here tells me there was a little – eh – a little episode at your shop yesterday?'

98

Carson glanced from Reilly to Regan, and then down at his feet.

Unperturbed Reilly continued quietly, keeping his voice calm and reasonable. 'I believe three men went into your shop but only two came out. I was hoping, Mr Carson, that you could explain this somewhat extraordinary situation to me.'

Gerry Carson decided to bluff. 'The three of them went out, Mr Reilly. Honest, the three of – '

Seamus Reilly held up his hand. 'No, Mr Carson. Two came out. And immediately after they came out Mr Regan went in. There was no sign of the other man. Now please explain.'

'Maybe – ' Carson started, but that was as far as he got with his hopeful hypothesis.

'Dammit, Carson,' Reilly snapped, 'don't try and treat me like a fool. I haven't all day to waste on the likes of you. Now what happened?'

Foolishly, Carson looked as if he might be about to attempt yet another diversionary tack. Immediately Reilly gave a little flick of his wrist and Thomas Regan moved forward menacingly. 'All right. All right,' Carson said, holding out both hands in a plea for restraint. 'This fella came in. Never seen him before. Then two of your men came in. They hit him on the head and knocked him cold. Knowing they were from you, Mr Reilly, I didn't like to say anything. I mean, I don't interfere where I don't belong. They said they wanted to dump him with me for a couple of hours so I told them they could leave him in the shed at the back. That's all I know. I don't even know when they took him away. All I know is that he wasn't there this morning.'

'The two men who you say were from me, did they say they were from me?'

Carson frowned, thinking. 'Well, no, Mr Reilly. But everyone knows that Eddie McCluskey and Pat Moran are with you.'

'Do they now,' Reilly said ominously. 'Did they happen to mention *where* they would be taking him after they collected him?'

Carson shook his head. 'No. Definitely not, Mr Reilly. I'm positive about that.'

Reilly fixed the man with a withering, prodding gaze. He decided to believe him. 'Right, Carson, you can go. Mr Regan will drive you back. Just one thing – and remember it well: you have not spoken to me. If either McCluskey or Moran should contact you again nobody has questioned you.'

'I'll remember that, Mr Reilly.'

'Do,' Reilly warned. 'Be very sure you do. And also, you get in touch with Mr Regan if they come back.' He turned away and walked across the shed to the enormous wooden scraping block that stood in one corner. 'Take him home, Thomas,' he said without turning round. 'Take him out of my sight.'

Alone, Reilly took to pacing the shed, his head bowed, his hands clasped behind his back. So far so good. McCluskey and Moran were definitely involved in some sort of kidnapping. Seamus felt a cold shiver down his spine. Already he suspected the reason and it horrified him: if correct it was a system of proving trustworthiness that he had always found repellent. And it was usually self-defeating in his experience: even those who could have been trusted veered away and became suspicious as hatred took over from the pangs of conscience, a deep-rooted loathing for those who had humiliated them and shown them their weaknesses, had demonstrated man's bitter attachment to himself even at the cost of another's life.

Reilly stopped for a moment and cocked his head on one side. He heard the car door slam, and he moved back towards the door. He was leaning against the wall, his hands now deep in his pockets, his ankles crossed when Jim Dowling pushed Sandy into the barn before him and into the centre under the light.

'Sorry to drag you here, Sandy,' Reilly apologized from the shadows.

Sandy swung round. He was sweating and he used his two pudgy hands to wipe his face. 'Oh. Mr Reilly.'

'Yes. Sorry about this. A few questions, that's all. This

deserter – Fisher – that we've been interested in . . . we haven't been able to locate him?'

Sandy looked relieved. 'You know, I was going to try and contact you about that, Mr Reilly. I said to myself last night when it happened "I'll have to contact Mr Reilly about that".'

'Very commendable, Sandy. About what?'

'Fisher. He was in the pub last night. Then about a quarter past eight Eddie McCluskey stuck his head in the door and told me to send him out.'

'And you sent him out?'

'I did, Mr Reilly.'

Reilly glared at Dowling.

'Why the hell didn't you tell me that last night?' Dowling demanded.

'I didn't get the chance, did I?' Sandy defended himself. 'You came out of the piss house and you were out the door like a scalded cat.'

'Do you know where they went?' Reilly interrupted.

'No idea, Mr Reilly. But I can find that out for you easy enough if you want me to. Someone's bound to know. Someone knows everything in my pub.'

'Thank you, Sandy. I *would* be obliged. Find out where they went and get in touch with Jim here, will you? I would like to know as soon as possible.'

'With a bit of luck I'll know by tonight, Mr Reilly.'

'That would be appreciated.'

'Anything to help.'

Reilly gave him a sceptical look. 'Take Sandy back, will you, Jim?'

Reilly waited until he heard the car drive away before leaving the shed. His driver was waiting, the car door open. He noted Reilly's satisfied look. 'Everything went well, Mr Reilly?'

'Yes,' Reilly said curtly, getting into the car, waiting until they were heading back along the country road before adding. 'Everything went well. At least, it went well for me.'

From another direction another car was heading for the city. It was a military car but unmarked. Colonel Maddox and Inspector Asher sat together in the back seat, each staring out of his own window. Some moments earlier Asher had asked the Colonel how he liked being back in Belfast, more by way of conversation than anything else, and was waiting for a reply. He had all but abandoned getting one when the Colonel said: 'You really want to know?'

'Well – yes.'

'I feel frightened to death,' the Colonel confessed.

'Things *have* improved since you were here last, Colonel.'

The Colonel gave a short laugh. 'Not that sort of fear, John. Not fear for myself. I am afraid for others. Every time I've been here I have been surrounded by tragedy and sorrow. It follows me. It haunts me. I'm afraid I'm the ill wind that bears nobody good.'

'Nonsense,' Asher said sharply. 'You are – '

' – surrounds you,' the Colonel was saying perhaps to himself.

'I wouldn't let it worry you, Colonel,' Asher said, trying to sound jovial. 'You're almost one of us now.'

The Colonel turned his head. 'That's what does worry me, John. I'm starting to look at death and tragedy through distorted eyes, seeing them as the norm rather than the exception. How *do* you live with it all the time?'

'The same way people live with other afflictions – poverty, disease, racist attacks. After a while you don't notice that they are in any way extraordinary. Indeed, here, when everything is quiet and peaceful we tend to worry since we know it only means the explosion, when it comes, will be all the worse.'

The Colonel was shaking his head. 'You make it sound as though you're fighting a losing battle.'

'Of course we are. Every schoolchild knows that. There is not and never will be a solution here.'

'How sad,' the Colonel remarked. 'How very sad.'

The car braked sharply and turned left: the men swayed in their seat. Suddenly Asher chuckled. 'They've given you your old office back. It will be like old times coming to see you there.'

'As bad as that?'

Asher's chuckle became a laugh. 'They weren't *that* bad, Colonel. I was talking to Reilly the other day and he's pleased you've come back. I'm damned if I know why, but he actually likes you.'

Perhaps Asher's humour was infectious because the Colonel tried a small jest. 'I'm a very likeable chap,' he said. 'How is the dreadful Reilly anyway?'

'As dreadful as ever. Actually, I think you'll find he's mellowed quite a lot. We get on very well together – unofficially, you understand.'

'Of course.'

'We sometimes joke that if the two of us were left alone we could come close to a solution. As Reilly always says, we're just a couple of old sods trying to do what we think is right. I suspect you'll be seeing quite a lot of him.'

'Oh? Why should that be?'

Asher sucked in his breath aware that he had gaffed. Using the driver as an excuse he said quietly, with a jerk of his head: 'Not here, Colonel. We can discuss that later.'

'I don't – '

Asher held a warning finger to his lips. 'Later.'

And later, in the Colonel's office, Asher was forced to return to the subject despite hoping Maddox would have forgotten about it by then.

The two men sat opposite each other across the desk, both with a drink in their hands. It was, indeed, like old times. The Colonel had insisted on going straight to his office, and had produced the bottle from his briefcase, holding it up mischievously. 'We always had a drink together, didn't we?' he asked.

'Nearly always.'

'Well, we better start off on the right foot.'

Now, sipping their drinks they allowed the room to grow dark about them. Asher was feeling rested and relaxed for the first time in ages when the Colonel blundered into his tranquillity. 'Why did you say I'd be seeing a lot of Reilly?' he wanted to know.

'Because we're – Reilly and me – we're co-operating . . . . Look, Colonel, we know quite well why you've been sent.'

The Colonel looked disbelieving and amused. 'Do you, indeed?'

Asher nodded.

'Tell me.'

Asher hesitated, but not for long. 'You've been sent so that a certain – shall we say person? – can contact you with information.'

Maddox now looked less amused.

'In fact, I can tell you quite a lot about what has been going on – all of which Reilly knows. Indeed, most of it came from him.'

Colonel Maddox looked decidedly worried.

'You want me to be frank, Colonel?'

The Colonel nodded.

'Fisher. Major Fisher. Mean anything?'

'My God,' the Colonel whispered. 'You *do* know. Nobody apart from myself is supposed to know about that here.'

Asher beamed. 'Don't look so worried. We've known for months. Fisher doesn't move without being watched. By the way – he's made contact. Things could be hotting up soon.'

Colonel Maddox stood up and clasped his hands behind his head. He stared at the ceiling and demanded: 'What in the name of hell am *I* doing here if everybody knows?'

'*I* can't answer that, Colonel. Mind you, the clever chaps in London don't know that we know.'

'They'll know damn soon,' Maddox snapped, and moved towards the phone on his desk.

John Asher reached out and caught his hand. 'Just before you do that, Colonel, there are one or two other things you should know.'

For what seemed a very long time the two men remained frozen, Asher still holding the Colonel's hand. The Colonel was the first to move: he withdrew his hand and straightened up, keeping an eye on Asher all the while, and then sat down heavily. 'It's starting again, isn't it, John? The intrigue.'

'It never stops, Colonel. Just listen to me a minute. Before you alert London I think you should speak to Reilly. I'll be speaking to him tonight about another matter – about a Corporal who has disappeared – and I can set up a meeting for tomorrow morning. When you've spoken to him if you still want to inform London –' Asher shrugged – 'I won't try and stop you.'

'Corporal who's disappeared?' the Colonel asked, bewildered.

'Don't concern yourself with that for the moment, Colonel. That's being dealt with. What about Reilly? Will you meet with him?'

Maddox sighed. 'You seem to think I should.'

'I know you should.'

'Very well. Tomorrow morning.'

At four o'clock the patrol moved into the Shankhill Road. Within minutes the area was saturated with troops, toms kneeling and lying in every corner, crouched in doorways, making sure the locals were aware of their presence. Major Fisher was in command of what all the soldiers knew was nothing but another futile, token exercise; they followed a procedure that would yield nothing and make them more hated than they already were. The Shankhill Road today, somewhere else tomorrow, democratically alternating their harassment between Protestant and Catholic so that it would appear they were impartial. It was always the same: line the bastards up against the wall in long rows, their legs spread, keep them there, waiting. The junior officers seemed to enjoy this: they strutted up and down the line of spreadeagled bodies, relishing their moment of power, their superiors not interfering, seeing the random pounding of someone's kidneys as harmless, as 'good training', as toughening the men up.

That afternoon was no different. Major Fisher moved down the line carrying out lengthy P checks and asking detailed questions, hoping someone would say something out of place. They never did. They were either defiantly dumb or exaggeratedly polite, and Fisher could see in their eyes the loathing and contempt, the smirky insolence that was a far cry from the fear and intimidation the military presence was supposed to induce. As he moved down the line he felt a terrible rage building up within him, a hatred for these incomprehensible people, for the army, but mostly for himself. For God, too, who had allowed him get conned into –

'Sir?'

Fisher swung round.

'There's nothing here. Can we let them go?'

Fisher nodded. 'Yes, Lieutenant, let them go.'

'You all right, sir?'

'Of course I'm all right.'

He watched the men straighten up from the wall, rubbing their hands together, filing away. When they reached the end of the street and out of harm's way the jeers and catcalls would come: 'Fucking English pigs youse animals, sons o' fucking bitches! Murdering Brit bastards!' Fisher winced.

And then it was the bumpy, uncomfortable haul back to the barracks, the men yawning and exhausted, talking to each other in undertones about what they would most like to do to the crummy shits who called them names; or just sitting there, their heads in their hands, longing to be far, far away from it all, away from the degradation and insults, away from the stupid wastefulness of it all.

Fisher threw himself on his bunk bed and covered his eyes with his arm. Suddenly, for the first time in his life although he had thought he had experienced it before, he knew the real meaning of loneliness, an isolation penetrated by appalling visions and shattered by terrible screams, his own silent, piercing screams melded with those of a short-necked ghost whose petrified eyes bore into his very soul and focused towards an unhearing God.

Reilly listened to Thomas Regan, his lips pursed, a satisfied twinkle in his eye that the little pep-talk he had had with Sandy in the morning had borne fruit so rapidly.

'– so I went out there with O'Neill,' Regan was saying.

'And?'

'Oh, he was there all right, Mr Reilly. Dead as a dodo. One shot did it. Bang in the heart.'

Reilly nodded. 'Poor bastard,' he said, sounding uncharacteristically sympathetic. 'What did you do with the body?'

'We have that. In the lock-up.'

Reilly nodded again, approvingly. 'Good. Keep it there. I'll tell you what to do with it.'

'That's what I thought, Mr Reilly. I was sure you'd have some use for it.'

Seamus Reilly ignored the statement. He drummed his fingers on his knee, frowning. 'I think,' he said finally, 'I think we better have this Fisher character in. But be careful, Thomas. I don't want them to know about it. Pick him up when you can – as soon as possible, but *do* be careful. They're bound to be buzzing around him now so it won't be all that easy.'

'Leave it to me, Mr Reilly. We're having him watched every time he leaves the barracks. We'll pick our time.'

'Good.'

Later, dressed suitably for the children's concert he had been invited to attend, Reilly met Asher. 'Your Corporal has been found,' he said.

'Where?'

'That's not important, John. He's dead. Shot.'

'Shit,' Asher swore, and made Reilly wince at his vulgarity. 'Where is his body?'

'We have it now. I want to talk to you about that.'

'I'm listening.'

'Not now. Tomorrow.'

'Ah, tomorrow. I've arranged a meet between you and Maddox for tomorrow, Seamus.'

'He's here?'

'You must be slipping. Yes, he's here. Came in this afternoon. It's important that the three of us talk.'

'If you say so.'

'Tomorrow morning. Eleven?'

'Yes. Where?'

'His office, I thought. Bring back memories for you. They've given him the same one he had.'

'You'll arrange things?'

'Of course. You'll be as safe as a match in a glacier.'

Reilly snorted. 'How is he?'

'The same as ever. Older, of course. But just the same.'

'He must be the only one who is.'

'He doesn't live here.'

Reilly gave a short laugh. 'Too true. Well, I must go. I'll see you in the morning. Who knows what will have happened by them?'

'What does that mean?' Asher asked, immediately suspicious.

'Just what it says.'

There was now no turning back; the murder of his colleague had seen to that. Chris Fisher trudged towards Sandy's pub. It had also broken him, wrapping his spirit in dread, his conscience branded and searing in pain. The only redemption lay, he now thought, in seeing the awful business through, if only to give his cruel act some meaning acceptable to whoever judged such things.

It was after eight when he arrived at the bar. Moran and McCluskey were waiting for him at one of the tables. McCluskey waved him over. 'We thought maybe you weren't coming.'

'I'm here.'

'Yea,' McCluskey agreed, staring hard at his eyes. 'You want a drink?'

Fisher nodded.

'What?'

'Anything.'

McCluskey grinned. 'A whisky here, Sandy,' he shouted. 'A double.'

Fisher lowered his drink in one swallow, shivering as the liquid burned its way down inside him, aware that the two men were studying him. It was time to start acting again. He put down his glass and smiled broadly. 'I needed that.'

'Yea, well, we had to be sure,' McCluskey put in. Then: 'Ready?' he asked, standing up.

They left the bar, McCluskey leading the way, then Fisher, Moran bringing up the rear.

As Moran started the car, McCluskey leaned across. 'Just another little precaution,' he said, producing a black scarf from under the seat and tying it securely about Fisher's eyes. 'We still have to be a bit careful, you know. Not that we don't trust you. But the less you know the less you'll be able to tell if the Brits find out.'

They drove in silence for about half a mile, taking a circuitous route into Andersonstown. Once Moran muttered. 'Shit!', his eyes flicking to the mirror above his head, then back to the road, then onto the mirror again. Then: 'It's okay,' he said, sounding relieved. 'I thought for a sec we were being followed, but it's turned off.' Without further incident they reached the sweet-shop and went inside. The door had been closed behind them a matter of seconds when a Range Rover drove past, turned down a side street, and parked.

Fisher blinked in the light, and rubbed one of his eyes, allowing Moran to guide him into a hard-backed kitchen chair. 'This is him,' McCluskey said.

The woman stood up and walked across the room, standing directly behind Fisher. 'So you're the one who wants to desert,' she said, not sounding particularly pleased.

'Yes,' Fisher said.

The woman made a clucking noise. 'What makes you think we'd want the likes of you?'

Fisher turned his head and looked up into the woman's face. 'I just hoped you would.'

'What good could you think you'd be?'

Fisher shrugged. 'I didn't think,' he answered, and made to stand up. 'If you can't – '

'Sit down,' the woman ordered. 'It so happens you might be useful. Stay on at the barracks for the time being. Just do what you always do. When we're ready for you, we'll let you know. You won't have to wait that long.'

Fisher nodded.

Now the woman walked slowly round until she was facing him. She leaned down and looked hard into his eyes. For several seconds she stared, saying nothing, almost as if she was daring him to flinch from her gaze. Still unblinking she said: 'And don't ever try and get cute, sonny,' she warned. 'One hint to me that you're playing us for fools and you're as dead as that bastard you killed yesterday.' Then she straightened up and moved away, arching her back, and caressing the nape of her neck with one hand. 'Take him back, Pat, will you. Let Eddie stay a while. I want a quick word with him.'

Patrick Moran guided Fisher out the door and closed it behind them. But he did not immediately start down the stairs. He lingered by the door, ostensibly to light a cigarette, taking his time about it, his head almost touching the woodwork of the door. Fisher watched him, and instinctively listened. At first there were just a few muttered words from McCluskey: nothing distinguishable. Then the woman took over. She seemed to be pacing the room as her voice came in waves although little of what she said seemed important at the moment. ' – do for Brighton – ' was one thing. ' – toffee Brit accent – ' was another. By then Moran, it seemed, had heard enough and he pushed Fisher ahead of him down the stairs.

'Where d'you want me to drop you?' was what Moran wanted to know.

'Anywhere. Near Sandy's will do.'

Moran obliged and dropped him outside the pub, driving off quickly without another word, without even noticing the Range Rover pulling into the parking space he had just vacated.

Seamus Reilly was peeved that he had to get dressed again. He had thoroughly enjoyed the concert, and had returned home at about nine-thirty, delighted with the opportunity of an early night. Twenty minutes later the phone by his bed rang. It was Thomas Regan. Did Mr Reilly want to see that soldier Fisher right away. Very well. Would he bring him round now? Right, Mr Reilly. Yes, he would take every precaution that the Major had no idea where he was taken to.

By the time Regan arrived, Reilly was dressed again. He had drawn the curtains in his sitting room, put the few family photographs into a drawer, switched on one bar of the electric fire, and poured himself a drink. Not that he wanted a drink: he wanted something for his hands to do. He would, under normal circumstances, simply have smoked, but he was trying to abandon the habit, albeit none too successfully. He opened the front door and signalled Regan to take the blindfolded Fisher into the sitting room by flapping his hand in that direction. Then he followed them in and closed the door. 'Take that thing off,' he told Regan. 'Yes, Mr – sir,' Regan said, and removed the blindfold.

Seamus Reilly studied the man before him. How inoffensive the poor creature looked! And probably, at another time, he was. Despite his innate dislike of the British Army, Reilly felt genuine sympathy for the young man. He was, he recognized, just a pawn. An innocent of sorts. He held out the palm of his hand indicating an armchair. 'Please, Major.'

Fisher looked taken aback, but sat down obediently.

'You've had a difficult few days,' Reilly observed. 'A drink, perhaps?'

Major Fisher shook his head. 'Thank you.'

Not offended, Reilly sipped his own drink for a few seconds, gathering his thoughts. 'Well, now, we have a problem here, do we not?' he asked in a chatty, friendly voice. 'I'm afraid you're rather in over your head, Major. And I'll bet they never told you in London that you might have to prove yourself by shooting one of your colleagues.'

A flicker of consternation passed over Fisher's face.

Reilly beamed. 'Oh you don't have to worry about the fact

that we know,' he explained. 'It's our business to know. It might set your mind at rest to tell you that we had a file on you before you ever set foot in Belfast. Dear me, dear me,' Reilly scolded himself, 'I haven't even told you who we are. Well, Major, let me just say that I am one of your real terrorists. Not one of those petty little gangsters you've got yourself mixed up with. I am the real thing,' he concluded dramatically, smiling happily at his little pomposity, pausing in case the Major wanted to say something, but not at all nonplussed when nothing was forthcoming. 'To come to the point,' he went on. 'As I see it you have two choices. One, you can help me. Two, you can, as they say, prepare to meet your Maker. And I suggest you consider the first as the better alternative. All *I* will want from you is information, and only information about the thugs you were with earlier. Nothing treasonable. You can't call that too unreasonable, can you?'

Fisher looked towards Regan as if for confirmation of Reilly's good intent, and was met with a blank stare. 'How do I – '

Reilly made a pained expression. 'You don't know, Major,' he interrupted. 'But let me put it this way. If I wanted you out of the way I could quite simply have you shot. If I wanted you discredited – well, you can believe me I have enough ways of letting the army know we're onto you to render you useless. And if *I* want information about the army I don't have to rely on someone like you who has just arrived.' Reilly let the message sink in, swirling the drink in his glass. 'For a start,' he finally went on, 'who did you go to see tonight?'

Fisher wet his lips. 'I don't know.'

'That's not an auspicious start, Major.'

'It's the truth. I don't know. Some woman.'

'Ah. A tall lady with long reddish hair, quite pretty?'

'Yes.'

'Excellent. There you are. That wasn't hard, was it? Now, what did she say to you?'

Fisher frowned. 'Not much. She wanted to know why I thought I would be useful to her. Then she said I might be useful and told me to carry on as usual until they were ready to contact me.'

'And that was all?'

'Yes.'

Reilly glanced towards Regan.

Regan nodded. 'He was only in there a few minutes – sir.'

'Did she say anything to the two men while you were there?'

'No – yes – not exactly.'

Reilly made a face to suggest his patience was running out. 'Which is it, Major?'

'Not when I was in the room. When the fat one – Pat – took me out of the room to drive me back he stopped outside the door to light a cigarette. I heard a few words. They didn't mean anything, though.'

'What few words did you hear, Major?' Reilly coaxed, leaning forward, his eyes dancing.

'Two things. The first sounded like "do for Brighton" but I can't be sure. And then "toffee Brit accent". That's all.'

'Now think, Major. Are you certain it was "do for Brighton"?'

'No. I'm not. I just said I wasn't sure.'

'All right. Was it definitely Brighton that was mentioned?'

Fisher frowned. Then he nodded. 'Yes. I'm pretty sure it was Brighton, but the rest – well, it doesn't make sense, does it, "do for Brighton"?'

Seamus Reilly was on his feet now, standing with his back to the fire, staring at the ceiling. Brighton. What in the name of God could be so interesting about Brighton? Suddenly he snorted. The bastards were probably planning a dirty weekend. Herself and McCluskey off to rut. 'Right,' Reilly said. 'From now on, Major, you'll be working for us. This gentleman here will be in touch with you regularly. I want you to carry on your little game with the others but you will tell us everything that transpires. I want to know every single word that you hear. In return we will help you. We will, in the first instance, see that no harm comes to you personally, and we will also allow you to pass on some of the information you glean to your superiors.

That seems fair to me. If you try to double-cross me, however – well, let me say that your lady friend will seem like Saint Bernadette, and her two henchmen as mild and harmless as Tweedledum and Tweedledee. Do I make myself clear?'

Fisher nodded. He was out of his depth and sinking fast. The imagined glories of espionage were rapidly becoming sordid and cruddy. There was no one he could turn to. The promised contact had not yet emerged, and he was suddenly gripped by the fear that he had been abandoned, that *they* already knew he had murdered Wilson and had disowned him. And it was possibly this dreadful sense of isolation that made him see Reilly's pedantic reasonableness in a new light. Somehow, the small, quiet-spoken man sitting across from him seemed totally trustworthy, the more so when he added. 'You can think of me as your guardian angel from now on. Just go about your duties and everything will work out in the end. One thing I can promise you: the end isn't as far away as you might think,' Reilly concluded.

· ELEVEN ·

SEAMUS REILLY WENT to early Mass, and was home again shortly before nine o'clock. He made himself a pot of fresh coffee, and settled down with the Sunday papers before he left for his meeting with Asher and Colonel Maddox. He found it impossible to concentrate, abandoning his reading, tossing the papers onto the floor beside him. He leaned back in his chair, his eyes closed. It was undoubtedly curious how Colonel Maddox and his paths continued to cross: their lives would touch briefly, the one never quite outwitting the other, yet forced, in the end, to call the game a draw. *The end isn't as far away as you might think.* For some reason his words of the night before repeated themselves in his brain. He shuddered. Dealing in death made it no easier to accept the imminence of one's own. He stood up and walked to the window, staring out. That was the saddest thing: death was so constant here, so familiar, that when someone died within days it was as if he had never lived, taking with him into the cold, unfriendly ground all memory of his life so that in the twinkling of an eye his existence was erased from the earth.

His mournful thoughts pursued him as he drove later

through the deserted streets. That was, of course, the most appalling aspect of it all: the wastefulness. The continuous, unrelenting wastefulness of young lives. The unlamented heroes — where had that phrase come from? Reilly looked puzzled for a moment, then brightened. Declan Tuohy. If only he had stayed! What was it he had written?

Like small unwanted creatures of the night
They crawl to hiding places in deep shadows,
There to curl in upon their loneliness and die
Not knowing why their screaming souls fly unheralded
Towards an angry Christ, then driven to an awful place
Devised for unlamented heroes.

'Will I drive in or stop here, Mr Reilly?'
' – ? What?'
'Do you want me to drive in or stop here?' the driver asked again.

Out of the window, Reilly spotted Mr Asher waiting for him on the footpath and noted the absence of obvious military presence. 'You can pull in here.'

Asher came across to the car, rubbing his hands as though to warm them. 'On time as usual,' he remarked. 'Parky this morning.'

Together they walked through the high, metal gates, and past the guards who made no attempt to hinder them. 'Into the lion's den,' Reilly remarked facetiously as they climbed the stairs.

'Hm. A dozing lion, however,' Asher said.
'Let's hope we don't startle him into full awareness then.'

Colonel Maddox, however, seemed bent on lending the lie to their approximation of him. He looked anything but dozy. His eyes were bright and excited. He rose to his feet as the two men came in, tapping the palms of his hands together as though applauding, then motioning Asher and Reilly towards the two chairs drawn up close to his desk. 'The terrible twins,' he observed lightheartedly.

Although not too amused Reilly managed a weak smile, while Asher looked embarrassed, hiding his feelings by lighting one of the black cigarettes he preferred. After a short cough he said, if only to break the silence: 'Not so terrible, Colonel.'

Maddox eyed them for a second. 'Perhaps not,' he conceded. Then, directing his full attention to Reilly, he continued: 'Mr Asher thinks we need to talk.'

'Mr Asher is usually right,' Reilly said.

'Indeed,' the Colonel agreed. 'That's why – that's why we're here,' he added, clearly changing his mind from what he had originally intended to say. He looked from Reilly to Asher and back to Reilly again, waiting for one of them to speak.

Asher took the initiative. Blowing a stream of cigarette smoke towards the ceiling, he spoke very deliberately. 'Well, Colonel,' he began but immediately glanced at Reilly for approval. Reilly bowed his head by way of signalling him to continue. 'I suggested we meet since there seems to have been an unmerciful cock-up at your end. The fact that Mr Reilly and I seem to know more about your reason for being here than you do proves my point. I asked you to refrain from contacting London until we had met because – ' Asher stopped again and turned to Reilly, hopefully implying that he should take it up.

Reilly did. 'Obviously London has recently become aware of something that we have known for a long time. We have had our problems. We have been forced to expel certain members, and some of these people have decided to – how shall I put it? – go it alone. There seems to be no doubt that they are planning some sort of action in England. That, Colonel, believe you me, is the last thing we want at the moment. We are trying to stop any such action, and we believe we are well on our way to doing just that. We've known about Fisher and his proposed activities for quite some time. We know you've been sent over to act as his contact. Quite rightly you feel you should inform London that Fisher's cover has been blown, as they say. But we, as it happens, need Fisher. We know he has been accepted as a deserter by some of our disenchanted brothers, the ones, in fact, whom we believe to be planning the attack in Britain. You

117

didn't know that?' he asked, noting the Colonel's flicker of surprise. 'Never mind. It is a fact. Now I had a chat with Fisher last night,' Reilly continued, keeping his voice casual, enjoying the amazement his information created, 'and I think we came to an understanding.' Reilly grinned. 'I made him an offer he couldn't refuse,' he said wickedly. 'He is going to continue his – eh – relationship with the splinter group but he will also be reporting everything that goes on to one of my men. If you inform London they will simply pull him out and our chances of finding out what is being planned and nipping it in the bud will be greatly lessened,' Reilly concluded solemnly, and filled the awed silence that followed by giving way to temptation and lighting one of his little cigars.

Unexpectedly the Colonel began to smile, shaking his head in something approaching admiration. 'You people never cease to dumbfound me,' he confessed.

'What he says does make sense, Colonel,' Asher volunteered. 'We've – we've been working together on this for some time now,' he went on cautiously. 'It's in nobody's interest to put a spanner in the works just yet.'

Colonel Maddox stood up, paced a few steps, then sat down again, studying his signet ring. 'So you're asking me to sit here behind this desk and do nothing, knowing that an entire operation has been blown?'

Reilly smiled. 'Something like that. We will, of course, keep you fully informed. Indeed, we have to. It may come to it that we will need the might of your influence in the long run. We have very limited resources,' he concluded coyly.

'Why not give me the names of the people involved? I can have them arrested. That would end the matter.'

'Mr Asher could have done that some time ago, Colonel,' Reilly informed him. 'Alas, it's not that simple. It would cause problems, you see. They do have considerable support still both here and in Dublin. The repercussions following any attempt to arrest them could be – well, catastrophic.'

'For you?'

Reilly nodded. 'For me. Whereas if we were allowed to deal

with them in *our* way, the solution would be final and there would be no waves.'

'And supposing you fail? Supposing they do whatever they're planning to do before you find out?'

Reilly shrugged. 'That is a possibility, Colonel. But *you* certainly won't be able to prevent it any quicker than us.'

'You've no idea what they are planning?'

Reilly hesitated. 'No,' he said finally. 'But whatever it is it will have to happen soon. The longer they delay the more face they lose.'

The Colonel put his elbows on the desk and buried his head in his hands. He knew Reilly was right; knew, too, he was about to capitulate; but not, it seemed, without knowing precisely where he stood. 'What is it you want me to do?' he asked.

Reilly raised his eyebrows and spread his hands. 'Why, nothing, Colonel. Absolutely nothing. Just relax and enjoy our fair city. We, Asher and I, will do all that is necessary. I should think that, given a little luck, we should clear the whole thing up within a couple of weeks.'

The Colonel looked at Asher.

'I think he's right, Colonel,' Asher said.

'And I have your word that you'll keep me fully informed?'

'Of course,' Reilly said.

'I was talking to Mr Asher.'

'Of course,' Asher echoed, giving Reilly a smug little look.

'Two weeks?' the Colonel now asked Reilly.

'Give or take a week.'

The Colonel pursed his lips and gave his ring a couple of twirls before coming to a decision. 'Very well. Meanwhile, though, what about Fisher?'

'No need to worry about Fisher, Colonel,' Reilly said. 'He is now under my protection. He's safer now than he would be in his own home.'

The Colonel looked sceptical but nevertheless accepted the assurance. 'How you seem to thrive on treachery.'

'I hope to Christ you know what you're doing, Seamus,' Asher said as they walked down the corridor from the Colonel's office. 'You mess this up and it'll backfire on me. I need my pension.'

'We'll look after you, John. We have an excellent pension scheme.'

'That's all I need.'

'What we all have to do now is the hardest thing of all: we have to wait. Wait for them to move. Wait for them to say a word out of place that Fisher can tell us. Wait for them to make a mistake.'

'Supposing they don't – make a mistake, I mean?'

'They will. Never fear. They will. They're being driven by revenge and humiliation. Anyone with those two things goading them will make mistakes. Damn! I forgot to tell Maddox to call in Fisher. The poor bugger will go scatty if he thinks London has deserted him.'

'Leave that with me. I'll tell him.'

Asher found the Colonel still sitting at his desk looking decidedly forlorn. 'You strike me as a man who could use a drink, Colonel.' Asher told him. 'Shall I?' he asked, indicating the filing cabinet, and without waiting set about pouring two stiff drinks. 'Reilly asked me to come back,' he continued, handing the Colonel his glass. 'He feels it's important that you call Fisher in for a chat in case he feels he's been abandoned. What you tell him and how much is up to you.'

The Colonel swallowed half his drink before speaking. 'Every time I set foot in this godforsaken city I am encircled by perfidy,' he said, frowning slightly, wondering if he had chosen the right word.

Asher sat down, and waited, the Colonel's observation seeming not to warrant a reply. But the poor old chap was right: he did seem to land himself in the midst of turmoil. For months, years on end nothing would happen, and then, out of the blue, some unheaval would occur and the unfortunate Maddox would inevitably follow in its wake.

'Have I done the right thing, John?'

'I believe so, Colonel. In any other place you would probably be mad to even contemplate such a thing, but here . . . ,' Asher let his voice trail away. He took a sip of whisky before continuing. 'Reilly is a shrewd bastard, you know. Devious, true, but very, very shrewd. And he keeps his word. Anyway,' he continued, 'there's no other option. Look on the bright side. It's a far better thing to have Reilly with you than against you. He *has* to work this thing out. It's a question of his own survival as much as anything else.'

'Hah. He's a survivor if ever there was one.'

'That's what I mean, Colonel. Reilly isn't going to let anything happen that would jeopardize his position. God knows he hates the British, hates us, the RUC, too, but he'd side with anyone if he thought he could help his cause by so doing.' Asher grinned suddenly. 'Why not tell London you have the IRA doing your work for you? That should impress them!'

Even the Colonel was forced to laugh. 'I imagine it would. God, John, can you imagine the consternation.'

'The mind boggles.'

'Yes,' the Colonel said, wiping away the laughter, 'I'll have Fisher in.'

'Good. I'll tell Reilly.'

Major Fisher felt the blood drain from his face when he was told Colonel Maddox wanted to see him immediately in his office, visions of a court martial and total disgrace looming into his bewildered mind. Worse still, the thought of his father's shame. Irrational solutions arose: flight or suicide. Immediately they were dismissed. Nothing could be worse than the torment he was currently experiencing. It would be bliss to get it all off his chest regardless of the consequences. So it was a bold, determined Major Fisher who confronted the Colonel, standing stiffly to attention, his eyes fixed on a crack in the plasterwork above the window.

'At ease, Major,' the Colonel told him, sounding tired, deciding the expression was too military, and adding: 'Do sit down, like a good man.'

The Major sat down, hunching his shoulders, his hands

between his knees, wearing the expression of a boy about to be chastised.

And possibly it was this very expression that made the Colonel feel strangely paternal. Unless he saw in the younger man an image of himself, the mind (like the shoulders) hunched against further bludgeoning, the eyes frightened and tired, mocking the brave, self-assured entrance. Another poor fool, the Colonel told himself, caught up in the whims of terrorism. 'A tricky kettle of fish,' he said aloud, giving a little start as though the words had been intended only as a thought.

'Colonel?'

The Colonel gave a weary smile. 'The first sign. Isn't that what they say? Talking to yourself. Have you ever thought about madness, Major?' he asked. 'I suppose not. Why should you? A strange old man once told me – here in Belfast – that madness lurked close to the skin in all of us. He was probably right. Look around you here and you begin to wonder.'

Major Fisher eyed the Colonel anxiously.

'But like every other adversity in life it can be overcome,' Maddox rambled on, or seemed to ramble, although he was trying desperately to get to the point. 'And we all have some lurking enemy to overcome, do we not?'

The Major blinked rapidly: this was a far cry from what he had expected.

'Take yourself, for example – Chris, isn't it? May I call you Chris? Take yourself for example, I hear you have landed yourself in trouble. Amazing. Here I am, not twenty-four hours in this dreadful place and already I know the – '

'Colonel – ' Fisher began, but stopped abruptly.

Maddox raised his eyebrows. 'Yes?'

Fisher shook his head and stared down at the floor.

'Oh for goodness sake don't be so despondent. Everything has been taken care of. We are, would you believe, under the protection of the great Seamus Reilly. Name mean nothing? Surprising. I understand you had a little chat with him last night. A nice man. Deadly as they come, but always the gentleman. He tells me you made an agreement. I've made agreements with him in the past. Very reliable chap. Never goes back on his word.' The Colonel stood up and moved around the desk. He pulled a chair across the room and sat down beside the Major, tapping him on the knee with one finger as he continued, his voice more caring than ever. 'Now listen to me carefully. I know what's been going on. I know why you were sent here in the first place. Believe it or not it's because of you that I'm here. I'm what they grandly call your contact. But be that as it may, there are intrigues taking place the likes of which you couldn't dream of. I know about them. I am being fully informed about them each step of the way. I want you to do what Reilly told you to do. Just carry on as if nothing had happened. See the people you've been seeing and tell Reilly what he wants to know. That's all.'

Major Fisher looked into the Colonel's face. 'But, sir, Wilson,' he blurted out.

Maddox straightened up, bewildered. 'Wilson? Who is Wilson?'

'Corporal Wilson, sir. I – '

A tiny light of understanding dawned in the Colonel's eyes. 'Corporal Wilson,' he repeated to himself. 'Someone mentioned a Corporal to me. Ah. Gone missing. A Corporal gone missing. Would that be the one?'

Fisher nodded, and before he could control himself, he was crying. His whole body shook with uncontrollable grief, a small whining noise created every time he took breath.

Colonel Maddox was mortified. He could, he liked to think, cope with most things, but an officer weeping before his very eyes and for no apparent reason was an experience he had yet to encounter, and, faced with it, was all at sea. He narrowed his eyes and peered through them at the shaking body. He stood up, walked away a few steps, turned and peered again as though by distancing himself it might make a difference. He cocked his head on one side, trying to pick up the mutterings that emerged from the tears. Suddenly he stiffened. He could have sworn the Major had said 'I shot him.' 'What was that you said?' he demanded.

The Major looked up. He took a handkerchief from his pocket and blew into it loudly. 'I shot him, sir.'

Maddox's immediate reaction was to think Fisher had taken leave of his senses. 'Don't be silly, Major,' he said. 'Pull yourself together,' he added more brusquely.

'It's true, sir. They made me. They said it was to prove I wasn't a plant. They said if I didn't they'd kill me and then kill Wilson anyway. I shot him, sir.'

Maddox was appalled. Strangely, however, the death of the unfortunate Corporal didn't enter his feelings. What horrified him was that anyone could be asked to do such a thing, that such savagery could still be countenanced. And there was more to it: forcing a man to murder a colleague was bad enough, but how could they inflict such torment? And what did he, Matthew Maddox, say to the young man now? Don't let that worry you? Just put it behind you? Forget it? Useless, insulting platitudes. 'You poor man,' Maddox heard himself say. 'What can I say?' Well, that was one way of getting out of saying anything. If only he had left it there. But he didn't. On and on he rambled, trying to disguise his own ineptitude in a flurry of words, plucking clichés from the air and tossing them hopelessly across the desk. And he got confused, kept repeating himself, losing track altogether of what he had hoped to say. It was, therefore, with bemused gratification, that he noted the Major looking at him kindly, and heard him say: 'Thank you, sir.'

'That's better,' he proclaimed stoutly. 'What's done is done. Dreadful for you, of course. But we won't speak further of this. Keep it strictly to ourselves.'

'But – '

'No buts, Major,' Maddox said, gaining control of himself again. 'Nobody else need know. I will take care of this. Or rather, I'll get someone to take care of it. Now, off you go. We'll be in touch soon again.'

Alone, Maddox considered the consequences of what he had just done, and poured himself a drink to drown the unpleasant thoughts that crossed his mind. Best to take his own advice.

What was done was done. He would, he decided, quite simply get Reilly to arrange things, make it look like a simple terrorist killing.

· TWELVE ·

THE MANAGER OF the Grand Hotel, Brighton buzzed about his domain. As far as he could judge, everything was ready to welcome the Prime Minister and the majority of the Cabinet. He had personally checked the Prime Minister's suite, removing a few objects of frippery put there for the honeymooners who normally stayed there, removing, too, tactfully the display of red roses and arranging for a bouquet of blue iris and white gypsophila to be substituted. He had run his fingertips along ledges to be certain the temporary staff had dusted properly: they had. The police had searched the hotel thoroughly; they had brought in their sniffer dogs; there were plain clothes men stationed in the foyer and on almost every floor.

Two streets away, back from the esplanade, in a small but clean guest house, Dermot Drumm lay on his bed, his eyes closed. Frequently he turned his head to study the little travelling clock on the table. The hour hand seemed to drag its way around the dial. Ten past bloody ten. Still far too early for those bloody Tories to be in bed. He propped himself up on one elbow and lit a cigarette, sucking the smoke deep into his lungs, bringing on a fit of coughing. For several seconds he was doubled up, his thin, wiry body racked in pain as he rasped the acrid fumes from his throat. 'Shit,' he said aloud, stubbing out the cigarette in a tin ashtray already filled with partially smoked Consulate. He went to the washbasin and drank some water, slurping it directly from the tap. Then he wiped his face with a towel and stared at his reflection in the mirror, twisting his face into a series of comic and sinister expressions, saying quietly to himself: 'Police have issued a photofit of the man they wish to question in connection with the Brighton bombing.' He was contentedly resigned to the fact that this would probably happen. He expected to be caught eventually. You didn't blow the Prime Minister of England to smithereens and get away with it. Not that it mattered. If they didn't get him Reilly would, and his chances of survival were infinitely better in one of HM's prisons. And prison held no terrors. He had spent more years inside them than out; should be in one now only he had been spirited away from Belfast and across the sea to bloody Scotland in a fishing boat. That had been Reilly's doing. Reilly was all right in those days. Gone soft now, though. Into fucking politics . . . .

At 2.40 a.m. Dermot Drumm shut the front door of the guest house behind him. He had taken the precaution of warning the landlady that he would be leaving very early, paying her in advance, explaining that as a traveller in farm machinery he had to make his calls at an ungodly hour.

'You poor man. I hope they're paying you well,' the landlady had sympathized.

'Not as well as they should,' Drumm quipped.

'They never do. You know my husband, God rest his soul, worked for the same company for the best part of forty years, and they retired him off with a pension that wouldn't feed a canary. Still, I expect you're grateful to have a job at all these days.'

'Indeed I am.'

He crossed the road, swinging his small overnight bag, and unlocked the door of the Audi. He threw the bag onto the back

127

seat, and got in behind the wheel. Then he leaned across and took a small metal device from the glove compartment. He glanced at the clock on the dashboard. He would wait a few minutes. As it turned out that few minutes' wait was to prove, from his point of view, a grave error of judgement.

At 2.53 the Prime Minister left her bathroom, closing the door. Immediately the bomb exploded.

One hour after the bomb had demolished the central section of the Grand Hotel, Seamus Reilly was awoken by the telephone. Without opening his eyes he grabbed the receiver and pulled it into the bed, hearing the rattle of excited words before he got it to his ear. When he finally got it there he heard only the tail-end: '. . . broken loose. Bloody pandemonium.'

'Who is that?' he asked sharply.

'It's me. Regan, Mr Reilly. They've done it. Blown up the hotel in Brighton where Thatcher and the Cabinet are staying.'

For a second Reilly felt he was in the throes of a horrible dream. Quite literally he froze, every nerve and muscle in his body seizing, his brain, still dulled by sleep, unable to grapple with the horrendous news.

'Are you there, Mr Reilly?' Regan asked anxiously.

'Yes. I'm here.'

'Did you hear me? They've blown up the bloody hotel.'

'I heard,' Reilly answered, slowly coming to grips with his thoughts. Regan was babbling on. '. . . least three dead. Christ knows how many injured. Jesus, Mr Reilly, this is – '

'Calm down, Thomas,' Reilly said quietly, aware that the advice was as much for himself as for Regan. 'Calm down,' he repeated. 'Start again. Tell me everything you know.'

'Only what I've told you, Mr Reilly. My contact called me from Brixton. I don't know where he got it from. A bomb went off some time around three o'clock and blasted the Grand Hotel. There's bodies everywhere.'

'Thatcher?'

'No news on that. No names at all. Jesus, Mr Reilly what – '

'Just a minute, Thomas.'

Reilly stared into the darkness. Bloody Brighton. Christ, he should have – 'Thomas. There's nothing we can do right now. Come round in the morning. Early. Eight o'clock. I'll talk to you then.'

'Right, Mr Reilly.'

Within seconds Reilly was dialling the number of his Commander in Chief. The phone rang and rang. He was on the point of hanging up when the receiver clicked and a tired, gruff voice asked 'Yes?'

'Seamus. Reilly. I've just been told someone's blown up the hotel where Thatcher is staying for the convention.'

Silence. The Commander was clearly as stunned as Reilly himself had been; he was also furious as Reilly could tell when he finally spoke, his voice crisp and cold and deadly, making the single word into a sentence of death. 'Who?'

Reilly's voice carried a shrug. 'Your guess is as good as mine.'

The Commander was in no mood for guessing. 'I want to know who,' he said flatly. 'Find out, Seamus. And fast.'

'Very well. I – '

'And deal with them,' the Commander added icily. Then, finally, he exploded. 'Jesus Christ! It's that fucking woman. Seamus I want that bitch hung drawn and quartered.'

'She will be if it *is* her.'

'It's her. I know it is.'

Reilly knew that too. 'Possibly,' he said.

'Meanwhile, I'll issue a statement claiming responsibility. I've got to. If *we* don't *they* will and make us look like incompetent fools who can't keep things under control.'

Reilly was shocked. 'We can't – ' he began to protest.

'We have to. We lose everything if we let them take the credit. They'll have those lunatics both here and in Dublin rallying round. Before you know it we'll be well and truly split down the middle. I've got to prevent that. I've no option. We have to claim responsibility and ride it out.'

Seamus Reilly wanted to protest again, but he knew it would

be futile. The decision had been made; and there was a grim, twisted logic to it. For a man who had always prided himself on his calm, detached, unemotional approach to things, Reilly was surprised and alarmed at the anger he felt rising within him, a hatred he had never before felt. That anyone should reduce his efforts for peace to so much rubble by such a stupid (and, more to the point, unsanctioned) action was more than he could stand. Borrowing the Commander's original tones of wrath he said: 'That decision is yours, of course.'

'Precisely.'

'And when I find out who was responsible I have your authority to deal with them as I wish?'

'You do.'

'Without question?'

'Without question . . . . You sound as though – '

'Without question?'

The Commander was forced to grin. 'Very well, Seamus. Without question.'

'Thank you.'

Seamus Reilly put the receiver back in its cradle and got out of bed. He put on his dressing gown and made for the bathroom. He was trembling. He tried to put it down to his anger but couldn't: he knew it was the sense of foreboding that made his nerves jitter. Again the words 'you are already dead' blundered into his mind. Damn them all to hell.

Five minutes later he was talking to John Asher. 'You won't have heard, John. Someone just blew up the hotel in Brighton. The one where Thatcher was staying.'

For a second Asher said nothing. Then: 'Holy Jesus. Is she dead?'

'I don't know. There are some dead, but I don't know if she's one of them.'

'Holy Jesus,' Asher said again.

'The reason I'm ringing, John, is to tell you that we have – that it has been decided that we must claim responsibility. You have my word we had nothing to do with it, but expediency dictates that we must say we did.'

'I don't under–'

'I can't explain now. Look, I have a meeting at eight in the morning. Can we get together around nine?'

'Yes. Yes, of course. You want me to come there?'

'If you can. I've got to be where I can be contacted.'

'I'll be there.'

'We'll have to move fast and I'll need your help.'

Asher hesitated. 'You're not – '

'You have my word. We had nothing whatever to do with it. I'll explain everything when we meet. We'll also need to see Maddox. I'll need him to . . . . I'll explain that in the morning also.'

Across the city Eddie McCluskey watched the woman anxiously as she paced the room like a cat, from time to time slapping her clenched fist into the open palm of her other hand, muttering to herself 'ring, ring, ring', and frequently stopping to stare at the phone as if she could mesmerize it into action. McCluskey was confused. He had been there since the evening before and had no idea why: he had simply been told that she wanted him there. It had, of course, happened before: several times. He was used to such summary commands. But this was different although he could not quite put his finger on it. Perhaps it was her uncharacteristic excitedness, a sort of semi-controlled frenzy that, to his mind, only made her more sexually desirable. Then there were her long silences when all she did was alternate her magnetic gaze between him and the telephone, seeming to find both equally fascinating. There was the way she kept wetting her lips, flicking her pink tongue in and out of her mouth like an adder. There was the occasional moan, not of pain but of, it struck him, longing. And it was all these with their promise of something that had sustained him through the evening and early morning.

When the phone did, at last, ring, she was across the room in three strides, grabbing the receiver. 'Yes?'

This was followed by a series of curt, chopped words. 'Yes. Yes. Good. How many? Shit. Yes. Right. Good. No.' Then the receiver was slowly, reluctantly replaced. 'We've bloody done it,' she exclaimed without turning round.

Suddenly she was waltzing about the room, her arms clasping herself in a tight embrace, her eyes dancing too. 'We've done it, we've done it, we've done it,' she kept saying, whirling about like a dervish.

McCluskey may have been impressed, but he was also confused. 'Done what, for Christ's sake?'

The woman stopped dancing abruptly. Then she rushed towards him, grabbed him by the hands and pulled him from the chair. She threw her arms about him, pressing her body hard against his. 'We've beaten Reilly, that's what we've done. We've beaten that smug little bastard,' she told him, her voice little more than a whisper but the venom in it screaming.

It was something of an anticlimax when all McCluskey could do was ask 'How?'

The woman stood back, holding him by the hands at arms' length. 'You know those trips to Glasgow?'

'Yea?'

'I was arranging the bombing of all time. And this morning it went off. Right under Thatcher's knickers.'

'Jesus. You *what*?'

'Months ago,' the woman exaggerated, 'as soon as I knew what hotel they were using for their convention, I had a bomb planted. This morning we set it off.'

'Christ Almighty!' McCluskey's mind skirted the horror of the bombing itself: such an enormous undertaking was way beyond his understanding. What took over his whole consciousness was the furious wrath of Seamus Reilly, and of that Eddie McCluskey was petrified.

'You should have fucking told us what you were doing. We'll have to get out – '

'What for?' the woman demanded, amazed.

'What for? Jesus God. Reilly, of course. What the hell do you think he's going to do to us? He'll crucify us, that's for sure.'

'No he won't,' the woman said firmly. 'He wouldn't dare now. He knows bloody well that we have our supporters and that they'll be right behind us now. It will take Reilly all his time to survive himself. He won't have a minute to spare on us.'

McCluskey was not convinced. 'You're wrong,' he told her mournfully, shaking his head. 'You don't know him like I do. You've made him lose face. That's something you can't do to Reilly.'

'To hell with Reilly's face. He's a nothing now. You just wait, Eddie,' the woman told him, moving away, staring into the distance as though in a trance or having a wonderful vision. 'You just wait,' she told him again. 'In a couple of hours when I announce that we did it, Reilly's power will be nil.'

'Yea, well, I'll tell you something. I can give you the names of eight different people who thought they had outwitted Reilly, and you want to know where they are now? Nobody fucking knows! They just bloody vanished.'

'We won't vanish, Eddie. Not us, I can promise you that.'

'Yea. The others said that too.'

The woman moved round in front of him again, and held out her hands. 'Come on, Eddie. Come with me. I *need* you now. Come on.'

Meekly Eddie McCluskey gave her his hands and allowed himself to be led into her bedroom, the aching in his loins for the moment obliterating his fears.

Perhaps significantly, Colonel Maddox was last to receive the news, reaching him through official channels, almost, it seemed, as an afterthought. His reaction was curious. Although naturally shocked and disgusted, he also felt an odd kind of satisfaction as though believing the outrage would inflict on his superiors the sort of unsolvable quandary they had inflicted on him. But he should have known better. That damned conniving Reilly. Lulling him into a false sense of trust while all the while he had been scheming to annihilate almost the entire government. Well, enough was enough. He would fix Seamus Reilly. He had been made a fool of once too often.

It was seven-thirty when Declan Tuohy learned of the bomb-

133

ing. The thirteenth was his day off, his first in quite a while, and he had determined to enjoy it, starting with a luxurious sleep-in. He had taken his phone off the hook, and drunk a little too much. So, it was in something of a haze that he went to investigate the hammering on his door. It went a long way to clearing his head when he saw it was the editor himself who was creating the ruckus. 'Where's the damn fire?' he asked, trying to smile.

Myles Cravan was in no mood for stupid remarks. 'Get dressed, Declan. And be quick about it.'

'It's my day off, dammit.'

'It was. Your friends have really gone to town this time. Tried to blow the whole damn Cabinet up.'

'*What*?'

'That's right. The IRA have claimed responsibility for a bomb that blew the shit out of Thatcher's hotel in Brighton. You get into the office and see what you can find out.'

'God above!'

'So much for your peaceful Seamus Reilly. Little bastard. He – '

'Hey now, hang on a minute. You don't know it was Reilly.'

'It was the bloody IRA, wasn't it? That's Reilly as far as I'm concerned. Come on, for Christ's sake. Throw some clothes on. I'll take you back with me.'

The woman eased McCluskey from on top of her and reached out to switch on the bedside radio . . . THE IRA HAS CLAIMED RESPONSIBILITY. A REPORT NOW FROM . . . That was all she heard. In an instant she was out of bed, wrenching the radio from the table and hurling it against the wall. For a second she stood still, her lips quivering. Then she started to scream. 'Fuck you Reilly,' she screamed, repeating the curse over and over again.

Poor McCluskey was scared out of his wits. He sat up in the bed, his mouth open, gaping. It wasn't until the woman had stopped that he dared ask: 'What the hell has happened?'

The woman rounded on him. 'What the hell has happened?

That fucking shit Reilly has claimed responsibility. He's grabbing the credit! He's making everyone believe they did it.'

McCluskey, for the life of him, couldn't digest the significance of all this. 'So what?' he was foolish enough to ask.

The woman looked as if she was about to physically attack him. Instead, when she spoke, her voice was calm and almost a whisper. 'Get the hell out of here, McCluskey.' Then she closed her eyes and yelled again: 'Get out!'

· THIRTEEN ·

Seamus Reilly had just turned off the early morning news when Thomas Regan knocked at the door.

'Sorry I'm a bit late, Mr Reilly. Bloody murder out there this morning. Saracens and foot-patrols everywhere,' Regan explained, closing the door and following Reilly into the kitchen.

Reilly dismissed the apology with a small gesture, and filled the kettle with water, plugging it in and switching it on. 'You take tea, don't you, Thomas?'

'I do, Mr Reilly. Thanks very much.'

'What more have you learned?' Seamus asked, sounding curiously vague as if he really couldn't care less, and setting about percolating himself some coffee.

'Not too much yet, I'm afraid. But I will. I've got everyone on it.'

'You've heard we've claimed responsibility?'

'I have, Mr Reilly,' Regan admitted, looking uncomfortable. 'And?'

'And what, Mr Reilly?'

'What did you think when you heard that?'

Regan began to fidget with his hands as his mind fidgeted with his thoughts. 'I didn't think anything, Mr Reilly. It's not my place to question something like that. If that statement was issued it was issued for a reason, and I just accept it.'

Seamus Reilly stared at Regan in quiet amazement, amazement and envy. 'How lucky you are, Thomas, to be able to do that. Ah,' he added as the kettle boiled. 'Your tea. I'm afraid it has to be a bag.'

'Grand, Mr Reilly.'

'Sit down, Thomas. And listen to me. We had nothing whatever to do with it. Nothing. But for – for reasons we had to claim we did. I, now, have been given the task of finding those who really are responsible and dealing with them – in any way I like, I might add.' Seamus paused to let that much sink in.

Regan nodded thoughtfully, adding milk and sugar to his tea, and stirring it.

'Whatever I do I want you to understand that I am doing it for a very good reason. I just want you to go along with me. I'll explain what I can – the rest you'll have to take on trust. The one major problem facing me is this: I cannot execute my orders in such a way that makes it seem we are taking our revenge for something done without our sanction. It will have to be done through other channels. For that reason I will be working with Inspector Asher.' Reilly paused again, and, similarly, Regan nodded again. 'Whatever I ask you to do I want you just to do it. No hesitation. No questions. I can promise you I will see to it that you come out of it unscathed – unharmed,' Reilly put in as he saw the squint of puzzlement.

Regan stopped nodding. 'You know I'll do anything you say, Mr Reilly.'

'That's all I wanted to hear,' Seamus told him, giving him a small, grateful smile, and pouring himself a cup of coffee.

Reilly carried his coffee to the table and sat down. 'Now,' he said, 'we don't know who actually planted the explosives but we do know who is behind it – '

'That bloody woman and McCluskey and Moran,' Regan said, if only to prove he was on the ball.

137

'Quite,' Reilly agreed, albeit a little testily. 'In your opinion which of them would break the easiest?'

'Oh McCluskey. No doubt about that, Mr Reilly. Everyone knows he's terrified of you.'

For an instant Reilly looked amused. 'Leaving me and my power to terrify out of it for the moment, Thomas – you still think McCluskey's the most likely to break?'

Regan took to nodding again. 'Yes. Moran's got family here. It wouldn't be easy for him to do a bunk if he gave anything away so they could get at him without trouble. McCluskey though could be gone before they laid a hand on him. Yea, McCluskey's your man, Mr Reilly.'

'Good,' Reilly said and tasted his coffee. 'Tell me this, Thomas. The place where McCluskey lives – what's it like?'

'Like? Well, he lives with his mother. Just the two of them. Not much of a place. Two up, two down. Dirty. The mother drinks a bit.'

'Any outhouses?'

'Oh I couldn't be sure about that, Mr Reilly. Probably there is though. Most of the houses on that street have a bit of a shed at the back. Used to be the piss house, the lavatories before they got inside ones. Most people use them as coal sheds now.'

'Find that out for me. As soon as possible, will you?'

'I can find out now if I can use your phone, Mr Reilly.'

'Good. Go ahead.'

Alone, Reilly finished his coffee and poured himself a second cup. Feeling guilty he opened the drawer at the end of the table and took out a tin of his small cigars and a box of matches. He argued with himself against lighting one but lost, and inhaled deeply, enjoying the nicotine.

'Yes, Mr Reilly. There is a shed. A lean-to thing.'

Reilly beamed. 'Fine. Can you get to it from the back?'

'Sure. There's a lane that runs right the way along. It's only a low bit of a wall. Easy to get at the shed if you want me to.'

'I do, Thomas. Tonight I want you to take Wilson's body and leave it in McCluskey's shed. Bring some sacks with you.

Cover the body up. Make it look as if someone was trying to hide it.'

Clearly Regan liked this idea. He grinned hugely. 'Sure I'll do that, Mr Reilly. No bother at all.'

'Good man. Just phone me when you have it done. Then we'll deal with Eddie McCluskey.'

'It's as good as done,' Regan said and finished his tea in one gulp. 'I'll be off, then, Mr Reilly, unless there's something else?'

'That's it for now, Thomas.'

'Right. And – well, good luck, Mr Reilly.'

Seamus Reilly was strangely touched: he looked almost embarrassed as he smiled at Regan. 'Thank you, Thomas. That's kind of you.'

'Yerra, you're worth any ten others, Mr Reilly.'

'Thank you, Thomas,' Reilly said again, making to open the front door, then changing his mind. He frowned. 'One other thing. You better phone me here this afternoon. About three. No, make it three on the dot. I might want you to pick up Fisher again. It depends how things go.'

'Will he be out, Mr Reilly? He's pretty scared now. He might just stay in the barracks.'

'He'll be out if I want him, Thomas. I'll see to that.'

'I might have guessed as much,' Regan said admiringly. 'Right then, I'll give you a buzz at three on the dot.'

So far so good. Reilly busied himself in the kitchen, putting the cups in the sink and the milk back in the fridge, running tap water on the butt of his cigar and tossing it into the bin. He had just finished when John Asher arrived. 'What a godawful mess,' he said by way of greeting.

Reilly grunted and led the way to the sitting-room. 'You could say that.'

'You should have been with me this morning and you'd know there's no supposing about it. The Chief Inspector's gone bloody berserk. You'd swear to God I'd put the bloody bomb there myself.'

Reilly could not prevent himself laughing.

'Huh, it's all very well for you to bloody well laugh, Seamus, but I'm telling you the laugh will be on the other side of your face if you're not damn crafty. You know what he said? He said he wanted every goddam Catholic in the province – the province, mind you – brought in for questioning before nightfall.'

'You'd better get a move on then, hadn't you, John?'

'What I'm trying to tell you is that we don't have a lot of time to sort this fiasco out.'

'I know, John. I know. I'm working on it already.'

'That's a relief.'

'By this time tomorrow I'll have someone for you to question.'

'Question!' Asher snorted. 'Seamus we have to nail someone for this, not bloody question them.'

'I'll give you someone to nail, as you put it.'

Asher squinted, immediately suspicious. 'You know who did this, don't you?'

Reilly shook his head. 'No. No I don't. I know who's behind it, just like you do. That's all. But – Look, John,' Reilly went on after a short pause. 'Later tonight I'll give you a call with a name, an address and something to look for. You can then arrest someone. From the questions you ask you should be able to find out what we both want to know. Mind you – you'll find out a lot quicker if I'm there,' he added with a twinkle.

'Why don't you just pick this nameless thing up yourself?'

'Not the same. We don't want to appear involved,' Reilly admitted. 'Far better for all of us that you be seen as the brains. I tell you what, though, if you just go along with me between us we'll soon have all the answers.'

'What charge am I supposed to use tonight?'

'Would murder do?'

'It would if I had proof.'

'I'll give you the proof.'

Asher shook his head. 'I've said it before and I'll say it again – you're a devious bastard.'

'I survive,' Reilly told him.

'You certainly do. So far.'

Suddenly Reilly went gloomy. 'Yes,' he agreed sadly. 'So far.'

' – Maddox to cope with,' Asher was saying.

'Sorry, John. I was – '

'I said I've also got Maddox to cope with. He was on to me at half eight this morning. He's convinced you deceived him and that you were behind the explosion. He wanted me to arrest *you* for Christ's sake.'

'Oh dear. What did you tell him?'

'I told him that I was seeing you this morning and if I thought you had anything to do with it I *would* bloody well arrest you.'

Reilly mockingly held out his wrists for handcuffing. 'I'll go quietly.'

'Very funny. He's damn jittery, Seamus, I can tell you.'

'Who? Maddox. Tell him not to worry. Tell him I have everything under control.'

'*That's* what he's afraid of.'

'You can say I'll phone him.'

'Better if you went and saw him.'

'I can't. I daren't leave home today. I've got to be within reach if any of my men want me.'

'I could bring him here,' Asher suggested hopefully.

'You can do that if you like.'

'I'll put it to him.'

'Just after lunch if possible,' Reilly said. Then he smiled. 'Actually, I might want him to do me a favour.'

'Just you do yourself a favour, Seamus, and stop buggering about. There's too many people in Belfast would like to see the back of you. They might just try and take their chance now.'

Reilly shrugged. 'Now or next year, what's the difference?'

'Twelve bloody months.'

Reilly stood up. 'Phone me if Maddox is coming.'

Asher, too, stood up now. 'I'll do that. And don't you forget: I need something by tonight.'

'You'll have it.'

'I'm banking on it.'

Declan Tuohy sat back from his desk, his feet balanced on the ledge of an open drawer, reading the first reports of the Brighton explosion. He found it all but impossible to concentrate. Something was wrong. It stank. Most of all the IRA claim stank. The bombing was sheer lunacy and, whatever else, the hard-core IRA were far from being lunatics. Especially Reilly. He would never in a million years have condoned such action, and he had the power to veto it. Besides, they had nothing whatever to gain except revulsion and appalling publicity which was certainly the last thing Reilly wanted, now that he was moving his section towards politics. Indeed, the whole trend of IRA publicity had been towards reasonableness, towards electoral success, towards, ultimately, peace.

Declan threw the reports onto his desk, and swung back and forth on his chair. Now, why the hell would the IRA claim responsibility if they didn't do it . . .? He looked at his watch. Then, from his inside pocket he took a small notebook, flicked through the pages, found what he wanted and reached for the telephone. When it was answered he stated: 'It's Declan Tuohy.'

'Ah.'

'Can you talk?'

'Of course.'

'Brighton. You've claimed – '

'I – Command claimed responsibility.'

'You knew about it beforehand though?'

Reilly hesitated. 'No.'

'Someone did.'

Reilly gave a small, tired laugh. 'Naturally.'

'What I meant was someone within your – '

'No.'

'Then you had nothing to do with it.'

'Nothing.'

'Well why claim – '

'There are reasons, Declan. Leave it at that for the moment.'

'Can we at least talk again later?'

'Perhaps.'

'Would it help if I came over?'

'Not really. Stay where you are. I'll be in touch. Who knows, you might even get that film you wanted,' Reilly said and hung up.

So that was it, Declan thought, and immediately burst out laughing as he realised he still had no idea whatever what *it* was.

'And I suppose you're going to tell me you believe him?' Colonel Maddox said.

Asher inclined his head. 'Yes. Yes, I believe him.'

Maddox threw up his hands in a gesture of exasperation. 'Well I don't,' he said.

'That's up to you, Colonel, but just think about it for a minute. Why should Reilly lie? Even if he was responsible, we could never prove it. He was in your office the other day. I've been in touch with him every day. How is that going to look if we charge him with something we can't even come near to proving?'

Maddox shook his head. 'I still think he had something to do with it. He's using us, John. He's twisting us round his little finger.'

Asher grinned. 'He would like to perhaps, but I don't think he is. Why not come and see him like I suggested. What harm can it do?'

The Colonel wagged a pencil at Asher. 'All right I'll come. But I'm telling you, John, if I'm not satisfied that he's completely innocent I'll have him arrested myself.'

So at 2.15 Maddox and Asher called on Reilly. Asher had already telephoned advising him of the visit, and had agreed to undertake the required security precautions, accepting Reilly's explanation that for him to do so would be 'tricky under the circumstances' meaning, presumably, that the streets were crawling with troops. When they were all seated, John Asher opened proceedings by saying: 'The Colonel is most displeased, Seamus. He thinks you're trying to hoodwink him.'

Reilly feigned surprise. 'Really Colonel?'

'Yes,' Maddox confirmed. 'There's too many coincidences. It reeks of your duplicity.'

'Oh dear,' Reilly sighed. 'I can assure you everything I told John this morning was the truth.'

The Colonel looked about the room as if hoping to find his next words painted on the wall. Seeing nothing, he stayed silent. It was all happening to him again. The damned intrigue was swallowing him. Already he was admitting to himself he could not cope. 'I simply want to know what is going on,' he said, perilously near to pleading.

Reilly was touched. One could not fail to like and be sorry for the unfortunate Colonel. Here was a man, he thought, who would have fulfilled his desires had he died heroically in battle. He was a brave man, and probably fearless when fighting anything he could understand. The trouble was his very decency and goodness left him naked and undefended in the face of the intrigue that was such a vital element in one's survival in Belfast. To him it was dishonourable, and life without honour was not something Colonel Maddox would wish for. Reilly appreciated that; he even admired the man for it; in truth he quietly envied him his goodness. 'Very well, Colonel, I will trust *you*. I will tell you what is going on. I will tell you on the condition that you allow me to pursue a solution without any interference, and with my promise that it will not involve any – eh – problems for the British forces here in Belfast. Do we agree?'

The Colonel surrendered. He nodded.

'What has happened is this. Some months ago we were forced to expel certain people from the IRA. They were thugs. Since then several things have occurred which made it clear they were going to take their revenge. They have, however, a following both here and in Dublin, and for them to survive as a viable entity it was vital that they prove their power by pulling off a coup, some grandiose action that would humiliate us and elevate them. We – John and I – are convinced they organized the Brighton explosion. They didn't *do* it themselves, but they were the brains, if that applies, behind it. In order to forestall the glory they hoped to reap among their supporters it was decided by my superiors that *we* should immediately issue a statement claiming responsibility. I had, and still have my doubts about the wisdom of this, but the decision was made and I must abide by it. For what it is worth I can tell you that we all are appalled and disgusted by the attack on the hotel. And that, Colonel, is the situation so far.' Reilly leaned back in his chair as if he had nothing further to say. But he had. He started speaking again almost immediately, keeping his eyes closed, and talking slowly, giving the impression he was reading the words from a screen somewhere in his mind; or it could have been that he was forging a plan as he went along. 'One problem that faces us,' he went on, 'is that we cannot be seen to be hunting anyone – that would simply put the lie to our claim. We have many members sitting on the fence, so to speak, members who could lean either way if it came to the crunch. If they got wind that we had *not* caused the explosion, that we were simply doing what we are, in fact, doing, they could very easily turn against us and make our future untenable. So, since I have been given the task of dealing with this matter, I have come to an understanding with John. I will supply him with the information he needs, but it will all appear to be an RUC operation. It starts tonight. Some time tonight, hopefully this evening, I will give John a man to arrest – one of those we suspect as organizing the bombing. John will bring him in for questioning. I will be there too.' At that point Reilly stopped, opened an eye and looked at Asher, who nodded. 'From this man we will, I hope, find out most of what we want to know. After that – ' Reilly sat up and spread his hands. 'After that who knows?'

'Who is this man you are going to question?' the Colonel wanted to know.

'Later. You'll be told later, Colonel. John, I'm sure will tell you. There are a few little arrangements to be made before he is arrested.'

'Does that satisfy you?' Maddox asked of Asher, clearly seeking an ally.

Asher nodded, 'I'm satisfied if everything works out as Seamus says.'

'Very well,' the Colonel said. 'I'll go along as long as John is happy.'

'Thank you, Colonel,' Reilly said politely, but in a tone that suggested he had known from the beginning he was going to have his way. 'There is one other thing.'

'Oh?' The Colonel didn't like the sound of that.

'Yes. Fisher. Your spy, Colonel. I may want to have another talk with him. He could be in danger now, and I gave him my word I would take care of him. If I contact you could you see to it that he leaves his barracks at a given time?'

'I could, but – '

'Thank you, Colonel,' Reilly interrupted.

Later as they drove home together Maddox turned to Asher, his shoulders heaving with mirth, but there was only a dry humour in his voice. 'You know what we've done, John? We've agreed to everything that damned Reilly wanted, and all he's given us is what is probably a cock-and-bull story about the righteousness of the damn IRA.'

Asher chuckled. 'I wondered if you had noticed that. Still, we'll know later tonight, won't we?'

As promised Thomas Regan telephoned Seamus Reilly at three on the dot. Their conversation was brief. 'No, Thomas, we won't need Fisher until tomorrow at the earliest. As soon as I know I'll get a message to you. Just you carry on and get Wilson's body into that shed. I'd like it done just after it gets dark if you can manage it.'

'I'll see to it, Mr Reilly.'

'Once you've done it get well away from that area and phone me. Don't phone me until you are well clear. Understand?'

'I understand, Mr Reilly.'

'Good man.'

It was well into the afternoon before Eddie McCluskey returned home. He was pretty drunk. He had spent several hours in a pub trying to drown the woman's screams that pierced his brain. And he was tired and scared, so the welcome he got was not what he wanted.

'And what time of the day do you think it is to be coming home?' his mother demanded, her hands on her bulging hips, her huge frame blocking the narrow hallway. Eddie ignored her question, pushing his way past her and climbing the linoleum-covered stairs.

In bed he shivered like an animal trying to warm itself. He was very frightened. He had thought of making off across the border but had soon realized the uselessness of such action. He curled himself up. No matter where he went if Reilly wanted him Reilly would find him, so bed, with its hope of oblivion, seemed as good a place as any to wait for the inevitable. And, indeed, he did manage to sleep, albeit fitfully. Once he opened his eyes and listened, trying to ascertain what had woken him. It was already dark, but there was no suspicious sound, only the laughter from the television downstairs as his mother watched some gameshow. Then, outside, a bin rattled, and he sat up, holding the blankets up to his neck, looking absurdly modest. There was silence again, and he slid back down in the bed, waiting to drift back into sleep.

Half an hour later Thomas Regan telephoned Seamus Reilly. 'All done, Mr Reilly.'

· FOURTEEN ·

FOUR RUC LANDROVERS and an unmarked car drove in convoy across the city. When they arrived at their destination they split up, one moving to each end of the street, blocking the entrance, the other two driving behind the car and stopping with as little noise as possible outside the dingy little house. Inspector Asher stepped from the car and directed the operation, not speaking, using only hand signals. But there was no mistaking his intent. In seconds the front door of the house had been smashed open and the security forces were piling in. Eddie McCluskey heard the rumpus from his bed. His reaction would have been comic were it not so pathetic: he pulled the blankets over his head and lay there, cuddled up, whimpering. Soon he was dragged from his bed and hustled down the stairs, his bare feet not once touching the ground. He saw his mother ineffectually trying to barge her way past two officers, heard her resort to verbal abuse. Then he was outside on the pavement. There was a strange eeriness about the place. Nobody spoke. The men's boots made no noise. The Landrovers, their engines cut, stood like grey, ghostly monsters waiting to be fed. He was kept standing on the pavement in his underclothes, and that was the worst part: waiting for something awful to happen. Then, far in the distance, an ambulance keened towards them. An engine was kicked to life and one of the Landrovers reversed, leaving the end of the street unobstructed. All the officers turned their heads and stared in the direction of the approaching ambulance, by now its blue winking light visible. Up the narrow street it came at full speed, looked, for a second, as if it was about to go screaming by, but in the nick of time skidded to a halt, swaying on its springs, the back doors already open. Asher pointed to the house with his hand, his arm at full stretch as though on traffic duty. Two men lifted a stretcher from the ambulance, and made for the front door, stopping for one stride to hear Asher's whispered instruction. McCluskey gaped. For a second he thought that perhaps, with luck, he was dreaming: when he saw Wilson's body on the stretcher he went to pieces, giving a long, high-pitched wail that belonged to a wounded animal.

Seamus Reilly waited at his home for Asher to pick him up as arranged. He sat at the kitchen table, a newspaper spread out in front of him. Across the top of the front page CONFERENCE HOTEL BLAST LEAVES 3 DEAD, 32 INJURED AND ONE MISSING was emblazoned, and under that, in even bolder print THATCHER DEFIES IRA BOMBER. There was a photograph of the damaged hotel, and scattered about the page were other headlines as though the editor had been unable to make up his mind which to use and hit upon the idea of using them all. TEBBIT AND CHIEF WHIP HURT AMID FALLING RUBBLE . . . FIFTEEN STAY IN HOSPITAL OVERNIGHT. . . JOSEPH SLEEPS THROUGH. . . CHIEF WHIP'S WIFE KILLED. . . INQUIRY ON SECURITY BLUNDER STARTS. . . FITZ-GERALD IS SHOCKED BY IRA . . . . And then, incredibly, with equal boldness the information that there was £22,000 TO BE WON in some oddity known as PORTFOLIO. Reilly smiled grimly, cynically wondering if it had anything to do with the price of death. It was something that had never ceased to amaze him: the view the British took of death. Of all the killings that had taken place in Britain the one that had most outraged them was the bombing in Hyde Park simply, it was clear, because of the injury to the horses. At that moment, John Asher arrived.

'No problems I hope?' Reilly asked as they sat together in the car, weaving their way through the evening traffic.

'None.'

'Where have you taken him?'

'Castlereagh.'

'Oh.'

Asher gave a little laugh. 'Don't worry. We'll let you out again.' Seriously he then asked: 'How do you think we should handle this?'

Reilly considered the question for a moment before speaking. 'I *think* the best thing would be for you to question him alone at first, John. I don't expect he'll tell you much. He wouldn't, you see, be all that afraid of the RUC. He might even have visions of martyrdom. Indeed, I can see that prison might seem very attractive to him – keep him out of my clutches, so to speak. And the longer you question him without result the more cocky he'll get. When he starts to smirk at you then I think you could bring me in,' he concluded with a satisfied, smug grin.

'And when you're finished?'

'When I've got the information I want you can do whatever you like with him. Charge him. Lock him up and forget all about him. Shoot him,' Reilly suggested, clearly joking. 'Any damn thing you want. He'll be no further use to me. Or to our plan of campaign,' he added thoughtfully.

As expected Seamus Reilly's prognostication was proved correct. McCluskey told Asher nothing. He sat on the wooden chair gazing glazedly at his interrogator. After half an hour his attitude started to change. He pretended to be bored, looking away and whistling through his teeth when posed a question. In an hour he was smirking. At his first smirk John Asher went to the door and whispered to the guard outside. Three minutes later the door opened and Seamus Reilly came in. Immediately he broke into a wide friendly smile. 'Ah, Eddie,' he said. 'You're just the man I want to see.'

Eddie McCluskey winced, but decided he might as well try and brazen it out. 'Hello, Mr Reilly.'

'Always the cool one, eh?' Reilly asked. 'And always the idiot. Well, I don't have time for any of your old crap, Eddie. You've had your little game with Inspector Asher here.' Reilly suddenly kicked the spare chair and sent it crashing into the wall. 'I've got questions, and I want the answers so you better come up with them.'

'Mr Reilly, I – '

Reilly's fist thumped down on the table, making McCluskey jump and cringe backwards. 'Shut up!' he shouted, then he turned away, licking the spots of saliva from the corners of his mouth, composing himself. When he faced McCluskey he was his calm, cold self again. 'First,' he said holding aloft one finger, 'in this – this – this coven of yours, how many are there besides you and Moran and that woman?'

'Nobody else, Mr Reilly. Honest to God. Just the three of us.'

Reilly nodded, accepting what he knew was the truth. 'Second, what do you know about the bomb in Brighton last night?'

Stupidly McCluskey tried to act innocent. 'What bomb, Mr – '

In a flash Reilly was round the table. He grabbed McCluskey by the short hairs on the nape of his neck and yanked him up (a painful but effective trick he remembered from his schooldays, a device perfected by the Christian Brothers), making him scream with pain. After a second Reilly released him, pushing him back into the chair. 'Second, what do you know about the bomb in Brighton last night?' he asked again.

'Nothing, Mr Reilly. I swear to God I know nothing.'

Reilly let that pass. 'Would Moran know?'

'Jesus no, Mr Reilly. Moran wouldn't know anything about a thing like that.'

'So we're left with your lady friend. She's the one, eh?'

McCluskey gritted his teeth, hesitated, but finally agreed, nodding.

'Now, wasn't that simple enough?' Reilly asked expansively. 'We're getting somewhere at last. She spoke to you about it then?'

'Only this morning. The first I knew of it was when she started cheering after a phone call.'

'Cheering, no less. Who was the phone call from?'

'I don't know.'

Reilly believed him, but there was something in his voice that suggested he might be able to make a pretty good guess. 'Make a guess, Eddie. Who do you think *might* have been on the phone?'

'Maybe someone in Scotland.'

'In Scotland?' Seamus Reilly feigned surprise. 'And why would you guess at someone in Scotland, Eddie?'

'She's been there a couple of times. By herself. I mean with kids. She takes kids over for a holiday. I was never with her. But she might have arranged something over there.'

'She might indeed. Names?'

McCluskey wilted again. 'I don't know any names. Jesus, if I did I'd tell you, Mr Reilly.'

'You might. You might. Where in Scotland?'

'Did she go? Glasgow. Always Glasgow.'

Now that he had capitulated Eddie McCluskey tried to ingratiate himself. He leaned forward on the table, looking intently at Reilly. 'You better watch that one, Mr Reilly. She really hates you. Especially now that you beat her to it and claimed responsibility for the bomb. She's mad you know. Crazy bloody woman. She'll kill you if she can.'

Reilly smiled. 'So would a lot of other people.' He glanced towards Asher who had remained leaning against the door through the entire inquisition. A silent affirmative message passed between them. 'Right,' Reilly announced. 'That's that. Now since you've been a good boy I'll give you a choice. Which would you rather do – live out your life peacefully if in somewhat restricted circumstances, in prison that is,' he explained as he saw McCluskey rummaging in his mind for an understanding, 'or be set free now and be dead within, say, ten minutes?'

Whether it was the lack of option or the precise, matter-of-fact manner in which Reilly offered them that made McCluskey

152

break into a sweat it was impossible to tell. 'Jesus, Mr Reilly, I don't want to die. I haven't done anything. I – '

'So you would prefer to go to prison,' Reilly cut him off.

'I could be killed there too. Jeez – '

'Not by me or anyone connected with me you won't. If you fart-arse around and get your fellow prisoners against you that would be your problem.'

'You mean you wouldn't have me – '

'Killed in prison?' Reilly sounded hurt. 'Certainly not. I've given you the choice.'

McCluskey shrugged. As far as he was concerned there was no choice now. 'Yes. Prison, Mr Reilly.'

'Now that is very sensible, Eddie. I mean you at least stand a chance of getting out one day, don't you? Doesn't he Inspector?'

'Oh yes,' Asher said.

'Now, Eddie, the Inspector will take a statement from you. And what you will say in that statement is quite straight-forward. You will say that yourself and Patrick Moran hit Corporal Wilson over the head and knocked him out. This you did *after* he had left Carson's shop. You put him in the back of your van. You drove him back to your house and put him in the shed at the back of your house. Clear so far?' Reilly asked, speaking very slowly and deliberately as he might have to someone not quite alert or someone very old. Without waiting for an answer he continued. 'After you put him in the shed at the back of your house you shot him. Afraid that he was not quite dead Moran then shot him a second time with a different gun. Then you were sure he was dead. You were going to dump the body only Inspector Asher got to you first. Perfectly simple.'

Eddie McCluskey was so bewildered that he would have agreed to anything, particularly if it was proposed by Seamus Reilly.

'Yes, Mr Reilly I'll swear to that.'

'Now that's being sensible.'

153

As they walked back along the corridor Asher said: 'Was that what you wanted?'

'Oh yes. You can pick up Moran any time after McCluskey has made his statement. The woman is best left to me. And don't forget, John – pop another bullet into Wilson's body. There's supposed to be two. We'd look a right pair of fools if after all this they could only find one bullet.'

Reilly gave a small shudder as he went out of the gates, and bestowed a wary smile on Asher.

'Glad to be out then?' Asher asked.

'Damn place gives me the creeps.'

'It's your guilty conscience, Seamus.'

Reilly opened the car door and got in. Closing the door he lowered the window. 'I suppose,' he said, flicking his thumb towards the driver, 'he knows I'm an innocent?'

Asher laughed. 'He knows he can drop you off wherever you want, if that's what you mean. Good night, Seamus.'

'Hopefully.'

Alone in the back seat Reilly lit a cigar. He was, so far, well pleased. Not that he had gleaned much new information, but he had had it confirmed, if by guesswork, that the actual bomb planters had been brought down from Glasgow. That was one thing. Something else that satisfied him was that Major Fisher would not be thought of as having murdered his colleague. Not that Reilly had a soft spot for the Major. He hadn't; but he knew Fisher would be more – more manageable when he learned of Reilly's kindness; he would be far more likely to look kindly on what Reilly was going to suggest to him; he would fulfil his role in the scheme of things – of that Seamus Reilly was certain.

Reilly might, however, have been rather less certain of Fisher's malleability had he overheard the conversation that took place between Colonel Maddox and Fisher the next morning. Fisher was looking dismal as the day was cold. Colonel Maddox made a great show of making him relax. 'Do you know what my grandmother used to say, Fisher? Eh? She lived to be a hundred and one, and she always said there were only two things in life that kept a person sane: reading *The Wind in the Willows* and several strong drinks of whisky every day. Actually,' the Colonel confided. 'she said tea, but a small transposition is valid, don't you think? Now drink that,' he ordered, handing Fisher a tumbler half-filled with Teachers, 'and the world will seem a different place.'

Fisher took the tumbler and drank; and for a moment it looked as if it might work. Alas, only for a moment. 'Sir, I can't take it any more. Can you transfer me back to England?'

Maddox, his glass half-way to his lips, looked pained, and put the glass back on his desk without drinking. As ever when upset and seeking words he took to turning the signet ring on his little finger, rubbing it as if this would bring forth its magic powers; but there was no sign of magic when he spoke. 'I'm afraid that is not possible, Major. I only wish it was. I wish we could all get away from this place. But we are here for a reason and here we must stay. You know, this is the third time I've been here? It gets no easier, no less bitter.'

None of which was what Major Fisher wanted to hear. His hands were shaking and he had difficulty getting the glass to his mouth; when he did he gulped the whisky down, the tumbler rattling against his teeth.

'It has often struck me,' Maddox went on, somehow feeling that by just talking he could calm the Major, 'that there are only two kinds of people – the manipulated and the manipulators. From time to time both change sides and reverse roles. For the moment we, you and I, are the manipulated, but this is not always a bad thing. You will have to believe me when I tell you that you must stay, just as I must stay. Because of the – ' Maddox hesitated, ' – the situation, we have been forced to form links with strange allies, people who many would regard as our enemies, as terrorists. That is the real horror of war, you know – the hypocrisy, the intrigue and treachery, the survival of the guilty and the death of the innocent.'

If Maddox knew what he was talking about, Fisher certainly didn't. 'Sir, I – '

Maddox held up a hand. 'Please, Major, don't make me refuse you again. You are needed here, now more than ever. The two men who forced you to – forgive me – to kill Wilson have been arrested – oh, don't be alarmed,' he said quickly as he saw the look of consternation in Fisher's eyes. 'Indeed no. They have been persuaded – Seamus Reilly's word – to confess to the murder of Wilson. What you did in that barn is your secret. Even I have forgotten about it. Only you now know – you and your God if you have one.' Maddox paused. Then: 'But the third person, the woman, is still at large. Reilly believes it was she who organized that bomb in Brighton. He wants her. He is, really, doing our job for us – oh, not out of the goodness of his heart: for his own reasons, but he can do it far more efficiently than we could. He has told me he may require your help. I told him he could count on it.'

'I don't understand, sir.'

Maddox smiled gently. 'You will. Please trust my judgement. Just make your peace with yourself. Be patient. Help me in this matter.'

Bewildered and frightened Fisher was touched by the Colonel's plea for help. It had a kindness and loneliness about it with which he could easily identify. It was as though the Colonel, too, felt abandoned. 'Very well, sir. I'm sorry, sir. Sorry for making – '

Maddox held a finger to his lips. 'Shh,' he whispered. 'You'll come out of this all right, Major. I'm sure of it.'

Two hours later when Seamus Reilly phoned him and asked if he could arrange for the Major to be available at three o'clock, the Colonel agreed.

'Thank you, Colonel.' 'If possible outside St Enoch's.'

'Very well. Just one thing. I'm holding you responsible for anything that happens to him.'

'That is understood. I've already told him he will be safe in my protection.'

'For your sake I hope he is. I can promise you, Reilly, if anything happens to him I will have you crucified. I promise you that.'

Reilly sounded amused. 'Thank you, Colonel,' he said and rang off.

'That's fixed,' Reilly told Regan as he returned to his sitting room. 'Maddox has agreed. The Major will be at St Enoch's at three o'clock. Have O'Neill pick him up and bring him here, will you?'

'Certainly, Mr Reilly.'

'You have the woman covered?'

'Oh yes. I've had men watching her house all day. She's still in there. They've seen her look out of the window several times but she hasn't set foot outside the house.'

'I'm going to have to send Fisher to her. We'll have to take the chance that she believes what he tells her.'

'Will she?'

'Huh. I wish I knew. She might. She just might. He'll be the only contact she has. I hope to God Asher got that report of the arrests into the evening papers. It's vital she sees that.'

'Suppose she doesn't go out for a paper.'

Reilly tutted, irked that he had been misunderstood. 'No. I want Fisher to bring one with him when he goes. If he can produce that as evidence it will give credence to the story he'll tell her. God, I hope Asher got it in.'

The woman had calmed down, although it had taken her the best part of the day to do it. At first, alone when Eddie McCluskey had been unceremoniously ejected, her fury had sustained her, keeping the danger of her own position in the background of her mind. But in the evening, still alone, her solitude less bearable in the dark, the first creeping apprehensions started to surface. She had failed, and failure was like a sentence of living death: she would, she now realized, be an outcast. But she hadn't failed, dammit. She had succeeded, only Seamus Reilly had out-manoeuvred her, and the promises she had made with such bravado had been brought to nought, leaving her exposed and fair game to be ridiculed.

She made no attempt to sleep. All through the night she paced about. She thought about contacting McCluskey and Moran but rejected the idea, fearing although unwilling to admit it, that they, too, would have abandoned her.

By dawn she was scheming again, the full force of her loathing directed at attaining revenge on Seamus Reilly. No easy matter at the best of times; even less now. But somehow, somehow, somehow she would bring the bastard down. The more her rage subsided the more she was prepared to concede that it was her pride urging her on. So what? For far too long she had been 'tolerated'. That's all bloody Irish men did anyway: tolerate their women. Useful but brainless. She fixed herself a large gin and tonic. Purposefully she stood in front of the mirror as she drank, watching herself, eyeing her image, wondering what the nuns would have made of the dear little Catholic girl who had been so sweet, so pretty, so holy at Mass, so good at her catechism: the demure, shy, alert girl who had spoken so often of joining the convent. That was so long ago. Brutishly she stuck out her tongue at her reflection, aware that the silly action was only to counteract the tears she felt welling into her eyes. So bloody long ago . . .

– They've killed your Daddy, Mammy told her.

She had not understood.

– They've killed your poor Daddy and taken your brothers away.

Still it had meant nothing.

– They've left only you and me to fend for ourselves. Oh, Holy Mother of God how are we going to manage?

It wasn't until months later when her favourite brother died from hunger in prison that the awfulness began to sink in. Then her second brother, Peadar, never the bright one but harmless and kind, came home. He had changed terribly. Always afraid. Hiding himself away in dark places. And Mammy having to try and find him and bring him out to eat; sometimes not bothering and bringing his food to him, putting the plate on the floor in front of him like he was an animal. That was when she knew about the awfulness.

– Don't you worry, Mammy. They'll never do anything like that to us again.

– There's no one left for them to do it to, girl.

– They'll be sorry. I promise you, Mammy, they'll be sorry.

And Mammy had looked at her fondly and stroked her hair, her lovely long and shining hair . . . .

She shook herself away from the dreams and moved to the window, peering out. It was drizzling and grey and unwelcoming. A car drove past, its tyres hissing on the damp street. Two girls, giggling, hugging themselves together under an umbrella, trotted along the pavement apparently playing at two-legged racing. The woman shivered and left the window. *Do* something, she told herself. But what was there to do? Whatever there was it could not be done now, she decided. Later. Tonight. When it got dark. She would do something then, and she had until then to think about what to do. She added a drop more gin to her drink.

Major Fisher felt much the better for Colonel Maddox's peptalk. He felt quite calm and at peace as the car drove him to Seamus Reilly's house, even to the point of asking good-humouredly: 'No blindfold this time?'

'Not this time,' Sean O'Neill told him. 'My orders didn't say anything about a blindfold.'

'And you always follow orders.'

'Yes. Yes I do.'

Seamus Reilly was waiting for them. He dismissed O'Neill to the kitchen with 'make yourself a cup of tea, Sean,' and, taking Fisher by the arm guided him into the sitting room. 'You'll never believe it,' he said chattily, 'but I got my first Christmas card this morning. From New Zealand. And you know something? I haven't a clue who it's from,' he admitted, finding this amusing and chortling away.

Encouraged by the friendliness, Fisher ventured: 'Perhaps it's one of last year's just arriving.'

Seamus Reilly enjoyed the joke. He threw back his head and

laughed. 'I never thought of that. You're probably right. I still don't know who sent it though.' Then, with a complete about-face of humour, his eyes darkening, he went on: 'Colonel Maddox has spoken to you?'

'Yes. This morning.'

'He explained that I need you to do something for me?'

'He said something about it.'

Again Reilly switched his humour, this time becoming paternal and concerned. 'You must be puzzled by the webs we weave,' he said. 'I certainly would be if I was you. The Colonel is – or he *was*, but I think he understands us better now. You see, we are not all monsters as some people would have you believe – the same people, mind you, who, for some unknown, perverse reason refuse to believe that we, too, only want peace. They think we *enjoy* killing.' Reilly stopped and shook his head as though still trying to fathom the reason for the folly. 'Nothing could be further from the truth,' he added, then paused again. Suddenly he became very businesslike. 'But you didn't come here to listen to me philosophizing, did you?'

Fisher managed a small smile.

'Of course you didn't. Right. You'll be wanting to know what it is I need you to do?'

Fisher nodded warily.

Reilly smiled. 'Still don't trust me? Never mind. Why should you? You don't know me. I never trust anyone I don't know. To tell the truth I'm not so sure I trust them when I *do* know them. But you can believe it when I say that I will take care of you. I won't ask you to do anything that might endanger your life.'

Fisher accepted this with another slow nod.

'Now, where was I? Ah. The Colonel will have told you about the two boyos? The ones who made you dispose of the unfortunate Corporal?'

'Yes. Thanks. He told you you made them confess to the shooting.'

'Well, in principle they did it, didn't they? Besides, it suited me that way. Which leaves us with one more to deal with.'

'The woman?'

'Exactly. That damned, accursed woman. A silly bitch really. Fancies herself as a sort of leader of the underdogs,' Reilly told Fisher scathingly. 'I'll tell you for nothing that she abominates me,' he went on, rubbing his hands together as though he relished being abominated. 'But I'm afraid she's bitten off a bit more than she can chew this time. With your help she is, so to speak, about to choke.'

Reilly rose to his feet and planted himself in front of the electric fire, warming his backside. After a few seconds he began to speak again in a slow, careful voice. 'What I want you to do is this. At eight o'clock tonight I will have you taken to her house. You will be given a newspaper in which there should be a report on the arrest of McCluskey and Moran – your two friends. If the report is not in the paper you won't have to bring one, but I am assured that it will be in there. She will be suspicious, of course, and the first thing she'll want to know is how you found out where she lives. You tell her – now listen to this carefully – you tell her that Sandy told you. She'll check on that but I'll have arranged that she hears what she wants to hear. The next thing you tell her is that you were hauled in before the Colonel – don't be specific – just the Colonel. If she insists on a name tell her Maddox. Now, the Colonel tells you he has reports that you have been seen associating – that's the word, isn't it? – with McCluskey and Moran. He further tells you that McCluskey and Moran have been arrested in connection with the bombing in Brighton. He also tells you that there is a woman involved and wants to know what *you* know about this woman. All right so far?'

Fisher nodded.

'Now, most importantly, the Colonel wants to know what you can tell him about certain people in Glasgow. He tells you their names but you can't for the life of you remember them since you don't know them in the first place. Clear?'

'Yes. I think so.'

'All through this you've got to look as though you're starting to panic. Try gibbering,' Reilly suggested with a little grin. 'I don't know how you gibber but try it. I am certain she will want to know the names the Colonel is supposed to have given you. I'm banking on that. I'm banking on her trying to jog your memory by suggesting a few names. She's no fool, though. She'll probably start off by giving you any old name. But I want you to memorize every name she suggests. Every single name. Got that?'

'Yes.'

'That's all I want. The names. When you've got those you can get out of there any way you can. You'll be picked up again on your way back to your barracks and brought here. But forget everything else. Just keep repeating the names over and over to yourself so that you can give them to me. As soon as you get here blurt them out. No hellos or how are yous or anything else. Just spit out the names. Can I count on you for that?'

'I'll do my best.'

Reilly shook his head. 'I'm afraid your best isn't good enough. I've got to have names,' he stressed almost vehemently.

'I'll get them.'

Reilly relaxed and smiled. 'That's just what I wanted to hear. Thank you, Major.'

From his tone of voice it was clear that Reilly considered the meeting over. Fisher stood up. 'Is that everything?'

Reilly nodded. 'Yes. That's everything. Enough I would think. You can, as we say, go in peace,' he said with a mischievous grin. 'Of course you would know that. You're Catholic, aren't you?'

'Yes.'

'Ah. More than ever difficult for you, then, this – what you've been through,' Reilly said, then his eyes twinkled and he added. 'Not that non-Catholics would have found it easy, but they're not quite as crucified to their religion as we are, are they? They seem to find it possible to escape now and then for a breather, for a breath of fresh heretical air. Whereas we – ' He shrugged. 'Go on. Off you go. You can make your peace with God in your own time.'

Fisher gave a hard, sharp laugh. 'You're the second person who said that to me. The Colonel said all I had to do was make my peace with God too.'

Reilly looked surprised. 'You surprise me. It's not something I would have thought the Colonel would say. Perhaps he *does* understand,' he added vaguely. 'Anyway,' he went on again, 'do what he says. It's always better to have the Lord on your side. And He's not as intolerant as He used to be,' Seamus pointed out, coming across the room and leaning close to the Major as if he was about to impart a deep secret. 'We've broadened His mind considerably,' he whispered in his ear.

Fisher looked as if he might be about to make some reply but was forestalled by the telephone ringing in the hall. Reilly excused himself politely and left the room; in no time he was back, beaming. 'The report I mentioned. It's in all the papers. That will help you no end.'

Fisher looked dubious still, but nodded none the less.

'Well, what can I say?' Reilly asked. 'Good luck and mind how you go. I'll see you later tonight when hopefully all this will be over and done with.'

'Yes. Hopefully.'

'O'Neill,' Seamus Reilly called, and when O'Neill came trotting from the kitchen he added: 'Take this gentleman back to where you met him.'

'Yes, Mr Reilly.'

Closing the front door behind them Seamus Reilly leaned his back against it and closed his eyes. That's all he had to live for, he thought. Hope.

It was with not much more than hope, too, that Major Fisher hammered on the door of the woman's house with his fist. He seemed to be left hammering for a long time, but he persevered, grinning once when he thought of Reilly's advice to gibber. There was a spyhole in the door and, though he could not be certain, he would have sworn he was being peered at. Finally the door opened. 'Christ!' the woman swore 'What the – come in for Christ's sake,' she whispered and dragged him into the hall by the sleeve.

Immediately Fisher began to blurt out his message. 'I didn't know what to do or where to go. When Sandy gave me your address I had to come round. What am I going to do? You've got to help me.'

The woman was taken aback by this onslaught, and for the moment the only thing she could think of to do was bring the wretch into her kitchen and give him a drink. 'What's the matter with you?' she asked absurdly as she started the kettle to boil.

'You don't know? You don't know those two blokes have been arrested?'

'What two blokes?' the woman asked still at a loss.

'*Your* two blokes. Look there's pictures of them in the paper,' Fisher told her and opened the paper for her to see.

Disbelieving and seeming to sense some invisible trap the woman came to the table and stared at the paper. 'Holy Jesus,' she whispered, her face growing pale.

'And that's not all,' Fisher went on, pushing his advantage. 'I've been hauled in to the Colonel.'

'What for?' the woman snapped.

'What for? For associating with those two,' Fisher said pointing to the photograph. 'You know what those two were up to, don't you? Only blowing up that hotel in Brighton. Not only them. There's a whole gang of them in Glasgow.'

The woman looked away. She walked to the far end of the table and sat down, ignoring the boiling water, allowing the kettle to switch itself off. 'Glasgow,' she whispered, possibly to herself.

'Yes Glasgow. He read me a whole list of names asking me which ones I'd heard of.'

The woman became immediately alert. 'Names? What names?'

Fisher put on a great act of exasperation. 'I don't know. I wasn't hardly listening. I don't know anyone in Glasgow,' he said. Then noticing what he felt might be her interest waning he added quickly. 'One I think I remember. Murphy, I think. Or Murray. Yea – Murray, that's it. Murray.'

'Any others?'

'I can't remember I tell you.'

'Jameson?' the woman suggested.

Fisher shook his head miserably. Jameson he memorized. 'Rourk?'

Again he shook his head. Rourk.

'Masterson?'

Better not be too dumb. 'What was that one?'

'Masterson.'

Fisher grimaced. 'That could have been one.' Masterson. 'Drumm?'

'No.' Drumm.

'Mulcahy?'

Fisher took to shaking his head again. Mulcahy.

The woman got to her feet and switched on the kettle again. 'What else?' she demanded.

'What else what?'

'Did they ask you.'

Fisher looked blank. 'Nothing. Jesus wasn't that enough? You've got to help me get out of this.'

Drumming her fingers on the worktop the woman said 'Yes, yes, yes,' but clearly without meaning it. 'What about me? Was I mentioned?' she demanded at last.

Fisher shook his head. 'I don't know. I don't even know your name, do I? There was nothing that sounded like a woman's name though.'

'I see,' the woman said, the fear in her eyes a little less.

'Yea, but what about *me*?' Fisher pushed on. 'What am I going to do?'

'You just sit still there a minute,' he was told. 'Make yourself some tea if you want it. I've a call to make.'

Alone Fisher ran through the names: Jameson, Rourk, Masterson, Drumm, Mulcahy. He repeated them over and over. He could hear the murmur of a voice coming from another room, and was on the point of going to the door to see if he could pick up any of the words when the voice stopped. Almost immediately the woman came back in. She looked, somehow, less tense, and when she spoke there was more confidence in her voice. Fisher was trying to make out the reason for this when she told him. 'That was Sandy,' she said. 'He says Eddie,' the woman pointed to the open newspaper, 'told him to send you here.'

Fisher looked at the paper. 'This one? Edward McCluskey?'

'Yes.'

Fisher shrugged. 'I don't know anything about that. All I know is that I went to Sandy's to try and find – eh – McCluskey after the Colonel had me in, and Sandy said I was to get round here as fast as I could.'

The woman smiled ominously. 'But what I can't understand is why the Colonel would let you wander off out of the barracks if he thought you were – '

Fisher decided to shout. 'He fucking well didn't. I *got* out. I'm not supposed to *be* out. I'm on the bloody run. That's why you've got to help me.'

For several seconds the woman stared into his pleading eyes without blinking. Then she blinked once. 'Well, you can't stay here, that's for sure. Can you make your way back to Sandy's without getting picked up?'

'I don't know. I expect so.'

'Well do that. I'll phone him again and tell him to expect you. He'll put you up for a day or two. Then I'll get you out.'

'You're sure?'

'Of course I'm sure.'

'You better. God knows what those two are saying,' Fisher pointed out, emphasizing his urgency by picking up the newspaper and shaking it.

'I said I'd get you out. Just you do what Sandy tells you to.'

'All right.'

'You better get moving. Out the back way. If you cut through the first street on your left it'll bring you back out onto the main road. You know your way from there.'

'Yes.'

Seamus Reilly had clearly been on tenterhooks. He opened the door before O'Neill had time to knock; and worried that Fisher might say something before giving him the names he took him by the arm and guided him immediately into the sitting room, all the while making a curious circular motion with his other hand as though he was winding an ancient, invisible phonograph. He sat Fisher in a chair and took a writing pad and ballpoint pen from the table by the fire. Holding the biro poised he said 'Now.'

Fisher closed his eyes and started the litany. 'Jameson. Rourk. Masterson. Drumm. Mulcahy.' He repeated the names again.

Reilly checked his list, his eyes shining. 'You did excellently,' he announced finally. 'No problems?'

Fisher shook his head. 'I'm supposed to be on my way to Sandy's now. He will get a call from the woman to tell him to hide me for a few days.'

'Good man,' Reilly told him. Then he turned to O'Neill. 'Get me Sandy on the phone.'

'I'm on the run from the army now,' Fisher contributed.

'Of course you are,' Seamus told him delightedly. 'Actually what you're going to do, Major, is stay in your barracks for the next few days. Colonel Maddox will see to it that you're relieved of all duties. He'll probably put you on the sick list.'

Fisher nodded.

'I've got Sandy, Mr Reilly,' O'Neill said, sticking his head round the door.

Reilly went immediately to the phone, coughing to clear his throat as he went. 'Sandy?'

'Yes, Mr Reilly.'

'Have you had a call from that woman yet?'

'I have. A couple of minutes ago. I'm supposed to stow someone for a few days. That Brit. He's on his way here now.'

'He isn't. He's here. Now listen. Give it ten minutes and call her back — you have her number?'

Sandy chuckled. 'Yea. She just gave it to me. I'm supposed to confirm that he's arrived.'

'Good. In ten minutes do just that. Tell her he's arrived safely and that you're sending him to the piggery later tonight.'

'Okay, Mr Reilly.'

'Now, at 10.15 exactly – exactly mind – I want you to call her again. I need her occupied for five minutes. What you say to her doesn't matter, just keep her on the phone for five minutes – got that?'

'Ring her at a quarter past ten exactly and keep her talking for five minutes. Yea, I've got that.'

'Fine. Now one more thing, Sandy. At 11.30 you're to call her again. This time you say that Fisher is causing trouble. Tell her he's refusing to stay at the piggery. Tell her he's going berserk and wants to get back to his barracks unless he can talk to her. You've got to make it sound desperate. I want that damn woman to go to the piggery.'

'I'll get her to go all right, Mr Reilly. You needn't worry about that.'

'She might just ask you to accompany her, Sandy. Don't. I want her to drive there alone. If she asks you to send someone else with her you'll have to wangle your way out of it. She's got to go alone. Clear?'

'Yes, Mr Reilly.'

'Good. I'll see to it that we don't forget this.'

'That's all right, Mr Reilly.'

'Thank you.'

When he came back to the sitting room, Seamus Reilly was his old businesslike self again; when he spoke his words were crisp and to the point. 'Right, O'Neill. Take the Major back. See him safely home. Then get in touch with Regan. Who's our mechanic?' he asked suddenly.

'Jimmy Doyle, Mr Reilly.'

'Tell Regan to pick up Doyle and bring him here. I want them here within the next hour. If you can't contact Regan, pick up Doyle yourself and bring him. You'll be able to find Doyle I suppose?'

'No problem. He's always in that garage of his in the evening.

Doing up some E-Type he got cheap. He'll be there without a doubt.'

'Good. Go on then. We don't have a lot of time.' Then Reilly turned to the Major. 'Thank you again,' he said, sounding sincere enough. 'I think you can safely say you'll be back in England before long. And don't forget what I told you – God is a lot more broadminded than they would have us believe.'

John Asher was peeved to be taken from his supper. His indigestion was bad enough without having his meals interrupted. But he soon forgot about his discomfort when he sensed the urgency in Seamus Reilly's voice. He listened intently, his eyes narrowing from time to time, then widening in surprise. He answered the few questions Reilly posed as briefly as he could, always in the affirmative. His longest statement came just before he hung up. 'I'll leave at once,' he said. And he did, throwing on his overcoat and leaving the house at the trot.

Colonel Maddox, also, was none too pleased to be called from the sparse comfort of his quarters. Indeed, when he came downstairs and confronted John Asher he was positively waspish. 'What is it *now*, John?' he asked.

'I'm sorry to disturb you, Colonel, but it is very urgent. I've just had Seamus Reilly on to me.'

'And what does *he* want?' Maddox demanded, sounding weary but keeping the sting in his voice.

Asher glanced about the hallway, obviously uneasy that he might be overheard. 'Could we – ?' he suggested, indicating a doorway.

'If we must.'

Maddox led the way across the hall and opened the door. Almost at once he backed out and shut it again. 'In use,' he informed Asher, now sounding thoroughly annoyed. 'We'll go in there.'

In there was the gents toilet, and Maddox strode towards it. 'Now what is so damned urgent?'

'The woman, Colonel. Reilly has arranged for us to pick her up. He's arranging for her to drive towards the border near Clones but he's had her car fixed so that it will break down before she gets there.'

'Well, pick her up, why don't you?'

'It had better be a military operation. To get sufficient men out I'd have to make too many explanations, and I don't have time to explain. '

'And on what excuse do I pick her up?'

'Not that you need one, Colonel, but Reilly has arranged that too. The boot of her car will be well stocked with explosives. If you could just have her taken in to Castlereagh we will do the rest.'

'And where is this car supposed to break down?'

Asher had been afraid of that. 'Reilly couldn't, of course, be absolutely sure. He thinks it should be about two miles this side of the border. You'd have to order her to be shadowed. A helicopter could do it nicely,' he concluded, slurring his concluding words upwards into a question.

'I'm sure it could,' the Colonel remarked sarcastically.

Feeling that time was being wasted and that he had not yet quite won the Colonel round, Asher went on. 'Major Fisher did everything he could to assist us in this matter, sir. He was most helpful. It would be cruel to have his efforts go to waste.'

'Very well,' the Colonel agreed at last. 'Wait in the hall, John, and I'll send someone down to you. Captain Young probably would be best. You can brief him.'

'Thank you, Colonel.'

'I just hope you two know what you're doing. The flak is already coming in from London. I'll have to give them something soon.'

'You can, Colonel.'

'You sound very sure.'

'I *am* sure.'

'Huh. I didn't think that was ever possible in this wretched place.'

170

The woman reversed her car out of the short, steep driveway. Sandy's phone call had been the final straw; although every instinct warned against going to the piggery, it was a risk, she told herself, she had to take: all she needed was that whingeing bloody Brit shooting off his mouth and then the shit really would hit the fan. She switched on the windscreen wipers as the rain suddenly bucketed down. Bugger Sandy for not coming. It was always the same: whenever you needed someone to help you in an emergency they always had excuses. Constantly she looked in her mirror as she drove through and out of the city. Nothing. All the good citizens were safely tucked up in their beds. Prods and Catholics alike needed their goddam beauty sleep. She slowed down at a crossroads and was about to curse as the engine coughed and almost stalled, but it picked up again grudgingly and on she went.

The nearer she got to the border the more relaxed she became, even dismissing the continued pinking of the engine as a minor hazard, putting it down to the damp: every year it gave the same trouble. When all this was behind her she would celebrate by trading it in for something more reliable. A helicopter flew overhead, quite low. More fucking Paras on their way to terrify the shit out of some poor unfortunate. She watched its winking lights veer away and disappear behind a hillock. Maybe it had turned back. Even the mighty fucking Paras hated the rain and the dark. Hopefully the bloody thing would crash.

She was about two and a half miles from the border when the car suddenly backfired loudly and came to a clunking stand-still. Steam poured from the bonnet, and there were small metallic cracking noises. At first the full extent of her predicament did not seem to strike her: she sat in the car, staring out, strumming the steering wheel with her fingers. The rain had stopped as suddenly as it had begun. She got out of the car and stalked around it. The hissing steam had subsided, and it was probably this that suggested that the engine might hopefully, miraculously have recovered. She was on the point of getting back in behind the wheel and attempting to start it when the

171

helicopter rose from behind the hillock, a glaring searchlight blazing from beneath its undercarriage, momentarily blinding her. Then a squawking megaphonic voice roared at her. '*Get out of the car. Put your hands on the roof. Spread your legs. Do not move.*' If further orders were given they were lost in the whirring whine of the descent, the great blades whipping up a storm, bending the bare branches of the trees that lined the narrow lane. She obeyed, still calm. They would search her, of course. They always started off by searching. And they'd take their time about it, their thick callous fingers groping about and lingering in all her nooks and crannies. They liked doing that, liked to cheapen people. Anything to humiliate. All the time making their lewd suggestions and sneering at one another, boasting of what they could do to her, already doing most of it in their minds. Oh, she'd been through all that. Several times. But she'd survive it yet again, using it to refuel her hatred. Fuck them all. They couldn't detain her. They couldn't do a damn thing. The car had simply broken down. Even here they could not make that an offence.

Three figures emerged from a gateway in the hedge, their faces smeared with black grease, their automatic-rifles thrust out before them. Two of the Paras walked round behind her, each of them grabbing one of her arms and twisting it behind her, yanking her away from the car. The third, seeming huge and sinister in the forged light of flashing torches, went directly to the back of the car and opened the boot. 'Corporal,' he yelled. 'Get that torch over here.'

There was a rustle behind the hedge. A radio crackled for a second and went dead. A fourth figure appeared and went to the back of the car. A flashlight was switched on. 'Take the bitch in.'

Immediately the woman went berserk. She tried to wrench herself free, screaming with the pain. She yelled obscenities and tried to spit at the two Paras holding her. 'You fucking Brit bastards. I've done fuck all.'

The Para left the boot, took two strides towards her, and hit her hard across the face. 'Shut your fucking mouth, you slut.

Done fuck all? What's all this then? Fucking Christmas presents?' He grabbed her by the hair and dragged her to the back of the car, shining the torch back into the boot.

The woman stared in total disbelief. At least half a dozen Armalite rifles. Hand guns. Grenades. Pounds of explosive. Suddenly it all became clear to her. A set-up. Seamus Reilly had set her up. It had to be him – nobody else could have manipulated everyone with such ease. Bloody Seamus Reilly. What a stupid goddam fool she'd been! Without warning she let her body go limp and started to laugh; a wild, crazed, hysterical laugh. And she was still laughing when they threw her into the helicopter and put their boots on her to keep her down.

'They've just sent her over here to Castlereagh,' John Asher told Reilly down the phone.

'Everything went according to plan?'

'Without a hitch.'

Reilly sighed. 'Good.'

'You want to come over now?'

'God no. I'm dead beat, John. Let her stew. She'll keep till the morning. Do her no end of good to wait.'

'Whatever you say. I'm done in myself. Goodnight.'

'Goodnight.'

· FIFTEEN ·

Late the following afternoon the woman was taken in an unmarked car to the docks. Her hands were handcuffed behind her back, and she was made to lie on the floor. She had no shoes, and a woollen cap had been put on her head and pulled down, covering her eyes. John Asher sat on the seat above her, ignoring her for the most part. He was preoccupied, wondering what on earth Reilly had schemed up this time. He obviously knew what he was about: everything had worked like clockwork thus far.

As they approached the main gates a klaxon sounded, signalling the end of the day's work. Immediately, as if they had been on their marks for some minutes, men came streaming out, mostly on foot, but some on bicycles, and a few in cars. John Asher leaned forward towards the front seat. 'Make for number four,' he instructed, peering out over the driver's shoulder. As the crowd thinned the place took on the eeriness engendered by huge, abandoned machinery. Arc lights had been switched on, the massive cranes casting geometric shadows, their criss-cross metallic structure giving Asher the impression he was being driven through penetrable, ghostly chain-link fencing.

Soon the driver brought the car to a halt outside an enormous, low warehouse, the figure 4 painted on its sliding metal doors. Almost before the engine had been switched off Asher was out of the car and making for the entrance. He peered inside, squinting. There was only one small circle of light in the entire warehouse: a high wattage naked bulb suspended over what could have been a rostrum or high desk. Beside this, one arm resting on it, stood Seamus Reilly, flanked by Regan and O'Neill, with Jim Dowling standing a little further back. Asher looked back towards the car and signalled his driver to bring the woman in. He waited for them by the door. As they approached he gestured that the woman be taken towards the light. Then he followed, keeping several paces behind. Nobody spoke. Not even the woman made a sound when the cap was removed; her eyes sought and remained fixed on the small dapper figure under the light. Then Thomas Regan moved forward and took her by one arm, raising it behind her back. The driver unlocked the handcuffs and pocketed them. Reilly leaned a little sideways and nodded to Asher. John Asher spun on his heel and marched from the warehouse, followed by his driver. When Seamus Reilly finally spoke, his tone did nothing to disperse the macabre tension. 'You were told what would happen if you defied our instructions and undertook any action without our sanction, were you not?' he asked, politely enough.

The woman ignored him, transferring her gaze on the bulb over his head.

'We know it was you who masterminded the Brighton bomb,' Reilly went on undeterred. 'We know you got either Drumm or Mulcahy to plant the device. You kindly told us that. Of all the names you suggested to Major Fisher only those two correspond to men we have in the field, both, funnily enough, in Glasgow. We know you made several trips to the city.'

At the mention of Drumm's name, her eyes flickered towards Reilly.

'I might regret having to punish you had you not made Major Fisher shoot one of his colleagues. That was a heinous thing to do. Hence I have no regrets whatsoever about the punishment.'

The woman stared at Reilly with undisguised hatred.

'Have you anything to say?' he asked, being absurdly democratic.

There was a pause. Reilly had half turned away when the woman screamed: 'Yes, Reilly I have something to say. I say fuck you and your likes. You're all full of shit. You think you can talk the fucking Brits into giving us back what is ours. You can't. But you're all too shit scared to put up a fight. They've beaten you, Reilly. They've made you one of their bloody lapdogs. Well the fight will go on no matter what you do with me. There are still some decent fighting men left who won't rest until we've killed every last Brit who has a foot on our soil.'

'Finished?' Reilly asked.

'Fuck you Reilly,' the woman screamed as though she had practised this chant. Then she spat at him.

Seamus Reilly turned to O'Neill and jerked his head towards the woman. 'You and Dowling take care of this, please,' he requested. 'You come with me, Thomas,' he added, and walked quickly from the warehouse.

As arranged John Asher was waiting for him by the dock gates. When he spotted Reilly and Regan approaching he had a quick word with the security guard who promptly closed the door of his little hut and buried his head in a newspaper, holding it with some exaggeration high in front of his face, only emerging when he heard the two cars start up: he came out, locked the gates and, shivering with the cold, returned to his paper. It was a sombre Seamus Reilly who spoke first, not looking at Asher who sat beside him, but fixing his eyes on the reflection in the windscreen of the headlights of his own car that followed. 'You can have your men find her tomorrow, John. A couple of days' silence, I think. Then a brief report.'

Asher nodded. 'Very well.'

Reilly sighed, making a rasping, gargling noise in his throat. 'It never ends,' he said, almost as if he were just thinking aloud. 'Just when it seems – oh, to hell with it,' he concluded abruptly, taking out one of his cigars and lighting it.

They travelled almost half a mile before Asher spoke. 'It's almost over,' he said, trying to be a comfort but managing only to sound wishful.

Reilly shook his head. 'It's never almost over, John. There will always be someone who thinks they know better. Someone who longs for power. Someone who feels we are getting weak. The trouble is a whole generation has grown up in the shadow of violence. For them it is the most normal thing in the world to kill in order to achieve their ends. They don't *think* any more. They simply cannot see that our strength for the future is in politics. Words frighten them. They are tired of words having no immediate, concrete effect.'

'They'll learn,' Asher offered.

'I'm afraid they won't until it is too late. I sometimes wonder if we haven't reared a generation of monsters. And they have youth on their side, with all its rashness. He paused. 'I just don't know what should be done.'

Obviously neither did Asher. 'We'll just have to do what we've done for years – ride it out,' was all he could suggest.

'No. No. No.' Reilly said sadly, pausing between each word to shake his head a couple of times. 'Those days have gone.' Suddenly he gave a short, bitter laugh. 'The glory days we used to call them. Glory!'

The car braked suddenly, throwing the two men forward. Then it moved on slowly, passing two cars involved in a minor collision, both drivers gesticulating wildly at each other. It seemed Seamus Reilly had not noticed. 'Those were the days when even death was glorious,' he continued.

Perhaps in a genuine effort to comfort Reilly, or perhaps, more likely, to relinquish responsibility, Asher said: 'Well, there's not much we can do about it, Seamus. The best we can hope to do is keep things ticking along until some genius comes up with a solution. Just keep things ticking along,' he repeated.

Reilly was still shaking his head. 'It's not enough. It's not enough. Someone has got to take a stand. Someone has got to be *forced* to take a stand,' he said vehemently.

Asher grinned. 'Well, take one,' he said, and was surprised at the sad, tormented look he got from Reilly.

'I might *have* to,' Reilly said. 'That is what frightens me, John. I might just have to.'

The car drew into the side of the road outside Reilly's house. Gratefully John Asher sidestepped any involvement in his friend's remark, by asking: 'What happens next? About the bombers, I mean.'

Reilly chewed his lower lip. 'I'm not altogether sure. I have to clear that. My – my jurisdiction does not cover Scotland. A decision on that will have to come from higher up.'

'Oh. Yes.'

'There's no hurry anyway. They think they're safe. They won't be going anywhere – not without my knowing at any rate.'

'You're sure?'

'Oh I'm sure. Give me a day or two.'

Nobody paid much attention to the small report in the papers a few days later. Who cared if the unidentified body of a woman had been found floating in the docks, particularly when the police did not suspect foul play? Probably another suicide. Some old tart who couldn't make it any more.

It was early December before Seamus Reilly was summoned to the Republic to meet with the Commander in Chief of the Provisional IRA. As soon as he received the summons Seamus knew something was wrong. He was certain of one thing: that the plan he had put forward had been rejected, perhaps not in full, but sufficiently for him to have a fight on his hands. Indeed, the fact that the meeting was to be held in the Commander's own home suggested that he might be fighting for rather more than the acceptance of his strategy.

'Ah, Seamus. An uneventful trip, I trust?'

'Thank you.'

'Come in and get yourself warm at the fire. It's the only

problem with Wicklow. Too much water about. Always damp. Beautiful but damp. Still, one can't have everything.'

'No.'

The Commander settled himself in his armchair and lit his pipe, eyeing Reilly through the haze of smoke. Between puffs he said: 'We've considered your plan, Seamus. It's very ingenious. I thought very highly of it. It showed your undoubted flair for the – shall we say the subtleties of bargaining.'

For a second Seamus Reilly felt he had misjudged the reason for his visit. His spirits rose, only to plummet again as the Commander continued in the same pleasant voice. 'Unfortunately, I am only one voice in the Council. In a word I have been outvoted.'

'I understand. So what happens – '

The Commander studied the bowl of his pipe as he said: 'Nothing.'

'Nothing?'

'That's it, Seamus. Nothing. Drumm is not to be touched. Indeed, he is to be commended,' the Commander explained, a hint of irony in his voice.

'You can't be serious,' Reilly expostulated, perhaps foolishly.

'I am. For the good of everyone we have been – we felt it was necessary to make certain concessions, certain allowances. At all costs we must avoid a serious split in our ranks. God knows there is enough dissent already. Many consider the Brighton bombing as a considerable coup and made it abundantly clear that should any further action be taken against the perpetrators they would feel obliged to disassociate themselves from us. We cannot stand another rift, Seamus. Besides, it will soon be forgotten. Everything will quickly return to normal and we can pursue our political objectives as before.'

'And when they decide to have another – coup?' Reilly asked, loading the word with sarcasm.

'They won't. That has been agreed.'

Seamus Reilly could not contain his laughter although aware that he was infuriating his superior. 'They *will*,' he said flatly.

'Don't you see? They have simply been testing your strength. If you give in to them on this they will see it as weakness, and before you know it they'll be blasting all hell out of what they consider to be legitimate targets all on the mainland.'

The Commander shook his head, trying to remain reasonable. 'They have agreed not to. They have been warned what will happen to them if they do.'

Seamus Reilly was dumbfounded at what he regarded as incredible naiveté. 'We gave them that warning before the Brighton bomb. They paid not a whit of notice. Why should they do so now? I'm sorry, but you're wrong, Commander. You've *got* to let me deal with Drumm and Mulcahy the way I suggested. I know the way they think. God Almighty I've been keeping people like that under control for the last fifteen years. You can believe me when I tell you they've – '

The Commander silenced him with a wave of his hand. He stroked his beard thoughtfully. When he spoke it was quietly, as though he was making an effort to be friendly and understanding, but his voice had a cold quality to it that Reilly recognized. 'Seamus, we've known each other a long time. We've been friends for a long time – far too long for us to allow something like this to destroy our friendship. As I have told you on many occasions, I admire you greatly. You are loyal. You are trustworthy. You are dedicated.' The Commander paused to let the compliments sink in. 'However,' he then went on, 'despite my admiration and fondness I must tell you that I will not tolerate your questioning the agreement that has been reached. I hope that you will accept the fact that we have decided it is for the best. Learn to live with it. I would grieve were it necessary for me to be forced to ensure your agreement. You understand what I'm saying?'

Reilly understood. For what seemed a very long time he just stared at the Commander, saying nothing, allowing his head to nod backwards and forwards. 'I understand,' he said finally.

Immediately the Commander cheered up, tapping his pipe vigorously in the ashtray. 'I knew you'd finally see things our way. We are only cogs in the great machine,' the Commander informed him in a mildly mocking way. 'Our destiny is determined by mere whims. We must adapt. Always be prepared to adapt, Seamus. Take my word for it. Adapt and you'll survive. Now, a drink?'

Reilly stood up. 'Thank you. No. I better be heading back.'

'Oh. You're sure?'

'Quite sure. Thank you.'

The Commander saw him out, even opening the car door for him. Just as Reilly was about to get in he felt a hand on his arm. 'We *have* reached an understanding, Seamus?' the Commander asked.

Reilly, bent to get into his seat, looked up. 'An understanding has been reached, Commander,' he said.

Seamus Reilly could never quite pinpoint the moment he decided he had to defy the Commander. Sometimes he believed it was the instant he had felt deliberately threatened; then again it could have been when the Commander had displayed a shocking misconception of the men he was so willing to barter with; or it might have been when it was declared that his destiny was determined by whims. Most likely, he ultimately thought, he had known from the moment he had received the message to visit the Commander, some small part of his mind tucking the defiance away for the moment it was confirmed that his plan had been rejected and a deal had been struck. Not that the actual timing made any difference: it didn't. What mattered to Seamus Reilly was why he had decided to choose his solitary, dangerous path. It was not vanity. Nor was it simply anger. When it came down to it Reilly knew his already exhausted spirit had rebelled at the prospect of continued violence, at the images of more and more maimed and crippled and dead people that haunted his mind. Innocent people. People who had simply tried to live out their lives, causing no harm to anyone. Perhaps a trifle too arrogantly, Reilly prided himself in the fact that he had never been responsible for the death of anyone who was truly innocent or uninvolved. Everyone had to accept the risks.

The evening of his return from Wicklow, Reilly went to bed early. He did not sleep. He did not want to sleep. He wanted to think. And in the quiet darkness of his room he allowed both the prosecution, so to speak, and the defence to argue their case, stating the pros and cons aloud. He was breaking the rule he had so vigorously enforced, and by so doing his death was a practical certainty. Oddly, this did not worry him for the moment. But the rule no longer applied, he decided. Not to him. And from long forgotten recesses in his mind he found a strange explanation for this. Something he had read, or had been told, but where he had read it or who had told him he could not, for the life of him recall – probably Arthur Apple. It sounded like Apple. Yet it was very clear '. . . *There seems to be no one to guide them towards human dignity, no one for them to admire, no one worthy of emulation.*' That was one thing. And having recited this, Seamus Reilly realized there was more to it, from somewhere else, some other voice was crying out, yet it was, strangely, the same voice. *Man dies in peace – reward enough; or with an awful darkness in the eye he dies screaming for the power of Shekinah to protect him, Alas, by then, it is too late for mercy, too late, even, for pity . . . .*

Seamus Reilly sat up and switched on the light, the evocative, frightening words echoing in his head. Too late for mercy. Perhaps that was so. He opened the drawer in the bedside table and pulled out his telephone book. He thumbed through it, then lifted the phone and dialled.

'Declan?'

'Yes. Who's that?'

'Seamus. Seamus Reilly.'

'Oh. What a surprise. How are you?'

Reilly ignored the question. 'Declan you remember what you wanted me to do? That film thing?'

'Of course.'

'I've decided to do it.'

'You – well, great. I wasn't – '

'There are conditions you might not agree to.'

'I've been told to agree to any conditions.'

'Perhaps not mine. Is there any chance you might come over for a day?'

'No bother. As soon as I tell – '

'You must tell no one, Declan. Not a living soul. Not until I've spoken to you at any rate.'

'I see. Okay. Fine. What's today? Say Friday next, would that do?'

'Yes.'

'I'll go straight to Rose's. I'll phone you from there.'

'Thank you, Declan.'

'Is something wrong, Seamus? You sound – '

'No. Nothing's wrong. I'll explain everything when I see you on Friday. Thank you again for coming.'

'Think nothing of it.'

So that was it. The first step completed, or almost. He could still change his mind, of course. He had a couple of days in which to do it. As though to eliminate such a possibility, Seamus Reilly now phoned John Asher.

'John. I'm sorry to disturb you. It's Seamus.'

'Yes, Seamus?'

'I need to meet with you. With you and Maddox. Tomorrow. Can you arrange it?'

'I'm sure I can. I'm free anyway, whatever about the Colonel.'

'I would prefer to see you both together. In the evening if that's at all possible.'

'I'll have to call you back on that.'

'Thank you. I would be grateful if you can organize it. It's important.'

'I'll phone Maddox now if you like and come straight back to you.'

'No. The morning will do.'

'Whatever you say. You sound – funny. What's happening?'

Reilly gave a little laugh. 'I'm not feeling very funny, John. Far from it. But nothing has happened. Well, not yet. I'll speak to you in the morning.'

The second step. Now he had dragged his self-imposed

ultimatum yet closer: only twenty-four hours, give or take an hour, to change his mind. He switched off the light and lay down again, pulling the blankets up under his chin. And he managed to doze.

If anyone had seen Seamus Reilly during the next five hours they would have thought, quite reasonably, that he was planning to move house. Methodically he went from room to room, clearing out drawers and cupboards, reading everything and stuffing all unwanted papers into a large black plastic bag, turning out pockets before consigning his old clothes to the sack also. Everything he wanted to keep he carried to the sitting room and stacked in a neat pile on the floor under the window. Fortunately he had never been a hoarder: there were few photographs in the house: nothing that connected him with his childhood, little to suggest he ever had a private life. There were some books (among them Declan Tuohy's single slim volume of poetry), an old tin box filled with foreign stamps, some magazines (dealing, mostly, with the tragic deaths of tragic men: Kennedy, King, Ghandi), and a collection of oddments he had picked up here and there: a meerschaum pipe, its bowl carved in the image of Lincoln, memorial cards held together by an elastic band, a tiny figure of a clown-like doll.

At six-thirty he was shaved and dressed ready for Asher and Maddox. He was wearing his black suit, the one he kept for funerals. He enjoyed the contrast of his scarlet tie and socks, an unusual urge to be devil-may-care triumphing. He was just checking that his hair was neatly combed when John Asher arrived.

'Ready?' he asked as Reilly opened the door. 'Maddox will be waiting for us at the barracks.'

Reilly gave him a twirl, coming to a standstill with a quick little tap dance. 'As ready as I'll ever be, John.'

Asher shook his head in quiet amazement at the antics, and grinned. 'I'm glad you're in such high spirits. Maybe you can cheer Maddox up. What I didn't tell you was that they're hounding him from London.'

As they settled themselves in Asher's car, Reilly asked: 'Why should they?'

'Because they want results. That's why. The only way Maddox could get Fisher back to England without too many questions was to tell them he had developed his own contacts – us, in case you don't know – and that he would have the names of the bombers within days. That was weeks ago. That's why they're hounding him.'

'Oh,' said Reilly, hunching his shoulders, and sinking lower in the seat. 'Well, that's part of what I want to talk to you both about.'

'He'll be pleased to hear that. So will I.'

Seamus Reilly looked at the clock on the dashboard. Time was almost up.

· SIXTEEN ·

WAITING FOR THEM to arrive, Colonel Maddox stared out of the window into the cold frosty night. He had chosen to wear his uniform, perhaps to stamp his authority on the meeting. Below him army vehicles reversed out and drove round the corner of the building and out of his sight, filled with young men who could possibly not return alive. Still, the city had been remarkably free of violence since the bombing in Brighton. It always was after a major offensive, but one could take nothing for granted: someone, perhaps from nothing more than boredom, could hurl a petrol bomb and the whole bloody mess would erupt again. God, how he wanted to be away from it all! He turned from the window and sat on the corner of his desk, swinging one leg. Life, he thought, had simply passed him by. It had used him. Like Seamus Reilly had used him. It was unfortunate that this thought was uppermost in his mind when Reilly and Asher knocked on his door and came in.

'You've arrived, then,' Maddox said gruffly, heaving himself from the desk and sitting down in his chair.

'As you say, Colonel,' Asher said. 'We've arrived.'

The Colonel put the palms of his hands flat on the desk in

front of him, looking directly at Reilly. 'You'd better explain what this is all about, Reilly. And I hope for your sake that it's not to suggest another damnable scheme. I'm in no humour for any more of that. From now on I want answers from you. And don't think I won't have you arrested if you try and play the fool.'

As soon as he had said it the Colonel realized he had made an ass of himself, had chosen quite the wrong approach, and certainly the wrong words. He felt himself start to blush as he noted Asher and Reilly glance at each other and laugh.

'I'm sorry, Colonel,' Reilly apologized as soon as he could control himself, waving his hand in front of his face as though to whisk away the last traces of merriment. 'It was just so unexpected – what you said.'

Maddox spotted his way out. 'Be that as it may, what is the reason for this meeting?'

'May we?' Reilly asked, indicating the two vacant chairs.

'Yes. Yes. Sit down.'

Reilly produced one of his small cigars, taking his time about lighting up, blowing out a stream of smoke before he spoke. When he did his voice was very quiet and tight. 'You will probably immediately object, Colonel, but before I tell you what I have to say I must first have your assurance – and yours John – that it remains within these four walls until I have completed all my preparations. You will not be able to use the information for at least another month.'

The Colonel jumped to his feet. 'No. No more deals, Reilly. I'm sick and tired of you and your deals.'

Reilly grimaced, shrugged and stood up also. 'I was afraid of that. I'm sorry that I wasted your time,' he said apologetically, already making for the door.

'Hang on a minute,' Asher said quickly. Then, turning to the Colonel, he went on. 'Colonel I don't believe this is another deal.' He swung back to Seamus. 'Is it?'

'No.'

Now Asher faced the Colonel again. 'No deal, Colonel. I think you should hear Seamus – Reilly – out. He has tried to co-operate with us. You know that. He needn't have taken care of Fisher the way he did.'

'No deal?' the Colonel demanded looking hard at Reilly.

'No deal. A request, Colonel. A request that you respect my confidence for one month.'

Nodding, the Colonel agreed. Annoyed with himself for being browbeaten yet again, he sat down and folded his hands under his chin.

'Yesterday morning I had a meeting with my Commander in Chief,' Reilly began, stopping there for a second to clear his throat. 'I was told that those who planted the bomb in the Brighton hotel were not to be punished, – that they were, in fact, to be commended. I think that was the word used. I was told that any plan I might have for effecting their punishment was to be scrapped. I was also told that should I attempt to disobey this order I would find myself as the one being punished.'

Reilly paused to take in another lungful of cigar smoke, to take, also, a look at the faces of his audience. It seemed that Maddox might interject so he continued immediately. 'I argued with the Commander. I explained why I thought the decision to let the bombing go unpunished was against everything I have fought for. I explained the devastating effect it would have on our chances in the elections. The Commander listened, but in the end he insisted that I accept the decision of the Council.' Reilly stopped again, this time to squash the remains of his cigar into the ashtray on the desk. Then he sat back. 'I have decided *not* to accept that decision.'

It took several seconds for the full import of what Seamus had said to sink in. Asher and Maddox looked at each other, one frowning, one with his eyebrows raised. Oddly enough, the realization of what had been said struck them both at the same time, and slowly they both turned their heads and gazed at Reilly. Reilly gazed silently back, faintly amused.

Asher was the first to recover. 'You mean you're breaking with the IRA?' It was as though he could hardly believe he was asking such a thing of Seamus Reilly.

Reilly shook his head. 'No, I don't mean that. I mean that I am going to make a stand against certain policies that have been adopted by the IRA. It is possible they will break with me, however,' he added wearily.

'You know what you propose to do will – ' Maddox began but stopped as Reilly held up his hand.

'I know,' Reilly told him.

'It is a far, far better thing,' Maddox decided to quote, and might even have finished the quotation had not Reilly winced.

'Nothing so dramatic, Colonel, I fear. Nor for such noble reasons.'

'Sacrifice is always noble,' Maddox countered, his tone distant, almost as if he was longing that the opportunity for sacrifice would step his way.

Reilly was cynical. He chuckled. 'You're still missing the point, Colonel. It has nothing to do with sacrifice. Years and years and years ago I swore I would do everything in my power to see to it that Ireland was united. And, from time to time, violence has been the only option.'

'I don't – '

Again Reilly held up his hand. 'You know that's true, Colonel. You won't – can't – admit it, but you know it's a fact. You saw for yourself how things worked when you were stationed here last time.'

The Colonel nodded. 'Yes. Yes, indeed I did.'

'Well,' Reilly went on, 'things have slowly changed. There is just a glimmer of hope that we can achieve our dreams by political means, so the violence has got to stop. Unfortunately there will always be those within our ranks who disagree. They see negotiation as weakness, terror as strength. Someone, finally, has to take a stand against the wasteful violence. Someone from within the IRA. So . . . .' Reilly smiled thinly and raised his eyebrows.

'Seamus you can't just barge blindly into a decision like that.' It was Asher who spoke, leaning forward and touching Reilly on the knee.

'Oh there's nothing blind about what I'm doing, John. I

shall be taking precautions. I'm a cautious bugger – as you've so often told me.'

Asher drew back, shaking his head.

'As to the bombers themselves,' Reilly went on, 'I'll give you the names I have soon, John. You know where they are; you can make your own cross-channel arrangements for their apprehension. But not until I say you can. It won't be long. Probably not as long as a month – that rather depends on a meeting I have tomorrow night.'

'To hell with that for the moment. What about you? For Christ's sake, Seamus, you can't just suddenly take on the role of martyr on us. We've worked together for too long for me to let you waltz into – '

Reilly stopped him. 'It's not a question of waltzing into anything, John. The probable truth is that I am just tired, tired of trying to maintain this interminable, uneasy peace when everyone around me seems bent on their own destruction. Besides, it is something I *want* to do; something I *need* to do.'

Asher protested: 'But – '

'And speaking of Christ – I remember reading once – it *is* strange the things you remember when you take the time to think – I remember reading somewhere that there is a legend among some tribe in Borneo – I believe it was Borneo, but maybe not – a legend, anyway, that God didn't really want to be bothered with us at all. It was up to *us*, you see, to attract *his* attention by whistling and dancing and singing. This, in an odd way, might be my little jig, my little hymn. But what I'll do if I ever do get His benevolent eye fixed on me I have no idea.'

Maddox and Asher seemed totally flummoxed, embarrassed even. Unabashed, Seamus was off again. 'It's the Irish Catholic circle, you see. At baptism you scream your head off and fight like mad to get away from the sacrament, but when death approaches you fight again but this time to partake of the sacrament that will give you at least a reasonable chance of a peaceful departure.'

Asher was shaking his head, completely baffled, but

determined to argue on. 'Look, so you don't agree with the decision. I understand that. But you don't have to – '

Again Reilly stopped him. 'But I *do*. I do. Won't you let me do one decent thing in my life?'

Declan Tuohy stopped the senior editor in the corridor. 'I won't be in tomorrow, Myles,' he said. 'I've got to go away for the day. Belfast.'

'Oh? Anything I should know about?' Cravan asked, smiling.

'No. Not really. Not yet at any rate. If anything comes of it we'll have to have a talk.'

'That means it could spell trouble.'

'It could. Well, not trouble. Controversy would be a better word.'

'That I can cope with.'

'I'll remember you said that.'

Now, still wearing his safety belt, a cup of lukewarm, weak coffee in a plastic cup in his hand, Declan stared out of the window at the sea below, thinking of the city they were fast approaching. The city of his birth. The city he feared. The city, as he had called it, of Moloch. The city he loved, too . . . .

It looms a far-off skeleton
And not a comrade nigh,
A fitful far-off skeleton
Dimming as days draw by.

. . . Well, perhaps Hardy was right even if Belfast had been the furthest thing from his mind. And it didn't dim either, for that matter. Far from it. That was the astonishing, the most admirable thing. Bombed and battered it might be, but there it still stood, sheltering its people. And what people! The most cheerful, friendliest people in the world, defying the world to beat you down with a laugh and a grin and a rose in your teeth and a clackety-clack-clack of your fingers.

Already the lights of the city were whooshing up towards

them. It could be anywhere, so peaceful and serene did it look. But it wasn't. It was Belfast, each tiny light like a candle lit to a personal tragedy, to a private agony. And, thinking of agonies, what agony, or, rather more likely, what devilish enterprise had made Seamus Reilly even consider putting himself at risk? Declan smiled to himself. God alone knew what he was up to! Well, he would be told too, soon enough. An hour at most.

Reilly could not settle. Even his beloved Mahler could not calm him down; *Das Lied von der Erde* sounded more than ever as if it was coming from the grave. Now that he had started the ball rolling he wanted desperately to get the whole thing over and done with. He walked from room to room, always returning to the hall and glaring at the phone, waiting for Declan to call. His tiredness made him irritable. All night long he had lain in bed, gazing at the myriad of tiny lights that seemed to flicker in the darkness, sometimes squeezing his eyes closed and opening them suddenly to intensify those lights. He had rehearsed, carefully, what he would say during the proposed interview. He was going to be open and frank. He would not hedge. He would answer every question as honestly and truthfully as he could: if retribution was to follow he would prefer to be hanged for telling the truth than for lying.

At last the phone rang.

'I've arrived, Seamus. Just this minute. I'm with Rose.'

'Ah, Declan. Thank you for coming.'

'You asked me to, didn't you?'

'How soon can we meet?'

'As soon as you like. Now if you want.'

Seamus jumped at the suggestion. 'Yes. Now. I'll come right over.'

'Fine.'

Declan was shocked when he opened the door to Reilly's knock. It was hard to believe that anyone could have aged so much in just a few months. He was no greyer, no more stooped, no less vigorous in his actions. His voice had the same crisp sharpness and he looked fit enough. It was only when Declan concentrated on his eyes that the trough of decline was indicated. There was no fire in them now, a veil of grey filtering the sparkle, leaving a residue of sadness. 'Come on in Seamus,' he invited.

'Thank you.'

'In here,' Declan said, leading the way to the small dining room. 'I've set a real fire in here. I thought it might be friendlier.'

Seamus followed him into the room, removing his overcoat as he went, hanging it on the back of a chair when he got there. 'Yes,' he answered.

'Can I get you anything? Tea? Coffee? Something stronger?'

Reilly smiled gratefully. 'Thank you, no. I've been drinking coffee most of the night.'

'Well, take a seat then. Rose is upstairs,' he added. ' "Doing" my room, as she puts it.'

'Ah.'

For several minutes they sat in silence, looking rather odd and uncomfortable side by side in front of the fire, perched on the straight, high-backed dining room chairs.

'Declan, I've decided to give you your interview,' Reilly said quietly at last.

'What made you change your mind?' Declan asked.

Reilly gave a tiny shrug, but did not answer.

Declan did not press the point. He leaned forward and poked at the fire. 'You mentioned conditions.'

'Yes,' Seamus agreed, and then laughed. 'I always make conditions, don't I? Habit, I suppose. I've done it all my life. Even with God. My prayers were always loaded with conditions. If *He* did this, I would do that. Even at school I tried to barter with Him. If He helped me pass such and such an exam I would – I think I promised a decade of the rosary every day. Anyway, yes, there are conditions,' Reilly confirmed and stopped talking again.

'Well, let's have them,' Declan said, trying to introduce a note of lightheartedness, putting a little laugh into his words.

Seamus Reilly held one of his hands out in front of him, palm upwards, and when he spoke he ticked off his conditions on his fingers. 'It will have to be done in absolute secrecy. You will have to vouch for everyone involved. It will have to be screened without editing. And, finally, it cannot be screened until I give you permission.' Reilly looked at Declan for his reaction.

Declan stared pensively at the flames. Finally he asked: 'Just one question – why the secrecy? That could be difficult.'

'Because, Declan, I have decided to do this without the knowledge or the permission of Command. So I need a certain amount of time. I have things to do. I have, as the poet said, promises to keep and miles to go before I sleep. Not too many miles, mind you.'

Declan stood up and walked across the room, turned, and stared down at the back of Reilly's bowed head. 'Why?' he asked, his voice suddenly strained. As he stood up he had thought about protesting, about saying he couldn't let Seamus do it, about insisting that he wanted no part of it. He had rejected these thoughts. He knew Seamus only too well. Reilly would not have undertaken such an action without very good reason.

'Why?' Seamus asked, turning and looking over his shoulder. 'You know, I wish I knew the *real* reason. Suffice it to say I believe it is the right thing to do. There is always a moment in one's life – everybody's life – when a single decision has to be made, and although we may not know it at the time, that decision is the one, vital, monumental task set to us. The result might be glorious or infamous. It doesn't matter. Destiny or fate or what you will has decreed that *you* must decide, and in deciding imprint your existence on the world. It makes not a whit of difference how insignificant it may strike you at the time, but if you fail to decide you are doomed.'

Declan walked slowly back to his chair and sat down again. He put his hand on Reilly's arm, but did not look at him. 'Seamus, Seamus, Seamus.' He was lost for words of comfort.

Reilly brightened. 'Sorry about that. I didn't mean to be so gloomy. Let's just say I *want* to do it. Now, can you meet my conditions?'

'I think so. I can get a crew who are used to keeping their mouths shut. It's back in London that worries me. I would have to tell my editor in chief.'

'And?'

'And – well, you know how the BBC feel about IRA interviews. They have to be cleared usually. And having you on film will be quite a coup. He might feel he *has* to go higher up . . . . I'll tell you what I *can* do. We could do the interview. When I have it in the can I'll tell him. If he doesn't agree to what we've agreed I'll destroy the film.'

'Can you do that?'

'I can do it. There'll be a lot of screaming, but I can do it.'

'And what happens to you?'

'Sent to the bloody Tower probably. Don't you worry about me. I'll ride it out. Maybe that is *my* monumental decision.'

Seamus Reilly patted the hand on his arm. He was just thinking what a strange thing friendship was when he heard Declan saying: 'You've split with them, haven't you?'

'No. Disagreed. Not split.'

'Same thing.'

'I suppose it is. The wrong people are getting too powerful again, Declan. Someone has to try and put a stop to that. I've elected myself.'

Declan shook his head. 'They won't like it, to put it mildly.'

Seamus managed a little laugh. 'I don't expect they will. But, you know, my friend, I've just realized that my usefulness is over. I may as well go out on a mildly human note.'

'When do you want us to do it, Seamus?'

'As soon as possible.'

'I'll make a few calls. With a bit of luck I might even be able to assemble the crew I want and get them over by tonight.'

'How efficient you are. That would be excellent.'

'I'll know by lunchtime.'

'Excellent,' Seamus said again. 'I'll be at home.'

'If you change your mind I'll understand, Seamus.'

Reilly stood up and put on his coat. 'No changing of my mind, Declan. The dye, as they say, is cast.'

At that moment, the Commander in Chief of the Provisional IRA was offering Thomas Regan a seat. He had driven to Clones the night before, and had slept badly in the unfamiliar bed. His humour was tetchy. 'Sit, Regan,' he said.

Regan sat, dropping quickly into the seat as though pole-axed.

The Commander was in no mood to beat about the bush. 'How long have you been working with Seamus Reilly?' he asked.

Regan cleared his throat. 'About ten years now.'

'Good. I have something I want you to do. I want you to keep an eye on him. We have cause for concern. If he does anything out of the ordinary, anything that causes *you* the least concern I want to know about it immediately.'

'Yes.'

'As from tomorrow you will stick to him like a limpet. And I want a written record kept of his movements. Who he sees, what time, where, and for how long. Is that clear.'

'Yes.'

'In particular I want to be informed as to any action he might be contemplating against Dermot Drumm or Joe Mulcahy in Glasgow. I can tell you that he has been ordered to take no action whatsoever. I want to be sure that order is obeyed. He might even instruct you to go over there. If he does, say that you'll go and let me know.'

'Very good.'

'And don't forget: I want to know *everything*. Every single detail of his movements.'

'I won't forget.'

'But be careful. If he suspects you *are* watching him, you could find yourself receiving the full extent of his wrath – and I need hardly tell you what that entails.'

John Asher was surprised when Reilly asked him to call round. He had not expected to hear from him just yet. He was even more surprised when Reilly told him the reason for the request, although he took his time about it, delaying it with a series of questions. 'How long do you think, John, it would take you to get the mainland police to react to information?'

Asher made a rather moronic face, indicating, more or less, that such a thing was debatable. 'That depends on the information, really. Depends on which branch would be dealing with it.'

'Anti-terrorist.'

'Oh they'd move on that.'

'Within hours?'

'Within bloody minutes.'

'Good. The name of the person who set off the Brighton bomb is Drumm. Dermot Drumm. You'll find him in a flat in James Gray Street, Glasgow. His accomplice is Joe Mulcahy. He lives in Shawlands also. With a woman. A Peggy Dunne. They actually planted the bomb. In three days I want you to get in touch with your colleagues in the special branch and pass on that information. But not for three days. I need that time.'

'Three days. And it's Dermot Drumm, Joe Mulcahy and Peggy Dunne.'

'Yes.'

John Asher wrinkled his brow, scribbling the names on his mind. Then he looked at Reilly, an uncharacteristic fondness in his eyes. 'This is it, Seamus, isn't it?'

Reilly gave a wan smile. 'Yes. I suppose it is.'

'I'll keep this to myself if you want.'

'Thanks, John. But no. Go ahead in three days. God alone knows how many lives you might save.'

'*You* might save.'

'Well, we might save.'

At the hall door but before it was opened they shook hands. It was a poignant gesture, a moment of shared sadness.

'If you need me – ' Asher began.

Reilly silenced him with an understanding nod. 'Thank you, John.'

No sooner had Asher left than Declan phoned to say he had

mustered his crew and that they would be arriving in Belfast at 4.15: where did Seamus want the interview done? His house would be fine. Yes, he understood why he would want to do it there. Yes, he would see to it that they did not all arrive at once. Yes, he, Declan, would be acting as interviewer. No, it made no difference: he would ask the right questions, be impartial.

Reilly spent the afternoon tidying up. He moved his stack of belongings away from under the window in the sitting room and put them behind the kitchen door. He hoovered and dusted. He arranged the furniture, pushing his favourite armchair back against the wall and under a copy of a print by Alken. Beside it he set his small table with an ashtray, a full tin of small cigars and a lighter. As an afterthought he put a couple of books on it also, giving it tone, as he gleefully saw it. Then he went upstairs and took a shower, humming to himself all the while, admitting that he was so doing to forestall the doubts that niggled at his mind. He took particular care in dressing, choosing a plain grey suit, blue shirt, striped tie. Nothing flashy, nothing too glum.

They started arriving at half-past five: Declan first, with the cameraman carrying his camera already loaded. Twenty minutes later, by taxi, came the lighting and sound men, each with what looked like an ordinary suitcase; and a quarter of an hour after that, in another taxi, an efficient young woman with a briefcase.

Seamus watched as they set themselves up, pleased when he saw the nod of approval at his arrangements. The curtains were tightly drawn and a single spotlight, produced from the suitcase, focused on the chair. He was asked to sit down. A small microphone was clipped to his tie. He was asked to say a few words, any words, for a voice level, it was explained. Seamus said: 'Where there is great power or great government, or great love and compassion, there is error for we progress by fault', and they all looked at each other, seeming to wonder if he had said something significant, but finally accepting it as just words and smiling with relief.

'Fine,' the soundman said and held up one thumb.

'Ready?' Declan asked the cameraman.

'Ready,' he answered putting his eye to the camera.

'Ready Seamus?' Declan asked.

Seamus nodded. 'As ready as I'll ever be.'

Declan smiled encouragement.

The clapperboard was clapped.

'Interview Seamus Reilly. Take one,' the young woman said brittlely, and went and sat beside the soundman, a clipboard on her knee, her pen poised, her ankles crossed.

The camera whirred.

Another thumb went up.

Declan Tuohy began to interview Seamus Reilly.

Driving home from Clones, Thomas Regan felt elated. That he had been summoned alone to the Commander was honour enough; to be his eyes and ears was more than Regan could have hoped for. Already the downfall of Seamus Reilly danced in his imagination and he saw himself taking Reilly's place in the hierarchy. Unconsciously he licked his lips as though already tasting the power. In a way, he admitted, he was sorry it was old Reilly. He quite liked him. Feared him, certainly, but liked him as much as that fear would allow. Still, one had to think of oneself first. Reilly had had his day. His was yet to come. As from tomorrow . . . that was what the Commander said. Regan toyed with the idea of calling on Reilly: he could easily find some pretext. It would, perhaps, show his enthusiasm if he could date his first report a day earlier than asked. On the other hand it might be seen as disobedience, and the last thing Thomas Regan wanted was to start off his mission on the wrong foot. No. He would go home. Have a nice meal. Play with the kid. Do what he was told. Tomorrow would obviously be time enough if that was the way the Commander saw it. Nevertheless he decided to drive past Seamus Reilly's house. Case the joint, he told himself, laughing at his little game.

He turned left and drove slowly down the street; even slower as he came close to the house. Not a light. The curtains tightly drawn. He must be out. Or gone to bed early. Probably out. Well, let him enjoy himself. Poor old bugger.

By ten o'clock they had finished, the equipment dismantled and stowed back in the cases.

'Is it safe to call taxis?' Declan asked.

Seamus shrugged. 'Does it matter now. Still, perhaps if you could – '

'Sure. I'll ferry them.'

They started filing from the house, each shaking Reilly's hand in turn. Declan was the last to leave. 'How do you feel now, Seamus?' he asked.

'Naked. How about you?'

'Frightened for you. The interview was terrific.'

'Don't you worry your head about me. Just see to it that you keep to our agreement.'

'I will. You have my word.'

'Good.'

'I'll have a transcript with you as soon as possible.'

'Thank you.'

'Well. That seems to be that.'

'Yes.'

Suddenly they embraced, patting each other gently on the back. Then Declan was gone.

· SEVENTEEN ·

FOUR DAYS LATER Seamus Reilly received a note from Declan Tuohy (a postcard of the Tower of London in an envelope, the significance of which was not lost on him), saying that the transcript had been sent to Rose, and would he collect it there, although for 'transcript' he had written recipe. Seamus smiled to himself at the silly subterfuge. It was proving to be a momentous day. Already the early morning newscasters had broken the story that two men and a woman had been arrested by the anti-terrorist squad, and, amid 'unprecedented security' had been taken to London from Glasgow to be charged with a number of IRA bomb incidents going back seven years and including the explosion at the Grand Hotel. They were to join two other men already being held in the special terrorist-proof unit inside Paddington Green police station. At the time of the arrest in Glasgow an unconfirmed report said police had found under the floorboards in a flat in the Shawlands district of the city a cache of weapons and enough explosive (estimates put as high as 150 lbs) to make between thirty and fifty bombs.

The next afternoon Seamus collected the transcript, at the same time giving Rose the money from her dead husband's supposed pension. As he was leaving he said quietly: 'Rose, I might have to go away for a while. I – '

'Oh good, Mr Reilly,' Rose interrupted, her eyes brightening. 'You need a little holiday. You haven't been looking yourself for quite a while now. A break will do you the world of good.'

For a moment Reilly thought of protesting. 'Yes,' he said finally. 'I'm sure it will.'

'You'll see,' Rose went on cheerfully. 'You'll be a new man when you come back.'

'I'm sure I shall. I just wanted to say that your pension will come in just the same while I'm away.'

'Thank you, Mr Reilly. Tell me, is it somewhere nice – where you're going?'

Seamus frowned. 'I don't know, Rose. I just don't know.'

Back home Reilly made himself a cup of coffee and carried it and the transcript upstairs. He went into the small back bedroom and shut the door. The mattress had been folded over on itself, so he unfolded it and sat down. There was no other furniture in the room: it looked for all the world as barren and impersonal as a cell. Appropriate, he mused grimly. Then he lit himself a čigar, and started to read. It was headed simply 'INTERVIEW' and the date of April 29th had been typed alongside. Seamus scowled and wondered what significance there could possibly be in the false date. Underneath that, in capital letters, was SEAMUS REILLY/DECLAN TUOHY. And then the actual interview began using his own and Declan's initials to identify the interrogator and his victim.

DT: Can we start by my asking you why you have decided to grant this interview.

Seamus chuckled. Grant, indeed! He recalled the sardonic glance he had given Declan and the almost apologetic look he had received in return. Well, why *had* he granted the interview. His official reply had been straight enough. He believed it was time someone explained certain facts about the IRA although, now, in the clinical loneliness that surrounded him, he found himself wondering if it hadn't been something of a last ditch stand by someone who was forced to admit that his life was a failure. He had pointed out that anything he said was a purely personal opinion although he believed those he labelled the 'majority of our right-thinking' members shared his views. Not that they would dare admit it. Certainly not now. Indeed, Reilly was only too well aware that by speaking openly about IRA affairs without the sanction of the Council he had alienated all those who might have reasonably been seen to be his supporters. And he could hardly blame them. He knew the rules better than anyone. He gave a small laugh. He had drafted many of the rules himself with youthful, uncaring eagerness. Once he chose to disobey them he automatically isolated himself.

Reilly stood up and walked across the room to the small window. He stared out at the neglected garden, watching an old tabby cat with a stiff back leg lopsidedly stalk a plump missel thrush. It was as though the bird was alert to the cat's incapacity as it managed to stay just out of reach, unflustered. Seamus smiled. That was what his own life had been like: just keeping one step ahead. That was all one could reasonably be expected to do, and he had done it adroitly.

Another of Declan's questions filtered into Reilly's mind. Most people would consider you a dangerous terrorist, he had stated. How do you react to that? He returned to the bed. This time he lay back. Terrorist. He winced. It was one of the more implacable aspects of his character that Seamus Reilly had never considered himself to be a terrorist. He believed himself to be a freedom fighter: the fact that the 'fight' had deteriorated in most people's eyes into an incomprehensible circle of murders and reprisals could not detract from the original well-meaning intent. Seamus ran his fingers across his brow. The truth was, he reflected, that governments only paid attention when violence disrupted the calm. Politicians could convince themselves that everything in the garden was rosy if people silently and submissively accepted oppression and hardship. He closed his eyes, sighing, feeling suddenly cold. Faces from the past loomed into his consciousness and then disappeared again, recoiling. His brother, pleading for his life, his eyes remorselessly accusing; Martin Deeley, a young killer nurtured on the hatred and violence that had surrounded his youth, still arrogant and cocky, winking at him, keeling over, toppling from life; Fergal Duffy, Declan's nephew, sprawled on the pavement, reaching out towards something only he could see, bearing an expression of total puzzlement. Seamus opened his eyes abruptly, dismissing for the moment his tormentors. Perhaps that was all death was in the end: a puzzle.

Thomas Regan was answering the Commander's questions as best he could: 'I've had someone watching him morning and night. He's not been out of the house once. Oh. Sorry. Once. He went to Rose Duffy's house, but that was nothing. He goes there once a week anyway to see her.'

'I'll decide if it's nothing or not,' the Commander snapped. 'And that's the only place he's been?'

'Yes.'

'Visitors?'

'None. It's like he's become a recluse.'

The Commander was furious. Damn Reilly and his meddling, righteous ways. It simply had to be him. It was too much of a coincidence. The Glasgow arrests had been too swift, too clean. Over and done with before even a hint of their possibility emerged. Worse still: his own tacit agreement with those who had demanded that Drumm and Mulcahy be kept active was being called into question; there were hints dropped that he was losing his grip on things. 'Go back to Belfast and bring Seamus Reilly here,' he said icily. 'I want him here this evening.'

Reilly sat up and glanced at the open transcript. He was amazed at how honest he had been in his answers to some of Declan's questions. He was, also, suddenly afraid. The more he read the more he realized the inevitable outcome of his replies. He let the pages flip through his fingers until, nearing the end, another question caught his eye. 'Could you yourself be killed for giving this interview without permission?' Declan had wanted to know.

Reilly gave a wan smile, recalling kindly Declan's gentle tone. His reply had been simple. He had nodded and said yes. You seem very fatalistic about it, Declan countered. Again Seamus had nodded. I am.

He threw the transcript onto the bed. If only they had known that the prospect of death terrified him. It had haunted him for years in a million guises. Dreams peopled by spectres who linked arms and prevented him from reaching God; pushing him away and downwards into an abyss. There had always been a glimmer of escape in the shape of a horny hand that reached down to save him from almost certain damnation; a hand, and above it that face, gaunt and haggard yet continually smiling, mouthing the words that Seamus Reilly had lived with for several years: *You are already dead*. It always struck him as particularly baleful that God seemed to play such a minor role. Perhaps, indeed, God had no say in the matter.

Myles Cravan looked particularly pleased with himself, grinning like the Cheshire cat. 'I've had it cleared,' he told Declan. 'The dear old DG likes the idea. *And* we get full treatment — coverage on the front page of the *Radio Times*.'

Declan was far less enthusiastic. 'You warned the DG we had to wait until we get Reilly's okay?'

Cravan hesitated. 'Sure,' he said.

'Myles,' Declan said, a warning of oncoming anger in his voice. 'Did you or didn't you?'

'Yes. Yes I did.'

'And you told him we couldn't even let a hint drop about the material we have in the can?'

Cravan looked away, his grin freezing to an embarrassed leer. 'Yes.'

'You're lying to me — '

'I told him we had to be careful.'

'Shit, Myles, that's not enough. We promised Reilly — '

205

'It's all right. It's all right,' Myles Cravan insisted. 'The DG just has to cover himself.'

'What's that supposed to mean?'

'He has to put the Governors in the picture. The IRA and the whole Ulster bit is too damned sensitive a subject at the moment.'

'Oh Jesus. You're a bastard, Myles. I promised Reilly – I gave him my word, dammit, that no hint of this would get out until he said it was okay.'

'Word won't get out, Declan. I'm sure of that. The Governors aren't going to blab to all and sundry about what we've got.'

'Oh, aren't they?' Declan asked sarcastically.

Reilly had nearly finished reading the transcript. It appalled him that at times he had appeared so ridiculously pompous, at times pathetically naïve. Still, what was done was done. He got up and carried the last few pages to the window, bending them towards the light.

DT: What in your opinion is the solution to the troubles in Northern Ireland?

Seamus threw back his head and laughed out loud. Solution! For whom? Britain? The Unionists? Sinn Fein? He remembered he had felt like shouting: 'There is no damn solution!' The possibility of agreement remained forever remote, but not unattainable. From time to time, it seemed almost within reach, there for the taking. Alas, something always went wrong. Bigotry, as the saying went, raised its ugly head.

Someone knocked on the front door, making him jump. Without hurrying he went downstairs. He was at first surprised when he saw Thomas Regan, but his surprise faded when he heard the Commander wanted to see him: now, 'I'm to drive you there myself, Mr Reilly.'

They drove rapidly towards Clones at a speed Regan would never have dared only two or three days before. Reilly observed him silently from the back seat, quietly, sadly amused. Poor Thomas. Illusions of power and grandeur were already getting the better of him it seemed. He would soon learn that there was a terrible price to pay for having power, but probably not until it was too late.

The Commander welcomed Reilly with a curt nod, and ordered Regan to stay by the car. So much for power, Reilly thought, and followed the Commander into the room.

'Just one straight answer, Seamus,' the Commander said immediately, not even bothering to be seated. 'The Glasgow arrests. Had you anything to do with that?'

For an instant Seamus Reilly felt like shouting out his involvement at the top of his voice. However, wily as ever, he decided to play a dangerous game of cat and mouse. 'I've only been out of my house once since we last spoke, and that was to visit a friend.' Irritation got the better of the Commander, who blurted: 'I know that.'

Reilly narrowed his eyes. 'Ah.'

Recovering, and seeming only slightly flustered, the Commander continued: 'That's not what I asked you.'

'My influence does not extend across the channel, Commander. The police, as we well know, are not stupid. Two and two makes four even in their book. You cannot expect to try and exterminate the entire British Cabinet and not have the police find you. Drumm, as I warned you several times, is a clumsy fool. Mulcahy isn't much better. They obviously gave themselves away.'

'And you had nothing to do with it? You didn't strike one of your deals with that RUC conspirator of yours?'

'You told me to do nothing. You said they were to be commended, I recall. Have you ever known me to disobey your orders?'

The Commander was forced to admit: 'No.'

Seamus felt the muscles in his stomach relax. 'That should answer your question.'

The Commander moved across the room and put an arm about Seamus's shoulder. 'I'm sorry, Seamus. I had to ask you.

We are under the severest pressure from our intelligence to find out what happened. The arrests were too – too clean.'

'I did warn you to have no truck with the hard-liners, Commander,' Seamus pointed out somewhat complacently.

'Damn it, Seamus, we had no choice.'

'There is always a choice,' Reilly told him, moving away. 'Always,' he repeated, almost to himself.

'Not always,' the Commander said, sounding sad.

'Always,' Seamus reiterated.

Three hours later he was back home. He decided to leave the final couple of pages of the transcript for the morning, and headed for bed. Once undressed, he put out the light and moved to the window, peering through a narrow gap in the lace curtains. The street was deserted. He was about to turn when he spotted a tiny movement of the curtains in the upstairs window of the house opposite.

'Jesus, I said I was sorry, Declan,' Myles Cravan protested.

'You're sorry? Well, that's just bloody great. *You're* sorry. What about Reilly? What do you think is going to happen to him when this breaks? He's going to be a hell of a lot sorrier than you I can tell you.'

'It couldn't be helped, Declan,' Cravan said lamely.

'Shit, of course it could have been helped. What a stupid fucking thing to say. It couldn't be helped! You know what we've done, don't you? We've killed Reilly, that's what we've done.'

Seamus Reilly was awoken by the phone jangling at his bedside. It was 2.30 a.m. 'Hello?'

'Seamus. It's Declan. Christ, I'm sorry, Seamus. They've cocked up everything over here.'

Seamus heaved himself up onto one elbow.

'It'll be in all the papers tomorrow. The fact that you gave us an interview. The government got wind of it. Someone must have told some gobshite looking to make points. Anyway, the

Governors have been got at. They've reversed the DG's decision to show the film. Seamus – you've got to get out.'

Reilly went cold, his muscles stiffened. 'Get out? And where do you suggest I "get out" to?'

'Anywhere. Over here for a start.'

Suddenly Seamus burst out laughing. 'Over there,' he said flatly. Then with equal suddenness he was serious again. 'And what would be the point of that?'

'Seamus you must – '

'I knew what I was doing. I knew the risks. To get out, as you put it, would be defeating the whole – '

'For Christ's sake, Seamus, will you wake up? Your name will be splattered across every front page in the morning – *this* goddam morning. You told me yourself what would most likely happen.'

'I said it *could* happen, Declan.'

'Could or would. Bugger the difference. We both know damn well what *will* happen. Jesus, Seamus, if you just stay there you're as good as dead already.'

'I am already dead,' Seamus replied, his voice curiously echoing. 'I am already dead,' he repeated as though recalling the words from long ago. Then abruptly and firmly he said simply: 'Goodbye, my friend,' and replaced the receiver in its cradle.

Alone, Reilly pondered what Declan had said. It was difficult not to distance himself from the truth; far easier to regard himself as someone else and commiserate with the plight of that unfortunate person, comforting him, telling him not to worry, that things could be worse. Not that they could be much worse, he admitted grimly as he came to himself, getting out of bed and slipping on his dressing-gown. What *was* strange was that all sense of fear suddenly vanished. It was as though he *was* already dead as predicted, patiently waiting for it simply to be confirmed.

· EIGHTEEN ·

O VER THE NEXT few days, the newspapers had a field day, delighting in the procession of incredible blunders that were made. HOME SECRETARY ASKS BBC TO BAN REILLY FILM. That was the start of it. BBC AGREES TO DROP IRA INTERVIEW — GOVERNORS BOW TO CABINET PRESSURE, soon followed. Then: STRIKE OVER BANNED PROGRAMME — BBC ULSTER CHIEF TO GO. Inevitably, next: BBC ULSTER CHIEF NOT TO RESIGN OVER BANNED PROGRAMME.

Seamus Reilly read the headlines in utter astonishment. He would never have believed such a furore could have resulted. If this was the Prime Minister's way of 'starving the terrorists of the oxygen of publicity' long may she reign. Most ridiculously of all came the news that the BBC TO SHOW IRA FILM — MY BOARD WAS READY TO RESIGN SAYS DG. Reilly knew now that he would be 'dealt' with, and for a moment he felt sorrow for those he had himself been obliged to punish. He recalled that his favourite tactic was to make them wait. It was, he now discovered, the waiting that was worst: the time to reflect on one's possible foolhardiness, to reflect, too, on the uselessness of one's life.

One week after the story broke an emergency meeting of the IRA Council was called. It was fully attended. The Commander sat at the head of the table looking tired and sad. 'There is no need to reiterate the reason we are here. I am sure I speak for all of us when I say how deeply I regret the decision we have to make.'

Everyone nodded.

The evening was filled with anticipation. The streets were deserted. Everyone was glued to their television sets watching young Barry McGuigan fight the fight of his life.

Seamus Reilly, too, decided to watch, but before settling himself comfortably in his chair he went into every room that had a mirror and turned each face to the wall. The sixth round had just ended and the boxers returned to their corners when the doorbell rang. He stood up slowly and deliberately: smoothed down his jacket and straightened his tie. He brushed a thread from his trousers, and flattened the hair on his temples with the palms of his hands. Then he walked deliberately to the door and opened it. Thomas Regan and Sean O'Neill stood there, looking solemn. 'Ah, Thomas – and Sean,' Seamus said without surprise. 'Not watching the fight? Come in. Come in. You can watch the finish from here if you've the time.'

He led the way into the sitting room, and sat down again in his chair. 'Sit down, sit down,' he invited, aware that he was repeating himself, aware, too, that neither man accepted his invitation but remained standing just inside the door. 'You see that man?' he asked quietly without looking round, pointing a finger towards the television screen. 'He's done what none of us could do. And without a word. It really is amazing when you come to think of it. Listen to them cheer! Every make and shape of religion, all together, cheering. Wonderful!,' he exclaimed.

That was when the first bullet hit him. He didn't move immediately. His eyes remained fixed on the screen. He felt no pain. He was just beginning to wonder if he had imagined the shot, was just rising from his chair when the second bullet ripped into him. Again there was no pain, but his knees buckled and he slid to the floor. He felt, suddenly, very tired. He could hear noises above him, noises he could no longer quite interpret. Someone touched him, feeling his neck, perhaps straightening his tie, making him presentable for whatever was in the offing which was kind of them. Then a mighty, uproaring cheer went up as Barry McGuigan pummelled his opponent sending him to his knees. For Seamus Reilly, now unaware of the impending victory, it was a frightening, hurtful sound, leaving him to slip into death bewildered that everyone should be so elated to see him die.